MW01116367

RIVER OF REMEMBRANCE

HEART ISLAND SANCTUARY SERIES

By

AnnaLeigh Skye

Inner Muse Publishing LLC

COPYRIGHT

River of Remembrance by AnnaLeigh Skye

Published by Inner Muse Publishing LLC

Hallstead, Pa 18822

Copyright @ 2024 AnnaLeigh Skye

First Edition August 2024

This book is a work of fiction. Any names, characters, companies, organizations, places, events, locales, and incidents are either used in a fictitious manner or are fictional. Any resemblance to actual persons, living or dead, actual companies or organizations, or actual events is purely coincidental.

NO AI TRAINING: Without in any way limiting the author's [and publisher's] exclusive rights under copyright, any use of this publication to "train" generative artificial intelligence (AI) technologies to generate text is expressly prohibited. The author reserves all rights to license uses of this work for generative AI training and development of machine learning language models.

This book is entirely written by AnnaLeigh Skye. No AI was used to create any portion of this book.

All rights reserved. No portions of this book may be produced in any form without permission from the publisher, except as permitted by U.S. copyright law. For permission, contact Inner Muse Publishing LLC.

Cover by Corinne Preston

ISBN: 978-1-957903-12-5 (paperback)

Playlist

When I wrote this book, these two songs were on repeat a good portion of the time as Danyka's story emerged.

"Wreckage," Nate Smith

"Messy," Chase Rice

Chapter 1: I Killed Him
   "Someone You Loved," Lewis Capaldi
Chapter 2: Hellhounds
   "Highway To Hell," AC/DC
Chapter 3: I Can't Lose Him
   "Help Is On Its Way," Little River Band
Chapter 4: It's Merely A Scratch
   "Who Knew," P!nk
Chapter 6: Choices
   "Knockin' On Heaven's Door," Guns N' Roses
Chapter 9: Missing Three
   "Faith When I Fall," Kip Moore
Chapter 10: Temper Tantrum
   "Hell Or High Water," Bailey Zimmerman
Chapter 11: Hangovers and NightMares
   "I Remember Everything," Zach Bryan, Kacey Musgraves

In memory of Bessie Brobst. I found you in a pumpkin patch and you immediately became one of my best friends. Your enthusiasm for life was infectious. You had the most giving heart and were a ray of sunshine and laughter everywhere you went. When I grow up, I want to be more like you.

I am eternally grateful for the day that you walked into my life. Your love and support helped me through some of my darkest days. Family meant everything to you, and I was so grateful to be an extended part of yours.

CONTENT WARNING

Dear Reader,

This book is intended for mature audiences eighteen and over. Some scenes may be uncomfortable for readers. Enclosed are scenes depicting:

Abduction
Parental neglect
Human Trafficking
Physical, emotional, and psychological abuse
Failed suicide attempt
Dragon tossing and munching
Well-deserved beheading
Graphic sex, which may include forced consensual encounters, attempted rape, references to past rape, castration, rough foreplay

RESOURCES

If you need help or know of someone else who does, please contact:

National Human Trafficking Resource Hotline -U.S.
call 211 or text your zip code to 891211

or call
1-888-373-7888

Also by AnnaLeigh Skye

HEART ISLAND SANCTUARY SERIES

RIVER OF REDEMPTION

RIVER OF REMORSE

RIVER OF REMEMBRANCE

COMING SOON

RIVER OF RESPECT

1

I Killed Him

Danyka killed him. The only man she'd ever allowed herself to feel anything for was dead because of her arrogance and neglect.

The peregrine falcon she had shifted into soared high above the earth, screeching with the pain that her soul was experiencing. Her high-pitched shrieks were heartbreaking. The updraft allowed her to glide long after exhaustion should have forced her to land and shift back into her human form.

Another falcon glided with her. Going by the name of Kerrygan, his flight was effortless, and he lazily circled above, protecting her from any potential enemies. Danny rarely flew with a partner, but today, she was grateful for his company. Her mind and heart were in so much turmoil that she doubted she would have paid any attention to potential danger.

"Land, Danyka," Kerrygan's voice filtered through their telepathic link, prompting her to use common sense and seek a safe place to rest.

Ignoring his command, she flew higher, pushing her exhausted muscles past their limits as she contemplated shifting and falling from this height, making sure the fall would kill her.

"Goddamn it, Danny," he snarled through their line. *"Shift, ye crazy bitch, and stop thinking 'bout doing something stupid."*

Another heartbreaking shriek pierced the air, but her end of the conversation remained silent.

"Well, just remember, hellion, if ye do something stupid, I promise I be doing it with ye. I not be leaving yer side in this form—or the other—so just remember, I be following yer lead all the way down."

Danny's body wavered in this form, and she knew Kerrygan well enough, the fucker, that he meant what he said. Gliding quickly toward the ground,

1

she landed on a cliff near the river. Isolated, it used to be one of her favorite locations.

The last time she sat here, the Earth Mother—her creator—had threatened to take the man she was falling for and give him to someone who would appreciate him if Danny didn't pull her head out of her ass. Time wasn't on her side, and fate had never been kind to her. Before she could affect change, fate took the choice from her altogether, leaving her with regrets.

Muscles twitching, her falcon form struggled to find the energy to complete the shift. She'd neglected to feed after shifting, and her body burned through too many calories during the long flight. Pulling her energy in tight and forcing herself to focus on the task at hand, she transformed back into her human form.

Crouched on all fours, her petite body curled into a ball and shook. Disheveled, short, black hair stood up in inky spikes on her head, and tears streamed down her face in fiery trails of despair.

The sound of wings beating behind her alerted her to Kerrygan's descent, but she couldn't force herself to look at him.

Kerrygan landed, his eyes piercing the darkness around them as he looked for any signs of danger. His moment of truth came as he attempted to return to his human form. Centering himself, he said a quick prayer and willed his body to shift. A heartbeat later, a man crouched where the falcon had sat.

Shifters were not meant to remain in their animal forms for long periods of time. Trapped in a cage too small for him to shift, he had remained a falcon for too long. As decades passed, his cellular structure changed. Ronan, a fellow warden, forced him to shift in a bid of self-preservation. The shift had not been complete. Shaggy, black, shoulder-length hair sported streaks of blue. His little fingers sported claws instead of fingernails.

The most unnerving change was the striking gold band around his dark brown eyes. This mutation told everyone who gazed into them that he was a failed shifter, stuck between both worlds and mastering neither. Most people were uncomfortable staring into them for long.

Rhyanna Cairn, a fellow warden and the Heart Island Sanctuary's healer, had warned Kerrygan against shifting too soon, fearing that every shift would leave him with less of his humanity intact. He attempted to follow her advice, but tragedy struck, and his intentions failed.

Danyka was one of his best friends and a woman he shared an intimate bond with because of their joint love of flying. Other shifters didn't understand the freedom of gliding on the wind any more than he understood their love of running on all fours.

Kerrygan had missed her the most while exiled in his cage. Seeing him in there had broken her heart, and in a sobbing goodbye, she had explained to

him one drunken night that she could no longer visit him in that form because it hurt too much to see him like that.

Anguish swamped him from the woman next to him. Ignoring the urge to look for further defects from shifting again too soon, he turned and gathered her naked body on his lap, tucking her head into his neck. Rocking her back and forth, he stroked his hand in small circles over her back while she sobbed.

Her nudity didn't affect him any more than it ever had. They had shifted many times together. It was simply another form to inhabit with no sense of shame or taboo when they sat on the cliffs in between shifts. Danny was a beautiful woman, but she wasn't a woman who called to the man in him, not sexually, anyway.

They were kindred spirits. He was grateful now that they had been nothing else because she would have refused the comfort he offered, and right now, they both needed it.

"I gotchye, luv," he whispered as he clasped her. "We don't know that he's gone."

Part of him was afraid to give her false hope, and the other part of him prayed that fellow warden Jameson Vance survived the night. Her silence unnerved him.

"They were still working on him when we left, lass."

Danny pulled back then, her light violet-blue eyes peering up at him with such haunting sadness that his deformed eyes misted over. "I've never seen anyone lose that much blood and survive. Have you?" Blood streaked her body from the man who had lain, bleeding out on her lap, when Kerry had arrived.

"Rhyanna and Ferg were still working on him when you took off, lass. I didn't stick around to see if he made it or not. I came after you immediately." His hand came up to stroke the side of her face. "I ken what he means to you, Danny. No matter how much you want to deny it, I ken that ye love him, and it fecking terrifies ye." Compassionate eyes bore into her as he said, "There's no shame in admitting yer feelings."

Danny's eyes locked on his for a long moment before she answered. "I've been in love with him for a long time, but nothing good will ever come of me loving him. I have nothing to offer him emotionally, and he deserves to be loved by someone who can do so unconditionally. The only thing I bring to any potential relationship is the promise of pain, disappointment, and a damn good chance of infidelity when I get pissed off or scared. Jamey deserves someone who is a match for him in every way. I'll never be the woman who can fill those requirements."

Kerrygan shook his head slowly at her statement. His fingers continued wiping the tears away as he bent down and kissed her on the forehead.

3

"Ach, Danny, why do ye always sell yerself short, lass? Ye've so much more to offer than ye'll ever realize, and so many people who love ye."

Her head shook, negating his words. "No, Kerry. I'm too fucked up for someone like Jamey to fix. I wouldn't wish that chore on anyone."

His gold-rimmed eyes focused on her intently, trying to see beneath the obvious. "We're all damaged to some extent, luv. Comes down to how much we're gonna allow that damage to rule the rest of our lives."

Hands constantly moving against her skin, soothing her as he did, he had one more thought to share before letting the subject drop. "Can ye honestly tell me it won't gut you someday to see him with someone else, lass?"

"Kind of moot point if he's dead, isn't it?" Voice wavering and tears falling steadily once again, she leaned her forehead against his chest and keened.

Not completely sure that it was a moot point, he reached out on his inner link. He found the one person who would give him an honest answer and sent his request. Danny needed to have hope, and he prayed he could give her some.

2

Hellhounds

Earlier that day...

Time slowed perceptibly and passed in a still frame of moments for Jameson Vance as the rogue hellhound charged at him.

Hellhounds. He hated the fuckers. Massive beasts, more than twice the size of a Great Dane, this was one of the biggest ones he'd encountered in the wild. The hound's head almost reached his shoulder. The animal launched forward as Jamey threw a titanium blade towards the big black bastard.

Glowing red eyes glared into his dark chocolate ones right before massive jaws, dripping ropes of toxic saliva, grabbed him around the left shoulder joint. A scream tore from his throat—a scream of agony and regret. Regardless of the shoulder injury, he would be dead within six hours from the saliva without the antidote.

Helpless, he hung there as the hound lifted him from the ground and shook him like a rag doll. Razor-sharp canines pierced his skin, and his muscles shredded from the ferociousness of the attack. Holding still, trying to mitigate the damage, he heard Danny screaming in the background as she raced toward them.

Out of the corner of his eye, he noticed streaks of silver arcing towards the animal as she tossed her daggers. Closer now, she vaulted onto the beast until she straddled his neck. "Mother-fucking demon," she screamed as she brought down both hands, plunging another set of daggers into the flaming red eyes.

Barely conscious, Jamey was aware of the ground slapping him, followed by the heavy hound crashing down across his damaged arm and chest.

Danny rode the beast to the ground, tumbling off at the last minute to prevent being trapped beneath the creature.

The shrill sound of her voice reached him beneath the animal. "Hang on, Jamey. You fucking hang on, damn you." She grabbed him from behind, heaving as she dragged him clear of the hound. The motion had him screaming in agony as she jostled his wound.

Yanking off the medical bag strapped across his body, she sought the antidote he desperately needed. She dug through the bag, chanting, "Please, don't be broken, please don't be broken." Dumping the contents to the ground, she found the undamaged syringe and looked for a location to inject him close to his heart.

Danny's stomach flipped when she looked at the damage to not only his upper arm, but to his chest as well. The fucker must have caught Jamey with his claws on the way down because deep puncture wounds and claw marks scored his skin. She inserted the needle below his collarbone and hoped there was enough antivenom to work. His normally caramel skin was a sickly gray as toxins flooded his system and he bled out in front of her.

Jamey heard her the moment she reached out telepathically on the community link. *"WARDEN DOWN. HELLHOUND bite. Assistance needed immediately on Singer Island ASAP. Hurry the fuck up!"*

To the Heart Island Sanctuary crew, she screamed, *"It's Jamey, and it's fucking BAD. He's bleeding out on me. Rhy, you need to teleport here from the closest portal. PLEASE HURRY; he doesn't have much time."* She couldn't help the sob that accompanied the next line. *"I can't lose him. Please hurry."*

Disconnecting as she felt their shock and disbelief radiating back to her, she turned all of her attention to Jamey. His breathing eased a little as the shot kicked in, and his body relaxed. She cut the other end of the leather strap from the medical bag and used it to tie a tourniquet above the bite on his arm. As she finished tying it off, she noticed blood running freely from the claw marks on his chest, soaking the ground beneath him. The gouges were deep, and air bubbles appeared in the blood, showing how deeply the tips had reached into his lungs.

Straddling his hips, she removed her vest and applied pressure, desperate to stop the bleeding. Her body weight on his chest would make it harder for him to breathe, but if he bled out first, it would be a moot point.

"On my way. Danny, give him the shot, stop the bleeding, and keep him awake until I arrive," Rhyanna shouted at her.

"We're coming!" Madylyn and Ronan said simultaneously.

"Don't ye let that fecker die on us, lass. I'll kick both yer asses," Ferg sent, and she could hear the concern in his voice beneath the threat.

"Almost there," said Roarke. *"I can transport him if he can't teleport out, and I'll pick up anyone who needs a ride at the closest portal."*

"I'm coming; grabbing help on my way," Kyran answered tersely.

Danyka sobbed, watching the color fade even more from his face. His eyes were drifting shut, so she hollered at him, "Eyes up here, buddy. You stay with me, goddamn it. Rhy's on her way, and she wants you awake and alert when she gets here. Gonna hurt like a bitch to put you back together, but don't you go to sleep, Jamey."

Jamey gazed at her with eyes struggling to focus as he weakly moved his head. She was such a tiny thing, barely five feet of ferocity. Pale skin, short, spiky black hair, and brilliant violet eyes completed the package. He wanted to reach up and touch her face, but he couldn't move his extremities.

His lips parted, but nothing came out. A second attempt to speak, and his voice emerged in a hoarse whisper. "I'm trying, Hellion… truly, I am… but I'm tired and cold."

Danny's heart was pounding in her ears, and she prayed she didn't pass out from lack of oxygen. She didn't feel like she could draw a breath through the sobs emerging from her chest and the tears trailing down her face. The Sanctuary needed him, and more important than that, Danny just realized she needed him so much more than she'd been willing to admit.

"Stay with me, Jamey. Damn it, don't you even think about leaving us. I need you."

"You've never needed no one, Hellion. Helluva time to change your mind now…" His eyes drifted shut as his breathing became more labored, and his chest moved shallowly under her bloody hands.

"Jamey," she shouted, trying to make him open his eyes. "Wake up, you bastard. There's no sleeping for the damned on my watch."

A sad smile crossed his face as his eyes focused for a moment and met hers. "But, what a way to be damned, Hellion, with you straddling my lap, the sun on my face, and the wind in my hair… I love you, Danny." With that last thought, his eyes rolled back in his head. He gasped once and blacked out.

In and out of consciousness, he traveled. One moment, unaware, and the next, Danyka was yelling at him as she increased pressure on his shoulder. There wasn't much pain, but he couldn't feel the fingers of his left arm, and he was so damn cold.

The next thing he was aware of was Danny's breasts right above him, clad only in a leather bra that barely contained her abundance. Focusing steadily on her breasts, he wasn't sure why he was so fascinated with them. T'wasn't the first time he'd seen them. Over nearly a century as partners, he'd seen her in many states of dress, or lack thereof. Must be the proximity to his face that made him want to reach up and bury his face in them. The attempt to follow through on that thought was pitiful and failed to yield even the slightest results.

7

Eyes gazing at them once again, he took in the black leather tethering them in place, then heard her yelling at him. Honestly, he couldn't blame her. His thoughts and actions were inappropriate at the moment, and they had been veering that way a lot lately.

"Goddammit, Jameson Vance!" she shouted at him. "Don't you dare leave me. You stay right here with me; do you hear me?" Arms straining, she leaned heavily on him, applying more pressure. He couldn't ignore the perfect globes nearly smothering him or the way her legs straddled his hips, putting her core right where it should be. God damn if that didn't feel amazing.

Odd though, he couldn't feel much of his body, but her warmth made sure that he was aware of every inch of hers. The heat radiated into him, and he was grateful for it because he was so damn cold and getting colder with every breath he took.

"Jameson, you fucking look at me," she shouted again, shifting one hand from his chest just long enough to slap his cheek. "Look into my eyes right now, or I'll lay a hurting on you like you've never seen before!" The vehemence behind her words brought him back out of the stupor he was in.

"That's right, eyes up here." Tipping her head to the side, she listened to an internal conversation he wasn't a part of. "Hurry, goddammit. You need to hurry, Rhyanna. I'm losing him here."

Jamey doubted she realized she had vocalized the last part of her conversation. His voice came out in a hoarse whisper, "I'm pretty fucked up if you're calling out the calvary." Coughing jaggedly, he tasted blood and watched as it splattered her pale breasts. "Yep, good and fucked up," he whispered before he felt his vision fade once again.

The clouds had finally drifted away, and the deep blue sky was clear, marked only by a red-tailed hawk soaring on the thermal currents above him.

The Earth Mother blessed Jamey with two spirit animals. His first was a grizzly, a form that he could shift into, and the second was the hawk—representing a sign when he needed one. "Perfect," he thought. His spirit animal was here to guide him to the nether world while the woman he loved tried to save him.

As that thought formed, he knew he must be ready to make his way to the other side. Sadly, he regretted not having the balls to confront her about the connection between them, and now he was running out of time.

Life hadn't been kind or fair to Danyka, but he rarely saw her cry or wallow in the circumstances she survived. Never a quitter, she was always in control unless her temper got the best of her. The effort to hold his eyes open was a losing battle. His gaze fell from the hawk to the blood covering her hands and splattered across her taut stomach and the soft, inviting cleavage of…

Crack! The feel of her hand snapping sharply across his face brought him back. Lids popping to half-mast, he looked up into her brilliant baby blues. A sad smile crossed his face as tears rolled down her cheeks, then over her chin before falling on him like a hard rain. The evidence of her distress was unchecked by this intensely controlled warrior woman.

"About fucking time," Danny said as he heard the faint sound of voices beyond her coming closer. The calvary had arrived.

Vision fading, his hearing held on for a while, and he listened to the hitch in Danny's voice as she explained what had happened and how this was all her fault.... The urge to argue was strong, but like his eyelids, his lips refused to cooperate.

Drifting on the edge of unconsciousness forced him to listen to her spewing the same bullshit. This situation wasn't her fault. Not in any way. Jamey was the one who couldn't keep his personal feelings out of the job, and he fully intended to tell them that as soon as he could speak. But the dark beckoned him, and he decided once he rested for a few minutes, he would tell them.

The grizzly shifter in him paced, trapped inside, but the urge to shift was strong. Shifting could help him heal, but he wasn't strong enough to fully shift on his own. Blood loss had seen to that.

Fury, and the need to protect Danny, warred with his animal's need to kill the hellhound again for nearly harming his mate. In a minute...he'd get to it in a minute... but he needed to rest first.

The man in him resisted sleep, terrified that if he let himself drift off, he would never wake again. This was an outcome he refused to accept, so he fought with both sides of his nature to stay with the people he loved for as long as his strength and adrenaline kept him going. He hoped sheer stubbornness would keep him going long enough to make a difference, but his hopes failed as everything went black.

3

I Can't Lose Him

Madylyn SkyDancer, Head Mistress of the Heart Island Sanctuary, pushed a long strand of her curly auburn hair back behind her ear as she giggled at a story her best friend, Rhyanna Cairn, was sharing.

Madylyn was small-boned and petite, with dark hair and midnight-blue eyes, while Rhyanna was voluptuous with honey-blond hair and emerald eyes. Both had quick wits and quicker tempers when pushed, and both had recently found the men they loved.

Madylyn had reunited with Ronan Pathfinder after centuries apart. Tall, dark, and brooding with shoulder-length dark hair and pale blue eyes, the man worked his way back into her good graces after she spent centuries despising him. They were happy together now and had recently welcomed Ronan's five-year-old son, Landon. The boy had joined them after his mother's death. The small family was continuing to expand as Ronan and Maddy anticipated the birth of their daughter this coming winter.

Rhyanna was head over heels in love with Kyran Tyde, a prince of the Court of Tears. Kyran was the first man she had ever had any form of a relationship with, and their courtship had been anything but easy.

The former Queen Meriel of the Court of Tears had done everything in her power to separate the pair by betrothing Kyran against his will to Princess Elyana of the Great Lakes Fire Clan. With the help of their friends and family, they dethroned Meriel. and Kyran and Rhyanna were reunited.

As a bonus, Elyana was now pledged to Kyran's younger brother, Kano. The couple had just returned to the Great Lakes Sanctuary to help rule while her father, King Killam, recovered from injuries sustained while dethroning Meriel.

"I wish Danny was here," Rhy said in a wistful voice.

"Me too," Maddy said, "but she and Jamey are on a mission on Singer."

Madylyn represented the Spirit Clan. Rhyanna, the Sanctuary healer, was Earth's Mistress. Missing this evening was the third member of their trio, Danyka, daughter of the Air Clan. She was also one of the best shifters, trackers, and self-defense teachers in the northeast. Centuries spent together through joyful times and difficult ones created an unbreakable bond between the women. The trifecta was magical on good days, formidable when necessary, and downright terrifying if you pissed them off.

Rhyanna was reaching for the pot of tea to top off both of their cups when she dropped the cup in her hand and clutched her head.

"WARDEN DOWN. HELLHOUND bite. Assistance needed on Singer Island ASAP. Hurry the fuck up!" The message came through on the community telepathic link from Danyka.

Rhyanna and Madylyn looked at each other in horror as another message came through on the private Sanctuary line.

"It's Jamey, and it's fucking BAD. He's bleeding out on me. Rhy, you need to teleport here from the closest portal. PLEASE HURRY; he doesn't have much time."

They sensed her anguish through their telepathic line as strongly as they felt it themselves. Jameson Vance was a well-loved, vital member of their family.

"I can't lose him. Please hurry."

Rhyanna was already up and moving. "This will destroy her, Maddy. The lass has fought so hard against her feelings for him. She won't recover from this loss."

"I know, Rhy. Ronan's on his way. We'll meet you there. Go ahead; you can teleport there faster by yourself. We're right behind you."

"Maddy, you can't help me with this," Rhy admonished as she reached the door.

"What do you mean, I can't help?" Maddy snapped.

"Yer bairn, Maddy. Ye can't afford the energy loss or the stress. Ye can join me, but I won't let ye endanger yerself or the wee lass yer carrying. I won't budge on this. There will be enough others to help." Her voice faded as she raced down the hall.

Maddy knew she was right, but she didn't have to like it.

Rhyanna reached out to Maddy as she left. *"If ye want to help, send a messenger to Kateri Vance on Wellesley. We need all the help we can get, have her gather the village elders and clan healers and meet us there. Also, request their strongest shifters."*

Maddy reached out to James, her best courier, and repeated the request. Heading out the door, she nearly ran into Ronan as he came for her.

"Ready?" he asked, reaching out to gather her close. Maddy's body trembled within his arms as fear for Jamey registered. He stroked her back, soothing her as much as he was able in the little time they had.

11

"As ready as I ever will be. Let's go." They stepped into the hall as Fergus Emberz, their red-haired giant of a fire mage, ran past them at full speed. "I'm meeting Rhyanna at the clinic to pick up supplies, then we be heading to the portal. She'll teleport us when we be closer."

Ferg never slowed, and before Maddy could answer, he'd left the building, hurrying to meet Rhyanna.

Descending the massive staircase, they departed through the front foyer. Ronan had brought Levyathan, her horse, and a mount for himself. Accepting the boost he provided, Maddy let her massive animal have the lead.

"Hurry, Jamey needs us," she encouraged him.

"I know he does. We all heard the common summons." Levyathan said.

The equine's answer still surprised her. Centuries together, and she was still learning about his magical abilities beyond the obvious. Telepathy and an incredibly long-life cycle differentiated him from the destriers of the past. He'd maintained their size and temperament, but gained wisdom, humor, and, to her chagrin, an attitude with his abilities. Until Ronan's return and redemption, he had been one of the few males who had never disappointed her.

Ronan kept up on a gray appaloosa. They made it to the stag portal and walked their mounts through the massive doors. Ronan leaned down and navigated the map and controls to work the portal, and they both waited for the sense of falling that accompanied portal travel. Neither of them minded this mode of transportation, but some suffered from nausea. Maddy was grateful that her pregnancy seemed to have no effect on her ability to use the portal.

"Mother of us all," Maddy said in a whisper, "help us stabilize and heal Jameson as best as we are able, for his highest good and your highest purpose. We need your assistance on this one, Mistress. Please, see fit to assist us in the coming hours and the long days to follow."

Maddy didn't know what they were walking into, but she felt in her soul that it was about to be life-changing for Jameson—and most likely for the rest of them. May the mother be merciful because their lives would never be the same if she decided to call the warrior home.

The creator's voice was no stranger to Madylyn, but today, her silence terrified her in ways she could barely conceive of. For the sake of all of them, she prayed she hadn't just received her answer because, like it or not, 'NO' was an answer, just not the one any of them hoped for.

4

It's Merely A Scratch

Jameson continued drifting in and out of consciousness. The blanket of darkness was welcome because, while under the weight of oblivion, he was no longer bone-numbing cold or hurting. In this place, the heartbreak in Danny's voice no longer haunted him.

On the flip side, when he finally pried his eyes open, he could trace the angles and contours of her face lovingly with his gaze. Hating the red-rimmed eyes and tears still falling at an alarming rate, he focused on her spiky black hair, long neck, and let's not forget about her other attributes currently on display.

Cursing silently because his lips still refused to participate, his eyes traveled back to her rare violet eyes. The pale blue bordered on purple in the right lighting and flashed at him in anger now.

"You've got to fight to live, Jamey. Please, for me, don't give up."

Eyes locked, he didn't glance away or close his eyes, even though, at the moment, it was harder than one would expect to keep them open.

Movement to his right caught his attention, and his eyes tracked the newcomers. Lovely Rhyanna—the heart of their band of misfits—and her inappropriately dressed sidekick, Master Fergus Emberz, arrived in style. As they reached him, Ferg looked like he was ready to hurl, and Rhyanna's color faded as she cataloged his injuries.

"Feck me, laddie, what've ye gotten yerself into this time?" Fergus asked while running a massive hand over his face.

Jamey tried to chuckle, but the sound was more like a gurgle.

Rhyanna gazed at him with such sorrow. He was pretty sure he was fucked, but he hoped he was misreading the situation. Pushing her sleeves to her elbows, she knelt next to him.

With a hand on Danny's shoulder, she looked him in the eye and spoke to him. "Jamey, luv, look at me now." Her voice was gentle. "I need to work on ye, lad, and it's gonna hurt like all the levels of hell at once, ye ken?"

The only thing he could manage was a slow blink, which she acknowledged with a nod of her head. Steel crept into her voice as she transformed into the renowned healer she was.

"Danny, put his head in yer lap and keep talking to him," she ordered like a battlefield general. "Keep touching him. Yer hands will help keep him grounded. The next few moments are going to be horrible, and he'll need something to focus on."

The sensation of Danny sliding off his hips should have been sensual, but he grimaced as her shift took the pressure off his chest and blood seeped down his sides again. As she positioned herself beneath his head, the warmth of her thighs was welcome. Strong hands cupped his head cautiously as she framed his face. Her thumbs kept up a gentle rhythm, stroking from his cheekbones to his temples and back. "Look at me, Jameson," she said in a hoarse voice, choked with tears.

The struggle to open his eyes was real and the effort harder to make each time she asked.

"Fergus," Rhy snapped, "if yer done gawking, get yer ass over here."

"Sorry, needed a moment, Rhy, darling," Ferg said in apology.

"A moment's all ye got ifn's we's gonna save him," Rhy responded silently, not wanting Jamey to realize how scared she was.

"Holy feck, he's lost a lot of blood."

"Aye, he has, and we have little time. His life force is fading as we watch. By all the Gods, goddesses, and the Earth Mother herself, I be damned before I lose him."

Jamey knew they were talking about him privately, and he understood why. He roared as Rhy moved his left arm, and pain finally announced its presence. The agony was like a red-hot poker going through the socket of his shoulder, into his chest, and radiating down his arm to his fingers. His nerves were on fire. Another shriek gurgled out of him. And why the fuck did he sound like he was drowning?

"From the bubbles I'm seeing in his blood and his labored breathing, I'm fairly certain it punctured his lungs." Rhy touched his chest gently, trying to determine the extent of the damage. "Burn this leather shirt off him so I can get a better idea of what we be dealing with."

Her gaze sought Ferg's. "Gonna pull all the energy I can tolerate from the elements, then I'll need to call on yer fire drakes for help. Do whatever ye need to boost yer energy stores, darling. Yer gonna need it."

Fergus used the tip of his index finger as one would use a knife, carefully burning a line down the boiled leather shirt Jamey wore. With the burning tip, he removed a large area of the leather a distance away from the wound to give them a better view and work area. A wince crossed his face, and he

struggled not to gag as he pulled the leather from his best friend's body and witnessed the amount of damage the hellhound inflicted. "Feck me twice," he muttered.

Eyes closed, he called on his element for help in saving this man's life. Lips moving silently, he called forth the Kings and Queens of the flames, urging them to supply him with the strength and endurance to help heal the man before him.

"This man is kindred to me. I beseech ye to spare his life. I offer a boon to ye in exchange fer yer divine help." Imploring them for help and compassion, he imagined the molten center of the earth and visualized hot, healing energy rising to his assistance. His energy swelled, and he felt the breeze of assent blow by him.

"We accept your boon, Fergus Emberz. Don't forget yer promise to us, for we shan't."

His gray eyes popped open in shock, surprised they had deigned to answer him so clearly.

A glance over his shoulder showed Rhyanna with her eyes closed and her hands fisted in the dirt, doing the same thing with her primary element, Earth.

Her melodic voice drifted to him as she chanted softly.

"Mother Earth and Father Sky,
Lend me yer help, lend me yer eyes.
This warrior kneels at death's door,
But death can't have him, as he's one I adore.

"Send me yer knowledge,
Yer strength and yer love.
Send me yer clarity,
Like the blue sky above.

"Give me all that I can manage,
Then give me more.
I'll return it, offering ye homage
Of this ye can be sure.

"Surround me with yer guidance,
Bless him with life
Give me yer strength so
That I can end his strife.

"Give me precision for me inner sight,
Me healing hands filled with yer light.

15

Me gratitude offered so you will see
As I will so mote it be.

"Thank ye, thank ye, Thank ye."

As her words drifted on the breeze, energy entered her body through her hands. With fistfuls of earth, she drew the life force from the surrounding grass, flowers, and even from the moss growing on the rocks. When her body filled to overflowing, she continued drawing energy, knowing Jamey would need every ounce she could spare.

Green leaves on the maple tree behind her changed color, fading to yellow, orange, and then to a rusty red before turning brown and falling from the tree.

Mouth dropping open, Fergus watched her in awe. "Holy hell, Rhy," he muttered to himself. "I've seen some crazy ass shite, but never did me think to witness our sweet li'l sister looking like that."

Danny's head popped up, surprised by his comment and sense of awe. The process only took moments, but in that time, Rhyanna had …expanded was the only word that came to mind. Her skin filled out. The golden halo of hair that usually hung nearly to her hips was standing straight up from her head. Energy crackled at the tips of her fingertips, and the elemental glow in her emerald eyes was terrifying. Rhy had never looked so damn fierce.

Returning her attention to her charge, Danny glanced down to find Jamey's eyes closed once again. *"Jamey, are you still with me?"* she murmured on their private link. *"Can ye hear me?"* Sobbing, she threw out, *"C'mon, you brawny bastard. Answer me!"*

Jamey's eyes lifted slowly, and there she was. A saucy li'l pixie with tears streaming down her face. The drops of despair trickled off her chin, falling to his lips. The salty taste of them motivated him, and he moved his left arm. Trying to cup her face, he missed until she grasped his hand and placed it against her cheek.

Unable to speak, he reached out to her the only way he could. *"Hellion, don't cry. It's merely a scratch."*

"No, you idiot, it's a bit more than that." She turned her head until her lips met his palm, placing a kiss on it before returning it to her face. *"You need to fight, you stubborn bastard. Fight to stay here, fight to live. Dammit, fight to stay with me."* The last part was so soft he barely heard her.

"I'd like that," he responded. *"Someone worthy to be with. I want to stay, Hellion, but I'm finding it difficult not floating away."*

The shaking of her body beneath him matched the sobs emanating from her. In the distance, Maddy's voice was faint as some of the other wardens arrived.

16

"Hold him, Danny. This is going to hurt!" Rhyanna yelled as she and Fergus fired up their gifts.

Danyka choked on the smell of burned flesh as Fergus cauterized his wounds. The process would stop Jamey from bleeding to death, but she couldn't help gagging. The damage was so extensive; she doubted he would survive. Fergus cursed, trying to work blind.

"No, Jamey, you don't get to float away. You hear me?" She kept stroking his face. *"We need you too much here. I won't let you leave us. Do you hear me, dammit... I need you."*

"Nah, Danny, you've never needed anyone. Don't be starting now."

His telepathic voice was fading, and Danny knew shock was setting in.

"Your wrong there, Jamey. As much as it pains me to say it," she took a breath before continuing, *"you might be the one thing I need the most."*

"Ah, lass, our timing has always been off, hasn't it?"

"Shh, don't waste your energy trying to talk to me."

"Danny, you need to know something." His words stopped, and she thought maybe he'd passed out again until a faint stirring on his line returned. *"You need to know that I love you. Have for a long time now, just been too much of a coward to admit it to you."*

"Bullshit. A coward is the one thing you've never been. This is going to get much worse before it gets better, but you hang on. You don't tell me something like that lying on the ground half dead like it's some twisted fairy tale."

His body arched away from the ground, protesting against the healing Ferg and Rhy were doing. Danny's fingers continued soothing him, stroking his forehead and his cheeks, trying to distract him from the pain. *"When you're better, you come tell me again, and maybe I'll believe you. Because I sure as hell can't when you're delirious with pain."*

"Will still be true... Danny." He faded away, and Danyka felt the loss of their connection like a slap. She leaned down and kissed his forehead. *"You come back to me, Jameson, because I will follow you into hell and drag you back kicking and screaming if you don't."*

"Goddammit! Rhy, I can't see what the feck I be doing in there, and I'se afraid I'se doing more damage than good," Ferg grumbled as he wiped sweat from his face with his forearm. Fire drakes—little dragon-like elementals who thrived on absorbing negative energy—raced up and down his arms and through his spiked Mohawk. "I've stopped most of the major bleeding, but I don't ken what to do next."

Rhyanna closed her eyes and studied the damage from the ethereal plane. In her mind's eye, she could view the damage to his body as a three-dimensional model. "So far, what ye've done looks good. We've still got two punctures in his lungs. Move yer right hand a smidge to the right." Watching

him critically, she waited. "No, ye've gone too far. Back it up… right there. Seal those and then work on the external wounds."

Fergus focused on the tasks she assigned him while watching her out of the corner of his eye. Rhy placed her delicate, blood-stained hands over the largest gash on Jamey's chest. Starting at the deepest part of the wound, she sent healing energy through her hands and into the innermost part of the wound. Intent on sterilizing the wounds, knitting the nerves and then the muscles back together, she worked quickly, but each wound took time to close properly.

Even though some were closed, the healing was far from complete. What they were doing was an attempt to stabilize him just to keep him alive. If he survived the blood loss, it would take weeks before he healed completely.

Danny's ragged voice pleading with Jamey in the background was breaking Rhy's heart, so she tuned her out. The only thing she could focus on was the next gash, seeping blood.

Exhausted, she sat back, wiping a bloody hand across her forehead in a half-assed attempt to push errant curls out of the way. A cursory exam told her his color was still horrible and his breathing much too labored. He was far from out of the woods.

Once again, she examined his aura, checking his vitals. They had finally stopped the bleeding, but his depleted life force concerned her. His body had little to nothing left to use towards replacing the blood loss and healing the damage properly. "Dammit," she swore fiercely, "I need more."

"What do you need?" Maddy's steady voice came from behind her.

Rhy had been oblivious to the others' arrival. A glance over her shoulder showed her a line of familiar faces. "I needs more healing energy just to sustain me levels… just more. I'm wrung nearly dry, and Ferg ain't far behind." She glanced around for Kyran, but he had yet to arrive.

Fergus nodded his head in agreement. "I'se got about enough left to maintain his body temp, but that's about it. I can't keep his organs functioning, and he's not gonna be able to do it for much longer on his own."

"Tis not enough!" Rhyanna exploded, near to tears. "We need *more*."

Madylyn dropped next to her and grasped her face in her hands. "WE ARE NOT LOSING HIM! I don't care if you drain this entire island of life and the river with it. Take what you need!" She took Rhy's hand in her own and placed it against her chest.

"I can't, Maddy," Rhyanna sobbed. "Not while yer pregnant. I'm afraid 'twill harm the bairn."

Kai Tyde, Kyran's youngest brother, approached her. "Rhyanna, I can channel energy from the river in the same way Kyran can with no harm to myself. Will you permit me to assist you?"

18

Luminous eyes glanced at him with gratitude. "Aye, I'd be mighty grateful, Kai. Thank ye."

Kai knelt behind her, placing his hands on her back as he siphoned energy from the water surrounding Singer Island. His body was a conduit for the onslaught of energy running through him and into her. Rhy gasped, and her back arched until her head rested on his shoulder while her body accepted every ounce of energy he provided.

Movement to Kai's left told him Kyran had finally arrived and was doing the same with Fergus. A cynical smile crossed his lips as he sensed the jealousy his brother was keeping at bay. Kai knew Kyran would have preferred to be holding the woman he loved rather than having his brother's hands on her, but he shoved his emotions aside and provided what Ferg needed.

A hand on Kai's shoulder told him his father, King Varan, had also arrived to lend a hand. A set of scuffed leather boots to his left meant his brother Kenn had also appeared. Stronger water elements, they channeled more energy from the water and from the emotional maelstrom drowning the island, providing an unlimited supply to Kai and Kyran.

With a gasp, Rhy jerked away, rejuvenated. Moving to Jamey, she shared the energy with him in a slow, steady stream. Moments later, Fergus joined her.

"If we could force him to shift, 'twould heal the worst of the damage," Rhy mused.

"He'd have to be conscious to do that, luv."

"I ken. I'm not daft, Ferg," she snarled, frustrated because this was one of the few cases she was afraid she couldn't fix. A contemplative expression crossed her face. "Can we force a shift?" She glanced to Kyran for advice because he was the Water Clan's equivalent of a shifter—a merman.

"Not unless we have a stronger grizzly shifter available to pull rank and force the change," Kyran answered.

"Maddy, is anyone in his family an alpha grizzly?" Rhy asked.

Maddy shook her head. "I'm not sure, but his mother will be here soon. Hopefully, they have someone who can trigger him."

"NO, NO, NO." Rhy chanted desperately, turning back to Jamey. "Ferg, his heart just stopped. He must have thrown a clot."

"Can we shock him?"

"There's too much damage. I don't think he can take it."

"What other options do we have?"

"Start chest compressions while I try something on the auric field to stabilize his organs."

Closing her eyes, she examined the puzzle pieces laid out before her. Her hope faded as she realized how much damage there still was to his body.

19

The lad had lost so much blood; she didn't understand how he was still alive. Near to tears herself, she couldn't think of anything else to do. The risk of shocking him might reopen his wounds, but they were out of options.

"Ferg, we have to try. I don't know any other way."

Two attempts with controlled energy failed, and they were out of options. Rhy laid her head on his bloody chest, trying to hear his pulse. Silence greeted her, and she sobbed against him. "Jamey, ye've got to help me. I can't do this alone. We can't do this alone. C'mon lad, ye can't leave us like this."

Danny's wail brought about the realization that she'd spoken aloud. Devastated violet eyes locked on her emerald ones. "No, Rhy, you can't be done. Fix him. God damn it, you fix him, Rhy." Danny's grief was turning to anger. She gently lowered his head, placed a gentle kiss on his forehead, then stood. "I can't stand here and watch him die. I won't."

Before anyone could speak, Danyka shifted into her Peregrine form and took to the sky. A devastated shriek came from the falcon as she raced away, unable to face the truth. Kerrygan hunched down and took Rhy's face in his hands. "Sorry, luv, but I can't let her go alone."

"NO! Kerry ye can't. Ye might not return to us again. We can't lose anyone else tonight. Don't go…" she keened, trying to get up to stop him until Kyran wrapped his arms around her from behind and held her back. She fought him, but exhaustion finally wore her out, and she collapsed back against his chest, sobbing.

"You've got to let him go, Rhy," Kyran said in a gentle voice.

Fergus was still doing chest compressions. Sweat ran down his face, and his arms were shaking, but he wouldn't quit.

"I'll take over, Ferg," Kai said as he put a hand on Fergus's shoulder.

Ferg wanted to argue, but his strength was failing, so he moved out of the way and let Kai resume. Genny had arrived with Kai and Varan, and she knelt near Jamey's head and blew air through his lips every few compressions.

Maddy dropped to her knees next to Jamey, the horror of the day catching up to her. Ronan caught her before she hit the ground too hard. Tears ran down all of their faces as they sat around Jamey's battered body.

Kai continued pumping his chest, refusing to give up, when a devastated voice came from behind them.

"Where is my son?" a woman's voice asked. Voice hoarse and red-rimmed eyes seeking her child, she said, "I can barely sense him tethered to me. Please tell me he still breathes."

The group gathered around Jameson turned as one. Kateri Vance was no stranger to most of them. She was a part of their extended family, too. A beautiful woman from an ancient indigenous line of gatekeepers, she was a

commanding presence in the Wellesley Island community and a powerful leader of their Earth Clan.

A sheet of long, black hair curtained high cheekbones in a delicate face. Timeless beauty usually masked the centuries she had lived, but utter devastation aged her now. Whiskey-colored eyes, just like Jamey's, demanded an answer.

The man whose hand she clasped was Jamey's father, Kuruk, a tall, muscular man. Kateri and Kuruk were a beautiful, devoted couple and pillars of their community. Jamey inherited his mother's eyes, delicate features, and her patience, but his broad chest, height, and sense of honor were his father's legacy.

The circle surrounding Jamey's still form parted as Varan and Kenn took a few steps back. They found Kai still doing chest compressions while a young woman breathed for Jamey every few seconds.

Rhyanna shook off Kyran's hold and pushed to her feet, trying to maintain her balance through her exhaustion. A raised hand encouraged Kyran to stay where he was. Staggering to the couple, she bowed her head deeply and said, "I've done me best by him, me lady. Please forgive me," her voice broke as a sob tore from her, "but it's not enough."

"Describe his injuries to me, Mistress Rhyanna."

Rhy collapsed to her knees. She wiped her arm under her nose as tears continued to fall and provided a clinical assessment. "Ferg helped me to try n stop the bleeding. We cauterized as many of his wounds as we were able, but he'd lost too much blood afore we arrived. He's in shock, and his hearts stopped. We shocked him multiple times, but we've gotten no response."

"How long has he been without air or a pulse?"

"Not long, me lady. We've been doing compressions since the moment his heart gave out, and we's providing him with air as well. I believe if he could shift, he might heal the worst of his injuries, but he's too weak, and we don't have a grizzly shifter powerful enough to force him."

"You do now." His father's voice was gravelly. "But you must all leave. We're not sure if it will work, and he's not safe to be around on a good day, let alone when he's confused and in pain."

"Neither are we," Kateri said. Helping Rhyanna to stand, she hugged her tightly. "Thank you, Mistress Rhyanna, for keeping him alive as long as you have. He wouldn't have made it this far without all of you." Her gaze landed on each of them. "I realize you want to stay, but I need you to trust me on this. We won't know for a few days if what we attempt heals him or kills him."

"May I join ye tomorrow to check in and help if needed?" Rhy asked.

"Nye," Kateri said. Her tone was final. "Not tomorrow, but I will keep you updated. Forty-eight hours from now, we'll welcome your assistance.

Your body desperately needs a chance to recover before you can do any more. Whatever boost you've received is only temporary. I'll not risk any of you in the state you're currently in." Her eyes beseeched the group. "Please, we're running out of time. You must leave us to this."

Jamey's father knelt next to Kai and replaced his hands on Jamey's chest. Kateri sat next to him, taking over breathing for him from the young woman with sad, scared eyes. A dozen of the Bear Clan's healers knelt around them, chanting the people's healing songs as Kateri locked eyes with her husband.

The wardens made their way to Roarke's boat anchored offshore. Rhyanna boarded as well, too weak to attempt teleporting back.

Kyran stood behind her, supporting her. She watched from the boat as the loved ones surrounding Jamey shifted into bears of various colors and sizes. When Jamey's parents shifted, it surprised her to note his mother was the largest of the gathering. Rhy prayed that she would have the strength to force his animal to come forward. His grizzly offered the greatest chance of survival. It killed her to leave, not knowing Jamey's fate.

The Earth Mother had plans for Jameson Vance, and like it or not, Rhy would have to wait with the rest of them to find out if Jamey's fate was here or on the other side of the veil.

5

Myranda

"You can't be serious?" Maryssa Belmont shrieked at her mother.

"And yet, you know I am," her mother, Myranda, said in a gentle tone.

"I'm not going, and you can't make me!" Maryssa stated, crossing her arms over her chest.

Maryssa, or Ryssa as her family called her, glared at her mother, daring her to push her on this. Sending her to Miss SkyDancer's House of Horrors for the entire summer was beyond absurd. After everything they went through this past year, she couldn't fathom this. The last thing she wanted was isolation from everyone she knew and loved for the coming eight weeks.

"No, you're right." Myranda's voice rose in warning. "I won't make you do anything. You're going to act like the young lady I raised—and that I still know is in there, somewhere. *She* remembers her responsibilities to herself, her family, and her clan." Myranda watched the anger change to hurt in her daughter's drop-chocolate eyes. She hated to stoke that hurt, but it was imperative that Ryssa accept the inevitable.

"If Dad were here, he would NEVER let you send me off to that place of horrors. He would…"

"WHAT?" Myranda exploded, interrupting her. "Tell me, sweetie, WHAT would he do? Do you honestly think he would go against the most important rule in our society just to let you have your tantrum?" Exasperated, she ran a hand through her hair. "I know you're not happy about this. I've known for a very long time. Screeching at me like the banshees three houses down isn't gonna change the fact that, come this time tomorrow morning, you will be down here and ready for your tour. This is NOT my decision. I wouldn't change this, no matter how much I might want to."

Myranda took a shaky breath before continuing, "The Heart Island Sanctuary is not a place of 'horrors.' This rite of passage teaches you how to control your powers. I can feel how close they are to emerging, and it fucking terrifies me. The anger and hurt you are experiencing because of your grief makes you volatile. You would never do anything intentionally, but it would be very easy to lose control of an element and harm yourself or someone else. The raw energy I sense in you is incredible and dangerous."

Ryssa glared daggers at her. Her dark eyes welled. When she tried to argue, her throat choked with impotence and unshed tears. Her mother never lost her temper, and she'd finally pushed her far enough to do so. A tear escaped as she closed her eyes, pissing her off even more. When she opened them, the only thing left was defeat. In a tortured voice, she asked, "How can you want me to leave? Why would you want either of us to be alone?"

Myranda wanted to weep at the sorrow etched in her only child's face. Recent events forced Ryssa to mature much faster than necessary. "Oh, baby, if I had a choice, you would never leave here." Her gray eyes welled with compassion as she fought back her own tears. "Honey, I'm not doing my job as your mother if you're not trained properly. Someday I may not be here to help you control your element."

Ryssa gasped at her choice of words and turned towards the door, slamming the heavy, carved piece behind her.

Myranda watched her stomp down the front steps and move animatedly across the front yard, arguing with herself. Hell, let's be honest, she was having a heated argument with Myranda, saying all the things she didn't dare voice in this house.

Ryssa was blue. Not blue like the small peacock feathers that covered the neighbor's yard, and thank you, Mother, not her hair, but her emotional state. The sweet young woman she raised was drowning in grief, struggling to stay afloat.

Myranda leaned against the wall for support. She should have phrased the statement better, knowing the sense of abandonment Ryssa would feel. As an adult, she was struggling to stay afloat, wandering alone in the world without her north star. How could she expect a teenager to manage her emotions when she barely made it through the day without losing her shit?

Her other half, Mathyas, had been her anchor to this plane. His loss devastated both the women in his life more than he ever could have imagined. There were days Myranda struggled to get out of bed. She forced herself to go through the motions, attempting normalcy for Ryssa's sake. Their argument slapped her with the fact that she was failing.

Why bother when Ryssa saw through her ruse, anyway? She tried to hide her grief and the anger. It might have been better for both of them to have embraced the hurt and rage of their loss. They should have ripped off the

emotional band aid and let the pain loose instead of wearing a mask just to get through every day.

"Oh, Mathyas," she whispered, "why, why did you have to go...why weren't we enough reason to stay?" She leaned against the wall for support, trying not to sink to the floor.

Ryssa asked her the same question months ago. Today—like that long-ago fall day—she still had no answer. She ached for him. Her consciousness still reached out to him, and her arms still reached across the bed to touch him.

Sighing, she pushed herself away from the wall. Pulling on his sweater—the one she wore over her sleep shirt every night—she stumbled off to the kitchen to make her first cup of liquid courage. Today promised to be a long, emotional day. Lost in memories, she put water on and waited for the kettle to whistle.

Long fingers traced over her favorite picture on the trestle table beside her. A drawing he'd made of her and Ryssa hiking on the River Trail. The wind blew their hair back, and they were laughing. Ryssa added the image of Mathyas after.... He stared out at her, so full of joy, so full of life.

Ryssa was happy here, so incredibly happy. The image could have represented any of the days in their life. Her daughter hadn't known a life without him, and it had been centuries since Myranda had either. She smiled at the image of the two people who held her heart and relaxed. Myranda knew where Ryssa was.

Her daughter would spend her last bit of freedom there. The trail was the one place she could still sense her daddy. She found tranquility on the banks of the Saint Lawrence. The trail was a place full of happy memories, and she could still connect with her father there. It gave her the capability to travel back in time to happier days.

The river trail's magic wasn't exclusive to Ryssa. Myranda knew the place intimately as well. Mathyas courted her on the banks of the river and pledged himself to her there. They spent all of their free time laughing, loving, and enjoying each other's company by the river.

Unlike now, when dark days descended on their happy home. Myranda lost her best friend and lover. Ryssa lost her hero. Their world today was a watered-down version of the life they once lived, like a primary color diluted with too much white—murky and lacking substance. Neither of them was navigating very well without him.

Her tea ready, she took her first sip of sweet, cream-laced earl gray. Myranda closed her eyes at the decadence. The silky heat warmed her inner core. Simple pleasures. Simple routines were the things that made her hamster wheel move a little smoother every day.

Carrying her mug into the living room, she settled into Mathyas's favorite chair. Snuggling here was like having him hold her. Eyes closed, she searched inward for a sign of him on their inner bridge—their telepathic link. Any sign would have worked. A flicker in the dark—anything to help her face her day without him.

Deep breaths centered her and floated unwelcome thoughts away. She waited for the feeling of peace and the inner connection she experienced in the silence. The simple fairy lights, energy transfers, and communion with the Earth Mother failed to greet her. She couldn't let go enough to receive any communication from her inner guides.

Lingering in the dark, she reached out to Mathyas's link, wanting something to cling to. Finding no sense of him, she gave up, disappointed once again.

Taking another sip of motivation, she unfolded herself from the chair. Slippers scuffing over the worn floor, she shuffled off to the bathroom on autopilot.

Turning the hot water on in the shower, she disrobed, carefully hanging up his sweater. She looked critically at herself in the full-length mirror on the back of the door. Loose brown waves hung over her shoulders, the tips barely reaching her breasts. She arched an eyebrow at herself cynically as her eyes lowered, seeing the passage of time life left on her. The stretch marks, droopy skin of her arms, crow's feet gathering at the corners of her eyes, and finally, the laugh lines at the corners of her mouth.

Her lips quirked at the physical evidence of the near-four centuries she'd existed. The wrinkles meant she laughed, the stretch marks meant she loved, and the droopy arms...well, hell, blame them on genetics—or chocolate cake.

Steam filled the small room as she stepped into the tile shower. Moist heat and a good body scrub, that's what she needed. Simple pleasures. The hot water turned her skin red as she washed her hair.

Myranda's thoughts wandered back to Ryssa. Mathyas's disappearance broke something vital and beautiful inside both of the women in his life. They replaced it with anger and sorrow so deep; she worried it would consume them. Ryssa was floundering, and she didn't know how to find her or bring her back. The distance growing between them was breaking what remained of her shattered heart.

Grabbing a towel, Myranda hummed to herself and prayed the tour would go well for Ryssa. This would be a change for both of them. There was no doubt about that. What Ryssa would make of the opportunity was yet to be seen.

6

Choices

Flashes of light crossed Jameson's eyelids like the flickers of light sneaking through the trees when he rode his favorite horse through the pastures of his youth. The light was brilliant against the darkness encompassing him. His chest was tight, and he struggled to take a breath while wondering if he still even needed to breathe? Gritty lids covered his eyes, and try though he might, his attempts to lift them failed.

Harsh sounds assaulted his ears as voices he should recognize rose to a shrill shriek in the distance. Sobs reached him, and he thought they might be from Danyka, but that didn't make sense. She cried for no one. His grizzly struggled to come into play, wanting desperately to shift to get to her, but Jamey resisted the urge, knowing he would endanger everyone around him.

His body was light, featherlike, as he felt himself drifting away from the chaos beneath him. Higher he flew, and the light filtering across his lids became brighter as he cleared the canopy of trees, found the warmth of the sun, and tasted salt lingering on his lips.

Prying his eyes open with a determined force, he realized he was floating. As he glanced down, he saw a silver cord tethering him to his damaged body. His head was in Danny's lap while she sobbed over him, cradling him tenderly. Her tears fell on his lips. Damn, he wished he was alert enough to enjoy the position he was in. Because he doubted he would get a second chance to get that close to where he truly wanted to be.

The heart beating in his chest belonged to her—had for months now—but he was too much of a coward to tell her. He doubted it would have done any good because she never committed to any relationship longer than the time it took to fuck someone.

Frustration roared through his grizzly at the thought. His animal had already claimed her as his mate, even though she didn't shift into a bear. No,

27

his Danny wouldn't be anything as cumbersome as a lumbering mammal. She needed the freedom and opportunity to flee at a moment's notice that flight gave her. Gifted with the ability to shift into multiple creatures at will, her favorite would always be the Peregrine falcon. Sleek and the fastest creature on earth, she loved taking to the skies. Dainty but deadly—like her human form, Jamey loved watching her fly. The sky was the only place she seemed carefree.

Life hadn't been gentle on his little hellion, but her experiences gave her a strength and resilience that no one should ever have to earn as a child. In a moment of weakness, she'd confided in him, sharing the horrific past she had endured. The knowledge of the sexual trauma she'd experienced horrified, then enraged him. The struggle to keep his raging emotions off of his face had taken every ounce of control he possessed.

Ashamed of her past, she compelled him to forget all about the conversation before the night was over, enraging him for entirely different reasons. Jamey played along, not wanting to distress her more or make things awkward between them as friends or partners. But Danny had forgotten compulsions didn't work on him.

Mirthlessly, he chuckled to himself. Playing along had gotten him into this situation. The longer he'd tried to ignore her confession and the rest of the feelings she let slip that night, the angrier he became. Anger was bad enough, but Kerrygan's reappearance tainted his already off-kilter emotions with a hefty dose of jealousy.

Looking back, he knew the petty emotion would cost him his relationship with Danny. Best-case scenario, he might lose the use of his arm or his life, and worst, he would lose her either way.

His hellion would never forget or forgive the way he'd acted over the past few weeks. Shame washed over him as he remembered his shitty attitude and his willingness to pick a fight with Kerrygan and with her.

Jamey didn't think there had been anything between the two but friendship, but the closeness and affection between them chafed after her confession. He'd believed she was finally going to let him in, and then Kerry returned, monopolizing her time and taking her away from him.

Jealous and furious, Jamey had been miserable to the man, and Kerrygan had enjoyed antagonizing him. They formed a truce of sorts at the Court of Tears when Danny needed comfort. Kerry encouraged Jamey to go to her because he knew Jamey was what she had needed. Jamey believed the man would back off from Danny, but he was wrong. Kerry's hands had been on her constantly, and he commanded her attention every chance he could, leaving no room for Jamey.

Thinking about it now, he realized how starved for human contact Kerrygan must have been. Danny was one of the few he tolerated. Jamey

had been such a fool. The man hadn't been trying to goad him; he had just been desperate to stay connected to his humanity through touch.

This morning, Madylyn gave Jamey and Danny a mission. They needed to capture—if possible—or terminate a rogue hellhound terrorizing Singer Island. After scouting the island, they landed and attempted to contain the threat.

Actually, that's what they should have done, but Jamey had fucked up in so many ways. They always worked so well together. Years of missions helped them anticipate the other's next move without speaking or telepathy.

With his panties in a twist, Jamey went against protocol and scouted ahead before Danny finished dressing. Her warnings were hollow in his ears as he pursued the big bastard. He didn't know what he had been trying to prove, but whatever it was, he failed miserably.

His arrogance and jealousy nearly resulted in her death, a fact he could never forgive himself for. Following the smell of brimstone made it easy to follow the fucker, and when he found the massive black beast with the glowing red eyes, his heart plummeted, and the rest of the bullshit faded away.

The hellhound stood between him and Danny. The situation was dangerous enough, but Jamey noticed the exact moment that the creature scented her. His head swung towards the back of the garden, and Jamey knew he was out of choices. The only acceptable course of action was to save his partner—to save the woman he was in love with.

Waving his arms to get the hound's attention, he moved closer, making sure the beast saw him as an easier target. Danny's voice in his head warned him to wait and not to do anything stupid, but he didn't listen. He couldn't listen. They were in this situation because of his carelessness.

Jamey knew the moment the demon from hell charged him, he most likely wouldn't survive. He could live with that as long as it meant Danny was safe. He didn't care. The only regret he had was the fact he would never feel her hands in his long chestnut hair again or experience her lips tantalizing his with her innocent kisses.

Danny was far from innocent. A flavor of the day was the rule she lived by. Never the same man twice, and never when she was facing them. She took her flavor of the night out behind the Rusty Tap—the bar the wardens frequented in Clayton. And Jamey had taken his share of women out back—most recently, Carsyn, his favorite barmaid.

Jamey's tastes changed, and his interest in anyone other than Danny waned. He craved her like the drunks sleeping on the docks craved another bottle. Unfortunately, he couldn't pursue her like he would another woman. Any interest he might have shown would have ruined not only their easy-going friendship but their working relationship. He valued her place in his

life too much to take a chance on losing her completely, so his feelings were unrequited.

Looking down, he watched her sobbing as she held his face, trying to get him to wake up and talk to her. Her tormented voice begged him to stay for her, and he wanted nothing more than to obey, but every time he tried to reach her, he floated higher. The tether connecting him to his body was weakening, and he wondered if blood loss would break his thin link or would the Earth Mother choose to reach out and snip his spiritual umbilical cord because his time had just run out.

As if his thoughts summoned her, a woman stepped onto a cloud beside him. Willowy, with bronze skin and dark eyes, she smiled at him, welcoming him home. Her mahogany hair fell in a long, dark sheet down her back. Warmth surrounded him as her presence soothed the uncertainty he was feeling.

The inclination to kneel was strong, but he struggled to get his body— even in this form — to obey. Bowing his head to her, he waited for her to speak. Long moments passed before she acknowledged him. A melodic voice came to him telepathically with a hint of humor mixed in with the soft tones.

"What am I to do with you, Jameson Vance?" She shook her head in frustration before continuing. *"Of all my wardens, I thought you were the most even-tempered and sensible of the bunch."*

Jamey's cheeks would have flushed at her displeasure if it was at all possible on this plane. *"Forgive me, for disappointing you, my creator."*

"You haven't disappointed me as much as you've surprised me. Unfortunately for you, the consequences of your actions are severe, and you have a decision to make before we go any further."

"What choices do I have?"

"You may move on to the next stop on your journey, knowing not what that may be, or you may return. Returning will not be easy on you or on them, Jameson. Your recovery will be fraught with frustration and with pain, and it will cost all of you. The energy they will need to expend to save you will be extensive, and the cost on their bodies and minds will be unparalleled."

"I don't want to cause them pain or anguish."

"You've already accomplished that, Jameson. However, your loss will cause more pain and destruction than your salvation will. There is not one member of your team who is willing to lose you, including those you dislike. Any of them would give their life for you and fully intend to. I can't guarantee they won't circle the outer reaches of their abilities to heal you or their ability to know when to give up. Your loss will be catastrophic to them. I don't know if she will survive it."

Jamey knew who she spoke of, and truth be told, he didn't want to leave her either. *"I've never been a quitter,"* he said in a steely voice. *"I'm not ready to leave this life I've made."*

"Even if the life you return to may not be the one you left?"

"Even if I only have the slightest chance of regaining their trust and love."

"Even if your body doesn't return to the state in which you were before?"

"Even then. My choice will always be to return to her."

"As you wish, Jameson. Remember, these choices don't come around again. You have much work to do and much trust to regain. I wish you well, and I'm sorry for the pain you return to."

Without another word, he was back in his body, and he felt every bit of the pain he hadn't been able to feel before because of the numbing cold spreading throughout his body. Every pain receptacle in his body was on fire now, and he couldn't feel the fingers on his shredded arm. Drowning in agony, he wondered if he'd made the right decision.

7

Maryssa

Maryssa's mother had lost her mind. There was no other explanation. Without looking back, she slammed the front door and made as much noise as possible as she descended the front steps. Throwing up her arms, she stomped off and refused to glance back. In her head, she told her mother exactly what she thought of her "adventure" as she called it. She thought it was in her head until the mail lady looked at her like she was a bit "tetched" in the head.

Cheeks burning, she made the next left onto Willow Lane and headed for her refuge. It was the one place no one knew about and where she could breathe. The wind blew her hair back as her stride lengthened. The need to enjoy as many hours of tranquility as possible before facing tomorrow's orientation was palpable.

"Ryssa," her mother's voice spoke through their telepathic link, *"be home before dark."*

Ryssa growled at the intrusion, then created barriers in her mind to keep her thoughts private. In addition to the stone wall she perfected as a child, she threw up a tangle of briars with huge blood-red thorns. Satisfied with the message she was sending, she shut down her link, knowing she'd hear about it later.

Following the lane for three blocks, she made a right onto River Run and then a left onto a footbridge that crossed the road. The bridge dead-ended on a trail running parallel to the Saint Lawrence River. One more left, and she stepped onto her favorite path.

Ryssa closed her eyes and relaxed with the sun on her face and her hair tangling in the breeze. The caress of her element against her face soothed her in a way that nothing else did.

Coming to a copse of trees along the river, she smiled. Weeping willows intertwined with the cottonwoods on the riverbank. She darted across

nature's emerald carpeting, arriving at her favorite haunt. A cottonwood with particular character wove its branches in and out of the neighboring willow seeking the sun.

Ryssa pulled herself up on the lowest branch of the cottonwood and moved towards the trunk. From there, she crawled under the willow branches, watchful of the spiders nesting there. Ryssa liked the eight-legged terrorists. They were nature's population control.

Climbing through the maze of trees, she reached an abandoned eagle's nest right over the water's edge. Long ago abandoned, the nest was still structurally sound. Ryssa loved the intricacy with which the predators wove it. Dead branches entwined with feathers, bits of bones, and other questionable debris became not only a work of art but a home.

Ryssa remembered the eagles that nested there when she was nine. Her father took her hiking every weekend, and they watched the family from the trail. The eagles hadn't returned for the past three years now, and Ryssa wondered what happened to them.

It took her a week of exploring the interconnected trees to make her way to the nest. On the verge of giving up, she made a map. Color–coded, it detailed the routes she'd already explored, and the ones left to try. She came close multiple times, but the nest was always just out of her reach. The branches narrowed the higher she went. More than once, an unstable branch nearly gave way, forcing her to find alternate routes. After days of climbing, she finally reached her destination.

The nest was massive. Three children could have easily played within it. Ryssa spent hours sitting here, sketching the structure and its hidden treasures—bits of colored glass and pebbles littering the bottom, along with the skulls and bones of small rodents and birds. This place became her sanctuary. When the pain of her loss became too much, the days too long, or when her heart just kept on breaking, the woven cocoon helped hide her from the world.

Comfortable on her perch, she gazed down on the trail from her hiding place. The summer foliage kept her hidden, and she watched people moving like busy little bees below her. Ryssa closed her eyes, absorbing the warmth of the sun and the wind on her face. The days were growing longer now as they neared the summer equinox. She looked forward to the longest day of the year and the celebrations that accompanied it. A part of her also hated it because it began the countdown to the shortest day. This year, she wasn't sure she could cope with another gray, gloomy winter.

The voices of two little girls carried around the bends of the river. They ran down the path, holding hands and giggling beneath her, their harried mother racing behind. Ryssa longed for those days. Yes, with only fifteen years under her belt, she'd lived long enough to miss the carefree days of

childhood and all that meant—bedtime stories and naps, playgrounds and ice cream, laughter, and endless love, carefree and cared for—she missed all of it.

Her heart felt like lead in her chest as she pondered what she now knew about life and what she wished she had never found out. Secrets abounded, and fear was ripe in the hushed conversations she eavesdropped on. Her mother seemed clueless, and Ryssa didn't want to talk to her most days, anyway. Mom was so critical of her nowadays. Nothing she did was right anymore. She missed the easy hugs and kisses and the days when all it took to make her parents happy was a hug or a silly drawing they would never throw out.

Eyes watering, Ryssa wished for a hug, a kiss, and an "Atta girl." Her life had been good—full of love and laughter. But that seemed so long ago now, she wondered if it had all been a dream. Mom was always quiet and sad, and Ryssa didn't know how to fix their failing lines of communication.

Wishing for their life back, she heaved herself to her feet. A tear escaped, and she wiped it away in disgust. Tears were a luxury she couldn't afford. Show some sass, but never let them see you cry. Emotions could be used as a weapon, and she couldn't afford to exhibit any weaknesses where she was going.

Ryssa stood in silence, watching the river roll by. Torrential rains and melting snow earlier in the month raised the water levels drastically. She watched the heavy rippling in the water—nature's warning of the strong current running close to shore. Broken branches sped by, along with other debris from the spring thaw. The chaos in the water matched the uncertainty in her soul.

Eyes drifting shut, she kicked off her sandals, settled back down, and took a deep, cleansing breath. The whisper of the river and the soft breeze on her face helped her find her inner Zen. This sacred place inside of her soul—her happy place—was the one constant that never disappointed her and the only thing keeping her from losing her mind.

Years of practice helped her imagine a tall, white, three-wick pillar candle. Pressed along the sides of the candle were last year's pansies and violets. Their happy little faces peered out at her through the wax, like trapped fairies—tragic and hauntingly beautiful at the same time. Carved runes danced along the edges of the wax for protection and clarity.

The image was easy to create in her mind because the same candle sat on her vanity at home. She helped her mother make cases of them for gifts and to sell at the Earth Clan's market. Each candle was unique in appearance and intention.

Hedge witches, or earth mages like her mother, connected with the magic the earth provided. They possessed the ability to harness the energy of living

things to heal and create. Many mages were also artists, producing beautiful, practical items laced with magical intentions.

The image of the candle held firmly in her mind, her inner self blew at the wick, lighting it. The small flame danced precariously as, in the real world, a dragonfly landed on Ryssa's hair, distracting her. Smiling inside and out at the visitor, she refocused her energy until her flame strengthened and grew. As it gained width and height, she fixated on the flames, watching the colors change. Relaxing her inner vision, she allowed the flame to smooth her shattered emotions. Body relaxing, she drew deeper breaths. The woven branches beneath her grounded her, helping her to draw strength and comfort from the Earth Mother's embrace.

Releasing the emotional overload that began her day, her muscles relaxed, and her mind calmed down with the exercise. Ryssa reflected objectively on the hurt and rage she experienced earlier. Deep down, she knew it wasn't her mother's fault, and honestly she couldn't change the path that lay ahead for Ryssa.

Ryssa recently passed her fifteenth name-day. 'Twas time to attend her mandatory training session. The Heart Island Sanctuary provided Elemental Training. The island was a safe place for teens to explore their elemental powers, shift for the first time, or learn the art of teleporting. Others would learn how to heal using the earth's generous gifts without killing everything and everyone nearby.

The Elemental High Court issued a decree stating *every* child, regardless of sex, race, social or economic standing, was required to attend basic Elemental Training.

Most students attended one or two of the sessions, while others with more unstable elements would need additional training. The Sanctuary offered two training sessions a year. One for new students began in the summer, and the other for more advanced students continued into the fall.

Reflecting on all of this as she meditated, Ryssa knew her mom wasn't being unreasonable. She would attend for a minimum of six weeks this year. This wasn't a surprise. She'd honestly forgotten about it with all the changes in her life this past year.

Losing her dad turned her world upside down. A sad sigh escaped her as she thought about how difficult this must be on her mother. Her parents had been the perfect couple. Every day, they showed her what the meaning of true love was. When her father disappeared, the rumor mill was ripe with opinions as to his whereabouts. She witnessed firsthand the pain this caused her mother.

Ryssa loved her mom, but her dad held her heart in his hands. Their connection went beyond words. Her flame flickered as her mind wandered to him, and her eyes welled up again. Her hand swiped at her angry tears,

tired of being sad and lost. She was so doggone tired of trying to pretend this didn't hurt. His disappearance shredded her heart.

With another breath, she steadied her flame and cleared her mind. She opened her mind to the source of all and sent out a prayer on the wind, as she did every time she came here. *"Tell him I love him, please,"* she said to whatever deity would listen, *"and tell him I miss him, and momma misses him, too."* She took another breath and whispered, *"And so it is,"* into the wind to carry her wish away.

The wind swirled her hair away from her face, and she could have sworn she heard his whisper in the breeze. *"I miss you, too, my little sweet pea... and I will love you... forever and always.... tell your Momma, too."*

Ryssa's eyes snapped open, and she looked around. Shaken, she jumped up, grabbing a branch to keep from falling. "Daddy?" she asked aloud.

Turning in a tight circle, she clutched the branch, not trusting her balance. The shock of hearing his voice on the wind stunned her. She'd heard tales of people communicating from the other side, other places, even other times, but she'd never experienced it.

Full of hope, she reached out on the inner link that should go directly to him, but she didn't receive a response. Her heart sank. She was wide awake, and she'd heard his voice clearly. Had she imagined it? Was she losing her mind?

Frustrated, she sat and nervously started braiding her hair. The simple rhythm of over and under, turn, over, under, turn soothed her nerves. As she grabbed a chunk of hair from the back, she felt something in the strands. Carefully picking it out, she found leaves—no surprise there—and then she pulled out a tiny peacock's feather.

It shouldn't have fazed her. She lived right next door to an entire flock. Her neighbors raised exotic, noisy, smelly birds in their backyard. Examining the feather closer, the depth of color and intricate pattern caught her attention. The indigo blue drew her eye, and she couldn't help but remember her mother's thoughts right before she slammed her mental door shut.

They never blocked their telepathic paths from each other. Ryssa doubted her mom thought about throwing up a wall when she stormed out of the house. Ryssa heard her comment about being blue. Looking at the gorgeous colors, she knew what she needed to do.

Life was changing tomorrow, whether or not she liked it. But, just maybe, Ryssa could try to make the transition just a bit easier on both of them. She gazed around one last time before making her way back down the tree.

Ryssa hurried down the trail, headed toward her favorite place—Artisan Locks, owned by her Aunt Gigi. Giggling, she quickened her pace, anticipating her mother's reaction.

36

8

Shift

A soft, melodic voice joined with Rhyanna's and Fergus's. His grizzly stretched, wanting to take over and heal their body. Jamey knew it was their best chance of survival. He willed his fingers to sprout claws, but his body wasn't strong enough, making him gnash his teeth in frustration until, once again, the sound of her voice soothed him.

Chanting surrounded him. Voices of ancient healers and his ancestors embraced him, trying to raise his energy to strengthen his failing body.

The alpha was summoning him. His mother's command was not to be ignored. A sharp tug on the invisible line that connected his soul to his mother—and his bear to his alpha—made him shriek in agony.

Forcing his bear to the surface was a painful procedure for him and an energy depletion for her, making her vulnerable. With muscles screaming, tendons popping, and skin shredding, he turned into the beast he struggled to keep chained.

His grizzly had saved his ass more than once, but just as many times, the animal had endangered him and those around him. When you turned into a violent monster nearly eight feet tall and over six hundred pounds, it wasn't safe for anyone or anything around you. There was no managing a rampaging grizzly, and Jamey's was a surly bastard on a good day.

His mother, Kateri, was the clan's alpha. Most of their clan were bear shifters, although different species existed within the clan. Black bears, grizzlies, Kodiaks, and even one polar bear. Kateri Vance was their queen, and they all respected and heeded her call if she forced them to shift.

Jameson was no different. This wasn't a request from his mother. No, this was a command from his alpha, and he could not deny her.

His ravaged body struggled to complete the shift. Shifting was always more dangerous when your human body wasn't at optimal health. Factor in

a fatal injury, and there was a terrifying possibility of getting stuck between forms if you fought the change.

As Jamey registered the command, he relaxed, letting the shift roll through him until it reached his chest and his arm. A tormented roar voiced the agony he was in. Another roar sounded right next to him, and he recognized his mother, reassuring him all would be well.

His heart raced in his chest, and he thought he was bleeding again, but he couldn't be sure. The shift ripped open the wounds Rhy tried to heal, but shifter magic would replace the blood loss and repair his injuries quicker. Shifter or not, the wounds he'd incurred were going to take a while to heal this time around.

His mother's voice came through their parental link. *"Sleep, my child, for you're still gravely injured, and your body needs all the healing you can allow it. Sleep."*

This time the command came with a compulsion, and he let the only person in this world who could successfully compel him roll him deeply under where he drifted into the dark, afraid he would never again see Danny's smile or feel her touch.

9

Missing Three

The journey from Singer Island back to Heart Island was the longest two hours of Madylyn's life. The wardens huddled on the deck, barely speaking.

Rhyanna sat in Kyran Tyde's lap, accepting the comfort he offered. Tears coursed down her face in a never-ending stream. His usual ability to absorb her emotions wasn't working because he was just as exhausted. Rhy was a phenomenal healer, and failure hit her hard when she couldn't help someone—especially someone she loved.

Kyran's brothers, Kai and Kenn, and his father, Varan, sat near them. They had provided additional energy and healing for Jamey, Rhy, and Fergus, but it hadn't been enough. Jamey's fate was in their creator's hands now.

Roarke brought around a tray laden with fruit and sandwiches. His chef, Treasure, followed with pots of strong coffee, black tea, and fresh-baked cookies. Grateful for the offerings, they accepted them, acknowledging the need for fuel even if they didn't want to eat.

Roarke tried to hide it, but Maddy recognized the longing in his eyes when he watched Rhy from a distance. She suspected Kyran noticed it as well by the way he glared at him when Roarke walked by. Kyran and Rhy were a beautiful couple who had survived their share of trials. Roarke had unintentionally been one of those trials. Even though Rhy chose Kyran, jealousy was still a hard monster for him to tame.

Genny, a ward of the sanctuary, sat on a bench with her knees clasped to her chest, staring across the water. Tiny of stature and hardly any meat on her bones, she was often mistaken for a child. Her mistrust of nearly everyone but Rhy and Maddy made it difficult for her to communicate with others. Rescued from a human trafficking ring, she still struggled with crowds of people, men in particular.

Kai approached her, offering cookies and a cup of tea. She gazed up at him for a long time before accepting the food and mumbling a shy thank you. A wee thing, she was fragile on the best of days. Trusting Kai was a big step for her, and Maddy's heart eased watching as Genny asked him to join her.

Ferguson was in the far corner nursing a bottle of whiskey Roarke provided. Another one was circulating around the deck, numbing the pain they were all feeling.

Maddy wished she had the option to numb the pain, but Ronan's hand stroking her belly was an unintentional reminder of why she didn't have that luxury. The ache in her chest wouldn't go away, but she'd attempted to calm herself when Rhy said her anguish wasn't good for the baby. After suffering a miscarriage centuries ago, Maddy wouldn't do anything to chance this child's healthy arrival.

"Do you think he'll make it?" she asked Ronan in a whisper.

"I think he has a good chance." He pressed a soft kiss to her temple. "The clan healers are the best thing for him now. We've done all we can. We have to trust in them and trust in his will to return to us. If nothing else, trust in his need to come back for Danny."

Her voice broke. "You saw her when she left. She thinks he died, and it destroyed her." Her hands tightened on his forearms. "I've tried to reach her, but she won't answer me. I can't lose her, too, Ronan. She's family to me, and so is Kerrygan. I can't lose all three of them."

"I know, darling. We can't afford to lose any of them, let alone three."

"Damn right, we can't," Fergus snarled, sitting down next to them. "Don't know what else we could've done, lass." He pinched the bridge of his nose between his thumb and forefinger. "Rhy was on top of everything from the second we arrived." He let out a shuddering breath, and his voice broke. "Jamey was a fecking mess. Ain't seen nothing that bad in a long fecking time."

"You both did all that you could, Ferg," Maddy said, moving to hug him. "There's no blame to assign. We just need to pray for the best. He's young, and he's strong."

"Aye, he is, and he's got the Pixie to return for."

"He does." She leaned her head on his shoulder. "Have you heard from her or Kerry?"

"Nye. From what I can tell, they haven't shifted back yet." He pressed a brotherly kiss to the top of her head. "Neither of the feckers have answered me."

"Please let me know when you hear from either of them."

"Right back atchya, Maddy. Danny's more likely to reach out to ye or Rhy than me."

Maddy nodded at him, then headed over to the Tyde men.

King Varan reached for her hand, clasping it between his. "How are you holding up, Mistress SkyDancer?"

"I'll be fine. Thank you for asking." Her gaze met all three of the men's eyes before continuing. "I wanted to thank all of you for responding so quickly to our distress call."

"It's the least we could do after your help a few weeks ago," Varan said.

Kenn nodded at her and said, "Happy to help. Wish we could've done more to help him. He's an excellent tracker, and a good friend."

"He sure is," she said with a sad smile. "Excuse me while I check on the others."

Maddy stopped in front of Rhy but didn't know what to say. Sorrow etched the healer's features. Rhy took her failures to heart, and there was no talking her out of it. Maddy knelt down and clasped her hands. Rhy could barely look at her.

"I'm sorry, Maddy, I can't talk right now. It hurts too much."

"I understand, honey. We're all hurting right now."

Rhy's head nodded. Her eyes shifted, continually tracking the people on the deck repeatedly.

"I can't stop counting."

"Counting what?" Maddy asked, furrowing her brows.

"After every mission we'se ever been on, I count heads, making sure everyone is safe." Her eyes met Maddy's. *"Like a mother with a newborn counting fingers and toes repeatedly to make sure there are ten of each."*

Maddy's heart broke for her, knowing where she was going with this now.

"I can't stop counting because we're missing three. So, I start all over again trying to account for everyone, but we're still missing three."

"Honey," Maddy knelt and took her hands, *"Jamey was still alive when we left. Danny and Kerry are together, and that's good that she's not alone. Right?"*

"Is it, Maddy?" She sniffled loudly. *"We couldn't keep Jamey's heart beating. Danny is a fecking mess, and I don't ken that she'll ever return the same after this—if she comes back at all. Kerry loses another piece of himself every damn time the lad shifts. What will he lose this time?"* Her gaze traveled around the deck again. *"This may be all we have left after today."* Tortured emerald eyes met hers. *"How do we move on without them?"* Shaking her head, she said, *"Not sure that I can."*

"Rhyanna Cairn, you stop this bullshit right now. You have never been one to see a glass half empty, and today isn't the day to start." Maddy took Rhy's face between her hands, ignoring Kyran's frown. *"Count with me."* She lifted her hand in front of Rhyanna and said aloud. "Until we know any differently, one is Jameson with his family's healers. Two, Danny, and three, Kerry, are gliding through the sky. Four, Fergus is getting drunk next to Ronan, who is number five and probably joining him. Six and seven, you and Kyran are

here, safe and sound. Eight is Genny, and nine is Kai, sitting together over there. I make ten. We're all accounted for, Rhy." She wiped the tears off the healer's face. "You need to rest, love."

Rhy nodded, then laid her head against Kyran's chest, closing her eyes. Her breathing deepened, and her features finally relaxed.

Kyran stared at her, gratitude shining in his eyes. "Thank you, Maddy. I've never seen her like this, and she couldn't tell me how to help."

"Be grateful for that. I've only seen her this way once before, and it took a long time to come out of it. She gets lost repeating an action obsessively until she can perfect it."

"Her way of coping with what she considers her failure?"

"Exactly. But we all know she didn't fail. She kept him alive long enough for his family to arrive. None of us could have done that. She needs to remember that."

"Sleep will help her," Kyran said, running a hand over her head and pressing a kiss to her brow.

"Sleep will help all of us. Make sure you get some, too."

A tired nod answered her as she moved away. And damn it to hell if she didn't start counting all over again, too. Even adding in the Tyde brothers, Roarke, and the crew, she was still missing three for a second set. Heart heavy, she made her way back to the bench and sat between Fergus and Ronan, trying to keep her eyes open and her hands off the bottle passing back and forth between them. Leaning against Ronan, she let her eyes close and prayed that when she opened them next, her family would be whole again.

10

Temper Tantrum

"Landon Pathfinder, ye get yerself right on back here with dem dere cookies," Mrs. O'Hare, the woman in charge of anything to do with the kitchen or running the Sanctuary, hollered down the hall.

Landon slid around the corner and scooted into the alcove beneath the staircase. His dirty hand clamped over his mouth to keep his ragged breaths from giving him away. The loud clomping of Mrs. O'Hare went by him and started up the stairs.

"She must shift into a dragon," he whispered to his pet rat, Tiny. Two fingers stroked the critter's back as he tried to calm him down. "I think she might have been breeving fire this time."

Tiny chittered, agreeing with Landon. The poor thing was terrified of the woman who attacked him with a broom every time they wandered into the kitchen. Landon didn't understand her dislike for his friends. It was bad enough they wouldn't let him bring his pet skunk inside, but she kept threatening Tiny, too.

"Shhhh," he told Tiny. "I'se got to listen for her." He propped the door open an inch, cringing as it squeaked. His dark head popped out, moving from side to side before he shuffled out, closing the door behind him.

His feet stuck him to the floor as he tried to decide which direction to run. He'd made sure the door shut, so he didn't reveal his hiding place, but he paid little attention to the crumb hitting the floor as he debated his next move. Tiny sat on his shoulder, nibbling on a cookie and offering no suggestions.

His hand brushed against his pants, wiping the rest of the mess from the cookies down the front of them. "We could try to get Tamas to let us ride one of the NightMares or go see if Uncle Ferg's magicked the drawer in Maddy's office with my watch." He gazed up at the massive staircase and

listened for the dragon. "She's up there somewhere, but we could be quick." A glance at Tiny made him frown. "I promise I won't get distracted, and then we'll go to the stables."

His mission decided, he ran up the outside edge of the stairs while hunched over, looking for trouble. When he reached the top, he ran full out toward Maddy's office, passing the massive carved tree on the wall. He stopped, brows nearly touching as the wall seemed to move. Too young to read the names, he couldn't help but notice a leaf seemed loose. His arm stretched as far as he could go, but he couldn't reach it to tug it down.

Mrs. O'Hare stepped out of the office, scaring the snot out of him. Her gaze darted to his hand, and her hand clamped over her mouth as tears filled her eyes.

"Laddie, please don't move," she whispered, coming behind him. Her hand stretched over the top of his and gently pulled it down. She turned Landon to face her and cupped a gnarled hand under his chin. "Do ye understand what this tree represents?"

"Looks like fall to me," he said, scratching his head. He pointed to the fallen leaves at the base. "See, some leaves have changed color and fallen. I was just trying to help that one up there. The loose one," he said, standing on tippy toe, trying to get closer.

"No, child. Please don't do that." Her voice was soft, sad even. He'd never heard her use that tone before. "Every leaf represents one of us, laddie." Tears hovered on her lashes as she met his gaze. "When ye see the ones that are hovering like that one," she nodded to the one that caught his eye, "Means somebody is struggling to stay in this world."

"Ye mean, they're sick?"

"Could be or could be they've hurt themselves." Her eyes moved back to the unstable leaf, paling as the color changed to a lighter shade of brown.

"Who is it?"

Her breath hitched, and she debated keeping her silence, but couldn't stop the sob coming from her chest. "That's Master Jameson, lad."

Landon stood still as stone for the first time since she'd met him. "He gonna die like my mama did?"

"Don't know, chile, don't know." She brushed a hand over his head soothingly. "Why don't ye bring Tiny down for a snack and some milk, and we can say a prayer to the Mother that he'll stay with us."

"That work?" he asked, gazing up at her dubiously.

"Sometimes, ifn the Mother ain't ready to take them away."

"I like Jamey."

"Aye, laddie. We all love Jameson. He's as good as they come."

The old woman held out a hand to the child and offered him a wobbly smile. "Come, keep me company. Maybe we can play a game."

"You're not gonna hit Tiny?"

"Nye, lad. Today he gets a free pass."

His hand, covered in chocolate and dirt, disappeared into her ancient one.

"I'm really good at poker."

"Are ye now?"

"Uncle Ferg says I'm a natural, but I'se not supposed to tell Maddy."

The dragon laughed—a sound so unexpected that a wide grin crossed his face.

"It will be our secret."

"Whatchya got to ante with? I ain't got no money."

"Think there might be a jar of jellybeans we could use. What do ye think?"

"Can we eat 'em?"

"When we're done, mayhap."

Hours later, most of the team dragged their way into the Sanctuary. Exhausted and emotionally spent, the rest made their way to their rooms.

Maddy and Ronan headed for the kitchen looking for Landon, but they found him sound asleep with Mrs. O'Hare on the sofa. A deck of cards and a jar of jellybeans lay haphazardly on the table. One of his favorite books rested on her chest, and Tiny was asleep on her shoulder.

"Seems like they've finally bonded," Maddy said.

"Was beginning to wonder if that would ever happen."

"Me, too." A smile crossed her face for the first time since Danny's call for help. "Should we wake them?"

"I think Landon will be fine, but she's going to be hurting tomorrow if she spends the night with him sprawled against her." He lifted the sleeping child in his arms. "I'll be back down after I get him settled."

Mrs. O'Hare stretched and gave them a bleary look. "Yer finally back." The fog cleared in an instant as she remembered where they had been. "Master Jameson?"

Maddy's face crumbled as it all came back. Wiping her face with her hand, she whispered, "We don't know. He's in the hands of his clan now."

"Gads, no." the older woman said as she deposited Tiny on the sofa and enveloped Maddy in a hug.

"Rhy and Ferg did everything possible, but it wasn't enough. His mother forced him to shift and is hoping it will help him heal. We won't know for a few days if it worked."

"By the Mother, I bet he be fine. He's a strong one, and he'll not go without a fight." Her eyes darted past Maddy. "Where's me Danyka?"

Maddy shook her head. "She couldn't stand to see him like that. When his heart stopped…"

"Now, now, child. We're not going down that path until the good Mother throws us on it." Strong hands shook her gently. "Ye hear me?"

Maddy pulled herself together and nodded her head.

"Have ye eaten, lass?"

"Not for a while, and this one's letting me know it." A hand rubbed her belly, trying to calm it down.

"Let's go then."

As they stepped out of the parlor, they heard Fergus's anguished shouts. The sound of breaking glass followed, and the walls of the building shook. The sound of anxious voices in the hall drifted down to them.

Ronan reached her, running his hands over Maddy. "Are you alright?"

"I'm fine. This is Ferg's way of coping. He'll settle in a moment."

"Lad's too old to be having these kinds of temper tantrums," Mrs. O'Hare huffed. "I'll reassure the staff that he won't kill us with this one."

"He has to find some outlet, and he never breaks down in front of us."

"If this isn't in front of us all, I don't know what is," she snapped as she walked away.

"Daddy!" A child's terrified shriek cut through the air.

They ran for his room. Ronan took the stairs two at a time and raced down the hall. Pushing open the door, he found Landon curled in the corner of his bed, sobbing.

"Hey, buddy," Ronan said, gathering him close. "I'm right here."

"Don't leave me, Daddy," the child sobbed, clinging to his neck.

"I've got you, Landon," he soothed. "We're not going anywhere."

"Can I sleep with you tonight?"

"Of course, you can." He stood and carried him from the room, rubbing circles on his back.

"Bad dream," Landon said in a sleepy voice. "Jamey's leaf fell from the tree, and Fergus was burning down the house."

"Go," Maddy said as she turned down the hallway toward her office. Not wanting an answer, but needing to look, she searched the tree for the Vance family branch. Jameson's leaf clung to the branch, still attached but faded. "He's still alive." Releasing a breath she didn't know she was holding, she leaned against the wall for a moment.

With steadier steps, she returned to her suite of rooms. Landon snuggled in the middle of the bed. Ronan sat next to him, gazing down at him with so much love.

"Jamey?" he asked.

"Still here."

"Fergus?"

46

"Seems to have worked it out of his system." Maddy moved closer until he pulled her in between his knees. "You, okay?"

"Yeah. Entire world drops out from under you when you think they're hurt."

"Yeah, it does." Wrapping her arms around his neck, she hugged him tightly. "He called you 'Daddy' for the first time."

A wide grin crossed his face. "He did. Twice." His hand rubbed her belly. "Can't wait to have two of them calling me that."

"I love you."

"Love you, too, darling."

As they settled for the night, Maddy's heart eased. She realized that having someone to hold your hand while you walked the darkest paths in life was a gift and one she would never take for granted.

11

Hangovers and NightMares

Fergus Emberz lay in the middle of his king-sized bed, waiting for the courage to move. Head pounding like a drum at a Midsummer's night festival, he couldn't even open his eyes. Bladder threatening to burst, he was out of options. With no choice, he faced the light and the chance that he was going to be puking his guts out.

Dragging himself to the side, he levered himself into a sitting position. Pausing with his head bent, he cursed himself for his overindulgence. Stomach queasy, he took a few deep breaths to calm the nausea. With a lurching motion, he bounced off the walls in the hallway leading to the washroom. He staggered in, covering his eyes with his hands at the bright light blazing in from the too-fecking-big window.

With a sigh of relief and his bladder thanking him, he found the sink and splashed cold water on his face with the vain hope that the water would wash away the past twenty-four hours like he was rinsing the sleep from his eyes.

A deep belch erupted from his sour stomach, and the taste of second-hand whiskey assaulted his already fragile senses. A glass sat on the countertop. He filled, emptied, and repeated twice more, trying to replace the fluid his body lost by combating the alcohol level in his system. Meaty palms pawed the glass shower door open. He stepped into the tile shower and turned the frigid water on full force to complete his misery. The shock shook the vestiges of sleep and sorrow from his system. The icy blast cleared his mind, allowing for a re-set. He attempted to view the situation they were in logically.

When his body shook from the water temperature, he adjusted the knob the other way, letting the hot water pummel his back, relaxing and releasing the knots in his muscles—and in his heart and soul. Fergus dried off, pulled on a kilt, and searched for a clean linen shirt.

Yesterday's events haunted him. Jameson was his closest friend, next to Danny, and the horror of seeing him laid out and bleeding to death when they arrived on Singer Island would remain with him until the day he died. Not knowing Jamey's fate was the worst part of the whole thing. Respecting his mother's request that they leave him in the hands of his clan and the healers of their village was one of the hardest things he'd ever done. Rhyanna did everything possible to save Jamey, and Fergus helped at her side, but they'd run out of options and energy. He only hoped that his alpha shifter forced him to shift. The wait for an update was bound to drive them all crazy.

Desperate for a little hair of the dog, he headed downstairs, hoping to find the remnants of breakfast still available and a potent drink to wash it down. Voices from the dining room made him hopeful brunch was still available. He stopped in the bar first, making his drink before joining the others.

His nearest and dearest surrounded a long mahogany table. Ronan and Maddy were at one end, with Rhyanna and Kyran to Maddy's left. They all looked as discouraged as he felt. Seems he wasn't the only one needing a hangover remedy from the looks of things. The buffet beckoned, so he filled two plates while shoving a piece of bacon into his mouth. He pulled out a chair next to Ronan and joined his fellow wardens. The air was thick with sorrow and uncertainty, and their unshielded emotions battered him.

Maddy nodded at him as she took a sip of her tea. With an eyebrow cocked, she asked, "You over your tantrum? Mrs. O'Hare will want a word with you. She didn't appreciate you terrifying her staff."

"I'm sorry, Maddy. There's no excuse. I lost control. It shan't happen again."

"Hmmm," was the only response he received in return.

"Funny thing," Rhy said, peering out at him from red-rimmed eyes. "Could've sworn ye rode past the lake on the back of that hell beast with her glowing eyes, laughing yer fool head off."

Fergus pinched the bridge of his nose, trying to decide how much to share. These were his people, so he shared the truth. "Sabbath called to me, and when I ignored her, she formed in the flames of me hearth and damn near torched me room until I agreed to come out and listen to her."

"That explains what I witnessed last night." Kai's voice came from behind him as the youngest Tyde brother joined them.

The humor in his voice sent Fergus over the edge. "Bloody Christ! Did nobody sleep last night?"

Five sets of eyes glared at him, waiting for his story to continue. "Aye, 'twas what ye saw. I confronted the beast."

"Sabbath let you ride her?" Ronan's voice was incredulous.

"Aye, she did. She surprised me by making a fair bit of sense." His gaze locked on Maddy as he spoke. "Ye might have an under-used asset in yer stable, darling."

"How so?" Maddy asked, remembering the reason they caged the beasts during the day.

Hell's steeds were black as night and half again taller than any workhorse they had ever seen. Eerie, glowing, red eyes were hypnotic and unsettling. Unrestrained, the NightMares preyed on the emotional and psychological weaknesses humans possessed. Upon their arrival, the island's suicide rate increased drastically. The need for residents to be institutionalized for their safety, and the safety of others, also skyrocketed.

"Wellna, their ability to manipulate one's mind also gives them abilities to help soothe emotional distress. They can consume the negative emotions as much as they can create them. She offered to take away our pain." He released a heavy sigh. "I gave her permission to assist some of us."

"Tell me yer joking," Rhyanna asked, outraged.

"Nye, lass. I'm not," Ferg replied, meeting her gaze without flinching.

"You allowed that demented animal into our minds without our permission?" Maddy asked in shock. "How could you?" The hurt and betrayal in her voice surprised and disappointed him, but he welcomed the anger layered beneath her words.

"How could I, Maddy?" he asked incredulously. The glass in his hand shook, so he set it on the table as his rarely seen temper came out to play. "I would do anything to protect any of ye." His eyes challenged them to deny it. "Ye all damn well ken that. I would do anything to protect the child yer carrying, Maddy," he fumed. "If letting our resident hell bitch help by siphoning off the hurt and devastation to protect ye and yer unborn bairn..." his eyes went to Ronan, seeking support. "Ye'll have to forgive me, but I think this was important enough to agree to."

His eyes snapped to Rhyanna. "I've never seen ye so depleted, Rhy." He drug out the syllable, dragging out the Rheeee to show his irritation. "Even with everything ye took from the earth and everything ye gained from the Tydes, ye were harming yerself." A slow perusal of her told him she still hadn't recovered. "I'd bet that man of yers spent most of the night channeling healing into ye as well." Her silence was all the answer he needed. "Ye still look like shite."

Rhy gasped at him while Kyran's fists clenched. Ferg pointed a long finger at her. "That white streak in yer hair is looking to be permanent. Excuse me if I believed easing the pain and devastation a wee bit might be a good idea."

Flames danced in his eyes as his primary element made itself known. Fire drakes—little bursts of dragon-shaped colors—raced up and down his arms,

gaining size as they feasted on his anger. "I'm not a bloody fecking, idiot. I set up boundaries with Sabbath. This be a onetime event."

"What was the cost?" Maddy asked in a cool voice, steely midnight-blue eyes meeting his. "And what about Danny?"

"It'll cost ye a parlay with the Queen of the Shadows, upon which ye may do as ye wish. I've promised nothing." Large hands ran over his face and through his wild hair before he continued. "Danny will still have to face her distress. Sabbath will only remove the raw ache. She needs to understand this lesson." He put his hands up at their outrage. "'Tis all I can tell you about the pixie. Speaking of Danny, any of ye heard from her?" Their silence and downcast eyes were answer enough. "I think I made the right choice, and as it stands, I'd do it again."

"I pray you haven't made a grave mistake, Fergus. We stand to lose an awful lot if you bet on a losing horse."

"Yer not usually one for puns, Maddy," he said in a sharp voice. "Give me a little fecking credit." With a shove, he pushed his chair back and stormed out of the room. Almost to the door, he cursed, remembering he wanted to ask about Jamey. He never got the chance, and he was too angry to return. Well, he'd reach out on his own. Mayhap he'd get the feck off this island, head to Wellesley, and check on the lad. 'Twas the least he could do for his best friend.

Until he heard otherwise, he refused to believe that Jamey was gone because it just didn't feel right. Sabbath gave him the impression that Jamey was going to need their support in the coming days. He intended to make sure they provided whatever he needed for a full recovery.

Last night, he'd allowed himself to dwell on the worst-case scenario. Today, he was feeling more positive. He believed Jamey would survive. His healing journey wouldn't be fecking easy. Ferg knew it would take time to regain his strength. Thankfully, Jamey was a scrapper. Ferg knew the lad would do everything in his power to return to them. Jamey loved Danny, and last night forced Danny to realize just how important he was to her. Time would tell if nearly losing him would make her do something about it.

12

S.O.S.

Rhyanna Cairn rested on the porch of her lake house. Nestled into an oversized rocker with a hot cup of tea in her hands, her mind drifted back over the past few days.

Long fingers reached up to pull the hair on the right side of her head forward. She ran it between her fingers, puzzled at the color and texture. The palest blond curls—almost white—contrasted with the rest of her honey-blond locks. The texture was coarse like a horse's mane, reminding her how close she'd come to harming herself in more permanent ways.

Kyran slept inside. Spending the better part of two days funneling energy into her exhausted the poor man physically and emotionally. The worry over Rhy's health exacted a toll on him as well, keeping him up nights as he monitored her.

A sweet smile crossed her face as she thought about the man she loved. They had conquered their own fears and obstacles over the past few months. In the honeymoon phase of their relationship, they lingered over kisses and sleeping in mornings, indulging every one of their fantasies and some that had never crossed her mind. Kyran was a generous lover and an even better friend. Rhy struggled to remember her life before him, single and celibate.

The wind blew her hair back, and she watched the light changing around her as night blew a kiss goodnight before retiring. Day was dawning cheerfully. Blue skies stretched as far as her eyes could see without even a hint of wispy clouds.

Clenched hands pulled the blanket tighter as the temperature dropped, and the earth waited for the atmosphere to resettle. The door opened and closed behind her, and her smile widened. Kyran stopped in front of her, greeting her with a soft kiss. Rhy set the mug on the table beside her and

looped her hands behind his neck. "Morning," she whispered against his lips.

"Morning, my lady,"

Strong arms lifted her easily, turning them so he claimed the seat with her tucked across his lap. "I missed you," he said, nuzzling into her neck.

"Ye were exhausted, me laird." A long sigh of contentment eased past her lips. "I was na the only one who needed sleep."

"You're right." His hands framed her face, and he studied her closely. Dark circles ringed her sunken eyes, but her color was much better overall. "Feeling better?"

"Aye." She nodded, reaching up to smooth the creases in his forehead. "Stop worrying. I promise I be fine."

His fingers worried the lighter lock of her hair the same way she had, but he said nothing.

"Does it bother ye?" she asked in a moment of insecurity. "I can have it dyed to match. Ye'll never ken it exists."

"Absolutely not," he said, tugging it lightly. "You've earned your stripes. Let it stand as a reminder to both of us how close we came to the tipping point." His hands clasped her face fiercely between them. "Promise me you'll never scare me like that again." His eyes were stormy as they locked on hers.

Her palms covered his. "I promise to try not to scare ye again." It was the best she could do. "Ye ken I would've done just as much or more had it been one of yer family members."

"I know. That's what terrifies me." Pressing a kiss to her forehead, he whispered. "I can't lose you, not when I've just gotten you back."

"Hush, na. Enough of this nonsense for today." She tucked her head under his chin and placed a kiss on his neck. "Thought I'd put a call out to a few of the other healers I trust to assist with Jamey in the coming days." She felt his body relax beneath her. "Will take some of the pressure off me, although I be going to see him regularly."

"I'd expect nothing less." With a push of his foot, he set the rocker in motion. "I think it's a wonderful idea."

Rhy's gaze lost its focus as she reached out to Myranda Belmont, Catalina Gallagher, Hadley Greene, and Fern Hollow on their group telepathic link.

"Ladies, the Sanctuary needs healers in the coming weeks. Jameson Vance, one of our own, is clinging to life. I'd like to set up a rotation of healers to head for Wellesley Island to give the clan's medicine people a wee break. We'll also need additional coverage on Heart Island to assist with the coming Training Session." She paused a moment as her emotions ran their course before continuing. *"Are any of ye in a place to offer assistance?"*

"I be dere," Catalina Gallagher said. *"I be 'onored to 'elp in any way dat I can."*

"*Aye, count me in as well,*" Myranda Belmont answered.

"*Yes, Rhy. Put me on a schedule and let me know where to start,*" Fern said.

"*Can't for a few days,*" Hadley responded. "*I'se got a set of twins that be breech, and I needs to stick close for a few days. I'll let ye know when me patients be stable.*"

"*'Tis understandable, Hadley.*" Rhyanna exhaled a sigh of relief. "*Thank ye, ladies. 'Tis more than I expected. If the three of ye could pop by tomorrow morning, we'll work out a schedule.*"

One by one, they signed off until Myranda was the only one who remained. "*Rhy, you're not the only one who needs a favor.*"

"*Name it, Myr. What can I help ye with?*"

The silence between them lasted, making Rhy uncomfortable and worried for her friend. "*Myr?*"

"*It's Mathyas,*" she finally said.

"*What's wrong with him?*" Rhy asked.

"*He's missing, Rhy.*"

A surge of overwhelming emotion came through the link, drowning Rhy's already fragile emotional barricades. "*What do ye mean, missing? For how long?*"

"*He didn't return from a mission last fall. He's presumed dead.*"

The heartbreak her friend was experiencing had Rhy unconsciously clinging harder to Kyran. His arms tightened around her, and his lips pressed to her forehead. "*Myr, I don't know what to say. I didna know.*"

"*There's nothing to say, Rhy, except that I believe he's alive. I can't explain it. I just know he is. No one will listen to me, and I was hoping mayhap Maddy would give me an audience.*"

"*I'll make sure of it. Stick around after the others leave tomorrow. We'll see what can be done.*"

"*Thank you, Rhy. I didn't know where else to turn. The High Court ignores my petitions.*"

"*Maddy won't.*"

"*Thank you.*"

"*We'll see you soon, Myr.*"

The link faded off, and she focused on the man holding her. His presence grounded her frail body and soothed her fragile emotions. "Help be a coming," she said, gazing up at him.

"I'm glad to hear it, for all our sakes."

"'Twill be a relief to share the load."

"Gives me more time with you." He nuzzled her neck, his lips tracing the edge of her jawline.

"Aye, 'twill." Her lips met his, and she let herself fall into the man who would always catch her when she fell. "I love ye, Kyran," she whispered when they came up for air.

"I love you, too, Rhy. Love you, too."

RIVER OF REMEMBRANCE

13

Hamish

Hamish leaned against the wall of the brothel across from Vulcan McKay's bar. Vulcan and his brother Brandell were the sons of Laird Killam McKay, the man at the helm of the Great Lakes Fire Clan.

Supposedly, the Laird was in poor health—if the rumor mills were to be believed. His daughter, Elyana, and her newly pledged partner—one of the Tyde bastards—were running things now. Vulcan and Brandell had been scarce at the bar they owned, pulling long shifts guarding the Laird. Hamish had been watching the joint for days, trying to avoid the brawny bastards who headed the Clan's guard.

At home, in the shadow he stood in, it was easy to miss him. Nondescript on the best of days, he was a slight man with stringy blond hair and a constant scowl. Deep lines etched his face from a lifetime of hard living. The tiniest amount of elemental blood flowing through his veins did little to halt the physical effects of his life choices. Calculating, soulless dark eyes watched the building and the traffic in and out of it.

He'd laid low the past few months. He'd snatched a girl near Heart Island, then tried to sell her to Jonah, a flesh peddler. The whole thing had gone tits up. Thieving bastard robbed him, kept the girl, and then the scarred fecker threatened him.

Hamish couldn't get past the slight. He intended to pay the bastard back, but he just needed someone else to get close to him so he could exact his revenge. Thought he might have found an ally here recently, and he'd been watching for the man to make another appearance. With no luck, he needed to leave a message for him. Dawdling, he studied the building for another half hour. He hated to bring attention to himself by doing this, but he was running out of time.

A soggy cigar drooped from his lips, and he inhaled deeply, letting the nicotine flood his system. Wishing for a joint, he took another drag and

stepped into the light. Two riders approached, and he waited for them to pass, cursing loudly when the closest horse nearly shat on him. Dodging the moist piles, he crossed quickly, not wanting to gain unwanted attention.

Pulling the door open, he cringed at the shrill sound of a bell announcing his entry. The room was well lit this time of day, but he'd never entered this early before. He preferred the cloak of darkness late night brought to him.

The anonymity of the corner table beckoned, so he headed that way. A heavily pregnant barmaid approached, resting her tray on her protruding belly. Cute, with short blond hair and a serene smile, she was easy on the eyes. Hamish kept his eyes on her face. The evil prick that he was, he cataloged her assets, calculating her value to the right buyer. Some men had a fetish for pregnant women. There was a market for everything if you knew the right buyers. Hamish did.

"Pick yer poison."

"I'll take a pint and a shot a whiskey." Hamish placed a ten on her tray, then watched as she waddled away.

The woman was pregnant more than not. The few times he'd been in here over the years, she was always expecting another. Lucky for her when others struggled for centuries to have just one. "Wish I had jest a pinch of the luck some get," he said to no one as he waited.

A pair at the next table gave him a funny look, but he gave them a crude gesture, and they turned away from him. Good. He didn't like the looks of them, anyway.

"Here ye go," the lass said, setting his beer and shot down. She reached for the change, but he held a hand up to stop her.

"Keep it, lass." His gaze fell to her belly. "Ye're gonna be needing it more than me."

"Thank ye, sir. I appreciate that, I do." With a nod, she turned to leave.

"Miss?" he called, stopping her.

The bar wench turned back with a brow lifted in question. "Would ye be willing to do me a favor, lass?"

"Mayhap," she said, agreeing to nothing yet.

"I'se told to leave a message here for a man I needs to meet up with."

"Who ye be looking fer?"

"Name be Cyrus. He's not around these parts much." He took a swig of ale, then wiped a dirty hand over his mouth. "Ye still taking messages for folks?"

Eyes narrowing, she gave him a strange look. "Ain't seen him in a while, but I can leave a message at the bar for him, should he come 'round."

"Tell him Hamish be looking fer him. Got some information. Be worth his while."

"How will he find ye?"

"Lad can leave a message for me in the last place we met. I'll be around for a few weeks, hoping he stops in."

"That's it? Nothing else?"

"'Tis enough." He pulled out a twenty and placed it on her tray.

"What else ye need?"

"Nothing. For yer bairn, missus, and yer discretion."

The barmaid gave him a grateful grin and a half curtsy. "Thank ye, sir. Ye shall have it."

Hamish watched her go, wondering who took care of all of them kids when she was working. Might be worth checking into. Could be easy pickings. His mind drifted to the proprietors of the bar, and he stopped his line of thoughts from ever taking off. Vulcan and Brandell would skin him alive if they ever caught him, and he wasn't sure a couple of brats would be worth the effort.

Finishing his ale, he lumbered to his feet and headed for the door, unaware of the eyes following him.

The barmaid, Aida, had delivered his message telepathically to the two men he'd least wanted attention from, then watched until he exited her bar. She knew who he was and what he was about. What the weaselly little man didn't know was that Vulcan was her partner, and they'd been patiently waiting for him to reappear.

Cyrus was the name Fergus had given Hamish when he overheard his conversation a few weeks ago. They'd all been on the lookout for this lil fecker—the one person who might get them closer to the dark gambling dens and the floating brothels catering to all kinds of depraved tastes. Mother willing, they were one step closer to ending the plague of disappearances on the St. Lawrence Seaway.

Aida gathered his glasses and wiped the table with a damp rag. A shudder ran through her—a delayed reaction to the creepy energy Hamish had emitted. She'd easily sensed the type of man he was the moment he walked into her bar.

Hands going to her aching back, she fisted her knuckles into the tight muscles. Disturbed by how much his presence still lingered near the table, she pulled a piece of sage and a piece of lavender from her pocket. She dropped them into the ashtray and struck a match on the stone wall, dropping it into the tray to smudge the negativity away. She never came to work without a supply in her apron pocket. The bar received its fair share of seedy characters, but most didn't disturb her as much as this one had. With the herbs wafting into the air, her mood cleared, and she headed to the kitchen with the dirty dishes.

Vulcan and Brandell's men would keep watch over him until Fergus made his way home. When they finished getting everything they could out of him, he would get his due.

Aida would sleep better when he did. She didn't like the way he looked at her or the way he'd been lingering in the shadows across the street. Vulcan had warned her about him, and now she knew why. The man was evil. Pure evil.

14

Where the Feck Are Ye?

Fergus fled the building, needing to escape the judgmental looks of shock and disappointment. He decided to the best of his ability, and he didn't believe Sabbath would wrong them. Only one way to find out, and he prayed he wasn't wrong.

"Pixie," he sent on their personal link, *"Where the feck are ye, lass?"* He waited a moment for an answer before giving up and pleading. *"I need to know yer all right, lass. Please."*

His gangly legs took him quickly to the stables, drawn to the object of his irritation against his will. A long corridor led to the section of the stables dedicated to Hell's spawn. Sabbath was in a stall at the end with her foals. A colt and a filly, born only a few months back, they were growing at alarming rates. The sight of the flames in their eyes and the smoke rising from their nostrils still caught him by surprise because, from the back, they appeared like abnormally large equines, not creatures that would possess you to kill yerself or others.

Elbows perched on the warded gate, he watched the two foals nurse. Sabbath ignored him, continuing to eat the grain in front of her. In her world, she was royalty, and she didn't deign to think she should jump because of his arrival. A few more mouthfuls of grain and she glanced his way. He would have sworn she raised one brow quizzically as if to ask what he wanted.

Phantom eyes stared back at him, and he felt like she was probing the depths of his soul. In barely a moment, he realized she had nearly rolled him with the ability to control his thoughts and propel his actions in ways that might harm others. Wiping his hands over his eyes, he broke the gaze and tried to examine exactly what her intention had been.

Sabbath's humor came through on her link with him. *"Maddy has reason to worry, does she not?"*

"Whatchye talking about?" he spoke sharply, intentionally misdirecting her, not wanting to admit to anything and way too fecking curious about how she knew what had transpired.

"You really gonna pretend that Mistress SkyDancer didn't just hand you your ass?" A hint of laughter floated telepathically to him.

"How could ye possibly hear what happened mere moments ago *inside* the sanctuary?"

A definite chuckle this time. *"Wouldn't you like to know?"*

If he weren't in such a foul mood, he'd find her entertaining. She was insanely intelligent and had a wicked sense of humor. Were she human, she'd be the kind of woman he'd find fascinating.

"A shame I don't go for gingers."

"For feck's sake, have ye no sense of personal boundaries? Royalty or not, ye need to ken when to stay the feck out of someone's personal thoughts."

"That's fair, if I were actively entering your thoughts, Fergus Emberz. However, I don't. You broadcast them loud and clear to me all the time. All of you do. Now, I've recently come to understand that none of you realize you do this. Please explain how I am to be blamed for something your kind are ignorant of?"

Fergus chewed on that for a bit and hung his head between his outstretched arms. Damn it, she had a point. "How can we wee mortals prevent this from occurring? Ye must tire of listening to our musings."

"You've no idea. Mortals are quite the whiny sniveling bunch on a good day. Most of the ones on this island are tolerable if ye keep them out of the bottle. Once they hit the liquid spirits, they've no filter at all in place, and I could tell you everything about everybody on this island."

"This might work to all our advantages. Is there a way for some of us to protect our thoughts? For our privacy and for your peace, of course."

"Aye, but until I meet with Madylyn, I'll not be sharing it with any of you. I wasn't joking when I suggested it. You brought it up to her this morning, but you need to reiterate the importance of this accord. This is an alliance you won't want to miss out on."

"I'm sure we don't want to have you as an adversary."

"No, Master Emberz, you most certainly do not."

"I'll talk to Maddy again later on." He scuffed his foot back and forth in the straw poking out from the stall.

"Out with it. Unless you want me to go probing for it. You're making me nervous." Snuffing flames out of her nostrils, she stomped her foot.

"Any way ye can tell me how Danny's doing? She took off yesterday and won't respond to any of us. We're concerned."

"Ah, yes, the pixie, as you call her. She's not alone, and the one she's with isn't a threat to her. He's too confused with his situation at the moment to be of any harm to her."

Fergus waited patiently for her to continue and bit his lip when she took her time getting there.

"Danny's mental frame is what you'd expect it to be. She's a chaotic mess. Guilt and shame mixed up with a lot of other unhealthy emotions that she really needs to get a handle on. They aren't helping her, and they won't help the feelings she has for young Jameson. He loves her. That's easy enough to see, but jealousy is a new emotion for him. His behavior scares her and makes her feel even more unworthy of his attention."

She snuffed again and pawed at the ground in a bored fashion. *"The guilt she's feeling now over his injury is tearing apart all the trust and love between them. She needs to be reminded of how they were good for each other. She needs to find her way out of the dark pit of despair and find her way back into the light. Jamey is going to need her before it's all done, and she'll never forgive herself if she lets him down again."*

"That's what I be afraid of and what I be trying to prevent."

"I can help her if she's willing to accept help. Can't help her otherwise."

"Understandable."

Sabbath walked towards him, her massive head looming over him. Leaning down, she nudged his shoulder, encouraging him to wrap an arm around her neck and stroke her softly. The smell of brimstone wafted from her, a subtle reminder that she could fry him with one breath.

"Thank ye, Sabbath."

"For what?"

"For helping me to understand."

"You're welcome."

With one last stroke, he turned and left the stables, striding towards the sanctuary. He and Maddy needed to chat. Taking a chance, he reached out to Kerrygan.

"Where the feck are the two of ye at, and how's she doing?"

"Not far. She's a fecking mess. How's Jamey?"

"We honestly don't know. Rhy couldna stabilize him. His parents and the healers from their tribe arrived and asked us to back off. They were hoping to force a shift."

"Was he strong enough to survive it?"

"I have me doubts. We couldna keep his heart beating on its own, and for all the magic I've seen and helped Rhy perform, she wasna able to keep it going either."

"Feck me. When will ye follow up?"

"They asked us to give them forty-eight hours. They'll call for help if they need it."

"Christ, that's gonna drive her mad, not knowing."

"I suggest ye keep her busy, then."

"I'll do me best. Any suggestions?"

"Take her to the Rusty Tap. I'll meet ye there later tonight."

"Will do."

For feck's sake, he wanted another drink now, but he needed to deal with something else first. His fire drakes snaked around his neck and through his beard, trying to cheer him up. Unfortunately, it wasn't working.

RIVER OF REMEMBRANCE

15

Find Out Who Your Friends Are

Danny knew from the look on Kerrygan's face that he was listening to a conversation she couldn't hear. To be honest, it was one she couldn't find the courage to initiate.

Kerry ran his hand through his hair when he finished. His fingers toyed with the coarser blue streak absently, a new habit he'd developed after years of being trapped as a falcon. Eyes closing for a moment, he took a deep breath before turning to her.

Her heart staggered in her chest.

Kerry's eerie eyes opened and focused on her in abject sorrow, not having the answer that she wanted. As tears filled her eyes once again, he reached out and grasped her face in his hands. "Don't go there, Pixie. Not yet." Thumbs wiping the tears away, he continued. "He's not dead, but he's still unstable."

"Are you sure?"

"Got it straight from Ferg himself."

"Define unstable."

"Rhy couldn't stabilize him. His heart could not beat on its own. They did all they could and were struggling to find something else to try when his clan showed up. His mother insisted they leave Jamey in the hands of her healers and to back off for the next couple of days. They will seek us out if they need additional assistance."

"You're sure he's not dead?"

"They forced him to shift. Now we have to wait for him to heal enough so he can safely shift back. It may take some time for him to reach that stage."

"But he'll live?"

"They're hopeful." Kerrygan refused to lie to her. It would do her no favors, and she'd been through enough the past twenty-four hours. Danny needed food and sleep in that order.

Her head hit his chest, and soft sobs came from her as she clung to him. He wrapped his arms around her once again, pulling her close as he offered her the comfort she sought.

His hand patted her awkwardly. He was out of touch with the emotional world and didn't remember if this was appropriate for what she'd been through. When she cuddled closer, he figured he was doing a decent job.

"Ye love him dontchya, lass?" His voice was soft, reverent.

"I'm not sure if I even know what love is, Kerry."

"Yer wrong, sprite. Ye fiercely loves yer friends and family. Ye've an inkling."

"There are so many ways for me to fuck this up. I have powerful feelings for him, but there are so many ways for us to go wrong, for me to hurt him, or make him hate me." Sad eyes peered up at him. "I couldn't stand for him to hate me."

"I donna think ye could stand to see him walk away or love someone else either. Can ye, Danny?"

"I don't think so, not anymore. Not since the Court of Tears. The way he held and touched me—the way he let me touch him." Her gaze held wonder now as she remembered their time on the beach.

Kerrygan knew what she was talking about because he'd encouraged Jamey to go to her when she was hurting. Kerry knew Jamey was the better man for Danny. He stepped aside to give Jamey the opportunity and to let her see him in a new light.

"Jamey adores ye, lass. He'll be good for ye, if ye let 'em."

"He is a wonderful man, Kerry. I doubt whether I can be what he needs. Some happy endings just aren't meant to be."

"Some endings are choices, Danny. Yer standing on a precipice. Are ye going to step back or step off and take a chance that the free fall will be worth it?"

"Perhaps I'll make another choice and just fly away from it all. I'll remove myself from the worry, guilt, and pain. I could just glide away on a current that takes me far from here with little effort on my part. Start anew as someone else."

"Ye could, Pixie. There's the easy choice. But I've never known ye to be a coward. 'Tis not a good look on ye, lass. I doubt ye'll be able to survive the other choice."

"That's all I've been doing for years, Kerry—surviving." She stared ahead, her gaze haunted. "Maybe I'm just terrified of trying and failing completely. There's too much at stake."

With no answers or words of encouragement left, he kept stroking her back, letting his hand glide from her nape down to her waist.

"We all fail. Just a matter if yer gonna stay down in the muck or keep putting one foot in front of the other."

"What if I'm too tired to keep moving forward?"

"Aw, lass, that's what friends and a bottle of booze be for," he said with a hint of a smile crossing his face.

A slight chuckle vibrated through her. "Good thing I've got those in my back pocket."

"Aye, 'tis a damn fine thing indeed."

16

Darkness My Old Friend

Pain caressed Jameson like a lover, stroking and stoking his skin and nerve endings into a fevered pitch. Instead of a climax that brought him unending pleasure, the waves rolling through his body brought him unending agony. The smallest movement woke the damaged nerves in his body like an angry fire god tap dancing on his skin with spikes attached to his feet.

Time had no meaning. Day or night, there was nothing to show him the difference between the two. Brief moments of lucidity teased him before the darkness rolled him under again like a wave, dragging him below the surface and suffocating him in the current.

Voices drifted in and out of his hearing, and the chanting never stopped, matching the pounding in his head. Different voices led the chants, but the drums and the voices were the one constant, tethering him to his people. His mother's voice and growl comforted him when he felt the healers tending to his wounds. His arms were bound to the table to prevent him re-injuring himself, and though the man in him understood, his animal did not and fought it every time.

Kateri's voice soothed him, and when the pain became too much for her to bear, she sent him into a deep, healing sleep. Soft sobs echoed in his ears as he faded away, and he knew this caused her as much pain emotionally as it did him physically.

Kateri's pain was the keen of a mother unable to help her child—unable to make it better, unable to shoulder the pain for him, unable to hold him because of his injuries. The guilt he already carried compounded every time she wept for him. This cycle repeated every time she forced him to shift from one form to the other so she could gauge his healing.

As his human brain drifted off, his soul wandered from his body. His spirit body rose far above the rough shelter they had created on Singer Island to protect him. He soared above the island, watching the people below scurrying like ants. Jamey glided on the currents like his red-tailed hawk, circling in ever wider passes over the river and islands below him. Searching. Seeking.

The farther he drifted, the less pain he experienced. As he glided, his gaze cast to the thin silver line tethering him to his body. The higher he climbed and the farther he searched, the more fatigued he grew and the thinner his tether became. His sole mission was to find her and make sure she was alright.

Danyka was all he needed, but even on this plane, he realized he might have messed up any chance he could have once had with her. His head canted to the side as his eyes picked up a familiar sight on the riverbank in the distance. Hopeful, he headed towards her—or rather he tried to. The harder he tried to get to her, the heavier he felt. With a frustrated shriek from his hawk, he gave in to the tugging sensation on his lifeline and allowed himself to be drawn back into his body.

As he descended, he studied the chalky coloring of the man below and struggled to see himself in the mauled flesh. His body was healing on the surface, skin neatly stitched, and his breathing more stable, but the extensive damage to his arm was obvious. Whether he would ever have full use of his arm again was questionable.

Jamey hoped so because he needed both arms to hold on to his hellion once he caught her again.

Kateri Vance sat back with an exhausted exhale, arms shaking from the effort it took to keep her son still. Dreams tormented him, and he thrashed in his sleep, trying to release the restraints.

Thankfully, his wounds were no longer life-threatening. Unfortunately for Jamey, though, his journey was far from over. The healers stopped the bleeding and repaired his organs, but the amount of damage to his muscles and tendons would take time and therapy to heal properly. The price for his impulsiveness would be boundless pain and hours of suffering.

"Tomorrow, we'll invite Mistress Cairn to join us," she said to Kuruk. "We've done all we can do, and we're exhausted. The Warden is an amazing healer, and her visit will give us an opportunity to rest and recharge."

Thick arms wrapped around her from behind, pulling her back tightly to his chest as he settled behind her. "That's all we can do, honey. His survival is up to the Creator. May she be merciful."

"Yes, may she grant us this favor." A laugh erupted from her. "And may he be less stubborn than he usually is."

Kuruk smiled against her neck before placing a soft kiss there. "He gets that from your side of the family."

An outraged gasp and the glare she shot his way made him laugh, but it was the laughter in his eyes that made her lean back and settle into his shoulder. "I can own that, but he gets his recklessness from your side."

"I've only ever been reckless in one thing, Kat."

"Really? What's that?"

"Same thing that has him in knots."

Turning so she could see him better, she asked again, her voice barely a whisper, "What's that?"

"My family." He kissed her on the forehead. "And my mate."

"So, you're reckless in love, then?"

"Yeah, but you've known that for a long time. Don't act all surprised."

"I'm not surprised, Kuruk." Luminous dark eyes held his for a long time before she palmed his neck and pulled his lips to hers for a soft kiss of gratitude born from a lifetime spent together. "I'm grateful you were reckless and loved me."

"No choice involved. First time I looked into your eyes; I was gone."

"Not gone. I found you and claimed you."

"Wouldn't want it any other way."

"Me neither."

Kateri turned, settling into the arms of the man she loved—the man who'd given her three wonderful boys to raise. Surrounded by his love and support, she studied her eldest son and wondered what it would take for him to claim the woman he loved. With a heavy sigh and an ache in her heart for them, she wondered if Danyka would give him the chance to love her, or if the little girl in her would trample over his feelings in the attempt to flee her past.

The answer eluded her, but a growl rumbled in her chest when she thought of the pain this woman might cause him. Restless, her mind contemplated the potential pitfalls these two souls were bound to encounter. A single tear tracked down her cheek as she realized there was nothing she could do to stop it or to help them. This journey was one her son would need to make on his own. Every painful, heartbreaking step.

Kuruk's arms tightened around her, knowing the dark paths her thoughts were traveling. "Don't worry, my love. We'll be here to help him every step of the way. Jamey won't go through this alone."

Kateri wasn't sure about that, but the feather-soft brush of his lips against her hair soothed her, and she knew that with him by her side, they would all survive this. Now if she could only convince Danny to be here by Jamey's side.

17

Be Right Back

"Can't stay here forever," Kerrygan said.

Danyka was curled up on his lap again. He was leaning against the massive trunk of an ancient maple tree. Their view of the St. Lawrence was unhindered, and he knew watching the waves and passing ships was therapeutic for her.

"Can," she said simply, curling up smaller.

Lips twitching into a half-assed smile, he tried reasoning with her. "I'm loving the feel of you in my arms, darling, but I'se just thinking it might be a little less awkward if I had a pair of pants on. Yer bony ass is digging into me sensitive bits."

Violet-blue eyes flew to his, and he could've sworn she blushed, but she'd never been the shy type. Body stiffening in his arms, she tried to jerk away, but he continued holding her. "Relax, just didn't want ye breaking anything off if it responded to yer position." A smile ghosted across her face, then was gone the moment he recognized it.

"I can't go back there yet."

"I ken. If I leave ye here jest long enough to fetch us clothes and some food, will ye promise to wait here fer me?"

Her eyes examined the ground beneath them. "Not sure I can promise that."

"Where do ye plan to go looking like that, lass?"

A quick glance reminded her of her nudity. A long sigh escaped her. Haunted eyes stared at him for a long time before she spoke. "You can't shift again so soon. Rhy will skin you alive."

"I ken, and I donna plan on it. I'll have a stable boy bring me a horse near to here so I can return quickly." He tipped her head up to meet his eyes.

"I be right back, I promise, lass. Alone."

A brief nod gave him her word.

"Clothes, food, water, drink—pick yer poison or suffer with what I bring back."

"Don't care. Not much of an appetite or desire to drink at the moment."

"Ye need to sleep, lass. Try n catch a nap whilst I'm gone." His lips brushed against the top of her head. "Mayhap later, we can go to the Tap and play pool."

A noncommittal shrug was all he received. Gently, he lifted her and set her against the tree as he stood and let the blood flow back into his legs. Waves of pins and needles assaulted him from his hips to his toes. He bit his tongue to squash any sound of distress he might utter and tried not to dance around from the agony. He didn't want her to refuse his comfort in the future because she caused him pain.

"I won't be long, lass. Wait here. Yer too exhausted to shift again until ye've fed and slept. Please don't do anything stupid."

"Good advice coming from you," she said.

A dark chuckle rose in him at her irony. Legs jerking, he hobbled away until he was far enough from her sight and hearing that he could bend over and attempt to encourage the blood to rush back into his extremities.

Needing assistance, he reached out to Ferg.

"Ye busy, Ferg?"

"Where ye two at?"

"Don't worry about that. I need yer help."

His words surprised Fergus because Kerrygan never reached out for help. The falcon had earned his reputation as a loner.

"Whatchya need, brother?"

"Meet me at the end of the western trail with a horse and supplies. Need changes of clothes for both of us, food for a few days, water, a couple bottles of something to kill the pain, coats, and blankets."

"Sounds like yer moving out."

"No, man, jest giving her the space she needs and the freedom she needs to take it. Danny's not ready to face any of ye right now."

"Understandable. Anything else we can do? She won't even respond to Rhy?"

"Nye. If she thinks yer close, she'll bolt. Give her some space for a few days to process and deal with the guilt she's drowning in."

"We won't make it worse for her—won't accuse her or any of that horse shite."

Kerry knew how close Danny was with Jamey and Ferg. Hurt radiated through the man's words. *"I ken, ye won't. She needs to put it right in her head afore she talks about it with anyone, including me. Don't go getting yer knickers in a twist."*

"Feck ye. Who do ye think was here for her all those years when ye sat trapped in a fecking cage?" He paused, daring Kerry to answer him. *"Me. I be the one who put her back together night after night. I kept her entertained and out of fecking trouble most*

nights. Some, I joined her in. So don't ye fecking dare be fecking condescending with me, ye li'l fecker, or next time ye trap yerself in a form ye can't shift back from, I'll clip yer wings."

Kerry almost laughed, but he did na trust the fire-haired mage not to put a hex on him. *"I hear ye, man. This isn't me choice, nor request. Remember, this is about what she needs, not what we want. This has torn her the feck up in ways I've never seen afore. Give her some goddamn space for a night or two. Tis alls I be asking. Have some fecking compassion. She kens what she needs to answer for, and she will. Just not today. Tell Maddy that for me, won't ye? She can get in line and holler at me later when Rhy's done beating the shite outta me. Ye ought to enjoy watching the show."*

A dark chuckle traversed their inner line, making Kerry smile despite the situation. *"Yer right. Much as I hate to admit it, yer right."* Silence settled for the next few minutes. *"Mrs. O'Hare is setting up food and beverages for the two of ye and providing decent bedding. She's sending Lily to retrieve clothing for Danny, and I'll go fetch what ye need. Any requests?"*

"Nothing pink, ye bastard."

"I'll be sure to find ye some na."

"Figured ye would."

"All right, I'll see ye soon."

"Ferg, thank ye. Yer helping her more than ye realize by just doing this. Thank ye."

Kerry stomped his feet until they lost the sense of pins and needles. A few tentative steps guaranteed he wouldn't end up on his ass, so he made his way down the hill to find the trail he was about to meet Ferg on, looking forward to some decent food, clothes, and a much-needed drink to soothe his dark, troubled soul.

18

Your Well Being is Important to Me

Kai Tyde knelt on the dock behind what was once a boathouse. The site currently housed a treatment center for injured river mammals. The water mages oversaw the facility and also used it as a training station for students during the summer.

At the moment, Kai only had a few charges to care for. A rather portly beaver was sleeping off a rough night after tangling himself in some fishing line near the shore. After a few more days of attention, he would be ready to depart.

The pen next to him on the left held a pair of muskrats the Romani patrol rescued from a poacher's trap. Dehydrated and nearly starving to death, they were making a slow recovery.

On the right, Sir Waddles a lot, as Kai dubbed the beaver, was accompanied by an elderly mink. His coat was various shades of brown with auburn highlights and a few gray streaks sneaking in around his muzzle. Shy most of his teeth and with a bum leg, he kept glancing at the muskrats and smacking his lips. They were his favorite meal in his younger years, but the only thing they had to fear from him today was wishful thinking.

Adopted as their resident pet, the mink relied on the kindness of the Sanctuary to provide him with sustenance. A tendency to hiss at anyone within hearing distance earned him the name of Grumpy—everyone, that is, except for Kai. He loved the young man and waited anxiously for the day to end so that he could perch on the lad's broad shoulders while they watched the sunset over the river.

River otters chittered at Kai from the dock. Frolicking in the morning fog, they encouraged him to join them for a swim. He tossed them some treats and looked around.

A prince of the Court of Tears, Kai was incredibly empathic and in tune with those around him. The gift was a curse more times than not, but he appreciated the ability to sense anyone nearby. Everyone emitted an emotional signature, and most people gave off a strong imprint.

He opened himself up psychically, and finding no evidence of early risers, he stripped where he stood behind the boathouse. The riverbanks were quiet this early in the morning. Sunrise was his favorite time of the day. He never missed the opportunity for a swim before the day began.

A light breeze scattered his wheat-colored hair. It hung below his shoulders in soft waves when it wasn't tightly braided. Lighter blond highlights were visible because of the time he worked in the sun. Sun-bronzed skin set off his deep–set, pale blue eyes. High cheekbones and a square jaw were more pronounced by twin dimples accenting the package. Oblivious to the effect he had on women and shy, Kai avoided them, even though he attracted more than his fair share.

Reaching over his head, he pulled off his shirt with one hand before reaching for the laces of his breeches. Stepping out of them, he stretched his arms overhead and executed a perfect dive. Midway to the water, his legs transformed into a single bifurcated tail covered in scales that matched the river's muddy green color.

Mermaids and their freshwater cousins, rivermaids, were common in water shifters. Of his four siblings, Kyran and his only sister, Klaree, were the only others in his generation blessed with the ability to shift. Not everyone was born with the ability or the magic to shift. The youngest of the Tyde boys and a grandson of Neptune, he was a merman, a much larger version of his freshwater counterparts. He could tolerate freshwater or saltwater when he shifted.

The north Atlantic was the playground he'd grown up in. He swam daily to assuage his need to commune with his primary element. Kai loved the feel of racing through the water as a merman. On a free day, he would spend hours in the river learning its secrets. He had mapped out miles around the Heart Island Sanctuary and was ready to scout farther out.

Working with his brother Kyran and representing the Water Clan at the Sanctuary, he was proud of the work they did. With the summer session about to begin, he was a little nervous about the teaching aspect. Shy, he didn't enjoy public speaking, but Kyran assured him he wouldn't have to do very much of it.

The St. Lawrence differed from the Atlantic beyond the obvious freshwater versus salt. The unique species and animals who called it home fascinated him. Every day, he learned something new and cataloged a new plant or animal species he'd found while exploring.

Moving easily and swiftly through the water because of his size, he covered the perimeter of the island, as he did every morning. He took his

time checking the sigils and glyphs of protection he and Kyran maintained for the safety of those who called this place home.

Besides educating the students who would arrive soon, water mages handled the security of the island from the water. Swimming around the east side of the island, he saw a small shape walking into the water.

A tiny thing barely five feet tall, Genny looked like a child standing in the shallows. Chestnut brown hair framed a heart-shaped face. A dimple accented her dainty chin, and the mysterious sorrows in the depths of her hazel eyes held your attention.

They'd only recently met. He'd accidentally terrified her in the Apothecary Shoppe when he'd stopped to see Rhyanna. Genny cowered before him, unable to move or stop shaking. Her reaction broke his heart as much as it stirred his interest. Her fear incited a fierce need within him to protect her and make her feel secure in the world she lived in.

No wonder he terrified her. Kai was nearly six-seven, with a heavily muscled chest and torso tapering into a narrow waist and thick thighs. He had a warrior's build and the training to match.

Wearing nothing more than a simple shift, she waded in facing him. With the sun rising behind him, he wasn't sure if she could see him yet. Trusting that she couldn't, he let himself float and studied her.

The water temperature this early in the year would be cold to her. His body temperature always ran higher when he shifted to protect him from hypothermia. For a non-shifter, it would be nippy this morning. A light fog rose from the surrounding water, giving her an ethereal appearance.

Kai studied her as his body responded to the sight of her slight body beneath the damp shift. Cursing, he pushed aside his physical attraction to her.

The wardens had rescued Genny from a human trafficking ring. He doubted she would have any interest in intimacy any time soon. And she was young—younger than him by a couple of years, but her circumstances didn't change the way he felt about her.

Kai was always good with things that required a gentle touch. Genny intrigued him, and he couldn't help wondering how she survived when so many others didn't. He wanted the opportunity to spend more time with her—get to know her better.

Loud chittering alerted him to his playful companions. He'd forgotten they were swimming with him. A mother otter floated on her back with her little one lying on her belly as she clutched her breakfast. She bit the head off a frog and then offered the rest to Kai. Chuckling, he declined. "No thank you, little mama. Your wee one will enjoy the rest." The otter scolded him and finished the meal.

Kai sensed the instant Genny realized she wasn't alone. Panic overwhelmed his senses as she froze in the water up to her chest. Her eyes darted towards the horizon and behind her to the shore, trying to decide where the laughter came from and which direction would be her safest option to flee.

Attempting to ease her mind, he spoke. "Mistress Genevieve, it's Kai. I'm sorry to have startled you. I thought you could see me."

A hand came up to shade her eyes as she sought him in the rising sun. A partial smile crossed her face, turning her features from ordinary into heart-stopping. Her smile welcomed him, and he couldn't help the wide grin that crossed his face. Taking a chance, he moved closer, wanting to spend some time with her.

"You're out awfully early," he said, stating the obvious.

"I love swimming while the sun rises." Her eyes darted shyly to her hands, twisting in the water.

"The cold doesn't bother you, mistress?"

"Never. I prefer it cool."

A playful splash sounded behind him, and a dozen little faces peeked around him at her.

"You have company?" she asked with a laugh, glancing up at him.

"They seem to have adopted me when I do my morning rounds."

"I've always wished to swim with the otters, but they never trusted me enough." Her eyes met his, and an electrical current passed between them. Kai knew she felt it as well because her cheeks flushed a deep shade of pink.

Her previous comments made him curious. "Mistress, are you, by chance, a rivermaid?"

"Please call me Genny," she said, gazing down at her hands in the water. "Once, long ago, my grandmother thought I might be, but so much has changed for me since then…"

Her voice faded, and there was an undercurrent of sadness that he heard in it. Empathetically, he could feel her sorrow for all the things she wouldn't get to do now because of the situation fate forced her into.

"Would you like to learn? I believe I could teach you." His words were gentle. He wasn't arrogant with the claim, just matter-of-fact.

Hazel eyes flew to his in surprise. "You'd be willing?"

Heart racing, he gave her a nod and said with all sincerity, "It would be my honor."

Genny felt the undercurrent of his emotions in the same way he felt hers. Her elemental training had been neglected during her incarceration, but her soul longed to move through the water as effortlessly as he did.

As quickly as her enthusiasm rose, it deflated. "I don't think I would be able to. I missed my session to train, and I'm too old to start now." Her voice cracked with sorrow.

Kai had been gliding toward her during their conversation. "It's never too late to learn, and it's not safe for you or those around you if you're not properly trained. When you have the time and want to try, all you have to do is ask me."

A hint of a smile returned, and her eyes flew to the otters playing behind them.

"Would you like to join them?" he asked her, holding out a hand and begging her silently to take it. What he was really asking was, *Will you trust me?*

A deep, shuddering breath left her body as her eyes closed tightly. Kai's hopes deflated, sure she was about to say no.

Luminous hazel eyes flew open and latched on to his. "Can you teach me how to be brave, Kai? Can you help me overcome my fear of almost everything?" A pitiful laugh accompanied her last request.

Kai's heart ached watching her struggle to face her demons. Slowly, he moved closer, close enough to touch but floating in place with enough space to make her comfortable. "I don't know if I can help you overcome all your fears, Genny. We all have fears we carry with us throughout our lives."

He stretched out his hand to her, palm up. "If you will take a chance on me, I promise to help you swim with the otters, and I promise to help you learn to shift if that's what you want." His hand lay between them, floating on the water, waiting for her to move.

His pale blue eyes filled with sincerity as he stared into her frightened hazel ones. "I can promise to never hurt you, Genny. Not by my words or by my deeds. I will never raise a hand to you in anger, and I will protect you with my life if necessary. Your well-being is important to me."

"How can I mean anything to you?" Honest confusion lingered in her eyes, perplexed that he would offer his friendship with no strings attached. "Until I came here, no one ever showed me kindness or bothered with me at all, until I possessed something of value…"

Involuntarily, she flinched. "What do you want from me in return?" she asked in a sad whisper.

Words softly spoken faded off as she finished, but Kai heard every syllable, every nuance, and the hurt in them. The effort to remain calm and not tense his muscles in anger at how life had treated her was a challenge. He wanted to reach out and stroke her hair or touch her face, but he didn't want to scare her. The question she asked was like a slap as he realized what she was referring to.

"I can't answer that, Genny, only that I long to see you smile more." An otter slapped its tail in agreement, and they both laughed at him. Kai raised his hand to her, trying once more. "I don't want anything from you. I was hoping we could be friends. Because other than Kyr, I don't really have

anyone my age to talk to. But I don't ever want you to feel pressured." With a sweet smile, he tried one last time. "Will you join us for a swim?"

Big hazel eyes held more than sorrow. A hint of hope shone through, warming him. She gazed up at him and, finding the courage to reach for his hand, trusted him to care for her.

Her tiny hand shook as she placed it in his, but she didn't pull back. His heart stopped at her simple act because he knew he was looking at his future. As Genny gave him her hand, Kai was on the verge of handing her his heart.

Giving her the full force of his smile, he pulled her farther into the river as the otters danced around them. The sleek creatures circled her, stopping for a moment and allowing her to pet them. Her laughter exploded, transforming her. The unabashed smile and sound unmasked her sheer beauty while holding his hand under the morning sky.

They frolicked for a while, still holding hands, his large one helping her to stay afloat without expending too much energy. She was still regaining her strength after helping with Jamey's injuries, and he didn't want to wear her out.

"We better head back. I still need to complete my rounds."

Instantly, she looked chagrined. "I'm sorry I've kept you for so long. It was purely selfish of me."

"Genny, it was my pleasure, and I left early, so no harm done."

"Did you mean it when you said you might help me shift?" Her eyes kept surreptitiously going to his tail. "It's so beautiful, you can barely see it in the water unless the sun hits it just right." Her eyes traveled over the scales coming up over his hips and dipping to the v beneath his navel. "I can't imagine what they must feel like."

Her free hand reached out, but then she caught herself, jerking it back tightly against her side. Kai reached for her free hand, but she shook her head, so he pulled her closer with the hand he still held until she was treading water directly in front of him.

Her gaze locked onto his as she tried not to hyperventilate. He let her drift there, not pulling her body any closer. Placing the hand he held onto his waist, he released it, wanting her to have complete control. "You're welcome to touch me if you'd like." Kai said softly, holding his breath and not moving a muscle as her eyes widened. Her tiny hand flexed against his side. "I can't quite describe the way it feels. They are just an extension of my skin," he said.

Still watching him, weighing his words and intentions, she moved her hand against the smooth skin of his waist. His muscles flexed beneath her hand, and the sound of his sharp inhale nearly had her fleeing, but he held still.

The movement of the water beneath him caressed her legs as his long tail moved slowly, keeping him afloat. Fingers spreading, she covered more surface area with her hand and let her fingertips trace the water trailing down his skin. When she reached the edge of his scales, the texture surprised her. They weren't rough like fish scales were. No, they were like touching heavy silk. Smooth and sensuous under her fingers, she watched as the colors changed, darkening beneath her hand.

Kai held his breath, willing his body not to react the way it naturally wanted to. Her innocent explorations were killing him, and he thanked all the sea gods that his cock was not in a position to react and scare her away. Heat pooled in his groin from the sensation of her touch, forcing him to chain his body's reaction to it. Reacting to her sexually would be the one thing that would make her run as fast and as far as she could, and he would not get another chance with her.

Fascinated, she moved her hand down the side of what would be his leg and watched the colors changing and merging. Biting her lip, she glanced up at him and saw the change in his eyes. One emotion she recognized easily was desire, and she could see the flames banked in his eyes. She froze, pushing her rising fear down as she assessed the situation.

Kai blinked, and the look was gone. A small smile emerged, and he asked her, "Not what you expected?"

"Nye, not at all. They are so soft and sleek. Do they change color with temperature or with touch?" She responded without having a panic attack, boldly asking what she wanted to know.

"They react to a variety of stimulation," he said. Needing to change the topic, he offered her his hand again, asking silently if she was ready to return.

Genny took it without hesitation, knowing deep down that she could trust this man with her well-being and wanting to find out if she could trust him with more.

19

Ain't Gonna Force This One

Fergus was heading in to confront Maddy when Kerrygan's request had him turning back to the stables for a pair of horses. Gathering the supplies, the Sanctuary's matron, Mrs. O'Hare, arranged for him, he made a quick run up to Kerry's quarters. He snagged a couple of changes of clothes, a leather duster, and a pair of boots.

Grateful to get away with no one seeing or stopping him, he made his way to the western trail. Kerry dropped like an evil little troll from the limb of a tree he'd been perched on.

Ferg handed him the reins of a spare horse, and Kerry hobbled the animal. A quick search through the saddlebags rewarded him with his clothing. Donning them, he tugged on his boots and opened a basket of provisions.

The smell of the fresh bread made his stomach growl. He ripped a piece of French bread off, then shoved a chunk of cheese into it. With a moan of pleasure, he devoured it. Kerry perused the flasks until he found the one with Irish whiskey. He finished his bread and followed it with a long swig of liquor. Sated, he leaned his head against the saddle and took his first deep breath since he and Danny had arrived on the cliff.

"Rough night?" Ferg asked in a somber tone.

"Ye've no fecking idea what it is to see her in such a state. It goes against everything ye believe her to be. Her strength and formidable personality don't prepare ye for her to just be a terrified woman worried about the man who owns her heart."

"She loves him, but will it ever be enough for her to give them a chance?" Ferg pondered.

"Don't know. She's still fighting against how she ain't good enough and how it's all her fault he got hurt."

"She needs to let that shite go," Ferg said, shaking his head.

"I ken that, ye ken that, but she needs to come around to it on her own. Ain't gonna force this one, Ferg. No matter how we might want to shove them along." His hand rubbed his tired eyes. "Any news on the lad?"

"Nye, not yet."

"Keep us posted," Kerry said as he swung up into the saddle.

"Will do."

Fergus watched him trot off, and he desperately wanted to follow him into the forest. Fighting the urge to see Danyka for himself, he cursed. The lass needed someone to make her see the foolishness she was feeling for what it was. He wanted to reassure her that Jamey would be just fine. Might gain a few fresh scars and a helluva story, but the lad would be fine.

The pixie, small though she might be, was one of the strongest members of their family. If she fell, the rest of them might damn well follow and then where the feck would they be?

Pulling on the reins, he turned his beast around and headed back the way he'd come. On the return trip, he allowed his mount to run, and he enjoyed the feeling of freedom it allowed him.

After his midnight ride on Sabbath the night of Jamey's attack, Ferg felt like he was standing still. The exhilaration of riding her had been indescribable, and he longed to do it again. He was fecked in the head to crave more time with the hell bitch, but his thoughts kept wandering to her, marveling at her deep intelligence and rapier wit.

Hell, she was the female equine version of him. Laughing out loud at that, he slowed as he neared the stables. Handing off his mount to the stable boy, he fought the urge to visit her because he'd put off his reckoning with Madylyn long enough. Might as well get this over with and take his whipping like a good boy. Damn good thing he'd never minded a little pain.

20

Decisions Not Yours to Make

Fergus sauntered into Madylyn's office as if he wanted to be there. Maddy glanced up at him from her desk. Her stern expression conveyed her irritation with him and with everything that had gone wrong over the past twenty-four hours.

"Help yourself to a drink and take a seat." She tipped her head toward the wingback chairs in front of her desk. Ronan sat in one, waiting patiently for the show to begin.

Ferg took advantage of the offer and poured himself a double. The whiskey burned all the way down, the way it should on a day like today. Another deep swig and his belly burned like his throat. A quick refill and he took his place as directed.

Steepling her hands under her chin, Maddy watched him with cool eyes. Fergus had been with her at the Sanctuary almost from the beginning. They might not always agree, but they held a deep affection and mutual respect for each other that they always tried to maintain.

"Tell me what happened last night," Maddy said in a calm voice that surprised him. He'd expected to receive the sharp edge of her tongue, which he was quite familiar with, but she threw him off guard with her cool patience.

"After I had a wee bit of a tantrum…" Ferg said.

"Which, before I forget, you need to apologize to the staff for your behavior," Maddy said, passing on Mrs. O'Hare's message.

"Yes, I be seeing to that in the morning." Head cocked, he waited to see if she was done with the reprimand. Steel-gray eyes gave her the same cool stare until she nodded for him to continue.

"Sabbath appeared—or rather, a miniature version of her appeared—in the flames of me hearth. I thought at first it was just another form of me fire drakes until I heard her voice in me mind."

"What did she have to say?"

"Ye gonna let me tell this or not?" Eyebrow quirked, he glared at her.

"Sorry. Go on." Maddy didn't look the least bit sorry.

"Ye need context to understand why I made the decisions I did, luv. I'se not be trying to avoid the conversation."

"Touché."

"I was raging at me gods, who were choosing to ignore me. Perhaps it was the disrespectful way in which I approached them, or mayhap they were napping or merely drunk. Who the feck kens?"

He ran a hand through his hair, pulling on the top until it stood up like a porcupine. "Regardless, I wasn't having one of me finer moments, as ye all were aware of. Not knowing if Jamey lived or died,"

His voice cracked, and he swallowed hard before continuing his tale, "it broke something vital inside me." The glass shook in his hand as he raised it to his lips. Finishing the last of the amber fire, he continued.

"She bid me to come down and join her. Curious—and in all honesty, because the bitch wouldn't back down and damn near caught me rug on fire—I went down. Her offer to diffuse the horrors of the day and absorb the negative emotions I was drowning in was beyond tempting."

Standing, he strode to the bar and returned with the bottle and another glass for Ronan.

"Shoulda done this from the get-go," Fergus said.

Refilling his glass, then draining it halfway, fortified him enough to continue.

"You ain't gonna fecking believe this, Maddy, but when I exited the foyer, Sabbath knelt down for me to mount her." He shook his head, still amazed. "The NightMare Queen kneels for no one."

"You're joking." Ronan couldn't conceal his shock. He and Maddy had helped Sabbath deliver a set of twins that were breech. Their relationship with the queen of the NightMares had improved since then, but the massive beast hadn't offered him a ride.

"Nye, I be fecking serious as can be," Fergus said. A broad grin crossed his face. "As I mounted her bareback, she told me she couldn't gain access to anything I didn't want her to see. I'se in complete control of what she could absorb."

"Did it work?" Ronan asked.

"Aye, I still could feel the sorrow and rage, but she muted it. I could reason through it as well. I could figure out a plan of action instead of wallowing in grief."

"What other privileges did you allow her?" Maddy asked in a sharp tone.

Ferg shuffled uncomfortably in his chair. "I gave her authorization to siphon from Rhyanna so that she could heal, should she need to. The toll of

not helping Jamey and her worry about Danny and Kerrygan were tearing her apart." He knew it sounded like he was justifying his actions, but he couldn't change the facts as they were.

"Who else did you give her permission to access?" Maddy's midnight eyes had blue flames showing her banked rage.

Ferg couldn't maintain eye contact. Ronan tensed in the chair next to him, and Ferg knew damn well that he was going to catch hell for this part most of all. Clearing his throat, he said, "To protect yer child, I allowed her to take a smidge from ye as well."

Maddy's face blanched as she looked over at Ronan. Fear crossed her face, and unease settled in Fergus's gut.

"I understand the choices you made for Rhyanna, although you should have gained her permission first. Fergus, you made decisions that were not yours to make."

Her fury was palpable, and Fergus knew she was keeping it in check by a thin thread. He hung his head, aware that this was not good for her pregnancy any more than her devastation over Jamey had been.

Voice rising, she continued, "You are never that irresponsible. We don't know what pathways you may have allowed that hell bitch to create with the three of us. You had no right to risk my unborn child in your experiment without at least consulting Ronan or me beforehand. If you wanted to experiment with this creature and take a chance on your mental health, that's your choice, but you had no right accepting for the rest of us. We don't know what you have unleashed or if she's able to warp our minds like she did to so many others when she first arrived." She shook her head in disbelief as tears pooled in her eyes. "How can you trust her?"

Ferg refused to look away from her. The biggest emotion emanating from her besides disbelief was fear, and he could understand why.

Maddy had suffered a mid-term miscarriage centuries ago, and he could understand her misgivings, but her mistrust in his decision stung.

Coming to his feet, he made his way around the desk to her. Maddy turned in her chair to face him. Tears she was fighting not to shed hovered in her midnight blue eyes. Ronan, God bless him, stayed where he was, giving Ferg the opportunity to redeem himself.

Fergus's eyes locked on hers as he lowered himself to his knees and took her delicate hands in his massive paws. "Do ye truly believe I'd do *anything* to endanger ye or the wee bairn growing inside of ye?" A gentle squeeze of her hands encouraged her to be honest with him. "Maddy, luv, ye ken me better than anyone else here."

The luminous gaze holding his wavered, and the first drop rolled down her cheek. Her head shook back and forth. "No, Ferg, I don't believe it would ever be your intention, but I've seen so many good intentions turn

into disasters and devastation. It's hard to believe anything good will come out of this nightmare."

"Ye helped deliver Sabbath's foals. She's already bonded with ye more than ye realize. I donna think she would endanger them either by harming ye or yers."

The sight of her tears replaced the anger and frustration he'd arrived here with, with an overwhelming sense of protectiveness for this woman who was like a sister to him—closer than a sibling could be. It hurt him to see her this way.

His large palms cradled her face, wiping away her tears. "I promise thee I will procure a guarantee from the lady that no harm shall come to any of ours or our allies. I believe the queen to be honorable."

Maddy nodded at him, then burst into sobs, throwing her arms around his neck. He hugged her tight to him as she tried to speak. "What are we gonna do if he doesn't make it, Ferg? I don't know if Danny will survive this. I don't know how any of us will ever be the same without either of them in our world."

Ferg wrapped her in his arms, letting her cry and realizing this was what was behind all her fears today. It was the same thing that was making him so volatile. His eyes cut to Ronan, and it was a testament to the man's control as he allowed Ferg to comfort Maddy when every inch of him was tense with the urge to do the same.

"I honestly believe that he will be well, Maddy. I do."

He rocked her against him for a few moments more before releasing her. "I do na want yer man offended by me hands all over ye, luv." He stood and gestured to Ronan. "She's all yers. Thank ye for yer self-control."

Ronan stepped to the desk, pausing toe to toe with Ferg. "You damn well better be right about Sabbath. If anything happens to either of them, I'll hold you personally responsible. You hear me?"

"Loud and clear, and I would na expect anything less from ye." They stared at each other for a few moments more, Ferg's height not intimidating Ronan in the least.

Ronan nodded sharply at him. "Good." He plucked Maddy from her chair, sitting with her curled up on his lap. His hand stroked her back while he placed a kiss on her forehead.

As Ferg headed for the door, Ronan sent him a private message. *"I agree with you. I don't think she would intentionally hurt any of us, but what worries me is not knowing what it would take to push her buttons and shift her from our ally to our enemy. Get that accord with her if you want my support."*

"Working on it. Might be interested to know that she doesn't need to link individually with us to know what's going on. When I sought her out after our meeting,

she told me nearly verbatim what we discussed in here. The power she possesses is immense and fecking terrifying if we can't harness it and keep her in check." Fergus said.

"You fucking with me?"

"No sir, just educating ye. That's me whole point, Ronan. We need to know how to collaborate with her, and we have to understand her abilities. I don't think she remains here because we've drawn a few glyphs around her paddock. She's here for a reason, and we need to understand and exploit how that helps the Sanctuary. Sabbath also offered her services to carry out Island Law. I'm curious to see what she has in mind. When Maddy calms down, I believe she will see the benefits of a parlay with Sabbath. Ye'll ken when best to approach her with it."

"I'll do what I can. Thanks for filling me in on what you found out." Ronan said.

"I intended to this morning until I went on the defensive."

"Well, now that your knickers are no longer twisted…" A chuckle floated through their line.

"Mayhap me balls can relax again since she's done squeezing the life out of them."

Ronan's laughter followed him out of the room. Taking the stairs two at a time, he headed for his suite, needing a shower, clean clothes, food, and a bottle of his uncle's finest whiskey. After a good night's sleep, he'd have a better perspective and, gods willing, news about Jamey.

21

Rosella Diaries
Seventh Entry

Rosella Gallagher gazed at herself in the looking glass, barely recognizing the young woman staring back. Months had passed since fate upended the life, she once took for granted, taking with it her innocence. Yanking a brush through her strawberry blond hair, she tried not to think of life before her abduction.

Ella—as she was now known—remained alert, always looking for a means to escape. She smiled and did as they asked, even if it meant learning the fine art of pleasing a man. Lessons so far provided Ella and the other young women trapped in this hell with an education in the subtleties of oral sex, art, and etiquette. Pearl, the woman who purchased her, prepared her girls for the life of a high-paid escort—or, as Ella thought of them, whores.

Pearl acquired virgins for her elite clientele. She provided young women and boys with unparalleled skills and discipline for those seeking unspoiled wares in the dark circles. With their training completed, owners displayed their wares in a showcase to tease interested buyers. Eventually, they auctioned off their young charges to the highest bidder.

Ella tried not to think about what came after the sale of her virginity or what the rest of her life might be like. Would she be nothing more than a vessel for nameless men to take advantage of?

The other reason she didn't dwell on the future was that she still possessed hope. She'd been able to astral travel to her family, and they knew how close she was to being auctioned off. Ella still had faith that her brother, Roarke, and her maman would save her. Her maman was a powerful elemental with assistance on both sides of the veil. Catalina Gallagher had successfully reached Rosella once before when she was first abducted. But the toll had been high, and she was still recovering from the

effort. Ella noticed the long-term effects on her when she last visited the astral plane.

A soft knock on the door brought her back to the present. It wasn't Shaelynn, her maid, because she never knocked. Braden, her guard, answered the door. A chill ran through her. Ella prayed it wasn't Pearl or Jonah, her owners.

Braden opened the door and let Gemma in. A lanky wisp of a girl with dark red hair, Gemma was the only girl who had ever spoken to Ella. Ella wasn't sure if they forbid friendships or if everyone was too terrified to bring any attention to themselves. This visit was a surprise, and Ella wasn't sure if it was a good one or not.

Startling forest green eyes with gold flecks caught her gaze, taking away from the slightly crooked nose and thin lips. She was an exquisite creature, even with imperfections, mayhap because of them.

With a shy smile, Gemma said, "I hope I'm not bothering you."

"No bother at all. Have a seat."

"I can't stay, but I wondered if you'd like to have tea with me after our lessons?"

Ella was stunned by the invitation. She glanced at Braden, wondering how to respond. A slight nod gave her the answer she needed.

"Yes, that would be lovely. Thank you for asking," Ella said.

A wide smile lit up Gemma's face. "It will be nice to have something to look forward to."

"Yes, it will."

Gemma turned for the door, waiting for Braden to open it for her.

Ella watched her leave, waiting for the lock to click in place before speaking. "Are we allowed to make friends?" she asked her guard.

"Pearl doesn't forbid it," he said neutrally, but his eyes cautioned her.

"What aren't you saying?" she asked, placing a hand on his arm. "Please." His arm tensed under her hand, and she heard the sharp intake of his breath.

"The only advice I can give you, Ella, is to trust no one."

Ella gazed at him, her expression a mixture of confusion and fear. "Not even you?"

His expression softened, and he cupped the side of her face. "I will never betray or hurt you, Ella. Never."

"Shaelynn?" she asked, questioning the loyalty of her chatterbox maid.

"I believe we can trust her as well."

"But you're not sure?"

"I'm as sure as one can be in these circumstances. She and I became friends before your arrival, and I do not believe she would do anything to harm me."

His thumb traced her jawline. "She knows I care for you, which puts all of us in danger. I doubt she will take a chance of spreading tales to anyone." He smiled tightly at her. "She genuinely likes you."

"I don't think she would either," Ella said. "I like her too."

Her hand came up and covered his. "I have feelings for you as well." She turned and pressed a kiss into his palm before stepping back. He hissed in a breath, and his hand fisted as it dropped to his side.

"Be careful who you confide in," he said once again. "There's too much to lose."

The rest of the day passed quickly. Lessons in paying attention to your partner's cues, followed by piano and French, were finally over. After lunch in the dining room, she returned to her suite.

Shaelynn had arranged a basket of chocolates and cookies for her to take to Gemma's. "So nice, miss, that ye can visit with Miss Gemma. A sweet thing she is. It will do ye both good to have friends here."

Ella smiled. "I'm glad to hear that you approve of her."

"Aye, she is kinder than most. The lass does na gossip or start fights like some of the other chits onboard. I think ye'll get along jest fine."

Ella relaxed, looking forward to the afternoon outside of her suite.

Ten minutes before the agreed-upon time, she gathered the basket and headed for the door. Braden opened it and fell into step beside her. "I hope you enjoy your visit, milady."

Ella glanced at him sharply. "Since when do we use titles?"

The look he gave her was a reminder of how dangerous it still was for all of them. "Since we are no longer in your quarters, milady."

"My apologies," Ella said, glancing down.

"Are not needed," he answered in a gentle voice.

They took two lefts and a right before they arrived at Gemma's sitting room. Braden waited outside while Ella entered. Her mouth dropped open when she saw the cotton candy pink wallpaper.

"What do you think?" Gemma asked, with her hands clasped together in front of her.

Ella stared, not sure what to say. The room was enormous, but hideous. "Well, it's big, and it's certainly bright," she said, trying to find a redeeming quality in the rose-colored space.

"It is, isn't it?" A giggle escaped, and Gemma clamped a hand over her mouth. "And it's absolutely disgusting!"

"I can't find anything nice to say about it," Ella chortled as they both laughed at the décor. "It's horrid. How do you sleep in here?"

Gemma laughed. "I have an eye mask to block it out. Sadly, come morning, it helps to wake me. I detest mornings anyway, and this," she gestured to the pink confection on her walls, "doesn't make it any easier."

She poured them both a cup of tea. "What's the rest of your suite look like?" she inquired, offering cream and sugar.

Ella pulled out the chocolates and cookies as she thought about her answer. "My room is more subdued than this. Smaller, but cozy. I actually like it."

Gemma took a bite of a cookie before asking, "And your guard, do you like him?" She wiped her lips with a napkin before continuing. "He's very handsome if you like the tall, brooding type." A long-winded sigh escaped her. "Mine is polite, but old."

"Braden is quiet, but kind. I'm just grateful I didn't end up with Saul full time."

"Aren't we all?" Gemma asked. "He's a miserable piece of shit who prays we will make a mistake and get tossed to him for punishment." Forest green eyes met Ella's. "I felt horrible for what you endured the night they released you from isolation."

A shiver ran through Ella as she remembered the smelly little guard, Saul. To prove her loyalty to her new owner, Pearl, they forced her to pleasure the guard orally the night they released her from isolation. Ella needed to prove her willingness to follow directions. Terrified of being thrown back into the cramped, dark cell, she did what she needed to be released. Hating every moment and trying not to gag, she followed instructions, touching a man's genitals for the first time.

Since then, Ella performed this act daily. Thankfully, none of the men they trained on were anything like Saul. Saul was the boogeyman Pearl threatened the girls with. Pearl would give Saul free rein with them if they disappointed her. Ella made sure she gave the woman no reason to punish her.

Saul was a cruel, small-minded bully. Ella knew that if he could get away with it, he would take what he wanted from the girls he oversaw. Braden, on the other hand, was a kind guard who had become her friend. As time passed, he was becoming so much more.

"Not one of my finer moments, to be sure." Ella looked at her hands, embarrassed by the memory.

"Don't feel bad, Ella. We all had to do the same thing our first night here."

Her words shocked Ella and unified them in the man's foulness. "How long have you been here?" she asked.

Gemma tapped her chin thoughtfully. "I'm not sure. Time seems different here, doesn't it? I'm not sure of the date, but it was late winter." Her gaze was unfocused as she remembered the day her life had changed.

"There was an early thaw, and I was gathering snowdrops near the creek. I was taking my time and not paying attention to anything around me when I had blinding pain across the back of my skull. When I woke, I was already in

90

chains." Her eyes filled. "I'm so ashamed that I never even fought to free myself. At least you fought the bastards."

"Aye, I fought, but it did me no good. I ended up bruised and battered for my efforts. I still ended up in chains, alone and in the dark. The cells are horrible. You can't even hear the prisoner next to you." Ella picked at her cuticles nervously. "I thought I was going to die in there." She glanced at Gemma sadly. "And in the end, I still ended up where you are, so all was for naught."

Gemma reached over and squeezed her hand. "All is not for naught." She took another sip of her tea, watching Ella like a hawk. "How did you end up here?" she asked in a gentle voice.

Rosella's eyes watered. She swallowed hard, trying to dislodge the lump in her throat. It had been weeks since she allowed herself to think about Manfri. Guilt twisted inside of her. How could she have forgotten him so easily? Braden was a beautiful new distraction, who had taken her mind off her loss.

Taking a sip of her tea to move the lump, she spoke. "I was on the river with my boyfriend, Manfri," she said in a choked voice. "We stopped to help an old man who said he was in trouble."

Her voice hardened as the images rolled through her mind. "He deceived us. When we got near enough, he killed Manfri and abducted me." She wiped at the lone tear running down her cheek.

"I was unconscious until right before we got here." She stared through the windows to her left. "Manfri died, and I ended up in hell all alone," Rosella finished in a whisper.

"No, my friend, you are not alone. You have allies, and I am only the first who will come to you." Setting her cup down, she clasped Ella's hands in hers. "We've been waiting to see if you'd survive the training." Her voice faded off. "Many do not. But you've already proved that you are a survivor."

Ella stared at her, not knowing what to say.

Gemma gave her a gentle smile. "You will make new acquaintances. Some are curious, some will become close friends or allies." Her tone dropped, and her brows furrowed. "Beware though because others are her spies." Her eyes pierced Ella's. "Be very careful who you trust."

Ella's big hazel eyes locked on Gemma, gauging her sincerity. "How am I supposed to know who to trust?" She cocked a brow at her. "How do I know I can trust you?"

"Honestly, luv, you don't. If you take away anything, let it be this. Each of us will do what we need to survive this hell hole. But until that day, I am your friend."

Gemma's eyes filled. "I don't want to be the friend who will lie and say I will always have your back and I will never betray you. But I've seen too

much deception here already. There are allies and games afoot. You must take care to trust only yourself. You don't know who's planted as a spy."

She wiped a tear away and continued in a harsher voice. "Is it your maid or your handsome guard? Am I the one who will trample you down in order that I don't suffer in your place?" Giving Ella a sad smile, she said, "The best advice I can give you is to trust no one."

Ella asked, "Then why did you invite me here?"

"Because I want to be your friend as best as I am able. And I want to begin with honesty." Her face flushed with shame. "I don't have the constitution for being beaten into submission. I know I will do anything to prevent it."

Ella laughed at her as she tried to track her winding path of logic. "So, we're to be friends as long as we accept that we may have to betray each other?"

"Yes. Exactly." Gemma said, clapping her hands together. "Can we do that?"

Setting her cup down after finishing her tea, Ella said, "I would love to be your friend. But I need you to understand that I would never betray you. Not even to save myself. Because that's the only kind of friend I know how to be."

Gemma's eyes welled again. "I wish I had your courage, Ella."

"Well, shall we work on finding your courage together?" Ella asked, smiling at her and looking forward to the challenge of helping this girl find her spine.

Gemma smiled back. It was a tremulous, hopeful smile that melted any misgivings Ella still had. "I would like to try."

"Now that's out of the way," Ella said. "What do you do to entertain yourself evenings?"

"Do you play cards?"

"Aye, I prefer poker."

"So do I." Gemma reached for a small box on the end table and pulled out a well-used deck of cards. "Shall we play?"

"What will we ante with?" Ella asked.

Gemma tipped her head towards the basket she'd brought. "I love chocolate, and my maid rarely brings it for me. She prefers cake, so that's what I get lots of."

"I love cake, and I get mainly chocolates," Ella said.

They giggled as Gemma dealt the cards. The played numerous hands. Chocolate was lost, and cake gained. By the time she packed up her winnings and hugged the other girl goodbye, Ella felt like herself for the first time since she'd arrived.

Shutting the door behind her, Ella caught Braden's dark eyes studying her. They walked the halls in silence until they reached her suite. She opened

the basket and removed the remaining sweets, along with some smoked cheeses and meats Gemma provided, then offered them to him.

Expecting him to reach for the meats, it surprised her when Braden reached for the chocolate. He took a bite, then popped the candy into his mouth, moaning in appreciation.

Ella's body responded to the sound with a flush running up her face. She wanted to be the one who made him moan like that. When his eyes popped open and stared into hers, she recognized the same heat reflected back at her.

With no thoughts of trust or betrayal, she stood on her tiptoes and pressed her lips to his. Soft, sweet, and tentative, she moved against the soft skin of his lips, needing for one moment just to be a woman in the company of a man she chose, a man she wanted.

Braden stood there, stunned by her bold move. A moment later, his arms caught her by the waist and hauled her against him. His hands traveled up her sides then cupped her face. Tangling in her hair and tipping her head back he explored her mouth. His tongue dipped inside, sliding against hers decadently before retreating. The taste of chocolate was sinful on her lips. Her arms slid around his neck, needing to be closer to him. Their panting filled the air.

The sound of the doorknob turning had them wrenching apart. Ella flew to the other side of the room, facing the window and trying to catch her breath. She couldn't look at him as Shae entered with an armful of pressed frocks.

"Didja have a good time with Miss Gemma?" she asked as she put the gowns away.

"I did," Ella said, grateful her voice didn't sound raspy. "We just returned." She walked to the basket and pulled out her winnings. "And I have cake!" She turned with a wide smile and offered the large piece to Shae.

"For me?" Her eyes were wide and filled with wonder. "I luv cake."

"I remembered you saying as much." Ella laughed loudly. "I won it in a poker game." They laughed together over that one, and even Braden smiled.

"Gemma's not a bad player, but I'm better. My brother Roarke taught me how to play before I could read. I'll make sure to bring back lots of cake for you, Shae. You deserve it for putting up with me."

"Milady, yer a pleasure to put up with." Impulsively, she hugged Ella. "Thank ye fer thinking of me."

"You're welcome, Shae." She glanced at Braden for the first time since Shae arrived. "You're the only real friends I have. I trust both of you with my life."

A shadow passed over Shae's face, but she quickly recovered with a grin. "We trust ye too, Ella. Thank ye for me cake."

Dear Diary,
Seventh Entry

I had the loveliest of days. I honestly can't believe I just wrote that. Gemma invited me to tea, and for just a fraction of time, it felt normal to laugh and talk like any teenager would. We played poker for chocolate and cake. I won lots of cake, and Gemma gained some chocolate. Her skills are fair. But if she plays with me regularly, she may show much improvement.

Gemma cautioned me not to trust anyone, including her. She has vowed to be friends until she can't be. I suppose that makes us frenemies. Braden has also warned me. Although, I do not think he intended to include himself on that list. It would destroy something inside of me if I could not trust him or Shaelynn.

I think his moan of pleasure while eating cake may have bewitched me because I lost myself and kissed him. It was decadently glorious. I wish to do it again. Braden returned the kiss with more passion than I've ever experienced to date. I'm trying to keep the smile off my face. I am not sure if I still recognize the joy bubbling inside of me.

Sadly, the joy mixes with twinges of guilt. I don't have the right to be joyful here after all that I've lost. Yet momentarily, I am. What does that say about me?

I'm stuffed with cake and kisses. For the first time since I arrived, I'm almost happy. How sad is that? I will reexamine the scene with Braden as I fall asleep because I'm allowed to have secrets in my dreams. I hope to dream of him kissing me…and more.

Always,
Rosella

22

What Gives You the Right?

Madylyn SkyDancer, Head Mistress of Heart Island Sanctuary, was fulfilling one of her mandatory duties today. Once a month, she wore the official costume of the acting Legal Guardian for the Elemental High Court. Thankfully, her pregnancy spared her the discomfort of a corset.

Madylyn's authority protected the residents living on and around the St. Lawrence Seaway and anyone who might pass through her district. Most of her cases were local disputes over fishing territories or drunk and disorderly patrons of the local bars.

Today had been a light day, surprising for this month. Warmer weather called in more tourists, and with them, more petty crime. Cases were down, and she was relieved because she desperately needed something to eat, followed by a nap. Her first trimester plagued her with fatigue, endless cravings, and an insatiable libido.

Ronan stood behind her left shoulder, her personal guard of the day. The guards used to rotate, but since he'd reentered her life, he'd made it his personal mission to protect her. She didn't mind, and she doubted the other wardens did either. They hated the boredom of court days. Ronan didn't seem to mind, and his presence was comforting behind her.

At her right shoulder stood Lachlan Quinn, the Law Guardian assigned to Heart Island. Lachlan provided files on each case, arrest records, and recommendations for sentencing. As court concluded, he recorded and enforced her sentences. He'd been a fixture in this court as long as she had, and she valued his advice and friendship.

As she glanced over her shoulder at him for the next case, he stepped forward. Leaning down, he asked, "Do you need a break, Maddy? Are you tired?"

Maddy stared at him, stunned. He'd never inquired about her health before. "I'm perfectly capable of doing my job, Lachlan. Thank you for your concern. Are we nearly done?"

"Aye, we are."

Quirking an eyebrow, she waited for an explanation of his bizarre behavior.

"Next case might upset ye a bit, is all. Just wanted to check."

Taking the file from his hand, she opened it, quickly scanning the contents. Her eyes flew to Lachlan's in surprise, understanding now why he was concerned. Heart racing, she took a deep, steadying breath as she realized her peaceful day was ending. A deep foreboding settled in her chest, and she knew this wouldn't be the only time this man would stand in her courtroom.

"Call him. Let's get this over with."

"The court calls Fisher Jordan."

The room was quiet until a movement in the back row caught Maddy's eye.

A mountain of a man lumbered forward. Shaggy brown hair surrounded his face, hiding his expression. He held his cap in his hands, and his eyes were downcast. His body language directly opposed the angry vibes his aura was radiating.

Maddy kept her voice even as she said, "How may we be of service, Mr. Jordan?"

"Ma'am, if it pleases ye, me daughter's been missing for over a year. Rumor's going round she might be one of those girls yer team rescued off Grindstone."

"We saved three girls from the shipwreck. What's your daughter's name?" Dread filled Maddy as she waited for the answer.

"Genevieve." A small smile crossed his face. "We call her Genny."

Maddy's heart sank. Genny was indeed one girl they'd rescued from the ship. Genny had begged Rhyanna not to contact her family. She said they would only sell her back into the flesh trade.

Without glancing at Lachlan, she sent him a message.

"What are my options?"

"Is this about who I think it's about?"

"Aye," Maddy said, *"Rhyanna's new apprentice."*

"How old is she?" he asked.

"I believe she's nearly sixteen."

"She'll need to become someone's ward, or you'll have to emancipate her. Then she will be your responsibility if she goes off the rails. Those are the only options that will remove his claims to her," Lachlan said.

"He can't forcibly take her from here?"

"Not unless he can get through your wardens. Alert the others."

"I will. Let's see what he has to say first."

"Describe your daughter for me, please," Madylyn said.

"She's a wee thing. Looks like a child. Waif like, a strong wind'll blow her over." He held a hand out just above his waist. "Bout this high. She's got brown hair and hazel eyes."

Maddy's temper flared, but she kept it in check. She gazed around the room. It had nearly emptied, with only a few citizens sitting patiently and the prisoners awaiting transport.

"We found a girl matching your description on the boat." Her tongue twisted in her mouth because what she wanted to say was that she had died on that ship. Maddy didn't want this man anywhere near that sweet young girl.

"She alive?" he asked, barely able to conceal the excitement or the greed in his eyes.

"Yes," Maddy said, hating herself for admitting it. "She survived and has been treated by our healer since her arrival."

"Why weren't we notified of her rescue?" he sneered, any traces of civility gone.

"That's a good question, Mr. Jordan," Maddy quirked a brow at him. "Why don't you tell me why you never reported your daughter missing?"

"I reported it to the local patrols."

"Check on that Lachlan," Maddy said without looking away from the man in front of her, "because it never crossed my desk. Why don't you explain to me why your daughter doesn't want you to know she survived?"

"Beg yer pardon?" he said with a mean glint in his eye.

"Why would your daughter choose to stay here instead of returning to your home?"

The man tipped his head and stared at her as if she were simple. "She's me child—me property. Why in the feck would what she wants even enter the equation?" His tone was sharp, impatient, and radiated barely controlled rage. "Get me daughter up here right now so's we can leave…mistress." He tacked on her title as an afterthought, and it sounded more like a threat than any form of respect.

Maddy reached out to her team. *"All wardens be on alert. Genny's father is here and thinks he's leaving with her. Stand by for further instructions."*

As an afterthought she reached out to Kai, *"I need you to escort Genny from Rhy's shoppe to my office. Do not stop anywhere along the way, and don't leave her alone."*

"Yes, ma'am. I'm on my way."

Maddy stood and addressed the room. "This matter is a custody issue, and we will discuss it in a closed courtroom. The rest of you are free to

leave. Thank you for your patience." She smiled at them. "Enjoy the rest of your day."

Her attention settled on the massive man in front of her. Her voice was like ice as she addressed him once again. "You never answered my question. Why would your daughter refuse to return home?" She snapped out, demanding an answer.

"That's between us."

"Not anymore." Maddy motioned with her hand to include the men standing behind her and the additional wardens lining the back walls. "It's between all of us."

"The feck it is."

"Never mind," she said, then stepped off the platform, avoiding the man before her by walking the perimeter of the room to her left. "I'll get my answers from Genny."

Fisher Jordan rushed towards her, but Lachlan and Ronan were quicker. When Maddy reached the back wall, Fergus met her and walked with her up to her office. The other Wardens kept the irate man in the courtroom.

Kai and Genny had just sat down when Maddy walked in. Kai stood, vacating the seat across from Genny.

Maddy took his seat and sat silently for a moment before reaching out and taking Genny's shaking hands in hers.

"Have I done something wrong, Mistress SkyDancer?" she asked in a frightened voice.

Maddy shook her head, squeezing her hand gently. "No, you've done nothing wrong. I just need to ask you something."

"Anything. I have nothing to hide."

"Your father has come to claim you." Maddy's heart broke as she watched the color drain from the young girl's face.

"I'll go anywhere, mistress, anywhere in this world, but I won't go with him." Her voice shook, and tears filled her hazel eyes. "I can't go back there."

"Why don't you want to go with him, child?" she asked softly.

Genny said nothing, but she glanced back at Kai standing stoically behind her. Maddy glanced at the young man and noticed how tightly he was clenching his jaw. Now she understood.

"Kai, can you give us the room for a moment?"

With a curt nod, he walked out into the hall.

"Genny, I won't force you to do anything you don't want to do, but I need to know what happened. We will protect you, but I need the ammunition to keep him away." She squeezed her hands again. "Do you understand what I'm saying?"

"Aye, I do. 'Tis just difficult to talk about." She pulled her hands away and wiped her eyes. Maddy handed her a handkerchief and gave her a moment to gather herself.

"My mam was never a strong woman, and living with my pa ain't ever been easy." She wiped the tears again before continuing. "When I was twelve, she started getting something from a man in the village to calm her nerves. Whatever 'twas wasn't very good for her cuz she could barely function while taking it." She sniffled before continuing.

"My pa, for all his poor qualities, loved her as much as he was able."

Her eyes held a faraway look as she remembered what her life had been like. "I started doing her chores and trying to cook." A harsh laugh echoed throughout the room. "I burnt more than we could eat, but I tried. The more she used, the meaner he got, usually taking it out on her, but as I got older, he started beating me, too."

She held out her arm and pointed to a jagged scar running down the inside of her forearm. "He tore me up good here and broke half me fingers the last time he hit me."

Maddy's eyes filled, but she held back the tears, owing the girl the strength to listen to her story.

"Ma didn't make it through the winter just before I turned fifteen. Her heart and body gave up on this world, leaving me alone with him." Her eyes grew distant as she remembered her personal hell.

"Pa was a gambler. Folk would tell 'bout how Fisher Jordan was the best damn card player in these parts." She scrubbed her face again. "When ma died, she took any luck he might have once had to the grave."

"Pa owed her dealer a heap of money and couldn't pay. One night, he showed up and beat 'em half to death. Pa laid there on the floor and saw me in the corner and offered him a deal." Her lips trembled as she worked up the courage to continue. "Pa gave me away to erase his debt." Her hand swiped angrily at the tears coursing down her cheeks.

Defiantly, she glared at Maddy. "Ye can send me back with him, but I ain't gonna stay. If I don't run away, I'll slit my wrists or leap off what's left of that bridge afore I ever stay with him again." She wiped her nose on the soaked piece of cloth and met Maddy's gaze once more. "Far as I be concerned, he forfeited his rights to me long ago."

Maddy barely concealed her rage and horror at what this child had been through. Seething inside, she pulled Genny into a tight hug. "I promise you will never have to return to him if that's what you want. Do you trust me to do what's best for you?"

"I do." Genny's body relaxed against Maddy. "Thank ye, Mistress SkyDancer. Ye won't regret it. I promise."

Maddy pulled back to gaze at her. "I know we won't." She wiped the tears from her cheeks and asked, "Are you comfortable with Kai staying with you?"

A look crossed Genny's face that was neither fear nor repulsion. Uncertainty defined it better. A hesitant nod followed. "He's been nothing but kind to me. I'm not afraid of him."

Maddy turned for the door. "Kai," she said, walking through it, "Protect her. She doesn't leave this island with anyone."

Kai nodded, glancing into Maddy's office. "She alright?"

"She's upset." Her gaze traveled over his handsome face, finding nothing but concern there. "I think she could use a friend."

"I'll take care of her, Maddy."

"Thank you. Now I need to go take out the trash."

Maddy returned to the courtroom. Taking her position at the head of the room, she took a moment to gather her thoughts.

"Me daughter best be packed and on her way," the arrogant man said, not waiting for her to begin.

"Mr. Jordan," Maddy said in a clipped tone, "Genny will be remaining here for the time being."

"For how long?" he snarled at her.

"As long as she wants," Maddy said in a deceptively calm voice.

"Ye can't keep me from me girl. I want me daughter returned right fecking now."

"Mr. Jordan," Maddy said. Her voice rose, and she infused it with the power of her authority. "Genny is no longer any of your concern."

"What the feck do you mean, 'not my concern?'" He stepped closer to where she sat at the table, but Ronan and Lachlan were already there.

"Genny is my ward and a ward of the Sanctuary. She has an apprenticeship with our healer, Rhyanna Cairn. This is her home and where she will remain until *she* chooses otherwise."

With a glance at Lachlan, she added for the official record, "I hereby emancipate Genevieve Jordan. I've offered her employment and lodging, which she has gratefully accepted, making her self-sufficient. Genny has the full force of this Sanctuary and the Elemental Court behind her. She no longer needs her father to speak for her. You have no control over this young woman in the future, and should you ignore this ruling, the consequences will be severe."

Fisher Jordan's face turned purple with rage. A mountain of a man, Maddy wondered whether Ronan could stop him in time if he lunged for her.

"What gives ye the right?" Fisher seethed. "She's me only flesh and blood. I don't even get to see her."

"That's her choice as well." Maddy's voice was steady as she continued. "You sold her into hell. What did you expect?"

A hint of sorrow crossed his face, and Maddy wasn't sure if it was because he missed her or because he'd lost another stream of income. "Ye ain't seen the last of me." His threat was heavy in the air.

"Fisher Jordan, you are no longer welcome on Heart Island. If you violate this ruling, justice will be swift and severe."

"Fuck ye. Ye don't know what severe consequences be."

"You'd be wrong about that," she said. Standing, she lifted the gavel and struck it on the table. "My verdict stands. Because of your neglect and poor life choices, Genevieve Fisher is no longer under your care. The Heart Island Sanctuary claims her as a Warden in training, which places her under the direct authority of the Elemental High Court." Maddy met the man's glare without flinching. "I advise you to accept my ruling. Court is dismissed."

Nodding at Fergus, Maddy continued, "See that Mr. Jordan leaves this island and gets off the boat on the mainland. Notify the harbor master and ferry captains, he is no longer welcome here."

Fisher Jordan's eyes followed her out the door, and she could've sworn she heard him mutter, "Ye ain't seen the last of me, yet."

Maddy ignored him and walked with her back straight and head high. She didn't breathe a sigh of relief until she reached the second floor.

Ronan was silent as they headed for her office. "This isn't over."

"I know. I'll have a word with the Romani patrols and increase security. We'll be ready for him if he tries anything."

Stepping into her office, she halted at the sight before her. Genny had fallen asleep on the chaise lounge, and Kai sat on the floor near her head with his back against it and eyes closed. Genny's fingers tangled in the long strands of his hair. It was the only place they touched.

Kai's eyes popped open as Ronan followed her in. "Is it over?" he asked in a soft rumble.

"For now," Maddy said, "but I'm sure we haven't seen the last of him." She gazed at the emotionally exhausted young woman. "I hate to wake her."

Genny sat straight up as she finished. "Sorry, mistress. Didn't mean to drift off." She pushed her hair back, not realizing her fingers held strands of Kai's hair. His back arched, and he hissed as she yanked on them. Mortified, she released the tendrils and faced Maddy. "What happened?"

"He's gone for now, Genny." Maddy sat on the opposite lounge and faced her. "I have emancipated you, which means he has no control over you. This means you are an adult, fully capable of taking care of yourself. You have a job here if you want it and are welcome to stay with us as long as you wish."

Genny gaped at her, and Maddy wasn't sure if it was in relief or fear.

Unsure of her response, Maddy said. "I hope this gives you some peace. He no longer has any power over you."

Still, Genny said nothing. Instead of speaking, she launched herself into Maddy's arms and hung on tight. "How can I ever thank you?"

Maddy hugged her back. "You've no need for thanks. You're part of our family now, and family takes care of each other."

"It's been so long since anyone cared 'bout me, 'cept for what I'se worth to them. Thank ye again."

"Why don't the two of you head on down for supper," Maddy said.

Ronan waited for them to leave before speaking. "He's good for her."

"I think so, too. He's one of the few men I've seen her around that she has no fear of."

"Ironic with his size."

"Aye, it is, but he'll protect her. There's a gentleness in him she recognizes."

"Kai will keep her safe," Ronan said, wrapping his arms around her from behind and resting them on her rounded belly.

"If she lets him." Maddy placed her hands over the top of his, knowing she was safe with Ronan by her side.

23

What Could Have Been

Danny awoke, snuggled into the cocoon of the warm, muscular man spooning her. She shifted closer, and, as always, he pulled her tighter to him, his hand tightening on her waist. Content, she sighed and melted into his hold, loving how he surrounded her with his heat and protection. But more importantly, he wrapped her in his love.

Groggily, he nuzzled her neck, his lips making her lean her head against his shoulder, giving him better access. Calloused hands drifted from her tiny waist up under her breasts. Cupping and tugging, he molded the sensitive skin between his talented fingers. Her back arched as she pushed her breasts further into his hands and ground her ass against his swelling cock.

The rigid length of him pressing against the soft skin of her ass always made her wet and needy. A greedy moan emanated from her as he pinched her nipples harder. Long, silky chestnut hair draped over her shoulder as he kissed her neck, tickling and teasing her skin. The erotic sensation of him surrounding her assaulted her senses. Rough palms, sleek hair, and the hardness pressing against her made all of her nerve endings light up with awareness.

Panting, she parted her legs, making way for him to stroke her wet cleft with his thick member. Broad palms grasped her thighs, spreading her legs as he drove into her with one stroke. She sucked in a breath at his intrusion and then sighed, welcoming him home, wanting—needing—more.

Hands traveled to her hips, pushing her torso away as he focused on thrusting himself into her and driving her higher and higher. When her inner walls fluttered around him, he reached around and strummed her clit, making her scream his name. A deep-throated chuckle rumbled from his chest. He loved the way his name tore from her throat when she came.

He pressed her torso into the bed as his hips thrust faster, and he chased his own pleasure while ensuring she reached hers again. His teeth found the soft spot between her shoulder and neck as he groaned and ground himself against her one last time. Releasing her neck, he kissed the mark he'd made and whispered, "I love you, Hellion."

Danny sat up in the dark, the forest silent around her as the dream drifted like mist in the morning sun. As she acclimated to her surroundings and the sound of Kerrygan's soft snoring beside her, tears filled her eyes as her heart broke again.

The dream had been so real. Sensual and beautiful. Tactile and tortuous. Her core wept, and her inner walls still fluttered from the orgasm she'd had in her sleep.

A dream, nothing but an illusion sent to mock her with how beautiful they could have been together, how their bodies fit together, and how perfectly he would have played her body. Like a master with a timeless instrument, Jamey had made love to her like a man who already knew her intimately better than she knew herself.

Violent sobs erupted from her as she remembered every moment of pleasure experienced through her dream. Her cries woke Kerrygan, and when he pulled her to him and wrapped his arms around her, she didn't stop him or push him away. She surrendered to what he offered, but it was more than she deserved. She didn't have the energy to refuse the comfort of his arms any longer.

Kerry let her cry, and when she had nothing left, he continued to hold her, saying nothing, just breathing with her. When she turned away and curled into a ball, Kerry sighed, then pulled her back to him, spooning her.

And when she cried harder because he didn't understand what he was reminding her of, she let him hold her. If she'd refused the comfort he offered, she would have let go of the tenuous leash that held her to this life. A life that continued to shower her with pain and heartache, longing and loss. A life that she didn't know if she wanted to survive anymore.

As sleep once again beckoned, she fought it. Her dreams had destroyed all of her defenses. The horror of it all was that her exhausted mind had given her the perfect glimpse of the life they would have had together. A peek at what could have been—but now would never be.

24

Welcome Back

The light was bright through Jameson's closed eyelids. His right hand came up over his face, forearm blocking the light streaming in through the window. A tired sigh escaped as he moved. His muscles were weak, as if he'd just slept off a long illness.

Stretching his legs, he kicked off the covers. With his left hand, he tried to push himself up on the bed. Stifling a scream as a white-hot poker of pain seared through his arm and into his shoulder, he collapsed back onto the cot. Black dots floated across his vision, and for a moment, he thought he would vomit from the waves of agony rolling through him.

Using his other arm, he heaved himself into a sitting position. Left arm dangling uselessly and throbbing like a bitch, he tried to remember what happened to him. He jerked as he remembered the hellhound lunging for him. A hiss escaped as the slight movement caused him immense pain.

When the throbbing slowed, he lifted his head, trying to pinpoint where he was. The sterility of the room told him he was in a clinic on Wellesley. This wasn't the first time he'd woken in this room. Last time, he'd been a boy and had broken the same arm. Talk about irony.

Jamey cleared his throat, trying to find his voice. Multiple sets of feet hurried his way. His mother was the first to enter. The tears of gratitude in her eyes made him feel guilty for making her worry. His father arrived next, and his expression was much the same. Jamey had never seen such relief on the man's face.

A vague fever dream of meeting his maker niggled at him, but it was just a dream. He hadn't been that bad off, had he?

A cough erupted from him. His right hand pressed against the left side of his chest protectively as the ache of a fresh injury made itself known. His mother handed him a glass of water, and he downed it without stopping. She

refilled it, and he repeated the action before shaking his head when she filled it again.

"Danny?" His immediate worry was about her. He couldn't remember if the hound injured her during his attack or not. But he'd felt her grief when he was floating away.

A look passed between his parents. "She's fine, Jamey." his mother said.

Jamey's brow furrowed. There was something she wasn't telling him, but he was struggling to stay focused.

"How long?" Trying to form complete sentences was beyond his capability.

"You've slept for five days. Your body desperately needed it," Kateri said.

Holy fuck. He'd never had an injury that required that much recovery time. One benefit of shifter magic was it reduced healing to a day at most for even serious injuries.

His father clamped a hand on his shoulder and said in a gravelly voice, "You nearly died, son. The only thing keeping you in this world when we arrived was one of Varan's boys pumping your heart and a young lass breathing for you. Ferg and Rhy did the best they could up til then." The stoic man cleared his throat and wiped his eyes as he finished.

In shock, Jamey was silent for a moment. The fact that he was sitting here talking to them was a fucking miracle. Even shifter magic had its limits. The dream of a choice flitted through his mind again, and he realized why he still lived.

"I'm sorry," he said, understanding now why they both looked exhausted and why his mother was wiping away tears. "I'm so sorry."

"Nothing to be sorry for," she said. "We just need you to get better."

A sluggish nod was the best he could do as he struggled to process everything that had happened. His right hand moved over his left side, noting the deep gouges in his shoulder, chest, and down his arm. More evidence of how close he came to not making it. Shifter healing rarely left scars—thin white lines, if anything. To have this much damage underscored how depleted his body had been.

"How bad is it?" he asked, trying to lift his arm.

"Why don't we let the healers have a peek at you first before you go moving it too much," Kateri warned. "We'll come back in after they've seen you."

Jamey ran his right hand over his face, pinching the bridge of his nose with his thumb and forefinger. His memory was coming back in fits and stutters. Fighting with Danny—the attack—blood covering her. Her tears and pleas for him to stay with her—Rhy and Ferg and the pain of them working on him—floating, should he stay or go...

"There he is." A familiar voice warmed his heart and stopped the chaos of his thoughts. "Thought I'se gonna lose ye, Jameson Vance." Rhy's voice brought him back to the moment. Her luminous emerald gaze met his, and tears slipped down her face.

Without thinking, he opened his right arm, inviting her in for a hug. Rhy stepped into him, squeezing his right side hard and avoiding the left. He held her tightly to him, knowing this woman was the reason he was still alive today. Without her knowledge and skills, he would've bled to death on Singer Island.

"I don't think I can ever thank you enough, Rhy," he mumbled against her.

"Well, na, she ain't the only one ye need to thank, lad," Fergus announced.

Rhy squeezed him one last time before making way for the fire-haired giant.

Jamey stuck out a hand, which Fergus took and then pulled him into a bro hug. "Don't ye ever fecking put us through that again, ye bastard!"

He stepped back, wrinkling his nose. "Yer in dire need of a shower, lad. Where's the closest one?"

Rhy pointed to the door leading to the en suite bath. "Think ye can walk?" she asked.

"Willing to try."

"I'll help ye, lad." Fergus waited until he pushed himself up with his good arm, then tucked a shoulder under him, wrapping his arm around Jamey's middle to keep him upright. With slow steps, they made their way first to the toilet and then the shower.

The enclosure was large enough for two. A bench made it easier for Jamey, and he took it gratefully. Fergus quickly stripped and stepped in to help him.

The hot water soaking into his muscles felt divine. He kept his eyes closed, not wanting to look at Ferg's dangly bits in front of him. The large man was surprisingly gentle as he washed Jamey's hair and soaped him up. All too soon, it was over, and he had to face standing again. His muscles were weak, and he hated how dependent he was on Ferg to stand and walk. Fergus dried him off and tied a towel around his waist before assisting him back to the bedroom.

Rhy had stripped the sheets and was finishing remaking the bed when they returned. Legs weak, Jamey sank down on it, grateful to be sitting once more.

"Alright, lad. Let's have a look at ye," she said, studying the deep scars on his shoulder and chest. Her fingers poked and prodded, causing him mild

107

discomfort. "Shifter magic be a beautiful thing, Jamey. Be grateful for yer heritage. Ye wouldna be here today without it."

"So, I've been told." A grimace crossed his face as she moved his arm, checking his range of motion. "Sorry to have caused you both so much trouble," he hissed.

"Just a wee bit of trouble, lad," Ferg drawled. "I mean I'd keep pumping yer heart again til me arms nearly fell out of me sockets anytime ye need me to, but I'd prefer to never fecking do that again."

Face losing all color, it was still hard for him to comprehend how close to death he'd been, even though the pain coursing through his arm right now was bound to be a damn good reminder for a while.

Rhy continued manipulating him even as tears leaked down his face from the agony. "Sorry bout this, Jamey, but there ain't no easy way to regain the movement without forcing it at first."

"Keep going. I can take it," he said through gritted teeth.

As she raised it near to his shoulder, he thought he might have overestimated his tolerance for pain when a wave of nausea rolled through him. Rhy gently lowered his arm, then placed a hand on either side of his injured shoulder. The pain subsided to an annoying throb. Tolerable, but much better than moments earlier.

"Ye still need lots of sleep. This much healing will take a lot out of ye for the next week. Ye move it as much as ye can, and tomorrow, I'll show yer ma and pa how to torment ye with pushing it farther than ye'll want them to."

"Thanks." He wiped the sweat away that was rolling down his face with his good hand. "I'm sure they'll take some perverse pleasure in torturing me."

"Can hardly blame 'em after what ye put 'em through, seeing ye like this."

"I know. I deserve everything they give me."

"Ye need to eat—as much protein as ye can manage." Rhy hugged him once more and leaned down to whisper, "I'm glad ye've rejoined us in the land of the living, Jameson."

His arm tightened around her. "It's good to be back. Thank you for everything, Rhy."

Fergus had been unusually silent, leaning against the frame of the door as she worked on him. When she left them, he came in and sat in a chair facing Jamey. The silence between them was unnatural and uncomfortable.

Clearing his throat, Fergus asked, "You remember what happened that day?"

"Bits and pieces."

"Wanna talk about it?"

"Not yet." Jamey squeezed his eyes shut as he tried to remember everything. "What did she say?"

"Ain't talked to her."

Jamey's head whipped up, and he met Fergus's gaze, worry clouding his features. "Why not?"

"She won't talk to anyone. Took off when she thought ye were dead."

"She's out there on her own? That doesn't concern you?"

Ferg grimaced, regretting his choice of words. "She ain't alone, lad."

"Who's with her?" Jamey asked, even though he already knew the answer to that.

"When ye stopped breathing, lad, she couldn't stay and watch ye die. With a shriek, she shifted and took to the sky. Only one of us could follow her, and he did, even though Rhy begged him not to."

"That was a helluva risk for him to shift again so soon."

"Aye, T'was, but he couldn't stand her hurting alone. I dropped supplies for them a few days ago. She still won't see me or answer when I message her."

"Fuck. I'm sorry, man."

"Not yer fault. Her choice to ignore me. Trying to give the lass the space she needs."

"If you get through to her, tell her I'm sorry."

"Nah, thinking that's something ye need to tell her yerself."

"You're right."

"Usually am. 'Bout time someone realizes it." Ferg chuckled, and Jamey smiled this time around. "Best get going. Rhy will want to get back soon, seeings how ye ain't her only patient today."

"Ferg," Jamey's voice was full of gravel as he tried to express his gratitude. "Thanks for saving my life."

"Yer welcome, lad. But me thinks ye gots some mighty powerful allies on the other side. Ye lingered in between fer a long time."

"I think you might be right."

Ferg clapped a hand on his shoulder. "I'll be back with her tomorrow."

"Thanks for the warning."

Fergus's chuckle echoed as he walked down the hall. Jameson sat there for a long time, processing just how close to death he'd come. He realized how lucky he was to have the people in his life he considered family. The realization that the one person he most needed to see, and to hear from, just might be the one who would have nothing to do with him crossed his mind.

Before he could think better of it, he sent a message out on his telepathic link, *"Hellion, are you alright?"*

Danny's line remained silent, but the rush of emotion that flared back on the line staggered him. Relief mixed up with guilt, then coupled with fear

and anger, assaulted him. Well, one thing was certain, the woman was pissed off at him. It didn't surprise him when she didn't bother to answer.

Jamey was going to have to earn Danny's trust again, and hell, after the way everything went down—he couldn't blame her.

25

Isabella's Brood

Mrs. O'Hare served breakfast in the private dining room for the wardens and their families every morning. She put on a breakfast buffet that could make anyone happy. Large pots of fresh coffee and tea helped the adults get off to a good start. Platters of fresh fruits and various cheeses sat between large trays of eggs, bacon, and sausage.

Freshly baked pastries filled with chocolate, three different kinds of muffins, and thick slices of bread were available all day long. They were a favorite for breakfast while they were fresh from the oven.

Maddy sat at one end of the table, with Ronan seated on one side of her and Landon on the other. Fergus sat next to Landon, trying to teach him how to do a bridge with a deck of cards. Kai and Kyran sat opposite of them, and Rhyanna was on the other end with Genny to her left and Grace tucked between her and Fergus.

Grace had been rescued along with Genny, and Roarke's niece Hailey earlier in the year from an abandoned ship used for human trafficking. The ship was sinking and only three of the girls on board had been alive when the Wardens found them. Grace was staying at the Sanctuary while she figured out what she wanted to do with her future.

Conversation was at a low hum while everyone caffeinated for the day.

"Ye almost got it, lad," Fergus said to Landon as he dropped the cards in frustration.

"My hands are too small." Landon puzzled it for a minute, then picked them back up again, not wanting to give up. His tongue peeked out as he concentrated, and Maddy hid a smile at how damn cute he was as he tried his hardest. This time, he got part of the cards to shuffle properly.

"I did it!" he yelled joyfully, in the way only a small child can make you feel their excitement.

A round of applause went up from the table, and he grinned broadly. "I'm very proud you didn't give up when it was difficult," Ronan said.

"It's not that hard," Landon said, then his jaw dropped as he listened to something on his inner link. "Daddy, c'mon, we gotta go…" Landon jumped from his chair and raced around the table, tugging on Ronan's hand.

Ronan quickly finished his coffee before giving him his full attention. "Hold up, what's the big hurry? I haven't finished my breakfast." He glanced across the table at Landon's plate and said, "Neither have you."

"We have to go," he insisted, still pulling. "The dragons are hatching."

"Isabella told you?" Ronan asked.

"Well, how else would I know?" Landon asked quizzically without an ounce of attitude.

"How long's she been talking to ye, chile?" Rhyanna asked in awe.

"Since the day I got here." He ran around the table and grabbed his chocolate croissant. "I'll eat it on the way. Please, I don't want to miss it."

"Does Alejandro talk to ye, too?" Fergus asked.

"Sometimes…when he's not growling or threatening to eat me."

A hush fell over the room at the boy's words. "Does he do that often?" Ronan asked with an edge to his voice that hadn't been there before.

"No. Only if I gets too close and don't follow the rules."

"What be the rules, lad?" Fergus asked, curious as to what the dragons would consider rules.

"The usual. Be quiet. No touching, and no questions, or Alejandro will eat me."

"Wow," Fergus said, impressed.

"Wait," Landon said, "there's a new one, too. You have to use your manners. Somefin 'bout not being rude."

"Sweet Mother," Maddy groaned, glancing at Ronan in near panic. "We need to discuss dragon visitations when you get back."

"You betchya," he said, giving her a quick kiss and taking Landon's outstretched hand.

"Can I come?" Fergus asked, looking as excited as the child jumping in place.

Landon paused and asked for permission.

"She said it's alright if yer not wearing too many bright colors."

The room erupted in laughter as Ferg glanced down at himself.

"Damn good thing I went with dark ones today, then." He snatched a couple of pieces of bacon and headed for the door.

"Wait!" Landon cried, heading back to the platters. He grabbed a napkin and put three chocolate pastries in, tying it up carefully. When he turned back, everyone was staring at him. "I always brings her a gift. She gets cravings like you, Maddy, so I take her chocolate." Cradling them to his

chest, he ran for the door, grabbing Ronan's hand. "C'mon, we have to hurry."

The boy didn't understand the laughter following them down the hall. He was too excited by the prospect of seeing the eggs hatch. Tugging harder until they were nearly running, the three men exited the building just as a groom arrived with Ronan and Fergus's horses.

Ronan mounted, and Ferg boosted Landon up into his waiting arms.

"Can we go fast?" he pleaded.

"You know the rules."

"As soon as we are far enough away from the house," Landon mimicked.

"That's right. Now, let's go see some dragons hatch."

They finally picked up speed. Landon squealed in delight, yelling, "Faster!" with his arms raised over his head and Ronan's arm tucked snuggly around his waist.

Ronan glanced over at Ferg, who nodded and shouted back, "Give the boy what he wants. There's nobody to holler at us." Both men grinned, nudging their mounts for more speed and laughing like the boy riding with them.

The distance passed quickly as they came up to the pasture before the cliffs. They slowed and tied their mounts off to a tree, then continued the rest of the journey on foot. Landon ran ahead, a frequent visitor to the caves on the cliff.

Chiseled stone steps led down to the mouth of the cave. Narrow and damp, they were slick, causing the men to go slower than the anxious child. "Landon, wait," Ronan called after him.

Landon peeked out of the cave with disappointment. "I come here all the time. They let me visit whenever I wants."

"I know they do, son. Today is a special day and may make Alejandro and Isabella more nervous than usual. Let's go slow and ask permission like you normally would before entering."

Landon glared at the ground and scuffed his boot against the rough stone floor. "Can I ask now?"

Ronan ruffled his hair and said, "Yes, you may."

Landon tipped his head, waiting for an answer, then said, "They're in the first room. I can take you there, but you gotta be quiet." His eyes were solemn as he gazed at both men. "Or Alejandro will eat you."

The light from the mouth of the cave let in just enough light for them to make their way through the uneven room. Ronan had only been here once to see the nest with Landon, but this experience was new to Fergus. The nervous excitement radiating from him nearly matched the child's. His fire drakes recognized his excitement and one of their own nearby. The wee

dragon-like lights absorbed Ferg's excess emotions. Their light helped them see in the near dark.

The space was enormous, with massive clearance overhead. Ten versions of the Sanctuary would fit in here and still have room to spare. At the back of the cave, the room narrowed as it split into two different tunnels.

Landon led them through the one on the right. For all the usual energy of a five-year-old, the moment he entered the nesting cavern, he settled down immensely, his energy respectful and full of gratitude. Ronan gazed down at him with pride, then up at Isabella with gratitude for bonding with his child. A moment of regret passed through him as he realized once again everything he had missed seeing with his son. Unaware of his existence until about a month ago, he couldn't imagine life now without him in it.

"Beastmaster," Isabella purred in a sultry voice in his head, *"welcome."*

Ronan bowed his head to the majestic creature. *"It is my honor to attend today's event, Isabella."* He turned to her glowering partner and said, *"Alejandro, congratulations on your growing family."*

The large onyx eyes observing him gave him a slow blink, and the massive head inclined slightly.

"I also want to thank you both for sharing this event with Landon. Your generosity and your patience," he glanced at Alejandro at the last part of that statement, *"will be remembered."*

Alejandro gave a low growl this time as his head whipped toward the child. Steam rolled from his nostrils, and the hairs on Ronan's arm stood on end. A deep rumble of a voice pushed its way onto Ronan's telepathic web, *"I have learned to tolerate the whelp like one tolerates rats in food storage. He makes her happy by bringing her sweets, so I allow it, and he follows the rules. She says it will teach me patience with our young. I'm not so sure about that yet."*

Ronan saw Fergus move behind Landon, placing both hands on his shoulders, claiming the child with the touch. Moving to the side, Ferg knelt before the pair. Two massive heads bent down to take in his scent and his intent. A long moment passed before they both blew a stream of steam and smoke over the fire mage, recognizing he was one of theirs and could tolerate the heat.

Fergus stayed stock still, not daring to move an inch. He was an all-powerful mage of the same element these creatures were born from, but they possessed the capability to unmake him as well. His fire drakes hid when they entered the chamber, terrified by the strongest elementals in their world. As the dragons expressed their approval, the mini-dragon bursts of light emerged from beneath Fergus's beard and under his shirt. They soaked up the heat and magic from the mythical creatures growing in size and lighting the chamber with their joy.

They abandoned Fergus and raced along the walls, working their way closer to the dragons until one was finally brave enough to touch her tail.

Isabella let out a deep rumble that may have been a chuckle. *"Do not fear us, little ones. We are all family. Come, say hello. We shan't harm thee."*

Three pairs of round eyes glanced at each other as Fergus whispered, "Did you hear that, too"

"Yeah," Ronan said. "She must have projected it to all of us."

"Holy shite!" Fergus said, astonished. "This is some trippy ass, mystical, magical shite even for an all-mighty fire mage such as meself."

Alejandro's head whipped towards the mage. *"Language."*

"Begging yer pardon," Ferg said, bowing deeply and trying not to chortle.

"There's no cussing in here," Landon said out loud in a way too serious voice. "His children will have a better vocabuarrry than we humans ever could deem to use," he said, quoting a lecture he'd heard at least once.

Both men coughed to choke back their laughter. Boys being boys, after all.

Isabella spoke to all of them, *"Little Ronan has been a great comfort to me during this time."* Bending her long neck down to his level, she asked, *"What do you have for me today?"*

Landon set his package on the ground and untied the napkin, displaying the chocolate croissants. "I asked Mrs. O'Hare to make yer favorites," he said aloud.

Isabella picked them up more daintily than one would think, and they were gone with one swallow. "Thank you, little Ronan. Do you want to see them now?"

"Yes, please."

"Yes," Ronan and Fergus parroted.

Landon tugged on both of their hands and peered up at them in solemness. "Use yer manners."

"Yes, please," Ronan said at the same time Fergus added, "If it pleases ye."

The creatures shifted slightly, revealing a massive nest behind them woven from small saplings. At least twenty feet wide and two feet high, the woven masterpiece displayed thirteen eggs of various colors. Isabella's pastel blues and greens mixed with Alejandro's dark blue and black in a tie-dyed effect on the outside of the eggs. The colors were gorgeous on eggs twice Landon's size.

In the stunned silence, they heard tiny peeps and growls coming from the moving eggs as the little dragons struggled to free themselves. Cracks formed on the sides of some of the jewel tones as little feet and snouts pushed, trying to escape the confines of their fragile prisons.

Landon's eyes were wide, and he pointed silently as the first leg popped through. Isabella leaned down and blew steam over the entire clutch. The

chatter of little voices grew louder. Some eggs rocked from side to side as their inhabitants became more motivated.

Ronan and Fergus watched with excited smiles on their faces. They both had seen birds hatch before, but watching a dragon come into this world was something else altogether.

An hour later, twelve out of thirteen dragons had emerged. An equal mix of male and female, but each one uniquely marked with the gorgeous combination of colors just like their parents.

As Isabella and Alejandro met their offspring, Ronan and Fergus watched silently. At some point, Landon dropped Ronan's hand. Glancing down, he realized the child was no longer by his side. Stunned, he glanced around to find the young man standing next to the nest, peering over the side.

"C'mon, little dragon. It's time to come out and meet yer momma and daddy," he crooned. "Yer momma's really nice and so pretty. You look just like her. Yer daddy isn't nearly as scary as he sounds." His hands were on the top of the nest as he leaned in to watch the last dragon struggle to make the first break in the egg.

To Ronan's horror, he saw the moment Landon forgot the rules and reached forward. His gaze swung over to the dragons and watched Alejandro's eyes narrow. Ronan ran for the nest, grabbing Landon seconds before his fingers touched the egg.

"Remember your rules, son," Ronan said, turning his back to the massive creature to protect Landon from his wrath. "My apologies, Alejandro. It won't happen again."

"No, it won't because he's not allowed to return."

Landon's face fell as he realized what his error just cost him. Tears ran down his face as he turned to Isabella. "I'se only reached out cuz she asked me for help. Her foot's trapped, and she can't move cuz of the way the egg is laying." He sniffled as he realized he'd lost one of the few friends that he'd had. "I didn't mean to break the rules, but she's struggling so hard to get out."

"She spoke with you?" The four adults spoke at once.

"Yes, like you do." The boy scrunched up his nose, confused, as if he weren't explaining it right. He tapped on his temple. "In my head."

Isabella leaned down and gently nudged the last egg until it rolled over. Moments later, a tiny leg poked out, and then another. When Isabella's miniature tried to stand, her front leg gave out from being pinned beneath her.

"May I help her?" Ronan asked. "If I massage her leg, it will help with the blood flow and relax the muscles. I've done it with foals who've been born in awkward positions."

Both dragons leaned down and blew a breath over the child so that she would recognize them as her elders and not think Ronan was.

"Please," Alejandro said, then turned to gaze at the troubled child. *"You may also help. She's chosen you already. There's not much I can do to stop it now."*

Ronan stepped into the nest, then lifted Landon in with him. "Hold your hand out like this," he said to him, "with your palm out and up. Let her smell you, so she'll recognize you in the future."

Landon did as told, giggling when the little she-dragon licked his hand. Ronan knelt next to her and began massaging her front leg and paw as gently as he could. She pulled away once or twice until Landon distracted her again. His laughter rang out as she head-butted him, causing a stampede from the other little critters tracking the source.

Ronan stilled as the nest filled with the hatchlings tripping over each other to meet their sister and her new pets. When the last dragon ran after her siblings, her gait was better, less stiff. His hand on Landon's shoulder kept the boy from running off after them.

"It's time to say goodbye, for now," he said to the child.

The disappointment was easy to read, but to Ronan's surprise, he turned to the dragons and bowed deeply. "Thank you for the honor of letting me attend the births of your children." Big blue eyes focused on Alejandro. "Thank you for not eating me when I broke the rules." He reached for his father's hand and turned to leave.

Ronan and Fergus followed suit, bowing and offering blessings on the recent additions and gratitude for the gift of attending. They left them there, surrounded by the evidence of their love.

"Ye tell him to say that?" Fergus asked.

"Nope," Ronan said, *"thought it might have been you."*

"Cheveyo, perhaps."

"I'll ask."

"Could just ask your son," Ferg said in a dumbass tone.

"Landon, why did you say that before we left?"

The child hesitated until Ronan stopped and hunched in front of him. "You can tell me anything, you know that, right?" Landon wouldn't meet his eyes. "I'm not upset by what you said. I just wondered who taught you that?"

Fidgeting in front of the men, he wiped his nose with the back of his hand before speaking. "My momma. She brung babies into the world, and she'd always say that when we left. It was her honor to help the next generation come into this world." He scratched his head. "Said it was a form of respect to thank them." A lone tear tracked down his face. "I still miss her, sometimes."

"I know you do, son." Ronan hugged him tightly. "Don't ever be afraid to talk about her to me or anyone else. She deserves to be remembered, and she loved you very much."

"I loved her, too." He glanced over at Fergus. "Can you time travel with your magic, Ferg?"

"Nye, laddie. I don't possess that particular gift."

"Not even with magic objects?"

"No, why do ye ask?"

"Because you could have taken me back in time to see her, and we could have saved her."

Both men were speechless for a moment as they processed his request.

"Even if we could go back in time, lad, there are rules," Fergus said, bending over to meet his eyes. "The number one rule is ye can't change the past."

"Why?"

"Because if ye changed the past, ye'd change yer present—right now. Ye understand?"

"Not really. Can we go back now? I'm hungry."

Landon reached for both men's hands, letting them swing him along. His laughter filled the air, quickly dispelling the pall that had settled over him. This was the first time he had spoken to Ronan of his mother.

"Ferg, you remember the time traveler's watch he found a while ago?"

"Yeah, Ronan, I do."

"Please tell me you magicked that away somewhere safe from him."

"Aye. 'Tis done."

"If I had my way, it would be out of this district and halfway across this continent."

"If it makes ye feel safer, I'll take it with me when I return home."

"I'd consider it a personal favor, and I'll clear it with Madylyn for you."

Landon's questions scared the breath right out of Ronan's chest because he had no doubts that his naturally inquisitive child would have no fear of trying to change history. Ronan had just gotten the boy to trust him. He sure as hell wasn't ready to lose him because he already loved him more than he ever would have dreamed possible.

26

Help Arrives

Rhyanna woke in the morning, feeling a little better. This was the longest recovery period she'd ever needed, and she still wasn't fully replenished. Even though she felt run down, it was a challenge for her to stay still and rest.

Kyran tried to help, staying close and keeping her company while she rested. Her sweet man was still worried about her, but this morning, she left before he woke, needing some time to process alone.

Hoping to appease him when he woke alone, Rhy left a note detailing promises for later. The only caveat was that he had to agree not to check up on her. A sultry smile crossed her face as she sensed the exact moment he read her note from the burst of lust rolling through their telepathic bridge.

"Don't overdo it, my lady. You have promises to keep later, and I fully intend to see that you do."

"I've never been one not to keep my promises."

"Thank all the gods and goddesses for that," he purred. *"I'll see you later."*

"Until then, me laird."

The smile remained on her face as she walked to her shoppe. Casting blue witch light into the lanterns and hearth, she headed through the clinic and out the back door.

Rhy slipped off her shoes and settled on the ground in her lush garden, taking full advantage of the beautiful summer day. A multitude of flowers were in full bloom, nestled alongside herbs and plants she used for healing. The heady scent of roses mixed with wild thyme and rosemary. She watched the buttercups, daisies, and blue chicory swaying with the wind. The sound of the bees and hummingbirds drifted on the breeze.

Letting her mind drift, she allowed the earth beneath her to soothe her soul and nourish her body. The hum of the earth's energy wound through

her body and comforted her as she opened herself up to the Earth Mother's greatest gift.

Grounding was one of the best ways to heal anything that ailed ye. Anything from an anxious mind, a broken heart, or a shattered soul could benefit from the earth coming in contact with bare skin.

As her body soaked up the delicious energy, her mind calmed, and she listened for the guidance of her inner voice. Her inner voice was silent today, letting her know that her body and mind were slowly coming back into balance.

The ferry whistle blew, and Rhy knew her guests would soon arrive. She raised her arms overhead, stretching her back. With her palms open, she drew in the heat from the sun, and let it flow into her body. Standing, she shook her skirt off and slipped into her sandals before heading back inside.

A knock at the front door announced her visitors. Rhy walked through the clinic and answered the door, greeting her guests.

"Welcome," Rhy said with a wide smile. "Thank ye all for taking the time. Please, come in." The three healers entered, each as different in appearance as they could be from one another.

Fern was near as high as she was wide, but with curves in all the right places. She'd pulled her black hair into a severe bun at the nape. Baggy men's trousers stopped two inches above heavy work boots. A short-sleeved, no-nonsense, gray smock matched her intelligent gray eyes. The stunning woman always downplayed her femininity. Rhy often wondered what caused her to hide behind the baggy clothes.

In a melodic voice, Fern said, "Rhy, 'aven't seen ye in a coon's age."

Rhy smiled back at her. "Aye, luv, 'tis been too long."

Catalina Gallagher stepped forward next. The woman was long and lean with wavy caramel tresses and warm hazel eyes. She opened her arms and hugged Rhy affectionately, then kissed her on both cheeks. Her voice was sultry and smooth like smoked whiskey when she spoke. "ma chérie, luv agrees wid yooo. I must meet dis mon of yers." Her eyes traveled up and down Rhy's form. "I take dat back; de mon be wearing ye plum out."

Rhy laughed. "Cat, welcome. Thank ye for coming so soon." Rhy examined her just as closely, then smirked when she saw the telltale signs in her aura. "I'm not the only one with a new man, na am I?"

Cat blushed prettily. "Mayhap. Dere is a mon who 'as me attention—for now. Mmm hmm, he be like dark chocolate wid sapphire eyes. Mouthwatering."

All three women laughed at her description. Rhy turned to Myranda, hugging her tightly for a long moment. "Ye've all met before, I assume?"

A chorus of "ayes" answered her.

"Good. I'll make some tea, and we'll get started."

The hearth flamed to life as they walked in, quickly heating the iron kettle that always sat ready over the flames. Rhy removed a porcelain teapot from a shelf and set it on a tray on the table with a small glass jar of honey. Gathering dried herbs from her cabinet, she combined rose hips, roasted chicory, and dried black cherries into a metal ball. Snapping off a small piece of a cinnamon stick, she dropped it into the teapot with the ball, then filled it with boiling water from the kettle. She covered the pot, giving it a chance to steep.

"That'll be ready in a few. Let's head into the clinic and figure out our schedule."

The clinic was empty this week, a fact for which bone-tired Rhy was grateful. A blackboard hung on one wall to track patients' needs and medications. They used another one on the opposite wall as a calendar.

"Tell me yer preferences, please," Rhy said.

"Evenings be better for me," Fern supplied.

"Mornings," Catalina and Myranda said simultaneously, laughing as they spoke in sync.

"Well, that works perfectly for us all, then."

"Jameson, one of our wardens, nearly died last week after a hellhound attack. He almost lost an arm, and his heart stopped from the trauma and blood loss he experienced. Only thing saved him was his alpha forced a shift." Rhy cleared her throat. "He's our number one priority."

"Mercy, me," Fern said, shaking her head.

"Cat and Myranda, if ye can both do mornings the first week, 'twould be a blessing. One of ye can focus on Jamey, and the other could offer his parents and the clan healers some assistance as well. They're all exhausted from this ordeal. I'll work on range-of-motion early afternoons, and Fern, ye can help soothe everything I'm bound to irritate come evening." Rhy used chalk to pencil their names into the daily blocks.

Brushing her hands off, she turned back to the women. "Tea?"

"Got any whiskey to add to it?" Fern asked.

"Jest might," Rhy said with a smile.

Cat, never one for subtlety, said, "I dink de tea needs da wait." She reached out and stroked the strip of faded hair framing Rhy's face. "I doan thinks dey be de only ones who overdid it, Chérie."

Myranda shook her head in sympathy. "You need some tending of your own, lass."

Rhyanna's cheeks heated. Embarrassed to be called out on her stupidity, she said defensively, "He's family. Not a one of ye would've done any different."

They all nodded in agreement. Cat pulled a stool over and pointed at it. Her eyes were snapping now as she told Rhy, "Sit down."

"That's not why I asked ye all to come today."

"Question is, little sister," Fern added, standing on the opposite side of the stool, "why did ye na call us to help sooner?"

"We could have been here immediately and would have been happy to do so," Myranda admonished.

"I been beyond thinking. Didna ken fer two days whether the lad lived or died."

Myranda joined the other two, and they placed their palms outwards until they touched each other. They surrounded Rhyanna with their healing, their friendship, and their love. As the energy from the earth women built, the front door slammed shut, and another voice piped up from the shoppe.

"Wait for me," Hadley Greene shouted as she rushed into the clinic. "I can feel the energy vortex you're creating, and I need a piece of this. It won't just benefit you, Rhy; it will help us all, and after last night, the Mother knows I need it, too."

Hadley was always a breath of fresh air. Average height and on the lean side, she was beautiful, with dark red hair hanging in a thick braid over her shoulder. Pale blue eyes twinkled at Rhy as she gave her a kiss on the cheek and took her place between Cat and Fern.

Hadley's hand went to her chest and said, "Not sure what's happened, but let's do this. I can feel how depleted she still is."

Once again, the vortex grew, only this time stronger than before. The women's hands touched palm to palm, letting the energy roll through them, taking their individual gifts, magnifying them, and weaving them with their sisters. The offering surrounded Rhyanna in a tube of healing energy that made the hair stand up on her arms.

Rhy closed her eyes and opened herself to the gifts her healing sisters blessed her with. The fatigue faded away, as well as the last of the dull muscle aches. As her inner well refilled to capacity, she sighed happily.

The women slowly lowered their hands and stared at Rhy in amazement. Cat reached out once again and picked up the strands before handing it to Rhy.

Rhy glanced down to see that they'd channeled enough into her to change the gray back to her normal honey blond. Tears threatened at the improvement. She was vain enough to enjoy seeing it returned to her natural color.

In a choked voice, she said, "Thank ye all for everything."

Hadley wandered over to the schedule board and said to Fern, "I can alternate nights with you if you'd like me to."

"Appreciate it."

Rhyanna stood, clearing her throat. "Cookies, anyone?" she asked, heading back to the shoppe. "Tea's ready."

The women gathered round a table full of freshly baked cookies, rich tea, and the joy of sisterhood. They talked about their patients, their families, and their men until they were laughing so hard their sides hurt. Rhy had forgotten that Catalina had a son, and to realize it was Roarke, made Rhyanna blush heavily. Catalina wisely ignored the reaction.

Catalina, Fern, and Hadley headed for the ferry midafternoon, but Myranda said she would wait for the later one. After hugging goodbye and promises to gather again when it wasn't necessary, the healers left. Rhy missed her Earth Clan sisters. They rarely were all together in the same place.

Looping her arm through Myranda's, she led her to the garden behind the shoppe. Wooden benches hid behind hedges throughout the healer's massive garden. Summer flowers bloomed everywhere. The heavy scent of roses opening for the first time wove a hint of nostalgia through the air.

Rhy led her to a small wrought-iron table with two wrought-iron chairs. Her eyes locked on Myranda, and she gave her a gentle smile. "It's yer turn, Myr. Tell me yer tale."

27

Big Girl Panties

Unable to stand the smell of herself, Danyka dove into the frigid waters of the St. Lawrence at the same time Jamey's link activated.

"Hellion, are you alright?"

Jamey's sexy growl of a voice rolled through her mind. Shock, coupled with so many other useless emotions, caused her to suck in a huge mouthful of water. Choking and pissed off about it, she jetted out of the water. Half in and half out of the river, she coughed up her lungs as she crawled to the edge of the riverbank.

Her mind was still processing, and her heart was beating in overdrive. The lucky bastard lived. Breaking down in sheer relief, she let the tears come and knelt there sobbing, "Thank you, thank you, thank you," she chanted to her creator.

Danny was so grateful he'd returned to them. Jamey was everybody's favorite, and with good reason. He was a damn good partner, the best kind of friend you'd ever have, and the sweetest and gentlest man she'd ever known. He'd do anything for anyone, and yes, he'd recently given her the damn shirt off his back.

Tears poured down Danny's cheeks. The relief she felt was palpable, and for a moment, she struggled to pull in a breath. Memories of the attack haunted her every time she closed her eyes. The horror of his injuries, his blood covering both of them, and the moment his heart stopped beating. Worst fucking day ever. The past forty-eight hours were a special torment, not knowing whether he lived or died. Not knowing if he would survive nearly destroyed her.

The devastation of his loss nearly drowned her in grief. She never believed he would survive the extensive injuries he received. Days trying to reimagine the possibility of a world he didn't exist in about drove her mad.

"Hellion, are you okay?" he repeated. Different word, same meaning.

Heart pounding, she wanted to answer him. Tried, actually. Failed. Because she didn't know what the hell to say. Did she apologize for her bitchy attitude nearly getting them both killed? Should she tell him what an idiot he was going in half-cocked and ignoring her command to wait? Maybe she should find the balls and tell him just how fucking grateful she was that he was alive. She needed to say something to the man. He deserved an answer. Didn't he?

Still, Danny floundered. Until the day he lost his shit and nearly died, she'd never seen this man out of control. Except for maybe those times she saw him fucking Carsyn. He'd lost control, and it was a thing of sensual beauty. What Danny wouldn't give to be the one who made him lose control.

"Don't even fucking go there," she whispered to herself.

Jameson Vance was the one man who could see right through all her smoke screens. He always had and always would. She couldn't bullshit him. He'd know the instant she answered that she'd been bawling, depressed— and if we're going with full disclosure—suicidal at the thought of losing him.

He was the one man she might actually love—if she stopped being a coward and forced herself to face her feelings.

But chances of that were slim to none. Life with Danyka was a losing bet. With a dumpster fire of a childhood, an inability to be intimate with any man without wanting to stab them, and absolutely no concept of monogamy, or goddess help her, celibacy, she had nothing to offer Jamey.

But the saddest part of the whole fucked up equation was, there was this itsy bitsy, teeny weenie part of her desperately yearning to try. Not just for Jamey's sake, but for hers.

This man evoked emotions and sensations in Danny that she could barely comprehend. No man gained access to her body without following her rules. They took her from behind, touching nothing but her hips, cept for what was necessary to penetrate her.

After watching him make love to Carsyn, she craved Jamey. In some twisted three-way, the man made her come from a distance while pleasuring the barmaid. Who the hell was born with that kind of telepathic fuckery? And sweet juniper, the man had the devil's sinful lips.

In a rare display of despair after someone had stabbed Rhy with a sword, Jamey comforted her. He'd waded into the surf and soothed her heavy soul. Then he'd held her with no inappropriate touching and allowed her to snot all over him. When her episode ended, the man honored her request and allowed her to take her first kiss from him. Oh man, the kiss when he finally joined in was…something she still fantasized about.

Yes, she'd been with way more men than she cared to remember or had fingers and toes to count them on, but she *never kissed anyone*. It was too

personal, and it wasn't safe for them. Danny had always been a fuck 'em and forget 'em kinda gal. She saw no point in the intimacy of a kiss—until she kissed Jamey and wanted to do it all over again. Kissing Jameson Vance was life-changing, and she wasn't sure she could ever change her life that much.

Danny loved being single. She could kick ass, take names, drink everyone else under the bar, find a flavor of the night, and not have to share the bed with anyone when it was all over. She *loved* her life.

So why did what he offered make all of that feel so threatened? Jamey made her wonder if, just maybe, she could love her life a little more with him in it. Because the fact of the matter was, she wanted Jamey to touch her. She wanted his hands and, goddamn it, yes, his lips on her and in places that she'd never found pleasure before. Thinking of his face between her legs made her wet. And after her dream the other night, the idea of waking with him spooning her was very appealing.

There was a part of her that longed to be his. That part had little influence over the woman whose mother sold her to a brothel. Raped repeatedly, she'd turned off her emotions to survive. To escape that life, she'd murdered a man because she was tired of being the only one bleeding. Dark, damaged Danyka couldn't take a chance on loving anyone because she was too much of a coward to let them see all of her flaws and scars.

When Jamey contacted her a third time, she dove back into the frigid water, drowning out his voice in her head, the pain in her heart, and the knowledge that the only reason he nearly died was because of her. He was better off forgetting about her because the only thing she could offer him was disappointment and pain.

When Danny returned to shore, her back was straight and her head held high. She reached out to Kerrygan, *"I'm on my way back. Let's pack up and return home."*

"Ye okay, Danny?"

For fuck's sake, why did everyone keep asking her that? *"Yeah, I'm fine."* Her tone was cool, offering nothing else.

"I'll be ready when ye get here." A moment passed before he said, *"By the way, Danny, he survived."*

Her tone was much less chilly when she responded to him. *"I know. It's time I put my big girl panties on and face the music."* There would be questions to answer and plans to go over for the coming session, and she would go through the motions and do her part. She took a deep breath and removed the blocks from her link.

"Maddy, I'm coming back. I'll be there for orientation tomorrow."

"I'm glad to hear from you, Danny. I've been worried." Silence lingered a bit too long before Maddy said, *"We need to talk."*

"I know. Just can't do it yet."

"You know where to find me when you're ready."

"I do. Thank you for understanding."

"Always."

When they returned, she planned to find a bar she'd never return to, get drunk, and find a stranger to fuck out back because she wasn't ready to face Jamey yet. A short-term fix at best. This would get him out of her system for tonight.

Jamey's confusion continued to bleed through their link, but she tuned it out, unable to deal with any more guilt. The man deserved better from her, but she knew the moment she opened herself up to him again, he would batter down all the defenses she'd just built up. Big girl panties or not, she wasn't ready to face him, and she wasn't sure she ever would be.

28

Myr's Tale

Rhyanna gave Myranda a gentle smile. "Tell me all about that lovely family of yers." If the sorrow oozing from Myr's aura was any sign, Rhy was afraid her tale was going to be a heartbreaking one.

Myranda gazed at Rhyanna with her soulful, dark eyes. "Mathyas is still missing," she whispered as the first tear slipped down over her cheek.

"Oh no, luv, tell me what's happened," Rhyanna said, reaching out and clasping Myranda's hand with her own.

Myranda drew in a ragged breath before she started her tale. "His team was called in to assist the Southwest District on a sensitive mission near Phoenix. From the little I've found out, someone ambushed them. Mathyas is officially missing in action. The men who went with him don't believe he's dead. They believe he was ambushed. There were no signs of a struggle or tracks to follow. Even the dogs couldn't find his scent, and they were there within an hour. They brought in hellhounds as a last resort since they're supposed to be better trackers. They couldn't locate him on this plane or any other."

Myranda wiped her eyes, then pulled out a handkerchief and blew her nose. "They asked me the most humiliating questions about our marriage. Have either of us had indiscretions or money problems? They've questioned our intimacy and tried to prove he left me." The waterworks started again. "We didn't have any problems, Rhy. I swear it. We bickered mildly like any couple does, but we loved harder than we ever fought. You know we did." Her eyes begged Rhy to confirm her words.

Rhy was happy to oblige. "Ye've always been a beautiful couple, Myr, and one I'se often jealous of. That man loved ye more than anything. Well, except maybe yer daughter." She offered a small smile, trying to bring a smile to Myranda's face.

"That's the worst of it," she said forlornly. "Even if we had problems, he never would have done this to Maryssa. *Never.* I would stake my life on it."

"Ye can't reach him at all?" Rhy asked, meaning their internal telepathic link or their lover's bridge. Those links lasted until one of them passed or until they mutually dissolved them. Lover's bridges were sacred, and you couldn't destroy them without significant damage to both parties. Rhy knew that well because, during a rough patch, she'd tried to destroy the one she and Kyran created. The only reason she hadn't caused irreparable damage to her heart chakra was that Kyran appeared and stopped her from taking it too far.

Myranda paled as she responded. "No, our link dissolved in seconds," she said. "I thought he died on the mission. Maryssa did, too." She swallowed the lump in her throat before continuing, picking nervously at her fingers. "The funny thing is, even though our link feels inactive, our bridge hasn't dissolved. I don't believe he's dead. I don't feel it here…" She tapped her fingers over her heart. "Neither does our daughter."

Rhyanna understood. It was entirely possible to lose a link and live. Someone very dear to her was living proof of that. "Let me reach out to Madylyn and see if she has time to see ye. I'd like to invite a few others as well. One who's endured a similar experience. The others might offer some insight."

Myranda nodded. "Thank you. We need closure. If he is gone, we deserve to know for sure so that we can finally grieve and get back to living again. Not knowing is making this ten times worse." She sniffled loudly. "It gives us false hope, which is much worse than no hope at all."

"Maddy, have ye time for a visit from an old friend in need of some help?" Rhy asked.

"Of course. Who is it?"

"Myranda Belmont. I'm calling in others to join us."

"Whoever you think is appropriate. My office or the parlor?"

"I think the privacy of yer office will be better today."

"We're on our way."

Rhy reached out to invite the others to join them as well.

"Maddy's available now, Myr." Rhy stood and said, "Shall we head on up?"

Myranda took Rhy's hand and squeezed it. "I can't thank you enough. With Ryssa leaving for the summer session soon, I'll have too much time on my hands."

Rhy squeezed her hand in support. "I can't imagine what ye both are going through, but I promise we'll do everything we can to find some answers for ye." Trying to give Myranda hope, she smiled. But a sinking feeling in her middle worried her. She was afraid that the answers they found wouldn't be the answers Myranda was seeking. She desperately prayed that

the Sanctuary's help didn't bring more heartache to the family. "If ye'd like, I could use help afternoons during the session. It'd give ye an opportunity to still be close to Ryssa while she's here."

"That would be perfect." Myr said. "She's struggling with leaving me after everything with Mathyas. I think this would be a much gentler way of sending her off."

"Aye, then the lass can see ye as much or as little as she wants. And I'll be grateful for the extra help. It's always twice the work with the clinic and classes."

They arrived at the front door of the castle.

"Why do I feel so nervous?" Myranda asked. "I've walked these halls hundreds of times."

"Aye, ye have. But none of those times carried the weight of yer heart as ye entered." She pulled the door open and followed Myr inside. "Let's head up and see what yer options are."

29

I Need Your Help

Madylyn waited for Rhyanna and Myranda to arrive. They'd met Myranda during warden training centuries ago, and they'd become lifelong friends. Myranda was a powerful Earth Mage whose healing abilities rivaled Rhyanna's.

The sound of female voices laughing in the hall had her standing to greet them. She stepped in front of her desk as Rhy and Myranda came walking through the door.

"Good morning Rhy," she said before turning to the other woman. "Myranda, you look fantastic. Family life suits you," she said as she hugged her old friend. "Our visits have been much too sparse."

"I've missed you as well," Myranda said. "I believe the last time I saw you, Maddy, was two summers ago."

"Sounds about right." Maddy laughed and said, "This is a pleasant surprise, but something tells me it's more than a social visit."

Myranda's eyes filled as she came to the reason for her visit. "Long ago, you stood with Mathyas and me during our Pledge Ceremony. You offered your assistance should I ever need it." She clasped Maddy's hands tightly as she said, "Sadly, that is my reason for this visit, Maddy. I need to redeem your troth. I need your help because I'm getting nowhere going through the proper channels."

Maddy's joy at the reunion shifted to concern at her devastated expression. "Myranda, we've been friends for a long time. You never have to redeem my pledge; just ask me for help. Please have a seat," she said. She led her to one of the wing-back chairs in front of her desk. "Rhy, please pour her a cup of tea. There's a pot on the sideboard."

"Thank you, Maddy. I didn't mean to offend. I simply forgot who I was talking to. Forgive me. Everywhere I turn, I keep running into walls. I've used up any favors I could call in, but I'm still not getting anywhere."

Rhy gathered the tea while Maddy took a seat across from Myranda. She handed Myranda a tissue as the tears overflowed and her face crumpled in despair.

Rhy arrived with the tea, and Maddy glanced up at her in shock. Rhy's expression was grim, and Maddy couldn't help but wonder where this tale was going to take them.

"Here, luv," Rhy said, handing a dainty porcelain cup to Myranda. "Light and sweet, just the way ye like."

"Thank you, Rhy." Myranda took a sip before setting the cup on the coffee table in front of her. Taking a deep breath, she wiped away her tears and tried to tame her wild emotions. "I'm sorry for the meltdown. But I keep my feelings reined in for Ryssa's sake. I guess being in the presence of friends was a safe space to release them."

"I've asked Ronan and Fergus to join us," Rhy said as she returned with a cup for her and Maddy. "I want Ronan to share his experience, and Fergus may have some insight into this as well."

Maddy raised an eyebrow at her curiously. She hadn't spoken with Rhy before the meeting, so she didn't know what to expect. "Ronan will be here any moment," Maddy said. His energetic link to her grew stronger as he approached, announcing his presence.

"How is your beautiful daughter?" Maddy asked.

"Maryssa is doing well, all things considered." Myranda sighed. "The past few months have been very difficult for her. Her elemental training is coming up. She doesn't want to attend, so it's been a battle recently. I'm hoping orientation will help her get excited to spend the summer here."

Maddy had been heartbroken to hear of Mathyas's disappearance. They were a tight-knit family that she'd envied before Ronan returned to her. The Belmonts had represented everything she once wanted.

Myranda and Mathyas had a beautiful relationship heavily steeped in love, laughter, and respect. Their relationship was the kind Maddy longed for before her reunion with Ronan.

A smile lit up her face as her soul's other half appeared. Ronan entered, grinning back at her. Warmth flooded through their link, showering her in love, appreciation, and ever-present desire. She was grateful to have found her version of their happiness.

Madylyn and Ronan's love story took the long way around, but after centuries apart and a lot of baggage to sort through, they were stronger than ever.

Maddy's hand moved to her rounded belly, which she rubbed absently as she thought of the miracle their family had become. She was just beginning to show, and beyond excited at the thought of a little girl.

Ronan leaned over and kissed her when he reached her side. Maddy beamed at him as he moved a chair closer. No matter where they were, he was always touching her. He took her hand in his, thumb rubbing absently over her fingers.

"Ronan Pathfinder," she said, pointing to the woman across from her, "Do you remember Myranda Belmont?" She turned as Fergus walked in, dressed conservatively for a change. "And this is Fergus Emberz, our Fire Mage."

"Pleasure to meetchya," Fergus said with a smile. He perched against Maddy's desk, facing the seating area.

"You're Mathyas's better half?" Ronan said.

Myranda's eyes lit up. "I am," she said. Her smile quickly faded as her eyes took on a haunted look. "Or rather, I should say, I was." She shook her head sadly. "I still can't think of him as gone forever."

Shock crossed Madylyn's face. "I couldn't believe it when I heard he was missing, but I wasn't aware they'd found him, Myr. I'm so sorry." Maddy's heart raced, understanding what she was going through because she'd gone through a similar situation with Ronan. Ronan's hand tightened around hers, sensing her distress.

"That's the problem, Maddy. They haven't found him." Myranda wiped at the moisture gathering beneath her eyes once more. "They want me to declare him legally deceased, but I can't make myself do it. Maryssa will never forgive me." She sniffled softly, reaching for a tissue. "I don't think I could forgive myself when it feels so wrong."

The room was silent. No one knew what to say. They waited patiently, wanting her to tell the tale in her own time. "I don't believe he's dead," she said. Her shimmering eyes beseeched them to believe her. "I *know* it sounds crazy—trust me, I do." She wiped her eyes again. "But I *feel* him. He doesn't answer me—he doesn't respond to either of us, but I still sense him."

Myranda looked at Maddy and Ronan's hands clasped in front of her. "You must comprehend what I'm talking about. I recognize the same connection emanating from both of you. When you've loved someone for more than half your life, you sense them even when they're sleeping. You *feel* them on the other end of your link. It's not active, nor intentional, but you always sense them there." Her fingers picked nervously at the damp tissue in her hands. "I know it sounds ridiculous, but I know he's still alive. Ryssa feels it, too, and it's destroying her."

Madylyn saw Ronan sit up straighter next to her as he listened to Myranda's tale. All his senses were on high alert. Maddy felt an anxiousness stirring inside of him. His hand tightened on hers.

"May I ask you a few questions, Mrs. Belmont?" Ronan asked gently.

"You may ask me anything, Ronan," she said. "I've nothing to hide. I need all the help I can get."

"Start at the beginning for me, please? I'm not aware of the circumstances of Mathyas's disappearance. Please take me through as much as you can."

Myranda reached for her tea, draining half of the cup before starting. She cleared her throat and began. "Mathyas went on a mission in the Southwestern District last December. It was special ops, so he shared little of the details with me. I was told they lost him in the Badlands. They were hunting a dark mage who'd escaped from a confinement center not far from there."

Her breath hitched as she continued. "He was communicating with me when it happened. He was in the middle of saying 'I love you' when our connection dropped. It was just gone."

Tears tumbled quickly as she continued. "Immediately, I went to the ethereal plane. I arrived just in time to see our bridge of oak branches burning from his end to mine. I tried extinguishing it. Then I tried repairing and rebuilding it from the cellular level. It was no use; nothing can withstand mage fire."

She sniffled loudly before she continued. "Nothing worked. I couldn't put the flames out or repair it. Where our bridges met is a gaping abyss. I can't find him, but I can still *feel* him in my heart and my soul, not as a spirit, but alive and breathing. Does that make any sense to you? Because it sure as hell doesn't, from my perspective."

Fergus sat up straighter, and his face was somber.

The color fled from Ronan's face as Myranda spoke. He knew Rhyanna was watching him and sensed Maddy's concern through their link. Myranda's story was hitting too close to home, and Ronan wasn't sure if he was ready to share his past again.

The only people he'd confided in were Maddy and his brother Damian. Damian mentioned it was still happening, but they hadn't investigated it yet. He sent a message to him requesting that he join them.

"Damian is coming. I want him here." Everyone nodded. "He's been trying to track the men who took me."

Ronan stood up and retrieved a glass of water from the sideboard. He drank the whole thing and poured another. For just a moment, he stood there with the weight of his guilt heavy on his soul. Would he never be able to walk away from his past for good?

A burst of love and support from Maddy pulled him out of his reverie. He returned to his seat, placing the water on the table in front of him. His hand shook as he set the glass down, so he clasped them both in front of him.

He peered up to see Rhyanna observing him.

"This be why I requested yer presence, Ronan," she said regretfully. She twisted her hands in her lap. "I'm so sorry to make ye go through this again, believe me, but I think ye might shed some light on this from yer experience."

Ronan nodded, accepting his role in this meeting. "You're also a healer, are you not, Myranda?"

"Yes, I am. Rhyanna and I trained together."

"In your combined experiences, when somebody you share a link with passes, what happens to their links from your end?"

Rhyanna spoke first. "I've lost a few family members in me time. Me experience be their links fade, are nearly translucent. I can still faintly see them, but they aren't animated like the living are. I ken their spirits have moved on, and there is no way for them to communicate through the links. They become..." She paused for a moment searching for the right word. "Dormant is the best I can describe them. How about ye?" she asked, glancing at Myranda.

Myranda nodded. "I've similar experiences. A faint shadow of a link, but a very clear knowing that it's no longer functional."

"Have either of you ever known of someone's link completely disappearing or self-destructing while they're still living?"

"Nye," Rhyanna answered.

"Never," said Myranda.

Ronan glanced over at Fergus, who appeared perplexed, but he shook his head no as well.

Damian walked in. "It's been a long time, Myranda," he said, kissing her cheek. He took the seat to the left of her on the couch.

"It sure has, Damian," she said returning the gesture.

Ronan sighed heavily as he leaned back in his chair, ready to continue. He gazed at Maddy and threaded his fingers through hers when she reached for him. Running a hand through his hair only delayed the process. Fuck him, but he did *not* want to travel through his past again.

It had been hard enough wandering through the wreckage with Maddy, but the cost was worth it to save their relationship. They wouldn't be together today if he hadn't found the courage to confront his demons.

"Mathyas was a good friend to me, Myranda," he said solemnly. "We met the night before he went out on that mission. I never heard about his disappearance, or I would have gone out looking for him immediately. I'm

truly sorry for that. Not sure if I could've made a difference, but I would've tried."

"I appreciate that, Ronan," Myranda whispered.

"I can't tell you where Mathyas is, but I think I might know what could have happened to him." Ronan scrutinized Rhyanna. "That's why you included me, isn't it, Rhy?"

Rhyanna nodded gravely. "I'm truly sorry to dredge up yer past."

Ronan cleared his throat, trying to figure out where to start.

"I'm so sorry, baby, that you have to relive this. I had no idea, or I would've warned you," Maddy said as she sent him an infusion of support and love.

Ronan glanced at her as he gently squeezed her hand. *"I know you would've, Maddy. It's taken both of us by surprise. I'm just trying to get my bearings before I start."* He met her eyes, and the support he found there made it easier to speak after their exchange.

Standing, Ronan moved to Maddy's chair. He picked her up, then sat with her on his lap. She leaned her head on his right shoulder.

Dainty fingers absently traced a pattern over his heart. Ronan wondered if she even realized she was doing it. Her fingers traced a scar on his chest in the shape of a star. It was where they branded him.

Ronan peered over at Fergus. "Have a seat. This will take a while." His eyes were bleak as he waited for the fire-haired giant to take the seat he vacated.

His arm rubbed Maddy's back slowly as he finally glanced at Myranda and Rhyanna. "My apologies. I need her support to tell my tale. Rhyanna knows some of my fate, how much I'm not sure, but Maddy's seen a lot of my lost years."

He cleared his throat before speaking to Myranda. "My experience may not be the same as what Mathyas is going through. You need to realize that. You also need to understand before we start that what I am about to tell you will make the unknown worse, not better. Are you sure you want me to continue?"

Myranda's eyes never left his. "I'm not afraid of what you're about to tell me, Ronan. My mind is wandering into enough depressing territory all by itself. If there is even a chance that something you experienced might help, I would like to hear what you went through."

"So be it," Ronan said. His fingers toyed with a piece of Maddy's hair as he gathered the strength to begin. Reciting his story didn't get any easier the more times he retold it.

Ronan pressed a kiss to the top of Maddy's head as his eyes claimed a spot on the mahogany table in front of him. He couldn't look at anyone as he spoke. The pain and shame were too great.

"I fell in love with Maddy while we were still in school. We were seniors, and I knew the first time I gazed at her, she was the one. My heart tripped,

and I would've done anything to get to know her. Fortunately for me, she felt the same way. We spent all of our free time together, shared our hopes and dreams, and planned a future."

Maddy peered up at him as he spoke, and the love shining back at him helped him continue.

"I was young and arrogant. Nothing could slow me down, let alone harm me. With two older brothers paving the way, I was popular. Our family was well-liked, and I believed I was untouchable."

He smiled down at Maddy. "I found the woman I loved early in life. Few couples find such a miracle that young. In the hubris of my youth, I thought nothing would ever come between us." His smile faded as he remembered the past.

"I headed out early one morning for a meal to break our fast when they abducted me off the main street in our little hamlet."

Ronan cleared his throat as his cheeks flushed. "The first violation I suffered was when one of their dark mages severed the links to my entire family."

Myranda and Rhyanna gasped as he finished. He saw Fergus's hands clench the arms of the leather wingback he sat in.

"How is that even possible?" Myranda said.

Rhyanna followed with, "I've never even imagined this being done." She glanced at Myranda and then over to Fergus.

"'Tis the first time I've heard any mention of it," Fergus said.

Ronan's hands clenched the arm of the chair. "When the mage found Maddy's link and realized it comforted me, he creatively implanted a subliminal response. Every time I pictured her, debilitating migraines and nerve pain exploded over my entire body. I stopped accessing our link, afraid he might sever it. I was also terrified of the repercussions if he recognized her."

"During my first week of captivity, they assaulted me physically, emotionally, psychologically, and sexually." The silence surrounding him was deafening. Shame heated his face, but then he sensed their outrage. They were all overwhelmed with horror, then rage. Their immediate response was like a living entity barely contained within each of them.

Damian's jaw clenched, but he said nothing.

Maddy stiffened in his arms. She'd witnessed all but the last when she merged with him, viewing his memories. She wasn't sure how he prevented her from seeing all of this. But then she remembered him taking over the tour of his private hell. Overwhelmed by the physical torture he experienced, she let him, understanding now why he wouldn't want her to see him being raped.

Maddy couldn't stop herself from connecting with him. *"I don't care what they did to you, Ronan. You must realize, the only thing I care about is you survived and returned to me. No one in this room will fault you for anything you did to walk out of there. They will not share your past outside of this room, either."*

The haunted look in his eyes wounded her soul. "I love you," Maddy whispered.

"I love you, too, Maddy," he said softly before switching to their private line. *"There's more, Maddy, and it's not pretty."* The remorse and regret swamping her line nearly took her under. *"Please remember, I only did what I needed to in order to survive. There was no pleasure in what they forced me to do. I still regret the things I did every single day."*

"For two and a half centuries, I was a prisoner. I became a shell of the man I once was. Scars crisscross my body from the beatings, whips, branding irons, and the magical weapons used on me."

Ronan ignored the gasps from the women and the curses coming from Fergus.

"He turned me into his servant, and eventually, my job was to execute the physical and sometimes other assaults on the other prisoners."

Silence greeted him after this statement. Maddy sat much too still against his chest, her breathing so faint she might have been sleeping.

"We all refused the first dozen times he tried to get us to perform in this manner. Then he used me as an example. With an incantation, he broke most of the bones in my body. I lay on the floor watching as, one by one, he brought in the prisoners I'd been assigned to fuck for the day. My master let his most ruthless men use them. He rarely let them play because they destroyed their playthings."

Ronan cleared his throat and wiped his eyes as he tried to continue. "They tortured and raped them, then left their dead or dying bodies surrounding me. They flayed some of them and left them to die slowly in front of the other prisoners. The strongest lasted for days."

His eyes defiantly glared at his audience. Myranda and Rhyanna both had tears streaming down their faces, and Fergus gaped at him in horror, but Ronan could sense the rage radiating off him.

A vehement "Fuck me..." came from Damian.

"I was one of many men he broke. Our minds were more resilient and able to withstand strong magical attacks after the torture and abuse. Our bodies survived horrific damage and still pushed on as if our pain thresholds were nonexistent."

"The master took us to the breaking point. Then he reestablished our tolerance and capacity for pain, endurance, and blind obedience. Many didn't survive his brand of reorientation. When they lost their minds or their hearts exploded from the adrenaline rush, they disposed of them like garbage."

His gaze lifted to theirs as he spoke, waiting for the condemnation he was sure was coming. Maddy's fingers started tracing the brand on his chest again, soothing him. Recognizing nothing but their compassion for him and the horror of what he went through, he continued.

"Our 'Master,' as he liked to be called, was running a breeding program. He was trying to combine our tolerance for pain and our stamina with the strongest elemental shifter women he could find."

"His example of what would happen when we defied him encouraged us to do as instructed. After watching what happened to their cellmates, the women willingly took part as well."

His voice cracked, dry from use. "We willingly performed, not for any sense of pleasure we might get out of the act, but because we tried to keep as many of them alive as we could."

Ronan leaned his head back against the back of the chair and sighed. "Even though fear made them willing, we always believed we were violating them."

Fingers toying with Maddy's hair, he let out a long sigh before continuing. "Our performances were 'somewhat lackluster.' That's what he called our half-assed attempts to fulfill our duty. They mixed drugs into our food, so we were ready to fuck on demand all day long. It was a nightmare, and fucking anyone at that point was a relief from the incessant raging desire. After months of trying, we triggered a Melding Cycle that resulted in half a dozen pregnancies."

"What happened to the children?" Fergus asked in a hoarse voice.

Ronan stared at him, expecting to see condemnation or disgust. The only thing he witnessed from the man he considered a friend was sorrow laced with a heavy dose of rage. To his surprise, the rage was not aimed at him.

"I can't say. They took the pregnant women to another holding area. We never saw them again." He rubbed his eyes, removing the moisture that had gathered.

"I don't sleep well most nights because the women he killed for my disobedience haunt me. I also wonder how many of my children I may've abandoned."

Fergus got up and went to Maddy's private bar. He grabbed a bottle of whiskey and five glasses and returned. Asking no one, he poured two fingers apiece. He chugged his, refilled the glass, and sat back down.

Rhyanna and Myranda picked theirs up and tossed them down like seasoned sailors arriving at their favorite port. Maddy picked up the fourth tumbler, sniffing it longingly before handing the glass to Ronan. He downed it, then handed it to Ferg for a refill at the same time Damian did.

"I can't imagine what you all must think of me now. That was the most shameful thing I've ever done, and this is the first time I've told anyone about this part of my ordeal."

Rhyanna spoke first. "Methinks it's pretty damn amazing that ye survived the horrors inflicted on ye." She refilled her glass and tipped it towards him in a salute. "It took a hell of a lot of courage to share yer tale with us. I thank ye fer taking a chance and sharing the hell ye been through."

Damian's face was a mask of compassion, having heard most of it before. "Thank you for trusting us with it, little brother."

"It was a brave thing to do, Ronan, and not an easy past to give voice to. You honor those you lost by remembering their sacrifices," Myranda said.

Fergus finished his second and set the glass down. "Ye've shined the light on dark mages who're misusing their powers. This fecking needs to be stopped. They need to understand their reign of terror is over because I will hunt them to the ends of the earth to prevent the feckers from doing this to anyone else."

Maddy stared up at him and cupped the side of his face with her hand as she communicated silently. *"Nothing you tell me about your time in captivity will ever change how I love you. I know you, and I believe that you only did what was necessary to survive."* Her fingers traced his jawline. *"I still love you the same way I did before you walked into this room."* Her midnight eyes locked with his. *"Now, I understand you so much better. I understand the scenes you sought to protect me from, and I thank you for the shelter you gave me from them."*

Maddy blinked and then gazed at the others, struggling to regain her composure. "Why don't we take a break? We'll continue when you drop Ryssa off for training."

They all nodded, needing some time to process. The space would give them time to ponder what Ronan had shared so far. Myranda would need the distraction when she left Maryssa for the summer, and Maddy wasn't ready to put Ronan through that again so soon.

Damian put a hand on Ronan's shoulder, then leaned down and kissed Maddy. "You know where to find me if you need me, brother."

They all nodded, then left quietly, but Maddy embraced the concern and support they were projecting to both of them.

Ronan sat there, stunned. He'd stopped trying to staunch the tears running freely down his face. He wasn't sure what he expected, but their calm acceptance and support surprised him. Unable to form a sentence, he pulled Maddy closer and buried his head in her hair.

Once again, they offered him redemption. He was reaching out and grabbing it with both hands while praying that no more of his past would be required to dance into the light.

Even though what he shared tonight was horrific enough, there were still things he didn't allow himself to dwell on. He was afraid if he were to look

too closely at his past, he would lose any self-respect he still had. And he never wanted to expose his family to the full extent of the depravity they forced him to take part in.

30

Kateri's Visit

Rhyanna, Damian, Myranda, and Fergus exited the study together.

"I'll say farewell here," Fergus said when they reached the stairs.

The others said their goodbyes and left through the foyer door. They walked silently down the path, each lost in their thoughts after Ronan's confessions. Before Rhy realized it, they were at her Apothecary Shoppe.

"Would ye like me to see ye to the ferry, Myr?" Rhy asked.

"That's unnecessary. Plenty of light left. I'll be fine." Myranda hugged her tightly. "Thank you so much for everything today. I'll head to Wellesley first thing in the morning."

"Yer very welcome, luv, and I appreciate the help."

"If you don't mind, Mistress Belmont, I'm heading that way," Damian said.

Myranda glanced at him in surprise. "I'd be happy for the company."

Rhyanna watched the two walking down the lane. Damian would keep Myr's mind off her worries for a little while.

"Are ye well, my lady?" Kyran asked.

"Aye, I be fine. Thank ye for checking on me. Ye made it to late afternoon without doing so."

"Only reaching out because you feel sad."

"I be teasing. Been a tough afternoon."

"Want to talk about it?"

"Nye, not me tale to tell."

"You nearly done for the day?"

"Aye, jest about to close up shop…" Her gaze picked up Kateri Vance coming up the lane. *"Might be a wee bit longer."*

"I'll meet you there. We can head home together."

"I'd like that."

Kateri stopped in front of Rhy's shop with a market basket in one hand and a fresh bunch of cut flowers in the other. She handed the flowers to Rhy and pointed to the basket.

"What's all this?"

"A thank you for saving my son's life."

The woman's gratitude warmed Rhyanna's heart. "Won't ye come in?" She opened the door and followed Kateri inside.

"This is lovely," Kateri said, wandering around her shoppe while Rhy put the flowers in water. Her gaze traced over the dried herbs hanging and the cabinets with tiny drawers covering one side of the wall. Rhy had neatly labeled each drawer with chalk on a slate tile that adhered to the front. "I need one of these! Who made this for you?"

"A man in Alexandria Bay who does custom work for me."

Kateri worked her way around the room before setting the basket on the table and pulling out a chair. "I am deeply envious of this room."

Rhy laughed, pulling up a chair and facing her. "Only an earth element or healer would say that."

"Makes sense then because I'm both." She pushed the basket towards Rhy. "Before I forget, this is also for you."

"Milady, the flowers were more than enough." She removed a piece of muslin covering the top and smiled in delight. Inside the basket were six pint jars of honey. She picked one up, marveling at how light the thick product was. "What kind?"

"Locust," Kateri said. "'Tis one of my favorites because of the delicate flavor. It doesn't overpower your teas or your baking."

"Who told ye this is one of me weaknesses?"

"I have my ways," Kateri said without giving up her sources. "Thank you for arranging nearly round-the-clock care for all of us. Fern stopped by this afternoon."

"Yer very welcome. Jamey is very important to all of us. We'd do anything to make sure he makes a full recovery."

Kateri's eyes filled. "You're the reason he's still with us, Mistress Rhyanna. He never would have made it without everything you did before we arrived. I can't imagine what it cost you."

Rhy didn't pretend to misunderstand what Kateri was saying. As a healer herself, Jamey's mother understood the amount of energy it would have required to keep him alive.

"Nothing a few hours of sleep and a visit from me clan sisters couldn't fix."

Kateri boldly reached across and pulled a piece of Rhy's hair from the side of her face. "They did a good job. Don't think I didn't see the white

streak before you left. I understand what saving him nearly cost you, and I am grateful beyond words."

Rhy sat quietly for a moment. "Jamey be like a brother to me. I'd a given all for the lad.

"That's what I was afraid of." Kateri cleared her throat before asking, "How's Danyka?"

Rhy paused, not sure how to answer. She didn't feel comfortable talking 'bout her sister.

"My son told me how he feels about her. I suspect she feels the same for him. I'm concerned about the woman who holds his heart."

Rhy let out a long sigh. How could she stay silent after that? Tears filled her eyes as she said in a choked voice, "I don't know how she is, milady."

Kateri reached over and took her hands. "I don't use titles, Rhy. Where is Danny?"

"Haven't seen her since that day. She flew off afore ye arrived and won't answer any of us." She sniffled, then stood to get a handkerchief from a drawer. "Kerrygan followed her, and he shouldna have shifted so soon after returning. I haven't heard from either of them, but I sense she's overwhelmed with guilt and shame. I'm not sure how she'll get past this when she feels like it's all her fault."

"No one is at fault," Kateri said firmly. "Jamey suffered from a senseless accident. There's no point trying to make sense outta something that will never be explained." She pulled her long hair over her shoulder and began braiding it. "He lives. That's all that matters to any of us."

The braid finished, she fished in her pocket for a leather tie. "He needs to see her."

"I'm sure he does."

"And she needs to see him…soon." Her tone was that of a clan leader, an alpha.

"I'll do me best to encourage her," Rhy said.

"I'd appreciate that, Mistress Rhyanna." She gave her a gentle smile. "We'd all love Danny—if she'd let us."

"She's easy to love, but she's skittish."

"Good thing Jamey's wonderful with skittish things, isn't it?"

They both laughed for a moment. When the alpha was gone, the mother returned. "Fern said to ask you for a massage oil to use on Jamey in the evening. She's going to show me how to work on him the days she might not make it."

"That would be a gift for ye, too. I promise ye, Kuruk would appreciate it after a long day, too."

"Then you'd better give me a large bottle of it."

"Yes, ma'am." Rhy took one from the shelf and put it in the basket.

The bell on the door tinkled, and Rhy's smile brightened as Kyran joined them.

"Mrs. Vance," he said with a slight bow.

"Prince Kyran, good to see you under better circumstances." Giving Rhyanna a hug, she gathered her basket and said, "I best be on my way. Thank you again, mistress."

"Thank ye fer the flowers and honey."

The moment the door closed behind Kateri, Kyran took Rhy into his arms. He pressed a kiss to her temple, asking, "Ready to go?"

"Aye. More than ready." After extinguishing the witch light in the hearth and the lights, she locked up.

Kyran took her hand in his, and they walked side by side up the path leading to the lake. He pulled her hand to his lips, placing a kiss on the back. "This," he said, "is my favorite part of the day."

"The walk?" she asked, thinking he was daft. She could think of many more favorite things they could be doing.

"Spending my evenings with you, my lady." His blue eyes flashed with heat, promising her a night to remember.

And with those words, Rhy fell in love with Kyran all over again.

31

Aftercare

"Fergus, can you see to Landon for a bit?" Maddy asked.

"Aye, I'd be happy to. Take yer time, Maddy. Ronan needs ye."

"Thank ye, Ferg."

Ronan's head was still buried in her hair half an hour later. His arms banded her tightly to him. She nuzzled against his face, trying to get him to talk to her.

Surprising her, he stood easily with her cuddled against him and strode from the room. He made his way to their suite in silence, looking straight ahead. Entering their suite, he kicked the door closed behind him and took her to their bed.

Setting her down gently, he finally glanced at her. "How can you stand for me to touch you, Maddy, knowing now what I was capable of and what they did to me?"

Maddy rose onto her knees so they were at equal heights. She framed his face between her hands and looked directly into his eyes. "You did what you needed to, Ronan, to survive. You took no pleasure in it."

He shook his head, disagreeing until she put a hand up to stop him.

"Let me rephrase. Your body may have found a natural physical release, but you found no pleasure being with those women. Did any of them come to mean anything to you?" Her voice held no censorship.

"No, there was no time for conversation or cuddling. It was a quick fuck, and then on to the next one."

Maddy's stomach rolled, and it was an effort to keep the horror off her face, but somehow, she managed it.

"Before the breeding program began, he used us to assault the male prisoners to break them quicker. I fucking hated being used like that. He castrated the first man who refused, making the rest of us much more amenable." Ronan tried to pull away, but she wouldn't allow it. "I can't make

146

you understand the amount of self-loathing I felt having to take another person against their will and the guilt that I did it selfishly for my survival."

Ronan yanked his head from her grasp and paced. "For fuck's sake, Maddy, they could have charged me with rape and implemented island law or executed me had we been living in normal society."

"You weren't in normal society when they forced this upon you, Ronan. There was nothing normal about the situation you were in. Everything you did was based on self-preservation. It wasn't your choice or your preference. You can't spend the rest of your life blaming yourself, or he wins."

"I try not to, Maddy. You don't know how hard I try." He ran a hand over his ashen face. "Do you realize, when I stand at your side during Warden's Court, and you hear rape cases, it's all I can do not to become physically ill? I am terrified someday one of those women or, the blessed Mother forbid, a man will stand and point at me, accusing me of rape in front of everyone."

Maddy gasped. "Ronan, don't even entertain those thoughts."

"What kind of example would I be for Landon, Maddy?" he whispered. "Some nights, I can't sleep. I can't stop thinking I have no right to be so happy after the harm I caused my fellow inmates."

Maddy's eyes overflowed as she realized how difficult it was for him to accept the happiness they'd finally found. "Don't you dare listen to your inner demons, Ronan. You deserve to be loved and happy as well."

"Do I, Maddy?" he scoffed before heading to the window. "You were all I could focus on getting back to. I pushed all the nightmares away in my pursuit to win you back, and now, in my dreams, they haunt me from their cells. Their bellies are swollen with children they didn't want and don't love. Their eyes blaze at me with hatred, and their fingers point at me while their lips whisper accusations."

"What do they say?" Maddy asked, even though she didn't want to know.

"'Rapist, murderer, enforcer, deviant,' they chant at me. As I back away, I brush against something, and I look down and realize it's Landon's hand I've walked into. He's staring at them, horrified, but understanding the things they call me. He looks up at me with disgust and backs away from me like I am something foul."

Maddy stifled a sob and climbed down from the bed. No wonder the man wasn't sleeping. The less sleep he got, the stronger the nightmares would affect him.

"I don't deserve any of you. I don't deserve the peace or the love you give to me," he said so softly, she nearly missed it. "I'm afraid I will taint anything good that comes to me. What if he finds out I survived and comes after you to get to me?" His overwhelmed mind was creating scenarios that were terrifying him and heartbreaking for her.

Madlyn walked swiftly toward him. "Look at me, Ronan," she demanded. She waited, and it was as if she hadn't spoken.

She grabbed his arm and jerked him towards her. "I'm sorry for this," she said.

His perplexed look slowed her for a moment, but it didn't stop her hand from swinging or the sting of her slap across his face. The shock on his face nearly stopped her, but she couldn't do this again. "I understand, as much as I can, the concerns and worries you are experiencing now. I understand the self-loathing and disgust you feel towards yourself. I can even understand your nightmares and the depths from which they spring."

She caught her breath and continued without breaking eye contact. "You listen to me, Ronan, and you listen well. You did nothing wrong but try to stay alive. As horrific as the things you did were, would you think less of me had I been one of those women who willingly participated?"

She waited for a head shake to continue. "Would you think less of me had they sent me in to force a man to fuck me who was tied up and drugged? If I entered a cell and sat on his chemically inflamed penis against his will so that I could live another day, would you hate me for it?"

His eyes bored into hers as she ranted at him. "No, Maddy, but-"

"Bullshit," she said crudely. "You did what you needed to. You came back to me and earned your right to stand at my side. We've created a good life together. It is a beautiful, wondrous thing. We are going to be happy. We are going to raise our children, and by the Mother, we will have our happy ending, and no one can take that from us."

Ronan tried to grab her wildly gesturing hands as she continued her rant.

"If I ever hear you speak like you are going to run away and leave me or leave our family to protect us again, Ronan, so help me, I will beat the shit out of you and let your son watch. You can explain to him the idiotic thoughts crossing your mind. Someday, when they are old enough, if you choose to, you can talk to our children and explain what you went through. Then if something arises, none of us will be shell-shocked. Until then, you are the rock our family needs. Do you understand me?"

He laughed aloud. Laughed, the bastard. Irritated and on the verge of tears, she stomped her foot and turned to leave the room. But Ronan caught her hand and stopped her.

The bastard pulled her reluctant body close and enfolded her in his arms. His hands rubbed her back soothingly as he kissed her forehead. "I'm sorry, darling, to have caused you such fear and doubts."

His palms framed her face. Her midnight-blue eyes still glared at him, but a sheen now coated them as well. "I'm sorry to have upset you, Maddy. I truly am." He rubbed his nose against hers. "Honestly, I don't know where those thoughts came from. I've never considered running from you before." His lips grazed hers. "I will never do that to you. You have my word."

Her hands gripped his wrists tightly, her nails breaking the skin. "You damn well better not, or I will hunt you down, and I promise you will live to regret it." Her angry tears escaped, and she clung to him still as he kissed them away.

When his lips reached hers, the delicate way he had been handling her erupted into an explosion of need. He took control of the kiss. His hands grabbed her ass, and he boosted her up around his hips. Her heated core found him swollen and ready. They both moaned at the contact. He turned for the bed, setting her down so she was kneeling facing him.

Their lips never parted as he unlaced his breeches and pulled them down over his hips. He raised her long skirt until his hands found the strings holding her panties. He tore them away, removing the barrier, blocking him from where he needed to be. With her skirt bunched up, he lifted her again and impaled her slowly.

She released his lips as her eyes locked on his, and he filled her. Her breath hitched, and her head kicked back at the exquisite feel of him throbbing inside of her without moving.

Using his shoulders for leverage, she leaned forward and glared into his eyes. "You belong to me, you bastard. Don't you ever forget it." His hands cupped her knees tighter as she lifted herself until barely the tip of him remained inside her sheath.

He watched the fire in her eyes blaze at him as he said, "I won't forget. Not with you to remind me, darling." Before her temper could flare again, he lowered her, slowly sliding back into her warm heat.

She rose back up, and they continued sliding against each other in an excruciatingly slow dance, building the pressure and the anticipation with each glide.

"More, Ronan," she begged.

"No," he said, holding her still this time and preventing her from rising. "I want this to last."

"I don't know how much more I can take," she chanted, her hormone-driven body already trembling into overdrive.

"You can take anything I give you, Maddy." He teased with little nips at her chin. "You always do and come back begging for more."

"We'll see who's doing the begging," she said as her inner muscles started fluttering around him. "How much of this can you take?" She taunted him as she focused on the muscle groups giving him the most pleasure.

"You don't fight fair, Maddy."

"Nope. I fight to get what I want."

"Tell me what you want."

"Move, you bloody bastard," she said again, trying to move.

149

His loud chuckle made its way through her core as he moved to the wall. He leaned her against it and watched as his body moved in and out of hers. Their eyes locked as his hips swung freely, finally giving her what she sought.

"Look at me, darling," he said as his speed increased. "I want to see you fall over the edge."

She whimpered as his cock stroked the special place inside that lit up her entire body. "Yes, right there," she moaned as he ground against her clit with each thrust. He never slowed, never missed a beat as she exploded into a million pieces with him watching her.

Her eyes dilated, and her body shuddered around him as he slowed down and watched her orgasm roll through her. She gasped as he pumped in and out of her, feeling her body winding up for another one.

"Ronan, I can't take much more," she whimpered as her over-sensitized body climbed once again to that magical peak. This one was stronger, and her hands reached for her belly protectively as the full-body contractions worked their way through her.

Knowing she couldn't handle much more with the boost of pregnancy hormones flooding her system, he picked up speed and joined her as her body milked him dry.

He leaned his head against hers as he endeavored to catch a breath. "Thank you for bringing me back to my senses."

"My pleasure, Ronan. My pleasure, every time," she wheezed out before kissing the fading handprint on his cheek.

They both laughed as he stumbled to the bed and laid her down gently. Kicking off his pants, he joined her, pulling a throw over them. They relaxed, wrapped up in each other, happy just to be together.

As Maddy drifted off, snuggled against his shoulder, he lay there thinking about how damn lucky he was to have found her again. He was going to do everything in his power to never scare or disappoint her like he had earlier because she deserved better from him.

After all the challenges they went through to be together again, she deserved everything she wanted, and he intended to make sure she received it.

32

Orientation

Myranda stepped out of the portal with a prickly blue-haired teen. Maryssa showed up last week with her straight black hair liberally streaked with peacock blue. Myranda loved it. They had talked over tea, and Maryssa apologized for her tantrum. She still wasn't happy about the impending elemental training session, but she would follow through on her responsibilities and make the best of it.

Rhyanna waved as she walked towards them. "I am so happy to see ye both. Maryssa, it's been too long." She gave the beautiful girl a big hug.

"Mistress Rhyanna," Maryssa said, hugging her tightly, "I forgot you were here."

"Aye, not sure I'll ever leave." Rhyanna laughed. "It made me day seeing yer name on our list this term."

"Knowing you're here makes it easier to leave home," Maryssa said.

"Anytime, anything, lass, ye come find me now, ye hear?" Rhyanna waited until she nodded. "Me door is always open to ye, and I'm always looking for apprentices at the shoppe if ye've any interest there as well."

"I would enjoy that. It will make me feel like I'm at home helping you," she said, looking at Myranda with a small smile.

"Well, orientation's about to start. We best be heading up," Rhy said.

They walked up the hill towards the castle perched above them. Maryssa stopped and stared in awe for a moment. "It's absolutely beautiful. I can't wait to paint it if I get a chance."

"Ye'll have lots of time to yerselves. Ye'll see, lass. Honestly, it won't be so bad."

"With you here, it won't be," Maryssa said in relief.

They reached the top of the hill and joined the small group of families assembling in the front garden. Maryssa looked around for a friendly face. So far, she only recognized two other girls from her school.

Amberly Briarwood smiled shyly at her. An earth element also, she was a tall, auburn-haired girl with glasses framing her mahogany brown eyes. She had a sweet smile and disposition. She wore a lightweight burgundy sweater over a long, flowing brown skirt. Maryssa smiled back, grateful for a friend in the crowd.

Colette Creek stood to the right, staring at her long nails in a bored fashion. As the local Water Clan princess, she was too good to speak to Maryssa. She'd pulled her long, wavy blond hair into a high ponytail, highlighting her sharp cheekbones and perfectly made-up features. She wore a short-sleeved, form–fitting, black knit dress that ended two inches above her knees where it met knee-high, cuffed boots. Silver bangles hung from her ears and adorned her dainty wrists. She raised one perfectly haughty eyebrow as she met Maryssa's eyes and turned away.

"Great, just like school," Amberly murmured next to her.

At least two dozen girls and a dozen or more boys, they didn't know milled around talking quietly.

A bell chimed, indicating orientation was about to start. Families shushed their children and found their table in the garden with light snacks and beverages awaiting them.

The Belmont table was in the middle, and Ryssa cringed to see Collette's family seated next to them.

Collette looked down her nose at her and said in a voice loud enough for the tables nearby to hear, "Let's hope we're housed by class and not by our elements. It will be difficult enough spending all day with them. We ought to get a break on our downtime." Her stepmother giggled with her and looked snidely at Ryssa's table.

Ryssa's cheeks flushed, and it took everything she had to keep her mouth shut and not tell the little snot off. Myranda's hand on her shoulder reminded her she was representing not only her family but her clan. She wouldn't embarrass either of them over that twit.

Light chit-chat surrounded them from neighboring tables. Myranda nibbled on a scone while Maryssa sipped her lemonade and tried to look for other students she might know surreptitiously. There were a few boys she thought she recognized but couldn't recall their names.

After everyone settled, a bell rang out, and the garden became eerily silent except for the buzzing of the bees.

Enormous French doors opened onto the stone porch along the length of the building. There were three large wooden chairs on either side of the door. A woman walked through the doors to the rail. Her powerful demeanor and sharp gaze captivated Ryssa as she stood before the crowd.

She instantly felt an affinity for this woman in the long midnight blue Victorian skirt and boots.

Artfully arranged dark hair formed a cluster of roses on top of her head. If Ryssa wasn't mistaken, those roses were a rare midnight blue. She fascinated Ryssa, and as if she had read her mind, the woman turned and looked right at her as she spoke.

"Welcome!" Her melodious voice projected out to the crowd. "I want to welcome all of you to the orientation for this summer's Elemental Training Session. For those of you who don't know me, my name is Mistress Madylyn SkyDancer, and I head the Heart Island Sanctuary. Thank you for gracing us with your presence. I'm looking forward to getting to know every one of you in the coming weeks." A warm smile soothed the crowd.

"I know it may not thrill many of you to be here, and some of you may even be frightened of what is coming. Please let me put your mind at ease. This island is a safety zone for you. This is a place for you to learn to use the elemental gifts you were born with while harming no one else. Some of you may have already noticed your gifts making themselves known, and without the proper instruction and defenses, you might accidentally harm your family, friends, neighbors, or yourselves."

Pacing the length of the stone porch, she let that sink in. "None of you would ever intentionally place the people around you in danger, but an untrained power is a deadly power in the novice's hands. Our mission is to help you find your strengths and encourage them. However, you also need to know your weaknesses and how to compensate for them. We will push you in the direction most suited for each of you to accomplish this. Our wardens will help you find the inner strength you need to open yourselves up to your true power. You will learn to awaken your senses and your skills for the highest benefit of all."

Her perky demeanor faded as she faced them. "I'll be honest, there will be times you will dislike us because of the way we push you to do your best. Mayhap, you might even hate us before it's over."

Madylyn stared at the crowd, her gaze locking on each of the students' faces. "That's all right." She gave a delicate laugh. "We'll help you channel that rage into a thing of beauty and hope, or of power and protection."

Her voice rose slightly. "You will form lifetime bonds here. Some will be with your instructors, others with your fellow students. We want to cultivate those bonds to strengthen you, making you healthier and more resilient than you've ever been. You'll walk out of here ready to face the adult challenges that are on the horizon."

Ryssa listened to the headmistress, fascinated with this woman and the power she was projecting with her voice. She was informing them, but she was also soothing the nerves of the students and the emotions of the

parents, many of whom would leave their children for the first time. Mistress SkyDancer wove a spell with her voice, and the magic floating throughout the garden was beautiful. Ryssa wanted to learn how to do that.

"The very definition of a sanctuary is a 'place of refuge.' That's what we offer you here. The class system that you might benefit from in your villages or towns does not exist here." She glanced through the crowd again. This time, her eyes noted parents who might have the mistaken idea that their children would be treated differently. "A few of you may believe that you were born with an advantage over your fellow students. That delusion will not help you here. Your elemental gifts don't care if you're rich or poor. Your power has nothing to do with your social standing, and if you think it does, you're sorely mistaken."

Her eyes landed on Collette, and it was all Ryssa could do not to turn and look at her, too.

Mistress SkyDancer let that sink in. "If your child attempts to leave without permission prior to the end of the term, they are committing themselves to an extra three months here for an unpaid work assignment. I promise you, they will not enjoy that part of their stay."

"I will expel any student caught bullying another. Expulsion from here will cause repercussions from your clans and your regional courts." Her eyes landed on every parent in the group, letting them know there would be no exceptions.

"Your time here will be best spent learning the true meaning of teamwork. The ability to think quickly and help others without hesitation is imperative. If you see someone fall, I expect you to help them back up, not kick them while they're down."

Her demeanor changed, and her voice softened, once again soothing her crowd. "This experience will be what you make of it. Every day can be a wonderful opportunity for growth and adventure, or it can become your nightmare. The choice is yours. Choose well."

That beautiful smile lit up her face again, taking the sting out of her threats. "Now that we have the formalities out of the way, let's get on with the fun part of your day. Let me introduce you to the wardens, who will assist your children on their elemental journey."

Madylyn turned towards the doors and said, "Mistress Rhyanna Cairn will be your instructor in earth magic. She has earned the highest rank among the Earth Clan's mages and has centuries of experience in the highest order of healers. Rhy will address any medical concerns at the Apothecary Shoppe down the hill from the castle."

Rhyanna stepped up on the stage in an ankle-length emerald silk skirt and peasant blouse. She'd partially pulled up her long, blond hair on the sides of her head, showing off her fine features. "Welcome! It be me pleasure to meet each of ye." She curtsied and moved to one of the waiting chairs.

Ryssa was happy to see the beautiful earth mage, who was also one of her mother's friends. She heard someone behind them commenting on her obvious lack of proper education because of her dialect. Ryssa stiffened in outrage until Myranda put a hand on her daughter's arm and mentally shouted, *"Don't"* Ryssa fumed, unable to understand the ignorance of some people. She treated everyone as an equal and expected others to do the same.

"Kai Tyde, our new Water Mage. And his brother Kyran Tyde on loan from the Court of Tears." Mistress SkyDancer continued, smiling at all the sighs of appreciation from the young ladies as the handsome young men gave them a casual wave.

"Fergus Emberz, our Fire Mage." Giggles ran through the crowd. His flaming red hair was out of control as usual, and his mismatched outfit was more serviceable than some she had seen. His fire drakes were larger than usual, putting on a show for the crowd. Ferg bowed and sent the drakes through the crowd, delighting the audience.

"Damian Pathfinder, an earth mage of the highest order, joins us as our Weapons Master and teacher of defensive training until Jameson Vance returns." Damian walked out to cheers from the young men who knew of his skills.

"Our Air Mage, Mistress Danyka, is also our expert on shifting." Danyka wore a leather vest instead of her halter today. She was as conservatively dressed as she would ever be, trying not to scare the parents away with all the weapons strapped to her petite frame or encourage the young men's fantasies.

"Last but not least, our Stable Master, Ronan Pathfinder. He is one of the most sought-after masters on this continent in the protection and care of rare and deadly creatures." Ronan's eyes lit up as they met Maddy's.

Madylyn faced the crowd once more. "My door is always open for every one of you. If you are struggling with your assignments, homesick, or being bullied by anyone—student or instructor—it is your duty to come to me or any of the wardens standing here today. I can't help you if you don't let us know there is a problem."

The wardens fanned out behind her. "At this time, students will gather in the garden to meet with the warden assigned as their advisor."

"Parents, thank you for trusting us with your children. While they enjoy their tour, we formally invite you to enjoy a luncheon in the formal garden. Afterwards, I will be happy to answer questions." Madylyn turned to a young woman who appeared at her side and said, "My assistant, Lily, will show you the way."

Madylyn watched as Lily led them off, grateful for a break from the group. Every year, there was someone who made it difficult for the rest,

thinking their child was special and entitled to tutoring or an entire suite to themselves. Maddy would quickly dissolve any notions they had that their children were on vacation. This season, she knew there were at least three who would challenge her before the day was over.

Maddy searched for Danyka, but she'd disappeared with her students. She'd hoped to talk with her before the council meeting tomorrow, but she'd skillfully avoided all the wardens since her return. They were trying to respect her boundaries, although Fergus was getting a mite testy about it.

A loud growl came from her stomach. Typically, she would take a quick break, grab something to eat, and toss back a shot to get through the questions and personal requests. Rubbing her growing belly, she sighed at her limited options. A tiny movement inside seemed to agree with her.

"All right, wee one, I'll behave," Maddy said as she headed for the kitchen. "But there damn well better be chocolate waiting for me—and lots of it."

33

Brass Balls

Danny flagged Carsyn down for another shot from across the bar. The usually friendly barmaid shot her a dirty look from where she stood and took her time making her way over. No surprise there. Danny understood why she was out of sorts and why she was pissed off directly at her.

Carsyn and Jamey had been...something. Not exactly dating, she supposed she could classify them as long-standing lovers out behind the bar on her break. Jamey didn't have a flavor of the night like Danny tended to. No, he was more settled and civil than she'd ever been. Danny had witnessed their sessions more than once, and the memories were still in the top ten of her spank bank. She realized Syn wanted more than the occasional fuck out back, but she also believed Jamey had recently ended things with her after their three-way orgasm a few weeks ago.

Jamey transferred the sensations from the orgasms he gave Carsyn to Danny empathetically while she fucked someone else at the other end of the building. The man had some mad skills to transfer the sensual assault Carsyn was enjoying to Danny through their telepathic link.

Danny experienced a rare and elusive orgasm. His eyes had remained locked on hers the entire time while he touched Carsyn, watching and ensuring both women were satisfied. It was hands down the best sexual experience of Danny's life and one of the worst for Syn when Jamey slipped and called her by Danny's name.

Carsyn took her time, but finally worked her way around the bar to refill Danny's shot glass. Hands clasped tightly around the neck of the tequila bottle, she stopped in front of her, topped off the double shot glass and glared at her. "How's he doing?"

Danny raised bleary eyes, wanting to avoid the question and get back to drinking, but Syn looked liable to hit her over the head with the bottle if she ignored her.

"From what I've been told, he's on the mend." She missed the flash in Syn's eyes as she reached for the shot glass and downed it, wanting to catch a refill before the angry wench wandered off again. Setting it down heavily on the polished bar, she tapped her finger down and pleaded, "Hit me again, wontchya?"

Carsyn's glare intensified. And it was just enough to piss Danny off and keep her from minding her manners. Orientation had taken for fucking ever. Danny took off immediately after because she wasn't in the mood to deal with anyone, and she sure the fuck didn't want to do it here, either.

"You're just pissed because he doesn't want you anymore." She should have paid attention to the outrage on the woman's face before she continued. "Not my fault if he wants someone he can't have." Her index finger tapped the bar next to the sticky shot glass again as a reminder.

Carsyn picked the shot glass up and slammed it to the side, out of Danny's reach, along with the bottle. Faster than she ever would have bet on, Syn reached over the bar, grabbed Danny by the front of her leather vest, and hauled her up and over it until their noses nearly touched.

Blue eyes blazing, she shook Danny like a terrier with a rat. "You think I'm pissed, li'l Danyka?" She quirked an eyebrow at her. "Well, lass, you got that much of it right."

Carsyn's actions stunned Danny. Thank God she was too drunk to reach for a weapon. The barmaid was a gentle lass, even on the worst of days. Danny hadn't thought she had this much strength or rage in her. Deciding she probably deserved whatever the woman had to say to her, she allowed it, needing to wallow in the guilt.

"You'd be right thinking that I can't comprehend why he'd want a trashy little thing like you. Why, when there are so many women who would cherish and honor him—myself included—would a man as kind and sweet as Jameson be pining away for you?"

Shaking Danny again, she continued, "I don't give a shite about how many men you feck out back, and 'tis none of my business that you don't enjoy being touched."

Danny's face blanched as the woman called her out. Carsyn was forcing her to face her deepest, darkest truths, and Danny couldn't defend herself or look away.

"I don't care that you can be a miserable li'l cunt to everyone around you when the mood suits. Any of us can have a bad day."

The hands holding her tightened, pulling her closer. Danny's fight-or-flight responses kicked in, and she grabbed Carsyn's wrists, trying to

dislodge them. She was ready to brawl until the barmaid's next words sent her reeling.

"What I can't fecking stomach is the fact that he saved your life, nearly died, and is suffering through healing now. And you're being a fecking coward." Carsyn spit the words at her in disgust.

Danny's face paled beneath the accusations Syn leveled at her. She didn't bother refuting anything because everything the angry woman said was true. Sagging in her grip, she waited for the guilt and humiliation to be over.

"I know you, Danny." Another shake ensued. "I *seeeee* you, and I recognize the hurt little girl screaming in your head that you try to drown out with the shitty attitude, the endless parade of men, and the rivers of booze. I know the pain you've endured and the reasons for it."

Compassion filled Carsyn's eyes. The thought of her pity made Danny want to puke.

"I understand and can damn well sympathize with your past. What I can't tolerate is the fact that for all your bravado and bullshit, you can't seem to pull out those big brass balls I keep hearing about and go check on the man I know you love."

Danny paled at her accusation, and her hands came up to jerk at Syn's wrists. Unable to listen to anymore, she found her voice. "Lemme go, Syn, before this gets ugly," she snarled.

"It's already fecking ugly, you twat. He loves you, and as much as it might gall me, I understand why. As pissed off at you as I am right now, I understand why he's drawn to you. You're fiercely loyal. You can be a lot of fun. Mostly, you respect and treat him the way he treats you."

Carsyn's brow quirked as she went on, "Never thought I'd witness the day that you were a fecking coward. You shouldna be afraid to face the consequences—whatever they might be—for anything that went down."

Her voice lowered as her eyes held Danny's hostage. "I also 'see' that the attack wasn't your fault, luv. Jamey was just as much to blame. Jealousy, misplaced emotions, and distraction on *his* part caused this as well."

One last shake, and Carsyn's eyes filled near to the point of overflowing. "I saw him last night. He's ridden with guilt because he almost got you killed. The poor man thinks this is all his fault and is terrified you'll never trust him again. Can you live with him believing that?"

Gentler than Danyka would have thought possible, Carsyn returned her to her seat and the reality of the silent bar around them. They hadn't heard what Carsyn said because her voice never rose above a loud whisper. The way they gazed at her spoke volumes. Syn didn't lose her temper, and she never laid hands on anyone.

As Syn released her vest, she reached up and gently cupped Danny's face, wiping the tears flowing down her cheeks.

"I know you love him, and that you're terrified of where that path leads. I believe you can be good for him if you want to be. You also have the power to destroy that sweet man. Choice is yours, Danny. What's it gonna be?"

Carsyn slammed the shot glass down in front of her and slid the bottle closer. "If you need to drink your way to the bottom of this to find your truth—or your balls…it's on the house." She refilled the shot until tequila sloshed over the side and set the bottle down next to it.

"I'll not apologize for a damn thing I jest said because I needed it off my chest, and you needed to hear me. Even through my disappointment, I can admit how good the two of you could be. It's a damn shame you can't admit what your heart wants as well."

Deflated, her eyes released Danny's, and she moved down the bar to the next customer as she shouted, "This round's on the house. What'll it be, folks?"

Danny hung her head, grateful for the distraction from the emotions still leaking down her face. Shaky hands reached for the shot, and she sloshed half of the drink over the sides. The gold liquid burned all the way down and did nothing to quiet the voices mocking her. Her inner voice piped up, adding her opinion to the chaos.

"What's it gonna be, twat?" Danny thought her inner demon might have chuckled for a moment. *"She had that part right, didn't she? Ye gonna be a coward and drown yerself in that there bottle, or ye gonna pony up and head to Wellesley?"*

Danny set the shot glass back down without a sound. Ignoring everyone around her, she slithered from the stool and headed for the door.

34

Warden's Council

Heading for her office to prepare for the council meeting ahead, Maddy telepathically linked with the sentient building she lived in—the Sanctuary's castle. Using images instead of words, she sent a request for her office to accommodate the number of people who would soon arrive. The Sanctuary housed the wardens and many of the island's residents on the second and fourth floors. They also housed students on the second floor for the duration of their stay in the summer. The third-floor housed classrooms and the first the common areas.

Maddy's office and conference room were on the second floor near her personal residence. When she reached her office, she knew the space would be larger, the conference table longer, and the extra chairs already in place. Full of gratitude, she offered the building her thanks and then reminded it of the number of individual suites she needed prepared. They needed a dozen rooms with en suite bathrooms in each elemental wing for the students arriving two days hence.

Maddy was excited about the group of teens who would be arriving. Every session was a new adventure and always challenging—for the students and the instructors. Rhyanna and Danyka would help monitor the girls in their respective wings of the building, while Fergus, Kai, and Jamey were in charge of the boys.

The thought of Jamey halted her mid-step. She assumed Jamey would be back in time. Most shifter injuries could heal ten times quicker than a human would. But Jamey's injuries were extensive, and Maddy didn't want him to push himself too quickly to return.

Maddy tapped into Mrs. O'Hare's link and reminded her to send hot and cold beverages, fruit and cheese, and sweets up for the coming meeting.

Landon was heading home with Tamas and Josyah, a pair of Romani twins who worked in the stables with Ronan. They had a heap of younger cousins Landon's age. He needed children his age to play with. This would keep him out of their hair during the meeting as well.

Maddy headed up the stairs to her study to go over the agenda for today's meeting. Rhy joined her at the top of the stairs, heading that way as well.

"You're early," Maddy said as they walked towards her office.

"Aye, figured I could check up on ye while I'se waiting. How ye been feeling, Maddy?" Rhy asked as they entered her altered office.

Maddy walked in first, appreciating the sense of magic that came with the sentient building readjusting to what she needed it to be.

"I've felt much better the past day or so. My energy is better. I don't want to sleep all the time."

"Nearly out of yer first trimester. Many women find their energy soars and their appetites are better."

"That's never been a problem," Maddy grumbled.

Rhy laughed. "You're barely showing. Sit for a moment. Let me take a peek at ye."

Maddy sat in a chair, giving Rhy enough room to walk around her. Rhy held her hands a few inches away from Maddy's body and closed her eyes. The energy coursing between them was invigorating. Opening herself up to the ethereal field, she could see Maddy's auric field. Her chakras were in perfect alignment, hormonal levels right where they should be, and her vital signs were perfectly normal. The bairn Maddy carried was healthy, safe, and warm inside of her.

Dropping her hands and opening her eyes, she grinned widely. "The wee lass is active. Ye should start feeling movement soon."

Maddy smiled as she glanced down at her growing belly. Her hand automatically caressed it as it did every time the child crossed her mind. This little girl was their miracle, and she couldn't wait to meet her.

Mrs. O'Hare entered, followed by five of her assistants carrying trays of food and urns of hot coffee and tea. Ice water, lemonade, and various bottles of wine and alcohol were available for their guests. Dessert tables sat in the middle of the enormous room.

Maddy eyed the tray of pastries and cookies, calling her name. Trying to decide on which one she wanted, she heard voices in the hall announcing their guests.

Ronan and Kyran walked in together, both smiling the moment they laid eyes on the women they loved. Behind them, Kenn and Kai entered, laughing loudly. Kano and Elyana trailed behind them with his arm around her possessively.

King Varan and the former Queen Yareli followed their sons. "It's nice to have them all in the same place again," Varan said to Yareli.

Her gaze flew to his, surprised that he initiated a conversation. "Yes, it's a rare gift and one that I treasure."

"As are you…" he said so softly, she didn't think she was supposed to hear.

Yareli kept her eyes straight ahead because falling for her ex a second time wasn't something she was ready to do. Turning to Elyana, she greeted her daughter-in-law with a hug. "How is Laird Killam?"

Elyana's smile faltered. "He's regaining his strength, slowly but steadily."

"Our healers are experimenting with seaweed wraps for burn patients. The rate of success has been impressive. I would be happy to provide some for your father if your healers approve."

"At this point, we'd be willing to try anything to ease the pain he is in."

"I'll have one of our healers meet you at the portal when you're ready to return. He can instruct your team on the techniques he has found most helpful." Yareli offered.

"That would be wonderful. Thank you, Queen Yareli."

"Don't use that title with me. I'm Yareli to you," she said with a smile.

Elyana nodded shyly at her. "It's nice to have another woman to confer with—and one who is interested in something more than fashion or men."

Yareli laughed. "I agree. We have brains and should be able to fully use them." Yareli gave her a hug. "Hopefully, when things calm down for you, we can spend some time together. I would like to get to know you better."

"I would enjoy that as well." Elyana glanced at Kano, laughing with his brothers. "Mayhap, your family can visit us, and we'll give you a tour of the lakes. I know he would love to see his family." As if he sensed her speaking of him, Kano turned and gave Elyana a smoldering glance.

"Not sure my son is ready to share you with anyone else yet." Yareli chuckled as Elyana blushed an adorable shade of red.

Cheveyo, a Hopi Shaman and Landon's grandfather, escorted Kani, Queen of the Rivermaids and guardian of the St. Lawrence River, through the door.

Maddy projected her voice into the low din. "Please help yourselves to some refreshments, and we will get started as soon as the rest of our party joins us."

The guests served themselves as Lachlan Quinn, Roarke Gallagher, Samson, and Damian Pathfinder completed the rest of their party.

Maddy and Ronan took one end of the table, with Rhy at her right and Kyran at his left. The Tyde family took up nearly the entire left side of the table, while the rest of the group faced them. Fergus and Lachlan took the end, facing Maddy and Ronan.

Conversation was low as they enjoyed the light brunch the Sanctuary provided. Pushing her plate away, Maddy took a sip of her tea and spoke to Elyana. "What news is there of Laird Killam?"

Elyana wiped her lips with a napkin, then spoke. "His prognosis is good. The healers believe he will be up and walking within the week. Pain management is his biggest hurdle to date. He's alert and aware, and fully on point with what's happening in his clan. I am stepping in as his emissary, only until he can fully return to the helm." Elyana's voice was soft, and she spoke quickly, uncomfortable with speaking in front of crowds. Kano took her hand in his, squeezing gently in a show of support.

With a glance at Fergus, Maddy asked, "Do you have any leads from your informant there?"

"Aye, Kano brought a message from me cousin, Vulcan. He and his brother, Brandell, own a bar. Me informant's in town and has reached out. I be heading back with them to try to meet up with him tonight."

"I'd like to join him—with yer permission, of course, Mistress SkyDancer." Roarke's eyes challenged her to say no. It was a power game they still seemed to dance around.

"I've no issue with that, Roarke. Remember that you shan't do anything without going through the proper channels first. You gave me your word, and I intend to hold you to it."

"Fair enough, Mistress, as I plan to hold you to yours."

"Touché," Maddy said before turning to Lachlan Quinn, her law advisor. "Any further problems with Mr. Jordan?"

"Nye. With threats of imprisonment, he went on his way. He tossed about a fair bit of venom towards the Sanctuary and ye personally, Maddy, but I'm not sure he's that ambitious."

"Wait a minute," Roarke said. "Are you talking about Fisher Jordan?" he asked incredulously. "The card shark?"

"The one and only," Lachlan said.

"He's a vile piece of shit. Don't trust the man, no matter what he promises you."

"We don't intend to, Roarke," Maddy said. "One girl we rescued, Genevieve, is his daughter. Mr. Jordan showed up in Warden's Court attempting to reclaim his property, probably intending to resell her."

A gasp of shock came from Rhyanna and one of outrage from Kai and Varan.

"She's a sweet girl," Varan said. "Always treated me with respect, even when I didn't deserve it."

"Genny fears everything, and I bet he's the reason," Kai growled.

"When she woke the first night we'd rescued her, she made me promise not to tell her family she lived," Rhy whispered. "She swore they'd sell her back into sexual slavery again."

Maddy's heart broke for the girl. Poor thing had never been treated well.

"The terrified lass threatened to run away or kill herself if I sent her back with him," Rhy said.

A shudder rolled through Maddy, making gooseflesh rise on her skin. "I emancipated her, promised her a home, lodging, and work if she wants it. I will never return her to him, but he didn't take it well when I stripped him of his parental rights."

"Wait a minute," Roarke said, a frown creasing his forehead. "If he sold Genny to a flesh peddler, he's one step closer to them than we are. We need to spend some time getting Mr. Jordan to trust us, and then we need to get information from him."

"What makes you think any of us can gain his trust?" Varan asked.

"I got this," Kenn said with a sly smirk. "He's a gambler. The only thing we need to dangle is his favorite game. We need a card game big enough that he can't stay away, and I'm just the person to set one up that he can't refuse." His wicked laugh rang out. "I know all the top players, and we," he glanced at his father, "could offer enough of an incentive for him to sign up for a tournament."

"I'll fund the operation," Varan said. "It will be less suspicious if we have it at the Court of Tears than if Heart Island sanctions it."

"I agree," Maddy said. "That would work better since I have banned him from Heart Island."

"Wait til I get back with Ferg," Roarke said. "I've got some loyal River Rats that can help pull this off. They'd be good for extra security and for keeping an ear to the ground to see if he suspects anything."

"I'm looking forward to making this man's life a living hell," Kenn said with an evil gleam in his eyes. "Best part is, he'll never see it coming."

"Well, with that in place, let's move on. Damian, have you found out anything from the Elemental High Court that will help us?"

"Negative. Whatever mage is running this show seems to prefer running from the Lakes to the Atlantic using the St. Lawrence Seaway to transport their forbidden cargo. Farthest west this is happening is in Laird Killam's territory. Don't get me wrong, there are always cases of missing people, but there are none as consistent as the ones we are experiencing."

"Thank you. Are you available to cover for my weapons instructor for the next week or two?"

"No need for that, Maddy," Danny said in a hoarse voice from the doorway. Her face was pale against the harshness of her short, spiky, ebony hair. Dark circles under her brilliant violet eyes highlighted her lack of sleep. Danny stood ramrod straight, but the sass and cocky attitude she usually exhibited were absent. She avoided everyone staring at her except for Maddy.

Clearing her throat, she said, "I'm back and ready to work. No need to trouble, Damian."

"I've other things to trouble Damian with if he's available." Maddy's eyes held hers for a long time, gauging her sanity, or lack thereof, and communicating silently that she wasn't so sure she believed her. "Welcome back, Danny," she said in a formal tone, leaving no doubt that they would speak soon.

"Good to be back," she said, sitting down next to Rhy. She accepted the hand Rhy offered, squeezing it tightly and ignoring Maddy's tone and the glare Fergus sent her way.

Maddy gazed at the people she most trusted and relied on and was so grateful for every one of them. Her child would grow up surrounded by people who loved her and would protect her with their lives. She couldn't imagine Genny with no one to put her first.

Pushing those thoughts away, she asked, "Does anyone have anything new to add or questions?"

Kani's ancient eyes found hers. The solemness in them was real, and the anger in their dark depths was palpable.

"My maids and men are hearing rumors of the man who poisoned my river trying to gain entry once again."

"McAllister?" Maddy asked on a gasp.

"The bloody arrogant bastard," Fergus added.

"Any waters he's contaminating comes under my jurisdiction," Varan said, seething.

"Get in line," Kani snapped. "I've got first dibs for the pain he caused my people."

"Yes, ancient one," Varan said, trying to soothe the first-generation elemental. "Neptune will have to be notified. He lays claim to all bodies of water on the east coast."

"Then, by all means, invite him to the party." Kani's voice was cutting, and pink stained her cheeks. "He wasn't here to take the pain from my people or to suffer alongside them." A sneer crossed her face. "But let him come. We have unfinished business."

Varan raised his hands in a placating manner. "I shan't get in the middle of this battle, my lady."

"Smarter than your father, ainthchya?"

Trying not to look at his previous queen, he said, "Depends on who you'd ask."

Kani's laughter was infectious, and they all joined in. "Humbler, too."

"Last call?" Maddy said, giving everyone a chance to pipe up. When no one spoke, she said, "We're officially finished here. However, I would like the ladies to stay a little longer. I have someone I'd like you to meet."

She gazed at the men gathered. "Thank you all for coming. We'll meet again in three to four weeks unless it's necessary to gather sooner. Please, grab some more food on your way out. You're welcome to wait in the parlor or the bar."

Rhy turned to Danny as the others mingled. "Ye alright, lass?"

Danny's haunted gaze met hers. "No, Rhy. I'm not, but I will be eventually." She let the healer embrace her. "I just can't talk about it yet. Sorry if I worried you."

"'Tis alright, lass. Just good to see that yer here and in one piece. Scared the hell out of me, ye did."

"I'll try not to do that again."

"I'll hold ye to that," Rhy said as Elyana approached her. "Excuse me for a moment," she said to Danny, standing to meet the woman who was nearly pledged to Kyran.

Elyana threw her arms around Rhy and hugged her tightly. "With everything going on that night at the Court of Tears, I never thanked you for saving my father's life."

"No thanks be necessary. Is there anything he needs?"

"I think we're covered. Yareli is sending a healer who uses seaweed wraps for burn victims."

"I hear they do wonders." Rhyanna said, "Let me know if there's anything else I can do."

"I will," Elyana said and then added, "Thank you for your blessing that night as well. It made an unpleasant situation a little more tolerable."

"A helluva mess it was." Rhy laughed. "At least we're both right where we want to be."

"I hope you'll visit sometime soon. I know Kano would love to see Kyran," Elyana said.

"After the summer session, we'll set a date."

"Wonderful," Elyana said, smiling as their men headed their way.

Danny gazed around the table at the couples surrounding it. They had all been loners up to a few months ago, and now two of the women she considered sisters had gone and fallen in love. You'd have to be blind not to see the sparks between Varan and Yareli, and there was something going on with Kani and Cheveyo...she wondered if Neptune would make that a nasty little triangle or an interesting one.

Fergus plopped down next to her, staring at his hands. "Pixie, if ye ever run off and leave me like that again, I'll blister yer hide." He cleared his throat. "Ye broke me fecking heart. Was bad enough young Jamey being a fecking mess, but we've always had each other's back."

"I'm sorry, Ferg. I truly am." Danny's eyes filled as she reached out to him, letting him take her hand and press it against his heart. "Forgive me?"

"Already did, lass." He pulled her up into a bear hug, whispering again, "Already did."

Danny clung to him as tightly as he did to her, then pulled away. "I can't do this right now. I can't do it here."

"Aye, lass, I hear ye."

"So, which one of these poor bastards do ye think will settle down next?" she asked, nodding towards the couples still sitting.

Ferg gave her a funny look, then said, "Not sure any of them are next in line. We'll have to see."

Danny didn't examine what he said too closely because she couldn't go there yet—if ever. Whichever one of them fell next, by the Mother, it wouldn't be her. The past week had been pure hell, and she was never going through that again. Not. Fucking. Ever.

35

A Safe Haven

Grace picked up her folder, took an excited breath, and headed for Maddy's office. Nervous, hopeful, and praying she would not puke, she raced up the stairs to the second floor. Dashing down the hallway she passed the men as they left. She recognized some of the Wardens. But there were other powerful men she'd never seen before. The Warden's Council had disbanded, and the matriarchs of their community were now waiting for her.

Rounding the last turn tightly, she smacked into a tall, lean male so hard that it knocked her on her ass. Head still racing ahead to her presentation, it took a moment for her to process what had happened. She sat there stunned until the male who had run her down squatted next to her and began gathering the papers she'd dropped.

His eyes met hers, and the humor in those strange orbs fascinated her until he opened his mouth and pissed her off. "Wanna be careful who you run into, li'l girl," he said with a cocky smirk, eyes taking her in from the top of her head to the tips of her boots. "I think the children are outside training, shouldn't you be?"

Ferg shook his head, chuckled, and said, "Careful, laddie. Grace here'll wipe the floor with ye."

Interest flared in his shifter eyes, and then the humor returned. "I wouldn't want to hurt the wee lass." He stood, offering her a hand.

Flames danced in the wee lass's eyes as she stood, ignoring his outstretched palm. Stretching every inch of her four-foot eight frame as far as she could, she craned her neck back and gazed up at the lanky man who had knocked her on her ass. Smiling sweetly even though she really wanted to knee him in the balls, she quirked a brow at Fergus. "Thanks, Ferg. Who might this arrogant asshole be?"

The cocky grin grew wider as Kerrygan quipped. "The wee lass has a mouth on her."

"And she bites," she snarled, baring her teeth.

Kenn chortled behind him. "Always had a way with the ladies, Kerry."

Ignoring him, she smiled sweetly at Ferg, the gesture lighting up her face. "Good to see ya, Ferg."

The glower returned as her gaze drilled back into him. "If you'll excuse me, I have business to attend to." She moved around the asshole and continued down the hall, ignoring the tingle moving down her spine.

"Kerrygan."

His smoky whiskey voice came from directly behind her. She stopped in her tracks and faced him.

"I'm sorry, I didn't get to introduce myself," the man with the fascinating eyes said.

Her gaze slammed into his, and in a frigid voice she said, "You needn't have bothered because I don't care." She turned on her heel and left him floundering behind her.

Kenn and Fergus chuckled behind them. "C'mon lad. Let's go afore she hands ye yer balls." Fergus said.

"What the fuck is her problem?" She heard him grumble in that sexy, deep voice as they walked away.

Fergus's voice was fading, but she heard him answer, "Men be her problem, laddie. Leave that one be."

An ache formed in her chest as she realized he was correct. Men were her problem and probably always would be. Not that she didn't want it to be different, but she was different now. Her captors groomed her to be something other than what she had once been. Something darker, desperate, and craving...

"Hello, Grace. Thought I heard ye out here," Rhy said, peeking out the doorway. "We be ready for ye, lass. Nervous?"

"A wee bit," she answered honestly. "I've never done this before."

"Yer gonna do fine, lass. Just a bunch of us chatting. Think of it that way."

Blowing out a deep breath, Grace stepped inside the lavish office and conference room. Maddy smiled at her, instantly putting her at ease. She knew that Mistress SkyDancer fully supported her project. She hoped she could convince the others to support them as well.

"Grab something to eat and take a seat, Grace," Maddy said. Turning to the other women, she said, please refill your coffee or tea and help yourselves to some more pastries.

Grace grabbed a cup of coffee, dumped in a heap of cream, and took a quick slurp for courage. She was too nervous to eat, so she took a seat next

to Maddy and waited for the others to rejoin them. With a nod from Maddy, she began.

"My name is Grace Brinley, and I am one of three girls who survived the shipwreck off Grindstone Island. The wardens from this Sanctuary rescued us and offered us a home for as long as we needed one. I had no urge to return home because my home life was not kind. I moved out on my own a year prior to my abduction because I didn't feel safe at home."

Hand shaking, she reached for her coffee, taking a sip while gathering her thoughts. "Although I am grateful for the welcome from the Heart Island Sanctuary, I long for a mission of my own. I want to make a difference in this world. And I need to be known as something more than one of the Grindstone survivors."

A finger tapped nervously against her mug. "I want to contribute to this community and help others who might need a safe place to go." Another deep breath and she found the courage to meet the eyes of every woman sitting at the table.

"I want to offer a place of sanctuary for any woman in need of one. There are many women like me who escape from hell but don't know where to go or what to do. I want to create a place where they have the time and space to regroup—to heal and figure out what their next step is without the pressure of finding housing or a job."

She cleared her throat, uncomfortable with the silence enveloping them. "My father never missed an opportunity to backhand my mother or one of his kids." Her face filled with shame, even though she knew it wasn't hers to carry. "I want women trapped in the cycle of domestic violence or sexual abuse to have a haven they can access if needed."

Kani's ancient gaze landed on her, and she asked, "What do you need from us, child?"

Grace didn't flinch when this ethereally beautiful woman called her a child because, in the sense of time, she was. Her gaze flew to Madylyn's, and the gentle smile and support she found there gave her the courage she needed.

Passing out a clipped bundle of papers to each woman sitting there, she explained. "This is my projected wish list for a shelter. Obviously, we need a structure to start. We will need a place large enough to house women and children indefinitely. It will need to be hidden—protected and warded from the community—so that the residents feel safe there. The supplies to house, feed, and teach would be a blessing as well—but only until we can provide for ourselves, of course."

"How will this place eventually support itself?" Elyana asked, as her eyes scanned over the projected budget.

Grace knew this would be the sticking point. "I would like for us to be as self-sufficient as possible. We would plant seasonal gardens to supply our fresh food. Eventually, we would build greenhouses for year-round produce. A creamery would be nice to make our own milk, butter, and cheeses—if we have enough pasture for cows."

She let out a ragged breath. "Again, space allowing. If the property is large enough to house a small herd of sheep, they could provide wool and meat. The river provides us with fish. Smoking surplus items would provide long-term storage, or we could sell them at local markets. If some of our residents' weave or knit, we could also sell any items produced from the wool." Her eyes glittered excitedly as she spoke.

The room was silent as those gathered scanned over her proposal. Grace's hands twined nervously, wondering if she was overreaching. Rhyanna gave her a gentle smile, encouraging her.

The River Queen Kani was the first to speak. "Our community has needed a place like this for a long time."

Her gaze met Madylyn's and every woman sitting at the table before continuing. "I know of a place that would be large enough. We own an island off Sackett's Harbor. The building is only accessible by a wooden drawbridge, so it would be easy to ward and need minimal protection. I believe the original structure housed an orphanage. The building has the space you would need, but it will take a lot of work to clean it up and make it useable."

Grace's eyes lit up with excitement. "I'm not afraid of hard work."

"The property sits on over a hundred acres. There are pastures for small herds of animals. But again, it has been a long time since they were used. You will need to clear fields and rebuild fences before you can add animals."

Her fierce gaze met Grace's. "I will give the Sanctuary this property—under your direction—if you promise me you won't turn anyone away because of their profession or ability to pay. Many women are just trying to survive. Promise me this place will be available to the meekest of our residents."

Grace met her gaze without flinching. "I would be the last person to turn someone away for that. I was one of those women. This place won't just be a refuge, but a place of healing. Counseling will be available to those in need." She glanced at Rhyanna, nodding for her to take over.

"Someone from me healer's guild will stop by once a week, or more if needed. I have a dozen women willing to donate their time for any form of healing. We have many healers who specialize in trauma," Rhyanna said.

Elyana spoke next. "My ore workers can provide wrought-iron gates warded for protection to surround the main structure. It will protect them from anyone seeking entry from the water. The wards will need to be

refreshed weekly, but any of your wardens can do that. None intending harm will enter the building."

"The Court of Tears can patrol and protect the perimeter." Queen Yareli said. "We will house a squadron off-site so that the women aren't uncomfortable with their presence. The patrol will be close enough if needed. We will also provide all the fresh fish you could want."

"This is a lovely plan. I am happy to support this endeavor," Kateri Vance said. "It's been too long since something like this has existed. I will provide a small herd of sheep and the cows you need. If the stable is salvageable, we will provide you with a team of horses and a wagon. I'll also send some of our gentler mares for those who like to ride. If it's a complete ruin, my boys will help rebuild it."

"The Sanctuary will provide laborers and journeymen for whatever needs to be repaired structurally," Madylyn added. "I'll also send our head gardener to help plot out a garden large enough to support the island."

"I will offer training twice a week to any woman who wants to know how to protect themselves," Danny whispered. "It will help empower them."

Grace's eyes filled. She struggled to speak through the lump in her throat. "This is so much more than I ever hoped for." She wiped her eyes. "I wish I'd had a place like this when I needed one. But I promise to put your donations to the best use possible."

The women began speaking excitedly, tossing out ideas and names of others who might help. Grace listened and created lists while praying she wouldn't let any of these women down.

"When the rest of you have time," Kani said, "we can plan an excursion to Sackett's Harbor to see how much work needs to be done. Then we can work on the funding and supplies needed."

Gratitude overwhelmed Grace. After her rescue, she had floundered, not knowing what direction to turn to or what she would be qualified to do. She had needed a purpose, and now she had one. Heart full and spirits lighter, she could not wait to get started.

The gaggle of women chattered like magpies as the suggestions kept coming. Full of hope, she gazed around at the powerful women who would help make her dreams come true. Grace jotted notes as quickly as the women offered them, but her mind wandered to the arrogant ass with the gorgeous eyes, wondering when she might see him again.

36

I *Miss* Him

Maddy returned to her office, surprised to find Danny sitting in one of her chairs. She was leaning forward, elbows on her knees, as she fidgeted with a tattered, braided leather bracelet dangling from her wrist. Maddy sat in the chair next to her, waiting for her to speak, understanding if she were here, there would be a damn good reason.

Danny ran her hand through her short, spiky, black hair, tugging on the longer bangs partially covering her eyes. "Do you have a moment to talk?" she asked softly.

Maddy's heart constricted for her friend. Things had been brewing between her and Jameson for a while. Nearly losing him because of their discord was weighing heavily on Danny. Hell, the day Jameson nearly died would haunt all of them forever. She gave her a gentle smile and said, "For you, always."

Danny took a breath, opened her mouth to speak, closed it, and cleared her throat. "I miss him." Her breath hitched. "I miss him so goddamn much. Some days I can't breathe. Does that even make any sense?"

Madylyn's eyes watered because she understood the sensation all too well. "Yes, honey, it does."

"Do you remember the day you found me?" Danny asked her in a hoarse whisper. "What they'd done to me?"

"I do," Maddy said with caution. This was something they had never spoken of. Danyka still had nightmares, and Maddy sat with her on the nights she suffered from them. But they never spoke of them in the light of day.

As far as Maddy was aware, Danny hadn't shared her past with anyone. Rhyanna knew about the trauma because she'd treated it, and Jameson knew because Danny had told him. She mistakenly believed she'd compelled him to forget, but Jamey couldn't be compelled. He spoke with Maddy

afterwards, trying to understand, but none of them ever mentioned her past to her.

"I don't know how to be with a man I care about," Danny continued in that harsh whisper. "I like to fuck, don't get me wrong, but I can't stand to look at a man when he's in me. I love the distraction, although I struggle to climax. I've only willingly had sex with most of my clothes on, leaning against a wall, so I don't have to look at them." A tortured sound erupted from her. "I'm fucking terrified that if I'm facing them, I'll kill them."

Maddy shuddered as she remembered the night she'd rescued Danny as a child. She'd found her chained in the basement of a brothel servicing darker fantasies. Two men were simultaneously raping her, and in self-defense, she'd torn the throat out of the man in front of her.

"I could have a different man every night, and sometimes I do." Danyka shook her head ruefully. "But I still can't chase away the demons in my head. I can't get past those fuckers raping me over and over. The looks on their faces, the smell of them, the weight of their bodies pinning me down. I can't fucking do it. It pushes something inside me until I reach for my knives." She stopped, still gazing at the piece of leather she worried between her fingers, unable to look at Maddy while they spoke about this.

Maddy sat silently, trying to listen without interrupting her.

"I met Jameson a few years after you saved me. Thank God he wasn't with you the night you found me. He would've never looked at me the way he does now."

Danny sniffled, absently wiping her nose with the back of her hand. "Best partner I've ever had. Whether it's been in the field or in a bar fight, he's always had my back." She laughed again without humor. "Hell, he's even walked out behind the bar and seen me with some of those men."

With a huff, she stood and walked to the windows, gazing out at the river. "Something's changing between us, Maddy. I'm not sure what to do or how to be with a man for more than an hour. He is a male of such worth, and he deserves someone equally worthy. I don't know how to navigate this relationship shit. I never wanted to."

The silence went on as she tried to find the words to convey the confusion she was experiencing. "The day the hell hound attacked him, I could see something in his eyes when he glanced at me. That big fucker was in midair, leaping for him, and all I could see was the regret in his eyes when he stared at me. I couldn't fucking move fast enough."

Glancing over her shoulder, Danyka gazed at Maddy with such sorrow, that Maddy's eyes filled. "He regarded me with such reverence, respect, and longing, Maddy…longing for me." A single tear slid down her cheek, hovering on her quivering chin. "I was so fucking horrible to him that morning, and he stared at me like I was everything to him."

Her forearm leaned against the window frame, and she pressed her forehead against it as a sob tore from her. "No man has ever looked at me like I was worth anything more than a few minutes of their pleasure." She laughed ruefully. "I've overheard people saying I'm no better than a common whore. Only difference is I give myself freely. No money changes hand."

"Danny," Maddy said softly, "you are equally worthy of him." She stood and walked to her slowly. "You know we all love you and value your contributions as a Warden." When Maddy reached her, she framed the other woman's face between her hands. "What happened to you as a child was nothing you solicited. Those men were sick bastards. I only wish I hadn't killed them, so you could have the pleasure of doing it yourself."

Maddy's eyes locked on hers. "You are worthy, loved, and treasured by so many people. Jamey would be blessed to have you by his side. The only thing holding you back, honey, is you."

Danny laughed raggedly. "What do I do about Jamey?"

Maddy wiped away the tears still running down her friend's face. "You told me what you glimpsed when he saw you. How do you feel about him?"

Danny's eyes shifted away, not wanting to face the truth. "The only thing I remember is when he lay there bleeding out in my lap, I would have given anything for him to live. I would have offered myself in his place. I can't imagine my life without him in it."

"How has it felt not communicating telepathically with him for almost two weeks?" she asked, her eyes daring Danny to be honest.

"I hate not hearing him or sensing his humor, his support. It's like a piece of my soul is missing." She pulled away from Maddy and sat on the window seat. "I wake up determined to go to him, and then I'm standing at the portal, and I can't step inside. I'm terrified I've imagined what he wants, or he's moved on to someone else." She shuddered, thinking of it. "I don't think I could face either scenario."

Maddy sat next to her. She gazed at the beautiful woman beside her, and her heart broke for everything life had thrown at her. "Well, I can tell you he hasn't been up to moving on to someone else." She waited until Danyka glanced up at her. "I can also tell you what you are experiencing is more than most partners ever feel for each other, and he's sensing it, too."

Maddy recognized the hope in Danny's eyes, and then it slowly withered away as she said, "I can't change my past, but I don't think I am strong enough to face it—not even for him."

"There's more strength in you, Danyka, than even you realize." Maddy brushed a hand over her shoulder. "You should reach out to him casually. Don't overthink it. You've been friends for a long time. If you keep avoiding him, you are going to ruin the relationship you had, and I promise that will destroy you just as much as if he'd died."

176

Maddy stood and headed for the sideboard. She poured herself a glass of water and Danny two fingers of whiskey. Danny took the glass gratefully. Maddy leaned against her. "Thank you for trusting me enough to come to me," she whispered to her.

Danyka nodded her head, drained the glass, and went for a refill, which she downed just as quickly. "Think he's up to a visit on Wellesley?"

"I know he would love to see you, Danny." Maddy said with a smile.

"I don't know how to do this," Danny said. Her face lost all color, and she was shaking.

"You've never been afraid of anything, Danyka. Don't start now. Jamey needs to see you. He deserves that much from you, even if you don't say a word."

"I owe him that." Danny's gaze turned inwards as she checked in with everyone else. "Rhy says he's up to visitors."

"Better get moving," Maddy said with a smile. "You've got this, Danny. You're not afraid of anyone, especially someone who loves you."

Danny headed out the door. Maddy was wrong. What Maddy didn't understand was disappointing someone who loved you was more terrifying than riding the hellhound to the ground had been. When she reached the split staircase, instead of going down and heading for the stables, she ran up to her room and packed a bag. She would saddle her horse, go to the portal, and ride as far away from Jamey as possible.

Danny realized she would disappoint Jamey and Maddy. Hell, she disappointed herself. But when she tried to imagine going to him, her heart seized in her chest, and she couldn't do it.

So, taking the coward's route, she hightailed it for the door. When she left, she would race for an out-of-town bar as fast as she could. Danny intended to drown her sorrows in silence, and then, when she could barely stand, she'd take some poor sod out back. Getting railed by some stranger who wouldn't care about her past, her secrets, or even her name sounded pretty fucking good right now.

37

Tell Me How to Fix This

Ronan went downstairs, needing to head for the stables and check on an injured mare. The foyer door opened before he reached it, and his eyes widened when Jamey stepped in, leaning heavily on a cane. His left arm was in a sling, but he looked a helluva lot better than the last time Ronan had seen him. He gave Ronan a weak smile. Kuruk stood by his son's side, there in case Jamey needed him.

"Damn, it's good to see you up and moving," Ronan said, giving him a bro hug and avoiding his injured side.

"Damn good to be up out of that bed," Jamey said. "Just needed to pick up a few things I'll need while I recover."

"I hope to see you back here soon," Ronan said as he walked out.

Jamey turned for the stairs and swallowed hard. He'd never realized how many stairs there were in each flight until today. Kuruk walked behind him, ready to catch him if he stumbled. He handed the cane to his father and grabbed the rail with his right hand. With a deep breath, he climbed the first step, clinging to the rail as his weak legs protested. Sweat dotted his brow, and the climb winded him. But it was good to be back on his feet and moving. When they reached Jamey's room, he sat heavily on the bed, catching his breath. Jamey urged his father to take a tour of the Sanctuary while he packed what he needed for the next few weeks.

"Hellion, are you on site?" he asked, hoping Danyka would answer. *"I need to see you."*

Jamey sensed her on the other end of the link tethering them together. Her chaotic emotions bombarded him. Fear, relief, guilt, longing, desire, and self-loathing were all mixed up into one intertwined mess. Like an emotional ball of yarn made up of so many colored strands. The strands tangled together in knots, fraying, and pulling each other tighter into chaos until the lines were so fragile, they were bound to snap.

178

"Come to me, Hellion," he sent to Danny, infusing his words with his need to see her. *"Please."*

Grabbing a large satchel, he headed for his wardrobe and packed enough trousers and shirts to work in and work out in. His brothers were looking forward to helping him regain his strength and mobility—most likely by beating the shit out of him while he was the weakest. They might not get this opportunity again.

A quick trip into the bathroom, and he gathered his personal care items. A leather toiletry bag under the sink filled quickly with everything he needed. He caught his reflection in the mirror. The harsh lighting over the sink made him realize how gaunt and tired he appeared.

As he examined his features, he felt like he'd aged decades from only a week ago. He would eventually heal, regain his strength and his vigor, but today he felt every one of the years he'd lived. The old timers talked about how they felt the seasons and the storms in their bones. He understood now what they meant. Rain was coming, and it made his shoulder ache like a bitch.

Jamey gazed around his room at the Sanctuary. This had been his second home for so long that he thought of the room as his. He intended to return, but he also knew Maddy would need to find a replacement for him, even if only temporarily.

Thinking of Maddy seemed to make her appear as her voice carried to him from the doorway. "This room will remain empty, awaiting your return."

A smile spread across his face as he turned to her, realizing she must have sensed his reluctance to leave. "Thank you. I need something to look forward to."

Jamey held his right arm open and welcomed the woman he considered a sister into his arms. Maddy clung to him as he hugged her tightly with his good arm.

"Don't you ever scare us like that again," she said, her breath hitching as she teared up against his chest.

"I promise to do my best to never do that again, Maddy."

Maddy stepped away, wiping her eyes. "Sorry, I just needed to do that once to get it out of my system."

Running his hand through his hair, he sighed heavily before sitting on the bed, looking forlorn. "Why won't she see me?" he asked despondently. "Or at the very least, talk to me?"

"I don't know, honey. I honestly don't," Maddy said. "Today's the first time any of us have seen her. The only thing I can figure is she feels responsible for what happened. Running has always been her way of coping,

and sadly, until she's ready to face whatever's chasing her, we can't force her."

"She won't even acknowledge me privately." His voice cracked as he spoke, showing his inner turmoil. "Beyond all the other crap, she's one of my best friends. My jealousy ruined that, and now she won't even talk to me."

Maddy sat next to him and put a hand on his back. "You did nothing wrong, Jamey. Danny doesn't have the emotional capabilities you and I have. When something scares her, all of her defenses come up, and she's unapproachable to any of us until she works her fears out. I can tell you, she's drowning in guilt over you nearly dying, and that's the main reason she can't face you."

"What happened to me wasn't her fault. I didn't follow protocol." He shook his head in frustration. "Danny meets everything head-on. She's never been afraid of anything."

"You're wrong there, Jamey." Maddy took his large hand in hers. "She's terrified of what she feels for you because you are the one thing she can't risk losing."

"Ignoring me doesn't make me feel that way," he snarled.

"I understand why you think she's avoiding you. Keep in mind that her emotional maturity stunted around the age of twelve. She's a woman in every way we measure what a woman is, but inside, she is nothing more than a little girl terrified of someone else she trusts and loves leaving her."

"I'll be back," he said. "I won't be gone forever."

"We both know you'll return. Danny trusts nothing until it happens."

"How in all the hells am I supposed to get through to her?"

"I doubt it will happen today. Give her time. When you return, she may treat you like nothing ever happened."

"That's bound to piss me off a bit." His amber eyes were backlit with his banked anger.

"Good, stay pissed off, and don't be afraid to let her see you're angry. She's emotionally fragile but not broken. Danny can take the truth when you call her on her bullshit. Make her accept responsibility for her behavior. When you see her, make her own her part in this mess, tell her your intentions, and give her the room to accept that she can't push you away as easily as she wants to."

Maddy gave him a saucy grin. "You're always so easygoing, and we love you because of your even temperament. But you also have steel in your spine, Jameson. Show it to her and meet her head-on. She'll respect you more if you do."

Jamey nodded, contemplating what she said. "Thank you, Maddy. I'll return as quickly as I can."

"You'll not return until Rhy says you're healed." Maddy used her headmistress tone, telling him she meant what she said.

"No, ma'am, I won't."

"I'll let you finish, then." Maddy hugged him once more and left alone.

Leaving the bag for his father, he walked down the hall to the staircase. He couldn't keep his gaze from searching the wing housing the Air Clan across from him, hoping for a glimpse of her, if nothing else. The hallway was empty, and the only sound reaching them was the laughter coming from downstairs. He could hear Fergus's bellow and Rhy's throaty chuckle. He didn't want to leave, but he wasn't any good to them in this condition. With the reception he was getting from Danny, it might do them both good to have a bit of space. Mayhap she would regain her sense of balance if he weren't around for the next couple of weeks.

He cautiously made his way down the stairs, then joined the rest of them in the parlor. Fergus clasped his hand and pulled him into a brief hug. "Ye get yerself well na, laddie, then get yer ass back here. Ye can't be leaving me here to wrangle this mangy bunch."

Jameson laughed with him and tried not to cringe when he slapped him on his sore shoulder.

"Ach, sorry lad, I forgots which one ye injured."

"Probably be the one with the sling," Jamey groaned.

Rhyanna came to him then. Framing his face with her hands, she searched his eyes. "Ye'll be taking it easy na for at least the next ten days. I'll be out to see ye daily, and if ye've done any more damage to your shoulder, I swear by the Mother, I'll box yer ears until they ring for a month. Yer brothers, too, if they've anything to do with harming ye."

She hugged him fiercely, her arms wrapped tightly around his back. "Ye come back to us, Jameson. Won't be the same without ye here. We need ye." Rhy hugged him tighter, sending him a private message. *She needs ye, too. She's jest not ready to admit how she feels. Don't give up on her yet. Give her some time to accept what nearly losing ye did to her.*

Jamey squeezed her tightly back and said, *Thank you, Rhy. She'll have all the time she wants because she won't talk to me. What am I supposed to think when she's shutting me out like this? What did I do to push her away?*

Nothing, Jamey. Ye did nothing but make her realize how important ye are to her, and that terrifies her.

Jamey released her and turned to Kyran, offering him a hand. "Thank you for everything you've done for me. Please thank the rest of your family for stepping in that day as well."

"My pleasure. I'll call on you in the future for help, so my assistance wasn't free." They chuckled, and Kyran offered Kuruk a hand when he

appeared. "My father's looking for some stallions for his breeding program. We'll be by in a few weeks to see what your family has available."

"I look forward to welcoming you to my home," Kuruk said with a welcoming smile as he shouldered Jamey's bag.

Jamey hugged Maddy once more and shook Ronan's hand. "Bring Landon for a visit. There are a bunch of kids his age running amongst the foals. They love to make new friends."

"We'd love to visit," Maddy said as Ronan nodded.

Jamey and Kuruk headed for the door, where a teary-eyed Mrs. O'Hare intercepted him. She let him hug her, then handed Kuruk a basket. "I've sent a few things for yer family, and there are some of those Scottish shortbreads yer so fond of."

Jamey gave her a kiss on the cheek. "Thank you, but I'm not sharing them with my brothers." A precocious grin spread across his face.

Mrs. O'Hare laughed and swatted at his chest. "That's why I made them something else, so ye don't have to." She wiped her face with her apron and left.

Jamey headed for the door. At the threshold, he looked back at the crew he was leaving behind. They were his coworkers and his friends, but they were so much more to him. The people gathered in this place were his second family, and he missed them already.

With a somber nod, he reached for the door. A choked sob behind him, and a surge of emotion on their link stopped him. His heart raced as he glanced over his shoulder and his eyes found Danny watching him from the shadows. Turning around, he faced her.

Without glancing away, he sent Maddy and his father a message, *"Can all of you give us a moment alone?"*

"Absolutely. I've ordered them to the dining room."

Kuruk clamped a hand on Jamey's good shoulder. "I'll wait outside," he said, shutting the door behind him.

Jamey's eyes met Danny's, and the torment and pain he saw in them took his breath away. *"Hellion, won't you come down and say a proper goodbye?"* he asked softly, extending his good arm to the side, welcoming her.

Danny had been in her room when his message nearly dropped her to her knees. Like a coward, she ignored him again. Waiting a few moments, she tried to sneak out without seeing him. She'd nearly succeeded until she heard his voice below and froze.

Expecting Danny to deny him again, he was shocked when she dropped her satchel, ran down the stairs, and threw her arms around his neck. His good arm wrapped around her waist as her legs wrapped around his hips. Her slight form quivered in his arms as he held her as tightly as possible. He turned, pinning her against the door, relieving the slight weight of her from his exhausted body. There was no way he was letting go of her this soon.

Jamey buried his head in her neck as she sobbed in his arms. "Shhhh, everything's going to be fine. You'll see. I'll be good as new in a few weeks." He kissed the side of her neck, wanting to kiss her properly but too aware of her volatile emotions.

"Can you talk to me, Hellion?" A brief shake of her head was the only answer he received, so he reached out on their inner link, where she couldn't avoid him forever. *"Won't you please tell me how to fix this? I'm so damn sorry, Danny, for not waiting for you, and putting both of us in danger. It wasn't fair to you. I want to fix this between us, but I can't if you won't communicate with me."*

Danny's voice was faint as it came through, and so damn sad. *"It wasn't something you broke, Jamey, so there is no way for you to fix me. This is something I need to deal with before I can move on. I'm sorry, but that's all I can say. I'm sorry for ignoring you, but I didn't think you would want to see me after I nearly got you killed."*

Another sob made him hold her tighter. *"I can't even think about you bleeding out in my lap without being physically ill. Give me time, and I'll be out to see you. Give my best to your family. Take care of yourself and then…come back to me."*

She pulled away to see his eyes, and what she saw reflected there devastated her. The longing and the love gutted her because she didn't deserve it.

"I will come back to you, Danny. You can count on that. This conversation isn't over, but you have to realize what happened wasn't your fault. The attack was an accident and could have happened to any of us who was being a dumbass and not following protocol. That's on me!"

His hand came up to cup her face, his thumb brushing away her tears. He kept communicating telepathically because she seemed less skittish when he did. *"It wouldn't have mattered who was with me. The outcome still would have been the same because I wasn't fast enough. Stop beating yourself up. None of us blames you. I miss my partner, but I miss my best friend more. Please stop avoiding me. You've never been a coward. Don't start acting like one now."*

Her head snapped up as his words echoed the ones she'd heard recently. *"You're wrong, Jamey. You're the one thing I'm afraid of. I'm not sure how to change what I feel because I'm not willing to let you go, although that would be the kindest thing I could do for you. You mean too much to me."*

"I don't want your kindness."

"What do you want?"

"Everything."

Danyka smiled at him sadly. *"And there is the root of our dilemma. You seek the one thing I will never give to any man, not even you, Jameson."* Releasing his neck, she dropped her legs and moved away, heading back towards the staircase. *"Safe travels, Jamey. May the road be clear and the weather fine as you return to your family."*

Jamey watched her until he couldn't see her anymore. His heart pounded as he replayed their exchange through his mind. Her words told him one

thing, but the haunted look in her eyes and the tone of her message on their link told him something else.

Danny wanted him. That much was clear, but she wasn't happy about needing him. A wide grin crossed his face because he could work with this. She hadn't run away, and she hadn't requested another partner. Jamey would take the advice given by the other women who knew her best. He'd bide his time while he gave her time to settle down.

Jameson came from a long line of horse whisperers, and he was damn good at settling skittish fillies. Danny wasn't any different, and he would treat her the same way. He'd earn her trust, sweeten her up, and when she least expected it, he'd surround her in love until she was so steeped in him, she couldn't imagine her life without him by her side—or her bed without him warming it. The second might take longer than the first, but Jamey was a patient man, and he fully intended to make sure by the end of the race, he won the girl.

Smiling to himself, he left the building and found his father waiting patiently, still talking to Ronan. They said goodbye and headed for the portal. Wellesley wasn't far by horse if you were in good health, but his arm would ache like a bitch by the time he got there, and he didn't want to strain the sore muscles. The scent of the buttery shortbread in the basket called to him, and he couldn't wait to bite into one.

With nothing but time before him, he operated the portal while planning on how he was going to wear down Danny's defenses. His sights were set on her, and he fully intended to get his girl in the end. Jamey loved a challenge, and he knew she would give him a good run for his money. Finally, finding some hope in their dilemma, he stepped out of the portal on Wellesley and embraced the forced downtime he had to heal. While he regained his strength and licked the wounds to his pride, he planned to figure out a way to break through her defenses. He would claim her heart because, dammit, even if she didn't realize it, she'd already claimed his.

38

Last Night Home

Myranda watched the sun setting from her kitchen window. Red and white buffalo check curtains blew gently in the breeze, bringing with them the fragrance of summer flowers in the evening air. Ryssa was nearby. Myranda could sense her proximity through her parental link to her daughter.

Elementals used telepathy as an intimate form of communication between close family members and lovers. Over time, they also formed similar bonds with friends and colleagues. Everyone could receive telepathic messages, but some people struggled to return them.

Myranda's ancestors were strong Earth elementals. The Earth Mother also gifted them with a powerful side of Spirit magic, making them extraordinarily gifted in telepathy. Her clan could send messages thousands of miles away and to people with no ties to them. This gift required a lot of energy and practice, but once mastered, it was a powerful asset for life.

For privacy, everyone learned at an early age to erect barricades to avoid unwanted communications. An imagined wall built of brick, hedges, or any dense matter worked. Myranda often erected barricades of apples or sandwiches. The only thing that failed her was marshmallows because too much air amplified the connection rather than keeping someone out.

Telepathy, for Myranda, was as natural as breathing. She'd also been blessed with the ability to sense a general proximity of her family through her bond. This made Mathyas's link dissolving mid-conversation with her even more devastating. Even with a damaged link, she still should've been able to communicate with her partner by creating a new one instantly.

Mathyas worked for the Elemental High Court, often taking jobs undercover and at significant risk to himself. But no matter how far his mission took him from her, Myranda could always sense him—always, with no exception.

Distractions on the job could be deadly, so she'd always waited for him to check in with her. The moment he was declared missing and presumed dead, she ripped open their internal bond and searched for him. Now, throughout her day, she tapped into the space he'd once taken up in her mind, seeking him to no avail.

Mathyas had been the man she had given her heart and her body to. They'd joyfully created another life together. Maryssa was the living embodiment of their love. Their daughter was a beautiful combination of both of her parents. She was the best of both of them.

Myranda doubled over as if struck. It was the first time she referred to him in the past tense, and it sucked the air right out of her lungs. She never believed he died when they didn't find his body in the southwest's Badlands. No trace of him existed anywhere, but her soul didn't accept that he no longer walked this earth. Every link he had to other members of his family and friends were also destroyed. So why couldn't she accept what everybody else so easily did? She still couldn't make herself believe he was gone—not when every cell in her body argued against it.

Something had gone horribly wrong on his last mission—no doubt about that. Even months later, Myranda refused to believe he was gone. She would *know*, and Ryssa felt the same way. The first lesson she'd taught her daughter was to trust her elemental instincts. She couldn't take that advice back now.

Myranda knew this was the major cause of Ryssa's anger at having to leave. Her daughter still believed she would return to their home to find her daddy in the garden, smiling up at her while he worked in the dirt. This image was what she clung to. Hope was the only thing keeping their baby girl going, and Myranda couldn't dissuade her when she felt the same way.

Ryssa wanted to be here when he came back, but missing the training session was not an option. Myr hated the thought of sending her last link to Mathyas away, terrified of losing her child, too. Elemental training was an arduous process for every child, and some struggled more than others. On rare occasion some participants failed horribly, resulting in their death or the death of their classmates.

Myranda felt a mental tingle alerting her to Ryssa's approach. Pulling herself together and pasting on a smile, Myranda prepared for her daughter to walk through the door. Watching her walk through the stag portal tomorrow and leaving her there would be one of the most difficult things Myranda would ever do.

Footsteps bounded up the stairs, the doorknob turned, and Ryssa walked in. Myranda laughed the same way she had done a few weeks ago when her daughter first walked in with blue highlights. Her daughter embraced the color from her hair to the short plaid skirt and tights. She wore nothing but indigo blue.

Myr smiled, realizing, for the first time in weeks, Ryssa was happy, and that's all that mattered. She also admitted to herself begrudgingly that the color suited her. Indigo blue was definitely her color and her child's way of reminding her to mind her runaway thoughts when she was angry.

Approaching Ryssa, she reached out and ran her hands down the length of her hair, marveling at how the indigo enhanced the natural ebony cascade of her hair. She'd layered the sides to frame her face, and it changed the shape of her face—matured her.

Her daughter's mischievous smile was a welcome sight. Myr had missed this side of her. Reaching up, she gathered the length of her brown hair up on top of her head and said, "Maybe I'll do mine, too."

Ryssa laughed. "Sweet Mother, no. Blue is not *your* color, mom. But don't worry; we'll find one for you when I get back." Impulsively, she reached out and hugged her mother, clinging tightly to her. "I'm sorry about the way I've been acting lately," she whispered. "I know it's not your fault. Somehow, I forgot about training, and I'm not ready to go. What if…"

Myranda clung just as tightly to her. "Shhhh, baby, I know. What if he comes back?"

She cupped her daughter's face tightly between her hands. I promise you if — no, when—he comes back, I will bring him to you immediately. Honey, you have my solemn vow, OK?

Ryssa gazed up at her, expression still haunted and lost, but she nodded in agreement. "OK, mom, I know you will." She sniffed the air. "You made my favorite dinner!"

Myranda laughed. "Of course I did. Did you honestly think I would let you leave without your favorite meal? Come on. The lasagna is ready. Let's eat and enjoy the rest of our evening together. I don't want to waste any more time on what we can't change. I want to enjoy tonight."

"Me, too, momma. Me, too," Marissa whispered back to her as they headed for the kitchen.

"Oh, I almost forgot to tell you," Myranda said through a mouthful of pasta. "You'll only miss me if you want to."

"What are you talking about? I'm going to be there for at least eight weeks, and you're only allowed to visit twice."

"You're right, but I just got an offer today to help Rhyanna for the summer. Would you hate it if I were around almost every day?"

Ryssa was speechless. "Are you serious?"

Myranda nodded. "I'll be helping afternoons in the clinic."

Ryssa's eyes welled. "That's the best news I've had in a long time."

They finished dinner and quickly cleaned up. With a pot of tea ready for dessert, they headed into the small family room and settled on the couch

together. Myranda had a book ready to read aloud, and Ryssa sat in the other corner facing her with her sketchbook and charcoal pencil ready.

Ryssa loved hearing her mother read a story. Sometimes she would draw pictures to go with the descriptions she heard, but tonight she sketched her mother. She worked confidently while her mom read an adventure story with trolls, halflings, dwarves, and elves. Her mother was wonderful with character voices, and Ryssa laughed as she impersonated a grumpy dwarf.

Lost in the story and in her sketch, she captured on paper the gentle slope of her nose, the angles of her cheekbones and chin, and the gorgeous shape of her dark wide-set eyes, framed by dainty eyebrows. Myranda had a full set of lips and gorgeous skin. Thick, dark hair framed her face with a full fringe of bangs. Ryssa stopped for a moment, her pencil between her teeth as, for the first time, she realized how beautiful her mother was inside and out.

Turning the page, she started another sketch. This one was of her parents dancing under the full moon—a tradition of theirs each month. Ryssa had often seen them through her window late at night when she should have been sleeping. They moved together perfectly, dancing to a tune only they knew. Her father looked at her mom with such reverence. He loved her so much—as much as he loved Ryssa, but maybe even more.

Heart strings entwined, the cords woven so complexly and tightly, nothing could ever come between them. Ryssa watched them enviously as a child. Someday she wanted that kind of love. The kind that blossomed and endured every challenge they encountered. Unaware, a tear slipped down her cheek and splashed onto the page.

"What have you created tonight, sweetie?" her mother asked, moving closer to her. Myranda took the pad from Ryssa and gazed at it for a long time. "Oh Ryssa, sweetie…" her voice cracked as she stared, mesmerized at the couple on the sketch pad. "You made me look so beautiful," she whispered, her fingers lightly touching her own face.

"No, mom, I didn't," Marissa said and waited for her mother to meet her eyes. "I only draw what I see. You are beautiful."

Now Myranda's eyes filled up, and the tears fell. "You did such a wonderful job with this. Your dad looks so vibrant and full of life and love." Her voice broke, and she swallowed hard. "We looked good together, didn't we?"

"Mom, you were perfect together." Ryssa gazed into her mother's eyes and told her the truth as she believed it to be. "You will be again. I have no doubts."

"I love you, sweetie," Myranda whispered, hoping she was right. She gathered Ryssa in close for a tight hug. "I love you so very much."

Ryssa hugged her back even harder. "I love you, too."

39

Don't Leave Me

Danyka turned down the hallway, walking away from the man who owned her heart. The weight of his gaze on her made her core heat. The sound of the front door opening and shutting was the sound of farewell. Her throat tightened, even though she'd sent him away.

Unable to stop herself, she ran to her window, needing one last glance of him. Kuruk waited with Jamey's bags at his side. Jameson stepped out into the sunlight with a picnic basket clasped in his good hand. Kuruk shouldered the bags, then shook Ronan's hand.

Jamey stopped, standing in place with the sun shining on his chestnut hair. He gazed up at her windows, but she doubted he could see her.

Danny wanted to call him back and hug him again. She could still feel the strength and heat of his body. The longing to have him hold her and soothe her was overpowering. She didn't want him to leave, but Wellesley was the best place for him to heal. With no one to blame but herself, she kept silent. She'd done nothing to encourage him to stay. Hell, she hadn't spoken to him or even gone to see him since the accident.

Jamey's gaze searched for her, settling on the corner she hid in. Danny held her breath, not moving a muscle as he stared up at her windows.

The room was dark. Danny stood to the side of the window, blocked by the heavy fall of velvet drapes. As his eyes sought her out, she moved forward, placing her hand on the glass, confirming her position. His lip curled up on one side in a lopsided smirk. He gave the barest of nods, acknowledging her.

The sight of the virile male below her made Danny's heart race. Her breathing was ragged as she studied him. He wanted her; he'd made that clear. She didn't know what she did to deserve him or what he might have done to be cursed with her. Mother, help her. She wanted him, too. That

fucking terrified her. The potential for them to be a disaster of enormous proportions was astronomical. And the repercussions were far-reaching if they couldn't make a relationship work.

Jamey believed she was worth more than a quick tumble. The other men she fucked expected nothing more because she offered nothing. They mutually used each other, seeking nothing more than the heat and rush of raw sex. She prayed for a quick release of physical tension and the mystical hope of the elusive female orgasm. When the deed was done, she barely acknowledged them as she dressed. She left unsatisfied, wondering what it was she kept chasing and why she even fucking bothered.

The sexual experiences she observed and shared with Jamey made her realize what she was missing. She didn't doubt that he would make good on his promise to take care of her properly and fuck her thoroughly. Every night since their last encounter, she fell asleep with Jamey's name on her lips. With her hand between her legs, she desperately tried to recreate the experience without him. It was another exercise in futility.

Danny craved the sexual pleasure she knew he would ring from her. More importantly, she loved the way he treated her like she was something he cherished. No one had ever believed she was worth the trouble before. Jamey made her feel worthy, and he wanted her for more than sex.

Jamey's eyes followed her when he thought she wasn't looking. When she walked away from him today, the intensity of his stare burning through her back left imprints deep in her soul, bringing tears to her eyes.

Now, once again, as his eyes locked on hers, he gave the barest nod at her hand on the window. The message she choked back because she knew it would make him turn around and seek her out was, *"Don't leave me, please don't leave me."* It was the message her heart radiated silently to him, beckoning him to hear it mixed in with the scattered beats coming from her chest.

Her soul's greatest wish was to belong to him, but she knew her wish wouldn't come true because Jameson Vance was destined for greatness. Danyka wasn't the right partner for a man so blessed by the Mother. Destiny must have plans for him with someone equally special. He deserved someone who treasured him for his kindness and would love him for his laughter and gentleness.

Danyka could find pleasure with Jamey. He'd already proven that. If pleasure were enough, she'd have jumped him already.

But she couldn't offer him the permanence his soul longed for when she was flighty, like a tumbleweed rolling across the desert. A strong wind would take her far from here without a moment's notice when the nightmares of her past hit hard and hungry. Drowning in shame, she couldn't face the people who loved her.

Danny often disappeared for weeks, and occasionally for months, until the drifter in her quieted, and she'd lulled the loner in her back to sleep,

allowing her to come home. When she returned to her family, they accepted her as she was—unapologetic and untethered.

Jamey would chase her until he corralled her, then he would try to fix her and make everything better. Eventually, he would resent the chase. Then he would stop following her. Finally, he wouldn't care enough to fix anything or if he even saw her again. The leash holding him to a woman broken too badly to settle down would chafe, transforming to resentment.

This honorable man would never give up on her. Hobbled, they would turn on each other like two wild dogs snapping and biting until they forgot the reasons they fell in love. Yes, Danny could finally admit that she loved him, but sometimes love just ain't enough.

Jamey would make that commitment to a woman only once, and Danyka wouldn't let him waste the most crucial decision of his life on a poor bet like her.

40

If I Have Me Way

Ferguson entered the Court of Luminosity with a heavy heart. Laird Killam, Fergus's uncle, nearly died from third-degree burns only weeks ago. Queen Meriel, the previous ruling monarch over the Court of Tears, attacked him at a pledging ceremony binding the two clans. Meriel lost the battle, her crown, and nearly her life because of her actions. Killam McKay clung to this world, although his body was struggling to recover.

The Court of Luminosity also laid claim to being the home of the Great Lakes Fire Clan—Fergus's boyhood home. He'd moved here from Scotland with his mother as a young boy after his father's death. His cousins, Vulcan and Brandell—fraternal twins—and their sister, Elyana, became his best friends besides family. Elyana currently ruled in Laird Killam's stead with her new consort, Kano Tyde, by her side.

Killam's tenuous grasp on life, and the story Ronan shared earlier in the week, weighed heavily on his mind. Turning right down the next corridor he came to, he stepped through the first open door and gazed into the laird's office.

The office was quiet and lacked the usual haze of cigar smoke drifting about. The drawn curtains and the wall of windows lit up the otherwise dark room. Burnished walnut bookcases carved with fire drakes and their larger cousins, dragons, lined three walls.

Elyana Tyde gazed out the windows at the far end of the room, lost in her thoughts. Ferg cleared this throat, trying not to startle her.

"How ye holding up, lass?" he asked as he approached her. The mantle of responsibility she'd accepted was visible in her gaunt features. A beautiful girl with red hair and hazel eyes and a renowned scholar. Politics had never been in her future.

Elyana turned to him with a sad smile. "Ferg, how good to see you again." She stepped into his open arms, accepting the bear hug he gave her.

Gads, the man knew how to hug. He hung on like he hadn't another care in the world and could do this all day. The visit from someone who knew her father nearly as well as she did and the warm embrace opened the floodgates. Try as she might, she couldn't stifle the sob that ripped from her.

"Hush, lass," Ferg crooned. One hand stroked her hair, and the other circled on her back. "Let it all out."

"I can't. There's no time for me to do this." She sniffled into his chest. "Kano doesn't know what to do with me when I'm emotional. I blocked him from this episode."

"I'd say it's a good time for the lad to learn how to soothe his woman. Don't start hiding yer hard times. If he truly loves ye, he'll want to see ye through the good and the bad."

Elyana gave a humorless chuckle, stepping away. Unsteady hands poured them both two fingers of whiskey. "He's been wonderful about everything. This relationship is a learning curve for both of us." Her gaze tracked around the room. "As is taking over for the laird." Voice dropping to a whisper, she continued, "I don't know where to start. His filing system is nonexistent, and the continuous requests about his health from the other clans are drowning me in paperwork."

"Where's your assistant?"

"What assistant?"

"Uncle Killam always had a scribe help him with the menial shite he couldn't bother with."

"I ain't seen hide nor hair of a scribe since we returned."

"I'll see about that, lass." Fergus took a drink, sighing in approval at the smooth liquor. "So, how's the old man?" he asked.

"Still in a mage induced coma," she said. "The seaweed wraps Queen Yareli provided are working wonders with his wounds. The damaged skin is regenerating at remarkable rates."

"Sounds like he'll live to fight another day."

"I believe he will. He's too damn stubborn to die."

"There's the truth of it, lass," Fergus said. "Did they take more of his forearm?"

"Nye. The healers have kept it from getting infected."

"Sure gonna piss him off to lose his drinking hand," Ferg said with a slight grin.

"Think he's gonna be more pissed off to need help lighting his cigars." They shared a laugh and finished their drinks.

"I take it this isn't a social visit, Ferg?"

"Nye. Have Vulcan and Brandell brought you up to speed about our lead with the missing girls?"

"Yes. They mentioned you'd befriended someone and were waiting for him to reach out with a job to get you closer to the inner workings of this nasty little network."

"Aye, that's the gist of it." Fergus refilled his glass and offered her more, but she placed her hand over her glass.

"As tempting as it is, I still have a full day of bureaucratic bullshite to deal with."

"I'll have one for ye." His grin faded as he continued, "Always gave the laird the courtesy of letting him know when I was walking the streets of home. I'm giving ye the same courtesy."

"Should I be concerned?" Elyana arched an eyebrow at him. "You planning on gathering the boys and starting trouble?"

"Nye, lass. Just like to have the support of yer office should I need to throw it around."

"Ye have my support, Fergus Emberz. I trust you implicitly to do what needs to be done for our clan and our world. You have full authority to make use of the guards. I'll let you work that out with Vulcan."

"Thank ye, Ely. 'Tis jest a formality—a dance we go through to cover the bases."

"I appreciate the consideration and keeping me apprised of your progress as well."

"Absolutely, me laird."

Elyana punched him in the shoulder. "Don't be getting used to me here. This is only temporary."

"Aye, I ken, lass." Fergus hugged her again. "Keep yer chin up; ye'll survive this."

A knock on the door announced Kano's arrival. Heading straight for Elyana, he pulled her from Fergus and kissed her before holding a hand out to the other man.

"Welcome, Ferg. How long you in town for?"

"Only a night or two. Need to get back afore the rugrats and curtain climbers arrive for the summer."

"Well, if you need any help, let me know. I'm ready for a night out, stirring things up."

Elyana rolled her eyes. "Just what we need."

The men laughed. "Come with me, lad," Fergus said, clamping a hand on Kano's shoulder. "I can see ye needs a night out with the lads." He steered him towards the door.

"Keep him out of trouble, Ferg, or you'll deal with your laird."

"But of course, lass. Cross me heart," he yelled back as they headed down the hall.

"Enough of the pleasantries. All bullshite aside, how's the lass really doing?"

Kano ran a hand through his short blond hair and then rubbed the shaved sides of his head. "Ain't been easy on her, Ferg."

"I'd be expecting that. She gonna hold up much longer?"

"Hell, I don't think the woman knows how to stop or how to fail."

"Ye've got a point." Ferg stopped and met the other man's gaze. "Ye ken she's blocking ye from about fifty percent of her breakdowns?"

"I suspected as much, but I was trying to respect her need to hide it and give her some space." His hand tugged on his hair again. "Am I making a mistake by doing that?"

Ferg scrubbed his hands over his face, contemplating the question. "As long as yer aware and willing to be there fer yer, I'd let it be. Just wanted to make sure ye ken what she's dealing with."

Continuing down the hallway, he punched the young man in the arm, making him sidestep. "Fer fucks sake, find out where the laird's scribe ran off to. Get the girl some help."

Kano nodded, rubbing his arm. "Done."

"Now that we've got all that outta the way, let's head down to the docks and grab a pint. I'se got something I needs to do."

Ten minutes later, they entered the dimly lit bar his cousins, Vulcan and Brandell, owned.

"Don't look like much, but they serve damn fine food and booze here," Fergus said, taking a table by the wall.

"Ely's told me about it, but we haven't had the time to stop by."

"Fergus," a woman's voice called, "'bout time ye showed yer face. Got a message fer ye," Aida said as she waddled toward them with a round tray, delivering two mugs of dark ale to the table.

"Vulcan told me ye had a message from the bastard."

"Aye, a right bastard he is," Aida huffed. "He's been hiding in the shadows, casing the joint since ye left. I don't like it, and I don't like him. Sooner he's gone, happier I'd be."

"Aye, that makes two of us." Fergus took a sip, pondering the situation he'd unwillingly put her in. The tavern rarely saw trouble. It helped that the owners were in the highest ranks of the laird's guard. "Ye don't let the little ones come in here, na do ye?"

"Nye, they're too much of a handful, and I don't want them turning into drunk sods like their father and the people he runs with." A saucy smile crossed her face, including him in that lot.

"Aww, lass, ye wound me," Ferg cajoled, hand over his heart. "We ain't all that bad."

"Hmmm." She glanced at Kano, then said, "Who's the new lad, and does he ken the trouble he's likely to find with ye?"

"Kano Tyde," Kano said, offering her his hand. She took it, and he kissed the back of it, making her eyes widen.

"Trouble. Hmmm," she said, but a blush stained her cheeks.

"Don't think I could get you into any more trouble," Kano said, nodding to her swollen belly with a smile.

"This un's the laird's new man," Ferg clarified afore she whacked the lad with her round tray. He turned to his companion, "Kano, this is Vulcan's wife, the lovely Aida McKay."

Aida attempted a clumsy curtsy made even more awkward by the fact she was near as wide with child as she was high.

"That's unnecessary, mistress," Kano said, standing and helping her right herself. "Won't ye sit and join us for a moment? Get off yer feet for a bit."

"Lad's, right, Aida," Ferg said, noting the dark circles under her eyes. "When was the last break ye had?"

"Bar donna run itself, lads," she said. "Half me staff be sick, the other half plum lazy."

Fergus moved in and patted the padded bench with his hand. "Sit while ye deliver me message, at least."

She arched an eyebrow at him, then blew her hair out of her face and lowered herself onto the seat. "Blimey, not sure I'll be able to get back up."

"We'll get ye up, donna worry 'bout that," Ferg said.

"How's the laird, milord?"

"Please don't treat me like that, mistress. I am as far from court as I can be and loving every minute. I don't want you to defer to me. Please."

"Alrighty then. How's Killam?" Aida asked Kano.

"Improving by the day, but he's got a long way to go."

Tears filled the young woman's eyes. "He's always been kind to me."

"He'll be up and bossing us all around afore ye ken," Fergus said.

"Aye," she wiped her nose on a rag and gazed at him, all business again. "The tosser outside wants ye to find him where ye last met."

"That's all he said?"

"Aye. But his eyes traveling up and down me body said a whole nother thing."

Fergus's fists clenched on the table, but when he spoke, his tone was calm. "Someone escort ye to and from work?"

"Nye, never needed that afore."

"I ken, but times be different, na. I'll talk to Vulcan afore I leave."

Aida's jaw clenched, and Fergus knew he was in for a fight with the independent woman. "I ken yer a scrapper lass, and ye be taking good care of yerself all these years. But this bastard is a flesh peddler who deals in young women and, I'm guessing, children as well."

Aida's face paled at the thought that she'd be leading him straight to her home and her hoard of children. "Don't want him in here again."

"I'll do me best to keep his contact here limited, but I may need to use the bar a time or two more. I trust ye lass—can't say that everywhere."

"As long as ye promise me, this ends with him off the streets," she said.

"If I have me way, he'll be off this plane of existence permanently." Fergus and Kano raised their glasses at the thought of evil taken down.

41

Magic, Drunks, and Whores

Fairfax McAllister emerged from the Wellesley Island Portal, happy to see he was alone. He walked up the flight of stairs to the upper deck of the gazebo and gazed across the night sky. The lights of the mainland twinkled across the water from where he stood. In the distance, the beacon of hope from the Heart Island Sanctuary shone brightly. 'Twas the island housing two of the women he hated the most.

Madylyn SkyDancer, the whore who ran the place, had the audacity to ban him from fishing on the Lawrence—as if the cunt had the right. During Warden's Court a few months ago, the whore threatened to take his ships and crew and toss him to the horrors of island law. Her time would come, and if he had his way, it would be sooner rather than later.

The other woman—a ghost from his past—went by the name of Danyka now. He'd never asked her name when he fucked her as a child in the filthy dungeon of a brothel, catering to a unique clientele. McAllister had many special tastes and enjoyed sampling the various delicacies available. How could one know what one truly liked if one didn't try them all? But this cunt destroyed someone he loved.

Fingers clutching the rail in front of him, he remembered the best and worst week of his life. He'd had some of the best sex of his life and lost his best friend and favorite brother over the course of a handful of days.

Shaking himself out of his reverie, he headed for the nearby town. A small tavern was within walking distance of the portal. The Drunk Stallion catered to the many stables on the island. A bronze statue of a rearing stallion stood beside the door. Hitching posts out front made it easy for the locals to drink, then ride home on their trusty steeds.

Claiming a seat at the bar, he ordered a stiff drink, and his mind wandered once again to the past.

Fairfax bragged to his younger brother, Max, about how tight the littlest one he'd ever fucked had been. His story inspired the young lad to seek her out. Max and a friend were enjoying her together when she tore his little brother's throat out with her teeth. The worst thing about the whole fecking rotting affair was that Fairfax had been drowning in ecstasy a few rooms down the hall at the same time Max bled to death. Too busy chasing his own pleasure and nearly choking another whore to death, he never recognized Max's screams.

Fairfax almost hadn't recognized her with the short, spiky, black hair when he saw her at the Court of Tears. In her youth, she sported long, gorgeous wavy blond locks. He closed his eyes as he remembered the time spent with her.

All that thick blond hair twisted around his wrist like a rope. He'd pulled her head back until tears leaked down her face as she choked on the full length of his cock. This angle helped him slide way down past her gag reflex. Startling violet eyes had glared at him defiantly as she did so, adding to the thrill as he wondered if she intended to bite it off when he came. Not wanting to take a chance, he pulled out, loving the sounds of her gasping for air. Roughly, he forced her against the wall while he grasped her hips, picking her feet off the floor as he slammed into her as hard as he could from behind. She was so fecking tight, he barely fit. Small and squeezing him like a virgin, his cock swelled more.

Tugging on her hair, he yanked her head back by her blond leash. She never made a sound. This infuriated him. He wanted her screams. Her tiny young breasts bruised and bled as he continued slamming her into the stone wall, and when he'd finally emptied himself, the li'l cunt laughed at him. Stepping back, he let her drop. She'd turned and slid down the wall, violet eyes daring to do his worst. "Ain't got much staying power, have you?" she asked, continuing to laugh at him.

Fairfax walked over to the guard outside his cell. "How much for another half hour?"

"Yer only supposed to get yer time slot, then get back in line behind the others if ye wants more."

Fairfax pulled a wad of cash from his pocket. "How much to get ye to break the rules?"

"Double the going price. But you only get one extra slot. Fifteen minutes, and ye tell the missus of this house anything—I'll find ye and fecking kill ye. Ye hear me?"

"I accept yer terms." Cash passed through the bars, and Fairfax watched him pocket half of it. "Now give me some fecking privacy."

Fairfax turned back to the wee thing. Fear finally appeared in her eyes, and his cock swelled once again.

"Just don't bruise her face. She needs to perform again in an hour." A loud cackle echoed off the stone walls as he walked away from the cell. "And don't damage the moneymaker."

"Gonna be the longest fifteen minutes of yer life, little whore," Fairfax said. He stroked his cock back into fighting shape as he approached her. "Gonna be the best fifteen minutes of mine."

flutter, he hit the nub again, and as she draped on the edge of consciousness, her sweet little pussy clamped around him, and she rode him like the whore she was, silently screaming as she came.

Feeling like a fucking champ, he dropped the belt, grabbed her hips, and slammed her on and off his cock repeatedly until the guard slammed the bars with his metal baton.

"Less than a minute left," the guard laughed, "but if you make it good for both of us, I'll give you two." A deep, dark chuckle floated in as the guard pulled his cock out. "Let's see whatchya got."

Fairfax always loved a challenge. Pushing down his rising orgasm, he slammed into her viscously, leaning down and biting her other nipple to bring her back around. Her back bowed, trying to escape his teeth. The view of her body lifting away from the wall, unintentionally tightening the belt another notch, made him blow his load violently into her.

Grunts came from the guard behind him, and Fairfax figured he'd given him a bonus along with the cash. Dropping her legs and sliding from her, he took a moment and enjoyed his handiwork.

Her nipples were raw and bloody, abrasions covered her chest, and when her body started bucking against the belt, he realized her feet were failing to hold her up. He liked the sight of her like this struggling for life—made him feel like a god with the power of life over death.

But alas, his time was over. Not wanting to push his luck with the guard, he unhooked the belt from her neck, tracing the bruises it left before walking away to retrieve his trousers. Threading the leather through the loops, he knew he would remember her every time he put it on.

Fairfax returned the following week, wanting to torment the child again. She was with someone else, two men if the guard was to be believed. So, he found himself a little brunette who was more fragile in temperament and took out his frustration and, ultimately, his pleasure with her until he heard the screams…

"No napping at the bar!" a gravelly voice snarled, bringing him back to the present. A yardstick slapped down next to him on the bar for emphasis. "We don't tolerate no vagrants in here, mister," the surly barmaid with a man's voice grumbled at him and gave him the evil eye.

"Not sleeping, ma'am. Just reminiscing." Fairfax slapped a twenty on the bar. "Yer tip, if ye can give me some peace."

The woman's scowl slipped as she pocketed the bill in her overflowing corset. "For another twenty, I'll give ye a bottle. Take yerself over to that corner booth, and ye can relive all the memories ye want outta me hair."

"Fair enough, me lady." Fairfax kept the smile pasted on his face as he resettled himself in the corner. This seat suited him just fine. He could see the entire room without moving, and he could listen in on many of the nearby conversations.

The group behind him was bitching about their boss. Two tables away, a man was leaving his wife for the working girl seated on his knee—yeah, that was gonna happen. With one eye on the door, he listened to the plight of the common man—the bitches and moans about the drudgery of their everyday life. The whores smiled, but their lifeless eyes lacked enthusiasm when they flirted, trying to fleece the dock workers out of their weekly paychecks.

His fingers toyed with the medallion around his neck. A sailor's charm for good luck and calm seas, or so it seemed. This one he wore was also a charm to alter his appearance. A glamour. It made him appear decades younger, with a fit body and a full head of thick blond hair. Witch woman who created it for him swore he looked like a local captain. What was the man's name…hmmm, he couldn't remember.

One of the younger girls wandered over with a pep in her step. "Roarke, it's been a while since I've seen you here." As she came closer, her brow furrowed, and her cheeks pinked. "Me apologies, sir. Ye reminded me of someone else."

"Who do I remind ye of, lass?" he asked with a smile, needing the information.

"Roarke Gallagher. Ye could pass for his brother."

"Makes perfect sense. We'se distant cousins," he said, taking full advantage of the situation.

Leaning against the edge of the booth, she leaned in conspiratorially, giving him a fantastic view of her cleavage. "Put a good word in for me. Name's Bethany and I've been wanting to take him for a ride."

"I'll do that if ye do one for me?"

"You betchya. Who ye aiming to take a gander at?" Her gaze wandered the room, tracking the working girls.

"No one in here. She's a warden at the sanctuary. Yay, high." He used his arm to indicate height. "Short dark hair, and violet eyes."

"Danyka?" she asked as her eyebrows got lost in her hairline. "That's a bold step, big man." A throaty chuckle came from her. "Words been she has a new flavor of the night most days at the Rusty Tap. Jest head round back, and yer likely to see her screwing some young thing. They all want a piece of her." A man at the bar flagged her down. "Nice to meet ye, but a girl's gotta eat."

Fairfax watched her striding away, hips swinging and enticing the entire room. He picked up his bottle and poured himself another shot. A mountain of a man in the booth beside him turned around and looked hard at Fairfax.

"Ye stupid or something?"

Fairfax bristled. "Beggin' yer pardon?"

"Why the feck would ye want to bag one of them female wardens? Nothing but a bunch of conniving little whores. Won't even return a man's daughter to him."

McAllister studied the man. It was obvious he was drunk. He needed a shower, too. The stench of him wafted from a booth away. But he might be useful. Picking up the bottle, he waved it at the mountain. "Drink?"

"Aye, done already gone through me coin for the day."

Fairfax filled the man's glass as he struggled to fit into the booth opposite him. Studying the bleary-eyed stranger, he said, "Tell me about your encounter with the wardens."

So, for the next ten minutes, he listened while his pathetic companion whined about losing his daughter to pay a debt. When the wardens found a shipwreck and rescued the girl, they never contacted him. He appealed to the court, and the presiding cunt refused him by emancipating the child. Fairfax smiled. This was perfect. He needed a distraction to grab Danny, and the mountain needed one for his daughter.

"I'll give ye work, but I needs ye to be sober." He glared at the man. "Take a shower, get yerself a good meal, and a couple of decent nights' sleep."

The mountain nodded, sitting up straighter in the booth now that he had a purpose. "What should I call ye?"

A wide grin crossed his face as he said, "Ye can call me Roarke."

"Ye can call me…" he trailed off as Roarke held up a hand.

"Don't need to know. This is a onetime offer and will come with a healthy bonus, should ye do as I require…" He waited until comprehension set in.

"Meet me a week from now, down at the pier. A man named Fairfax will find ye at sundown." He took out a pouch and emptied a few gold coins on the table. Pushing two towards the mountain, he said, "Don't be late. There's two more if yer on time and a bonus if ye follow directions."

The mountain looked uneasy. The stranger had gold, but something didn't sit well with him. It was too easy, and anything too easy usually ended up with someone dead. The gold shone in the dim light of the bar. Licking his lips, he thought, *"Fuck it,"* and reached for the coins. Life was too damn short anyway. "I'll be there sober and well rested."

Fairfax lifted his drink. "Here's to getting our girls, then." They clinked glasses and chugged the whiskey.

"And here's to desperate men when you need them," he thought. Because this man would never live to sell the daughter he was "rescuing." Fairfax would consider her a bonus for the dangerous mission they were undertaking. He would get his little Danyka to play with, and his men would get a little plaything to motivate them as well. Refilling his glass, he chuckled and stroked the magic pendant. He'd have to see about getting the shelf life extended permanently on this glamour. Being young wasn't much of a hardship. Life was good. Thank the gods for magic, drunks, and whores.

42

Deal With the Devil

Fergus entered the brothel with his glamour firmly in place. His normally scrawny form was saggy from the beer belly he now exhibited. Wild red hair was now a nondescript brown, lank, and greasy looking. His eyes peered around the dimly lit room, made even dimmer by the lingering cigar smoke.

Wondering if he'd been sent on a wild goose chase—he wouldn't put it past the man he was meeting—he finally found Hamish tucked in the back corner behind a massive palm plant.

Ferg made his way to the bar, purchasing a pint of dark ale and a bottle of cheap whiskey. Tipping the barmaid heavily, he took the long way to the booth Hamish sat in.

"Took ye long enough, Cyrus," the vile little man sneered, using the name Fergus had given him the first night they met.

"Got here as soon as I'se able," Ferg said, raising a brow.

"Not very professional."

Halfway to planting his ass on the bench, Ferg stood and glared down at the miserable excuse of a man. "I can take me bottle and leave if yer gonna be a prick about it." His no-nonsense attitude told the little man he had no patience for his bullshite.

"Nye!" Hamish said much too quickly, showing Ferg exactly how desperate he was for a partner. "There's a showcase coming up and an auction on the solstice."

"How's that help us?" Fergus asked.

"Yer gonna get a job onboard for the event."

"Who do I talk to for this position?"

"Tain't that easy, lad. Ye should ken that," Hamish said.

"Aye, I do. So, what kind of miracle ye gonna work?"

"I got a friend works in the kitchen of this boat. He'll sneak ye on, give ye a uniform, and ye can find out if Jonah is showing girls or not." Hamish smiled widely, showing his rotting teeth.

"Then what?"

"If he has any lasses in this showcase, we knows they be in the following auction. Then I can hire a crew and do what I wants while they're busy selling their wares."

"Ye make it sound so simple," Fergus said with a frown. "What's yer end goal? Thought ye planned to scuttle his ship?"

"Ain't decided yet exactly what's I'se gonna do. Prefer to reclaim me property."

"What property? I don't like surprises," Fergus said, grabbing the bottle as Hamish reached for it.

Hamish glared at him. "Worked me ass off to get him a pretty young thing, and he never paid for her. I wants her back or I wants proper compensation. I'll have to get a glamour to make ye..." he frowned as he looked Fergus up and down, "a mite more attractive, and mayhap less of ye. Then ye can work as a bouncer—can't see ye as a waiter—and observe the buyers. Mayhap we can even get ye in as a dealer on the next show."

"It better be a damn good glamour. Those cost a pretty penny. Ye be paying for that?"

"Yeah, and I only buy the best. I have a mage who likes to barter."

"What's he barter for?" Fergus asked.

Hamish's eyes narrowed and moved closer to the table. "Yer asking a lot of questions fer a man needing work."

Fergus filled his glass to the brim with whiskey, remembering how chatty the man was when drunk. "Might need to hire him meself."

Hamish drank half of the glass down with one gulp, wiping the back of his hand across his thin lips. "Lots of men like pretty young things," he said in a voice so low that Fergus struggled to hear him.

"Sorry to be doubting ye. I needs to trust the man I be working for. And what will ye be doing while I risk me hide on this scheme of yers?"

"Trust be earned." The hard glint of suspicion still lingered in his eyes as he stared without blinking at Ferg. "I'll be on the water, placing a tracker on his ship."

How in the fuck could this maggot afford a spell like that? Fergus kept his thoughts to himself as he sipped at his whiskey, keeping his wits about him. "What do I needs worry about on this ship I be stowing away on?"

Hamish gave him a rough appraisal, his eyes traveling over him from head to toe. "Glamour will only do so much. Clean yerself up and wear some decent clothes. Ye should have something that will make ye blend in better." He rubbed his hand over his stubble and sighed. "Ye'll only have one shot at this."

206

"I won't feck it up."

"Best not." Dangerous, beady eyes stared hard at him. "'twill be to yer disadvantage if ye do."

The thinly veiled threat amused Fergus, but he'd take the deal with the devil because he had some tricks of his own. This lil pissant thought he had the upper hand, but Ferg didn't trust the slimy bastard. He was looking forward to showing his true self when the time came, and he would make this man regret he'd ever been born.

43

Come Back Home Baby Girl

Jameson leaned over the fence, chest heaving. He tried to convince his lungs to relax and draw a breath, but the pain radiating down his left arm overrode all other bodily functions. Spots formed behind his eyelids, and he knew he was only moments away from passing out. Might be for the best. Once he hit the ground, his muscles would relax, and his body would remember how to breathe.

Soft hands on his shoulders grounded him, and the throbbing in his shoulder diminished in a slow, steady slide. Gulping in a deep breath of air irritated it, but only for a moment. Resting his head in his hands, he allowed the oxygen he needed to circulate through his exhausted body.

"You overdid it again," his mother, Kateri, said as she worked the knots of his muscles with a gentle massage.

"The only thing I did was try to saddle the damn horse," he grumbled.

"And that was obviously too much."

Jamey swore creatively under his breath, keeping his voice low because, injured or not, she would still box his ears for being vulgar.

"You've never dealt with an injury this serious before, Jamey." Her voice continued soothing his frayed nerves as she berated him. "This injury is going to take more time than any other you've experienced. You shredded your muscles and your nerves. They are still knitting back together, creating new pathways and avenues for sensation—pain included."

The sound of her voice soothed his soul and quelled the queasiness in his stomach. He might just be able to keep lunch down. "I know, but I don't have to like it." His head dangled like a pendulum as he allowed himself a few more moments.

"Want to talk about what's really bothering you?" Kateri asked.

Jamey let out a groan, knowing who she was referring to. "Not really."

"Hmmm." A smile touched her lips as she thought about the woman her son was in love with. "Danny would kick your ass right now if she saw you like this."

"That would require her making an effort. I'm not foreseeing that anytime soon." He regretted the words the second they left his mouth, knowing he'd revealed too much.

"Why do you say that?" Kateri asked, stepping down off the stool she'd stood on to massage his shoulder. "Has she spoken to you?"

"Nada."

Kateri shook her head in frustration. Though she tried to hide it, she was pissed. "I'll let you make your way back to the house. I've got some errands to run."

"Mama?"

"What, Jameson?"

Shit, his full name was being used, which meant she was getting angrier by the moment. "Don't."

Kateri tipped her head at him quizzically and asked, "Don't what?"

"Please don't interfere."

Her most terrifying emotion appeared as an angelic smile lit her face. She walked away and tossed over her shoulder, "I wouldn't dream of it."

"Fuck me…" he trailed off as she walked off, admonishing him.

"Heard that." Her voice popped into his head, and he couldn't miss the humor entwined with the words. She might not appreciate the vulgarity, but the one thing she understood was the three men in her life when they were hurting.

Jamey was hurting physically, but the greatest damage was to his heart. Kateri had waited long enough for Danyka to pull her head out of her ass. Her son was due a visit, and she was damn well going to see that he got it.

"I'll be back in a few hours," she hollered as she shut the door behind her and made her way to the stables. Giving her horse the opportunity to run, they quickly made their way to the portal. Passing her animal into the care of the stable hand, she entered the portal and selected the location where she knew she could find the woman who was hurting her son.

Danny was like a daughter to her, and it was about time she called her on her bullshit like she would any of her children.

Moments later, Kateri exited in St. Vincent, briskly walking towards the courtyard in the town square where self-defense classes were about to begin.

Kateri smiled at Grace, the young woman who introduced the shelter initiative. She received a smile in return and a cheery wave from her.

A dozen women of varying sizes and ages awaited instruction. They gathered at this shelter twice a week for lessons in self-defense provided by the Wardens.

The four o'clock bell rang in the town hall, and people appeared out of the woodwork. Women of all ages, and a few young men, wandered into the yard and stood in lines.

Danyka came in and stood in the middle so they could all hear her when she spoke. "Welcome, one and all." A rare smile crossed her face as her eyes took in the crowd.

"It's wonderful to see how many of you have returned, and I think I spy some fresh faces in the crowd as well." She gave them a nod and said, "We will try to teach you some basic moves that we hope you'll never have reason to use. Grace will be my assistant, and I'd like to introduce a few others who've volunteered their time today."

Pointing to two tall, dark-haired men, she said, "These are the Pathfinder brothers, Ronan and Damian. Wardens at the Sanctuary, they are very proficient at self-defense. The tall, gangly redhead is Fergus Emberz, our resident Fire Mage who has a few tricks up his sleeve."

Kerrygan emerged from the back of the crowd. "I'd like to offer my assistance as well, Danny."

Danny nodded her appreciation at him. "This man is Kerrygan, also a fellow Warden. He will be wonderful working with our youngest members."

Kerry's eyes flashed at Danny, but then he noticed Grace's surprise and confusion behind her. Giving her a nod, his lips quirked into a smile when she narrowed her eyes at him. Hell, this just might be fun.

A smattering of applause sounded in the courtyard following the introductions. "We'll take groups of six to practice with each instructor."

People quickly broke into small groups and worked through the exercises with their individual trainers. Danyka circulated throughout, offering advice and helping each group.

Grace was working with a beautiful Indigenous woman when Danyka approached them. The timeless woman had braided her hair and pinned it up on her head. Grace tripped the woman, sending her sprawling onto the ground. Danny reached out a hand to help her up, and when their eyes met, her face lost all color.

Releasing Kateri's hand and jumping back as if her touch burned, she mumbled an excuse and moved on to the next group, thoroughly pissing the older woman off. Kateri watched Danny escape and smiled. She wouldn't be ignored so easily, but she was a patient woman and could wait until everyone else left.

Danny was rolling up mats and storing weapons in a duffle when she felt the powerful energy move in behind her. Kateri was an alpha shifter, and Danny knew a predator by the feel of her energy.

This woman had been nothing but kind and generous to her. She'd opened up her home and made Danny feel like part of her family every time she came by. Today was different, though, and they both knew it. Kateri's son nearly died because of her negligence. This was a reckoning that Danny had been avoiding.

Tying the bag shut, she took a deep breath, stood, and faced this mother's wrath. She was gobsmacked when Kateri reached out and pulled her into a powerful hug. Then, Mother help her, she started sobbing as she clung to Danny.

Danny's eyes were wild as she glanced around, looking for someone to save her from this awkward situation. No one was around, trapping her with this normally stoic alpha. Awkwardly returning the hug, she patted her shoulder, remembering Maddy and Rhy doing that for her when she had nightmares. Silently, they stood there as Kateri finally released her pain and fears.

The tears slowed, and Kateri wiped her nose on her shirtsleeve, then took a seat on the grass. Pointing to the ground across from her, she pointed and said, "Sit."

The word wasn't a request. Danny plopped her ass down as directed and waited for her to begin.

"Where've you been?" Kateri asked, narrowing her eyes at Danny.

Swallowing hard, she cleared her throat and tried to produce something—some line of bullshit—to excuse her avoidance of Jamey. One glance at the woman's expression, and she couldn't pull it off. Kateri was here as a mother. She had questions and deserved answers. "I can't," she finally whispered in a hoarse voice.

"Why?"

"It hurts too much."

"What hurts? Seeing him in pain or knowing you're causing it?"

Danny reared back as if the woman had struck her. The statement was a matter of fact. No accusations, just plain truth. How was she supposed to justify that?

"I'm so sorry," she said in a hoarse whisper.

The perplexed look on Kateri's face gave Danny pause.

"Sorry for what exactly?" Kateri asked.

When she opened her mouth to speak, all that emerged was a pained croak. Closing her eyes, she willed her voice to work and her eyes to not overflow. But this time, when she opened her mouth, all the pain and fear poured out instead.

"I'm sorry for being the reason he almost died," Danny choked out.

"What the hell are you talking about?" Kateri's expression was as puzzled as the question she'd asked.

Danny shook her head, not wanting to confess her sins to this woman. This woman, whom she respected tremendously, would never look at her with kindness again.

"I was horrible to him that day. Actually, I'd been horrible to him for weeks; since we returned from the Court of Tears, I'd been distancing myself from him." Her eyes stayed on her fingers, worrying at the frayed ends of a braided leather bracelet she'd worn for years. This was one he'd made for her long ago, she realized with a jolt.

"Why did you feel the need to distance yourself from him, Danny?"

Danny shook her head, not wanting to tell her the truth. She didn't want Kateri to know how used and unstable she was.

Firm fingers gripped her chin, forcing her to gaze at the other woman. "Tell me why, Danyka." Kateri's voice held a primitive power that compelled her to obey. She wondered if Kateri did it intentionally or if being an alpha made all shifters want to comply with her.

Tears filled her eyes, overflowing and slipping down her cheeks in a steady stream as she clamped her lips shut and shook her head.

"TELL ME!" This time there was no doubting the compulsion was intentional.

The need to confess everything to this woman was intense. Fighting it caused Danny physical pain, which she could live with, but the disappointment in Kateri's eyes made her give in. Maybe if she told her, his mother could shift to hating Danny, and the entire family would finally leave her thoughts.

"Because I'm in love with him, and I'm the farthest thing from what he needs. He deserves someone who would be easy to love," Danny sobbed aloud. "I'm a fucking mess, and I come with a shit ton of baggage that I have no intention of ever unpacking." Her voice rose as rage rolled through her for being forced to have this conversation.

"He loves you and wants you exactly as you are," Kateri said.

"He says that now, but what will he think when I hit a rough patch, and he doesn't like the way I deal with it? When old habits kick in—and I guarantee they will—he'll fucking despise me, and so will the rest of you."

Danny's eyes flashed dangerously at Kateri, no longer caring what the woman thought. She'd tried so hard to forget her past, but it never worked. It was always there in the cobwebs of the attic of her mind, waiting to remind her of what she'd done.

"You're not the only one with a past, Danyka. We all have them. We all have things we're embarrassed of—ashamed of. You don't have the corner market on that."

"I'm sure you've got some tawdry secret hidden about your perfect family." Danny's sarcasm came out caustic and thick.

212

Kateri's lips quirked as she answered the accusation. "My grandmother ran one of the biggest gambling dens and whorehouses this side of the Mississippi. My mother was her bestselling whore, and I don't know who my father was. But you know what...I don't care. I loved those two women more than anything because of the way they loved me. Their life choices and careers were minor choices in otherwise beautiful lives."

Danny gaped at her in shock, then shook her head to make sure she'd heard her correctly. "You're fucking with me."

"Nope." Kateri grinned. "Ask Jamey or Kuruk; they'll concur." She took Danny's face in her hands, wiping tears away that were still racing down her cheeks. "He loves you, Danny, knowing everything he knows, and he doesn't care." She leaned over and kissed Danny's cheek. "That's a rare gift, and not one you should squander."

Danny shook her head again. "Your ancestors made choices. I respect that. My mother threw me into that life as a child. Kateri, I have such a deep well of rage, and I'm not sure I want to let it go."

"I know, honey, but that rage is going to destroy you eventually. It will eat away at you from the inside until you're willing to let it go or it destroys you. Are you willing to give it that much power over you?" She stood and offered Danny her hand. "Don't you think you deserve to live without the weight of that hatred dragging you down?"

Danny took the hand, pondering her words. She'd heard similar versions from Rhy and from Maddy. "I'm not sure I know how."

"Fair enough." Kateri wrapped her in a hug, and Danny returned it fiercely. "But it's an awfully lonely life once you drive everyone else away and only have yourself to deal with at the end of the day."

They walked side by side in silence. When they reached the main lane, Kateri reached out and clasped Danny's hands in hers. "We love you, Danny. You are already a part of our family. We would love to make you a more permanent part of it. But those are decisions you have to make for yourself."

Kateri reached out and brushed Danny's long bangs to the sides. "Remember this. You'll find no one who loves you as much as Jamey does or who will dedicate his life just to making you smile. If you don't love him, tell him that." She released her hand to point a finger in her face. "But don't you dare lie to him. He deserves better than that." She released her hand and walked away. "Remember that you deserve to be loved just as much as anyone else does."

"Thank you, Kateri," Danny said with a half-hearted smile.

"Come back home, baby girl. We all miss you."

"Yes, ma'am," Danny said as her eyes misted once again. Gathering the weapons she'd brought with her, she replayed their conversation in her

mind. The woman had given her a lot to think about, but she wasn't ready to do it right now. Right now, she wanted a beer and a friend. She hoped Fergus hadn't left yet. Maybe they could grab a pint on the way back. She owed him one for putting up with her surly ass lately, and she felt like being generous.

Danny knew Jamey loved her. She'd never doubted that. The thing holding her back was, did she trust him enough to hand over all of her past? Could he still love her when he knew all of it?

Shaking her head, she knew what her decision would be. Losing his respect was a chance she wasn't willing to take, or had she already lost it?

44

Last of Our Solitude

"Come in, Kai," Rhyanna said with a smile, holding open the door to their lake house. "I'm so glad ye can join us for dinner."

"I was looking forward to it," he said, handing a bouquet of wildflowers to her.

"Thank ye. Daisies are one of me favorites, and what gorgeous shades of columbine ye've found." Standing on her tiptoes, she gave the young man a kiss on the cheek.

Kai flushed and took a step back, uncomfortable with the display of affection from his oldest brother's woman. Rhyanna was one of the sweetest women he'd ever met. He wondered how his grumpy brother had landed her.

"Kyran's out back if ye'd like to join him while I finish dinner."

"You cook?" he asked, surprised, because the chef at the Sanctuary usually took care of all meals on and off campus.

"Aye, I enjoy it, but rarely have the opportunity. The kitchen staff be a mite territorial."

They both laughed. "I'm gonna put these in water. Go on and join Kyran."

Kai walked down the hall to the screen door leading to the back porch. Kyran stood gazing into the distance, his hands clenched at his side. He turned at the sound of the screen closing. A grin quickly spread as he clamped Kai on the shoulder. "Glad you could make it. Are you all settled in?"

"Yeah. The rest of my trunks arrived yesterday. Although I doubt there's much I need. Been without them for weeks and didn't miss anything."

"Come winter, you'll be grateful for the warmer clothes," Kyran said. "That is if you're intending to stay." Kyran poured two glasses of ale, handing one to Kai, and then keeping the other for himself.

Kai gazed out across the lawn to the forest beyond. He could hear waves from the lake hitting the shore and understood why Kyran chose this location for their home. "I see now why you like it here—besides the obvious allure of Rhyanna."

"It's a beautiful location, and the Sanctuary has enough work to challenge me. I'm happy for the first time in a long time."

"And she cooks," Kai added with a gleam in his eye. "Thank the gods we're not counting on you to feed us. We'd go hungry tonight."

A deep chuckle erupted from Kyran. "You're right. It's definitely not my skill set."

"Skill set? Hell, how difficult is it to boil an egg? We were picking them off the ceiling for hours after that fiasco."

"Who canna boil an egg?" Rhy's melodious voice drifted to them as she backed through the screen door with platters of food.

Both men moved to assist. They carried the platters to the table set in the middle of the porch while she returned for more. Kai took in the simple taupe linen tablecloth with cream-colored napkins. A hand-carved walnut bowl was already there, filled with early spring greens. Walnuts, dried raspberries, and chunks of goat cheese were sprinkled on top. The raspberry vinaigrette drizzled over the salad smelled amazing. His stomach growled, reminding him he hadn't eaten since lunch.

"Kyran," Kai replied, wincing as Kyr cuffed him upside the head.

"We'll have to work on that," Rhy said, gazing at him.

"Rather not," he mumbled as she returned to the kitchen.

"That Ken's work?" Kai asked, nodding to the carved bowl.

"Yes, it was a gift for Rhy."

"It's beautiful. He should focus on what he loves doing. Each piece is always unique."

"He's not ready to settle down yet," Kyran said with a smirk. "Not for a job or for a partner."

"I think that be everything," Rhy said breathlessly as she joined them with small loaves of bread straight out of the oven.

"Everything looks wonderful," Kai said, taking in the feast.

Poached trout covered in lemon slices and dill sat atop a bed of wild rice mixed with almond slivers and green onions. Roasted asparagus and cauliflower rested in a garlic herb butter.

"Dig in," Rhy said, "before it gets cold."

Rhy enjoyed listening to the brothers talking throughout the meal. They discussed the upcoming training and the tournament Kenn was organizing to lure in Genny's father.

After cleaning his plate, Kai wiped his face with his napkin. "I can't eat another bite. It was wonderful, Rhy."

"That's a shame," she said. "You haven't seen dessert." She winked at him and headed back into the house.

"If you ever screw this up, she's fair game," Kai threatened his brother. "Any woman that can cook like that…is worth fighting for."

Kyran gave him a cocky grin. "She has many fine qualities, of which cooking is only one."

Kai grinned back, not goading him for more information. He truly liked Rhyanna, and he'd never seen Kyran this content before. Envy crept in, and he realized he wanted this someday. With the right woman, he'd be content coming home to dinners, laughter, and loving at the end of a long day. Unbidden, Genny's face flashed through his mind. He reached for his ale and took a gulp, trying to return to the present.

Rhyanna returned with slices of yellow cake laden with blueberries, blackberries, and raspberries. A heap of whipped cream sat on top, teasing him. Kyran must have told her they were his favorites.

"Mistress, you don't fight fair."

"Then ye'll have a slice?" Rhy asked with a smile.

"Or two," Kyran added with a chuckle.

"There's always room for dessert," Kai said, reaching for the slice she offered him.

When dessert was polished off, they helped her clear the table and wash the dishes, chatting the entire time. Afterward, Rhy made them mugs of cocoa.

"Let's take these on the front porch," she said. "I want to watch the sunset over the lake."

They moved to the front of the house and out onto the large stone porch. Kai leaned against the rail, assuming they would take the two rockers. Kyran sat in one, placing his mug on the table between the chairs, then taking Rhy's mug and setting it next to his. He pulled her sideways onto his lap, then handed the mug back to her.

"Please sit, Kai," Rhy said. "We rarely use both. One is big enough for both of us. You'll miss the view."

He settled into the other chair, surprised by how comfortable it was for his large frame.

"We have a proposition for you," Kyran said.

"What would that be?" Kai asked suspiciously, taking a sip of the creamy concoction.

"We'll be staying at the Sanctuary for the summer session. We thought you might like to stay out here. It will give you some privacy from the hordes of young women who will be fawning all over you."

"I doubt there will be hordes," he said, clearing his throat.

"Yer an attractive young man, Kai," Rhy said. "Ye'll be surrounded by impressionable young women who also know yer a prince."

Kai sighed heavily. "Don't remind me. I forget my titles when I am here."

"We'd appreciate having someone we know to watch over the place while we're gone," Kyran said, approaching it from a different angle. "We won't be able to come out and check on it as much as we'd like."

"I be worried our more adventurous teens will be out in places they shan't be at night," Rhy said.

"So, you don't want them taking advantage of your love nest?" Kai asked with a smirk.

Rhy blushed, burying her face in Kyran's shoulder. Kyran grinned back at him. "Hell no."

Kai considered their request and realized they were right. The house was far enough from the Sanctuary to be private, and he would appreciate that at the end of the day. He watched the sun dipping low in the sky, hovering over the water. The colors reminded him of home, and the proximity to the lake was perfect. It certainly wouldn't be a hardship to relax here. "I'd be happy to stay here in your absence."

"Wonderful," Rhy said. "I be mighty relieved to have someone I trust here. There are guestrooms upstairs. Take yer pick."

"Let me know if there's anything I need to take care of while you're gone."

"We'll leave a list. Thank you for doing this," Kyran said, grateful he agreed. They both would feel better leaving their home with him staying in it.

"It's getting late. I'll put my mug in the kitchen and let myself out," Kai said.

Rhy moved to climb off Kyran's lap, but Kai stopped her by leaning down and kissing her cheek. "Stay there, little sister. Relax." He nodded at Kyran and made his way out the door.

"Thank you for inviting him," Kyran said, pressing a kiss on the top of her head. "I'm glad he agreed to join the Sanctuary staff."

"No need to thank me. I like the lad, he's intelligent and hardworking. But more importantly, there's a gentleness in him this world needs. Beneath his imposing physical size and strength, he's a kind, generous man."

"Good thing I'm not the insecure type...or I'd be jealous of my brother," Kyran said with a grin.

Rhy laughed aloud at that. "Good thing," she echoed in a mocking voice and raising an eyebrow at him.

"Do you want to go in? It's cooling down?"

"Nye. Yer keeping me warm enough and I love watching the sky changing this time of night."

Kyran and Rhy sat in silence, enjoying the last vestiges of light as the sun abandoned the day. Her head rested on his shoulder, her soft breath against his neck. His hand drifted up and down her back, trailing lower with each swipe. She let out a breathy little sigh, and his cock hardened. She tipped her hips, causing her ass to grind against him. When her arms wound around his neck, pulling his lips down to hers, he moaned.

Starving for the taste of her, he delved inside, his tongue stroking against hers. His hands moved over her, finding the hem of her skirt, searching for her silky skin.

Rhy pulled away, gasping as his palms traveled from her calves up over her knees. Supporting her back with his right arm, his left pulled her legs apart. He traced intricate little designs up the inside of her thigh, dancing over her core, but offering no form of relief.

A whimper left her lips as she arched tighter, and he inched closer to his destination. His lips caught her next sigh, and his fingers traced her folds, gathering moisture and dragging it up and around the perimeter of her clit. Trailing kisses down her neck, he nipped at her along the way until he reached her ear. "Tell me how badly you want me, Rhy. I want to hear you begging before I take you."

A shocked gasp of outrage snuck out before he recaptured her lips again. When they parted, she gave him an evil smile. "I willna be the only one begging afore the night is out, Kyr. Remember that." This time she nipped him, drawing blood.

His forefinger stroked her clit once, then slowly slid into her. Withdrawing and adding another, he set a slow rhythm, sliding in and out, then occasionally grazing her clit with his thumb. When her hips tried to meet him, he held her in place with his free hand, tormenting her.

Waves of pleasure built in a slow, steady wave until she screamed his name in frustration. She was so damn close, but she needed more. "Kyran, inside me now," she whimpered against his lips.

The feel of his lips curling into a smile under hers was a challenge. Well, if he wanted to play, she would be happy to play. Kyran continued his tortuous pace until she gave in and screamed his name. Kissing her thoroughly, he released her. She stood and dropped the skirt she was wearing to the floor while he unlaced his breeches and shimmied them off his hips.

The sight of him aroused was always impressive. She licked her lips, a wicked smile forming at the sight of him stroking his cock.

Eyes taking in her every move, Kyran groaned, watching her tongue. "Come here, my lady. I'll give you what you want."

"Will ye na?" she asked as she straddled his hips. She was so grateful that they'd found these extra wide rockers because she could do this comfortably with her thick thighs and have room to spare.

Large hands kneaded her buttocks while she kissed him. Her hands tangled in his long hair, then pulled his head back. Her flashing emerald eyes locked on his blue ones, darkening with desire. They always reminded her of storm clouds when he was angry or aroused. The blue swirled and changed colors with his moods. His hands shifted to her hips with gentle pressure, encouraging her to lower to his cock. She pulled his hair harder, remaining where she was.

"Place yer hands on the armrests, Kyran," she ordered. Her emerald orbs challenged him to obey.

Because of his experience, Kyran usually led their dance while making love. Rhyanna was catching on quickly, and she reveled in teasing him just as much.

"Hands, Kyran."

His fingers were digging into her hips as he contemplated obeying. He squeezed her tighter, then his fingers relaxed, and he massaged the skin he had been clenching. Drifting down her legs in a slow caress, he released her and reached for the armrests. His gaze never left hers, and the desire in them made her feel so sensual and alive.

"Good lad," she whispered against his lips, kissing him thoroughly. They both were panting as she finally lowered herself onto his lap.

Kyran clenched his jaw. Rhy looked so fucking beautiful as she claimed her sexual power from him. He loved the confidence she exuded and wanted to encourage her as she explored their power dynamic. He moaned as she lowered herself because it just might kill him to sit here and not touch her in return. She rested on his thighs, her wet core mere inches from where he needed her to be. Although he tried to talk himself out of it, his hips punched up of their own volition, wanting her to wrap her sweet pussy around his aching cock. Her hands tightening in his hair once more warned him not to move.

Rhy tipped her hips forward so that her pussy slid against the length of his cock without allowing him to enter. His gaze never left hers, and she'd never forget the way he was looking at her right now. The reverence and heat in his eyes made her feel like a goddess. She released his hair and pulled her blouse off, leaving her only in her corset. His nostrils flared, and the muscles in his arms corded as he gripped the armrests tighter. She slid back and forth, teasing them both.

The head of his cock bumped her clit with every glide, making her gasp and making him groan beneath her. A throaty chuckle tore from her as her fingers unlaced the corset she wore. "I see na why ye like to be in control, me laird." She dropped the laces when it was loose enough to free her

breasts. The large globes filled her palms while she kneaded them, then pinched her nipples.

"Fuck," Kyran said, "I can feel you rippling against me." Their moans echoed across the lake. "Please, Rhy, let me feel that while I am buried inside of you."

A sultry smile emerged. She reached up and released her long hair, letting it fall around them. The long strands moved in the slight breeze, teasing them both. Silky strands floated across Kyran's hands. Without thinking, he trapped it beneath his fingers just so he could touch some part of her.

Hands stroking her breasts and hips, tormenting him, Rhy captured his mouth. Lips bruising and tongues clashing, they drove each other higher. As much as she wanted him begging, she wasn't sure how much longer she could hold out. On the next stroke, she whimpered as he groaned and thrust his hips, trying to gain the right angle.

"Please, Rhy," Kyran whispered again. "You win. I'm not beneath begging, my lady. Please, put us both out of our misery."

"Put yer hands on me, Kyran," Rhy whispered as she changed the angle of her hips and slid down on him.

She didn't have to ask twice. One hand fisted the hair at the base of her neck while he pulled her lips to his for a bruising kiss. The other clenched her hip, guiding her up and down on his over-sensitized cock.

"I'm not going to last long," he said, his voice thick with lust.

"I willna take long either," she said in a keening tone. "Right there, Kyran. Harder."

The rocking chair made it hard for him to get any leverage. With a muttered curse, he mumbled, "Hold on." Wrapping his arms around her, he stood and walked to the railing. He set her on the edge of the wide stone slab, which, thank all the gods, was the perfect height for him to fuck her.

Kyran pushed her knees wide and drove into her over and over until her inner walls shuddered around him. The change in position helped him regain control over his body, and selfishly, he didn't want it to end just yet.

Rhy was supporting herself on her arms, lifting her hips to meet him. She was close, but he knew her body well enough by now to know what it would take to send her over the edge.

"Yes, yes, yes…" Rhy chanted desperately, seeking her climax. She felt his cock swell and knew he was ready. She leaned forward and caught his nipple between her teeth, nipping.

"Oh, fuck, Rhy." His thumb found her clit, applying just the right pressure. "Come with me."

His shout and her cry drifted across the lake. Rhy clung to him, gasping. Kyran's head was on her shoulder, and his ragged breaths were loud in her ear. His hand cupped her cheek, and his lips found hers for a gentle kiss.

"I love you, my lady." He pressed a soft kiss on her neck. "This wasn't the worst way to spend the last night of our solitude."

"I love ye too, me laird." Her head rested on his chest, and her hands stroked his sides. "This was the best way to spend our last night here. I'm going to miss it."

"'Tis only for a few months, and we'll return." His lips grazed hers again. "I'll still be in your bed every night."

"Right where ye belong." She yawned and snuggled closer to him. "Take me to bed, Kyran. I be tired, and it's cooling down."

"As you wish, my lady," he said, picking her up and cuddling her closer as he walked toward the door.

45

What Else Does This Day Have in Store for Me?

Myranda lay awake as night transitioned to the wee hours of the day. Her head was heavy and her stomach queasy as she wiped a tear from her face. Though it was only temporary, Ryssa living somewhere else for the next few months was devastating to her. This house would be too big and lonely with her daughter gone.

Trying to shake off her melancholy, she showered and dressed before heading downstairs. Cooking was always a great distraction. Today called for waffles. They were Maryssa's favorite and the one thing she might take a few bites of herself.

Fresh flowers from her garden sat on the lace-covered table, and her favorite china awaited the waffles. A fresh pot of tea rested on a trivet. As she sliced strawberries, her mind wandered to the many mornings that had begun with a breakfast like this. Beautiful memories of family breakfasts served just like today's, but back then, there were three people to enjoy them. With a shuddering breath, she focused on the red berry in her hand, determined not to show Ryssa how difficult this was for her, too.

Footsteps on the stairs told her Ryssa was up and moving. A muffled curse, and she raced back up them to get something she'd forgotten. Myranda removed the last waffle from the iron as Ryssa sat. She poured a cup of tea for both of them, then doctored it with generous servings of cream and sugar.

Myranda carried the waffles, strawberries, and freshly whipped cream to the table. Ryssa filled a plate with waffles, fruit, and the fluffy goodness. Thankfully, her daughter's emotions rarely affected her appetite. Myranda wanted to send her off with a full belly.

"You have everything you need?" she asked as Ryssa filled her plate.

"Yep," Ryssa uttered around a huge bite of her waffle. "Toothbrush, check. Clean underwear, check. Corsets, check. Art supplies, check." She took another bite before continuing. "What else could I need?"

The sarcasm she answered her mother with made it better. It was also a reminder for Myranda of how much she would miss the snark while she was gone. She took a small bite of her waffle, pushing the pieces around on her plate to make a good show of it. Her stomach was rolling, and her eyes still burned with unshed tears.

Ryssa sipped her tea. Her mother was staring at her plate and playing with her food. Even across the table, she noticed the tears pooling in her eyes. Pushing back her chair, she tossed her napkin on the table and walked to the other side. She wrapped her arms around her mother, hugging her from behind.

"It's ok, mom, really, I swear." She kissed the side of her head and continued, "This is the way it has to be. I'm resigned to getting it over with."

Myranda hugged her back and wiped her eyes. "I'm fine. Just had something in my eye."

Ryssa let the fib go. "I'm gonna head upstairs until you're ready to leave, if you don't mind."

"Go on, honey, while I clean up." Myranda washed her face and put her kitchen back in order before stepping outside. A daughter of the Earth Clan, she knew where to release her frustrations, fears, and heartbreak.

Kicking off her sandals, she picked up her shears. She wandered through her garden, pruning and purging weeds and strays as she sealed the cracks in her heart. With her feet connected to the ground, she called on the Earth Mother.

"Mother of us all, hear my plea. I don't want to do this today. I *know* it's what I need to do, and it's what she needs to do. Thank you for the blessing of this child I have nurtured for over fifteen years. Please grant me the ability to let my daughter begin the path of her destiny with courage and strength. Help me say goodbye with grace. I can visit her daily. Other parents don't have that luxury. Grant me the patience to give her the first taste of independence. I will allow her to find me if she needs me. Please help me let her go."

Blood pulsed in her legs as the energy of the earth washed through her, leaving her hollowed out and clear-headed once again.

Gathering her shoes, she entered her kitchen. "Ryssa, are you ready?"

A cool breeze blew in through the window, reminding Myranda to grab a light shawl. One matching the pale-yellow flowers on her sky-blue skirt hung near the door. She wore a cream-colored peasant blouse embroidered with the same tiny yellow flowers along the neckline and sleeves. The outfit would help lift her spirits. A had carved bowl on the trestle table held crystals of every color. She picked a small piece of raw rose quartz to slip

into her pocket. A worry stone for her to play with when she felt overwhelmed. The stone would also soothe her heart chakra.

Ryssa clambered down the front steps with two more bags in tow. Myranda slung her other bag over her shoulder, and they headed out the door. Walking past the peacocks next door, Myranda ran her hand along the blue streaks in Ryssa's hair.

Ryssa smirked at her and said, "Admit it, mama, you love it. Just come out and say it."

"It definitely suits you, honey," Myranda agreed with a smile.

They arrived at the lighthouse, which also served as the portal gate for their town. Expecting a rush to use the portal today, they assigned each family a departure time. As they waited to be called, Ryssa studied the other families patiently waiting. Typically, they only used the portal a few times a year when they visited her father's clan.

Glancing around, she saw boys and girls her age looking as nervous as she felt. Amberly Briarwood's cheery smile helped Ryssa relax. They'd been friends since they were toddlers. Ryssa felt better with an ally in the mix. Amberly looked different today. She'd pulled her long brown hair back from her face. Plaited into multiple tiny braids and pulled up into an intricate design on top of her head, she looked older. The style highlighted her high cheekbones and dark brown eyes.

Glancing through the crowd to find anyone else she might recognize, she heard a squeal behind her. She turned just in time for Willow Lakeshore to launch herself at her. Long and lean, like her name, she had fine blond hair that frizzed easily in humidity. Today, she had it pulled back into a ponytail. Tiny strands had already escaped and were curling around her face.

Willow was her best friend, and it was a testament to how depressed Ryssa had been that she'd forgotten Willow would join her on Heart Island for training. Any other time, this alone would have made her excited to go.

"I'm so glad you're here," Willow gushed. "I wasn't sure if you would be with, well, you know…" she paused awkwardly, not sure how to finish.

"Unfortunately, the disappearance of a parent does not excuse you from attending," Ryssa said softly, not wanting to talk about it anymore. "When I didn't see you at orientation, I forgot you were going to miss it. I'm so glad you're here, too." Ryssa glanced around. "Did you notice Amberly?"

"No, I didn't. She's always so sweet to everyone," Willow said. "Even if they don't deserve it." She glanced over at her mother, glaring at her from across the square. "I better go."

Myranda pulled her into a hug. "I've missed you, Willow."

"Missed you, too, Mrs. Belmont." Willow pulled away, racing back to her parents.

Life had become socially awkward for the Belmonts with Mathyas's disappearance. Myranda would have never expected her clan to treat them this way. Their Earth Clan had always felt like her second family until recently. The Elders weren't sure how to interpret the circumstances of his disappearance. Some members avoided them like the plague, as if what happened was contagious. Others treated her like a widow, assuming he'd died. Not knowing what to say, some gossiped incessantly about it. Was he cheating? Was she? Did he leave her? Did she kill him? Myranda learned long ago to ignore those who weren't intelligent enough to mind their own business.

"Mama…" Ryssa started, then stopped.

"Yes, honey?"

"What was it like for you when you attended training?"

Myranda put her hand on her daughter's back and leaned closer so she could hear her over the din of the crowd. "It was scary at first. I'd never been away from home, except with family. I won't lie. The first week was tough for me. The entire experience was intimidating and very challenging. They will ask you to do things you aren't familiar with and challenge you in ways that might not seem to make sense. You just need to remember that this is new for all of you. It doesn't matter who is rich or poor. At the Sanctuary, everyone is on equal ground."

"It doesn't seem that way when the same bullies I've had to deal with my entire life are here."

"I understand, honey. The entire purpose is to find your strengths and hone them. Everyone is different. Some will shift easily, while others will struggle. The earth will call to a fair few, and others will kill everything green they touch. Working with fire will come naturally to part of the students, while many will never light a candle."

Myranda smiled at her, trying to ease her nerves. "You will have at least a little grace with your clan element. But latent genes from both sides of your family tree can alter your strengths and weaknesses. Mayhap you'll be a lucky one. Spirit might come naturally to you. In that case, you will control all the elements easily."

"Mama, don't wish that on me," Ryssa said in mock horror. If she exhibited even the slightest hint of controlling all elements equally, she would have to return in the fall.

"You'll make new friends and allies that will last you a lifetime. Be careful and watch your tongue and your temper because enemies you create there will last a lifetime, too."

"Great. Already found some of them now."

"On a positive note. The island is beautiful. I remember the yacht and carriage house well. You can enjoy the river in your spare time. Take a boat out on the river for me, Ryssa. That was one of my favorite things to do."

The portal operator called their name, and they entered the lighthouse. Selecting their destination, the portal shuddered. They experienced the free fall until they arrived at their destination.

Stepping out onto the end of a long dock, Ryssa understood why her mother enjoyed being here so much. The glare of the sun on the river and stone castle at the top of the hill gave it a magical glow. Little cottages peeked through the pines and maples across the river from them. Peace rolled over her for the first time in weeks. She wanted to paint this view.

Families gathered in small groups, waiting for everyone to arrive. The teens arriving represented clans from all over the northeast. When the last family joined them, they walked up the hill to the garden they had been in for orientation.

White folding chairs awaited the guests. Everyone took a seat and waited for Mistress SkyDancer to arrive. A low hum of conversation filled the air, mainly from the parents. Most of the teens were too nervous to talk. Ryssa's stomach was queasy as she looked around at the strangers in the crowd.

"Welcome!" Mistress Madylyn SkyDancer's melodious voice projected loud and clear throughout the garden.

"I want to welcome all of you to the first stop on your uniquely personal elemental journey. We are so excited to have you for the next few months. I realize leaving home for the first time is terrifying for many of you. Others might not know anyone here, and that can be uncomfortable for you." Madylyn's gaze searched the crowd. "I challenge you. Introduce yourself to someone new today. Make a friend. Be a friend.

"I'm sorry to say this, but it's time for your parents to say goodbye for now. They are welcome to join you in a few weeks for our Summer Solstice Festival."

Ryssa's heart was beating out of her chest. She knew this was coming, but she wasn't ready yet. Holding back tears, she stood and realized her mom was doing the same.

Myranda saw the near panic in Ryssa's eyes as she embraced her. "You are going to do fine, my sweet girl. You've got this." She kissed the side of her head and stepped back. Ryssa begged her with her eyes not to leave her here. "You come find me at the clinic if you need me. I won't seek you out because I want you to focus on your lessons. But I'll be at the clinic most afternoons. Rhyanna is there for you, too."

Ryssa nodded, unable to speak. She squeezed her mother's hand, then let go even though she was screaming inside.

Myranda framed her face in her hands. "I love you, baby. Your daddy is so proud of you for going through with this."

At that, the control she was tenuously holding onto snapped, and tears slipped down her face. One shuddering sob left her, but she reined in the

227

rest. *"I love you too, Mama."* Wiping her eyes, she stepped back and gave her a crooked smile. "I got this."

Myranda's eyes pooled with tears. "I am so proud of you, baby." Without another word, she turned and walked away.

Ryssa straightened her back and looked around. They weren't the only ones in tears. Somehow, that made her less self-conscious.

"Maryssa Belmont?" a soft voice asked behind her.

"Yes," she answered, turning around. A petite woman with straight blond hair was smiling up at her.

"My name is Lily," the young woman said. "Are these bags yours?" she asked, pointing at the leather satchels surrounding her.

"Yes," Ryssa answered. "I may have over-packed."

Lily laughed. "Not even by a long shot." Her gaze traveled across the garden, and Ryssa couldn't help but follow it. Multiple trunks and bags surrounded Collette.

"Well, that makes me feel better," Ryssa said.

Lily tagged the bags as hers and sent them with a valet, who was waiting patiently behind her. "If you'll follow me, we'll gather the rest of the lasses."

Having no time left to even think about her mother, Ryssa followed her, wondering what else this day had in store for her.

46

Temporary Home

Lily finished checking Ryssa in and headed for the next trainee, tagging bags and sending them ahead with a valet, as she had done for her. One by one, they gathered the girls who were still in the garden until there were nearly two dozen young ladies waiting in an awkward silence.

Amberly made her way over to stand by Ryssa. "I'm not sure whether to be excited or terrified," she said in a whisper.

"Me neither," Ryssa agreed, gazing at the other girls waiting. She recognized two others near Collette. "Great, her minions are here too." She nodded in their direction at the same time Collette glanced at her. Their eyes held, and though she didn't understand why, Collette's glare unnerved her. They'd rarely spoken, so she couldn't imagine why the girl disliked her so.

"Never leaves home without them," Amberly said disgustedly under her breath. "I wonder if they wipe her ass for her, too.

Ryssa covered her mouth and coughed to cover up the laugh threatening to burst past her lips. Amberly's sarcasm and humor were only a few of the reasons Ryssa loved her. Amberly was brilliant at everything, but also the most down-to-earth teen she'd ever known. Neither of them thrived in the drama girls their age seemed to revel in.

Willow bounded up beside them.

Lily rang a bell to get everyone's attention. "If ye'll all line up two by two and follow me, we'll tour the castle, and then I'll show ye to yer rooms."

They lined up as directed. "I'm so glad you're both here with me," Ryssa said. "I don't think I could've managed this alone."

"Of course not," Amberly piped up. "You need us. Just think about how much fun and trouble we can get into along the way with Willow."

"That's kind of what I am afraid of," Ryssa added dryly.

Willow chuckled, glancing over her shoulder at them from the row in front of them.

Ryssa gazed around the massive granite building. It seemed larger today than during orientation. But that didn't make any sense. The main door took them into the foyer. They squeezed in around the base of the massive stairwell, waiting for Lily to begin.

"On the right, you'll find the formal parlor for welcoming guests." She pointed to the room with Victorian furniture and heavy velvet drapes. "Next is the Wardens' parlor, which speaks for itself, followed by the game room. Ye are all welcome to use the game room anytime ye don't have class or additional duties."

"Duties," Collette sneered. "What duties would we need to complete other than those pertaining to our education?"

Lily smiled patiently. "Good question. Should we assign ye one, ye might find yerself working in the kitchens, housekeeping, or the stables. We may assign them as punishments or to teach valuable lessons. For example, lessons in humility." Her cool gaze landed on Collette as she finished. The girl's cheeks flamed, and she glared back at their tour guide.

"How dare you?"

"How dare I what?" Lily asked, sounding honestly perplexed while maintaining her angelic smile. "I simply answered yer question and gave an example. Any personal affront ye may have taken must stem from guilt or recognition of a trait that ye lack." She gazed at all the girls, her eyes meeting each of theirs. "There's not a one of us standing here that couldna benefit from a dose of humility. Meself included."

Someone snickered in the back. It was all Ryssa could do to keep the smile off her face. From the elbow jab Amberly gave her, Ryssa knew she felt the same way.

Lily continued the tour as if nothing had interrupted her. "On the left is the Wardens' dining room and the one for the students and staff. We serve breakfast family-style from six to nine every morning. Ye'll always find an array of fresh fruit and snacks available in here throughout the day if yer hungry. Feel free to help yerselves."

"We eat with the staff?" The stage whisper was intentional, and Ryssa shot a glare over her shoulder at Collette's little crony, Blaze. Named for her shocking mane of red gold hair, her personality was just as spicy. She was petite, with curves in all the right places. If she'd been able to think for herself without deferring to Collette, she just might have been a decent person.

Lily's smile remained firmly in place as she turned, but her body language was screaming something else. "If ye don't care to eat with the staff, there's a picnic table behind the stables. Ye're welcome to join the horses. Can't promise how clean it'll be, though."

"I think we'll need to speak to management," crony number two piped up. Chantal Van den Berg's curtain bangs swung over her face as she nodded her head. The black silk sheet of hair reaching her waist was her pride and joy. With her caramel-colored skin and exotic black eyes, she was uniquely beautiful. She was also arrogant, cruel, and brainless.

Lily's head tipped to the side as if she were having a conversation with someone. "I scheduled ye an appointment with Mistress SkyDancer. Ye can tell her 'bout yer concerns regarding the harsh living environment yer being forced to accept."

Without waiting for a reply, she turned and headed back to the foyer. The girls followed behind. The line had gotten jumbled, and Willow was several rows ahead of them. Ryssa and Amberly were in front of Collette and Chantal now. Blaze stood in front of them with a timid girl who made her look tall—a rare occurrence.

Ryssa noticed the space the other girl gave to Blaze. She clutched her elbows as if to make herself appear even smaller or invisible. Wavy auburn hair cascaded over her shoulders, hiding her face from those around her. Her clothes were ill-fitting and too big for her. She was thin—too thin—but what startled Ryssa the most was the irrational amount of fear in her aura. She was terrified, and standing next to Blaze was making it worse.

Maryssa sent a message to Amberly, trying to get her help. *"Did you notice how terrified the girl in front of you is?"*

"'Tis hard to miss."

"Switch places with me, please."

"Ryssa, what are you doing?"

"She shouldn't have to be terrified standing next to anyone. Can you stand being around Blaze?"

"She doesn't bother me because she knows I won't put up with any crap from her," Amberly said with a smirk.

"When we line up again at the next stop, switch, and I'll stand with her."

"Okay," Amberly said.

The opportunity came sooner than either of them expected. The group gathered at the bottom of the staircase, waiting patiently for the others to walk up. Ryssa and Amberly swapped sides, and Ryssa took a step forward next to Blaze, who was bitching with Collette and Chantal.

Ryssa glanced at the young woman beside her. Her eyes were downcast, and she took a step to the right but bumped into the wall. "My name is Maryssa," she said, holding out a hand to her. "But everyone calls me Ryssa."

The girl stood still, staring at it in surprise. Enormous hazel eyes gazed at her, confused.

"I don't know many people here. I thought it would be nice to make some new friends," Ryssa said. The statement was partially true. Amberly and Willow were the only girls here she liked.

Ryssa was thinking she wouldn't answer her when she stuck out a hand and said in a whisper, "Genevieve, but they call me Genny."

"Well, Genny, it's nice to meet you," Ryssa said with a smile.

Genny nodded. "It's nice to meet you, too. I don't really know anyone here either."

"Do you live nearby? I'm from St. Vincent."

Genny glanced over her shoulder at the other girls and said so softly Ryssa almost didn't hear her, "I live here now."

Ryssa's eyes widened. She knew the Sanctuary housed strays when needed, and the Romani encampment was on the island as well. "That must be so cool to be here all the time!" she said enthusiastically. "I'd love to work here someday, preferably with Mistress Rhyanna. It would be wonderful to be so close to all the magical creatures. I would love to sketch them." Her cheeks flushed before she said, "I'm sorry, I get excited by the prospect."

"It's fine. I don't mind being here. It's better than anywhere else I've ever been." She glanced away. "The line's moving. We better get going."

Ryssa got the distinct impression that she didn't want to talk about her past.

When they reached the second floor, Lily stopped. "Ye'll find the classrooms, library, and sparring rooms on the third floor. Additional housing is on the fourth. If ye need to see Mistress SkyDancer, her offices are here on the second as well as yer rooms." They moved to the right of the landing down a long hallway. Doors lined either side of the hall.

"Each room will be as unique as ye all are. For yer security, we require a drop of yer blood to bond ye with our sentient structure. She will create a room for ye based on what she believes ye need and will enjoy here. The bonding process will be complete after lunch. Yer handprint will be required to enter the room, and no one else will have the ability to gain access."

Lily looked at Genny and asked, "Are ye sure ye don't mind showing us?" At Genny's nod, she explained. "Genny will show you how to access yer rooms when they're finished."

Uncomfortable being the center of attention, Genny kept her eyes on the floor as she crossed the hall to a white door. Placing her left hand on the wall at the same height as the door lever, she waited until a dim glow flashed under her palm. Once it did, she pushed the lever down and opened her door.

The room was larger than expected—sixteen-foot square, painted white, and absolutely beautiful. A large canopy bed occupied the middle of the room with a dresser and vanity opposite. A cotton bedspread and matching

sheer curtains in a soft lavender gave it a dreamy quality. Bookshelves chock full of romance novels and craft supplies lined the walls. Deep window seats waited with fluffy throw pillows. The room was serene.

As beautiful as the room was, it made Ryssa sad because it didn't feel settled in yet. She wondered how long Genny had been here because, from the brief glimpse she got, there wasn't one personal item on display.

"Thank ye, Genny, for being willing to share yer space with us," Lily said, placing a hand on her arm.

Genny tried to match her smile while she subtly flinched and pulled her arm back. She was still uncomfortable being touched. "Yer welcome, Mistress Lily."

Lily glanced around at the group of girls and asked, "Who wants to go first?"

Collette's voice rang out loud and clear. "I want to be the first," she said as she pushed her way through the crowd.

"Pick a door." Collette glanced at Genny and her nose twitched as if she smelled something bad. "I want to be farther down the hall."

Lily followed her then said over her shoulder, "Everyone pick a door and stand next to it. When I tell ye to, place yer hand to the left of the doorknob until ye get a flash of light. Wait until the light flashes, or ye'll have to do it again. There will be a slight prick on yer ring finger, and then it will be over once the property recognizes you as one of ours." Lily placed her hand above Collette's and said, "Ok, ladies, I be starting with Collette and working me way down."

Ryssa picked the door next to Genny. This young woman called to her compassionate soul. Amberly took the one on her right, and Willow the one next to her. The remaining girls each found their own door.

A brief shriek from Collette made it sound as if she were dying. Lily ignored it and moved on to the next girl and then down the line. No one else made a sound, and Ryssa barely noticed it when her time came, wondering what Collette was whining about.

"All right, ladies. Tis time for lunch. Please head down to the dining room, and we be meeting afterwards to reveal yer rooms."

Amberly waved at Genny. "Hi. I'm Amberly, and this is Willow" She indicated the other girl who gave a friendly wave. "Would you like to sit with us for lunch?"

A small smile crossed Genny's face as she said, "I'd be grateful to sit with you." Her gaze met theirs. "I could use some friends."

"Then it's settled!" Amberly said, nearly skipping towards the landing. "Is the food any good here?"

"Best I've ever had," Genny said.

"Thank God," Willow said. "I'm starving; I couldn't eat anything this morning."

The three of them headed for the dining room. Genny kept glancing at them from the side, wondering how she made friends so easily. This was a skill that had previously eluded her. They seemed really nice, and it had been so long since she'd had a friend. But now that she found some, she wasn't sure what to do with them. Could she ever really confide in them about her past? Would they judge her for it?

She clenched her palms as they walked, her nails digging into her palms as self-doubt chimed in with, *"You're a fool. Do you really think they would be so nice to you if they knew what you've done?"*

"STOP it!" she screamed back in defiance. Genny wasn't sure how long this would last, but until they rejected her, she intended to enjoy the girls who were offering her friendship as long as she could.

47

Puzzle Pieces

The chairs in Maddy's office were occupied once again. Ronan sat with her at his side as they waited for Fergus, Myranda, Damian, and Rhyanna. He stoically met everyone's eyes as they entered.

"I want to thank all of you for your compassion and support the last time we spoke," he said brusquely. It was the only acknowledgment of the horrors he'd shared that he allowed. Today, he was relaxed and easy-going as ever with his arm draped over the edge of Maddy's chair.

Fergus spoke first. "First things first, Ronan, thank ye for yer brutal honesty. I admire the faith ye have in us to share yer story. I have a few questions, if ye don't mind."

Ronan nodded his head and said, "I expected you would."

"They took ye from the Eastern Districts, but ye ended up in the Southwestern one. Do ye ken how long it was afore they transferred ye? And how did they move ye?"

"I can't tell you that, Ferg. They always sedated us before we were moved. It kept us off balance."

"Is there anything ye can tell me about yer confinement? Any clues where ye were being held or by whom?" Fergus asked.

"The summer before my abduction, I apprenticed with a master fire mage. He claimed the northeastern tower in the village keep for his experiments. I remember the worn stone steps and how smooth they felt as they circled up and around the stairwell. I traced the texture of the small river pebbles in the mortar on the wall to keep my balance in the dark because the old mage was too cheap to buy candles for the sconces."

"The damp, musty stench of the place they kept me in the first few days reminded me of that, but it was more pungent. I'm sure it was a mage's

tower because I recognized the scents of the chemicals and the lingering hint of old power."

"Was he alone, or did he have others collaborating with him?"

"There were quite a few of them—powerful mages in their own right. The leader was someone special, though. The man possessed the strongest powers I've ever encountered. He had phenomenal control of all four of the elements." Ronan said, clearing his throat. "But spirit was his playground. The bastard excelled at mind games and torment."

Maddy poured him a glass of water from the pitcher on the table in front of them. She handed it to Ronan then sat back down.

"Can ye tell me anything about him physically? Distinguishing features, height, weight, or the sound of his voice?" Ferg prodded.

"Not much," Ronan said. "I wore a hood or blindfold when it was his turn to play. The others weren't as cautious. They were cockier, like they knew I'd never be able to challenge them in the future. Some of them wanted me to see their expressions as they tormented me. None of them expected me to leave there alive." Closing his eyes, he ran a hand over his face as he tried to remember more. "The leader was a tall man. He towered over me when standing, and I'm not short."

Ronan met Damian's eyes, not sure what he was looking for. Pity? Disapproval? Condemnation. But what he found was pride mixed with rage. Damian nodded at him, and Ronan knew that when the time came, Damian would be by his side, taking the motherfuckers down.

"Close yer eyes, Ronan, and listen to me voice," Fergus said in a soothing voice.

Ronan did as asked. Fergus glared at Maddy when she opened her mouth to question his methods, but she stopped when he put a finger over his lips in the universal sign for silence.

"Try to go back to the first night you met the leader, Ronan," he said.

With his eyes closed, Ronan tried to remember the details of his captivity, no matter how small they were. When he spoke, his voice was younger–the sound of memories dancing through the dusty corridors of his mind.

"His hands are enormous. They're the only part of him I can glimpse with the blindfold. He has large knuckles swollen with age. Scars mar the back of them. He's missing the first joint on the little finger of his left hand, but it doesn't seem to trouble him much as he backhands me."

His brow furrowed as he found himself once again in front of the man who beat him. "He wears a wide ring on his left hand. It has a raised sunburst pattern on the top that rips open my cheek. I can feel the blood running down my face."

Rhyanna and Myranda's faces were pale. Rhy glanced at Madylyn, knowing how difficult this would be for her to endure a second time. Rhyanna had found them merged on the Spring Equinox so that Maddy

could witness why he vanished from her life. Connected during the merge, they experienced his captivity together. The experience had devastated both of them.

Today, Maddy was newly pregnant, and the healer in Rhy was concerned about the stress this would place on her.

"Are ye all right, Maddy?" she inquired.

"I hate doing this to him, Rhy. You don't know how horrible it was the first time."

"I have a pretty damn good idea, Maddy. I came upon ye before he tranced ye, love. Would it be easier if ye left while Fergus takes him through it again?"

Maddy's eyes met hers in a fierce glare, challenging her. *"I won't leave him Rhy, and don't you dare suggest it!"* Her hands tightened on the arm of her chair as she waited for Rhy's response. She knew Ronan would stop if he sensed it was too much stress for her or the baby.

"As ye wish, Maddy. For now," Rhyanna said, meeting her glare with a hard stare of her own. *"The second I think it's gone too far for either of ye, I'll stop this. Ye can bet on that. I care too much about the two of ye to take a chance with ye or yer wee one. Ye should, too."*

Her admonition surprised Maddy and hurt her heart. Rhyanna had never spoken to her so harshly, and the thought that she would put her child at risk was a mental slap.

Maddy beseeched Fergus, begging him with her eyes to stop this. She'd seen the hell he survived, and hated putting him through it again. *"Ferg, please..."* she begged.

"I'll be delicate and quick, Maddy, love," he said. *"I doubt ye'd prefer that we need to do this multiple times, would ye?"*

Ferg had her there. Maddy quickly blinked away the tears, feeling betrayed by two of her closest friends. She knew they were doing what they believed best, but she was helpless and completely out of control of the situation they suddenly found themselves in.

Closing her eyes, she sought her inner haven. Finding it quickly, she located her link to Ronan. She sensed his unease, but more importantly, his concern for her. Realizing her emotions were upsetting him more, she channeled love and peace into him through their link.

Opening her eyes up again, she peered at Fergus with a question.

Fergus held up a hand, preventing her from speaking. His voice was melodic, and Maddy could hear the faint thread of compulsion weaving through the room as he asked Ronan another question.

"What kind of scars does he have on his hands, Ronan?"

"Burns, splatters, and splotches on the right one, and a tattoo on his left one."

Ferg cursed under his breath before continuing. "Can ye describe the tattoo to me in as much detail as possible, please?"

237

Ronan's brow furrowed as he tried to focus on the distant image surfacing from his memory. "Red ink in the shape of an equilateral triangle. The point is at the base of his middle finger. Intricate patterns of flames in assorted colors make up the sides." He shook his head, confused. "Sometimes, when I look from an angle, the flames are changing color and moving. They look like they are alive."

The color drained out of Fergus's face as surely as it had drained earlier from the women in the room. Every one of them, except for Ronan, was a high mage or mistress in their own right and knew what the symbol he was describing meant.

Each element had a unique tattoo to mark the highest members of their order. The symbol Ronan had seen was the Fire Clan's highest-ranking mage. Fergus had one of his own started on his chest, but it wasn't yet complete. He'd tattooed the base pattern, but the different colored flames for each side were something he had yet to earn.

This mage was cocky enough to wear the sigil where all could see. Arrogance in its purest form. Fergus had never met this man, but he had an inkling of who might help him locate the bastard.

"Is there anything else memorable ye can think of?" Fergus asked.

"His voice was rough like he drank or smoked too much, and he wheezed when he laughed." Ronan paused, thinking. "He was barrel-chested."

"Do ye remember anyone else," Ferg prompted, "or anything else that might be identifiable?"

Ronan was silent while he sifted through his memories as Fergus instructed. "There were so many of them..." his silence filled the room, pregnant with nightmares about to be unleashed. "Every couple of weeks, our guards and mages changed. They rotated frequently so we couldn't form attachments. The ones I remember the most were the most vicious. They always made the most lasting impressions." His voice was a monotone as he told them about the men who violated him repeatedly.

Fergus cleared his throat, hating to push this line of questioning but wanting it over with for all of them. "What do you remember about them?" he asked in a neutral voice, not wanting to incite Ronan's fear or violence.

A sneer crossed Ronan's face. Maddy was glad she couldn't see his eyes because she didn't think she could stand watching them turn glacial as he recited his abuse from a third-person perspective. She knew that beneath his everyday calm exterior, he buried an incredible amount of rage.

Maddy dreaded the day the scab covering his emotional trauma tore open. She was terrified to think of the man who might emerge if all his barricades were torn down. Never knowing him like that, she never wanted to meet the man they forged through their abuse of power.

Two centuries stood between her and the man who finally escaped, choosing to die in the desert rather than live another day as a prisoner or an implement of their pain.

Ronan crawled his way out of a pit of despair and reclaimed part of who he used to be. The man who loved her reemerged, and he rebuilt his life around his need to return and fight for her.

Maddy sensed, deep down, that if he ever needed to return to the monster they created, he would lose all the self-respect he'd fought so hard to regain. Once he lost that, she would lose the man she loved all over again.

The grandfather clock in the corner ticked on loudly, and they all wondered if he would answer Ferg's question. As Ferg opened his mouth to try again, Ronan's voice poured forth in a long, agonized keen before he spoke.

"I remember them," he said in a gritty whisper. "I remember every one of the motherfuckers. The sound of their voices and the touch of their hands bruising and abusing me still haunts me in my dreams. I remember the smell of them up close as they knelt in front of me, branding my thighs, or behind me, doing things of which I will never speak. I remember them all," he said in a voice Maddy didn't recognize.

"If I ever come across one of them on the street, I will kill him with my bare hands and laugh whilst I finish him. There will be no remorse. I'll gladly face island law, knowing I have left this world safer for those who come after me."

Maddy stared at Ferg as tears cascaded down her cheeks. *"Please end this. Please, for the love of the Mother, and for any love you have for me, Ferg, end this and make sure he doesn't remember what we talked about."*

As she wiped her tears away and placed a glamor on her splotchy face, Rhyanna and Myranda did the same. Silently, she said a prayer of thanks as she heard Ferg's voice.

"Ronan, I need ye to listen to me now. Are ye still with me, lad?"

"I'm here, Ferg. What do you need?" Ronan asked, his voice once more conversational.

"I need ye to forget about everything we just talked about. Can ye do that fer me, man?" Ferg's compulsion was stronger now. The silent women could sense the energy vibrating around them.

"Absolutely, Ferg. Anything else?"

"Yer going to open yer eyes and have a pressing need to check on Landon and the Stables. Ye'll kiss Maddy, say yer goodbyes, and then head on out without looking back. We'll gather for dinner, and ye'll have no recollection of this meeting. Do ye understand?"

"Yes," he said calmly.

"Open yer eyes."

Ronan's pale blue eyes sprung open. He didn't look around at his surroundings, but stood, brushed a kiss over Maddy's cheek, and turned back to the others.

"If you'll all excuse me, duty calls."

A chorus of goodbyes followed him down the hall. When they all heard the front door shut, they let down their guard. Maddy went to the window and watched as Ronan crossed the lane, heading for the stables.

Her shoulders shook as sobs escaped. She sensed Damian beside her and let him enfold her in a tight hug.

"Let it out, Maddy, love," Damian crooned. "Let it out." His body was shaking as he held her. Maddy wasn't sure if it was from shock or rage.

"I've blocked your link, Maddy, so that he can't sense yer distress," Rhyanna said. She placed one hand on Maddy's back and one on Ferg's as Myranda did the same from the other side.

"Let us help calm you both," Myranda said as they channeled healing energy into them.

Moments later, Maddy's crying subsided, and her breathing evened out. Damian's grip loosened. He kissed her on the forehead as he released her. "Ye all right, lass?"

Maddy nodded. "Are you?"

Damian nodded. They both looked at Ferg sitting in a chair, elbows on his knees and hands clenched so tightly they were white.

Ferg felt their gaze on him. He closed his eyes, knowing what his next words were going to be.

"You recognized his description, didn't you, Ferg?" Damian asked.

Ferg nodded, looking traumatized in a way they'd never seen before.

"Who is the motherfecker?" their mild-mannered Rhyanna asked.

Ferg looked at her, his eyes pits of pain. "Feck me, I think it's me great-grandfather."

Four shocked gasps echoed off the walls of the study as Fergus pinched the bridge of his nose. "It's not fecking possible, though. As far as I ken, the evil bastard died long afore I existed. That was hundreds of years afore Ronan was taken."

"I'll check into all of this, Maddy, ye have me word." He looked her in the eye and said, "I'll never lie to ye, lass. Ye've always known that, and I'll not be starting now. Whatever I find, I'll bring it straight to ye."

Maddy hugged him tightly. "I'd never question your integrity, Fergus. Never."

He hugged her back. "I need to speak with the Keeper of me order before I go any further. We need to see how deep the decay goes before we confront them, because I don't want to give any of those bastards a chance to escape."

240

Releasing her, he turned and took Myranda's hands in his as he searched for the words he needed to say. "I'm not sure how Mathyas's disappearance is connected, but I fear tis might be like Ronan's and the disappearances up and down the river. Ye have me word that we will do everything we can to find him and return him safely to ye."

His face was pale as he said, "After everything we jest heard, I don't think he's dead, and I don't think ye do either."

The three women shook their heads. Both were in shock from Ronan's revelations, and Myranda's fears escalated.

Ferg felt Damian's gaze on him, and it didn't surprise him when the man contacted him privately.

"Ferg, while she's pregnant, you will bring anything you find out to me first. Do you understand what I'm telling you?"

"Loud and clear. Seems yer saying ye'll beat the shite out of me if I do anything to jeopardize her pregnancy."

"You've got that right. Unless they are in immediate danger. This can wait until she's in better health. I held her while she lost her first child. I won't see it happen again on my watch."

"There'll be hell to pay when she realizes what you've done," Ferg said.

"Then she can scream at me or beat the shit out of me later. I'll deal with it." Damian said.

They'd wanted answers, and now they had some. The answers they received would give them all nightmares for weeks to come. Their exhausted subconscious minds continued to try to put together the pieces in the puzzle they were trying to complete.

The harder they tried to make the square pieces go into the round holes, the more frustrated they were bound to become, but this was one battle none of them were willing to back down from. Too much was at stake, too many lives hung in the balance, and all their futures were too precariously perched on the knife's edge of destiny's madness to give up.

241

48

Acceptable Risks

Ryssa sat between Amberly and Genny at a round table they claimed in the dining room. Willow sat to Amberly's left. Two empty seats remained across from them. The overloaded table offered heaping bowls of sandwiches, cold salads, fresh fruit, and vegetables.

"I'm starving," Ryssa said, taking a ham sandwich from the pile. Thick slices of smoked ham, Swiss cheese, tomato, onion, and lettuce were barely staying inside of a crusty artisan roll. A honey mustard sauce melded the flavors beautifully.

"Me too," Amberly chimed in, reaching for smoked turkey and gouda piled high with vegetables. Her mouth barely fit around the sandwich. Somehow, she managed a big bite, then dropped it on her plate and reached for the bowl of fruit salad. Slapping a scoop next to the sandwich, she passed it to the others.

Genny grabbed a roast beef with provolone. She nibbled daintily at it, wiping her face with her napkin when the horseradish sauce dribbled down her chin. She closed her eyes, enjoying the sandwich and taking a moment to be grateful for having food to enjoy. Accepting the fruit bowl from Ryssa, she scooped two spoonfuls onto her plate as well. Willow chose a grilled portobello with pickled red onions and moaned with pleasure when she bit into it.

The dining hall filled quickly. Everyone found a seat. Most tables still had seats available after everyone settled. A low hum of conversation echoed throughout the room. But the four girls were more focused on eating than chatting.

Kitchen staff moved through the tables refilling glasses with water or tea, and the wardens wandered in from time to time, checking on everyone.

Genny nearly jumped out of her seat when an enormous shadow fell over her. Eyes wide, she glanced over her shoulder, then relaxed, smiling up at Kai.

Kai returned the expression, then nodded at the other girls. "Afternoon, Genny. How are you today?"

Genny twisted her hands in her lap, glancing down shyly. "I'm good. How are you?"

"Better now," he said with a wink. "Who're your new friends?"

Genny pointed to the two girls and made the introductions. "Ryssa, Amberly, and Willow, this is Kai Tyde, a prince from the Court of Tears."

"I'm just Kai to all of you. Welcome, ladies. If you ever need anything, please don't hesitate to find me for help. I'm usually at the marine rescue center—the brown and white building across from the docks." He nodded at the empty chair across from them and asked the group, "May I join you?"

Genny glanced at the girls, wondering what they would say. Eyes wide, they all nodded, encouraging him. "Of course, you may, but wouldn't you prefer to eat with the wardens?" Ryssa asked.

"Nah, I typically eat with the staff. I'm not a warden—more like an apprentice, I guess."

"But you're a prince," Amberly gushed before slapping her hand over her mouth. Her cheeks turned scarlet, and she giggled when he smiled at her.

"It's only a title. I don't think of myself that way." His lips quirked to the side. "Trust me, collaborating with my brother doesn't make me feel that way either. He works me harder than any other supervisor has ever done."

Amberly's jaw dropped. "There's two of them here?" she said, glancing at Genny with a raised brow.

Genny thought she might swoon.

Ryssa answered her, "Yes. His name is Kyran, and he's the water mage. Mistress Rhyanna is his partner."

Amberly fanned herself theatrically. "Please tell me there's no more. How are we supposed to focus on learning anything if they all look like you?"

Kai's cheeks flushed. He ducked his head, taking a bite of a roast beef sandwich and avoiding the young woman's gaze. His eyes widened, and he reached for the glass of water, nearly knocking it over. Gulping half the glass, he turned accusing eyes on Genny. "You didn't tell me how spicy the horseradish is."

Genny lowered her head and then caught herself. Rhy had challenged her to work through her fears. This was an opportunity to do just that. She met his gaze and spoke softly, "You didn't ask."

Ryssa and Amberly's eyes widened. She was talking to a *prince* like that. *"Holy shit,"* Ryssa sent to Amberly. *"That was ballsy."*

"No shit! I couldn't have done that."

Kai stared at her for a long moment, and then his lips parted into a wide grin. "Guess that's on me, then. Next time, I'll ask."

Genny stared at him for a moment, and then her face lit up with unbridled joy. She'd won a round of verbal sparring, and it felt damn good. But her mood quickly took a nosedive when she heard Collette's high-pitched laugh near them.

"Aren't you going to introduce me to your friend, Genny?" Collette's sugary sweet voice suggested they were friends.

"Why would you be interested in my friends?" Genny asked in a curious tone. Her clasped hands were on the table in front of her, clenched so tight that her knuckles were white. Out of the corner of her eye, she saw Kai glance at her in concern, and that was enough to make her second-guess her reaction.

"Kai Tyde, this is…" she trailed off, realizing she didn't even know her name. The trio were not nice people. She'd picked up on that immediately and intended to avoid them at all costs. Yet here they were, and she didn't know how to finish the introductions. She needn't have worried because Collette took it from there.

"Tyde?" she asked, arching a perfectly groomed eyebrow. "Are you related to the royal family?" Her lips quirked in a sly grin.

Kai cleared his throat, looking uncomfortable. He'd hoped to remain anonymous for the training session. That had been his goal this morning, but his firm sense of integrity wouldn't let him lie or be rude, so he stood and bowed at the waist. "I'm the youngest Tyde prince, but I would prefer if we kept this information between us, ladies." His gaze took in everyone at the table except for Genny to his right.

Collette batted her eyes at him as she executed the perfect curtsy, as did her cronies. "Collette Creek," she said. And then, without losing eye contact, she gestured behind her, "Blaze and Chantal."

"A pleasure to meet you," Kai said politely. He picked up his plate and said, "If you will all excuse me, I've got to get back to work." He took a step away before glancing back at Genny. "I wanted to ask you if you had time this week to work on our rivermaid theory?"

Her hazel eyes lit up as she answered him. "I believe I'm free in the evening. I'll let you know."

His grin made her heart beat faster. "I look forward to it."

"Prince Kai," Collette said, taking a step toward him. She placed her hand on his forearm and stepped closer.

Kai froze, staring at her hand on his arm as his brow furrowed. "How can I help you?" His voice held none of the warmth it did when he spoke with Genny. The tone was cooler and much more formal.

Collette batted her eyes at him, and Ryssa tried not to gag.

"I thought you might grace our table with your presence for the evening meal. Perhaps you'd enjoy more civilized company." Her nose scrunched up in disgust as she glanced pointedly at the other girls.

An audible gasp came from the young women he'd been sitting with. Genny turned away, tipping her head until she was hiding behind her hair.

Kai knew Genny well enough that he sensed her withdrawal like a slap. Frowning, his gaze fell on Collette's waiting expression and he struggled to keep his tone civil as his temper simmered. He'd spent most of his life around spoiled little rich girls trying to get their claws into one of the Court of Tears' princes. The Sanctuary offered him anonymity, and as far as Kai was concerned, it was one of the biggest perks of this job. He didn't have to spend half his day avoiding them, and he got to do something that actually made a difference to the marine life in this area.

Giving Collette his full attention, he said, "Thank you for the offer, but Genny and I usually take our meals together."

Genny's head whipped up, and her wide eyes met his. For a moment, he prayed he hadn't made a mistake, but then her eyes lit up, and she gave him a tremulous smile.

The expression on Collette's face made him want to laugh, but he didn't. Aware that her type wasn't very good at taking hints, he gave her brutal honesty. "I'll take the company of someone who is kind over civilized any day." Biting his cheek at her gasp of outrage, he gave her a sharp nod and said, "If you'll excuse me."

Collette glared at his back as he retreated, and then her gaze shot to Genny. Studying her from head to toe like she was a bug, she sneered, "What are you offering a man like that to make him so damn loyal to you?"

Genny's face blanched, and tears filled her eyes. Unable to speak, she tried not to cry.

Ryssa was stunned at the vitriol spilling from Collette. She'd always been a bitch, but this was beyond her usual scope of nastiness. "Maybe he doesn't want to spend his free time with a viper who has an agenda."

Collette's eyes snapped to hers. They'd always been competitive at school, but they hadn't been full-on enemies. Ryssa never tolerated bullies, and Collette had the predisposition to be one. Ryssa met her gaze as she gathered her plate and stood.

"What would you possibly know about men or about politics?" Collette hissed at her.

"I know no one likes to be treated like a pawn," Ryssa retorted, raising her voice.

Genny's eyes were wide, and Amberly's mouth hung open as they watched the two girls face off.

"You're too stupid to understand the way the world works," Collette sneered. "Maybe that's why your father left you."

Their voices had risen as they verbally sparred, and neither of them noticed the silence surrounding them. A collective gasp echoed at Collette's horrible accusation.

As Ryssa's face drained of color, she heard a ringing in her ears. She clenched the plate so hard it was a wonder that it didn't break.

"Too far, Collette," Blaze said, shaking her head.

"Low blow," Chantal followed up with.

Both girls took a step back from their friend when a sharp voice entered the void. "Show's over. Your guides are waiting in the foyer to show you to your rooms." Danyka stood in the doorway, staring at Collette as if she were a piece of shit under her shoe. She pointed at her. "You. Stay."

Everyone shuffled out without a word, although most of them kept peeking at the shit show in the corner.

Danny glanced at the three girls at the table, saying, "Go." As Ryssa passed her, Danny said, "You come see me in the pit after you get settled in."

Ryssa gave a curt nod and left.

"Don't make me come looking for you," Danny shouted after her.

Danyka waited until the last student was gone. Collette stood, vibrating with fury and humiliation.

"Sit down," Danny snapped.

Collette pulled out a chair and slammed herself into it. She gazed at the wall, refusing to give this woman the time of day.

"You want to give me one good reason I shouldn't take you down to the pit and beat the shit out of you while we're sparring?"

Collette's mouth dropped open, and when she met Danny's eyes, flames danced in her pupils. "I'll have your job if you lay one hand on me."

Danny laughed at her so hard she bent over to catch her breath. "Kudos on the full-blown aristocratic bitch attitude. You've got it down pat." She ran her hand through her spiky hair. Her violet eyes locked on Collette's flashing brown ones as she said, "I'm giving you one warning, and only one. We don't put up with that kind of bullshit here. You are no better than any other student in this room."

Indignation radiated from every pore in Collette's body. "You have no idea who you're speaking to, do you?"

"Nope." Danny winked at her, "Wanna know a secret?" She waited, and when no answer was forthcoming, she continued, "I. Don't. Give. A. Fuck."

The girl's face flushed with shock and fury, but wisely, she held her tongue.

"I don't give a flying fuck who your daddy is. What I do give a fuck about is the way you treat other people when you are on this island."

246

Danny let that sink in for a moment. "Should I choose to make an example and beat the ever-loving shit out of you in the guise of self-defense training, he won't be able to do a damn thing about it. I have the authority to do just that with any of you stuck-up little princesses."

Danny's glare never relented, even when the young woman's eyes filled with furious tears. "You don't come here to hold court. You come here to learn. Weapons training falls under my jurisdiction, and with that training comes certain risks. Humiliation, bumps, bruises, and potentially death all fall under those acceptable risks. You embarrassed your little posse with your behavior." She tilted her head and asked, "Who do you think would step in and stop me?"

Tears slipped down Collette's face as Danny hit her with the stinging truth.

"If you are fortunate to have parents who give a shit about you, you're truly blessed—not by how much money they have or what kind of house you live in. A family who loves you is a gift many of your peers don't have.

"Maryssa Belmont had two parents who adored her. She's lost one of them and is struggling just to get through the day without wondering what happened to him. If this had just been some catfight over Kai, I would've ignored it. But if you ever use her father's disappearance as a weapon again, I'll make you regret it."

Collette's eyes hit the floor as shame hit hard. Her voice wobbled as she whispered, "I'm sorry. It was a low blow."

"Sure as hell was, but I'm not the one you owe an apology to. Think about that. I think a little humility would do you good." Danny moved away from the teen as she said, "Catch up with the group. Find out what the Sanctuary thinks you deserve for a room."

Collette clenched her fists and kept her head down as she exited the room. As she made her way down the hall, she heard Danny chuckling.

How dare she laugh at her? She tried to imagine a punishment for the petite bitch. As she passed the window in the foyer, she glimpsed a pair of majestic white tigers cuddling in the sun. Fury swirled in her abdomen, and she silently wished the warden was their plaything.

49

Hell's Therapist

Ronan dutifully left Maddy's office and headed for the stairs. He made his way outside, smiling at the staff he passed while clenching his teeth so hard, he thought he was going to break a molar.

"Hello," Ronan said gruffly as he passed Tamas feeding the horses.

"Hello, sir. Anything special ye need me to do today?"

"No, lad, but thank you for asking. Finish feeding this lot and take the afternoon off."

"But I'm supposed to be here all day."

"You work for me, lad, and I'd kind of like the place to myself for the afternoon. Go ahead. Enjoy it. I swear, I have the authority to give you time off." He chuckled at the look on the young man's face. The boy was afraid Miss Maddy might not agree. "Do ye want me to call the head mistress to come down here and approve it?" he asked, wanting to set the young man at ease.

"No, that won't be necessary. You surprised me, that's all. I've never had a Stable Master who didn't expect twice the work they contracted us for."

Ronan laughed. "Well, if it makes you feel better, you can work twice as hard tomorrow."

"I'll do that," Tamas said, grinning ear to ear.

Ronan was sure the lad was already reaching out to the pretty little kitchen maid he'd been seeing. Most likely, he was trying to get her to take the afternoon off as well.

Ronan smiled, thinking that's what he would have done with a free afternoon. Yep, he would've been chasing after Maddy, trying to steal a few kisses and perhaps a little more.

He wandered into the eyrie, intending to dump all the emotions rolling through him onto his resident therapist. As he cleared the archway and

gazed at the empty cage that once held the shifter, Kerrygan, he realized the error in his plan.

In his irritation, he'd completely forgotten that Kerrygan was no longer trapped as a peregrine. For months he'd talked to the falcon, laying out all his fears and concerns while trying to regain Madylyn's trust. His one-sided conversation nearly bit him in the ass when he finally forced Kerrygan to return to his human form.

"Goddammit!" His voice echoed through the room. The other birds of prey were silent in their cages, warily watching the agitated man in front of them.

Ronan took a deep breath, trying to calm himself. He'd spent a lot of time making these creatures trust him, and he didn't want to piss it all away with his nasty mood. "My apologies," he whispered, slowly backing out of the room while projecting his regret.

"Kenn, you on site?" Ronan asked.

"Nada. I'm watching a pretty lil thing wearing a very skimpy bikini on the beach."

"Gotchya. Never mind then."

"Whatchya need?"

"To blow off some steam. Was gonna offer to thrash the shit out of you in the ring. But I'll find someone else to terrorize."

"Would have enjoyed watching you try Ronan."

Kenn had at least six inches on him and seventy-five pounds. Ronan would have worn himself out doing little damage to the Court of Tears' prince.

Kenn's humor bled through their link. *"You sure you want to do this?"*

"Hell yeah. You've promised me a match."

"I'll hit you up tomorrow and take you up on that offer."

"I look forward to it," Ronan said, disappointed. He hadn't had the time to spar with Kenn yet and was fairly certain he would regret this conversation come tomorrow. His agitation would have given him the edge. Now, he'd better hope his survival skills kicked in.

Temper still smoldering, he headed for the wing housing the most terrifying predators on the island. He wouldn't scare them. They would take his pissy mood as a challenge. A dangerous part of him hoped they would, and they would see how fucking scary he could be.

Reaching the locked gate leading into the hellhound enclosure, he slowed long enough to press the sequence of runes on the side of the door to open it. The locks were a recent addition since Landon's arrival. His son was smart and very motivated to get into places he shouldn't. Add that to the fascination he had for the vicious animals, and that made him sneaky. Ronan wouldn't take any chances on him working his way into a potentially lethal

situation. He'd only just found out about him, and he was going to do everything in his power to keep him safe.

The caustic smell of brimstone had him scrunching up his nose and letting out a sneeze, then a cough. So much for intimidating them. He didn't think a sneeze was going to cut it. Leaning over the side of the gate, he gazed at the hellhound king.

Nearly the size of a small horse, the massive hound glared back. Red malevolent eyes stared him down, challenging him to put his hand in the pen. Ronan knew better. He enjoyed having two hands to please Maddy with, and he intended to keep them. Resting his head on his hands, he tried to unravel the knots this morning's confessions had formed in his shoulders and his stomach.

"Beast Master," a voice in his head called. *"It's been too long between visits. Stop challenging the pup and come see someone who will aid you in your needs."*

The king growled low in his throat, bored and needing a fight as much as Ronan did. Maddy and Landon's faces projected into his head, and feeling guilty, he lowered his eyes, letting the king take this round.

Long strides took him past the hounds and into the equine stables. There were two rooms housing horses. The first one—closest to the hounds was where they boarded the Nightmares.

Hell's steeds were dangerous in an entirely different way than the hounds. The hellhounds would destroy your body, causing catastrophic organ failure from the toxins in their saliva. The NightMares, on the other hand, destroyed you psychologically. They shredded your self-esteem, your ability to know right from wrong, and your will to live.

Sabbath was their resident NightMare queen. Ronan had formed a delicate alliance with her when he aided in the birth of her twins. A breech birth, he had to turn them and pull the foals out of her to save all their lives. The balance had shifted between them when he realized he could communicate telepathically with them.

A grudging respect formed between the two—a delicate balance of push and pull. After Fergus's stunt the night Jamey nearly died, Ronan wasn't sure how he felt about her powers. He hadn't been in to speak with her since.

"You've been avoiding me, Beast Master," Sabbath scolded.

"Needed time to process," Ronan answered.

"Has Madylyn agreed to my terms? Courtesy dictates that she should at least acknowledge my request."

"Your request was forced. We tend to call that a bribe."

"Hardly a bribe. I offered emotional relief and mental stability in exchange for an audience with her…"

"And here you are, stuck with—"

"An errand boy," she said, sulking. *"And one who is too busy drowning in his own self-pity."*

250

"You don't know what you're talking about, Sabbath."

"Don't I, Ronan?" Her glowing red eyes stared him down. They were even more eerie against her sleek, black coat and the steam rolling from her nostrils. *"You going to share what the problem is, or are you going to make me go digging for it?"* She neighed softly. *"I guarantee you don't want me doing that."*

Ronan ran a hand through his hair, making it stand up all over. "We delved into my past—a place I hate fucking going. There are things I've done that I'm not proud of." His head hung, ashamed once again of his past.

Her breath on his neck made him jerk back slightly as she leaned down, brushing her head against his. *"Tell me what happened."*

"I'm surprised you don't already know," he snapped. Hot breath fanned his neck while she stomped her hoof against the floor. His shoulders sagged as he gave her the truth. "I was laid bare by Fergus to help another warden who is missing."

"Laid bare?"

Ronan understood her confusion with the phrase and sought to clarify his meaning. "I took them back to places I never wanted to return to. When Ferg finished his inquisition, I walked out, letting them believe they compelled me to forget."

"Are you angry at the fire mage for his methods or because you didn't have the courage to tell them you were aware?"

A long pause ensued as he pondered her question. He shook his head. "I don't know. I guess both. The whole time, I was wondering what the fuck I was doing. I got so caught up in the charade that I didn't know how to get out of it. So, I did as Ferg suggested and left without looking back."

Ronan paced, agitated once more. "I knew how upset Maddy was, but I couldn't offer her comfort because I wasn't supposed to remember. I fucking hated not being able to reach out to her. And I detest her seeing my weaknesses."

His body vibrated with emotion. He'd already laid most of it out there and thought, *"Fuck it, might as well finish."* Inhaling a deep breath, he admitted, "I never wanted her seeing how fucking depraved they made me. Maddy saw enough when we melded. She didn't need to see the degenerate they turned me into."

Sabbath remained silent, letting him spew the vitriol that was suffocating his self-esteem and his soul.

Ronan kicked at a pebble as he stopped pacing and leaned his head on his arms again. "But like a dutiful dog, I did what they asked, and smiled, kissed her on the cheek, and left as if it all was fine. I don't even know if anything I told them will help them find Mathyas."

"'Tis the only reason you did it, isn't it?"

251

"Yes. I would do anything to prevent anyone else from going through what they subjected me to."

"There is no shame in that." Her voice was gentle as it drifted through his mind, calming his anxiety and anger.

"Fergus compelled me to forget about the entire thing and to leave the room." Ronan hung his head in defeat. "I wanted to be there for Maddy—to answer any questions she had about my confessions. And now…I don't know if she'll even be able to look at me, let alone let me touch her."

"Now, you don't know what you're walking into or how she's going to react." Her voice was matter-of-fact as she stated the obvious. *"Reach out to her, Beast Master. She's concerned about you. That's all I can sense."*

"She'll know I remember everything we discussed."

Her hoof stomped in a display of her confusion, sending little sparks flying. *"I don't understand your hesitancy to admit such a thing."*

"I'm not sure your kind fully comprehends failed morals or shame."

"I know it tastes sweeter to my palate than joy and love." A soft neigh of appreciation filled the stables. *"Yet, I also sense the pain it is causing you."*

"Is that not appetizing to you as well?" he asked, genuinely curious.

"Not when it's someone I respect." Her head nudged his shoulder in a caress. *"You are one of the few who've earned that from me."*

A spark of pride shimmered in his soul. Just a tiny one, but enough to remember his worth in this world. "Thank you, Sabbath."

"You're welcome, Beast Master." This time when her head collided with his, she knocked him back a step. *"Stop being a coward and be honest with her."*

"Yes, ma'am," he said, turning to do just that. "Sabbath, if you're going to be my new therapist, next time, we need to discuss personal boundaries."

Her neigh this time might have been a chuckle or the equivalent of *"It ain't gonna happen."* He wasn't sure. As he left the stable, she sent him one more message. *"Make sure you tell her I'm still waiting to hear from her."*

Ronan chose not to answer that command but made his way out without a backwards glance at his unconventional therapist.

Following their link, Ronan found Maddy in the garden, creating a new topiary creature. She'd just begun the piece, and he wasn't sure what it would become. One glance at her splotchy face and red-rimmed eyes told him she'd been crying. She glanced up at him as he approached and gave him a tremulous smile, trying to pretend all was well. "How was your afternoon?" Her voice broke, betraying how hard she was fighting to remain calm, as if she hadn't learned the most horrific things about him earlier.

Taking the shears from her hands, he set them on the table beside her and pulled her into his arms. Her delicate hands gripped the fabric of his shirt, nearly untucking it. He rested his forehead against hers while rubbing circles on her back. The garden was silent around them as they grounded each other.

"Stop pretending, Maddy," he whispered on their link, unable to speak yet. Maddy jerked in his arms, but he held her tighter, pressing a kiss to her temple. *"Their mind games destroyed my ability to be compelled."* A stunned silence followed his statement.

"Why did you pretend?"

"Maddy, I needed a few moments to myself before I could face you. Do you honestly think I ever wanted you to know the vile things I'd done?"

"I understand why you didn't want to share those details, but Ronan, the truth is, I don't care. You did what was required to survive. I'm grateful you're still here."

"You sure about that?" Ronan lifted his head to meet her eyes. *"When I touch you—when I'm inside of you—your mind won't drift to the ways I used sex as a weapon or as a punishment?"*

Tears shimmered in her eyes as she gazed into his. *"Nothing will ever change how I love you, Ronan."* A lone tear slipped down her cheek. *"When you touch me, all I see is you. Nothing else exists but the passion and love between us."*

"You say that now, but a week or a month from now, when horrors I shared keep circling through your head…"

"I will still love you. I promise if it rears its ugly head, we will talk about it." Her hand caressed the side of his face. *"Is there anything else that you want or need to tell me?"*

Ronan shook his head no, then tipped his head into the caress, desperately needing the comfort. He pressed a kiss into her palm before saying, *"If you ever need to talk about anything I said today, please ask."*

"I promise. I will." But Maddy would never ask him to relive that pain again. The only thing she wanted was for him to put it behind them once and for all. Stretching, she put her arms around his neck and gave him a soft kiss.

His arms pulled her as close as her swollen belly would allow. Their daughter promptly gave a hefty kick, as if to chastise them for squishing her. Laughing, he kissed the tip of her nose and said aloud, "Is she hungry again?"

"Yes, she never lets me forget meals." Maddy linked her hand in his and they headed inside for lunch.

"Ronan?"

He quirked an eyebrow at her, waiting for her to finish her thought.

"Thank you for being honest with me about the compulsion." Gazing into his eyes, she continued, "We can overcome anything as long as we're always honest with each other."

"Yes, we can." He brought their clasped hands to his lips and kissed the back of her hand, grateful once again for the gift of redemption she offered him.

50

Touche!

Danny watched Collette stomping off and smirked. Little Miss Hoity-Toity would be a challenge and one she was looking forward to. The next thought she had was *"Holy fuck!"* as nausea hit her, and she landed between the two enormous white tigers they'd recently rescued. The massive beasts were sleeping, and as they turned their heads to see what had disturbed them, Danny stopped breathing. She wasn't sure how much time she had, but she needed to maintain control and shift instantly to flee this unhealthy situation.

The male's nose twitched as he caught her scent. *"Focus, goddammit,"* she thought as he drew in a deeper breath. A rolling growl reverberated through her back, tightening her bowels. With one deep breath, she transformed into her falcon and darted out from between them as their hot breath fanned over her feathers.

"Touché, Collette," Danny thought. The little twit had a bite. Danny wondered if she'd even realized what she'd done. Teleportation was an air clan power. Collette was from a water clan.

Danny landed on the tallest branch of a tree over the kitties and observed the beautiful beasties shredding her leathers. Collette had impressed her with a special power this early in the training. However, she wasn't so impressed with losing her favorite vest.

"Ronan," she called, reaching out to the man she prayed was the closest available assistance.

"Whatchya need?" he asked, forgoing the pleasantries. She rarely reached out to him, so he figured there was a good reason.

"Your kitties have something of mine I'd like returned."

His humor came through before he answered her. *"I see they're playing tug of war with your pants."*

"Can't you drug them or lure them out with a live snack?"

255

"Not till I hear the full story." His chuckle was audible as he stepped out of the barn.

"I pissed some little twat off, and she must have imagined me somewhere else, because I blinked and found myself snuggled up between them."

Ronan doubled over in laughter. "Well, I'd temper your attitude around that one."

"Ain't gonna happen. We'll work through it, but she'll probably still hate me when it's over."

"Use your falcon speed and agility to entice them to the other end of the field. When they're distracted, I'll grab your stuff."

"That's the best you've got? No dart guns. Magical naps?"

The exasperation in her biting tone amused him, but he bit his tongue. "I'm not drugging them unless somebody's life is at stake. Get out there."

"Mine could be," she whined, really not wanting to get too close to them again.

"You're the fastest animal on the planet. Move your ass. I've got shit to do."

"Yes, sir," she snapped back. Without another thought, she dove from her perch and swooped right under the beastie's noses, getting their attention.

A roar sounded behind her as she swooped low to the ground to keep them engaged. She banked hard to the left and back to the right, zigzagging across the twenty acres of pasture. Her sharp eyesight caught Ronan running across the pasture behind them. He knelt, gathered her things, then sprinted for the gate. She continued playing with the cats for a few more rounds because she was enjoying the flight. When they dropped to the ground, panting, she cleared the fence and transformed behind Ronan.

He'd taken off his button-down, handing it to her as she approached. He held up the shreds of her outfit. "Want to fix them?"

"I'm not into wearing patchwork quilts, so I'll pass," she said, buttoning up the shirt. It came to her knees, but at least she wouldn't be flashing her students.

Ronan stared straight ahead as she dressed. "How're you doing, Danny?"

The question from anyone else would have pissed her off, but they'd been friends for a long time. Ronan had helped her through a rough patch years ago. The man understood more about her than some of her friends.

Her bare foot scuffed at the dirt, unable to meet his eyes. "I don't really know," she said, giving him the honesty he deserved. The others had left her alone, as she'd requested. This was one reason they'd become such good friends. He pulled no punches.

"This," his hands indicated the torn outfit and the weapons he still held. "This reflecting normal, bitchy Danny, or the Danny who's still reeling over Jamey's injury?"

Her gaze flew to his. She blew out a huff of breath, moving her long bangs out of her eyes. "A little of both, I think." Her hand moved through the top of her hair, leaving spikes in its wake. "She's a rich bully, and I have no patience for them. I watched her pushing Genny's buttons, and that poor kid just shrank into herself. Then she taunted Ryssa with her father's disappearance."

"That's fucking low."

"Yes, it is." Danny sighed. "I called her on it and threatened her with repercussions coming from me. She was near to tears when she left and vibrating with fury."

"And," Ronan said, "she obviously wished you somewhere else—somewhere unpleasant."

"Shocked the shit out of me," Danny said. "I was nauseous, and then boom, I was snuggling the beasties." She shook her head. "It happened in seconds. I've never seen Rhy teleport that quickly before, and she is always touching someone when she moves them."

"Ask Rhy about ways of controlling it and make sure your students know my animals aren't their playthings." His voice was icy. "Had she done that to another student without your gifts, they would be dead right now. I'm going to talk to Fergus about a magical leash for her."

"A shock collar might work better," Danny snorted.

He laughed with her as they headed for the castle.

"Ronan," she said in a somber voice.

"Yeah?"

"Thanks for saving my ass."

"Welcome. Let's get a drink."

"Absofuckinglutely," she said with a sigh. "Fuck me. It's only day one."

51

The Biggest Fool

Jotting a quick note to Myranda, Rhyanna thanked her for covering the shoppe and clinic. With her bag slung over her shoulder, a wide-brimmed hat on her head, and food for the journey, she set off down the lane to the harbor, hoping to catch the ferry. The portal was always available, but it was a beautiful day to be on the water. Her soul needed the mist on her face and the wind in her hair the brief journey by boat would provide.

The dock was uncharacteristically barren of ferries. With her hands on her hips, she gazed around for any other vessel that took passengers. Not seeing anything but larger vessels at the dock, she headed for the harbor office to see when the next ferry was due to arrive. Lost in her thoughts, she collided with a man exiting the office.

"Pardon me, ma'am," said a sexy voice full of gravel that could still curl her toes.

Tipping her hat back so she could see him properly, she found the sea captain, Roarke, gazing back at her. "Hello," she said, keeping it simple. Their last conversation had been awkward.

Dark chocolate eyes drank her in, and he gave her a lopsided smile. "Mistress Rhyanna," he said with a nod, "where might you be off to this early in the morning?"

Returning his smile, she said, "I meant to be off to Wellesley to check on our lad, Jameson." Glancing at the empty dock, she said, "But alas, it appears the ferry has not arrived."

"Portal?" he asked, quirking an eyebrow in surprise. Most people would take the quickest route.

"Guess I needs be heading that way." She sighed in disappointment. "Jest longed to be on the water this morning."

Roarke nodded, understanding her longing. He lived on the river, and it suited him. "I jest let the harbor master know the ferry collided with a private vessel and will be out of commission the rest of the day."

Rhy's face fell in disappointment. Her luck was bound to be shite for the day. "Well, it's been nice to see ye, Roarke. I won't keep ye any longer. I've got a hike to the other side of the island to use the portal." Part of her was grateful for the excuse to leave, and another part missed this man in her life. "G'day."

Not three steps later, she heard him say, "I'll take you to Wellesley, Rhy. I'm headed that way to deliver supplies to the tavern."

Rhy turned, surprised that he would offer. "The last thing I want is to make ye uncomfortable, Roarke."

Two long strides positioned him in front of her. "The last time I saw you, my behavior was uncalled for. I've regretted it ever since. I took out my pain and anger on you, and it wasn't fair. Believe me, I deeply regret my behavior, and I hope someday you will forgive me."

"Oh, Roarke," Rhy said, stepping closer and taking his hands in hers. "I forgave ye the moment you showed up to support me at the Court of Tears." Her eyes filled. "I hoped someday ye'd forgive me for being so insensitive."

His large hands framed her face. "There's nothing to forgive. I knew how you felt about Kyran and was a fool thinking I could change that." He pressed a chaste kiss on her forehead. "Can we start over as friends?"

Releasing her face, he held out a meaty palm to her. Rhy placed her dainty hand in his and nodded. "I would love that."

His eyes twinkled as he said, "As your friend, I would like to provide you with transport to your destination."

"In that case, Roarke, I accept yer offer. When are ye leaving?"

"As soon as we board?" He offered his arm, and Rhy took it, glad they were on better terms once again. "Will Kyran be alright with this?"

With a cocky glance up at him, she said, "Of course he will be. He's no reason to not be alright with this."

"You've told him then?" Roarke asked, cocking an eyebrow.

"As soon as we're on our way, I'll inform him," she said, following him up the ramp to his ship. "Haven't exactly had a chance yet."

"Right," Roarke said, but his smirk said something else entirely. He was pretty damn sure the oldest Tyde prince would not be happy to hear the woman he loved was with him. His recent infatuation with her had caused some issues with the couple. "If you need anything, send one of the deckhands for me."

"Thank you," Rhyanna said, watching him walk away as she settled on a bench.

Everyone's path had different forks of possibilities. Roarke had been a potential fork in hers. She chose Kyran because her heart belonged to him first, but had she met Roarke first, her choice might have been different.

"Kyran," she sent telepathically.

"Yes, my lady." The warmth of his love flooded their lover's bridge. *"Are you on Wellesley already?"*

"Nye, I wanted to take the ferry and enjoy the river today."

"I don't blame you. What's wrong?"

"Ferry had an accident, but I found another ride and wanted you to be aware of it."

"Who's taking you, Rhy?" His entire mood changed, and she knew she'd made a mistake not checking with him first.

"Roarke's boat was leaving, and when he realized I couldn't catch the ferry, he offered to take me because he had business there anyway."

Butterflies in her stomach that had been silent for the past month fluttered, and she pushed them down, refusing to feel guilty about this. *"I'm sorry, I should've checked to see if ye were comfortable with it first..."*

The three of them had a complicated history, and she didn't intend to add fuel to the fire.

Their line was silent for a long span before he answered her. *"Enjoy your day."* His love flooded the line once more when he added, *"I love you, Rhy. Tell Jameson I said hello."*

Letting out a tremendous sigh of relief, she said, *"I love ye, too, and I will."* She sent back her own infusion of love and gratitude. *"Kyr, thank ye fer not being upset with me."*

"I have no reason to be upset, Rhy. I know you love me, and I trust you to be away from me for any length of time. Give Roarke my best."

"As ye wish," she said, smiling.

"Me lady," a gruff voice said on her right.

Rhy glanced up to find Treasure, Roarke's cook, with a tea tray laden with fruit, cheese, and cookies. "Oh my, what is all this?"

"Captain said to bring ye something for the trip." He set it next to her on the bench, then removed his hat and gave her a half bow. "Hope this be sufficient."

"'Tis more than sufficient," Rhy said, giving him a wide smile. "Would ye care to join me? Ye've provided more than enough."

Treasure blushed, shaking his head, "Nye, me lady. Best be getting back to prepping fer the noon meal."

"Thank ye again. Please thank yer captain fer me."

"Be happy to, me lady." He shuffled off, slapping his hat back on top of his head.

Rhy poured a cup of tea and nibbled on a cube of cheese while watching the beautiful homes lining the banks of the river. They passed by small towns settled near the water and small islands that barely passed for more

260

than a piece of stone with a scraggly tree sticking out of the water. The sky was cloudless, and the water a dark blue.

Much too soon, they were docking by the massive Wellesley Island gazebo. Rhy picked up the tray, intending to return it to the kitchen, but she didn't know where to take it.

A deckhand approached, saving her the trouble and preventing her from following through on the urge to see Roarke just once more.

"Please give the captain my appreciation for the transport and for the tea. I'm very grateful," she said.

"You're very welcome," a deep voice said behind her, startling her.

Turning, she found Roarke behind her. "Ye startled me. I didn't expect to see ye before I disembarked."

"Were ye trying to avoid me, darling?" His cocky grin was in place, showcasing his dimples.

"Nye! I assumed ye were busy and didna want to distract ye."

"Never too busy for you, Rhy." His eyes twinkled mischievously.

"Kyran sends his best," she said, blushing at the reminder of the other man in her life.

"Tell him I return the sentiment," Roarke said as he took her arm and walked her down the ramp. "Will you require a ride back? I'd be happy to wait for you."

"Nye. Unfortunately, I don't have the luxury of time this afternoon. How's Hailey settling back into life at home?"

The lightheartedness he'd shown earlier faded, and his face fell at the mention of his niece. "She's struggling to adapt and to fit in. She's become a recluse, and her powers are more volatile than ever."

A hand rubbed the back of his neck. "I'm worried about her, Rhy, and we don't know how to help. She won't talk to her parents or her siblings about her ordeal. She's a shell of the person she was before."

His eyes glossed over, and she knew he was thinking about his sister Rosella, who was going through the same damn thing.

"May I make a suggestion?" Rhy asked, placing a hand on his forearm.

"Of course. We're open to any suggestions."

"Bring her back to the Sanctuary," she said. Her words were full of compassion for his family's struggle. "We'll help her manage her powers and give her a purpose. She enjoyed working with me in the shoppe. I'll offer her an apprenticeship."

"I don't know," he said in a thick voice. "I'm not even sure she'll listen to the offer."

"Genny and Grace are still with us. It might do her good to have the option to talk to someone who went through hell with her."

261

Roarke cleared his throat, still indecisive. "Would it be asking too much for you to come talk to her? I think she bonded with you."

"I'd be happy to come for a visit. Shall I bring Genny with me?"

With a grateful nod, he said, "That might work out the best."

"We'll be out as soon as we get a chance."

"I can't thank you enough, Rhy," he said, pulling her into a quick hug.

Rhy returned it, offering him much-needed comfort.

Brushing his lips against her cheek, he whispered in her ear, "It's been lovely seeing you, Rhy. I've missed you."

Rhy blushed. "I've missed ye, too, Roarke." She turned her head to kiss him on the cheek, but her aim was off, and she met his lips. A quick peck and she jumped away as if scalded.

Their eyes met, and the heat that was always between them flared to life. Horrified at her reaction, she backed quickly away, apologizing. "I didn't mean…"

With a sad smile, he brushed it off. "I know what you meant, darling. We're good." With a wave, he turned and headed for his ship.

Rhyanna watched him go, wondering why she felt a tug on her soul—a moment of longing for this man. Kyran gave her everything she'd ever wanted and more. Damn it all, she would use the portal next time.

Renting a horse at the stables, she headed for the mountain path, carefully making her way. The sun was high as she removed the light jacket she'd needed for the morning. Temperatures climbing, she was glad she'd settled on riding breeches today instead of her heavier split skirts.

The path climbing the mountain spiraled up and around until she finally emerged on a wide plateau. Enjoying the spectacular view from here, she couldn't imagine Jamey settling anywhere else.

Behind her, she could see the Vance's horse farm. Before her sprawled the valley below, bordered by the St. Lawrence, winding its way like a ribbon through the islands and mainland.

Jamey's large two-story cabin was impressive. A wrap-around porch provided the ability to enjoy the view on all four sides. A large red barn with pastures fenced in on either side beckoned her with the sound of metal clashing.

Metal screeching against one another warned her they weren't using staffs anymore. Dismounting, she shook her head, ready to throttle the two of them if they'd done more damage than good to his arm.

Walking through the barn, she entered a large, cleared arena where two handsome, shirtless men were beating the ever-loving hell out of each other. Silently watching, she observed Jamey as he swung his sword in controlled strikes. Sian met him and beat him back occasionally, but Jamey had

regained most of his mobility and met his attack head-on. In perfect form, he outweighed Sian by about fifty pounds and had a longer reach. His younger brothers rarely beat him.

Today, Sian was keeping up and keeping him on the run. From where Rhyanna stood, they were going to end in a tie. Sian proved her wrong when he swept Jamey's feet out from under him and pressed his sword to his neck. "Do you yield?"

"Do you?" Jamey asked with a dark chuckle.

Sian glanced down to find Jamey's blade too damn near his crotch for his liking. "You fight dirty, big brother."

"Sometimes, you fight to stay alive. No clean or dirty, just survival."

Rhyanna's clapping made both men glance up. "Well played, both of ye."

Sian gave her a wide grin as he reached down and pulled Jamey to his feet. "Mistress Rhyanna, didchya come out to watch me beat him into submission?"

Rhy laughed. "Think ye ended on a draw there, laddie."

Jamey enveloped her in a massive bear hug. "Missed you, Rhy. Please tell me you're here to free me from my prison."

Rhy swatted at him. "Release me, you sweaty beast."

Jamey twirled her around before setting her feet back on the ground. Grabbing a towel from the fence rail, he wiped himself down while Sian gave Rhy a hug.

"I'm heading back," Sian said to Jamey. "Good seeing you, Rhy."

"Aye, 'twas good seeing ye as well."

"C'mere, ye big oaf," she said to Jamey with a smile.

His hair was tightly banded, making his sharp cheekbones and deep-set eyes more intense. The lad was devastatingly handsome and one of the sweetest men she'd ever known. Danny was lucky to be the one he loved.

Jamey plunked his ass down on a bench in front of her. Rhy examined the wounds on his chest, happy to see the redness and inflammation had receded. She lifted his arm, rotating it as far as he could tolerate.

"Yer goddamn lucky yer a shifter, Jameson."

He chuckled. "You're like my mother, Rhy. The full name only comes out when you're about to ream me out."

"Damn right, I am." She took his face into her hands, peering into his eyes. "Do ye remember how damn close to death ye came, Jamey? Cuz I'll never forget it till the day I die. T'was one of the worst days of me life. When yer heart stopped beating and knowing there was nothing I could do to fix it."

Tears threatened, and Jamey stood, pulling her into his arms. "I know how bad it was, and I'm grateful for everything all of you did to keep me here."

"If not for yer ability to shift, lad, ye'd have left us, and that would have destroyed us as a team, not to mention what it woulda done to me personally."

Somber eyes met hers. "I truly understand how bad it was, Rhy. *She* gave me a choice to stay or go. I had unfinished business."

Rhy gasped, stunned at his mystical experience with their creator. Hugging him fiercely, she growled, "Dontchya ever do that to me again!"

Digging into her bag, she pulled out the poultice. "Use this again tonight. How's the pain after ye and Sian beat the hell out of each other?"

"Burns like a bitch, but otherwise tolerable."

"With or without whiskey?"

"Some days with. Most without."

"Mix a teaspoon of this with water if ye need something to get you through the nerve regrowth."

Rhy put pressure on his shoulder and his chest. "Any pain when I press?"

"No, just pressure."

"Fatigue?"

"Getting better every day. Please tell me I can come back to the Sanctuary. I miss…working."

"Hmmm." A quick peek at his auric field for anything she might have missed, and she realized she couldn't keep him protected forever. "I be back in a few days and then I be talking to Maddy about it. She'll make the final decision."

Jamey's face split into a huge grin, and luminous eyes showered her with gratitude. "Thank you, Rhy."

"Ye have to promise me ye'll come to me if anything is off. Pain, pressure, dizziness, fever—anything. I need to be aware of it. And I want ye to stop at the leather works in town. I've already spoken to him 'bout creating a leather brace for your shoulder and arm that will help ye from overdoing it with students who don't ken when enough is enough."

"I promise to come see you if anything's off, and I promise to stop in town," he said solemnly, although he didn't look thrilled about the brace. Clearing his throat, he couldn't stop himself from asking, "How is she?"

"Scooch over," Rhy said, waiting for him to make room for her on the bench. Plopping down, she toyed with the ends of her hair, not sure how to answer.

Jamey knew her tell as well as she did his. "It's ok if you don't want to talk about it with me. I understand." The disappointment was obvious in his voice, but he was giving her a way out.

"It's not that, lad," she said, shaking her head. "I don't know what to tell ye." Deft fingers pulled her hair over her shoulder and started braiding without even realizing she was doing it.

"Since…she's been distant. Kept to herself first week. Kerry's the only one who ken where she was. Appeared at the last council meeting, and we've barely seen her since. Oh, there's one girl challenging her authority already."

"Damn, not even through the first week."

"Nope. Think she's about to make an example out of her."

"There's always one," Jamey said and chuckled. His laughter quickly died. Scuffing the toe of his boot against the ground, he asked, "Do you think she'll ever forgive me for nearly getting her killed?"

The anguish and guilt in his voice broke her heart. "What I can tell ye, from reading her the way I do, is, tain't ye she can't forgive. 'Tis herself."

Exploding into motion, he paced in front of her. "But why? I was an arrogant asshole, proceeding without backup. That's not her fault."

"Nye, 'tis not." Rhy let out a long sigh before continuing. "She believes yer head was up yer arse because of her actions earlier in the week. That's what she can't get past, Jamey. Ye nearly died cuz she was afraid of her own feelings."

"How do I fix that? How do we move past this?"

"Give her time to make peace with it herself, and don't give up on her, lad." Emerald eyes pierced his amber ones. "Did ye ever think loving a hell cat would be easy na?"

"Hell, no," he said as a half-smile made an appearance.

"Then settle in and plan and prepare, the same way ye would if ye went to battle. Meet her where she is and don't let her run away or push ye away cuz she's bound to try."

"Not the first time someone's given me that advice."

"Then bloody well listen!" Rhy growled, bumping into his side. "I've missed ye, Jamey." She leaned her head on his shoulder, sighing as she looked at the view. "This is a beautiful place ye've got,"

"It sure is. Think she'll like it?"

"She'd be a fool not to love it." Rhy wished she could promise him Danny would come around, but she didn't like to mislead anyone. He knew her as well as Rhy did. There'd be no sugar coating the situation.

"I think we both were fools."

"Aye, love can make a fool out of the best of us. I be guilty of it meself," said Rhy. "Gods know the mess I nearly created between Kyran and Roarke."

"Rhyanna Cairn," he said, jaw dropping, "You created a love triangle? Tell me more."

Her deep chuckle filled the yard. She filled him in on the last six weeks of her relationship. Rhy hadn't spoken of it to anyone, but after seeing Roarke today, it was good to take it out and discuss the foolishness that nearly

occurred. Jamey had always been a good listener, and she trusted him implicitly.

As they sat there enjoying the afternoon, Rhy hoped Danny wouldn't be so stubborn that she let this beautiful man go. Because if she did, that would make her the biggest fool Rhy had ever met—and there was a long line afore her.

Rhy prayed she was wrong, but she feared Danny's foolishness would disappoint all the wardens if she broke Jamey's heart. Worst of all, it would destroy Danny and Jamey both.

52

You Get What You Need

The students shuffled out of the dining hall, whispering about the altercation they witnessed during their first meal.

Cheeks flushed with embarrassment, Genny stared at the floor as they walked, unwilling to meet anyone's eyes.

"Are you all right?" Maryssa asked her as they walked down the hall to meet Lily.

Genny shrugged noncommittally, and Ryssa looked over her head to Amberly on the other side of her. Amberly's eyes were wide, and she shook her head, not knowing what to say either.

"I wonder what Mistress Danyka wants with you, Ryssa," Willow said.

"I don't know." Her shoulders sagged as she walked. "I shouldn't have engaged with Collette. I know better."

"She started it," Amberly pointed out.

"My mother would remind me I should be above petty squabbles," Ryssa said.

"You want me to go with you?" Willow asked.

"Nah, I got this." A wry laugh erupted from her. "Not like they are going to penalize me by sending me home."

"True."

Genny listened to the comfortable banter between the girls. She liked them. "Danyka's bark is worse than her bite," she said in a soft voice.

"You've already worked with her?" Willow asked.

"What's she like?" Amberly rattled off.

"She's always been kind to me. She trains students, but she also teaches self-defense on the mainland and on some of the other islands," Genny said.

"Does everybody have to train?" Willow asked, looking distinctly uncomfortable. "I don't like conflict."

Genny gave her a sad smile. "We don't have to like conflict for it to find us." Her smile slipped. "And sometimes we don't have to go far to find it."

They reached the foyer and took their places in Lily's line. Maryssa was in the back of the line with Amberly when Collette joined them. Her face was splotchy, and she was shaking. Ryssa wasn't sure if it was from rage or fear.

"Are you all right, Collette?" Ryssa asked, genuinely concerned.

"As if you care," Collette snapped at her.

"We don't have to be enemies," Ryssa said.

"We sure as hell don't have to be friends either," Collette said. Tipping her chin forward, she refused to meet Ryssa's eyes. "Line's moving."

Ryssa turned around and made her way up the stairs with the rest of the students. As much as she hated what Collette said to her earlier, she felt sorry for her. She always seemed angry at the world. It had to be exhausting to carry that load everywhere she went.

On the second-floor landing, each group went down one of the four hallways leading away from the landing. Ryssa's group and the mean girls followed Lily with four other girls from different districts.

Lily turned to face the group of girls. "Remember when ye reveal yer rooms, 'tis not a punishment. The Sanctuary knows what ye most need, even though ye may not agree with her choice. There are lessons to be learned and opportunities for yer soul to grow if yer open to them."

"'Tis yer choice to share yer room with others. We'll not force ye to." Her gaze landed on each of them. "Yer journey begins here. Find yer door."

Ryssa headed for the last door, the one she had chosen before lunch. Her brow furrowed as she stared at it, not understanding what was going on. Her door sported a name in the middle of it. Glancing around, she noticed they all did. The perplexing part was it wasn't her name painted in scrolling letters. It was Chantal's.

"I thought we could choose our rooms?" she asked Lily.

"Ye are," Lily answered. "The Sanctuary chooses who yer most suited to be next to. Keep looking."

Disappointed that she wouldn't be near her friends, she moved down the hall until her feet refused to move any further. Collette stood staring at the door next to hers—the one with Maryssa written on it.

"Is this some kind of cosmic joke?" Collette asked.

Lily stood behind her, and Ryssa could read from the woman's expression that the girl's reaction didn't surprise her. "Me thinks the two of ye have some things to sort out."

"I don't see that happening," Ryssa said.

"Hell. NO," Collette said. "This is unacceptable."

"This is what it is. Lasses, this is the one place you don't get what you want. This journey is about giving ye what ye need to survive the trials ahead. The trials ye will encounter here, and the trials ye'll encounter in life."

Collette and Ryssa shared similar expressions as they stared dumbfounded at her.

"Lesson one, lasses," she said as she turned towards the others, "is the ability to adapt to what life throws at ye. We shall see how well ye adapt." Standing in the middle of the hallway, she said, "Ye have part of the afternoon to unpack and settle into yer new rooms. Enjoy the downtime ye have, for there will be precious little of it in the coming weeks. Three hours from now, ye'll meet with Mistress Danyka in The Pit."

The girls grumbled as a group. "Ladies, open yer doors."

Grudgingly, Ryssa placed her hand on the wall and turned the latch for her door. As the door swung open, she snapped her eyes closed, terrified for a moment about what she might deserve. A shriek from next door made it worse.

Ripping off the bandage, she pushed the door the rest of the way open, opened her eyes, and gasped. Tears filled her eyes as she stepped into a familiar place. High ceilings allowed interlocking tree branches to form the walls. In the farthest left-hand corner, her bed nestled in an eagle's nest high on the wall. A retractable ladder led to a pallet on the floor of the nest. A dark duvet and pillows blended in with the background. She climbed the ladder and lay on the bed.

Ryssa sighed. She felt like she was lying on a cloud as her eyes took in the details. Above the bed, she found a skylight above her that would allow her to gaze up at the stars at night. She sniffled when she rolled over and found a sketch of her parents on a built-in shelf next to the bed. Her fingers traced the images, missing them both so much.

The opposite shelf held a small sketchbook and pencils. Climbing back down, she found a desk cleverly built into the wall beneath her bed.

In the right-hand corner stood an easel made from branches. Neatly stacked art supplies rested on shelves below the window. A glance out the window showed her a beautiful view of the St. Lawrence River. As she took in the details, the view changed, and she was looking at her part of the river on the river trail. A tear fell down her cheek. She was so grateful for this room, providing her with all her happy memories in one place.

Shelves covered the upper half of the wall the door was on. Books from her favorite authors filled the shelves. A built-in dresser covered the lower half. Two dark brown woven baskets on top of the dresser were full of the wonderful soaps and candles her mom made. A card rested on top of a smaller one with *Welcome* neatly written on it. This one held snacks.

Fingers trailing along the rough edge of the dresser, she walked to the corner, studying the left wall. Something was off in the center of the wall. She was too close to it to understand what it was, so she took a few steps back.

"Holy shit," she muttered as she recognized the outline of a door. Where did it lead? Moving closer once again, her fingers traced the outline, trying to open it. A small chalkboard dangled from the middle of the door. Her eyes widened when she saw the words *Be polite and knock three times to go where ye might.*

Unsure of the meaning or of where she would go, she stepped back. Turning, she faced the last wall and found the doorway to the en suite bath and walk-in closet. A deep copper tub sat in the middle of the room, inviting her to soak away her sorrows. Trailing plants formed a curtain on the window behind the tub.

The Sanctuary had given her a private oasis with touches of home. She absolutely loved it and couldn't wait to have the time to paint and soak in her free time.

Wrapped up in her own little world, she hadn't noticed the commotion outside. Opening her door, she stepped out and walked down the hall. The open doors showed her a peek into rainforests, deserts, and starlit nights. One looked like a library, while another was a music room lined with instruments. The Sanctuary tailored the suites to each student with their passions woven into the room itself.

A hammock hung in a meadow for Amberly. With a fire pit on the floor and a shower hidden in the trees, it evoked memories of sleepovers they'd had in her yard. Massive clusters of clear quartz formed a bench in a patch of wildflowers. Various crystals filled round baskets in the corners of the room, begging one to meditate with them.

Willow's bed was a canoe floating in a small pond. Bluestone lined the perimeter, and a small fountain in the pond aerated the water for the massive Koi swimming around the canoe. Ryssa thought she could hear peepers in the distance.

The size of each room was enormous. Ryssa struggled to understand how they all fit in the parameters of the castle.

Chantal had a cave with torches on the wall. A pallet heaped with furs sat on the floor in the center of the room, but otherwise, the room was sparse. Goblins Glow lined the floor and walls. The luminous moss emitted a soft, golden-green light to the room. Chantal stood slack-jawed, but Ryssa wasn't sure if she expressed joy or displeasure.

Blaze's room was at the base of a volcano. Smoke drifted throughout the room. Thick beams of basalt created a bed frame that sat a safe distance away from the molten heat. A duvet dyed in an ombre pattern gave the appearance of flames licking up the sides of the bed. In the corner, a sunken hot spring bubbled, but nothing else existed in the soft volcanic glow.

Ryssa caught glimpses of igloos on frozen tundra and beaches with white or black sand. Some girls had dainty beds made up with lacy spreads and

fluffy pillows; others were painted black with a goth feel to them. Every room was unique, with different accessories and en suite bathrooms.

Reaching Collette's door, she slid to a halt. The room was the blandest she'd come across so far. Even the Goth room she passed by had an elegant quality to it.

Collette's walls were the drabbest gray Ryssa had ever seen. Too murky to be soothing and too dingy to look like steel. It was hideous. A dingy blanket lie on the floor. Ryssa wasn't sure if it was dirty or if that color was intentional. Narrow, cell-like windows near the ceiling let in barely enough light to see the room. Glancing from corner to corner, Ryssa couldn't find any other form of light. Collette's extensive collection of trunks towered haphazardly in the corner. The room lacked furniture, and from the quick glance she got, it lacked any form of decoration. On the wall opposite the door, carved in rough letters, were the following words:

"Thoughts create your reality, and deeds create your world. To create a more beautiful world, change your thoughts and your deeds."

Collette stood stock still in the middle of the room, vibrating with fury. As she turned full circle, she noticed Ryssa standing there and screeched, "What are you looking at?" As her voice rose in pitch, the light dimmed, and the color darkened to an even uglier color.

"I'd like everyone to gather in the hall," Lily said. She waited until all the girls wandered out. Most seemed happy, but there were a handful like Collette that were miserable. "I ken, some of ye are not keen on yer new lodgings."

"I demand to see Mistress SkyDancer," Collette said. Her voice wavered with her indignation. "This is unacceptable, and I refuse to stay in there. I will stay with Chantal or Blaze first."

"Yer welcome to see the Headmistress, but I guarantee ye that her answer be the same as mine." Her gaze took in every student standing there. "Even those of ye who are happy with yer accommodations have the power to reverse them in a moment with an unkind word to another student or an unkind deed."

"If ye don't care for the rooms yer assigned, I suggest ye examine the truth written on yer walls. Think about what ye can do to change yer circumstances because that be the only way to improve yer lot."

"What did we do wrong?" one girl asked in a defeated voice.

"I can't tell ye that, lass." Lily glanced at the sour faced students and said, "The Sanctuary values teamwork, humility, and, more importantly, kindness. Remember that."

Lily gazed at each of the girls, and her gaze hardened. "The Sanctuary monitored yer behavior from the moment ye gave her a drop of yer blood. Think on yer behavior today and find the moments ye could've made

another choice. When ye recognize and atone for those slights, ye'll see a difference in yer lodging."

Collette was still furious, but Ryssa could see the hurt on her face and felt sympathetic toward her. Not sure that Collette wanted to speak to anyone, she turned as Lily began handing packets of papers to each girl.

"Ye'll find the rest of today's events and yer weekly schedules. Make sure yer on time for meals and classes, and don't dally outside past ten o'clock in the evening, or ye'll remain there 'til morn. Hellhounds patrol in the evenings, and ye'll not want to give them a reason to chase ye."

Handing the last packet out, Lily said, "It's been me pleasure to give yer tour. Ye've a few hours to settle in, and then ye'll meet at The Pit for an introduction to self-defense. Enjoy yer stay with us."

Lily left them to their own devices. The girls glanced at each other, looking lost after she left. Amberly, Genny, Ryssa, and Willow headed towards their end of the hall, stopping at each other's rooms along the way.

With a bit of time before she met Mistress Danyka, Ryssa finally climbed into the nest for a brief nap. She couldn't help thinking about Lily's words earlier, "Ye get what ye need." This room was exactly what she needed—a reminder of happier days. It offered her a place to relax, study, create, and to remember. Some of the anxiety she arrived with drifted away as she closed her eyes and slid into the peaceful dreams of her family.

53

Rosella Diaries
Eighth Entry

Ella reclined on the window seat in her room. A book lay open on her lap, but she couldn't focus on the print. A small window beside her teased her with a peek at the outside world.

The sun was setting on the horizon, her only indication of time passing quicker than she wanted. Waves gently lapped at the distant shore, making her long to be on land once more. With one last longing look at the shore, she sighed. Closing her eyes, she dreaded what tonight would bring.

Ella and two other young women were to be exhibited to potential buyers this evening. At a later date, they would auction the girls off like chattel to the highest bidder. These strangers would purchase the privilege of taking their virginity and anything else they wanted from them. Dwelling on this evening's events made her nauseous, and she tried not to let her mind wander into the unknown.

The only sources of comfort she'd found on this floating hell had been Shaelynn and Braden. Braden's mission was to keep her safe and keep her in line. They had developed a fragile friendship over the past few months. Opening her eyes, she allowed herself the luxury of watching him while he was unaware.

Braden sat on the floor near the door with his back against the wall. His dark eyes were almost closed, but Ella knew he was always alert. A form of waking meditation provided all the rest the Romani guards needed. As she watched him, his eyes opened and his gaze locked on hers.

Ella found herself drawn to the somber man. Braden had shown her kindness. There was a strange energy building between the two of them. They both fought against the futility of giving in to that energy. T'wasn't safe

to get attached to anyone in this world. Everything was so unstable. Trust was hard-earned and still questionable.

Shaelynn came bustling through the door in a flurry of movement, a long yellow gown draped over her arms. Hanging the dress on a hook, she turned towards Ella with sad eyes.

"Forgive me, milady, but I've specific instructions to prepare ye for this evening." She wrung her hands. "None of this is me choice, milady. Please remember that." Shae looked as devastated as Ella felt.

Ella tried to give her a reassuring smile. She failed to keep the nervousness from her face. "'Tis all right, Shae. We all do what we have to. Every moment we're still breathing is a moment we might change our circumstances."

Shae gave her a terse smile. Talk of escaping made her nervous, even though her maid wished they had other choices. She'd reminded Ella more than once that she was one mistake away from finding herself in the same circumstances.

Setting up a screen in front of a large copper tub, Shae drew a bath for Ella. The scent of lavender was heavy in the air as she tossed a handful of petals in along with grains of pink salt.

Ella stepped in, settling into the warm water. Wrapping her arms around her knees, she leaned forward, allowing Shae access to her back. Their chatterbox, Shae, was somber tonight, except for the soft tune she hummed under her breath. Finished with her back, Shae reached for her right arm and then her left before letting Ella lean against the copper back. Ella extended her right leg and then left, allowing Shae to perform her duties without comment.

Ella rarely allowed Shae to bathe her. She could complete the task herself and preferred it that way. Tonight was different, and they both allowed for the change in routine. Shae handed her the cloth for her to finish her breasts and between her legs. Ella went through the motions. Shae rinsed her off, and she stepped out of the tub onto a thick cotton towel. Ella dried herself and then settled on a stool while Shae slathered her skin in coconut oil.

Clean and moisturized, Ella stepped into the chaste undergarments held before her. A white chemise covered her bust, while white satin panties covered little. White lace stockings snapped to a ribbon of white satin roses that trailed up her thighs before attaching to a whalebone corset of the same color. The corset was snug on her, but bearable.

Shae pulled her hair back on each side with small pins, leaving soft curls dangling to frame her face. As Ella looked at her reflection, she cringed, knowing the intention was to make her appear as young as possible. She wore no makeup except for a clear beeswax gloss that made her lips look moist. Diamond studs glittered in her ears.

Ella stepped into a pale-yellow chiffon dress that complimented her coloring. The style was more suited for a girl of ten than for one in her mid-teens. She'd have been grateful for that if she thought it made her appear less desirable, but she knew the entire show they were putting on was to encourage degenerates who preferred having sex with children.

Pearl needed their desire heightened and teased. The entire charade was to make these men crave the young women presented. This left them time to fantasize about which delicacy they would spend a small fortune on for the evening.

Ella didn't want to do anything to encourage them to focus on her. But she knew luck wasn't on her side. There was no hiding from her fate. This was inevitable. If nothing changed, next month, she would give away something precious—something that should have gone to a man she chose.

Unfortunately, that option was no longer on the table. Ella would have to settle for surviving the man fate chose for her and pray that she didn't humiliate or displease her owner while being raped. Because Ella knew, as afraid of the unknown as she was, disappointing Pearl terrified her a thousand times more.

Dear Diary,
Eighth Entry

I have been bathed, primped, and dressed like a doll. May I keep my mouth shut like one, so that I am not punished upon my return.

I leave this ship for the first time since I've arrived. I long for the caress of the wind on my face and for a view of the night sky.

I pray to any deity that will listen to give me courage and strength, for I am in desperate need of both.

Rosella

54

Time Will Tell

Ryssa left early to meet Mistress Danyka as instructed. Her palms were sweaty, and her stomach was queasy. She followed the map that was included in her welcome packet and made her way to The Pit.

Walking down the knoll towards the weapons shed and sparring area, she understood why they called it The Pit. The knoll sloped into a low basin. A wooden fence surrounded the perimeter of the basin. Crude benches sat behind the fence on the first side you came to. On the opposite side was a shed Ryssa assumed held weapons.

Ryssa stepped into The Pit, then turned a small circle, surveying the space and the ground.

"Heads up!" came a shout from behind her.

On instinct, Ryssa turned in a crouch and caught the staff headed for her head. Catching it out of the air, she started twirling it between her hands, waiting for the inevitable charge, knowing it would come.

Danyka stalked towards her, twirling her own weapon. In the blink of an eye, she charged Ryssa. Ryssa raised her weapon, blocking her attack. Two more strikes came, and she avoided them. Pissed off at the unexpected attack, she went on the offensive, moving Danny back half a dozen steps.

The maniacal grin on the instructor's face concerned Ryssa. She wasn't sure if the look was a compliment or a challenge. Back and forth they went. Ryssa continued holding her own.

"She's holding back," Ryssa thought. For an unidentifiable reason, this pissed her off. Her offensive strikes came faster, harder, and more unpredictable until Danny yelled, "Cease!"

Ryssa's hands immediately went to her sides. She held the staff upright until Danyka reached for it. Ryssa handed it over, bowing her head in a sign of respect to her instructor.

Danyka returned the bos to their rack and tossed Ryssa a glass bottle of water. "'Twas a pretty shitty thing for that little twat to say to you earlier."

"That's why you were toying with me?"

"Not at all," Danyka said with a deep chuckle. "I knew you'd be good, just wanted to see how damn good you were. I've sparred with your father before. He was one of the best I've ever seen." She took a long drink. "He handed my ass to me more than once."

"He had a habit of doing that," Ryssa said with a smirk.

Danyka watched her, noting the smile didn't reach her eyes. "Sorry 'bout what happened to him."

"Thanks," Ryssa said, trying to keep her shit together. Tears were burning in the backs of her eyes, threatening to run down her face.

"He was a friend of mine, and I won't tolerate anyone being disrespectful." Her violet eyes captivated Ryssa, and she couldn't look away from them. "Your father loved you very much. He often spoke about his family. He never would have intentionally abandoned you. Don't let anyone make you doubt that."

Ryssa cleared her throat, trying to find the words to tell her how much this meant to her.

"Thank you, Mistress. I needed to hear that today."

"When we're alone, it's Danyka. You can drop that *Mistress* bullshit."

"Yes, Mist…Danyka."

"You mind if I make an example out of you today?"

"No, ma'am."

"Good. Have a seat. The others will be here soon."

As if Danyka conjured them, Ryssa heard the whisper of voices in the wind. Five minutes later, the benches were full of young men and women who appeared equally excited and terrified.

Danyka moved across the packed dirt, twirling her staff faster and faster as she moved. She spun in circles, dancing across the arena.

Ryssa smiled, studying her, anticipating her next moves. The woman was mesmerizing to watch.

"Ryssa, pick a staff and join me."

Ryssa headed for the rack and pulled out the one she'd worked with earlier. It was lightweight and perfectly balanced for her. She met her in the middle, blocking the first parry that came at her. Back and forth, they traded blows in what could be a deadly game.

Danyka didn't hold back this time, and Ryssa welcomed the opportunity to work out her frustrations and rage over the loss of her father. When Danyka yelled, "Cease," sweat was dripping down her face. Her shirt clung to her back as she bent over to catch her breath.

Danyka faced the class. "Your first lesson today is this…we work together on this island. We don't tear each other down. If I hear anyone being disrespectful or antagonizing a fellow student, you'll work your anger issues out in there." She pointed to the arena behind her. "With me." An evil smirk crossed her face as she added, "Trust me, I won't hold back if it comes to that."

The silence was staggering. Ryssa could see the fear on Collette's face and tried not to smile. Danyka had made her point.

"Everyone find a partner and grab a staff. You're going to learn the basics." Danyka headed for the bench with her water, taking a drink and wiping her face. "Collette, you're with Ryssa."

Collette's eyes widened, but she did as she was told. Moving cautiously toward Ryssa, she gripped the wood tightly as she stared at the ground. When they took their places in the line facing each other, Collette glanced at her. Regret in her eyes, she said, "I never should have said that about your father. Please accept my apologies."

Ryssa stared at her for a moment in silence. As tears pooled in the other girl's eyes and her bottom lip quivered, she spoke. "No, you shouldn't have. It's been difficult enough without the gossip and hate we've experienced."

"I am truly sorry." Collette sniffled. "You were lucky enough to have a father that actually cared."

Her voice trailed off on her last thought, but Ryssa heard her clearly. She couldn't help wondering why the local Water Clan princess was so unhappy. "I accept your apology, Collette."

Collette's eyes snapped to hers in surprise. "Thank you." She glanced away, then added, "You're great at this. Please don't beat the shit out of me, even if I deserve it."

"We're good," Ryssa said with a grin. "Now, if she'd thrown us in here earlier, it would have been a different story."

"Listen up!" Danyka shouted so that all could hear. "Our goal isn't to damage anyone today, so go through the motions slowly and carefully. The weapons are awkward when you first handle them. I need every other one of you to take ten steps back. Turn the wand so that you can appreciate the reach you have and how much space it will affect."

Danyka turned the wand in a slow circle. "The piece of wood you are holding is a bo. We also refer to it as a staff. Now, extend it from one arm. Pay attention to the additional reach you have gained, and make sure you know where your classmates are."

She walked around the students while she spoke. Her bo continued spinning as she moved. "This weapon gives a weaker opponent power. As Ryssa and I demonstrated, with speed and agility, you could prevent an attacker from getting close to you."

Using one arm, she began spinning her bo faster. "With training and practice, this becomes a deadly weapon. If I ever see you raise this against a fellow student anytime other than during practice, you will regret it."

Reaching the beginning of the line, she stopped the spinning bo and held it in front of her. "This is one of many weapons you will learn to wield. Some are easier than others, but you will try them all until we find the ones that best suit each of you. Then we will split you into groups to focus on your strengths. You will meet here twice a day."

Danyka greeted a tall, dark-haired man who joined them. "This is Damian Pathfinder. He will assist me for the next few weeks. You will work with him first thing in the morning for strength training and hand-to-hand combat. We will reconvene here after lunch to work with weapons."

"For the rest of this class, I want you to familiarize yourself with the feel of your staff. Try different ones. Find the one that's comfortable in your hands. Pay attention to the length, weight, and balance of the staff until you find one that seems custom-made for you."

They spent another quarter of an hour working with them. "Line up if you've found one that feels right for you," Danyka said. As each student approached her, she placed her hand on the staff until magic etched their names into the wood. "If you didn't feel comfortable with the ones you tried, don't worry. You can try again tomorrow. Remember your partners. You will start each session with them."

Pointing to the rack, Danyka said, "House your weapons and head in for the evening meal. Enjoy the rest of your evening. This will be the easiest day you have for a while. If you have questions, see me after classes."

Ryssa and Collette replaced their staffs and ambled to the other group of girls.

Chantal and Blaze stood to the left of the gate, waiting for her. With every step, Collette's bearing changed. Ryssa could feel the chill returning to her disposition. Walking off without a word, she reclaimed her place in their hierarchy.

Amberly arched an eyebrow at her and asked, "How the hell did you refrain from braining her with that stick?"

Ryssa shrugged. "She apologized."

"Hell just froze over," Willow said in a whisper.

"About time someone held her to task for her miserable attitude," Amberly said as they walked up the knoll.

"Wonder if it will change anything?" Genny pondered.

"What do you mean?" Ryssa asked.

"I just wondered if her change in attitude will affect her room. You know, the message on her wall about changing her deeds," Genny clarified.

"Do you think the other girls will figure out how to fix their rooms?" Willow asked. "Will she tell them?"

"Have to wait and see," Ryssa said. "But she likes power, and why would she share something she can hold over them? I still don't trust her—not even after the waterworks display."

"She didn't!" Amberly gaped.

"She did, and I might have believed her until I saw her transform back into her old self just now," Ryssa said. "Time will tell."

55

Rosella Diaries
Ninth Entry

Rosella and Braden took their places at the end of the line, with eight other mismatched couples in front of them. Young women with their hands on the bent elbows of their escorts. No, that wasn't quite right or fair to the girls—with their guards. Beautiful young belles stood in line with men who received gold and sexual favors to keep them detained and well-behaved.

Fury rolled through Ella's belly, making her more nauseous than she'd originally been. Fending off her fight-or-flight urges was getting harder by the minute, especially when she caught her first glimpse of the night sky in months. The compulsion to dive into the river was intense, but she pushed it down.

The night was clear, and the summer sky was full of stars. Her eyes charted the constellations. Memories of her brother, Roarke, teaching them to her brought tears to her eyes. If he could see her now, he would be livid. There would be no controlling his fury if he were to witness her humiliation. And when he found her, there would be no controlling his wrath.

Braden squeezed her arm, bringing her back to the present. Karyn, a petite, dark-haired beauty from the Southern Seas, stood in front of her in a pale green copy of the yellow dress Ella wore. In front of her, Tryna, origins unknown, wore pastel pink. Ella could see her fingers worrying the fabric on the side and hoped Pearl wouldn't swat her for it.

Pearl, looking elegant as always, faced the line of young women arrayed for their first journey into womanhood. "I know many of you hate me right now. I expect and deserve your hostility." Her gaze met each of theirs, accepting the silent accusations and the pleas for mercy in their eyes.

"Tonight is a steppingstone for the rest of your life. Should you please your owner, they may choose to make you a permanent acquisition. You

might serve as pets or live in a private harem. If so blessed, your master will cherish you if you please him. He may reward you with lavish gifts."

"Your only requirement in these lifestyles is to provide pleasure for a few hours a day, or if you're really lucky, on a weekly basis. Think of tonight as an interview for a job you really want. A job where there are no threats of Saul to haunt you."

Pearl turned away, then gazed over her shoulder at them. Her voice chilled, and her eyes flashed dangerously. "If you exhibit any tears, hysteria, or attempt to flee," her soulless dark eyes met Ella's, "you will only make the evening harder on yourself and on your guards."

She paused for a moment to let that sink in. "Your guards will face financial repercussions, and they will have my permission to punish you as they see fit." Her gaze wandered the line.

"For some of you, that isn't much of a threat. But when they've finished, Saul and the sailors below decks will enjoy you for the next week as a lesson in obedience. I will give them free rein with your bodies if you disappoint me tonight."

Saul was enough of a threat, but the unknown world of the sailors below deck made Pearl's point hit home. The girls shifted nervously. Ella's eyes dropped and her grip on Braden's arm tightened.

Pasting a perfect smile on her face, Pearl turned and led the line, her arm on Jonah's. Her voice carried on the wind. "Let's go girls. Your temporary owners are excited to meet you."

Their temporary owners would purchase a twenty-four-hour block of time to play with their new toys. They were free to take what they wanted—gently or brutally. They paid for the anonymity of the auctions, the promise of a new toy to break in as they saw fit, and the freedom from repercussions the dark market provided.

All eyes were on the new arrivals as a small craft took them to a paddle boat anchored in the middle of the river. As they reached the floating bordello, their guards helped them cross over a temporary bridge attached to the side of their smaller vessel.

Rosella and the two other girls before her wore pastels, while the six girls in front of them wore white from head to toe in body-hugging satin. The color of purity proclaimed their value and position in the evening's entertainment.

The guards led the girls in white up a platform. They found their places amongst dozens of other candidates. It horrified Ella to realize how widespread this nightmare was. The local authorities should notice if dozens of girls disappeared regularly. Shouldn't they?

Ella memorized their faces, horrified to realize that Gemma was the last girl led on stage. She had been the only girl who had been kind to Ella since

her arrival. Standing on the platform beneath her, Ella witnessed the panic in the young woman's eyes.

Ella's heart broke for what they expected these young women to endure tonight. Sending a nod and tight smile in Gemma's direction for support, Ella clenched her teeth, praying Gemma would keep her emotions hidden. Gemma locked eyes with her and nodded, lifting her chin higher.

A man dressed in a black and silver brocade topcoat took center stage. He began the evening's entertainment by introducing the owners. Then, in intricate detail, he listed each girl's or boy's assets as if he were going over their family pedigree. He categorized and enticed the buyers, whetting their appetites for the auction to come.

Giving them time to peruse their options, he moved on to the showcase of coming attractions. One by one, the guards brought forth the offerings for the next auction. Alternating by owner, Ella was the last girl to be displayed.

As she stood there doing her best to appear demure and malleable, she couldn't help but let her eyes wander over the ensemble. Curious, she examined the people in the crowd.

Appalled to see nearly as many women as men holding auction paddles, her jaw clenched. Immediately, she regretted being so bold when she caught a few of the men sizing her up. Eyes hitting the deck, she bit her tongue and hoped a flush didn't dust her cheeks. She wasn't supposed to meet the buyer's eyes unless they requested it. Ella prayed Pearl hadn't noticed.

The auction officially began, and Ella watched in horror as three or more buyers at a time fought for the honor of raping a child. The bidding was fast, and the line dwindled quickly.

When the spotlight landed on Gemma, Ella saw the terror in her eyes when four men set their sights on her. Two heavily muscled men had similar features. A third was taller and wore a beautifully tailored suit. Last but not least was a vertically challenged older gent with wiry white hair.

Ella was certain the older man would win the bid. But when the two brawny men realized the suit could outbid either of them, they joined forces. Ella realized in horror that they intended to share Gemma if they succeeded. The old gent dropped out when the bid continued to rise, and the suit doubled his bid, causing gasps throughout the crowd.

Ella lost track of the bidding as quickly as it changed. Her hand tightened on Braden's elbow. She tried desperately to keep her face neutral, but she failed, and the horror she felt for Gemma was on full display. Braden took a step closer, acknowledging her distress.

The bidding halted, and the barker cried, "Going once. Going twice. Sold." Pointing to the pair of men leering at Gemma, he said, "Gonna be a long night for this wee lass."

The sales completed, Ella watched in horror as they attached a leash to a delicate chain around each girl's neck. Gemma's face was pale and her eyes much too wide as her new owners led her by them. She caught Ella's gaze, and her luminous eyes begged her to intercede.

No matter how much Ella wished she could, they both knew it was futile to believe anyone would assist them. The die was cast, and this was their life now.

The man leading Gemma tugged hard on the leash, making her follow quickly behind him. The other man wrapped an arm around her waist, his hand grazing her breast as they walked down the stairs. Her neutral faced guard followed two steps behind them.

This was only one of hundreds of degradations they would suffer before it all ended. Ella prayed for the strength to accept her fate as gracefully as Gemma had on stage.

Then she prayed for Gemma to survive the night with the two animals who purchased her. Holding back tears, she followed Braden's lead. They returned in silence with twelve fewer people on board their vessel. Pearl sat next to Jonah, her head resting on his shoulder.

Ella wondered if Pearl could feel the heat of her glare in the dark. Heartsick and horrified, somehow she made it back without dishonoring Braden or herself. But she couldn't help but wonder if she would dishonor them all when it was her turn to be sold.

For a moment, she wished fire was her element. For if she were an elemental with that kind of power, she would have incinerated the boat they left behind, sparing only those who were innocent.

But alas, she was merely an untrained water element. She feared if she tried to tap into anything in this frame of mind, the only thing she would accomplish was drowning them all, herself included.

Taking a chance that her link to her mother might be open, she reached out, seeking comfort. *"Maman. Are you there?"*

Mere seconds passed before her mother's voice made it harder for her not to cry. *"Rosella, ma chérie?"*

"'Tis me."

"Where you at, love?"

"I don't know, maman. I just watched dozens of young girls and a few boys auctioned off. Next time, it will be me." She couldn't suppress her internal sob. *"I'm not strong enough or submissive enough for this life, maman."*

"My sweet chile," her mother's voice hitched, and Ella knew she was trying not to show her fears. *"Be strong and brave. You are my warrior. We be coming for you. 'ang tight chile. I promise you dat we be coming."*

With those words, their connection broke. It took everything Ella possessed to walk back onto Jonah's boat and not drown herself in the river. With her head held high, and her fingers digging grooves into Braden's arm,

she walked the length of the ship to her suite, with Pearl and Jonah by her side.

Ella stared at the floor, afraid that if she met anyone's gaze, they would punish her for the hatred simmering there. But she would be strong, and she would be brave because they were coming for her. And hell, hath no fury like Catalina Gallagher.

Dear Diary,
Ninth Entry

I glimpsed my future this evening, and it is bleak. But the stars were out, and I heard Maman's voice. These two things should bring me joy, but they make me feel even more caged and alone.

Pearl sold six girls like chattel to the highest bidder. A barker proclaimed their virtues against the background noise of giggling and champagne flutes tinkling on trays.

It took everything I possessed not to scream or attack. Yet at the same time, the weakest part inside of me wanted to give up and leap from the side of the boat, allowing my frilly confection of a dress to drag me under. I would have welcomed the solace of the cold, dark water embracing me, and the eternal silence it would have offered.

But Maman counseled courage, and hope, and though I have less now than I did this morning, I will continue to survive. I will be her warrior, and one day this warrior will have her due.

Rosella

56

Reconnaissance

Fergus's lanky stride took him to the harbor in no time flat. He'd stopped off at the Rusty Tap before leaving for some liquid courage. A forty-five-minute ferry ride delivered him to an undisclosed location.

Well, to some, it would be undisclosed, but to a man who'd spent a few centuries on this shore, let's just say…he wasn't lost. Leaving the ferry, he made his way to the enormous riverboat docked farther down. Guards stood at all four ports of entry, and Fergus knew better than to try his luck at the one intended for guests.

"Reconnaissance," he whispered to himself. *"That's all tonight be about."*

A rope ran across the servant's entrance with a guard on either side. Both guards were massive motherfuckers with no nonsense expressions.

"State yer purpose," said the one on the left, in a voice full of gravel.

Fergus removed his hat and worked it in his hands. "I'se told ta report ta the kitchen tonight. Needs to earn some extra fer me kids ta eat." His voice was pitiful, and he spoke in a raspy whine.

"Don't look like much of a chef."

"I might not seem like much, but I'se a helluva prep cook and dishwasher."

The man on the left unclasped the rope and handed it to his counterpart, allowing Fergus through. "Make a right when ye enter, then two lefts. 'Twill take ye to the kitchens."

Fergus bobbed his head gratefully and gave them a half-assed bow as he lumbered up the ramp. He hadn't expected it to be this easy, but he wasn't complaining.

Following the directions, he made a right, noting every room he passed. Garbage and laundry on the left, mess hall and restrooms on the right. Next left took him past cold storage for smoked meats and magically lit growing rooms for fresh produce. His last turn dead-ended in the kitchen.

Glancing down to make sure the charm Hamish provided was still working, Ferg was happy to see everything was still active. The glamour he used when he dealt with Hamish responded to the one Hamish gave him to appear leaner and more attractive.

He'd just finished confirming his disguise when a woman hollering like a fishwife caught his attention. Glancing up, he saw a formidable ole gal headed his way with a metal spatula raised.

"Ye filthy wretch. Whatchya be doing in me kitchens?"

Fergus hunched in a low bow, hat in his hands as he murmured, "Sorry, mistress. I'm seeking Jasper."

Hand still at the ready, she examined him from his head to his feet. "What kitchen experience ye got?"

"None, missus," Ferg said, taking a step backwards. "I'se supposed to get a uniform from Jasper and head upstairs fer extra security."

The woman raised a brow in speculation, then screeched, "Jasper, when ye gonna stop offering the riff-raff jobs?"

Jasper, a thin man with a glossy, bald head, slunk towards her, staying just out of reach. "Boss's orders, missus."

"Best be. I be checking after we be through." She gave him a side eye and headed back into her domain, ladle raised and voice shrieking.

"Hamish send ye?" Jasper asked in a whisper.

"Aye," Fergus whispered back. "Name's Cyrus," he said, offering a hand.

Jasper took it briefly and led him back towards the laundry. A closed door marked "staff only" held uniforms of every sort. The man stepped in and fumbled around until he found a lamp. With light restored, he sorted through the different sizes of black shirts and pants until he found something he thought would fit Cyrus's body. "Changing rooms across the hall. Ye can stash yer things in there 'til ye leave."

"Thank ye, sir." Cyrus scraped and bowed.

"Best get moving, event's about to start." He pointed a long, thick finger down the hall to his right. "Follow that hall until it dead ends into a stairwell. Go up four flights 'til you hit the upper decks. Muscle's s'posed to blend into the sidelines in case there're any problems or if anyone who t'aint supposed to be here shows up."

"How's I s'posed to ken who belongs?" Cyrus said, scratching his head in confusion.

Jasper went back to the closet and picked up a box. Nestled inside were a variety of lapel pins. Handing Cyrus one with a piece of black onyx on the pinhead, he said, "Affix this to yer left lapel. Shows yer staff." He picked up a handful of other pins with various gems. "Sapphires represent guests, and rubies represent owners. The only diamonds ye'll see are on the approved buyers—and there t'aint many of them. Each pin is identifiable by the

number of gems on it. The more important the guest or buyer, the fancier the pin." Cocking a brow, he asked, "Ye got it?"

Cyrus nodded with enthusiasm. "Aye, wear mine on the left. Guests and buyers have them on the right, and the more stones, the richer they be."

"Close nuff. Alls ye need to know to be the muscle tonight."

"Who hands out the pins?" Fergus asked.

Jasper gazed at him as if he were daft. "Why wouldchya give a feck? Ye've got all's ye need to make some fast cash tonight. Don't be asking too many questions, or ye'll be feeding the fish come the end of the shift."

Cyrus raised his hands, trying to placate the man. "No offense intended. Jest wondered if someone was missing a pin or needing one, who I should send them to."

"Anyone makes it topside without one don't belong there," Jasper said with a mean gleam in his eyes. "Speak to the man in black wearing a ruby on his left lapel, and he'll be along to escort the offender off permanently."

Cyrus nodded his head to show he understood. With clothes in hand, he found the washroom and changed into the uniform. The silk button-down and black trousers fit him perfectly. After stashing his clothes in a locker, he headed for the stairwell. Fingers fidgeting with his pin, he took the stairs two at a time.

"Bloody fecking hell," he groaned as he hit the last flight. He didn't think he was that out of shape, but the stairs mocked him in disagreement.

The night was clear as he stepped onto the deck. Bright stars illuminated the midnight sky. He assessed the platform, the security, and the guests making their way towards the raised dais in seconds.

The extravagantly decorated deck was pure elegance. Hundreds of candles cast a soft glow amongst pale-colored roses. The heavy aroma of the summer blooms was overpowering to Fergus's senses. Lace-topped tables held crystal-cut champagne glasses for the champagne fountain in the center.

A red velvet carpet led the participants through the crowd and up the two steps leading to the display platform. Numbered gold stars marked positions for the young men and women to stand on, with only a railing separating them from the gathering crowd.

Trembling bodies already occupied six spots. Five young women and a very young boy stood terrified under the audience's hungry stare. Dozens of additional stars patiently waited to be claimed.

Fergus clenched his jaw and tried to relax his fists before his rage gave him away. A man dressed in black and wearing a ruby on his lapel nodded at him and pointed to an empty space on the perimeter of the room.

Making his way to his assigned position, Ferg noted black circles painted on the outside of the deck. Scanning the perimeter, he noted security stationed every six feet. The spacing of guards along the back rail prevented the terrified property from escaping by jumping ship.

A dozen men in black wove through the crowd besides the wait staff serving drinks and appetizers. The event was heavily staffed, which surprised him. How could they afford to have this many people knowing about their perverse business?

Head cocked to the side, he pondered how they managed the anonymity needed for this kind of invitation-only auction. The dark circles were rife with those searching for young flesh, but the penalties, if caught dealing, were lethal.

Heavily cloaking a tendril of his magic, he sent it on the wind as he sent it in search of nearby mages. His brows furrowed as he detected one representing every element, including spirit on board.

But wait, what was that he sensed? His head tipped to the side as a wave of similar magic slipped by him. Yanking his thread back, he absorbed it, then buried his abilities beneath a barricade no one could penetrate. "Feck me," he said under his breath.

Fergus wasn't the only powerful mage here. Another mage, nearly as powerful as he, was on this vessel. The hair on his arms rose as he considered the repercussions of this intel.

The formally dressed crowd conversed as if attending a ball. An orchestra played softly in the background while the guests drank from crystal champagne flutes. Surprisingly, a third of the crowd was women. Their enthusiasm shocked him more than anything else he had witnessed so far.

Hands clasped behind his back, like the other hired men, he studied the crowd. Trying to understand the type of person who thrived in another's misery, he observed the group while making a list in his head.

One - Money. Resources ran deep. Nothing shabby about this group of people. From their clothing to their attitudes, they had an air of confidence that only the extremely wealthy exhibited. But they weren't all old money. Young entrepreneurs rubbed elbows with families who had bought and sold empires.

Two - This was definitely a much larger network than they'd originally expected. Foreign accents and formal wear represented four of the eight continents. He overheard more than one interpreter explaining the bidding process.

Three - Guaranteed anonymity. These people were fearless. Not a one of them was concerned to be seen here. Island Law was fecking brutal. If captured and convicted, there wasn't enough money to avoid the creative death sentence Madylyn would impose.

Another seller arrived, catching his attention. The crowd's excited anticipation as more options appeared was disgusting. A beautiful woman with long dark hair and pale skin led her offerings on stage. Big, dark eyes dominated her delicate features. Wearing green silk, she was absolutely

stunning. Fergus's eyes traveled to her companion, and he sucked in a breath and whispered, "Gotchye," under his breath.

The massive escort was bald with a scar the shape of a lightning bolt traversing his wide features. As unattractive as she was beautiful, they made a powerful couple. This was the man Hamish sought, Jonah. And if he was Jonah, then she was the elusive Pearl. Pearl led six young women to gold stars on the dais, while three others took their place in a line in the front.

The evening's master of ceremonies arrived. Like a carnival barker, he began his spiel to the crowd, making Fergus's stomach clench. His smoky voice advertised next month's coming attractions one at a time in lurid detail. The way he ogled the girls and described them was fecking creepy. Especially when the majority of them were under fifteen.

Ferg tried to memorize faces, but he couldn't see them clearly. One girl near the end was familiar, but the crowd in front of him made an identification impossible. *"Feck me,"* he thought in frustration.

"Remember, asshole, this mission is merely for informative purposes. Tonight's not a fecking rescue." His inner voice chided him, understanding how badly he wanted to sink this ship and everyone but the innocents on it.

Tonight might not be the right time, but by gods, the next time he set foot on this vessel, it better be. His eyes tracked the crowd instead, committing to memory the men and women taking pleasure in this indecency. Picking out the buyers by their diamond pins, he kept his eyes on them.

A muscle ticked on the side of his clenched jaw as the auction commenced. The energy surrounding the ship was rife with unadulterated fear and the heavy tang of lust. His stomach rolled, but he kept his shit together by digging his nails into the palms of his hands.

Time dragged on as he bore witness to children being auctioned off to enthusiastic buyers. Choking on the taste of their anticipation and their victim's terror, this was one of the most difficult things he'd ever endured. The coming horror and his inability to prevent the buyers from leashing their trophies nearly destroyed him.

"Fergus, I know you are struggling with this," Maddy said, reaching out on their link. *"I sense the fury and pain this is causing you. Stay the course. We have to see the bigger picture. Keep it together, my friend. The end is near."*

Fergus shook his head, trying to clear it. Maddy was right. He'd never make it out of here alive and save all of them. But he would return with reinforcements, and he'd take the feckers down.

When the barker cried "Sold!" for the last time, the new owners stepped forward, connecting ornate leads to the collars of their prizes. The leads were unique to each buyer. Some were made of leather and others of precious metals and jewels. They proudly led their acquisitions off the stage for the crowd to appreciate up close.

Eventually, the crowd dispersed, making their way to the private rooms below. If Fergus accidentally stumbled and bumped into a few of them as they stood in line to descend, the diamond pins in his pocket were worth touching the sick fucks.

The deck finally cleared, and the head of security came around. The burly man handed a hefty wad of cash to each man in black. When he reached Fergus, he stared at him for a long time.

"Yer new here, ain't ye?"

Fergus nodded. "Aye, me first night."

"Remember, lad, yer paid well for yer discretion." He clamped a hand on Ferg's shoulder. "And we'll hunt ye and yer family down and kill ye slowly and painfully should we hear ye talking to anyone about tonight's events."

The hand tightened on his shoulder, and Ferg fought the urge to shake it off. "Ye understand?" the burly man asked.

"Yes, sir," Fergus answered bowing his head in acknowledgement.

"Good. Get changed and get the hell outta here."

Ferg nodded and joined the others as they descended to the lowest deck. Herded quickly below deck, there was no time to wander on the other floors.

The quick pace didn't prevent him from listening, though. Sadistic laughter rang out from multiple rooms, and his steps faltered when the screams began.

A middle-aged man walked next to him. As Fergus paused, the gent glanced his way. "Pay no attention to anything. Ye hear me, laddie? Won't do ye no good to intervene," he said in a gravelly voice full of regret and resignation.

Ferg cocked a brow at him.

"Others 'ave tried." Swiping a hand through his wavy, salt-and-pepper hair, he continued, "'Tain't never seen nor heard of again. Lost me best friend that way."

"Why ye still doing this?"

"I'se got me four daughters. All beauties and younger than twelve." Eyes shifting around them, he said, "They know where's I live, and I tain't bout to give them any reason to take a shine to me bairns."

Ferg's eyes were wide as the man confided in him.

"Came first time cuz I heard 'bout easy money. Didn't know they'd own me fer life." His head shook ruefully. "And they sure as feck don't tell ye that ye'll lose a piece of yer soul every time ye stand there and do nothing. No, sir, they don't." A meaty paw swiped through his thick mane again.

Ferg said nothing as he pondered the information the man gave him. "How do they track ye?" he asked.

"On yer way out, the mage takes a drop of yer blood. He's like a fecking bloodhound." He met Ferg's eyes. "Try to get out without doing that if ye can. Might save yerself."

"Why ye telling me this?" Fergus asked him.

"Cuz I sees the fury and disgust in yer eyes. Ye mustn't be much of a poker player."

Ferg's head dropped to his chest in disgust. He knew better than to let it become personal. "Na, not me game." Peering at the man, he asked, "Ye gotta name?"

"Horace. I'll distract them while ye slip outta the staff exit."

"Why ye helping me?"

"I'd be anywhere else but here if I could, laddie. I be trapped, but I don't want ye to be, too. Get out of here and don't ye ever come back."

One last turn and they were in the men's restrooms. Changing quickly, Fergus took his time with his boots, waiting as the room cleared out.

Probing the pins for magical trackers, he was grateful to find nothing attached to them. With careful folds, he turned his shirt sleeves up, tucking a pin in each one, making sure they lined up with the seam. Even if they searched him, they wouldn't be easily detectable.

A quick glance over his shoulder and he saw the older gent who'd walked with him was nearly ready. Dark eyes met his, and the man gave him a nod, getting in line for the door.

Ferg followed, allowing two others between them. Not sure what the plan was, he didn't want to be too close and have nowhere to go.

The line moved slowly as they methodically searched the departing men. Two of the men at the front of the line had their fingers pricked. Fergus watched as the mage carefully stored their samples in a small wooden box.

"Feckity, feck, feck, feck…" Fergus thought as he moved closer. A blood mage would recognize the power in his blood in seconds, bringing unwanted attention. Horace had better put on a bloody good show if he was going to get out of here in one piece without blowing his cover.

Horace's turn came. He raised his arms and allowed the head of security to pat down his body. They chatted amiably, but Fergus couldn't hear what he said. Believing the man had scammed him, sweat pooled under his arms. Cleared to go, Horace stepped through the door.

What ensued next was a bloody miracle. Horace walked through the door, chatting and laughing with all the senior security officers and the mage. Next thing Fergus saw was his arms pinwheeling as he lost his balance. He bounced off both security officers and then fell into the mage, knocking his box to the floor and scattering samples everywhere.

The mage shrieked and pushed Horace off of him. Horace grabbed his chest and yelled, "It's me heart," as he clutched his chest and fell into the officers again. The guard searching the men after him turned to help.

Fergus jostled the two in front of him as he said, "Don't jest stand there. Help the man."

Confusion reigned as they bumbled into the hallway and got in the way. Fergus snuck to the left. Shrouding himself in shadows, he made his way to the door he'd come in earlier.

A glance back showed Horace being helped to his feet while the head of security dismissed the two men standing in the hall without searching them. The mage was still gathering pins in a frenzied fashion as security hollered, "Hurry the hell up! There're others here needing to get through."

"I am hurrying, ye prick," the mage snarled at him. "Ye'll finish no faster than I allow ye to. Just cuz ye got tight young pussies waiting downstairs, don't mean I've any need to rush."

"Might share those tight, young holes if ye'd hurry the feck up."

"Deal." With a wave of his hand, the mage pulled all the pins from the floor and deposited them in the box. "I can organize these later."

"Not if I have anything to say, 'bout it," Fergus thought. Carefully, he attached a spell to the box that would cause it to burst into flames an hour hence. The fire would destroy any blood inside the box and no one the wiser.

The mage wasn't a very good one, or he'd have noticed Ferg tampering. Distracted with promises of forbidden sex, the mage either didn't sense him or didn't care. Either way, Ferg made his escape, blood intact.

Hitting the docks, he noted the other day workers disembarking. Two of their fellow employees assisted Horace to a wooden bench.

From the corner of his eye, Fergus noted a grubby figure beside the last warehouse. Heading that way, he came up behind Hamish. "Jonah's on board. Saw the ugly fecker meself."

Hamish cackled. "Good." He tossed a brown leather pouch at Ferg. "Ye done good. Ye up for another job?"

"No," Fergus said firmly. "I wants no part of this in the future. Yer on yer own."

"'Tis a shame. We made a good pair." He swiped a hand under his runny nose. "Gots ta go. I've gotta get a tracker on his boat."

"Then what? Ye track him, and then how ye gonna get on?"

"Not yer problem, laddie."

Ferg wanted to argue that part, but he wasn't willing to continue collaborating with this weasel. "If I change me mind, I know how to reach ye."

"Yep. Little Miss Aida's the best way." A crooked smile crossed his face. "Now there's a pretty li'l thing. And she produces pretty li'l things, too."

Ferg's control was nearly gone as he forced a smile on his face. "Think she'd hurt ye. That barmaid's a feisty one."

"Jest the way I likes them." Hamish was nearly drooling at the prospect. Tipping his hat at Fergus, he slithered off into the night.

Fergus immediately reached out to his cousin Vulcan. *"Keep men on Aida and the little ones. 'Tis not safe for her right now."*

"I'll double her security. Give me fecking names." Vulcan's fury came at Fergus like a fist to the jaw. The man was incredibly protective of his family, and someone had just threatened them.

"That piece of shit that's been lurking in the alley. Next time ye see him, take him into custody. But don't fecking kill him. I need more info from him."

"Can't promise that, not even for ye, Ferg."

"Don't make me drag the laird into this," Ferg said.

"Me wee sister don't scare me. She'd skin him alive if he touched me family."

"Aye, she would. After what I seen tonight, I want in on that man's justice and will take it as a personal slight if ye kill him without me."

Ferg sensed Vulcan's laughter through their link and relaxed.

"I'll wait. Might as well make it a party. Brandell will want to be there, too."

"Aye. He will. I'll be in touch."

Their link slammed closed as Vulcan disconnected. Ferg opened his senses, searching for anyone nearby. A few drunk sailors staggered on the dock, and Horace still rested on the bench.

Ferg walked back the way he'd come, the opposite direction which Hamish had taken. As he stepped into the open, he saw Horace sitting with his head in his hands. Fergus sat next to him in silence.

Horace leaned against the back of the wooden bench, watching the paddleboat leave. He let out a raspy sigh. "Was afraid you didn't make it out."

"I made it," Fergus said. "I'm in yer debt fer yer help."

"Ye owe me nothing as long as ye save those girls." Horace turned to him and stared straight into his eyes. "Warden."

Fergus blanched. There was no way the man could have known who or what he was. "Pardon?" His voice quivered as he spoke.

"I spent all night watching ye. That's me job, checking out the new hires. Ye were too damn intent on the buyers and less on the exposed flesh that was visible."

"Might jest not be to me taste."

"Bullshite." The man stared him down. "There was something for everyone's taste up there."

"Yer a fecking undercover warden, ain'tchya?" Fergus said with awe as he ignored the urge to stare at the man.

"I'll neither confirm nor deny," the man said, staring straight ahead.

"How close to bringing them down are ye?" Ferg tried from another angle.

"No where's close enough," he rasped.

"Thanks fer the help on board." Ferg tugged on his beard thoughtfully. "Can ye get word to me if the venue be changing?"

"Yer welcome. Doubtful. But I sits on this here bench every couple weeks 'round this time. Be creative with your appearance if you decide to visit. Now make yerself scarce before ye bring suspicion down on me."

"Yes, sir," Fergus said as he stood. "By the way, in another hour or two, that mage won't be able to track anyone through their blood."

Gratitude filled the old man's eyes, and he gave him a nod.

With the tip of an imaginary hat, Fergus walked down the dock. A ferry to somewhere far from the Sanctuary would be the safest way for him to depart. He'd portal his way around the islands to confuse anyone following, then make his way back to the Rusty Tap. This had been one helluva night, and he sure needed a fecking drink…or ten.

57

The Kindest Thing You Can Do

Myranda shook out the top sheet for the bed she was making in Rhyanna's clinic when the bell on the front door jangled. "I'll be right with you," she hollered, wanting to finish the task she was doing.

The door between the shoppe and clinic opened, and Ronan walked in. Crossing to the opposite side of the bed, he grabbed the sheet. He pulled it tight before tucking in and squaring off the corners with military precision.

"I can finish this; you don't need to help," Myranda said with a smile.

"I don't mind a bit. I've made my share of beds over the years." He returned her smile as they straightened the coverlet over the pillow. "Let's start on the next one," he said, moving to the next unmade bed. "How long are you covering for Rhyanna?"

"Just until tomorrow. What can I do for you, Ronan?"

"I've been wanting to talk to you since we met the other day." He scrubbed a hand over his face, unsure of how to begin. Clearing his throat, he took the half of the bottom sheet she held out to him.

"If the same group of men who held me took Mathyas," he said, meeting her eyes, afraid that what he shared would make her worry more, "he won't be in very good shape when you find him." Running a hand over his face uncomfortably, he cleared his throat and continued, "He may be nothing like the man you lost—the man you remember."

Myranda's hands balled up her section of the sheet while he spoke, and the color drained from her face. She took in a shuddering breath before speaking. "I'm perfectly aware of that possibility, Ronan."

Meeting his gaze, she gave him a sad smile and said, "But I'm also standing here with you. I see a man who survived, became a useful member of society, and was able to find love again."

Snapping the wrinkles out of the sheet, they continued making the bed. "I understand your concerns, and believe me, I also have them, but I will never give up on Mathyas until his lifeless body is in front of me."

Her eyes flashed at him as she spoke. "I need to believe he will find a way back to us because it's not just about me losing the other half of my heart. My daughter has lost a father who adored her, and I will *never* believe he would do anything less than claw his way back from hell to be with her."

Viciously shaking out the top sheet, she continued. "We had a good life. Our bond was incredibly strong, and he wouldn't abandon me—not without ending it first. I can't imagine any circumstance that would make him intentionally stay away from either of us."

Ronan hesitated a moment before responding. "Mathyas might if he believed he was protecting you, Myr. If he thought coming home would lead them back to you and Maryssa, I'm sure he would trade his freedom for your safety."

Myranda's hands shook as they finished making the bed and moved on to the last. By the time they finished, she was steadier. As they pulled the last quilt into place, she finally spoke. "I understand your concern about getting our hopes up, and I'm grateful you came to me with this. However, I beseech you not to mention any of this to Maryssa."

Ronan nodded. "You have my word. It's not my place to tell her."

"I, on the other hand, am a realist. The same thoughts have already occurred to me, but I don't have the luxury of wallowing in them. I have to believe we'll find him—or have closure of some sort. The possibility of the man I love returning home to me is what keeps me going because I can't imagine a world without him in it. Until I'm proven wrong, I won't."

Myranda walked around the bed, taking his hands in hers. "Ronan, you give me hope and help me believe in the possibilities of a reunion. I understand the odds are stacked against us. But every time I see Maddy glowing while carrying your child, I cling to the thought of his return. So, as much as I appreciate your concern, let me believe for a little longer."

Myranda's eyes filled with tears. "If I'm wrong, all of you can help me pick up the pieces and grieve, should that be our outcome. Please, give me this." Her voice wavered then.

Ronan pulled her into his arms, rubbing her back while he held her. "We will all be here for whatever you and Maryssa need. You're not alone in this, Myranda. Allow us to help shoulder this burden."

Her body shook as she released the tears she'd held back for months. Ronan let her cry, soothing her gently as she sobbed. As the storm subsided and finally passed, he released her.

Myranda wiped her face and apologized. "I'm sorry…"

"Don't be sorry, darling," he said gently. "There is no shame in allowing yourself to grieve for the time you've lost.. Tears are the soul's way of letting go and fortifying us to make it through another day."

She gave him a tremulous smile and asked, "Would you join me for a cup of tea?"

Ronan put his arm around her shoulders as they walked out to the shoppe. "I would love a cup. It's actually the reason I stopped by. I need more of the tea Rhyanna provides to help me sleep better."

"I'll set you up. Have a seat while I put the kettle on."

She moved easily around the room, gathering the supplies he needed and a tray for their tea. Pouring them each a cup, she sat opposite him at the small table by the front window. She took a sip before asking, "Is Maddy aware Fergus didn't compel you?"

Ronan jerked, and the hot beverage sloshed over the side of his dainty porcelain cup. "Yes, he confessed," drying his hand on a napkin. "I didn't think anyone else knew, not even Fergus."

"They don't," she said in a soft voice. "There was something in your eyes when you stood that told me. Fergus and Rhy focused on Maddy and the baby and didn't notice." She reached over and put a small hand over his large, scarred one. "I won't tell anyone, as long as you give me your word."

Ronan looked at her suspiciously. "What is it you want from me, Myranda?" His tone was icy, suspecting she was trying to blackmail him.

Her eyes widened at his tone, and she put her hands up in a placating manner. "No, I don't want *anything* from you, Ronan. I just wanted you to know if you need more help, you can come to me. It's obvious your past haunts you, and if I can be of any assistance with herbs, teas, or charms, please visit me."

"I'm sorry," Ronan said, grinning sheepishly. "I'm just so used to everyone having an agenda. Forgive me."

"Forgiven. But please, don't wait until your nightmares spill over into your days because I promise you, eventually, they will. The lack of sleep and the demons riding you will wear you down. They will appear as anger, frustration, or fear. I know you would never intend for it to affect Maddy or Landon."

Running his hand over his face and into his dark hair, he shook his head. "No, I don't want that."

"I'm offering you an alternative. If you don't want to go to Rhy, if you don't want anyone else here to be aware of your struggles, you can find me on the mainland. I have a shoppe there." Rifling through her bag, she pulled out a hand drawn business card with her address on it.

Ronan glanced at the card and smiled. "Ryssa make this?"

Myranda returned his grin. "Yes, she did."

"She's very talented."

"Art is her passion." She took a sip of her tea and said, "Anytime you need to talk, or if you need a new remedy, come see me, Ronan, even if it's just to visit."

She gave him a moment to process her offer. "If I suspect you're struggling and it will endanger others, my choices become limited."

Ronan watched her carefully, judging her intentions. "I appreciate the offer, Myranda, I do. I also understand the predicament it puts you in. Drugs aren't my first choice because they forced them on me too many times during my captivity. I work out my demons the old-fashioned way; I work my ass off until I'm ready to drop."

"That is one way to do it, but it can catch up with you, too."

"I'm used to it. Now I have Landon to keep me busy days," his eyes twinkled mischievously, "and Maddy to keep me busy nights."

Myranda chuckled with him, and the conversation turned to safer subjects as they finished their tea. By the time he left, she'd regained a friend, and one she was grateful to have on her side in the coming days.

Ronan's concerns about Mathyas were valid, and Myranda struggled to keep her mind on the shoppe. She was grateful it was a slow day. The unknowns circled in her mind, conjuring up images of all the horrible things Ronan endured.

As terrifying as it was to think—and she would never say it aloud, but if Mathyas was in the same place Ronan had been, it might have been better if he'd died in the desert months ago. Because no one deserved to be treated like an animal.

Mathyas would have fought with everything he had to escape, and she now knew the punishments he would have endured each time he fought. As much as she loved her man, she worried about how he could have kept his sanity under extreme duress.

Myranda liked Ronan. He'd been a student when she, Maddy, and Rhy trained together. She'd watched them fall in love, and the bond he shared with Maddy today was beautiful. But she would closely monitor him. Rhy and Maddy were too close to the situation to recognize how unstable he might be.

Even sitting here civilly drinking tea with her, she sensed he was a powder keg ready to go off. If Mathyas returned as Ronan had, would he still be the man she loved?

A shiver ran through her as she sent a prayer to the Mother. *"Mother of all, please protect my man, and help Ronan maintain the life he's so carefully rebuilt. Please don't force us to make any decisions that will destroy our friends and families."*

Horrifying as it was to consider, sometimes the kindest thing one could do for a wounded animal was to put them down.

58

FerguSyn

Fergus sat on his favorite stool at the Rusty Tap, halfway through his seventh beer. A line of abandoned shot glasses littered the mahogany surface in front of him. He smiled at them, adrift in the river of alcohol that missed his mouth. It was a slow night, but the barmaids had yet to clean up in front of him. Mayhap they figured it was a lost cause as he became messier the longer he sat there. He reached for another shot, but everyone he picked up was dry. Desperate, he contemplated licking the bottoms.

A foul mood had descended on him after his meeting with Hamish. He wanted to drown out the little prick's voice. The way the fecker went on about "pretty little things" made Fergus want to kill him.

Slamming the shot glass down in disgust, he looked around, contemplating his possibilities for companionship. The ladies were scarce tonight. Inclement weather kept many at home. Catching Carsyn's eye, he motioned in front of him for refills. She nodded in acknowledgment, then took her time working her way back around.

Fergus knew she was pacing him before he face-planted from the stool onto the floor. It had been a few years since he'd last done that, and they still hadn't let him live it down. Damn Danny and her bets to hell and back for drinking him under the table. He still thought she cheated and spiked his drinks with something much more potent than alcohol.

Carsyn finally arrived and set about cleaning up his mess.

"Lass, ye think ye can refill one of these first?" he slurred, motioning to his empties.

"No. I think you need a clean area for your next round, Ferg, darling."

"That's mighty considerate, Carsyn, but me's a mite thirsty is all," he said, looking pitiful.

She walked away and returned carrying a large mug.

Ferg gave her a grateful smile and took a deep swig, barely restraining himself from spitting it back at her. The evil wench had filled it with water.

"What the feck, lass, I thoughts we'se friends?" he sputtered.

"We are, luv, and this is how friends help friends. Bottoms up now," she said as she sauntered off. "Ye'll thank me tomorrow."

"Ye won't be thanking me when I forget to tip ye," he hollered after her.

She stopped, turned around, and came back to him, eyes flashing. "You've always been a generous man, Fergus, and I've always been grateful for that. You go right ahead and start throwing yourself a fine tantrum because I care enough to keep you from getting tossed out of here by management for an entire month. Go on then; that's alright with me. I'm used to dealing with nasty drunks, and I've already dealt with too many tonight. If you choose to do that, be sure and remember why you get nothing but watered-down beer and bottom shelf whiskey at top shelf prices for the next six months from me."

Carsyn waited, watching him in silence. "Or maybe we can talk about the bug that's crawled halfway up your ass instead of sitting there moping about it?"

Fergus looked at her through bleary eyes. He wasn't sure he was ready to confide in anyone. Carsyn was a peach. Fergus had always been fond of her, and she was always good to the wardens when they were in town. However, he didn't make it a habit to discuss his magic. If everyone knew about his premonitions and his other gifts, he would become a walking fortune teller, with everyone wanting to know what he could "see."

"I be sorry, lass. I know I be making more of an ass of meself than usual." He ran his hand over his face and through his shaggy hair, leaving it standing in crazy tufts on the top of his head. "Aw, feck me. There're things that are difficult fer me to speak of, ye ken?"

"I ken," she said as she picked up her rag and continued wiping the bar off, glancing away, giving him time to gather his thoughts or ignore her altogether.

"And then there're things we shouldn't speak of in such a crowded location." His voice trailed off as he eyed the miserable-looking man two stools down and the Tap's token prostitute off in the corner having a slow night herself. A lost soul, she was. But she was also more than willing to sell herself, her mother, or any other piece of information that might come her way.

"I'm about done for the night, Fergus. Why don't you walk me home? It's not far, and I'd rather not have to deal with the class of men on the streets this time of night by myself."

With a bleary look, he released a heavy sigh.

"I've got a very nice bottle of Irish whiskey if you're interested in a nightcap," she offered.

"Lass, ye sold me at the opportunity to walk ye home. The whiskey's jest a bonus."

"I'll get my things," Carsyn said as she turned and waved goodnight to the other bartender.

Fergus stumbled to the door. Wrestling it open, he stepped out into the cool, damp night. The pitter-patter of rain dripping off the roof from a thunderstorm earlier irritated his hypersensitive ears. His fire drakes slithered around his neck, warming him from the drop in temperature. He lit a cigar and wondered why he'd accepted her offer. His eyes traveled over the heavy fog blanketing the area, and a shiver ran down his spine.

Their relationship wasn't sexual—never had been. They'd always been good friends, and he liked a girl who'd stand up for herself, even against him. He respected it. It was because Carsyn was neutral, he decided, staring out into the thick mist that clung to the shore. She wasn't tied to the Sanctuary, and she was well-versed in discretion. The woman respected her customers and their privacy.

The door opened, and soft golden light from the barroom filtered through the gloom. Carsyn stepped out with a lightweight hooded cape to protect her from the weather. The lass was even more beautiful in the soft light. Fergus gave a deep bow and offered his arm. "Where to, me beautiful lady?" he asked, seeming much more sober than he had inside.

"To the left, kind sir," she said as she accepted his offering. They walked, content in the silence for a long way.

"Why has no one snatched ye up, lass? Ye've many interested in ye," he said as she steered them to the right at a fork in the road.

"Aye, I've many interested after one too many, or after a fight with the missus, or for those after one more notch on their belt. There's very few worth taking seriously." She paused, gathering her thoughts before continuing. "I've had my share of drunks and fools in my life. I try my best to steer clear of both if I can." Her voice held a sad note as she whispered in a voice so soft, he almost missed it, "I want more…"

"Yet yer out here walking the streets with the likes of me?" He chuckled. "So, truly, none have caught yer eye for more than a tumble?"

"Aye, one did, but I believe his heart belongs to another, even if he's not quite ready to admit it," she said, with a hint of longing in her voice.

"Jameson?" Fergus said with a raised brow. It wasn't a secret that the pair had hooked up occasionally, and to their mutual benefit, he was sure.

"Aye, he is a handsome man, a considerate lover, and an overall decent human being." Disappointment radiated from her voice, even as her demeanor was trying to play it down. "But alas, he longs for someone else,

and I can't change that. So, I enjoyed it while it lasted, and I hope someday she can make him happy."

"Ye've a bit of true seeing, don't ye, lass?"

"Not sure how true it is," she said with a tired sigh. "It's frustrating to see what you cannot change. I'd hand him my heart with a ribbon around it if I thought it would make a difference, but I see how he looks at her. It's quick, and it's confused, then it's hopeful, and he shuts it down the second he recognizes it." An ironic laugh bubbled out of her. "That's when you see him rubbing his chest right over his heart."

"Aye, lass, ye've got the right of it. Doesn't stop ye from caring or from hurting, though, does it na?"

"No, Ferg, it doesn't. I'm not one to judge others, but I just hope someday she will appreciate him and not devastate him. Their souls are tangled and broken in places. Their future is very murky, like an old bottle under the river for decades. It's dirty, scratched, and full of so much sludge mucking it up from the past that it's become fragile as if the slightest bump will shatter it." She shook her head in frustration.

"I see possibilities, and none of them are pretty for either of them. And then, just when I think their future is hopeless, I get a glimpse of hope. Their road will not be easy."

"Christ, lass, ye've just confirmed some of me own concerns and visions. Do you ever get any definite warnings of the rest of us, lass?" His eyes bore into hers, desperate to know. "If ye don't mind me asking, that is?"

Carsyn turned and faced him, her brows climbing into her hairline. "Ye've seen it too, haven't ye?"

"Ye tell me yers…" He quirked an eyebrow at her and waited.

"Ronan?" she asked, her face losing all color in the faint light at his nod. "I could be wrong. My visions aren't always correct," she said frantically, searching for an alternative.

"Aye, it happens," he said as his heart grew heavy. "Let's not worry any more about it tonight, lass. Premonitions aren't foolproof, and I refuse to dwell on what I can't change. You should, too."

Carsyn turned towards a small stone cottage set near the river. A long lane led down to the water's edge, and a small stone path led to the front door. "This is mine." Her eyes gazed at him for a long moment. "Won't ye come in and join me for a bit?" she asked softly as she held out a hand to him.

Fergus looked down at her and couldn't refuse. His large hand dwarfed hers. She was lonely, and right now, so was he. "Yer long ways from town, lass. Anyone ever bother ye way out here?"

"No. I learned how to ward my home against unwelcome guests and uninvited spirits long ago. I like my privacy, and I love being near the water.

My Grammy raised me here, and I couldn't stand to leave when she passed. She also taught me how to defend myself." A laugh burst from her. "Now, that woman could tell your future, and more than you'd want her to, about your past."

Carsyn unlatched the door. "C'mon. I'll tell you all about her. You would've liked her, Ferg—few who didn't, except for the usual heretics."

Casting a ball of witch light into the stone hearth and the lantern on the table, she took off her cloak and hung it near the hearth to dry. Fergus took off his wool coat and did the same.

Opening a small curio cabinet, she took out some fine glasses and the bottle she'd promised him. She handed it over for his inspection.

"Now, that, lass, is some damn fine whiskey. How did ye get yer hands on this bottle?"

"I've my ways, Fergus. One benefit my job provides me with is contacts on both sides of the law. I take advantage of them when needed."

"I'll keep that in mind," he said, licking his lips as she poured him a generous serving. Accepting the glass, he raised it to his nose and took a good, long sniff, appreciating the rich aroma. He took a small sip, rolling it around in his mouth before swallowing and wincing a mite as it went down. "Damn, lass, I forgot how potent this shit was." He took another healthier sip. "But it's well worth it."

"Sit," she said as she placed the bottle betwixt them on the table. "Alright, Fergus, enough about me. Stop deflecting and tell me what the hell is wrong with you tonight."

"But ye were about to tell me of yer Grammy," he said, trying to avoid this discussion.

"And I shall when we're done with this conversation." Her fierce look gave him no room to wiggle out of it. "I've known you a long time, and I've never seen you like this. What gives?"

Fergus ran his hands over his face as if seeking the answer. His hair stood up in tufts as his hands tugged through it. He scratched his beard, and his eyes traveled around the room, avoiding hers. Sighing heavily, he downed his drink and muttered, "Feck me. Guess there's no getting out of it."

She cocked an eyebrow and refilled his glass, giving him the time and space to come out with it.

"Ye've heard about the fecking nightmare we found on Grindstone?" he asked, raising an eyebrow at her.

"Rumors abound about a shipwreck full of dead girls, but none seem to know if it's true."

"It's true, lass, and as bad as ye might think it could be, it's fecking worse." He rubbed his jaw and then clenched his hands together. "One of the most horrible things I've ever seen—and I've seen a lot of shite in me

time." His face paled as he stared down at his hands, picking absently at his nails.

Carsyn placed a small hand on top of his massive ones. "You don't have to tell me if you don't want to, Ferg." Her eyes radiated sympathy when his luminous gaze met hers and quickly glanced down. "I'd like to help if I can."

She watched a tear roll down his face as he stared, unseeing, at his hands.

"They chained them to the wall like bunches of dead herbs gathered to dry. Their hands were shackled above their heads, limp bodies swaying with the movement of the boat. Their sightless eyes haunt me every fecking time I close mine to sleep. They're staring at me, accusing me of doing nothing to avenge them, nothing to stop it from happening again." His breath hitched, and it took him a moment to continue. "They won't let me fecking sleep, lass." His voice broke, and his chest heaved. The man she'd always thought of as their jester took a shuddering breath.

Stunned, she sat there for a moment, watching as his shoulders heaved. "Then fecking Jameson…" his voice was thick as he continued. "I thought the li'l shite was gonna bleed out in front of me… and when his heart stopped, I couldna stop doing chest compressions even when me arms went numb." He leaned forward, head hanging low, elbows on his knees.

Without a second thought, she stood and went to him, pulling his head to her chest and wrapping her arms tightly around him. "Shhhh. It's all right, I've got you. Just for tonight, Ferg, let it all out."

One hand rubbed circles on his back as she said, "Lean on me. Let me carry some of the pain and sorrow for you." Her hands stroked his hair where she cradled his head against her bosom, surprised by how soft the wiry mess was. She whispered into his ear, "I've got you. You're safe here, and this goes no farther than the two of us-ever."

His hands came up and banded around her waist, clinging to her like a lifeline in a winter storm. His body shook as she held him, offering the support he needed. Eventually, he pulled her onto his lap, and she allowed it, straddling him, knowing he wasn't ready to let go yet.

In time, his breathing regulated, and his tears dried. When his bloodshot eyes next met hers, they weren't bloodshot from alcohol but from the horrors he'd witnessed and the grief he'd held in.

Carsyn moved in slowly, giving him the opportunity to refuse her as she kissed his eyes and removed the traces of tears from his cheeks with her lips. They held each other for a long time before she pulled back and met his eyes once more.

Sharing his sorrows changed something between them. Gazing into his eyes, she understood him more than she ever had. She realized there was so much more behind the man than his jovial behavior, horrible fashion sense, and bad luck at betting.

Fergus was more than the pied piper the ladies followed. Carsyn knew the burdens he carried for his Sanctuary, his friends, and for all those on the river they were trying to save.

Deep down beneath all of his bullshit was a man dying to be loved for who he was. It was the same thing she kept searching for. She felt the flush roll through her as she stared into his eyes. For the first time since she'd met him, she saw him, truly saw him for the man he was.

As she got lost in the sorrow and loneliness in his eyes, flames of desire flared, mirroring hers. She felt the change in the air around them and in the way he held her. He no longer clutched her like a dying man might cling to the last shred of life. No, now his hands stroked her gently, soothing circles on her back, but going nowhere they shouldn't. Unconsciously, she moved closer to him, seeking the heat he offered and the end to the torment they were both experiencing.

His hand cupped her cheek, and his thumb wiped away the moisture she didn't know was there. "Why are ye crying, lass?"

"I'm not," she said, unable to look away from him. Her head tipped, and she squinted her eyes at him. "You're not magicking me, Ferg, are you?"

"Yes, ye are lass, and no, I'm not." His deep voice was gravelly. When his lips came down and erased the moist trails with whisper-soft kisses in the same way she had done for him moments before, she moaned. His beard brushed against her skin in an erotic caress, and she tried not to clench her thighs tighter around him. When his thumb traced her lips, he paused, looking into her eyes once more and then retreating, disappointment clouding his gaze. As his hands relaxed and released her, his rejection was like a physical blow.

Carsyn knew this opportunity wouldn't present itself again. If she turned away, he wouldn't try again. Reaching for her courage, she found her voice and asked, "Do you want me, Fergus?"

59

Rosella Diaries
Tenth Entry

Rosella staggered into the room, clawing at the neckline of the dress. "Get it off of me, get it off of me." Her voice rose as she made her way behind a screen to undress.

Shaelynn made quick work of the buttons and stays, stripping her with sure movements and handing her a long robe to put on instead.

Ella paced, biting her nails and trying to pull herself together. Hysterics weren't a luxury she allowed herself very often.

Braden had been called away as they returned, replaced by that bastard Saul, and she'd be damned before she let him see how upset she was at the moment.

"Ye want me to fetch ye some tea, milady?" Shae asked in a formal tone.

"Yes," Ella said, "and perhaps something stronger as well."

"I'll be right back, ma'am."

The second the door nicked shut, Ella regretted letting Shaelynn leave when she noticed the way Saul was leering at her.

"Yer a pretty li'l thang all cleaned up, na aintchya?"

Ella ignored him, pacing to the other end of the room and staring out the window at the churning river. The angry water mirrored her fragile emotional state.

"Don't ignore me, ye li'l cunt. Ain't nothing that makes ye any better than the rest of us. Ye's just the makings of a high-class whore."

When his voice came nearer, she reacted on instinct as his hand clamped down on her shoulder, yanking her around. Without thinking, her knee came up and caught him in the groin, doubling him over.

"Don't you ever touch me, you bastard," she spat at him. "Without a direct order, I will never touch your nasty cock again."

Face purple and breath heaving, he lurched to his feet, swaying. One hand held his swollen balls while the other supported his weight against the wall as he leaned over, gasping.

Breathing raggedly, he righted himself, then turned to Ella with such hatred that she flinched and took a step back.

Saul stalked her until he backed her against the wall, with nowhere left to run. His free hand closed around her throat. He leaned forward and whispered in her ear, "Someday yer gonna feck up and meet Mistress Pearl's wrath. When ye do, I'se gonna be the first in line to takes whatever's I wants from ye, lass."

His tongue snaked out and licked the side of her cheek. "Pretty li'l Braden won't protect ye forever. When he's on leave, who do ye think will watch ye then? Mights want to think about how's ye're treating me, lass."

Braden's voice boomed from behind him. "You're no longer needed here, Saul. They're expecting you in the galley." He kept his tone even, but Ella picked up on his irritation. Saul, on the other hand, was oblivious.

"Remembers whats I said, li'l miss," he said in a sinister whisper. Turning on his heel, he walked by Braden, staring him down the entire way.

When the door latched shut, Ella let herself react. She went to the washbasin and soaped a cloth. She wiped her cheek with rough movements of the cloth, needing every inch of him off of her. Tears streamed from her eyes as she thought of the possibility of Braden being gone and what she would do without him to protect her.

Hands on her shoulders grounded her, and she dropped the cloth into the basin before turning to him.

"Did he hurt you?" he asked at the same time she said, "When are you leaving?"

"You first," he said, stroking her cheek with his thumb.

"I'm fine. He makes me uncomfortable, and he threatened me, but he didn't touch me." A shudder ran through her. "He licked my cheek." The memory made her want to gag.

"They give us the opportunity to return home twice a year to see our families. It's optional, and most times, I choose to remain so that I can send more money home. They pay us better if we don't take our leave."

The relief crossing her face was obvious. "So, you won't be going?"

"No time soon." A hand came up to cup her cheek. "Are you all right?"

The full aspect of her looming future slammed into her. "I can't go through with this, Braden. How am I supposed to allow a complete stranger to touch me, knowing he has permission to brutalize me at will?"

A sob slipped out. "This should be my choice, a gift to a man that I care about. I can't fathom having it taken from me against my will. They just expect us to walk out there with a smile and accept our fate."

Her eyes begged him to understand. "I'm not that docile. My nature demands that I fight back, but I know that will make things worse."

His hand continued stroking her cheek. "I'll never lie to you." He let out a defeated sigh. "I've seen girls return broken in ways I'd never imagined because they fought back. Some men enjoy the challenge of breaking the strong ones more than I think they enjoy the sex."

His tormented eyes locked on hers. "Please," he whispered. "Please, don't give them a reason to torture you, Ella. I can't help you when you're there." His lips brushed against her forehead.

Ella shook her head. "I don't know that I can promise you that." Their connection calmed her. "I promise I will try to submit. That's the best I can offer."

"It's enough." His voice was tight, and she could feel the tension vibrating through his body.

The doorknob jiggled. Braden released her and hurried to open it for Shaelynn.

"Passed Saul in the hallway with a scowl like a rabid dog. He's walking gingerly, holding his balls with one hand." She set a tea tray on the small table. "Ye know anything about that?"

"No." Ella cocked an eyebrow at her. "Should I?"

"Hmm," she murmured under her breath as she poured them all a cup, added three lumps of sugar to each and then some cream.

"Not one ye want to make an enemy of, luv." Her gaze locked on Ella's. "Alls I'se saying."

"I understand," Ella told her with all sincerity. Hands shaking, she drank her tea and grabbed a cookie from the tray, praying the sugar would settle her stomach.

The future was dark and dangerous. Even though she didn't want to face what was coming, it was time for her to accept her reality and stop whimpering about her fate.

Because no matter how much she didn't want to go through with this, time was running out. Ella intended to survive the trials coming her way. She needed to so that she could make the bastards running this organization pay for the horrors they inflicted on their victims.

An hour later, she crawled into bed, grateful the day was done. As her lids grew heavy, she added another diary entry.

Dear Diary
Tenth Entry

After the horror of my first auction, I had another run-in with Saul. It is one he shan't soon forget. Caught alone with him, he put his hands and his tongue on me. It took all I had not to vomit.

I kneed him in the balls and am sure he will seek revenge the first chance he gets. He's the only person I've come across here that truly frightens me. He's always disgusted me, but I think he would defy Pearl to put me in my place, and that makes him dangerous.

And yes, I know that makes me stupid for poking the bear, but I couldn't stand his hands on me for another moment.

Braden and Shae were wonderful upon my return. I am grateful for their concern and guidance.

Sleep eludes me because every time I close my eyes, I wonder what Gemma is enduring. I hope she survives unscathed.

Rosella

60

A Crack in the Door to Me Heart

Fergus gazed at Carsyn for a moment, surprise competing with desire. "More than you ken lass, but I wouldn't ever want to ruin our friendship or fer you to have morning-after regrets."

Carsyn framed his face as she leaned in and brushed her lips over his. "I want you to kiss me, Ferg. Tonight, I want your hands on me. I want to fall asleep wrapped around you so that I know you'll get a good night's sleep, and I want to wake with you inside me once again, reassuring me I didn't just dream this up."

His gray eyes widened in surprise. The banked desire she'd glimpsed flared, and she could see tiny flames in his irises. She felt him swell beneath her thighs and she gasped at the size she felt there. Unable to stop herself, she rocked against him.

"If you don't want me, Ferg, I'll go back to my seat, and we'll finish this bottle. Then you can head on your merry way with no hurt feelings or emotional entanglements to deal with. The choice is yours, big man."

Fergus's eyes widened in disbelief. He'd wanted her since the first time he saw her, but he knew she was different and required more than what he'd been able to offer back then. His hands moved to her hips, and he pulled her tighter against him.

She gasped, surprised that he might actually take her up on her offer. His hands clasped both sides of her face in a fierce grip, and he leaned down, his lips a breath away from hers. "What happens, lass, if me wants more of an emotional entanglement?" he asked, dead serious.

"I guess we can take that one day at a time," she whispered as she met him in the middle and their lips crashed together.

Fergus kissed her with a fierceness she'd never experienced and with great finesse. He claimed her mouth as her hips writhed against him. His

311

hands traveled under her blouse, caressing her breasts through the corset she wore. He bit her lower lip, watching her expressions as he teased her nipples. Her hips moved against him in a restless roll.

"Gods, Ferg, you already have me so fucking close." A whimper escaped as she arched against him.

His left hand found its way under her skirt and pushed her panties aside, finding her slick, warm heat.

"Please, please, please," she chanted against his lips as his long fingers found their way into her body, stroking all the right places.

"Please what, lass?" he growled, making her say it.

"In me now."

"Happy to please, and even happier that I wore a fecking kilt today." Both hands grabbed her panties and ripped them off of her. She lifted enough for him to raise his kilt, and then his enormous cock was prodding her entrance.

Carsyn gasped in surprise at the actual size of him, then moaned as she took more of him. His hands on her hips stilled her. "Easy, lass. I want to take this slow."

His lips claimed hers, and as he once again mastered her mouth, her body welcomed his presence. He kept the pace painstakingly slow, loving the feel of her shuddering around him as she begged him to move. While his lips teased her, his thumb found her clit and feathered light caresses across the sensitive bundle of nerves. The onslaught of sensation had her rising again and then sinking more fully on him. She leaned her forehead against his, finally understanding his earlier reasoning. "That's it, luv, take me." His hands continued kneading her ass as he controlled the speed.

Tortuously, he lifted her until she growled at him, desperate for more. Her body shuddered around him as he filled her again. His hands guided her as she rose above him and then sank down.

"Holy fuck, Ferg, I don't know how much more of you I can take." She gasped as she gained ground, her head kicking back at the sensations they were creating.

"Trust me, lass, you're going to take a lot of me afore the morning light crawls through this window, and it will only get better." His scrawny ass stood with her impaled on his length. "Where's yer bedroom, lass?" he asked while burying his head in her neck.

"Hall... end," was all she could manage with a whimper.

He walked stiltedly toward her room. Every step jolted and rubbed her in the most erotic way. When he reached her room, he laid her out across the middle of the bed, pushing her skirt up so that he could appreciate her beautiful body. He pulled her blouse over her head and released her breasts over the top of the corset so that he could lean down and feast on them as

he withdrew and then reentered her tight sheath. Her body shuddered underneath him, trying to match his rhythm and failing to keep up.

Carsyn watched him moving over her and in her, amazed at the way he was making her feel and the way he appeared to her now. She didn't see him as scrawny or pale. His chicken legs seemed thicker and more trunk-like than normal. His features filled out more, his cheeks no longer hollowed, and his eyes, his gorgeous flame-filled eyes entranced her.

She reached up and touched his face, then lifted her upper body up to kiss him. Supported by his arms, she stared up at him, brows furrowed and said, "I don't know what's real with you, Fergus. Is this truly you, or is the other?"

"Ach, lass, it's all part of me, though this one is more than the other. Different looks suit different roles I need to play, but I promise ye, yer seeing all of me. The way I'm luving ye right now, I'm holding nothing back."

"I bet you say that to all the girls," she panted with a smile as her hips once again rose to meet his thrusts.

"You'd lose that bet, lass." His voice trailed off as his speed increased. "Aw, feck, ye feel amazing."

Fergus pulled out to her sharp cries of disappointment, then rolled her onto her stomach. Straddling her hips, his nimble fingers unlaced her corset, punctuating each move with a kiss. When she was free of her clothing, he removed his. Sitting on his haunches, he pulled her to her knees, molding her back to his front. Her head rested against his heart, her long hair tickling his thighs.

Ferg took the muscle between her shoulder and neck in a possessive bite. His massive paws banded her from behind, stroking the underside of her full breasts. Angel kisses scattered across the pale flesh. The light smattering of freckles enhanced her pale skin, and her skin flushed prettily beneath them as he pinched her nipples.

She ground her ass against him, needing him inside of her again. Unable to voice her complaints as his lips captured hers, she followed his lead as he guided her hands down to the bed. He propped her on her elbows, kissing the back of her neck and working his way down her spine. When he moved lower, he encouraged her to spread her legs wider so that he could fit between them. His fingers teased up and down her thighs, and he smiled at the tremors that followed their trails. His large palms massaged the globes of her ass as his cock strained towards her warm haven.

Sliding his cock back and forth in her moisture, he coated his length before reentering her. Carsyn sucked in a breath as he breached her, then moaned as he moved half his length in and out of her. As her hips pushed

back, seeking more, he bent over her shoulder and whispered, "Feel good, lass?"

"Gods, yes," she panted.

"Ready fer more?"

In answer, she slid to his tip, then all the way back down, slowing when she reached the base of him.

"Wait," she whimpered, "just a moment."

"Take all the time ye need, luv. Ye set the pace and take as much or as little as ye want." His hands stroked over her back, soothing her with his touch. "Feck me, but ye feel amazing, twitching around me jest the way ye are, Syn."

"Why'd ye call me that?" While she waited for an answer, she raised up off his cock, then descended and repeated the motion several times, each time slower than the last.

"Because anything that feels this good must be a Syn, luv," he growled at her as she ground down flush against him again.

"Bet ye say that to all the girls, too," she gasped.

He grasped her hips and stopped her momentum. Bending flush against her back, he set his teeth into her shoulder then said, "No, lass, I don't. I can promise ye that. And there aren't as many others as ye might think. Many a time, I jest see them to their door with a suggestion of what might have happened while I was there. I rarely sleep with them, but don't tell anyone. I've a reputation to keep intact."

"Is that what this will become in the morning—a suggestion or dream that I had?"

The sadness in her voice destroyed him. Fergus pulled out of her, turning her to face him. He captured her face between his meaty palms. "That's not anything like what this is, lass, not by a long shot. I don't want to be just a dream to ye, lass."

"What is this, then?"

"I don't know yet, but I'm willing to see where it takes us if ye are."

She kissed him soft and slow in answer and then more fiercely as she climbed his body, wrapping her legs around his waist.

"I'm willing. Now fuck me, Ferg."

"Yes, ma'am," he murmured as he laid her down and held her hands over her head with one of his. With the other, he pulled one leg up and around his hip to change the angle as he seated himself inside of her welcoming heat. With each thrust, he increased his tempo, challenging her body to accept him.

Carsyn met him thrust for thrust, each time harder than the last. Her body's response allowed him to unleash his control. Releasing her hands, he grabbed her hips, pulling her against him as he pounded into her. His thumb

found her clit throbbing and begging for attention. Moments later, she screamed his name while her inner walls squeezed him tightly.

A satisfied grin crossed his face, glad she'd found her release—her first one, at least. Her voice was ragged as he pulled out and flipped her back to her stomach, intending to finish in this position. She had such a fine ass, and he wanted to watch it as he buried his cock inside of her.

The night was just starting, and he had no intention of stopping until they were both limp with exhaustion and delirious with pleasure. His massive hand lightly slapped her ass as he growled, "Hang on, lass. Time for a real ride."

Hours later, when both of their bodies quivered from exhaustion, he pulled her close, her head resting over his heart. He pressed a soft kiss to her forehead and felt her smile against his skin. Her arm lay across his chest, and her leg over his hips, teasing his semi-hard cock. A cocky smile appeared because he knew when the first rays of sun came through the window, he would honor her request and be inside of her when she woke. He wouldn't be able to help himself.

"Sleep, Ferg. I've got you tonight," she said in a voice hoarse from screaming his name. "I won't let nothing bad keep you from sleeping, luv."

Carsyn's hand traced patterns over his chest, tangling in the wiry hair. It soothed him, and his eyes struggled to stay open and enjoy it. The feel of her in his arms and the smell of her on his skin were potent, and he wanted to remember every nuance of this.

His hand stroked the length of her blond hair as he held her tighter, trying not to notice the tug in his chest at her words. The past month had reminded him of the fragility of life, and there was a large part of him that was fecking terrified of feeling anything for this woman, or any woman. But after tonight, he knew he wouldn't be able to keep himself closed off from her for long.

This sweet woman had just found a crack in the door to his heart without really trying, and it wouldn't take much for that crack to rip wide open, welcoming her in. And if she broke through all of his defenses, where would he be then?

61

Never Want Someone Ridden so Many Miles

The sun in her eyes woke Maryssa earlier than usual. Languidly stretching, she went over the first day in her mind. Overall, it hadn't been as bad as she'd expected. Except for Collette's nasty comment, she had actually enjoyed herself.

The relief of having Willow and Amberly along for the ride made all the difference in her attitude. With them nearby, it was like an extended slumber party. Each of their rooms were so different, they could change their environment with a visit down the hall.

Blinking into the light, her eyes traveled around the four walls of her room. Spacious, it held everything she held dear—everything that would help her find peace when she needed it, except for the people she missed.

A thump from next door had her glancing at the wall she shared with Collette. When they'd returned after the evening bonfire, Collette found a thick mattress on the floor with a soft white duvet on top. Her surprised shriek brought the others running.

"I can't believe it worked," she said to herself in awe, glancing at Ryssa, then looking away quickly as she flushed in shame.

"It's sad that being kind is such a foreign concept to you," said one of the new girls. She was from a clan north of them, near the Arctic. Black hair touched her shoulders, and blunt bangs hung over her guileless dark ebony eyes. She didn't intend her comment to be rude; it was just an observation. "We're raised from toddlers to put others' happiness ahead of our own." Tipping her head, she considered this and said, "I assumed it was that way everywhere."

Collette looked fit to be tied. This newcomer had innocently called her on her behavior, and Ryssa imagined she was biting back a retort. Collette glanced over her shoulder at the mattress on the floor and took a deep

breath before pasting a smile on her face and trouncing into her room. If she slammed the door harder than was necessary, no one pointed it out.

"Did I say something wrong?" the young woman asked, glancing at the group of girls with Ryssa.

"No," Amberly piped up. "She's just not used to having anyone call her on her inappropriate behavior. Little Miss Queen Bee was just put in her place by pure common sense and needs to dust herself off before we can be in her presence again."

"Why is everyone ganging up on her?" Chantal asked, clenching her fists. "She's not always like this."

Ryssa was close enough that she could see little sparks dancing in Chantal's eyes, making her volatile until she had control over her minor element.

"She might not treat you like this," Amberly said, "but this is all we've known of her."

"Maybe if she had just once offered any of us kindness," Willow said softly, "we could be more sympathetic to her." She gestured towards Ryssa and Amberly. "We've been her target for so long that it's a mite difficult to want to stand up to or for her. You don't know what it's like feeling like an outcast."

Chantal's eyes swept over Willow from head to toe before speaking in a scathing tone. "Well, maybe if you did something with your frizzy hair and found some clothes that gave you some shape, we would see you."

Gasps rang out down the hall until Chantal's door lit up with a dark red glow. Chantal's mouth dropped open as she mouthed, "No." Running across the hall, she slammed her hand on the wall and pushed the lever. Horror crossed her face as she found her furs missing and only half the bioluminescent moss glowing. Her fiery gaze settled on their group again. "We'll all make mistakes here. I doubt we'll be the only ones punished."

"Being mean isn't a mistake, Chantal," Ryssa said softly. "It's a choice."

A bell rang, signifying they had only fifteen minutes before lights out, effectively ending the conversation.

Reflecting on it in the morning light, Ryssa wondered how much worse their attitudes could get before the summer was over. She cringed, thinking about it.

She performed her morning ablutions and dressed for the day. The uniform was very basic. Blue leather breeches with a matching shirt and brown vest were comfortable enough. Ryssa braided her hair into a fishtail braid over one shoulder, banding it with a piece of leather. Glancing at the clock, she only had ten minutes to make it to the dining hall. She peeked at her schedule and saw she needed to be at the Apothecary Shoppe with

Mistress Rhyanna until lunchtime. A smile crossed her face as she looked forward to this session.

A cacophony of chattering teens accosted her as she stepped into the dining hall. Her friends sat at the table they used yesterday. Ryssa poured a cup of tea and joined them.

The breakfast offerings were as delectable as lunch and dinner the day before. Ryssa chose a hot pastry filled with eggs and sausage and a bowl of fruit to break her fast. The first bite of the pastry made her roll her eyes with delight. Fluffy and light, the pastry housed perfectly seasoned eggs smothered with cheddar. Starving, she finished it and reached for a chocolate puff pastry.

Half awake, she listened to the other girls chattering.

"Will Kai be joining you this morning?" Willow asked Genny.

"I doubt it. Mornings are busy for him. He checks the perimeter of the island and swims with the otters."

"That's my favorite thing in the world," Willow said, clasping her hands together in delight. "We have an otter family in the river near us. We often join them."

"I'm jealous," Amberly said. "I have little time to swim," she took a bite of her toast, then added, "and I'm not very good at it. I can barely keep myself above water."

They all chuckled at that. A bell sounded, urging them to head for their classes. "Where are you off to?" Ryssa asked the girls.

"Fire," said Amberly.

"Water," said Willow.

"Earth with Mistress Rhyanna," said Genny.

"Well, it appears we all start our week with our clan element," Ryssa said. She glanced at Genny and said, "I'm heading that way, too. Want to walk together?"

Genny's face lit up, and she nodded her head. "I would like that."

They cleared their plates and headed for the door, saying goodbye to Willow and Amberly when the path forked.

"Have you learned anything about our element?" Genny asked. "I mean, has your clan worked with you?"

"Had little choice," Ryssa said with a laugh. "My mother is a healer, and I've been by her side in the garden since I could walk."

"Oh," Genny said, deflating a little. "I've never worked with anyone other than Rhy. I hope I'm not too far behind."

Ryssa glanced at her and couldn't miss the anxiety she was experiencing. "I doubt that. My situation was unique. Most have learned very little. I'll be happy to help you if you feel the need to catch up in any area."

"Thank you. I may need to take you up on your offer," Genny said, giving her a brilliant smile. "Thank you for reaching out to me yesterday. It was awkward not knowing anyone here."

"I'm glad I did, too. I think we're all going to become great friends. Amberly and Willow are really nice. You'll love them when you get to know them."

"I already like them." Genny laughed, "I love Amberly's sense of humor and Willow's fashion sense."

Ryssa smiled at that. Willow's fashion had a sense of its own, but it always suited her, regardless of what anyone else thought.

The Shoppe door was open when they arrived. By the time Mistress Rhyanna walked in, there were a dozen students waiting—eight girls and four boys.

Ryssa glanced around, recognizing one of the young men, Galen Hill, from their village. Galen was tall for his age, with broad shoulders and narrow hips. Blond, wavy hair fell across his forehead in soft curls, partially obscuring his piercing blue eyes. When his eyes met hers, he nodded in acknowledgment.

Mistress Rhyanna stood in the middle of the room, gazing at the youth gathered in her shoppe. "A good morning to ye all. I'se trusting yer first night here wasn't too traumatic," she said. "For those new to this region, me name be Mistress Rhyanna, and this be me shoppe and clinic. Should ye have need of a healer, me door be always open. If I be out, the bell by the door will alert me to yer need, and someone will be here momentarily."

"Some of ye be here for yer mandatory training, some are making up for training they've missed, and others be here because yer powers are manifesting early. Whatever the case, yer all in this together. I expect ye to help each other in this class. I'll tolerate no unkindness under me roof nor inside me garden gates. Is this clear to all of ye?"

Mistress Rhyanna waited for them all to nod. With that out of the way, a beautiful smile lit up her face, and she clapped her hands together in front of her chest. "I've introduced meself. Now, let's take a moment to introduce yerselves. First names, town yer from, and if yer beginning to manifest your birth element."

They took turns going around the room as instructed. Ryssa counted four who had already begun manifesting, two who were unsure, and six who hadn't yet. Ryssa, Genny, and Galen were all in the not-yet group.

"Let's head through the clinic and out the back into me garden for our first lesson," Rhy said, leading them through a door. Halfway through the clinic, she turned and faced them. "This clinic serves the island and the people who call this part of the St. Lawrence their home. For those of ye who present healing abilities, ye will spend some of yer time here. This will

give ye the opportunity to fully understand the responsibilities and options available should ye choose to become a healer."

"Follow me," Mistress Rhyanna said, leading them from the room. Outside, they followed a flagstone path to the garden behind the shoppe. A wrought-iron gate led into the lush botanical display.

Orderly beds full of flowers, herbs, and healing plants of all kinds competed with ornamental kale and other fruits and vegetables. The visual display was stunning. Stepping stones led between the beds to a circle of grass in the center. Black pots stood equidistance around the perimeter, holding various saplings.

Rhyanna stepped into the center and said, "Pick a plant that appeals to ye for this exercise. We're going to learn what energy feels like." Waiting until everyone had claimed a pot, she said, "Take off yer shoes, and plop yer arse on the grass."

Ryssa removed her boots and sat down on the ground. Shoes made her feel stifled, and she was grateful for the opportunity to let her feet soak in the regenerative powers of the earth. Genny sat between Ryssa and Galen. A young man to Ryssa's right lowered himself to the ground more gracefully than she would have imagined for his size. Tall and muscular for his age, he had the grace of a cat.

Dark brown eyes caught her gaze, and he smiled, showing dimples on either side of his cheeks. Offering a hand, he said, "I'm Tobias, from Wellesley."

"Maryssa from Clayton. Nice to meet you," she said, shaking his hand. His grip was firm, and she could feel the callouses on his hand. This boy was used to working. His long dark hair had auburn highlights from being in the sun.

"Place your hands on the grass beside ye, palms down," Mistress Rhyanna said as she walked through the inner circle facing them. "Close yer eyes and sense the power of the earth beneath ye. Feel the blades of grass beneath yer fingers teeming with life, and the dirt neath the grass, warm from the sun."

Rhyanna's voice trailed off as she moved away from Ryssa. Her voice was melodious as she continued instructing them. She soothed them with sound and helped to wipe the distractions from their mind by giving it something to focus on.

"Take a deep breath and fill yer lungs with the fresh air. Release it slowly and let yer shoulders relax. Sense the power of the earth beneath ye. Pay attention to the place where yer body comes in contact with the plane we exist on. Notice the pressure of yer body where it comes in contact with the grass and the way the earth always supports ye. Continue taking deep breaths and feel the rhythm of the Mother's song as she speaks to us through the ground."

Ryssa smiled as her soul connected with the earth and the Earth Mother. Palms throbbing, she could distinctly feel the energy radiating through the crust of the earth to the grass beneath her palm, and then into her. Acknowledging the energy, she could sense the health of the plant life beneath her hand.

"As ye feel the energy the earth is sending ye, imagine sharing it with the plant before ye. See the cells of the plants soaking in that energy and thriving even more than they were when ye arrived," Rhyanna said in a soft voice. "Picture the energy in yer mind as a living moldable thing and then envision sharing it."

As her voice trailed off, Ryssa imagined her mother walking through their garden and touching the plants before her. Myranda's touch helped limp, wilted stalks stand straight, and flowers on the edge of dying last another day or two.

"Raise yer hands from the ground, palms up, then imagine cutting the energy between ye with a crystal knife in yer mind's eye. Place the knife down, then rub yer hands together and place them over yer heart chakra to absorb the beautiful energy received."

Eyes closed, Ryssa could still feel the moment Mistress Rhyanna walked past her. The hair on her arms stood up as the powerful Earth Mage moved in front of her.

"Take another deep breath and open yer eyes."

Ryssa heard gasps and excited giggles as she opened her eyes. Eyes wide, she realized her plant had grown nearly a foot with her help. A glance around the circle told her that wasn't the case for everyone.

Genny looked horrified as she gazed at a plant so dried beyond recognition that Ryssa was sure it would crumble if you touched it. Galen didn't fare much better. A dark green fungus covered his plant.

Tobias's had neither grown nor withered. It remained in the same condition it started in. The results were split into thirds. Rhyanna was quiet as they examined their attempt.

After a few moments, their instructor stopped in front of Genny. Gazing down at the timid young woman, she gave her a wink. Mistress Rhyanna knelt before her, cupping her hands on either side of the stick, and moments later, the plant was once again healthy. As she moved around the circle, healing the damaged foliage, she spoke.

"Contrary to what ye might believe right now, ye were all successful." She waited for the shocked looks and whispers to die down. "I asked ye to send energy to the plants before ye, and ye did."

Genny and Ryssa exchanged confused looks.

"Who kens why ye were all successful?"

321

Tobias raised his hand, speaking after her nod, "Because you didn't specify what kind of energy to direct to the plant. Not sure which to use, I sent equal degrees of both."

"Exactly!" Mistress Rhyanna said, clasping her hands together in front of her. "Pushing energy will give ye the results similar to Ryssa's plant and several of the others. Pulling energy results in…"

Genny raised her hand, "A dead stick."

"Well, na, not dead, but definitely not at peak health."

"Every one of ye channeled energy. I saw it and felt it as well. There are proper times for their usage, which ye shall learn about in yer journey through this class."

Galen's hand shot up. "If I may, Mistress?" He waited for her to acknowledge him before continuing. "When would we need to destroy the life force in anything? And why did mine grow something that would damage it?"

"Excellent question, Galen," Rhy said, picking up a large plant that sat in the center of the circle. Within seconds, the leaves wilted, drooped, and then withered on the stalk. "I can draw the energy from this plant," she pointed to a tree next to the circle, "trees, bushes, and even the grass beneath yer feet."

Following her words, everything she mentioned wilted instantly. The grass was dry and brittle beneath their hands and feet. "The only time we borrow energy from anything is when someone direly needs aid. AND we always promise to return and heal what we've injured."

Gracefully dropping to her knees, she placed her palms on the crunchy grass and chanted,

"With air all around us,
and the soil beneath,
With heat from the sun,
and water from underground springs.

"I return what I borrowed,
with a blessing and sigh,
Giving more than I took
before saying goodbye."

When Rhyanna stood, the grass was lusher, and the tree and bush fully revived. "In Galen's case, he sent energy, but there was already a hint of a fungus on his plant. He didn't focus the energy on what he wanted to enhance. So, everything was affected. A harmful organism grows much quicker under the right circumstances."

A round, dark-haired girl raised her hand. "Is it possible to take too much?"

"Aye, it's possible to overextend, and that can harm ye as well as the living thing yer drawing from." Several short paces around the circle brought her in front of the girl. "Ye must never go beyond what ye can repair, or the cost will be yers to pay. Nature will take its price. Ye can be sure of it."

"Have ye ever gone too far?" A thin boy with a pinched face asked.

"Aye, and not too long ago it was. I paid with my health for quite a while until my fellow earth sisters healed me." The solemn look on her usually cheerful face convinced them she wasn't telling a faery story. "Had me fellow healers not been available, me skin would still be wrinkled, and me hair half gone white. If yer not careful and prepared, it very well might kill ye."

"For the next week, we'll work on fine-tuning our power and the ways in which we may use it. I want ye to think about how it felt when ye were doing this exercise. Were ye pushing or pulling from yer energy stores? If ye were pulling from the plant, ye weakened it. Next time ye will try to send energy to the plant for it to store in times of drought or damage." She beamed at them. "Ye've done well today. Go on and head off to yer next class."

Mistress Rhyanna took her time walking around the circle, speaking with each student as she passed. She gave each of them encouragement and compliments as she spoke. Ryssa watched her closely. Not once did she utter a negative word.

Ryssa waited for her for a moment after everyone else headed for the shoppe. Rhyanna gave her a big hug and asked, "How are ye holding up, lass?"

"So far, so good. We've been busy, so that helps."

"It does. Don't forget to come find me if yer ever in need of company. I see ye've befriended our Genny. I'm glad. Ye lasses will be good for each other."

"I really like her," Ryssa said with a wide smile. "She's quiet and unsure of herself." Her voice was sad.

"Aye, she's been through a lot in a short period. Lass be well on her way to getting over it, but it's na been easy. She'll be mighty grateful for some new friends."

"She's found some. Willow and Amberly really like her, too. I'm glad for that..."

"Someone giving her problems?" Rhy asked with a sharp edge to her voice. Ryssa could tell how much she cared about the girl.

"Nye, nothing too badly yet. Collette is a spoiled brat, but Genny handled it well."

"I'll trust ye to let me know if it's too much."

"Promise."

"Ye best get on yer way, don't want to be late na."

"See you tomorrow."

"Aye, lass. Til then," Rhyanna said, ushering her out the door.

Ryssa walked down the steps just in time to hear Genny speaking with Kai.

"So, I'll see you this afternoon before dinner?" he asked, his deep voice eager.

Genny's face lit up with joy. "Aye, I'm looking forward to it."

Kai walked away, but not before Collette's voice pierced the air. "I found out all about your sordid past this morning, Genevieve. The boys on the dock told me about your adventures. You're nothing but used trash from the wrong side of the river."

Rage spiraled through Ryssa as Genny's face lost all color, and she gasped. Ryssa's gaze fell on Kai, who stopped and was listening as Collette spoke.

Collette tossed her hair over her shoulder and gazed down her nose at Genny. "A prince of the court will never want someone who's already been ridden so many miles. You'll be like an old nag no one wants anymore. Prince Kai will get bored before long, and you'll be put out to pasture."

Ryssa's mouth dropped open as she searched for words to defend a devastated Genny. It was bad enough that Collette did this in front of them and with their other classmates listening nearby. Worse yet, Kai stood there with his fists clenched, hearing the whole thing.

Tears filled Genny's eyes, but she straightened her shoulders and lifted her chin as she faced her bully. "You may be right. He might want nothing to do with me, and that's his choice. But I can guarantee you this. He will have nothing to do with you, whether or not I'm in the picture. Kai will never be with someone as petty and mean as you are. You might be beautiful on the outside—that's all a matter of taste. But on the inside, where it really counts, you're ugly, Collette, and there's no getting past that flaw or covering it up with makeup or money."

Genny stepped away, but not before throwing one more barb over her shoulder, "Thank you for telling everyone about my past. Now I don't have to worry about them finding out." Her eyes met those gathered around. "What happened to me wasn't my choice or my fault. I won't apologize nor feel shame for it. Think what you will."

Head held high and fighting tears, she turned to leave and was stunned to find Kai waiting with his hand outstretched, reaching for her. "Walk with me?" he asked with a gentle smile. His eyes told another story as she stepped towards him and put her hand in his. He pulled her close, under his shoulder, before facing the crowd gaping at them.

Kai's eyes were molten blue fire as he pinned Collette with a glare and said, "Don't presume to know anything about me or what I want."

His gaze traveled around the entire crowd before saying, "Genny's under my protection. I will tolerate no one speaking to her like that again. Am I understood?" His eyes pierced Collette's. She dropped her gaze and mumbled, "I'm sorry," under her breath before gathering her cronies and slinking away.

Kai tugged gently on Genny's hand and asked, "Are you ready to go?" Genny nodded, needing to escape the rest of the gawking teens.

As they walked away, Willow fanned herself and sighed. "Oh my, that was so romantic."

"My gawd, he's hot," Amberly uttered. "He just staked his claim."

"Put your tongue back in your mouth, ladies. He's definitely got eyes for someone else. Lucky her," Ryssa said in a wistful tone.

Galen and Tobias shook their heads. Galen quirked a brow. "I'm glad he stood up for her. I was just about to say something, but Genny was holding her own."

"Collette has always been a bully," Tobias said. "Ain't about to change now."

"No," Ryssa said, "She won't. Her good behavior lasted less than twenty-four hours. I just hope she doesn't ambush her with anything else."

"'Twon't tolerate it if she does." A sharp voice came from behind them. Mistress Rhyanna stood there, eyes spitting fire. "Ye all get on to yer next class and don't let me hear you gossiping about what you overheard. I guarantee she'll think twice before messing with Genny again."

They walked away, following the others who'd gathered to watch the show. "That's one healer I wouldn't want mad at me," Ryssa said, garnering four nods of agreement.

62

Sea Dogs, River Rats, and Busty Barmaids

Kenn Tyde sidled into the Rusty Tap wearing his version of the monkey suit required to represent the Court of Tears. The actual formal attire was head-to-toe turquoise and black velvet. Black was his favorite color—but in fucking velvet? Hell would freeze before that happened. The icing on the shit cake that made it even worse was they topped it off with lace fringes on the neck and sleeves. That made it a hard NO for him.

Black leather breeches fit his muscular body like a glove, leaving nothing to the imagination. A turquoise silk button-down was the only splash of courtly color he wore. The black studded collar around his neck matched the studded vest he wore over the shirt. In cooler weather, he would have finished his ensemble with a long, worn, black—of course—leather duster, but it was June.

As his eyes adjusted to the smokey gloom of the bar, he perused the clientele. Sailors just into port were getting rowdy at the corner table. Barflies and day drunks were in their usual rickety, wooden stools at the bar. Individual ass prints dimpled the thin leather covering their seats like a label.

Sweet little delectable Carsyn lingered too near the fire mage he sought. Fergus's eyes traveled possessively over the woman in a way only a water element would pick up on. He tasted the thick tang of lust between the new lovers. Thank fuck his elemental gifts saved him a shit ton of time and effort when picking his fuck buddies.

Goddamn, Fergus Emberz was fucking Syn on a stick. *"Kudos to him"*, Kenn thought jealously. Tipping his head, he examined them on the auric field. His brow lifted in surprise to see how well they fit. Her heartache over young Jamey was healing well, and Fergus's hollow spot was brighter and healthier than Kenn had witnessed in a long time.

A psychic slap from Ferg told him to mind his own business, making Kenn chuckle darkly. Joining the man at the bar, he ordered a drink and one for Ferg as an apology.

"Too fecking early for ye to be that rude, laddie," Ferg drawled, removing the cigar that dangled from his lips and tapping the ash into a glass tray. "For that matter, it's too fecking early for ye to be seeing the sun."

Ferg gave him a look that should have curled his short hairs, but Kenn loved riding the razor's edge. Giving him a cocky grin, he said, "I'se just checking on the lass after Jamey broke her heart. Couldn't help but see your ties. I'd high-five you, but then she'd think you kiss and tell."

"I ain't toldchya a fecking thing, you arse," Ferg said with a glare as he inhaled the pungent smoke.

"Of course not, but you're well aware of what I speak."

"Ifn's yer so worried about the lass, why ye got yer sticky little fingers in me business?"

"Just followed the trails and couldn't help but notice the improvement," Kenn said with a saucy grin.

"Are ye me fecking therapist, na?"

"Fuck no, man. My kind of therapy wouldn't work on a stubborn prick like you."

"Thank fecking god," Ferg said, and they both chuckled. "Whatchya doing up this early, night walker?"

Kenn grinned at the nickname. "Got to get sign-ups started for the poker tournament. Solstice is not far off, and there's plenty to be done prior to it."

"Ye find the fecker yet?"

"This is my first stop." Kenn gazed around the room surreptitiously. "He ain't here." He chugged his whiskey. "Hmm, thought this would be one of the best places to pin down the little bastard."

"Probably not after Maddy handed him his ass and threatened him," Ferg said, drawing hard on his cigar. He held it until his lungs burned, then blew the smoke in the prince's face.

Kenn ignored him, wrapping his knuckles on the bar surface to get Carsyn's attention. She finished pulling a beer from the tap, then took payment from the cash on the bar before sauntering their way.

"Morning, Kenn," she said with a wide smile.

Kenn gave her a grin that would have gotten him almost any woman he wanted. "Why hello, sweetness," he said as he leaned over the bar to kiss her cheek. Wasn't the first time he'd done it, but hearing Fergus growl made it ten times more fun. "Seeing you makes it worth being up at the ass crack of dawn."

She returned his grin and then glanced at Fergus. "What can I get you boys?"

"Whiskey on the rocks and make it a double," Kenn said, tossing more cash on the bar. He motioned to the rest of the room. "And buy my fellow day drinkers a round on the Court of Tears."

His eyes followed her hips as she wandered down to the end of the bar. Fergus's hand connecting with the back of his head smarted, but he'd been expecting it when he antagonized him.

"Keep yer eyes off her arse before I kick yers out the fecking door."

"I'm more of a tit man, Ferg, so I'll save my lascivious looks for when she works her way back down here." He sucked back his whiskey, trying not to spray it from his nose when he saw the flames in Fergus's eyes get bigger. Fire drakes, Ferg's li'l pets, ran up and down his forearm, hissing at Kenn.

"Call off yer wee lizards, now, Ferg." Kenn said, "I don't want to drown any of the little buggers this early in the day."

Carsyn picked up a metal striker and beat it on the side of a cowbell that hung at the end of the bar. "Next round is courtesy of the Court of Tears and Prince Kenn at the end of the bar." The bar erupted in mugs thumping on tables and hoots of thanks from the regulars.

Kenn stood and walked to the middle of the room, working with his audience. "Listen up, all you crusty old sea dogs, river rats, dock workers, and fellow day drinkers." He waited for the noise to die down. "King Varan wants to show his appreciation to the working men on the St. Lawrence."

Having their full attention, he continued, "Rumor has it the king is a gambling man, and that rumor would be accurate. The man loves a game of poker or a decent challenge at the pool table."

He heard murmurs of agreement and glasses raised to the king's choice of games and his generosity. "The summer solstice is nearly upon us, and King Varan is hosting a tournament at the Court of Tears for any man interested. Sign-ups are free, and the Court will spot every participant fifty dollars to play." Excited rumbles echoed around the bar.

"Official sign-ups will be at Court this weekend. No one may enter the games without going through official clearance. A ferry will be at the docks for transportation if needed. Just let Carsyn know to add you to the list." He winked at her as she caught his eye and ignored Fergus's glare.

"Make sure and tell all the heavy rollers you know. King Varan will play in the final round. Let's make it a challenge for him this year. Get the word out to Sea Dog Sal, Fisher Jordan, Rum Running Roarke, and any other card sharks you can think of. The prizes are heaps of gold. As a bonus, the winner will enjoy the Court of Tears' hospitality for an entire week."

Voices rose as they excitedly talked about the upcoming tournament. Kenn grinned, knowing the word would get out quickly before the day was over. "Drinks are on me while I'm here, but remember to tip the girls well for the extra work they're doing today."

Kenn worked his way around the room, shaking hands and reassuring them that the tournament wasn't a poor joke on his end. If he mentioned bonuses for any high rollers encouraged to sign up, no one would care. The promise of easy cash was always the best way to a working man's heart.

Finally, making his way back to Ferg, he found a refill waiting. Tossing it back, he winked at Carsyn. "Think it will work?" he asked Fergus.

"Me thinks some of these men be desperate enough to make sure 'twill work."

Kenn raised his glass and tapped Fergus's in salute. "Here's to salty ole sea dogs, rum-running river rats, and busty barmaids." Without glancing at Ferg, he tossed his drink back and clamped Ferg on the back.

"Carsyn is a damn fine woman, Fergus. I know you will appreciate her more than most. I'm happy for you both," he said with all sincerity.

"Thank ye, Kenn. Not sure what I did to deserve her, but I'm going to do me best to make her happy."

"All you can do, my man," Kenn said, trying not to notice the ache settling in the expanse of his chest where his heart should be. He'd often wondered if he'd been born with one.

Part of him wanted desperately to have a partner he cared about as passionately as Ferg did Syn. Another part of him wondered if there was a person out there who could ever accept all his dark ways. Could they love him with all his sexual predilections and his lack of empathy?

This was the question he could never honestly answer. If the situation were reversed, would he be able to accept a partner he had to share with the Court, with his family, and with other lovers? Was there anyone out there who could deal with that and meet his dark needs?

"Fuck it," he thought. He had too many bodies to enjoy to even think of settling down. The variety his lifestyle offered suited him, and he had absolutely no intention of changing it now.

Shaking off his somber mood, he clinked his glass on the bar and waited for a refill with a smile on his face, a twinkle in his eyes, and a hole in his chest where his heart should be.

63

Spoiled Lil Bitches

Danyka stood in the shadows of the garden, listening to Collette humiliate Genny. Blood boiling, she was just about to step in when Genny straightened her spine and stood up for herself. Danyka was so damn proud of her; she could've danced a jig.

Since her arrival, Genny had been their meek little mouse. Danny understood why she was that way, but it made her crazy watching her apologize constantly and duck her head when she thought she'd offended someone.

The friendship blossoming between Genny and Kai was good for her. Whether he realized it or not, Kai had just staked a claim. Danny couldn't be happier. The youngest of the Tyde princes, he was the kindest and gentlest of them all. He was older than Genny, but that child had aged well beyond her years while in captivity. They would be good together someday. Danny knew Kai well enough by now to know he wouldn't rush things with her, and she was grateful Genny had found someone like him as a champion.

His patience reminded her of Jameson, and not wanting to go there right now, she allowed her anger full reign as the three li'l bitches stormed by where she stood.

"You didn't have the sense the Mother gave you to take me seriously when last we spoke, didchya?" Danny asked, stepping in front of them.

Collette paled considerably, and the other two looked down their perfect, aristocratic noses at her. Blaze scoffed, and Chantal looked Danny up and down and said, "We don't have self-defense training now. We're on our way to lunch."

"You don't think I have the authority to turn your day into a shit show? That's what you are saying?"

Chantal's eyes widened, but she didn't back down. "What I am saying is that I think you're crass, uneducated, and dress inappropriately for your

330

position." Her eyes took in Danny's bosom-hugging, red, leather vest and painted-on leather breeches.

Danny's jaw clenched, and her eyes narrowed. "Well, honey, I take that as a compliment." The leash on her barely controlled rage was unfurling. "Lunch today is that way," she said, pointing toward the pit. "Mrs. O'Hare is packing your lunches and having them delivered. Unfortunately, you won't get to enjoy them until after I'm done with the three of you."

The three girls gaped at her until Danny snapped, "Get your asses to the pit right now! You're holding up my noon meal now, and it ain't pretty when I haven't eaten."

Noses in the air, the trio headed for the pit, but they took their sweet time. Wishing she had a hellhound for a pet to chase the wretches, she took matters into her own hands.

Tapping into her primary element, Danny channeled gale-force winds and focused them in a steady stream behind the young women. The controlled burst didn't bother anyone else, but it forced the girls to pick up their pace or get knocked flat on their faces. When they reached the berm of the pit, she increased the force, knocking them to the ground and rolling them down the hill. It was her reminder to them that her elemental power didn't give a shite about what clan family you came from or how much money your daddy had.

Power needed to be controlled by the user, or it would consume you from the inside out. Danny was in perfect harmony with her element, and she was in a bitchy mood, all of which boded ill for them but promised to help her blow off some steam.

The girls landed in a heap in the pit's bowl, as three staffs clattered to the ground in front of them.

"Pick them up," Danny said, grabbing her favorite bo. It was one that Jamey had hand-carved for her. Made of oak, he'd carved falcons in between the runes and symbols covering it for protection. The carving was faint enough to prevent interference when using it as a weapon, but it was beautiful to behold. Ferg magicked it with just enough weather proofing to protect the delicate carvings. This gift meant more to her than almost any other she'd received as an adult.

Twirling it at lightning speeds, she circled the girls. "Pick them up." Her voice was cool, demanding they respond.

"This isn't fair," Blaze whined. "We did nothing wrong."

"Exactly," Danny said scathingly. "You did nothing, and that's why you're joining her here."

"There were dozens who didn't step in," Blaze wailed. "Are they going to be punished, too?"

"You are Collette's best friends," Danny said, circling closer. "You stood behind her, supporting her claim."

The girls stood there, stunned into silence.

"In the dining hall, you stood up to her and called her on her bullshit," Danny continued. Her staff stopped spinning, and she slammed it in front of them, making them all jump. "You best pick one up because the next strike I make will be against one of you. You're going to want something to defend yourselves with."

They scrambled to obey as Danny explained their punishment to them. "Today, you stood there and smiled while she tore a sweet young woman's already fragile self-worth to shreds. Collette shattered her reputation and the self-esteem she has been fighting so hard to regain. You can't imagine what it cost her to stand up to you."

"Well, then she ought to thank me for helping her," Collette said in a snarky tone.

Whap, Danny's staff hit Collette's fingers, knocking the staff out of her hand.

"Good, then when we're done, you can thank me for teaching you some compassion and decency splashed with a bit of humility."

Her staff twirled, then lashed out, catching Blaze on the side of her thigh. Blaze yelped and grabbed her leg with a squeal. Chantal's wail followed when Danny caught her forearm.

"If you don't want me to hurt you, then make a fucking effort. Break a goddamn nail if you have to," Danny taunted. "If you're so goddamn sure you were in the right, then fucking prove it to me."

The girls spread out in a triangle with their backs facing each other. Every time Danny circled around the trio, her staff connected with one of them. The order varied, keeping them on their toes and giving them no break.

Students arriving for the next session drifted down the hill, watching the show.

Humiliated more by an audience, the girls tried harder. She'd give them that. But in the end, they were no match for Danny's years of skill and a lifetime of hard knocks. With each strike, Danny knocked them down off their pedestals until they were even with the rest of the school.

For the crowd's benefit, she amplified her voice. "I will not tolerate bullies, mean girls, or miserable li'l bitches like the three of you on this island." Her swings came harder as she drove her point home.

Damian arrived to assist with the next lesson. Leaning against a tree with his arms crossed over his chest, Danny sensed his disapproval at her methods.

With a scream of fury, Collette rushed her, swinging wildly. Danny let her land a few hits, which she blocked easily before sweeping her feet out from

under her. Chantal and Blaze came at her together, giving Collette an opportunity to get back on her feet. They landed a few minor strikes, but Danny's staff came faster and found soft, painful spots that stung a hell of a lot more.

When she'd completely exhausted them mentally and physically, and bruises decorated their skin, Danny asked, "Do you yield?"

"Was that an option all along?" Blaze asked, incensed.

"It's always an option once you've learned the lesson," Danny said.

"I yield," Chantal gasped, tossing down her staff. "I can't take anymore." Tears streamed down her face.

Blaze joined in with a whispered, "I yield," as she bent over, trying to catch her breath.

"I hate you, and I hate this fucking place," Collette screamed, rushing Danny again, refusing to give up.

Danny allowed the furious girl to flail at her, easily blocking the strikes—but no longer returning them. Tears and snot were running down Collette's face as she screamed in rage and frustration, making Danny wonder who at home was bullying her.

When Collette finally wore herself out, Danny knocked her staff to the ground, sending the young woman hurtling behind it. Angry bruises covered her arms, and she'd broken at least three fingers on her right hand. A cut on her face was bleeding, and her cheekbone showed hints of purple and blue bruising. Danny knew her hand had to fucking hurt, and a part of her admired the girl's perseverance despite the pain.

"Do you yield?" Danny asked softly, hoping she would.

Collette's shoulders shook with sobs, but stubbornly, she reached out for the staff once more.

Blaze jumped up and stood between Danny and Collette. "I'll take her place until she's willing to yield."

Chantal limped over, standing shoulder to shoulder with Blaze. "So will I. She's too stubborn to yield."

"So be it." Danny's staff twirled as she locked eyes with Collette. "Are you so stubborn that you will allow them to take your pain for you?"

Collette's glare dimmed as she glanced at her friends, and she shook her head, "I yield, mistress."

"Finally. I wondered if you had any common sense. Be grateful for the loyalty of your friends. It's a rare gift." Her eyes pinned each of the girls with a glare. "Mayhap it's one you should learn to share with those who are less fortunate than you are."

Her staff twirled faster as she glared at them. "You have no comprehension of what Genny endured, so you don't have the right to judge her or comment on it—ever. Keep that in mind with everyone you meet

here. You don't know their backstories any more than we know yours. We all have things we've done that we aren't proud of. Would you want your darkest days drug into the light in front of your peers?"

In synch, the girls shook their heads. No.

"Have the balls to stand up to each other, especially when you know what is going down is wrong. Remember this lesson in humility, and don't make me have to give you another. Because if I have to, it will make today feel like a fucking spa treatment."

Danyka glanced at all three of the girls. "The kitchen staff brought you bagged lunches, and Mistress Rhyanna is awaiting you in the clinic. Have your wounds treated, and then head to your next class."

The trio stood and staggered up the hill, grateful to be leaving hell. Danny watched them leave, then hollered after them. "Almost forgot, Ronan's expecting you at the stables after dinner every day for the next two weeks. Mayhap shoveling shite will give all three of you some perspective."

To the rest of the crowd observing, Danny said, "Grab your staffs and find your partners. Go through the first set of warmup exercises."

Danny joined Damian by the tree, dropping to the ground and leaning her head against the rough bark. She uncorked a skin of water and drank deeply. She felt his eyes burning into her head. "You got something to say?" Her violet eyes challenged him. "Just fucking say it."

Damian met her glare and shook his head. "Don't you think you were a little harsh?" His eyes darted to the trio walking away.

"Did you hear her verbally attack Genny?"

As he shook his head, Danny said, "Collette threw her ordeal in her face in front of half the students. Then she all but called her a whore in front of Kai, no less."

"You've got to be fucking kidding," Damian said, clenching his fists. They all had a soft spot for the young woman who had endured so much. "In that case, they got off pretty fucking easy. I'll make sure Ronan knows why he's gained stable hands. He'll get creative with their assignments."

Danny grinned at him. "That would be great. Nice to see we agree on this one."

"I do, Pixie." He offered her a hand, tugging her from the ground. Running his hand through his hair, he asked, "Do you think they will remember this lesson twenty-four hours from now after Rhyanna heals them?"

"Honey, they will remember this for at least the next week. She witnessed it, too. I doubt she will do more than reset any fingers I broke. She just might mete out some additional punishments of her own."

"I'm glad I've never pissed you ladies off. You're fucking ruthless."

"No, we're not," Danny snapped, her eyes flashing at him. "We stand up for the underdog. We're trying to stop bullies in their tracks by turning them

into decent fucking people." Jaw clenched, she glared at him. "That's not ruthless. This is our way of making this world a better place to exist in."

"I understand your reasoning," Damian said, conceding her statement. "But it's also a way of creating future enemies if you push them too hard."

"I take that chance every fucking time I walk out the front door. Why should this be any different?"

Damian laughed, slinging his arm around her shoulder. "God, I love your ability to make friends, Pixie."

"Yeah, I just bet you do. Got all the ones I need." She brushed her pants off, then cocked an eyebrow at him. "If you need to work off any of that frustration you've been carrying after losing your lover to your brother, come see me."

"That was low, Danny." His eyes glittered dangerously at her, but he didn't deny the accusation. "If you want a match, you don't need to antagonize me."

"Offer stands." Danny walked away but not before tossing over her shoulder, "Think it might do us both some good to beat the ever-loving shite out of each other."

"You might be right," Damian said, following her. "Tonight, after lights out?"

"I'll see you then," Danny said with a smile. "Looking forward to a real challenge for a change. Haven't had one…" She trailed off, and they both knew she was thinking of Jameson. "No fucking crying when I hurt your pride," she snarked, stopping her train of thought.

"Challenge accepted. I don't want to hear any when I kick your ass. I'll see you tonight."

Letting out a long sigh, she headed to find herself a meal. Reflecting on the sparring match, she realized that once the trio found their footing; the girls fought well together. She winced, rotating her arm. The blows they landed were making themselves known.

She hated having to prove a point. But sadly, this was a lesson she gave nearly every session. Sending out a plea to any deity that would listen, she said, "Let this teach them all some fucking compassion, please." She prayed she wouldn't have to repeat the point she made because, no matter what she said, she fucking hated doing it.

64

Honor Among Thieves

Fairfax McAllister sat at a chipped wooden table on the docks while waiting for his informants to join him. He'd donned his impersonation of Captain Roarke again because he had hired them under this guise. Not that it was any hardship to appear young and virile. No, he was enjoying every moment while trying to hustle enough to make it a permanent change.

Hocking up phlegm, he spit it in front of a handsomely dressed couple who cast him a glare of disdain. Fairfax didn't know who Roarke was, but he was adding his own flourish to this role. A wide—brimmed, leather hat tipped down over his face, hid his eyes and added to the mystery.

With his feet hooked around the rungs of his chair, he tipped it back, balancing it on two legs. A bottle of whiskey and half a dozen shot glasses scattered across the scarred table. A glass with ice clinking the sides was half full of amber liquid. It dangled casually from two fingers of his right hand.

He jerked, nearly tipping the chair past its balancing point, when a lad too young to be drinking took it right out of his hand and danced out of reach. Looking him in the eye, the lad downed the whiskey with a wink. *"The little bastard,"* Fairfax thought. He had been drinking the expensive shite, not the watered-down swill he was offering his informants.

Four had already been by. They were a fucking waste of his money and time. They knew she worked for the Sanctuary, hung out at the Rusty Tap and was ornery as hell. For fuck's sake, McAllister could have told them that. He needed specifics—at the very least a half-assed schedule.

But this bunch wasn't ambitious enough to do the work and earn the bonus he'd offered. The sun dipping low in the sky told him he was nearing the end of the time for the reward he'd offered. He took a sip of his whiskey and tried to plan how he would gain access to Heart Island. Hopefully, it would be one that didn't get him killed.

A middle-aged gentleman with thick, silver hair framing his face ambled over, taking the seat directly across from McAllister. Pouring a drink into the last clean shot glass, he slid it across the table. With a nod, the man picked it up, tossed it back, and slammed it down in front of McAllister.

"This time, I'll take a shot of what you're drinking, not this watered-down swill you gave the other idiots," he said in a gravelly voice.

McAllister tipped his head, admiring the man's forthrightness. Leaning down, he picked up his bottle from the floor and refilled the glass. The man sniffed the whiskey and gave McAllister a sly smile. "That's more like it." Tip, swallow, slam. His eyes closed, and he let out a moan of appreciation, then grinned. "Nothing like the good stuff."

"Ye damn well better prove to me yer worth it," McAllister sneered.

A throaty chuckle had the man wiping his eyes. "Yer full of piss and vinegar camouflaged in that young captain's skin, ain'tchya?"

McAllister's eyes snapped to his at his implication. Only two others knew about the glamour, and this asshole wasn't one of them. "What's yer point?"

"Point is, we've all got secrets, hopes, and dreams." With a finger, he flicked the shot glass closer to McAllister. "I see through yers, Fairfax."

Fairfax refilled it again, his shaking hands sloshing some over the side. "Whatchya want?"

"Nothing ye've got, but a way we might help each other."

"I'se listening."

"I'll tell ye when to get the girl and show ye a way in."

"What's the catch?" McAllister asked, lifting a brow.

"Besides the bonus ye offered, I wants transport on and off the island with ye."

"If yer so knowledgeable, why do ye need me?"

"Light on funds at the moment and need transport." A dirty hand wiped over his broad brow. "Ye interested, or shall I find another buyer who'll provide what I needs?"

"Depends on how helpful the info is."

"I gots nuff to get ye in and out safely. Word is, there's still a bounty on ye if yer found in this area. Something about dumping toxic waste into the River. Mighty fine reward they be offering fer ye, too." His voice grew steadily louder so that men at the next table glanced their way.

"Shut the fuck up before I gut ye from here," McAllister sneered through his teeth. Reaching under the table, he grasped the short sword he'd stashed there. Aware of the crowd on the docks, he wanted this bastard out of here and quick. "Tell me what ye got or feck off."

"Hands on the table, motherfucker, or I'll toss the dagger hiding in me palm." The man's eyes glittered with a dangerous light. "Ain't no reason this should get nasty."

Fairfax placed his hands on the table, his fingers clenched tightly into fists. "I be listening."

"Solstice coming up quick. The island's usually open to more residents than usual. Public's encouraged to join in the festivities. Security is predictable most days, but that night they will be too busy celebrating. Kids be round, so no one wants a scene. She be a Warden."

"Knew that, not sure how it plays into what I need."

"She be there in the evening for the celebration. Mandatory shite."

"What will ye be doing?" McAllister asked, not sure he could trust the bastard.

"I'se be taking something rare. I needs transport and a cage high enough for a horse."

"Whatchya stealing?" McAllister was curious. He also wanted to know how much it was worth, intending to take advantage of any opportunity that presented itself.

The stranger stared at him for a long time. "I got something on ye, and now ye'll have something on me. Should make us thick as thieves." A crooked grin crossed the man's face before he said, "I be helping meself to a couple of hatchlings."

"Holy fuck," McAllister said. "Yer crazy nuff to steal from the fecking dragons."

"Crazy as a fox. Ye ken what they're worth to the right buyers."

"I ken 'twill get us both killed in very slow, painful ways."

"So ye want in?"

McAllister sat there, studying the man across from him for a long time. He'd known his fair share of loons, but this man took the batshit award. Pouring himself another round, he tossed it back, contemplating his options. Refilling both their glasses, he raised his in a salute. "Ye, I be in. Ye must be one stupid mother fucker to risk yer life over this." His long fingernails tapped on the table. "But…" he waited until the man met his eyes so that he knew how fecking serious he was. "If yer willing to risk it, ye bring me one, too."

The stranger's eyebrows rose into his hairline before a sinister smile crossed his face. "So, yer gonna journey to the dark side with me, then?"

McAllister tossed him the bag of coins. "Ye earned this for the information. Should've thought of the Solstice meself, but it was decent intel." A sinister smile of his own matched the man opposite him. "Ye brings me a hatchling to cover the cost of the cage and transportation to and from, or I'll leave yer arse there."

McAllister stood from the table, kicking back the chair as he went. "And for the record, the dark side is me fecking playground. Meet me here at sundown."

The man stood and offered him his hand. McAllister spit on his palm and slapped it into his. He pulled him close and, in a savage whisper, said, "Ye cross me and there won' be nothing recognizable left of ye."

The man looked him square in the eye and said, "The same applies, cept I'll torture ye for days afore I kill ye."

Fairfax chuckled. He appreciated a man with guts. "Ye got a name?"

"Only thing ye need to call me is... Sir."

Tipping his hat at the cocky man, Fairfax said, "Make damn sure yer ass is here at sundown on the Solstice."

"Wouldn't miss it." Tossing the bag of coins in the air, he stood and sauntered away.

Fairfax watched him go, then drank the last shot straight from the bottle. Grudgingly, he admitted to himself that he respected the man. Another time and another place, he might have made a good friend or a partner in crime.

Unfortunately, the only thing this fucker was gonna be was dead when this was over. The one thing in his line of business he couldn't stand was loose ends. It was how he'd lived this long. He'd absolutely no intention of leaving anyone involved in this mission alive because there was no honor amongst thieves.

65

Bottoms Up

Thick steam coated the windows and billowed along the floor of the bathroom as Jamey showered. Standing in water as hot as he could handle, he leaned against the far wall, supported himself with his hands, and let the blistering water pound against his tired muscles.

Head hanging, he replayed the conversation he'd had earlier this week with his mother and worried about where she'd run off to. Kateri Vance wasn't a woman to ignore, and Danny had done just that. Even if she hadn't come to check on him, his family had taken her in as one of their own. She was hurting them just as much as she was him. His mother had disappeared for the afternoon and returned in a better mood, but she hadn't said a word to him about where she'd gone.

The water cooled as he stood and wiped his large hands over his face, preparing himself to begin the ordeal of washing his hair. He never could have imagined such an ordinary task could take so long or be so fucking painful. But God damn, it hurt to raise his arm over his head. Even though it hurt, he continued to push his limits, holding it as far as he could reach until his arm shook and his teeth clenched against the pain.

This was the price of saving someone you loved, and he would pay it all over again in a heartbeat. Danyka was worth going through this every day for the rest of his life. The healers assured him that the pain would pass, and his range of motion would fully return, but it would take time.

'Twas the most time he'd spent with his family in a few years, and he was enjoying this part of his confinement and recuperation. His younger brothers were fun to be around. There were two centuries between him and Sian and another one and a half between Sian and Tobias. He'd missed them. They joked and pushed his limits, but it was good to have someone to laugh with and at. Tobias had left for Heart Island for his Elemental Training, but Sian was still here to torment him.

Sian worked the family farm alongside the rest of the extended Vance family. He hadn't wanted an apprenticeship after his education. Working with the horses and in the fields gave him a sense of fulfillment few seldom found. Being a farmhand kept him in shape. He was a bit leaner than Jamey, but just as ferocious in a fight.

Nearly the same height and weight made Sian the perfect sparring partner to help Jamey recuperate. There was hardly any difference between the two when sparring, except that Jamey, at peak fitness, was much quicker because he trained daily.

The damage Jamey had sustained left him clumsy and slow. His left arm tired quickly, and the pain when he jarred it nearly made him puke. The Earth Mother warned him that his recovery would be difficult, and she hadn't been sugarcoating the truth. Sian was good for him because he didn't baby him when they practiced. He was aware of the importance of a full recovery for his older brother. Jamey's response time could mean the difference between life and death for him or a partner.

The shock of the cold water brought him back to the present. Toweling off, he stepped out of the shower, drying himself. Combing his long, dark hair, he left it unbound for the evening. It was too damn hard to band or braid it, and he had no intention of asking his mother to do it for him. She would, but she took too much pleasure in causing him pain while she did. She often reminded him that pain was a reminder that he was alive. Whenever she spouted that wisdom, he kept his opinions to himself, knowing how difficult this ordeal had been for her.

Jamey pulled on leather breeches and knee-high boots. With some effort, he worked himself into a short–sleeve, burgundy cotton shirt. He painstakingly buttoned the damn thing up with fingers that didn't want to cooperate. His fine motor skills were slowly returning. Too slowly, in his opinion.

Forcing himself to use his left arm to brush his long hair shouldn't have been challenging, but somehow, he tangled the brush three times. Carefully, he set the brush on the dresser, fighting the urge to fling it across the room in his frustration. With a sigh, he glanced at the mirror and spun away, wondering if going out was worth the effort. His sunken eyes betrayed the nightmares that kept him from sleeping, and his skin tone was much too pale.

Afraid he was going to back out, he called on his partner in crime.

"Ferg, where the hell are you at?"

"Jamey, my lad, is that ye?"

"Yes, it is. Forget me already?"

"Never, laddie."

"Where are you drinking tonight?" Jamey asked.

"Sadly, I'm not. I've got some indoor activities in mind tonight, laddie, but I be free tomorrow."

"I'll take you up on that, old man."

"Who the feck ye calling old, laddie? Didja bump yer noggin when ye played with the wee hound?"

"Wee, my ass. See you tomorrow," Jameson said, ignoring him and dropping the link.

Discouraged, he once again debated staying the hell at home. Although this was one of his favorite places to be, claustrophobia was creeping up on him. Not wanting to drink on an empty stomach, he made himself a sandwich and considered his options.

The usual gathering place, the Rusty Tap in Clayton, was never as much fun without Fergus, and he hadn't faced Carsyn since their last awkward night together. She was a good lass. He felt bad for the way their mutually satisfying friends-with-benefits status had ended. But he couldn't give her what she longed for. He wasn't up for the guilt trip he'd lay on himself if he walked in there tonight.

Mentally he went down the list of taverns in the region, considering and rejecting a dozen until the Seaway Brewery came to mind in Sackets Harbor. He hadn't been in that establishment in years. Quiet and out of the way, he wasn't likely to run into anyone he knew well.

Gripping his left shoulder with his right hand, he massaged the tight muscles and scar tissue. Unlike most shifter injuries, this one was going to leave him with one hell of a nasty scar. Thick ropes of scar tissue ran across his shoulder and down the side of his ribcage. The healers Rhyanna sent daily massaged a lineament into his skin to reduce the thick tissue. The oil smelled fucking horrible, but he thought it might actually be working. His skin was growing more supple, and the angry, rough seams were slowly smoothing out.

A tall glass of milk topped off the sandwich. He headed for the door just as Sian was coming in after his evening chores.

"Where you off to?" Sian asked, his eyebrow quirking as he took in the clean clothes.

"Need to get off the island for a bit. Thought I'd head over to the Seaway for the night."

"Want some company? I could use some time away from here."

"Sure. I'll meet you later. Got something to do first."

Sian gave him a grin and headed up the stairs to shower. Jamey felt bad for not waiting for him, but he needed a few minutes alone and was going to take them.

Jamey closed the door softly behind him as he stepped onto the porch. The days were longer, and the sun was just beginning to descend. The equinox would be upon them in no time, and then the amount of light

would begin decreasing once again as they headed toward fall. He headed for the barn, pulling a deep breath of warm summer scented air into his lungs.

Jamey pulled a mounting block over to his horse, a rare chocolate palomino. His mother often joked that his horse was almost as pretty as he was. The joke prompted him to name her Nizhoni, which translated to beautiful inside and out. And she was beautiful all the way through.

Nizhoni lowered her head to his injured shoulder and nickered softly, instinctively knowing not to lean too heavily on him.

"Hey girl," he said, scratching behind her ear. "I know it's been a while. You want out of here?"

She huffed loudly, stomping her front foot for emphasis and tossing her head.

"I hear you," he said, stepping onto the block. "Take it easy on me, girl. It's been a while, and I'm out of practice."

Settling onto her back, he took the reins in his good hand and brushed his other one down the side of her neck in a caress. Using his thighs to encourage her to move, they walked out of the stables and took the road toward town.

Her gait was smooth as they moved, giving his body time to adjust to the jarring of her footsteps. Braver, he nudged her into a trot and immediately regretted it. "Sorry, sweetness, I don't have it in me to go that fast yet."

Since they were taking their time, his gaze fell on the fields they passed. Daisies and buttercups were blooming everywhere, the yellow cups nearly done for the season. Hay was heavy this year, thick and ripe, blowing in the light breeze. It was ready to be mowed, tedded, raked, and then formed into square bales to provide fodder for the cold months. Most of his clan spent the past week in the hayfields, and they were nearly halfway done with their property.

A farmer's life was never easy. Long fucking hours in the dog days of summer and blistering cold ones during the shortest days of winter. Animals depended on their owners to feed them, so you only got days off if you found someone to take over for you. Jamey had the utmost respect for anyone who worked the land. The Earth Mother was fickle, and the blizzards and torrential rain they occasionally received reminded them of that regularly.

The Wellesley gazebo was in sight. He guided Nizhoni into the livery next door and made arrangements for her care. The pounding of hoofs sounded behind him, and Jamey smiled, expecting Sian to round the corner and meet him any second now. Another exhale, and his brother pulled his gelding to a stop right in front of him.

"You didn't have to damn near kill your horse to catch up with me," Jamey said, patting the sweating beast.

"I didn't. You were just moseying along. Didn't take much for us to catch up with you," Sian said, tossing a leg over the horse's back and dropping effortlessly to the ground. He tossed some coins to the lad as he handed over the reins and wrapped an arm around the right side of Jamey's neck. "Let's go, big brother," he said with a laugh, "the whiskey and women are awaiting."

The two men walked the short distance to the gazebo housing the portal on Wellesley.

"I'll take the whiskey, and you can have the women."

"You trying out celibacy?" Sian asked with a disbelieving grin.

"Hell no. Just waiting for the one I want."

"Aww, finally told Danny you loved her, didchya?"

Jamey's head whipped around, and he glared at his younger sibling. "What makes you think it's Danny?"

"Hell, you've always had eyes for her. You hide it well enough, and I doubt Tobias notices." He clapped Jamey on the shoulder and grinned. "Whenever she's around, your eyes follow her every move. You finally work up the balls to tell her?"

"None of your fucking business, wise one," Jamey snapped. "Never realized I was so goddamn transparent."

"Only to those who've known you your entire life, dumbass."

"You could have stayed home," Jamey said to him, wondering why he came if he was going to bust his ass the entire night. They entered the gazebo and walked down the stairs to the portal access. Entering, Jamey pulled up the map and picked the location closest to the Seaway.

As soon as they arrived at their destination, they exited and walked down the street to where it dead-ended into a small marina. The brewery sat along a bend in the river.

Loud music from a local band assaulted their eardrums as they walked in. The locals were singing and clapping along throughout the chorus. A barmaid jumped up on a table, hiked up her skirt and did a little jig, earning a few coins from the men gathered round.

The place was rowdier than the Rusty Tap, but Jamey liked the anonymity it afforded him. He could claim a table or seat at the bar and ignore everyone without offending them.

"I'll grab drinks. Find a table." Sian said, pointing to one of the few left on the far side of the building.

Jamey worked his way through the crowd and sat down, barely fitting into the small booth. His eyes traveled through the crowd, looking for acquaintances, women, and trouble. He didn't recognize anyone. Most of the women were working girls, and trouble was lurking in every corner in the guise of a mean drunk, a sore loser, or a fight over a woman. Jamey wasn't

interested and intended to give it a wide berth tonight. He just wanted to drink in peace.

"Wanna talk about the problem between the two of you?"

Any thoughts of peace faded away when Sian slid into the booth and opened his mouth. Jamey sipped the ale his brother placed in front of him, then tossed back the shot, wincing at the nasty shit Sian had picked.

"Hard pass."

"C'mon. You know I won't say anything to her."

"I know. That's not it. Not much to say."

"I'm calling bullshit on that. Danyka is one hell of a woman, and she must be one hell of a partner for you to fall for her as well. Hell, we've all had a crush on her at some point.

Jamey's head snapped up, and he pinned his brother with a glare.

"See! You can't even take me talking about her. We know what she means to you. Why won't you talk to me about her?"

"For one, she and I need to talk first. Two, it's not my story to tell. And three, it's none of your damn business."

Sian raised his hands in front of him. "Message received loud and clear. As long as you realize that you can talk to me if you need to…"

"I know. Thank you for that." Jamey upended his beer and finished it, wanting to change the subject. "So, tell me about your love life, if you're feeling the need to share."

A grin crossed Sian's face. His head rested on the booth seat behind him, and a dreamy expression appeared on his face.

"What's her name?" Jamey prompted, trying not to gag at the look on his face.

"Sheera," Sian finally answered.

"And…" Jamey quirked an eyebrow at him. "How did you meet her?"

"Works at the feed store. One responsibility they've assigned me lately is to fetch wagon loads of grain for the stables."

"Our mother?" Jamey laughed.

"What's so funny?" Sian asked, looking ready for a fight.

"Calm down," Jamey placated. "She set you up to meet the girl. She's always been a matchmaker."

"True," Sian said. "But I don't think she'd even met her yet when I first saw her."

"What's she look like? Your usual blond with blue eyes?"

"Nope, this one broke my mold. Wavy chestnut hair to her shoulders and soulful dark eyes that have bewitched me. Curves everywhere," he said with a wicked gleam in his eye. "You know I don't like tiny petite things. I'm too afraid of breaking them. That's more your style."

"So, you've already bedded her?" Jamey arched an eyebrow at him, ignoring his accusation and wondering if he'd kiss and tell.

"Hell no. She ain't like that." Sian glared at him. "This one's different. She's one of the sweetest lasses I've ever met. I'm taking it slow because I want to keep this one more than a night or two."

"She feel the same?" Jamey asked, finishing his ale. "Have you spent time with her?"

"Of course, I have. We had a picnic down by the river last week. I'm seeing her again on Saturday." Sian folded his arms across his chest and mirrored Jamey's arched brow as he said, "Enough deflecting by asking about my love life. This is the reason I came with you. I'm surprised she hasn't been out to check on you." He waited for a comment and when one wasn't forthcoming, said, "Tell me what's going on with the two of you. You need to talk to someone other than Mama."

Jamey closed his eyes, wanting to ignore the question, but Sian was right. He needed someone to talk to other than Ferg and Maddy. Since Danny wasn't giving him much opportunity, he might as well get another opinion on his inability to connect with his woman.

Running his palm over his face and tangling his fingers in his hair, he looked at Sian, wishing he could change the subject. But his brother sat silently with a determined set to his chin, arms crossed and waiting.

"Danyka and I...it's complicated," he finally settled on. Huffing out a breath, he continued, "Danny is..."

"Here..." Sian finished for him in an apologetic voice. Eyes widening, he was looking over Jamey's shoulder. "Sorry, bro, but she just walked in, and she ain't alone."

Jamey's fists clenched until his left arm let him know it was too much. "Motherfucker," he said under his breath.

"You can't really be mad at her if you haven't told her how you feel," Sian said sympathetically, glancing over his shoulder again. "You want me to wave at her?"

"Hell no," Jamey said vehemently. He needed his temper under control before he saw her. "She can't see us back here. Most likely, she'll head for the pool table in the opposite corner and ignore the rest of the room, make a couple hundred bucks, and head out back to get laid."

"And you're okay with that?" Sian asked in disbelief.

"Fuck no. But I told you, it's..."

"Complicated," Sian scoffed.

Even though Jamey tried to hide it, the vehemence in his voice told the story. He hated everything about this situation. It made him want to hurt the man who was going to have her. But he understood what she was doing. Danny was trying to forget her problem with a random, unsatisfying fuck. There was a time when he would have done the same.

So, he swallowed his judgment, flagged down a barmaid, and ordered two pitchers and half a dozen shots for the two of them. Jamey knew of more than one way to adjust his attitude.

"You're going to be hurting come morning," Sian said as he watched the bartender unloading her tray. He tossed her a hefty tip and told her to keep their pitcher overflowing.

"No, little brother, *we're* going to be hurting come morning," Jamey said with a dangerous smirk. "When was the last time you tried to drink me under the table?"

"Been a while, but I think I'm more up to the task than I was years ago," Sian said with a saucy grin.

"Bring it on." Jamey picked up a shot glass, tapped it against Sian's, and tossed it back, then reached for another. Alcohol would dull the pain in his arm and kill the pain in his chest. It was the least harmful choice overall. Two of the barmaids had been eyeing him, but his cock didn't want to respond to anyone but his Hellion.

Fuck it. "Bottoms up!"

66

River Maids

Genny's mind wandered as she walked the mile to the lake to meet Kai. Still in shock over this morning, she couldn't help but hear the words Collette had said to her on repeat. There was only the slightest bit of truth in Collette's accusations, but she couldn't help but wonder if her words would end up being prophetic.

It had taken every ounce of self-esteem she possessed—and let's be honest, she didn't have much—to straighten her backbone and not burst into tears at the verbal attack. Her mind struggled at how quickly her past had come back to haunt her and how much the ache in her chest had grown, knowing that Kai was witnessing her humiliation.

Heart breaking, she'd turned to leave, believing that he wouldn't want anything to do with her. Knowing where she'd been and the abuse she'd survived would turn any man off, even one as kind as Kai. But his outstretched hand and the simmering blue fire in his eyes said otherwise. So, she took his hand and let him pull her under his arm as he declared she was under his protection.

They'd walked away, and somehow, she'd kept her head held high. His body was vibrating with barely controlled anger coursing through it. Halfway back to the castle, she was shaking uncontrollably. He pulled her off the main road onto a footpath she'd never noticed before. When they could no longer see or hear the road, he turned to her and opened his arms, offering her comfort. "Come here, Genny."

No man had ever offered Genny kindness and expected nothing in exchange. As her eyes met his, she realized his fury had abated, and the only thing she could sense emanating from him was his concern for her. Without another thought, she stepped into the shelter of his arms, grateful for the offer. When his massive body folded around her protectively, the floodgates burst open. Everything she'd held back since her imprisonment surfaced. With one choked sob, she let out all the pain, horror, and frustration from her time in captivity.

Collette's cruel actions pulled down every brick in the wall Genny had erected to help her survive hell. Now, she didn't have any defenses left to cling to.

Kai stroked her back for the longest time, holding her and allowing his presence to be enough. His large hands were tender as he stroked her hair and rubbed her back. He offered no platitudes and promised no happy endings. The kindest thing he could do was to give her the space to acknowledge the horror and fear of her ordeal. He allowed her the safety to release all the rage and frustration she'd buried at having all of her choices taken away. It was the greatest gift anyone had ever given her.

When the sobs subsided into soft, hiccupping breaths, she took a deep, shuddering breath and asked, "Why did you speak for me earlier? Why did you offer your protection?"

With her face still buried in his chest and her fists clenching his shirt, she struggled to understand what was happening between them and how to navigate it.

Clearing his throat, he said, "I couldn't stop myself after her vile accusations."

Her fists clenched his shirt tighter. "They might be vile, Kai, but they're the truth." Another ragged sob erupted from her as she admitted that to him.

Kai's gentle eyes were tumultuous as he lifted her chin to meet his gaze. His hand cupped the side of her face. Thumb brushing back her hair and caressing her cheek, he said, "I know, honey. But I forget that when I'm with you." He pressed a gentle kiss to her brow. "I don't care what came before. It doesn't matter to me."

"Just because you don't remember it doesn't make it go away," she said. Another tear fell down her cheek.

"I want to be whatever it is you need to survive this world, Genevieve," he said fiercely. "I've wanted to say that for weeks now and have been terrified of scaring you away." His thumbs wiped the still-streaming tears away.

"I hate what she did to you in front of all those people," he said in a growl layered over a heavy dose of rage.

"I only hate that you were there to hear it all," she whispered. "Why did you defend me?"

"I didn't need to defend you. I was so damn proud of you for standing up for yourself. It was the reason I remained. You have always been so timid." His free hand brushed the hair away from her face. "I wanted to see the warrior I knew was hiding inside."

Genny tipped her head to examine him. A wry laugh escaped. "I didn't recognize my inner warrior at first, but I was so furious at Collette for placing me in that situation."

"You should've been. She had no right to do that to you. It was cruel and meaningless."

"On the contrary, it was very intentional. Collette deliberately tried to destroy…" she motioned between them, then flushed and glanced away, not knowing what to call it. Settling on, "our friendship," she shook her head vigorously. "I don't understand why. I don't know her. We've only had half a dozen verbal exchanges."

"I, unfortunately, understand her all too well," Kai said with a heavy sigh. "My family attracts women looking for a way into the Court of Tears. I've been fighting off women like her for a long time. Never had one this young, but I know the type."

"If that's what you prefer…"

"If you listened to what I just said, you already know better. Don't disrespect both of us by implying otherwise."

"But..." Genny said, unable to comprehend why this man wanted to be with her.

"I enjoy spending time with you," he said simply. A frown crossed his face before he added, "I can be myself with you without the usual stress that comes with my family name." His brows nearly touched as a thought occurred to him. "Might be easier for you if I stayed away. It would cause fewer problems for you with the other students if I kept my distance."

"No, please don't. Our friendship is important to me, too," she said. "I'm not willing to give this up. I've never had a friend of the opposite sex before, and the only girls whose opinion I care about won't be a problem."

A lazy grin crossed his face. "Are you afraid to call me a boyfriend?"

"No, no." She was so flustered she could feel her cheeks heating. "I never could date before... so I'm not sure how to do any of this."

Her voice held the echoes of innocence lost, and it broke his heart. "I'm sorry," he said. "I didn't think."

"Don't apologize. It's not your fault." Her voice rose and tears threatened again. "I never expected to escape from hell, and when I did, I couldn't imagine any man would want someone used like me."

"Now you know better," he said. Hating to see her this way, he took her hand and tugged her farther along the path. The trees thinned out, and the path opened up into a small private garden. Full to bursting with summer blooms, it was wild and exotic at the same time. Vibrant reds and deep golds blended with royal purples as far as the eye could see. A twelve-foot living hedge of red and white rose of Sharon formed a privacy fence around the garden.

Hidden by the hedge, he walked towards the secret garden's center feature. A bronze fountain in the center portrayed a mermaid stepping out of the sea. One leg was human, while the other formed half of a tail. The leg appeared dry while a massive conch shell on her opposite shoulder spilled water down her right side, keeping the sparkling blue scales wet. The artist depicted the duality of the mermaid's nature beautifully as she reached towards the blooms in front of her while still clutching the shell on her shoulder. Her longing for land and her need to be in the sea were etched in her features.

Long waves of dark hair covered her breasts and trailed over her shoulders to her hips. The exquisite details on the subject's face clearly exhibited her wonder. Wide eyes took in the new world before her. Her sensual lips formed an O.

The mermaid-woman's sensuality was unmistakable, and Genny couldn't stop staring at her. Her eyes were wide as she pulled away from Kai and examined the details of the fountain. Upon closer inspection, she found her own features gazing back at her. Whipping around so fast her dark hair covered part of her face, she demanded, "Explain this to me."

Kai had taken a seat on one of two wide benches positioned on either side of the fountain. Spaced to allow for intimacy and far enough from each other to afford additional

privacy. "I can't," he said simply, "I didn't create her." His face was open and honest, as always.

"We could be sisters…" Her voice trailed off as she circled the figure.

"Twins," Kai agreed.

"What do you think it means?" Genny asked, frowning as she took in the fine details of the bronze.

"I think there's a significant chance you can shift into a mermaid or a rivermaid. Mayhap both." Kai ran a hand through his wind-tousled hair. "I've heard this island gives you what you need. Mayhap this is her way of convincing you of your ability to shift."

"Surely this has been here for ages…"

"I've never seen the path we took before today. It appeared when you needed to get away from everyone else." Standing, he joined her in front of the statue. "She's magnificent," he said, then glanced down until he was staring into Genny's eyes. "Just like you."

A blush stained her cheeks, but Genny met his gaze, and her chin raised a bit as she stood in her own power. Hearing the truth in his words, she leaned in to him and said, "Tonight, we'll find out."

Tonight had finally arrived, and Genny was terrified and excited at the same time. A stirring in her soul over the past few weeks made her long to be in the water as much as she could. Thankfully, her schedule prior to training had allowed for it. Now, her days were full, and the opportunities to swim would be few.

Palms sweaty, she was nervous for another reason as well. She would need to collaborate closely with Kai. She would have to touch him, and he might touch her as she tried to shift for the first time.

Over the past few years, men touched her repeatedly against her will. This was the first time that she wanted a man to touch her, and that fact terrified her just a little.

Circumstances beyond her control forced her body to perform the acts of a woman at an inconceivably young age. When she was around Kai, she longed for physical contact, but was terrified to initiate it. She didn't want him to think she had no morals, but her body and mind were no longer on the same timeline as most young women her age.

A cotton skirt covered her legs to the ankles, and she wore a bikini top beneath a summer blouse. In a large, jute bag worn across her body, she carried an oversized towel, a lightweight shawl, and a glass jar of black cherry tea.

Figuring they'd be starving and missing dinner, she'd asked Mrs. O'Hare to pack a light meal for her and Kai as well. The picnic basket she carried was heavy, but Genny was strong for her size.

Genny had agreed to meet him at the lake house he was staying in, and as she climbed the path up to the lake, she opened herself up to possibilities. Possibilities of another form, of shifter magic, and of a blossoming relationship.

She sought the Earth Mother's blessing and asked for the strength to move past her ordeal and to seek a future that would bring her happiness and joy. With each step, an affirmation filled her mind, reminding her of her worth and of her innate elemental gifts—gifts just waiting for her to open them up and play with them.

Climbing the steepest section of the path, she found herself on a plateau overlooking the glacier lake before her. A house sat on the edge. Built of wood and stone, it was a beautiful accent to the forest behind it. As she took in the breathtaking view, the front door opened, and a shoeless Kai walked out.

He was facing the lake, and she doubted he saw her arriving. But sensing her presence, he turned towards her with a broad grin. Jogging down the stone steps, he met her, relieving her of the basket. "What's this?" he asked in surprise.

"Thought we might work up an appetite, and I didn't want to face an audience tonight."

"Don't blame you, neither did I." He led her to the edge of the lake, where a small beach led to a dock. "Where do you want to set up?"

"I'll leave that up to you," Genny replied, not knowing what to do now that she was here.

Kai set the basket on a large, flat stone close to the lake. "This is a pretty spot."

Genny nodded. The lake drew her attention, and she felt a tugging in her soul. She needed to get into the water. "I want to swim for a bit before we begin. It will help relax me." Her hazel gaze sought his. "Do you mind?"

"Not at all. Go ahead, and I'll join you in a bit," he said, sensing her need to be alone for a bit.

"Thank you," she said. The gratitude in her voice was clear as she turned away and unbuttoned her blouse, then removed her skirt. Her modest, two-piece green suit was simple. The top fit like a tank top, and the bottoms were shorts that reached mid-thigh on her.

Kai tried not to stare at the scars on her back as she cautiously made her way into the water. But he couldn't keep his eyes off her. Her thick, chestnut-brown hair hit the middle of her back and was tangling in the breeze. He'd only noticed the whip scars when the wind moved her hair. Her frame was slight, but she was strong and becoming fearless in her claim for her independence.

The timid mouse he'd met in the Apothecary Shoppe earlier in the summer was fading away. This beautiful young woman was reclaiming her

power as she acclimated to her freedom. Standing up for herself against Collette was the first step. He was so fucking proud of her. Kai couldn't wait to see who she became as she followed her heart's desire.

His breath caught as she dove into the water, wondering if her newfound strength and independence would take her away from him. Once she got her legs under her and was used to standing on her own two feet, she wouldn't need him. He rubbed a hand over his chest as he realized that in helping her find herself, he took the chance of eventually losing her.

Releasing his breath on a sigh, he realized it was a chance worth taking. He was a few years older than her, but her situation was unique—as was she. Unwilling to let fear take hold, he headed back inside to change into his swim trunks. He would swim with her for a while in his human form before trying to help her find her inner mermaid.

The first step in the water's temperature took Genny's breath away. After a moment to acclimate, she dove in, wanting to get the shock over with. Allowing the embrace of the water to close over every inch of her, she felt like she'd come home. Arms propelling her forward, she went deeper, skimming against the shallow bottom. Silky strands of underwater plants tickled her belly and legs as she moved through them. Hair forming a halo around her, she took a moment to settle cross-legged on the rocky bottom, where a ray of light filtered through the water.

The underwater habitat was teeming with life. Largemouth bass chased perch minnows. A snapping turtle propelled itself by. The ungainly body moved elegantly in the water. A few feet above, a pair of loons drifted through her sunbeam, their lonesome calls muffled but still hauntingly beautiful.

Lungs burning, she placed her feet on the bottom and pushed off, making her way back to the surface. Breaching the place where water met air, she came halfway out of the water, gasping for breath, with a smile on her face.

Slicking her hair back and wiping her face, she opened her eyes to find Kai watching her from shore. His expression bordered on adoration, and deep inside, a spark kindled.

With a wide grin, she waved at him. "Are you going to join me?" she yelled.

Not bothering to answer, he fisted the back of his shirt and pulled it off in one motion. Running into the waves, he dove in, disappearing beneath the dark water.

Genny waited for him to emerge but couldn't see any evidence that he was below the surface. No bubbles emerged to track his breaths, and the

water was still between where he'd entered and where she treaded water. Turning in circles, she continued looking for him but found no sign. Five minutes went by, then another five. Concerned, she turned faster, seeking him in the tall reeds around the perimeter. "Kai," she called in a loud voice laced with concern.

When nothing but the call of the loons responded, she grew even more worried. Pivoting back around, she frantically searched the shore, thinking that he might have returned while she faced the other way.

"Kai!" she yelled.

Near to tears, she was about to go down and see if he'd become tangled below the surface when something soft grazed the arch of her foot. Pulling her feet up, she tried to see beneath the water.

When he emerged beside her, she shrieked in surprise and relief. "Where were you?" she demanded, slapping water at him. "I was worried about you."

His grin slipped when he realized her distress. "Genny, I'm sorry," he said, holding out his hand. It was a long moment before she took it, her luminous eyes still glaring at him.

Dragging her closer, he used his hand beneath her chin to get her attention and force her to meet his eyes. "Honey, you need to remember I have a water god for a grandfather. I breathe just as well below the surface as above it."

Tugging her hand to the side of his neck, he let her feel the slight rise of the gills lined up in rows. "I partially shifted because I wanted to make sure there was nothing in this part of the lake that would startle you when you shifted."

"It would've helped if you'd told me that before you went under," she said.

"Understood." His somber expression let her know he took her words seriously. "Would you still like to try?"

"Yes."

"Well, first off, you're going to need to be nude below the waist."

Genny blanched, not having considered this before. "Why?" Her voice rose uncomfortably.

Kai's tone was patient as he explained. "Your legs will touch when you transform them into a tail. Fabric can hinder a shift and be very painful if absorbed during it."

"Oh, I see." With pink coloring her cheeks, she headed back to shore. "Let me remove these, then."

"I'll give you some privacy," Kai said, swimming in the opposite direction.

Uncomfortable with the scars on her nude body, she pulled her skirt over her shorts and then slid them down. Kai was quite a distance away when she

headed back into the water. Lifting the fabric up as the water climbed, she pulled it up over her head and tossed it to the shore as the dark water covered her nudity. Swimming towards him, she called his name. "You can come back now."

He swam towards her until only a few feet remained between them. Eyes steady on her face, he said, "It takes an incredible amount of courage for you to trust me, and I'm humbled that you do." His dark blue eyes never strayed from hers. "I'm going to explain the process, and then you can try to shift."

Kai waited for her nod before continuing. "You're going to need to imagine every aspect of what it would be like to have a single appendage. You need to envision the way it would feel to have your legs melded into one. Imagine the strength you will need to use that appendage in ways your muscles have never moved before. Envision bending your legs at the knees to propel yourself forward or back. Feel the texture of your scales and notice the colors of the water you're in so that you blend your tail with the natural hues in the water."

Genny's eyes widened as he spoke. "That's a lot to remember."

"It is. Remember, if you partially shift, it's not a failure. We just need to get you back and start again. I can pull you back if you turn into something else, so don't be afraid of that."

"You mean if I turn myself into a fish or a turtle, or gods help me, a frog?" The pitch of her voice rose with each creature she mentioned. "You can fix that?"

His eyes crinkled with suppressed laughter at the panic in her voice. "Well, I could leave you that way if you prefer…put you in an aquarium and feed you crickets and flies."

She gave him a horrified gasp. "You, Kai Tyde, are evil. And to think I thought you were a gentleman." She swatted water at him, and he let out a deep chuckle.

"I usually am, but you seem to bring out the mischievousness in me."

"So, how am I to stay afloat as I press my legs together and fall into the devilish timbre of your voice while you lead me into a shifting meditation?"

"If you're comfortable with it, I will support you with my hands on your waist."

He cocked an eyebrow, asking her if she would allow him to touch her.

Genny drew in a ragged breath and blinked rapidly. Men had touched her, used her, and abused her. But none of them had ever looked at her the way this young man did—with kindness, respect, and care. Knowing she was safe with him, she nodded, then offered her hand, allowing him to pull her closer to him.

Kai spun her around so that her shoulders rested against his torso. His hands rested lightly on her waist as his lips whispered, "Honey, I need you to relax and breathe."

Genny tried. Honestly, she did, but the feel of him behind her and the sensation of his breath in her ear were overwhelming.

"Let your legs drift in front of you, Genny," Kai said. "Close your eyes and focus on matching the rhythm of my breathing." His chest moved as he inhaled deeply, held it for nearly a minute, and then released it. He continued the breath pattern, holding it for longer periods of time with each inhale. "Your lung capacity will increase, and you will find you can store large amounts of oxygen every time you inhale. Eventually, you'll need to breathe less because your body stores oxygen for long journeys beneath the water. These stores will feed your cells while you are in this form."

His voice faded as they took in longer and longer breaths. Her body relaxed against him. Continuing to hold her steady, his hands never left her waist, although his thumbs stroked back and forth over her skin in a soothing pattern.

Closing his eyes as he imagined the process he used to shift, he did his best to ignore the feel of her skin beneath his hands and her head resting against his chest.

Genny lost herself in the deep rumble of his voice beneath her head. She soon forgot that she wore nothing on her lower half and just focused on the sound of his voice lulling her into another plane of existence.

Breathing in sync with him, every time his chest moved on an inhale, she couldn't help but follow his example. For a moment, her mind drifted, and she wondered how many other women he'd helped do this. Her body tensed at the thought, but his voice quickly soothed her again.

"Focus on the feel of your legs sliding against one another. Notice where they meet at your thighs, your knees, and your ankles. Sense the weight of the water surrounding you, blanketing you in warmth. You are safe here with me, Genny. I won't let anything harm you in this form or any other."

A small smile crossed her face at his declaration, and she rubbed her head against his chest, snuggling into him for more. When he spoke again, repeating the instructions again, and then a third time, the only thing she was aware of was his voice and the feel of the contact points in her legs.

"Now, I want you to imagine your thighs melded together painlessly. They are no longer separate but melded into one solid appendage. That's it, honey. Keep your eyes closed and keep listening to my voice."

Genny felt a spark of something inside of her stir. Her inner shifter reached out and grasped her hand. Standing opposite her in her mind, she faced a version of herself with a tail—identical to the statue in the meadow. Allowing her to take over, Genny stepped back just a smidge and let her inner shifter loose. Kai's voice continued, reassuring her.

"Now, Genny, I want you to picture the colors of the water when you stepped in and when you were sitting on the lake floor. Imagine overlapping scales cascading down from your waist and covering your joined legs. Where your ankles meet, you now have a bifurcated tail to help you swim faster and be more agile in the water. See the shimmering blue-green of the water merging and imbuing your scales with an iridescent glow."

Kai stopped speaking, and for a moment, she lost her train of thought until the fingers of his left hand interlaced with her left. "Keep your eyes closed and maintain the image of what you want to become and how you want to move."

His hand moved hers over her belly and down along her hip. Genny sucked in a breath as her fingers grazed over her scales. His hand continued sliding hers down the outside of her leg. "Practice moving it back and forth, just a little," he said as he moved his other hand from her hip to take her hand. He turned her body until she was facing him. "I've got you, honey. Just let yourself sink into the water. I promise I won't let go."

Genny trusted him completely. Clasping his hands tightly, she let her body sink into the water. Closing her eyes, she marveled at the weight of her tail and the way the water flowed around it. Flexing it slowly back and forth, she allowed her body to drift with it. A harder movement put her fully against Kai's body.

Eyes snapping open, she opened her mouth to apologize, but he shook his head. "It's alright, you're adjusting to it. Get your balance before you let go. You'll know when you're ready." His encouraging smile made it easy for her to fall into the rhythm of her body's movement.

"I want to try letting go," she said in awe.

"I'm right here if you need me."

The pride in his eyes warmed her and gave her the courage to go out on her own. With a nod, she squeezed his fingers. His hand relaxed, and he allowed her to set the pace as she moved away from him.

With her arms free to balance her weight, she soon had the hang of moving forward and back. Wanting to try the movement underwater, she dove in, slapping her tail on the water as she did. Being fully underwater took more effort at first. The challenge was worth it when she finally understood the undulating movement needed to propel herself.

Genny moved through the water at incredible speeds, loving every minute. She rolled and twirled in the water, feeling graceful in a way she never had on land. An enormous shadow shot past her, and for a moment, she was afraid. Unaware of what threats might lurk in the depths, she headed for the surface. Out of the corner of her eye, the shadow reappeared, and Genny realized Kai had shifted and was protecting her from a distance.

Returning to the surface, she took a deep breath, filling her lungs to full capacity repeatedly. Unsure of how long she'd been under, she stayed there, marveling at the gift he'd given her.

The sun hovered on the horizon on the brink of sinking into its nighttime bower. Pink and purple splashes of color reflected off the clouds onto the water in front of her. It was one of the most beautiful sunsets she'd ever seen.

Kai emerged silently beside her, observing the painted sky without speaking. The night was perfect, and Genny had never been so happy. She reached over and laced her fingers with his. Her eyes welled, but she refused to shed a tear, even if it was a happy one. Tonight had been perfect, and she wouldn't ruin it. Squeezing his hand, she whispered, "Thank you for the gift you've given me."

He squeezed back and said, "You're welcome," so softly she nearly missed it. "You deserve to have everything you want, Genevieve." He rarely used her full name, but when he did, his voice deepened and became huskier.

Genny's eyes found his, and the way he gazed at her stirred something inside of her. The reverence and longing she saw when they locked eyes made her want a future she'd never allowed herself to hope for. His friendship had slowly become a lifeline for her as she became addicted to his kindness. The feminine part of her who once swore she would never willingly want a man stretched and yawned inside, making herself known.

"You're being silly," a little voice inside mocked. *"He's kind to everyone. It doesn't make you any more special than every other woman on this island."* This small voice warned her not to get too comfortable because fate had a way of knocking her down just when she thought things were going great.

With one more glance at the glorious sunset, she enjoyed the last moments of this day. Clinging to this gorgeous man's hand, she formed a protective layer around her heart. Because if the day came when Kai found another lost cause to rescue, he would break her heart.

67

Dealer's Choice

Jameson lost count of the rounds of shots they consumed, and the barmaids kept the pitchers overflowing. Sian was listing to the right across from him as he spouted poetry about the young woman who held his heart—this week. And it was terrible poetry.

Jamey wanted to bitch slap him to get him to stop. "Do you still have a pair of testicles?" he asked after the fifth stanza. "I can't take any more of the hearts and flowers bullshit...please stop. I beg you."

Sian clasped his chest as if Jamey had wounded him. "Do I have a pair? You have some nerve. The woman you've been in love with for years is less than thirty feet away, and you're fucking hiding from her like a coward.

"Fuck you, it's..."

Before he could finish, Sian held up a hand and beat him to it. "Complicated, yeah, I know. And you know what else? That's nothing but a fucking excuse."

Jamey's right hand fisted. He'd never wanted to cold cock his brother as much as he did right now. His control was slipping, and he wouldn't be held accountable if Sian kept running his mouth.

"Just fucking drop it, Sian."

"Or what? What are you going to do? Hit me?" He scoffed and picked up his tankard of ale, tipping it back to finish the dregs before reaching for the pitcher and slopping some more back in. "We both know that for the first time in our lives, I can kick the ever-loving shit out of you. So, please, make the first move. Take a swing at me, big brother."

Even though he knew he couldn't win, it was fucking tempting. Following Sian's example, he emptied and refilled his mug and drained half of it again. Trying to keep his mouth shut, his eyes drifted over to the corner where Danny was holding court.

Danyka was born to run a pool table. It was one of her gifts. She took Fergus's money regularly, and he used magic to try to win. He'd seen no one beat her. The men didn't care about the money they lost, they just loved watching her play.

Her body responded to the increase in testosterone around her, and her hips swung more freely, accentuating all of her curves. She moved like a cat. Purposeful and sensual as she stretched her body over the table while balancing her stick for a perfect shot.

And fuck him. The smile that lit up her face when she did so successfully went straight to his cock every time. She was in her element, playing the table and the men betting against her. Anyone who'd watched her play in the past knew to bet on her.

His eyes observed the men surrounding her, watching as one casually draped an arm over her shoulder and another casually brushed her hip or her ass. A hand cracked up against his temple, causing blinding pain and rage to roll through him simultaneously.

"Knock it the fuck off, Jamey," Sian hissed. "Your eyes are glowing, and you're growling. She's going to see you if you shift in the middle of this bar, you imbecile."

Jamey shook his head until the ringing stopped, then glared at Sian. "Don't hit me again, you little shit."

"Stop acting like an idiot and I won't have to." Sian pushed his mug away and sighed heavily. "I've had enough. Are you ready to leave? It's going to be a bitch throwing bales tomorrow in the heat."

"Nah. Go on. I'm not far behind you." Jamey cleared his throat and said, "Thanks for coming with me."

"Welcome. Don't do anything stupid, and get your ass home before dawn."

"Yes, mother."

"It's your fault I have to act like one," Sian grumbled as he staggered away.

Jamey ignored him as he sat there, surreptitiously watching the pool game from his seat. Danny leaned over and, for the Mother's sake, her boobs nearly popped out of her vest. His body responded as if electricity had just hit it.

When she stood up, her ass ground against a man who was standing much too close behind her. Expecting her to cause bodily harm, he was disappointed to watch her rotate her hips and back tighter into him. She'd obviously made her choice for the night.

His grizzly paced in his mind as he watched their mate being touched by someone else. With a clear idea of where the night was heading for her, he struggled to keep his beast in check.

A conversation he had with Maddy recently went through his head. *"Can you tolerate her repeatedly trying to compel you to forget and move on from her, or using other men to disgust you?"*

Glancing back over at her, he realized that was exactly what she was doing. Drowning him out with booze and men. Could he handle this shit? His eyes examined her face as more than one man groped her. Danyka's body moved in a sexual heat, but her face told another story. As his eyes found her face, he noted how drawn and exhausted she appeared. He wondered if she'd slept much at all over the past few weeks.

When his eyes found hers, he muttered, "Oh, shit," because her haunted eyes locked on his. The shock of him witnessing her behavior was obvious. Disappointment crossed her face for a moment before she locked her jaw and lifted her head, tipping him a nod and letting him know that she'd seen him. With one last heartbreaking glance, she took the hand that was wrapped around her from behind. Threading her fingers through the asshole's, she tugged, and they headed for a side door.

Danyka made her choice and was taking her flavor of the night out back to fuck him while the man who loved her sat there shitfaced, devastated, and ashamed.

As Jamey fought the hurt and anger sifting through his body, his mama's advice from before his attack echoed in his head.

"Keep loving her with everything you've got. Let her know that you will always be there for her, no matter how she lashes out. Show her that her past doesn't matter. Remind her that she is worthy of being loved."

Tossing back the rest of his drink, he carefully set the tankard on the table and gathered the shattered shards of his self-esteem and confidence around him. He was a Warden and a man of worth. Even though he might be half in the bag, he was sobering up by the minute.

As he stood, Jamey was grateful his legs were steady, and his eyes were clearing. Fighting his animal had sobered him up considerably. He needed to be clearheaded when he walked outside and found someone buried up to their balls inside of her. Taking a deep breath, he ran his hand over his chin and headed for the side door.

Pushing it open, the silence surprised him. The well-oiled hinges provided the illusion of privacy to the couples who stepped out for a quickie. His eyesight was better in the dark, and it didn't take long to find her halfway down the building. Her pants were down to her ankles, and she was leaning against the building.

The asshole behind her had his pants part way down his thighs, and from the rocking motions, he was enjoying her sweet little pussy right now. Jamey's nails dug into his palms as he watched the woman he loved being fucked by another man. He doubted she even knew his name.

361

Eyes stuck to the point where their bodies joined, he almost walked away. Then he heard her sob. "Stop. I don't think I can do this."

"Baby, you're doing just fine," the man's gravelly voice retorted as he picked up speed, wanting to finish before she changed her mind.

One look at her face told him she needed something, but this asshole wasn't gonna get her there. So be it. If she needed to come, he would get her there, and they would use this asshole until he couldn't walk when he was done.

Since tonight seemed to be the night to relive previous conversations, he pulled up one they'd recently had and reached out telepathically.

"Are you getting anything out of that?"

Danny's head swung around, and her gaze caught his. A slow, sad smile crossed her face, and her eyes filled with tears. *"No, but I was hopeful in the beginning."* A small sob escaped from her lips. *"I wish you hadn't come out here, Jamey. I don't want to hurt you."*

"You're not hurting me, Hellion. You're hurting yourself because you don't really want this. But I understand why you are out here. Whether you realize it or not, you're showing me exactly what you need."

Jamey managed a sad grin and tried to infuse their link with humor and love. *"Hellion, compel him to slow it down and to not even think of coming until you give him permission, okay?*

"Jamey, you don't have to do this. You don't have to watch me humiliate us both." Tears tracked down her face as she pleaded with him. *"Please forget about this and just go."*

"Not going anywhere, Hellion. Not until you get what you need. Now, do what I said. Compel him to go at the pace you need." She did what he asked and then blanched when he said, *"Tell him someone is going to join you."*

Her tears fell harder as she realized he wasn't going to abandon her. *"Please..."*

"You asked him to stop, and he didn't, Danny. Did you even register that? He's fucking clueless that you are not enjoying this. I'm not leaving you alone with him, and I'm not leaving until you're satisfied." His eyes never left hers. *"Hellion, if you ever trusted me before, please trust me now."*

"No regrets tomorrow?" Her voice sounded haunted as she asked him what she was most afraid of.

"No regrets. I will still love you come tomorrow, Danny. That will never change. Now, do as I ask, please."

Danny stood and turned to look into the stranger's eyes. He couldn't hear what she said, but the man immediately slowed his thrusts and glanced at Jamey curiously.

Jamey stalked towards her slowly, purposefully, letting her see every ounce of desire and emotion in his eyes. When he reached her, he stood in front of her where she had supported herself against the building. His

362

massive hands framed her face, his eyes searching hers for a long time before he asked, "Do I have your permission to kiss you, Danny?"

She sucked in a gulp of air and nodded. His thumbs brushed away the tears on her face before he bent down and kissed the trails away. When his eyes met hers again, he said, "Nothing but pleasure from here on, Hellion. The next tears I see better be because you're coming so hard you can't control it."

The shock on her face at his words was worth it, but he wasn't giving her time to think about it. His mouth crashed into hers, taking her on a heady ride with just his lips. His tongue caressed hers, and she whimpered, trying to move closer but unable to do so with the man behind her gripping her hips.

Jamey moved into her, sandwiching her between the two of them. His lips kept hers busy, and his hands slowly roamed over the front of her body. When his body was flush against hers, pinning her between them, he felt the change in her posture instantly.

Lips that had been kissing him passionately clamped shut. Her body tensed and arched like a tightly pulled bowstring. Fingers that had fisted his shirt, pulling him closer, now felt like claws piercing his skin—and not in a good way.

Jamey pulled back to see her violet eyes. The panic and deeply buried rage greeting him was devastating. "Asshole, you need to leave right now," he growled.

The man behind Danny barely registered his words, still caught in her compulsion. Danny's fingers released him, and when his eyes met hers, they shimmered with rage. Realizing she was reaching for her knives, he grabbed her wrists and reached out to her on their link.

"Hellion, I need you to look at me, honey." His voice was the soothing tone he used with skittish animals. *"No one is going to hurt you, Danny, but you need to focus on me. NOW."*

The snap of his tone caught her attention, and her eyes finally met his, seeing him. Jamey gave her a soft smile and said, *"We're going to let your partner here go on his way. Okay?"*

It took her a moment to process his request. Glancing over her shoulder as if she'd forgotten he was there, she shuddered. Soft words and a mental nudge later, and the man behind her withdrew his cock and put it away.

"Night, y'all." The stranger said. "That was fucking amazing. Thanks for letting me join you." The door shut behind the asshole as he reentered the building.

Danny's shoulders sagged, and she leaned her head against his chest. "I'm sorry, I'm sorry, I'm so sorry…" she chanted against him. "I'm bound

to disappoint you every time, Jamey." Her ragged voice was so sad and lost that he struggled to hear her.

"You didn't disappoint me, Hellion. I didn't think you were enjoying yourself. I just wanted to make sure you got something out of it." He ran a hand over his face ruefully. "I think I made it worse."

"No. You didn't," she said fiercely, glancing up at him. "If you hadn't come by, I might have hurt him."

"You only seemed dangerous when I stepped too close and pinned you against him." One hand stroked the top of her head while the other rubbed slow circles on her back. "Wanna tell me what happened?"

"Not really. But I guess I owe you that."

"You don't owe me anything, Hellion," he whispered in her ear. "I just don't want to make the same mistake again.

She pierced him with her icy stare. "Why do you even want me after finding me with another man?" She shook her head, puzzled. "Who does that?"

"I told you before. You're not scaring me off, Danny. I love you and will do whatever it takes to prove that to you."

Her hands fisted in his shirt, and the look on her face fluctuated between confusion and humiliation. "What if I don't want you to love me?" she asked in a whisper.

"You don't have to return the sentiment, but you can't force me to change the way I feel about you."

"How many times are you willing to forgive scenes like this, Jamey?" she asked caustically.

"As many times as it takes to convince you, I will still wait for you."

"Stubborn fool."

His eyes burned into hers with the same fierce stubbornness. "Been called worse," he said. In a softer tone, he reached out telepathically and said, *"Hellion,. What triggered you?"*

Eyes still locked with his, a shuddering sigh escaped her. She closed them for a long moment, and when she opened them, she stared at the middle of his chest. Her fists released his shirt, now smoothing the wrinkles out as she searched for the words. *"It reminded me of the night Maddy rescued me."*

"Tell me about it."

"I can't," she wailed in his head. Her head dropped and rested against his chest.

"Hellion, it will help to get it out of your mind if you can share the burden."

"Why, so we can both have nightmares?"

"No. So that I can absorb some of your pain."

"I wouldn't do that to anyone."

"I'm not anyone, Danyka."

Jamey rarely used her full name. Surprised, she glanced up at him. His dark eyes held more compassion and love than she had ever received as a child. She shook her head as a tear rolled down her face.

Kissing it away, he stroked her cheeks with his thumbs and cupped her face as he said, *"Let me carry this for you, Danyka."*

Another tear rolled down her face before she answered. *"I can't tell you, but I'll show you. And then you will never want to be this close to me again."*

Jamey bent down and placed his forehead against hers, needing the contact. "I'm ready," he said aloud as his hands circled her waist and pulled her closer to him.

A sob tore from her as images flickered through their link.

Flickering images of a dark room skittered through his mind's eye. Seen from her perspective, he watched a man in front of her pounding into her with her legs wrapped around his waist. Blood ran down her legs and dripped steadily onto the floor. Another set of large, beefy hands gripped her waist from behind.

The horrific scene she shared with him made him want to puke. It horrified him, as he witnessed her child's body being raped by two men. As the scene continued, he saw her lean forward and grasp the head of the man in front of her. Initially, she appeared to nuzzle his neck. Her actions confused him until he saw the arterial spray hitting the walls of the stone room. She clung to the man until the man behind her beat her off of him. The other rapist stood paralyzed in front of her with his erection jutting in front of him. Jamey watched as Madylyn stepped in behind him, grasped his hair, then drew a knife across his throat.

The scene cut off, but he held her tighter, not wanting to lose the feel of her skin against his. Dainty palms framed his face, and the feel of her wiping his tears away made his eyes pop open. Large, tear-filled violet eyes looked at him in horror.

When her fingers released the tension on his face, he grasped her wrists, holding them there. *"Nothing's changed, Hellion. You can't scare me away. Let me battle your demons with you. I just wish I could have done it then."*

Nuzzling his nose against hers, he said, *"I'm going to kiss you now. If you don't want me to, say so."*

Expecting her to push him away, he interpreted her nuzzling back as permission.

His lips grazed hers in a light caress. Playing and gently plying hers open with his, he took his time before introducing his tongue to the mix. Her arms wound round his neck as his hands hooked under her legs, lifting her up and around his waist.

365

Danny's sharp gasp popped open his eyes, and he saw the fear in hers. Again, he nuzzled her before asking, *"Do you have the urge to rip out my throat, Hellion?"*

Tipping her head, she surveyed him for a moment, and he was sure she was inspecting her inner feelings. *"No, but…"*

"If and when that changes, all you need to do is say stop. It's that simple. I will always put the brakes on when you use that word. If that one doesn't work for you, you pick our safe word, hellion."

His lips brushed against hers in a soft kiss. "I will always respect your request to stop—instantly," he said aloud. "You will never have reason to doubt that."

Large, luminous eyes stared at him for a long time before she responded. "I know you will always respect me. Never doubted it for a moment." A resigned sigh escaped her while her hands drifted through the silky length of his long hair. "You're not going away, are you?"

A wide smile crossed his face at her concession. "Hellion, I don't know how to give up on you—or on us." His teeth nipped at her chin. "Now, shut up and kiss me like you've wanted to all night—without the guilt."

He'd barely finished when her lips took his. Her tongue stroked his in a delicate dance that heated his blood. His lips traveled over her chin and down her neck. "I will take care of all of your needs, Hellion. All you have to do is ask."

"Jamey," her breathy exhale of his name was all the request he needed.

He turned, pinning her to the wall of the bar, then immediately checked in with her. *"You good, honey?"*

"I'm good, but I need…" Even telepathically, she couldn't ask for what she wanted.

His amber gaze met hers. *"You want me to make you come?"*

"I know it's selfish to ask, but I don't think I'm ready for more tonight."

"Danyka, bringing you pleasure is never one-sided. I will enjoy every fucking moment of watching you come apart. Tell me what you want. My tongue or my fingers…or both?"

A flush appeared on her cheeks as her chest heaved in anticipation. "Dealer's choice."

Her whispered words had him grinning broadly. He set her legs on the ground and adjusted her pants, pulling them back into place.

A gasp of outrage or disappointment, he wasn't sure which, came from her as her fists clenched at her side. With a laugh, he kissed her again. "I wasn't teasing, Hellion. I just don't want to share your pleasure with anyone else who might come along."

He offered his hand, palm up. "Come with me, Danyka. If you still want this, take my hand."

The doubts were still warring with her needs, but in the end, trust and her desire won the battle, and she placed her dainty hand in his massive one.

Tugging gently, he pulled her away from the bar and down the road. They headed towards the center of town until they reached the portal. Pulling her inside, he took them to Wellesley Island. They emerged on the bottom floor of the enormous town gazebo.

Built for the community, the beautiful structure could easily hold a hundred people. The town used the main platform for community gatherings and pledge ceremonies. Picnic tables and benches surrounded a dance floor. The bottom floor housed the entrance to Wellesley's portal.

Jamey pulled her up the steps and across the wooden floor to the main rail. Their steps echoed on the scarred wood until they reached the side facing the water. Staring out at the dark river flowing by, he stepped behind her, wrapping his arms around her waist.

The night had cleared, and the stars were so close this time of year.

"How many other girls have you brought here, Jamey?"

"None. I always liked to come here when I needed to think. Everything winds down at this time of night. I enjoy the peace of the water and the view of the sky."

With a soft kiss on the side of her neck, he swayed with her to the rhythm of the waves battering against the shore. Their bodies moved fluidly together to a beat only they could hear. Hips connected and moving in sensual circles together, his hands caressed her abdomen. His thumbs brushed the underside of her breasts, making her arch against him. Her hands traced patterns down his forearms as she leaned back against his chest.

A throaty purr erupted from her throat as his one hand pinched a nipple and the other one snaked down her abdomen into the front of her pants. Her ass ground into his erection, making him moan where he found her slick center waiting for him.

"I thought you didn't want anyone to see us?" she panted.

"They won't. My grizzly will sense anyone approaching. This area doesn't get the traffic the bar does."

His mouth closed on either side of her shoulder, and he nipped lightly. "Stop distracting me from my task."

Two of his fingers sank slowly inside of her an inch at a time, making her squirm in his arms. Her breath came in short bursts when he pulled out and used his slick digits to draw large circles around her clit.

"Touch me, Jamey," she panted.

"Hellion," he whispered against her temple. "I am."

Her hand covered his and pushed him closer to where she needed him.

"Show me what you like," he said, and the gravel in his voice made her wetter.

367

"I don't know what I like…" she groaned. "I've never been able to do this easily." Her pants came quicker, and she pushed her hips into his, making him pant right along with her.

"We're going to spend all night finding out what makes you whimper, tremble, and sob." His teeth sank into her earlobe, making her twitch. Grazing her clit, he continued, "Then I'm going to find out what makes you scream for more."

His other hand continued caressing her breast, occasionally pinching her nipple lightly. When she bucked against him, he increased the pressure. His fingers found their way back to her entrance, skimming and circling without entering.

Danny's hand coaxed him further down, pressing his fingers firmly against her entrance. Her pressure on his fingers pushed the tips into her pussy. She arched back against him, trying to sink them further in. "Jameson…"

"Tell me what you need, Hellion."

The gravel in his voice was rougher, and she loved she could do that to him.

"Tell me what you want," he growled.

"I need them deeper inside of me. Finger fuck me, Jamey," she said in a tortured voice.

"Your wish is my command," he said a moment before he slid two fingers in to the palm. Withdrawing at a slow, steady pace, he circled his thumb around her clit then sank three fingers into her and pumped in and out. With her pussy pulsing around his fingers, his thumb stroked her clit with firm pressure. Circling around her over-sensitized nub ceaselessly, he drank in her moans. "That's it, honey. Fall into the pleasure I'm giving you, knowing you're safe. I'll catch you when you freefall. I promise."

Danny's head rested on his shoulder, pushing against him, trying to get away and trying to get closer to the explosion threatening to occur. Arching against him like a cat, she placed her right foot on the rail, trying to give him more access. This position amplified the sensations he was creating. His voice was far away as he encouraged her to fall, and she wanted to. His arms around her made her feel safe. She knew she could trust her wellbeing with him. Jameson Vance would never fail her.

Unexpectedly, he removed his hand, garnering him an outraged gasp. In record time, he removed her boots and pants, then took up his position behind her again. Placing her right leg back up on the rail, he said, "Spread your legs more for me, Hellion." Jamey said, wanting better access. Without hesitation, she responded, and his heart raced at the level of trust they had reached tonight. "That's it, Hellion," he said as his fingers skimmed over her soaked pussy, and his lips brushed against her neck.

Her body responded to his voice and his touch by flooding his hand. "Let's see what happens when we go faster." Sinking two fingers back in, he moved in and out of her pussy faster while scissoring his fingers inside of her. With each stroke, the heel of his hand bumped into her clit, and she moaned.

Erecting a bubble of air around them for privacy, he finger fucked her until she was bucking against him and screaming his name. Her body was slick with sweat as she clamped her thighs tightly around his hand. Jamey rode out the orgasm, slowing his hand down to draw out the sensation. When her breathing settled and she was moaning long and low, he picked up the pace again.

"I don't think I can take anymore," she cried as she came again. Tears rolled down her cheeks from the pleasure he pulled from her.

Waiting until the tremors in her legs stopped, he slid his hand out of her, loving the shivers that ran through her body. He turned her in his arms, tipping her chin to see her eyes. The amethyst orbs were hazy with pleasure, but the heat returned when he kissed her languidly.

"How are you able to do that every time you touch me?" she asked in wonder. "No one else ever has."

"Trust, sweetie." He pressed a kiss to her temple. "You never really gave them a chance because of your fears. Maybe if you did, they would've done just as well."

"No, they wouldn't have." Her sharp denial pleased him. "You're right. I do trust you, and very few people have earned the privilege of claiming that."

Jamey framed her face in his hands. "If you would give me the honor, I will happily provide you with all the pleasure you need, Hellion. You don't have to keep wasting your time out back with strangers who leave you disappointed every time."

Sad eyes told him she couldn't promise anything. He could live with that, but right now, he wanted to hear her screaming his name again. Taking her mouth in a rough kiss, he had her panting and begging in minutes.

Hooking his hands behind her knees, he lifted her to the wide ledge over the railing and sat her there. Pointing to the posts on either side of her, he said, "Hang on to them."

Danny quirked a brow in confusion, but comprehension dawned when he dropped to his knees and placed her legs over his shoulders. "Hellion, you better hang on tight. I wasn't kidding when I said we're going to spend all night finding out what works for you."

"Jamey," she began, but he'd taken a long swipe up the full length of her cleft with his tongue. Her words faded into a moan as he buried his tongue inside of her, thrusting in and out with it. Kissing his way up to her clit, his

fingers found her pussy again as he latched on to the bundle of nerves with his lips.

Sucking without ceasing and using his fingers to prod her g spot, she quickly screamed for him again. When her body was boneless and listing, he cradled her in his arms and shifted his back against the railing. He was content to hold her curled up against his chest. Her head rested over his heart, and her hands toyed with the ends of his hair as they both caught their breath.

Kissing the top of her head, he said, "It brings me great joy to see to your needs, Danny."

"Hmmm," she murmured against his heart. "But what happens if the time comes, and I can't reciprocate fully?"

"If a time comes when either of us is dissatisfied with our arrangement, we will talk about it together."

Jamey sat there, happy just to have her in his arms. When she stifled a yawn and shivered, he grabbed her pants and helped her into them. Danny allowed it, leaning against him as exhaustion crept in. He stood easily with her, slowly letting her legs drop to the floor.

Danny looped her arms around his waist and leaned against him. He stroked slow circles on her back, not wanting to let her go.

"I'm going to go home now," she said, staring at her feet.

Kissing her temple, he said, "I'm going to take you back. I want to know you got there safely."

"That's unnecessary," she grumbled.

"I know," he said, kissing her head. "Please indulge me."

Danny gazed at him for a long moment and then nodded. When he held out a hand, she took it, letting him pull her under his shoulder. She leaned against him, grateful for the support.

When they arrived at the stag gate, she pulled away. "I've got it from here," she said.

Jamey kept his protest from escaping, not wanting to ruin the time they'd just spent together. "Good night, Hellion." He turned to step back into the portal.

"Wait!" Her voice caused him to pause. She flew into his arms and hugged him tightly. His arms instantly banded around her.

"Thank you, Jamey."

"For what?"

Danyka stood on her tiptoes, cupped his face, and pulled his lips to hers, giving him a soft kiss goodnight. "For never giving up on me."

"Never, honey."

She gifted him one of her rare smiles—the kind that lit up her entire face. Without another word, she headed up the hill towards the Sanctuary.

Jameson smiled, watching her walk away. Tonight gave him desperately needed hope, and he wasn't about to second guess it.

"Hey, Danny," he said.

She never stopped walking, but he sensed her pleasure at the contact. *"Keep in touch, Hellion. I've missed the feel of you in my mind."*

"I've missed you too, Jamey." Her steps paused for a moment, and she glanced back over her shoulder at him. *"I'll take down the wall."*

"Thank you, honey. Good night."

He closed the portal door, smiling when he heard, *"Good night, Jamey."*

68

Shifter Senses

Danny grabbed a bottle of whiskey and headed for the back porch. It had been a long fucking twenty-four, and she was beat. Stretching out on a long wooden swing with her back against the arm, legs extended, and feet crossed, she plucked the cork and took a deep swig of the burning liquor. Closing her eyes, she let the burn roll through her veins.

Tapping on her boots made Danny pop one eye open. Kerrygan stood there with one hand reaching for her bottle and the other tapping, encouraging her to move her legs so that he could join her.

Danny shifted with a long-winded sigh as her muscles screamed and protested the movement. She handed him the bottle without question, grateful for the company.

Leaning her head against his shoulder, they sat in silence, watching the sunset. Kerry shifted, putting his arm around her, letting her snuggle in against his chest. The two shifters had always been close, but his love and care after Jamey's incident brought them even closer.

"So, how is the lad?" he finally asked when she offered nothing.

Danny peered up at him with one eyebrow raised.

Kerrygan tapped at the side of his nose. "Ye forget me shifter's sense of smell is as good as yers, Danny girl." He ran his nose up and down her neck. "I ken what the two of ye were about."

Danny flushed, realizing she'd been too tired to shower last night after the many mind-blowing orgasms, and woke too late to do so this morning.

"He seems well." She didn't bother telling him it hadn't gone as far as he assumed because she doubted he'd believe her. Body chemistry told a good part of the story but not all of it.

Kerrygan was kind enough to let the matter drop. "Heard ye made yer first statement of the season."

"Aye, I did."

"Be nice to have one season without having to," he said in a wistful tone.

"Aye, it would."

"Heard ye did some damage, and Rhy did little to fix it."

"Yer the town crier tonight, ain'tchya?"

Kerry chuckled, then squeezed her tightly against him. "Sounds like the little twit deserved it."

Danny was silent for a moment, examining her motivations for the attack on the trio of twits. "When I arrived here, I needed to attend my Elemental Training early because my elemental powers and rage were out of control."

"Understandably so," Kerry agreed. "Your rage at what you'd been through would have amplified your emerging elements."

"Yep, it did. I had a group of tormentors, too. They were worse than the ones Genny has, and Maddy made a helluva statement that year. She broke two of their wrists and one of their ankles." A sad smile crossed her face as she remembered.

"No one said anything unkind to me for the rest of my training." She coughed out a rueful laugh. "Hell, hardly anyone said anything to me at all." She nudged his ribs with her elbow. "I broke a few fingers on the meanest of them, but the rest are bumps and bruises. Rhy probably healed them completely."

Kerry laughed out loud. "Not this time. Our sweet little sister had a bee in her bonnet over this one. She splinted it, stitched a few cuts, and sent them on their way with nothing for the pain. She didn't take away any of it. Told them maybe they'd think twice before they said anything they wouldn't want said about them."

Danny snickered. "Stop, you're making me feel sorry for them."

"I'm calling bullshite on that," Kerry said with another squeeze. In a more somber tone, he said, "I'm glad ye went to see Jamey. Ye needed it."

Danny tucked her head down, not wanting to meet his eyes. "I didn't exactly go to see him. Let's say I ran into him."

"Out the back door of the bar with another man?"

"Now you're just being an ass."

Kerry tapped the side of his nose again and winked. "He ain't the only man I smell on ye, Pixie." He tipped her chin up to meet her eyes. "Seems to have worked itself out, na."

A sad smile crossed her face. When she thought of them together, it was the first time she didn't want to run away from the possibility. "Aye, I think it just might have…"

The night air made her shiver. She snuggled closer to his chest for warmth while allowing herself to examine how she felt about last night. When she thought about Jameson, her body came to life, and her heart rate increased.

If she was honest with herself, she'd admit she missed him and longed to see him again—she longed for the serenity she felt when she was with him. It was a sensation she rarely experienced, but she craved more—more of his smile, more of his kisses, more of everything the man offered her. Danny wanted it all, and if she could get out of her own way—mayhap she could have it.

69

Ye'll Heal on Yer Own

Rhyanna glanced over her shoulder at the virile naked man in her bed. Kyran lay on his stomach with the blankets pooled at his hips. His muscular back made her fingers itch. She wanted to strip, straddle his hips, and trace each muscle with her fingertips…and then her tongue.

With a regretful sigh, she shouldered her bag, took one last hungry look, and left him as he was—warm, naked, and all hers. She'd never been possessive about anything until he entered her life. And after everything they had been through, she would stake her claim in blood.

His sleepy voice echoed in her head as she walked toward the steps leading to the foyer. *"Don't go, my lady. I was dreaming of you, and…"* He sent her the image of him fisting his cock and moaning.

"You don't fight fair, Kyr." She paused and set an image of her own, replacing his hand with her lips. *"I'll make it up to you tonight."* His sexy moan and a healthy dose of lust came through their lover's bridge, heating her core and making her take a deep breath before heading out again.

Every step down the stairs was sensual torture, as her thighs rubbed together and increased her sensitivity. *"That's just being mean, me laird,"* she said, adding the sensation of her deep-throating him. *"Enough. Let me get me work done, and I'll return that much quicker, luv."*

Kyran backed down the heaviness of the lust and replaced it with the warm glow of his love, making her smile. As sexy as the man was, she loved his sweet, romantic side even more. Every day, he made sure she knew she was not only loved but cherished and appreciated as well.

Grabbing tea, a fresh hunk of warm, just-out-of-the-oven bread, a thick slab of sharp pungent cheese, and an apple to break her fast, she headed for her shoppe.

Dawn was barely breaking, and the night was making way for what appeared to be a glorious day. The lane was quiet, and the songbirds were just beginning to sing as she neared her building. It was cool this morning, but the temperature would be warm by this afternoon.

Rhy needed to gather supplies before she went to check on Jameson. Myranda was covering the shoppe for part of the day while she was gone. The shoppe wouldn't keep her too busy today. The clinic, however, might. T'would depend on how mean Danny was feeling or how out of control the fire clan students became.

Nearing the front door, her oversized mama cat wove in and out of her ankles, seeking attention. Picking her up, Rhy gave the kitty some proper loving until her purring vibrated through her arms. Dropping her to the ground, she magically unlocked the clinic and cast pale-blue witch light into the lanterns around the room.

Jars of scented massage oil she'd made the day before sat on the counter next to pouches of powders for pain relief and teas that helped induce sleep. Grabbing a large, leather satchel off the wall with padded sections for the oil, she loaded up everything she would need for this visit. A few extra herbs for the clan healers fit nicely in an inside pocket. Rhy picked out some lavender scented candles she'd made. She'd pressed pansies into the wax around the edges.

A soft knock on the door surprised her. She rarely had visitors this early. "C'mon in," she called as she continued loading fresh bandages and poultices to her bag.

The door slowly opened, and it surprised her to find Collette Creek standing in her doorway. "What can I do for ye, lass?" she asked in a sharper tone than she would've used for anyone else.

Collette hung her head, and her voice was hard to hear as she closed the door and said, "I wondered if you would consider healing the marks on my face, Mistress Rhyanna?"

"Come into the light," Rhy said, pulling a chair for Collette to sit in. Taking the teen's face in her hands, she examined the gash high on her cheekbone. T'was far enough from the eye not to be a worry. The edges were raw, and the bruising had spread a palette of blues and purples to the surrounding area. Pressing on the surrounding area made the girl hiss, but nothing appeared to be broken.

"You're a renowned healer. I'm sure you are capable of finishing the job today."

Rhy paused with her hands on either side of the girl's head and stared into her eyes. "Yer quite right, Collette. I be quite capable of healing this in a matter of moments."

Collette gave her a brilliant smile. "Thank you so much, mistress."

"I said I was capable, lass. I didna, however, say I'd fix it fer ye."

Eyes blazing, the girl gave her a stupefied look. "You're the healer. This is painful and looks horrid. Why won't you help me? I'll see that my father hears about this."

"Ye go right ahead and do that, lass. I'll have the pleasure of explaining to him that although it may be a wee bit uncomfortable, the biggest discomfort yer feeling is to yer pride."

"How dare you!"

"Seriously, lass. How dare I?" Rhy asked, her sharp tone putting the twat in her place. "How dare I share a truth with ye? Well, get comfortable in yer chair, chile, cause I'se about to share a few more."

With a gentle pressure of air keeping her in place, Rhy gave her a piece of her mind. "I held me tongue yesterday because I was afraid of what I might have said to ye lasses."

Her eyes met Collette's, and the furious indignation was still there. "How dare *ye* humiliate Genny the way ye did? Ye never once gave a thought to how much yer statement could've harmed that girl, didchya?"

When no answer was forthcoming, she continued. "None of ye cared that ye were flinging accusations at her fer *everyone* to hear because that was intentional." Rhy came up for a breath and went right back at it. "Ye implied she was a whore, and that she wasn't good enough for the prince to waste his time on."

Emerald eyes flashed dangerously at Collette. "What gives *ye* the right to determine who's good enough for Kai? You ken nothing about his preferences or her circumstances. Do ye ken what led up to her lifestyle? Ye have any inkling what that poor chile endured? Because I sure as hell do. I ken the abuse she experienced, physically and emotionally, because I was the one to heal it. Ye ken what I can't heal?"

Collette's face flamed with her shame, and she shook her head no, turning away as tears tracked down her face. Rhy grasped her chin and forced her to meet her eyes. "Ye donna get to hide from yer shame, Collette, when ye didn't have the grace or mercy to let her keep her past to herself."

Staring into the willful lass's eyes, she continued. "I couldna heal her sense of self-esteem or her sense of shame. I couldna take away the sense of betrayal by the only person she thought loved her. And I couldna give her back the one thing that a woman possesses that shoulda been her gift to a man of her choice."

Rhy glared at the young woman as Collette's tears turned into sobs. "I couldna give her back years of her young life that are long gone, never again to be viewed through the lens of innocence and joy. The wee lass never makes it through a full night of sleep without nightmares, and now ye've made her waking hours a nightmare, too."

Rhyanna handed her a handkerchief to wipe her nose with and said in a milder tone, "Ye think on all that while yer minor blemish heals. In nigh two weeks, ye won't even be able to see it existed. Genny will carry some of her wounds for the rest of her life—especially when there are miserable lil twats like ye in this world."

Collette sat there as tears dripped down her face to her chin and then splashed to the floor. "Genny's not the only one with demons here," she whispered. "She's just one of the few you could actually save."

The statement was so low that Rhy nearly missed it. Meeting her haunted gaze, she handed her a cool, damp cloth to wipe her face. Sneaking a quick peek into Collette's auric field, she wanted to vomit. Someone was abusing this girl as well. "Ye'd be right," she said, pulling her rolling stool over. Taking a seat, she reached for the girl's hands.

"I ken someone is hurting ye, lass. Anything ye say to me stays with me. I can't offer ye help if ye don't ask me fer it. Ye ken?"

This time, when Collette met her eyes, she saw nothing but sympathy. Straightening her spine, she gazed down her nose at the healer. "I've no idea what you are talking about."

"Yer welcome to play it that way, lass. I'll not force it from ye. Remember, me door be always open should ya need it." Rhy stood, understanding the moment had passed, and Collette wouldn't confide in her.

Collette was at the door when Rhy spoke again. "Lass," she waited until the teen glanced over her shoulder at her. "I wish ye'd consider the fact that most bullies hurt others because someone's hurting them. If the cycle doesn't end, ye'll be no better than they are. Someday, ye'll leave this world with nothing to remember ye by but the damage and pain ye've inflicted on others. Is that the legacy ye wish to be known fer?"

All the color drained from the lass's face, and her eyes filled once again. Stoically, she straightened her spine and gave Rhy a nod. "Good day, Mistress Rhyanna. I'm sorry to have wasted so much of your time."

Rhyanna let out a long sigh as Collette left the building. The sound was full of frustration and sorrow for what this poor little rich girl was going through. All her family's money and power hadn't protected this child when it damn well should have. But without Collette's testimony, there was nothing she could do about it...yet.

Rhy finished gathering supplies, but the encounter with Collette dimmed her enthusiasm for the day. The lass could be miserable, but the behind-the-scenes glance into her auric field helped the healer in her understand why.

The poor lass was in trouble and lashed out at everyone else in her path. Rhy believed she set her sights on Kai in a bid for self-preservation. She was looking for a man to protect her, and the prince was a big man, one most people wouldn't try to antagonize. He also provided the type of pedigree her family could hardly refuse.

Ethically, Rhy felt conflicted. Without Collette coming to her directly for help with this situation, she could not have Warden's Court step in to protect the lass. Some would argue that she had no right peeking into aspects of the lass's life without parental authorization. Although, others would agree that checking her for a concussion or shattered cheekbone would allow her access to her entire auric body.

If Rhy brought it to Maddy's attention, it would put the wheels of justice into motion. The Creeks were a prominent family, and the scandal would make waves all the way to the Elemental High Court. If she confided in Danyka, Danny would eliminate the threat, thereby creating an entirely different set of problems.

Shaking her head, she set her concerns about Collette to the side. She had other matters to attend to today. Taking the portal she arrived on Wellesley Island mid-morning. Renting a horse at the stables, she rode like the wind, getting the cobwebs out of her mind and her heart. Of all the thousand islands, Wellesley was her favorite. Lush vegetation and large farms maintained much of the natural beauty of the island.

The gelding she rode needed speed as badly as she did, and they quickly approached the Vance farm. The main gate was open, so she slowed him to a walk and made her way to the home of Kateri and Kuruk Vance.

After tying her horse to a post with a watering trough nearby, she made her way to the door. Before she could knock, the door popped open, and Kateri threw her arms around her. "Rhy, what a lovely surprise."

Rhy hugged her back. They'd known each other for many years but had grown closer since Jamey's accident. "Kat, how are ye?"

"I'm wonderful. Want a cuppa?"

"Nye, jest here to check on our Jamey, and then I needs be off."

Rhy couldn't miss the look of disappointment on Kateri's face, so she removed her bag and said, "Actually, I'd love a cup." Reaching into her bag, she carefully removed the candle she'd packed. "For you. May it brighten your nights and help solidify yer intentions when manifesting."

"It's beautiful, Rhy," Kateri said. Picking up the fat, three-wick work of art, she examined the tiny wildflowers pressed into the sides. "It's like having a tiny piece of the spring meadow with me all year long. I won't want to burn it."

"Nye, ye must. That's why 'twas created. I'll make ye another whence this one's done." She sipped her tea and asked, "How's yer lad coming along?"

Kateri met her gaze, raising an eyebrow. "Physically, he's doing well, gaining strength and range every day. Emotionally…"

"Danny?" Rhy asked, knowing the heart of his hurt.

"Yes. He loves her, and I'm pretty damn sure she loves him." She laughed and added, "But they're stubborn as mules."

"That they are, and she more than he."

"May I ask you something, Mistress?"

"Must be serious if ye be tossing out titles on me."

"No, just a mother's concern."

Rhy took a deep breath, not knowing how far down this path she could safely tread. Danyka was one of her oldest and dearest friends, and she wouldn't be gossiping about her. "Ye can ask me anything ye'd like, but there's only so much I will answer."

"I respect your discretion." Long, delicate fingers traced the rim of her cup as she put her thoughts into words. "Jamey has given me some of Danny's background. I understand more than you realize the trauma she experienced."

Rhy's eyes widened at her statement. "I'm sorry that ye have personal knowledge of her suffering," she said, trying to confirm what Kateri was telling her.

"'Twas a long time ago, and I rarely allow it to take up space in my mind or my life." Her fingers tapped on the edge now. "Since our conversation weeks ago, I've had a few nightmares."

Rhy listened, allowing her the space to share her story. "I wish Danny would come see me. I might help her navigate a relationship." She cleared her throat. "I know how easy it is to believe you don't deserve someone good."

"I'll do me best to encourage her to seek ye out, Kateri. But that's all I'se can offer."

"I'm being silly, but I just hate to see both of them suffering when they might heal each other instead." Kateri wiped her eyes.

"I agree. Avoiding him breaks her heart and makes her bloody miserable to be around." They both laughed at that.

"Speaking of Jamey, where can I find him at this hour?" Rhy asked.

"He and Sian are sparring up at the cabin."

"Perfect, then I can see how well his range of motion has improved since me last visit."

Rhy stood and gathered her things. "Thank you for the tea, and sorry I couldn't share more…"

"No worries. A healer's oath prevents you from sharing some things, and a friend's pledge prevents you from sharing others. I understand and appreciate your integrity, Rhy." Hugging her tightly, they said their goodbyes.

Rhy headed for Jamey's cabin, praying she could clear him for active duty. His future as a Warden would then rest in Madylyn's hands. Rhy hoped changes wouldn't be needed to keep the entire team safe from the emotional fallout of this couple. Because if they were needed, it would only add

another layer of guilt and shame to an already volatile couple, and she didn't know if they could tolerate anything else.

70

I Hate This Place

Collette stumbled away from the healer's shoppe, weighed down with guilt, shame, and so much rage she didn't know where to go with it. Running as fast as she could, she made her way to the far side of the island, as far away from the docks and animal rehab center as she could.

The last thing she needed after Mistress Rhyanna's rejection was to run into Kai or Genny. She'd already botched up any attempts to get that man on her side.

She didn't understand it. Why was the pitiful little waif with a shit ton of baggage worth helping, and she couldn't even get him to look at her?

The girls were polar opposites in appearance and personalities. Dark-haired Genny with a waif-like figure devoid of curves—or breasts, if we were being honest. The little mouse trembled if you raised your voice. She was from poor breeding stock and the wrong side of the river. Rumor had it her family sold her to the traffickers. Who did that to their child?

Collette had overflowing curves in all the right places, accentuating a tiny waist and long, lean legs. Born into privilege, she had no problem standing up for herself or putting someone else in their proper place. Unfortunately, her family wanted her. She was receiving entirely too much attention from one of them for all the wrong reasons.

Mistress Rhyanna saw her shame. Collette refused to face it, discuss it, or seek help from anyone. No one would understand how she, of all people, could end up in this situation. Collette wouldn't become fodder for the gossips and shame mongers.

Guilt ate at her for the accusations she leveled at Genny. She made certain everyone's attention was on the rescued whore's horrific life so that they wouldn't examine hers too closely.

Running out of island, she stopped on the edge of the cliff overlooking the river. Bent over with her hands on her knees, chest heaving and legs burning, she thought she was going to puke. Unable to catch a breath, she wheezed as she processed her options.

Collette couldn't go back to classes looking like she got the shit kicked out of her—which she had. She refused to be humiliated again by the pixie-like woman who beat her with a stick. "I hate this fucking place!" she screamed into the wind.

When she left here, she intended to file a formal complaint with the Elemental High Court. She would go into detail regarding the barbaric conditions she experienced. While her burning lungs sucked in air, she drafted it in her head.

Intending to call for Mistress Danyka's job and Mistress Rhyanna's for refusing to heal her when she could do so, she might just add Headmistress SkyDancer to the list as well. The woman obviously had no control whatsoever over her employees.

Letting herself live with the fantasy of ruining their lives for a few moments longer, the anger evaporated, and she burst into tears. Knees hitting the ground, she curled up and sobbed. Collette didn't know what to do, and she had no one to confide in.

Blaze and Chantal had been her friends since they were children. Their families moved in the same circles. But, were they really her friends or just her social equals? Did she even have one person who would have stood up for her like Ryssa did for a girl she'd just met?

Collette didn't inspire that kind of loyalty from anyone. She couldn't think of one person in her life that she would have done that for either. Her life was fucking pitiful. She was a horrible person and deserved everything that was happening to her.

Who would she have become had her mother survived her birth? It was a thought that plagued her lately. If only one person in her life had shown her kindness or love, would she have become this cold, shallow bitch?

Sobbing harder, she realized how close to the cliff she was. *It would be so easy*, she thought. They couldn't hurt her anymore and she would stop hurting everyone around her. Crawling to her knees, she knelt on the edge, gazing down at the waves crashing on the rocks below.

In the early morning light, the distant campfires of the Romani village below her were burning brightly, welcoming those near and far. If she had any hope left, she might have sought shelter there, but she knew she didn't deserve mercy or forgiveness.

Collette was tired of fighting to be perfect. Tired of keeping secrets and trying not to fucking scream; she had nothing left to give.

Wiping the tears from her face, she stood up, straightened her clothing, fixed her windblown hair, and tipped her face into the breeze. Smiling because she knew she would finally be free of everything and everyone that tormented her in this world, she spread her arms and stepped off the edge.

71

Hosting A Tournament

Queen Yareli stood, glaring at her former partner and her son, Kenn, as if they had lost their ever-loving minds. "You've arranged a tournament *here* in less than two weeks' time and now expect me to pull off a miracle?" She'd mistakenly thought they were joking when they suggested it at the Warden's council meeting.

Two heads nodded eagerly, glad that she'd finally caught on.

"Imbeciles," she muttered under her breath. "These things take time and planning. I'm still trying to straighten out the mess this court is, and you think this is a good idea?"

Varan drifted towards her, making her heart race traitorously in her chest. She didn't want him to affect her in any way—but he did. The treachery that separated them for years hadn't been his fault, but the damage done wasn't so easily forgiven.

Taking her hands, he kissed her knuckles, causing a flush to rise in her cheeks. "If anyone can pull this together on short notice, it's you." Lost in his gaze, she was drowning in his presence.

Kenn barked out a laugh. "I'm sweating from the heat the two of you are generating and need to cool down. I'll be back…"

"Don't you dare walk out that door, Kenn." Yareli's maternal tone snapped his spine straight, and he felt like he was ten, not wanting to disappoint her.

"Leave us," his father said in his most official tone, which, thankfully, didn't have the same effect on him.

"Hell hasn't frozen over yet," Yareli said, yanking her hands away. "If you want this to happen by the solstice, you both are going to sit your asses down and help me figure this out."

"We could just go through with the sign-ups and cancel when we apprehend the bastard," Varan said.

"Like hell," Yareli said at the same time Kenn chimed in with, "You won't earn any points with the locals that way."

"You need to reestablish yourself, not just to your family and this court, but to the community at large," Yareli chided.

"I busted my ass spreading around good cheer from the Court of Tears, and we are going to honor the promises I made on your behalf. I don't get up that early for nothing," Kenn snarled when she finished.

Varan raised his hands in a placating manner. "Forgive me, please, for my insensitivity." His gaze locked on Yareli's. "I'm well aware of the things I need to atone for and the penances due. I will pay the price for my failures until the day I die because they cost me years with you."

Yareli's breath caught at the sincerity of his words. It was the first time she'd allowed him to speak of the past, and it hadn't been intentional on her part. This was why. Varan's golden tongue could always convince her of anything, even against her better judgment. She couldn't afford to play the fool again.

The king's gaze moved to his son's, sharpening as they did so. "I am also painfully aware of the ways I've failed my children. The formative years when my attention might have made a difference are gone. I'll never get that time back, and with the loss of watching my children grow, I've lost any form of credibility in your eyes."

Kenn's gaze never faltered. He met his father's frustration head on, refusing to make this easier on the man whose choices made their lives hell.

"Maybe someday you will find it in you to at least give me the courtesy of trying to get to know me as an adult. Form your own opinions of me without the drugs in my system or that bitch by my side."

Varan took a shuddering breath. "I sincerely appreciate the time and effort you have put into this tournament, Kenn, and I will not disappoint you or the citizens you represent. I was merely thinking of the information we are desperate to gain and the women we need to rescue."

Kenn nodded his head slowly, pondering his words. "I think the king should offer to meet Fisher Jordan when he shows up. Invite him to a private game between the king and his sons. A lesson for them in the fine arts of poker. We'll play a game, and at the end, when he's ready to claim his winnings, we'll lead him to one of the finer rooms in our dungeon. Tristan can get the information we need." An evil smile crossed his face. "I wouldn't be averse to assisting him."

Yareli shook her head. "Kenn, really. I'm not sure I want to know about the depravities you enjoy."

"Sorry, Mama," he mumbled, but his voice was anything but sincere.

A servant entered with a letter on a silver platter that he delivered to Kenn. Breaking the seal, he read the message and headed for the door. "Gotta go. Will check back in later."

Yareli's heart pounded as she watched her son leave. She'd made damn sure she wasn't alone with Varan over the past few weeks. Turning back to the king, she bowed, ready to leave, but found he'd moved directly in front of her. Already in motion, she lost her balance and stumbled into his chest. Her hands grabbed two fistfuls of his shirt to keep herself upright as his hands grabbed her hips, steadying her.

"My lady, he said, gazing into her eyes."

"Varan…" her voice trailed off as his gaze dropped to her lips, and gods help her, she couldn't move and couldn't speak.

"You are so damn beautiful, Yar," he said as a hand came up to cup her face. His thumb brushed against her lips, and as she sucked in a breath of surprise, he lowered his lips to hers. His eyes flashed back to hers, daring her to stop him.

When she didn't put on the brakes, he brushed his lips against hers, whisper soft, afraid she would run away. But she didn't run. She leaned into his hand, meeting his kiss. Still, he kept his touch light, teasing her senses, making her want more.

Yareli didn't know what came over her. Maybe it was the passionate way in which he'd spoken to her and Kenn. Maybe it was the sensual dreams she had of him nightly since she'd returned to court, or maybe it was the constant reminder of their chemistry. She didn't know and right now; she didn't care. It had been so long since she'd wanted a man. Yareli wanted his lips on hers.

Releasing his shirt, she threaded her hands through his long hair, tangling her fingers in the heavy strands and pulling him closer. When he continued to tease her, she bit his lower lip to get his attention. "If you're going to kiss me, Varan, then by God, get to it."

His lips smirked against hers. "As you demand, my queen."

This time, there was no teasing, no playing. There was nothing but unending heat. His lips scorched hers, and his tongue demanded she keep up. One arm pulled her body tightly against his while his other hand cradled her neck, holding her still while he pillaged her mouth.

Just as she was getting lost in the taste of him, a discreet cough sounded behind them. Varan reluctantly released her with a curse and a gaze of longing and regret.

"This better be damn good, Tristan, to interrupt us," he barked, still not looking away.

"Aye, Your Majesty, I wouldn't have interrupted you if it wasn't."

"Don't go…" he said, trailing off as he turned to the captain of his guard. But he was too late. As soon as he'd turned, Yareli quickly headed for the door.

"Excuse me," she said to Tristan as she walked by, needing to be anywhere but here when Tristan left.

She didn't understand why she'd encouraged Varan, but she didn't want to pick up where they left off. Heading straight for the gardens, she left the two men behind her, observing her.

"My apologies, Your Majesty. I shouldn't have interrupted the two of you," Tristan said.

Varan brushed off his apology. "Don't worry about it, Tristan. She would have bolted soon, anyway. I'm surprised she allowed me to kiss her, and I'm damned because all I can think about is doing it again." he brushed a hand over his face, trying to get her flushed face out of his mind. "What do you need?"

"Well, my lord, 'tis about the queen."

An arched brow encouraged him to continue. "It's a man, and he's here to see her." Tristan let that sink in before asking, "How should we proceed?"

"What's his name?"

"Kendall Winslet."

Varan winced, rubbing his hand over his beard.

"You know him?" Tristan asked.

"Of him," Varan growled. "He was an old suitor of Yar's."

"I see."

"Do you now? And how would you advise I deal with this, wise one?"

"Well, wiseass," Tristan said drolly. "You have three choices. Welcome him, turn him away, or throw him in an oubliette."

Tristan enjoyed watching Varan mulling it over. "Two of those choices stand to show her you are no better than Meriel. Allowing his visit indicates a level of trust."

Varan stalked to the liquor cart and poured two fingers of bourbon into a glass for each of them. Handing one out to Tristan, he swirled the amber liquid in his and contemplated not what he wanted to do but what was the right thing to do.

"I'll allow it." He tossed back the whiskey, wincing at the burn. "Bring him here first. I don't want him to have any delusions as to the health of the king."

"Smart move. Both of them. It's what I would have recommended."

Casting him a side glare, he asked, "Are you never wrong?"

Tristan barked out a laugh. "I'm wrong a good portion of the time. Usually in matters concerning women, not common sense." Again, the droll sense of humor was like a slap.

"Well, I can't wait to see the woman who knocks you on your ass, Tristan. Because when she does, I intend to laugh at your expense."

"Gonna be a chilly day in hell, old friend," Tristan said as a scowl crossed his face. "I loved once and lost. I have no intention of putting my heart out to be trampled on again."

"Haven't you learned yet? Love doesn't wait for anyone's permission."

Varan's laughter followed Tristan out the door. "I wish you luck on your journey with love, Your Majesty, because you've got a long road to go."

"Fuck you, my friend," Varan called after him, hating that Tristan was right. A nagging in his gut made him wonder if she'd ever really give him another chance.

The kiss this morning might have been a fluke, but it gave him hope. All he needed was an ounce of hope and he'd fight to the death for Yareli. They were soul mates. Even though another woman had insinuated herself between them and made a fool out of him, he intended to get back in his queen's good graces—and her bed.

But first, he thought as footsteps neared, he was going to show this pompous ass that it was good to be king. It would take more than this man possessed to insert himself between Yareli and him.

Kendall gave a curt bow, acknowledging his station, then gave him a charismatic smile. "King Varan, it's wonderful to make your acquaintance."

Varan's hackles instantly went up, but he offered his hand. The man's handshake was steady, surprising him. Tristan stood at the door, waiting. Varan gave him a nod, indicating he should fetch the queen.

"Mr. Winslet," Varan said with a predator's grin. "How can the Court of Tears be of service today?"

Kendall's smile only grew bolder. "Yareli sent for me. I'm to be Klaree's tutor."

The fuck you are," he thought instantly. One thing was for sure, he didn't want this man near his queen, and he sure as fuck didn't want this young peacock near his impressionable daughter. *"We'll see about that."*

Turning the wattage up higher, he met Yareli's eyes as she returned. "My darling, you have a guest."

Her quirked eyebrow told him she didn't trust his behavior for a minute, and her side glare entreated him to behave. Then his woman had the audacity to meet Kendall in the middle of the room with a sincere embrace. As the man kissed both sides of her cheeks, Varan's fists clenched, and he strode to the window, doing his best to behave.

Yareli took the man's hand and said, "Come with me to the parlor. It's much less stuffy than this room." As Varan's head whipped around, she caught his eye and openly dared him to challenge her.

Instead, he gave her a brilliant smile. "Sounds like a lovely idea. Come, I can't wait to hear how Kendall intends to tutor our daughter."

As they headed for the door, Tristan shoulder-checked him and said, "You're laying it on pretty thick. Might want to back off."

Varan's growl made him chuckle as he stalked down the hall behind the woman he loved and the one man who might come between them. Tristan's footsteps behind him mocked him, and he had the childish urge to break something.

But Varan Tyde was the Court of Tears King, and it was about time he acted like it. Pushing down his petty jealousy, he followed like a dutiful puppy to see what this man's role in their lives would become.

72

I've Been Waiting For You

Expecting the sensation of falling and a moment of excruciating pain, Collette shrieked in frustration when a body wrapped around her. Strong limbs clamped tightly around her, dragging her back from the ledge.

Pulled back against a muscular chest, she screamed and thrashed in his arms. "Noooo," she wailed. "Let me go, please let me go."

Ignoring her request and her screeching, he picked her up. Despite her thrashing limbs, he carried her away from the ledge, through the meadow and back into the forest. Settling against an old maple with her in front of him, he wrapped his long limbs around her and rocked her. Collette cried and fought his confinement.

"Release me, you bastard. You have no right to stop me. You understand nothing about my situation. Go the fuck away and leave me be." Her words fell on deaf ears. When her body tired from the fight, she collapsed against him, weeping inconsolably.

His lips pressed against her temple as he rocked her to a rhythm she couldn't hear. A deep baritone voice sang her a song in a language she didn't understand. She didn't know the words, but she recognized a song of healing and soothing for her soul.

When she finally stopped fighting him, his hands ran long caresses down her arms. Interlacing his fingers with hers, he whispered in her ear. His exotic voice was a caress against her frazzled emotions. "I don't comprehend what yer running from, lass. But there is nothing we can't face together."

Sniffling, she wiped her nose on her sleeve. "You know nothing about me." A sad laugh erupted from her. Her voice was nearly gone from yelling when she added, "And trust me, you don't want to. The best thing you could have done for this world would have been to have let me fall."

"Nye," he said fiercely. "I wouldn't deprive the world of something as beautiful as you. Then I would never learn what makes you smile."

His words destroyed any walls she had left. On a hiccuping sob, she said, "Someone told me recently that I was beautiful on the outside but ugly on the inside. You don't want any part of my world."

Strong arms tightened around her, and he pressed a kiss on her neck. "That's where you're wrong, lass. I've spent my whole life waiting for you. I want to learn everything about you so that I can help fix your problems and hunt down your tormentors."

He gently squeezed the hand he held. Collette looked at his long fingers and the gentle strength in them. The callouses on his palms rubbed against the top of her hand. She liked the way it felt, and the way it soothed her.

His arms had relaxed and were loosely encircling her. She pulled her hands free and used her shirt to wipe the tears and snot from her face.

Pulling her knees to her chest, she swiveled to look at the man who refused to let her die. Her jaw dropped when she viewed the handsome young man who'd saved her.

A mop of loose curly black hair framed the face of a fallen angel with eyes so black she couldn't spot his pupils. A double row of lashes framed those eyes, giving him an exotic appearance. High cheekbones and a dimple in his chin made him appear even more so. Broader and much taller than she was, her head barely met his chest.

"What do you mean you've waited a lifetime for me?" she asked him with her brows drawn together and arms crossed over her chest.

Reaching towards her face, he halted when she jerked her head back out of his reach. It would have been comical with her settled between his legs if he couldn't sense the sorrow radiating from her.

Eyes locking on hers, he said in his rhythmic, soothing voice, "I'd never harm you, Collette, because I've been waiting for you."

When he reached for her again, she allowed it, watching him warily while he pushed a strand of her hair behind her ear. His other hand did the same thing until he was cradling her face with his hands and examining her with his dark, piercing eyes.

"I don't understand." Her voice was raw, raspy. "Why have you been waiting for me, and how do you know my name?"

"I've dreamed about you for the past month. My nights were tormented as I watched you jump from here so many times, I've lost count. I'm always chasing you, trying to stop you from falling." He cleared his throat before continuing. "Every single time, I've been too late. I find your broken body on the rocks below."

His voice was hollow as he recounted his dreams. "You've haunted my nights for weeks. Today, when I saw you running…" He paused, closing his

391

eyes against the horrific images she couldn't see. "Because I've failed you so many times, I almost didn't bother trying." A shudder ran through his body. "You would have succeeded once and for all."

Leaning down, he rested his forehead against hers. "I would've lost you before I'd even found you, and it would have destroyed me." His voice was rough when he finished.

The sincerity in his statement shocked her. She couldn't believe that anyone would have cared if she'd disappeared. Tipping her head up so that she could see his eyes, she asked, "But why?"

His gaze was somber as he framed her face and said, "You're my destiny, Collette." He took her hand and placed it over his racing heart. "Can't you feel the ties between us—the lives between us?"

Shaking her head in denial, she tried to pull her hand away.

"Trust me just a little more, baby. Close your eyes for me, please." He kept her hand on his heart, and when she closed her eyes again, he placed his forehead on hers and shared images of her that made her body arc away from him.

His arms banded around her as images of them in another time and place rolled through her mind. Growing up together, falling in love—then making love. Images of his hands on her body—her other body—and the feel of him inside of her as they screamed in pleasure together had her moving closer to him.

When she opened her eyes, she was straddling him and panting. His hands tangled in her hair, and hers held his face. A sob left her as she asked, "Where have you been? I've needed you to find me."

His lips moved over her face, kissing his way to her lips. When he brushed against hers, softly and sweetly, she returned the kiss—her first until a sob ripped from her.

This was too good to be true. Maybe she was lying broken on the rocks, and this was some dying dream she was having. Collette couldn't make sense of any part of this experience. Shaking her head, she said, "You're not real, you can't be..."

"Shhhh, baby, I'm here now, and I promise I won't be far away the entire time you're on this island. I'll protect you."

Tears poured down her face again as she let out an ironic laugh. "I'm safe here. The only thing I need protection from is my own stupidity." The laughter died off as she spoke in a hollow voice, "And then what? Home is where I need help."

"We'll figure that out. For now, I need you to live for me, baby. Can you do that?" He kissed her again, not pushing for more, but needing the connection. "Please, give me your word."

Kisses on her forehead and temple pleaded silently for him, "Please, Collette, I believe if you give me your word, you'll honor it."

"You know nothing about me," she snapped, thinking she'd run him off easily. "I don't even know your name."

His deep laugh was rich, and she melted inside. "That one's easy. You can call me Lash," he said with a cocky grin. "Now, give me your word. If you're struggling, come to me first. Don't give up on us before I have time to make you fall in love with me again." His dark eyes captivated her, making her hope there was something better.

"I probably should get back," she said in a small voice, not wanting to leave him.

"Yeah, they'll be searching for you soon." His hand came up and traced the bruise on her cheek. "You hurt yourself," he said, and she didn't correct him. "Allow me."

Collette grabbed his hand and said, "No. Don't. It was a lesson learned, and one I needed." If it hadn't been for the humiliation of this wound, she wouldn't have found him. They stood, and he took her hand, leading her back the way she'd come.

"When can I see you again?" she asked him.

"They like to keep the students in training close by. But the longest day of the year is nearly here. The entire island celebrates. I'll find you." His lips brushed against her fingers.

"But what if I need you before then?"

"Take this." Lash pressed a gold coin into her palm. "Keep it on you. If you are in danger, I will know, and it will lead me to you."

"You know this entire day is feeling very surreal to me, don't you?" She glanced at him through the curtain of her hair.

"To me as well. I thought I was losing my mind and didn't believe you existed." A deep chuckle made her feel warm inside. "My family believed something was wrong as well."

"Perhaps they're right and we've lost them together," she said, glancing away, suddenly feeling shy.

"I'll find you again soon," he said, giving her one last soft kiss. Releasing her fingers, he faded into the forest.

When Collette turned around, she found herself once again in front of Mistress Rhyanna's shoppe. Students were coming down the hill for their first classes. If she hurried, she could still grab something to eat and make it in time.

Later, when she was alone, she'd examine what happened because a part of her still didn't believe Lash was real. But when she opened her right hand, the antique patina of the gold coin mocked her, slapping her with the truth.

73

Dangers of Shifting

Students sat cross-legged in The Pit's hollow. Everyone sat except Collette, who scampered in late. Bruises covered her face, and leaves tangled in her hair.

Ryssa and Amberly shared a surprised glance. Collette always had her shit together. She never had a hair out of place, and she'd just slunk in looking like something the cat dragged in.

Amberly raised a brow, and Ryssa shrugged her shoulders. Collette dropped to the ground on the outskirts of the students, away from her usual friends. Ryssa wondered if she was just trying to avoid pissing Mistress Danyka off again.

"Nice of you to join us, Collette," Mistress Danyka's voice rang out from the front.

"My apologies, mistress," Collette said with her eyes cast down.

Now Ryssa was curious. Nothing cowed this girl, and here she sat, pale and meek. What the hell happened to her this morning?

"All eyes up here, if you will," Danyka snapped. She and another of the wardens sat on stools before them. "Most of you probably haven't had the pleasure of meeting Kerrygan, another one of our air mages." Her hand pointed towards him. It was as much of an introduction as they were going to get.

"I realize, typically, this is hand-to-hand training, but today, we are going to delve into the world of shifting. Some of you are already showing indications of having the ability to shift, and we don't want you caught unaware or caught between forms," she said.

Danyka stood and paced before the students. "Many of you will have the latent gene allowing you to change the shape you inhabit. Some of you will possess the ability to take several shapes, like I can."

Wandering through the students, she continued, "Others won't possess this trait at all. However, they may have other specialties, such as teleportation or invisibility. Or they may communicate with other forms of life better than they can telepathically with humans."

"You will all share some abilities, but the beauty of our elemental powers lies in our body's ability to be unique. Our greatest strength as a species is our ability to capitalize on our strengths with each other." She gave them a minute for that to sink in.

"I am blessed with the ability to shift into multiple forms."

One moment, she stood there as a woman, and the next, her clothes dropped to the ground, and she flew over the crowd in her peregrine falcon form. On her next pass over the students, she dropped to all fours and roamed through them as a white tiger.

She sauntered over to Collette, sniffing her hair and rubbing against her cheek while the poor girl stiffened in fear. With a low growl, the tiger wandered up to the stage, and the warden stood before them nude for a moment as she quickly dressed.

"Nudity is a part of shifting. You will never return to your human form fully clothed. This is something you learn to accept. Eventually, as you mature, you will stop gawking at other shifters." Her gaze landed on several of the young men in the front row. Cheeks flaming, they studied their hands or the ground beneath them.

"Larger shifters learn to take their clothing with them, tied around their neck or on their back. Smaller shifters are unable to carry their clothing. If you have a partner who shifts into a larger animal, they can carry your belongings for you."

"Should you accidentally shift the first time on your own, we beg you to just lie down, or sit down wherever you are and wait for help to arrive so that you harm no one. For example, if you shifted into a tiger, a grizzly, or a hellhound, you might unwillingly become a threat to your fellow students."

Danyka paused for a minute, letting that sink in. "Stay where you are, and your fellow students will call for help. Try to stay in touch with your human thoughts and emotions. Fight to stay focused and clear-headed. If we have to tranq you to force a change, you will have one hell of a hangover the next morning."

"There are a few of you who will easily shift and who may prefer to stay in your favorite animal form." Danyka turned her gaze on her fellow warden. "Kerrygan will explain to you the dangers of shifting for too long."

Kerrygan sat on his perch, his slit pupils taking in each of the students before him. He took his time meeting their gazes, letting them see the distortion in his eyes.

Standing, he paced before them. "Through no fault of me own, someone trapped in a cage much too small to allow me to shift. I spent decades there."

Whispers and gasps worked their way through the crowd. "When Ronan released me a month ago, I returned to my human form with some alterations."

Running his hands through his hair, he plucked a blue feather from his scalp, letting it drift to the ground. "Me eyes be the most obvious transformation, but this be another adverse effect." Splaying his hands in front of them, he displayed the fingers that now held claws instead of nails.

"That's really cool," one of the louder boys in the front yelled.

"How cool do ye think it would have been if ye returned with a prick the size of your fingernail?" Kerrygan asked. His deformed eyes drilling into the little asshole. "How cool would it be if ye could only shriek instead of speaking? If ye laid eggs instead of bearing human young?" He sneered at him. "Real fecking cool, huh?"

Walking back towards Danny, he said, "This class is called the dangers of shifting because it's fecking dangerous. It ain't a fecking game. If ye don't listen to us, ye could plummet from the sky while flying a mile above the ground. Ye could end up challenging another animal of yer species that doesn't realize ye're human. A grizzly will attack on instinct, uncaring that ye fecked up when ye shifted too close to her cub. She will kill ye, and there's no bringing back stupid when he's dead."

"Form a line," Danyka said, waiting for the students to fall in. Leading them towards Kerry, she said. "Look at him. Really look at him. Touch his hair; he won't bite. Feel the claws on his hands, and look him in the eye, knowing that anytime he shifts in the future, he risks losing what little of his humanity remains."

Mistress Danyka paced as they studied Kerrygan's changes. "And who could blame him if he did for having to deal with your dumb asses?"

Nervous laughter joined hers. "There are enormous risks with shifting. It is your responsibility to learn everything about the species you feel a kinship with prior to your first shift."

Danyka paced through the students, speaking somberly, "Only shift when a warden is nearby. If something goes wrong, we can help you. At the very least, we will keep you safe and contained until someone else can arrive."

Collette was last in line. As she walked by Danny, she met her eyes bravely, earning her a nod. When she stopped in front of Kerrygan, she peered into his strange eyes, tipping her head thoughtfully. Reaching towards him, she hesitated until he nodded for her to continue. Her hands reached into his hair, assessing the difference in textures.

Taking his hands, she traced his claws with a finger. Releasing him, she stared into his eyes and whispered, "I think you're beautiful." Dropping her gaze, she walked away.

Kerry's eyes followed her as she walked away. He cleared his throat, suddenly struggling to blink quickly. No one other than Rhy and Danny had touched him since his return. This young woman made him feel less repulsive than he had since Ronan forced him to return to his human form. Perhaps there was hope for him after all.

"Questions?" Danyka asked. When no one spoke, she said, "You got lucky and get out early today. Class dismissed." Turning back to Kerry, she asked in a low voice, "You alright?"

"Yeah," he said in a strangled voice. "I didn't expect kindness."

"I didn't expect it from her," Danny said. "But she's right, Kerry. You are beautiful, and there are lots of women out there who are going to think so if you give them the opportunity."

"Maybe."

"You afraid things won't work properly?" Her eyebrows met near her hairline. "Or did your pecker shrivel up?"

"Shut the fuck up," he said in disgust.

"I see," she said with a smirk, punching him in the shoulder. "You've already tried it out."

"Wouldn't tell you if I did." A blush stained his cheeks.

"Aww, c'mon tell me. Now, I'm curious."

Kerrygan shoved her away. "Go away, freak."

"Nope, you're stuck with me."

Tucking herself under his shoulder, she gave him a hug.

"Wouldn't want it any other way, Pixie."

"Me neither."

74

My Solemn Vow

Madylyn dismounted her horse and headed for the door of the Vance family cabin. Before she could knock, it opened, and Kateri welcomed her.

"It's always a pleasure to find you at my door, Madylyn," she said warmly. "Come in."

"Thank you Kateri." A man built nearly the same as Jameson, but taller, nodded at her from where he leaned against an archway. "Kuruk, good to see you both."

"Tea?" Kateri asked.

"I'd love a cup." Madylyn smiled and took a chair Kuruk pulled out for her. "Thank you. Tobias is doing well with his training."

"Has he shifted yet?" Kateri asked.

"No, we haven't begun yet. We like to get them settled with the basic elements first before encouraging their first shift."

"Makes sense. Ensures they have greater control over their emotions and primary element."

"Exactly." She took a sip of the tea Kateri poured, then asked, "How's our Jamey doing?"

A shadow crossed the other woman's face, and Kuruk made a sound behind her. "I'm going to get to work," he said, giving Madylyn a nod and Kateri a kiss on his way out.

"Was it something I said?" Maddy asked.

"No. He's just frustrated with him. He thinks Jamey should fight harder for Danny." Her gaze met Maddy's. "But you and I know the battle for Danny is much more difficult than it would be for most women. The journey will be fraught with frustration and anguish for both of them before this is over."

"I'm afraid you're right. Between her stubborn streak and the memories that haunt her, their relationship will not be easy for either of them."

Maddy took another sip of her tea.

"I nearly forgot," Kateri said, jumping up. "These just came out of the oven before you got here." She laid a plate of fresh shortbread on the table in front of Maddy.

"One of my favorites!" She bit into the buttery cookie and mumbled, "Thank you," around the crumbs.

"So, tell me how your pregnancy is progressing."

Maddy beamed. "Everything is going as planned. Rhyanna says the babe is healthy, happy, and growing steadily."

"The Mother has blessed you and Ronan. A boy and now a girl. Your family and hearts will be full."

"Damn near to overflowing!" Maddy said with a laugh. She snagged another cookie and got down to the reason for her visit.

"Rhyanna was out earlier this week. She reported Jamey has improved tremendously, and she thinks he is ready to return to light duty." Her eyes never left Kateri, examining her reactions, trying to read any doubts the woman might have about her son's return to duty.

"You don't trust her opinion?" Kateri asked skeptically.

"I do. But I also wanted to hear your opinion. You know Jamey better than anyone, and if you have any hesitations, I trust you to be honest with me. I know you wouldn't do anything to put him, or the rest of my team, in jeopardy again."

"No, I wouldn't," Kateri's voice was matter-of-fact, but her gaze showed her concerns even when she didn't say them.

"Truth is, the Sanctuary has become his home now, and all of you have become his second family. You know him as well right now as I do. You'll need to speak to Jamey yourself to gauge his state of mind."

"Of course," Maddy said. "I just wanted to run it by you first." She finished her tea and then stood to let herself out. "If you can, direct me where I might find him."

Kateri turned inward, locating her son instantly. "He's in the stables."

Walking Maddy towards the door, she said, "I appreciate the consideration, Maddy. Even if I can't give you the answers you seek, I'm grateful for the courtesy."

Maddy gave her a wide smile. "I wouldn't have done it any other way."

Making her way down the stairs, Maddy crossed the dusty road and headed for the enormous, whitewashed barn standing across from the house. Centuries old, the building withstood the passage of time gracefully, and the family kept it well maintained. The freshly whitewashed boards and clean floors spoke of something that was well taken care of.

She found Jamey in the back of the building, brushing down his horse. "Maddy," he said, giving her a wide grin. "What are you doing out here? I'm surprised Ronan let you out without a guard."

"That's probably because I didn't bother asking permission." They both laughed. "He's gotten even more protective with the little one on the way." She rubbed her belly, loving that she could sense a prominent bump forming.

"Can't say as I blame him at all," Jamey said, picking up the curry comb again.

Maddy stroked Nizhoni's nose, rubbing her hands down the front of it and along the sides of her neck. "I know, but sometimes it's better to ask for forgiveness than for permission."

Jamey chuckled. They stood there in silence for a few moments while he finished brushing the horse. "C'mon girl, I know you want to be out in the pasture with your friends." He led her out the back door, through the gate and into the pasture.

Maddy followed him. Folding her arms on the fence, she rested her chin on them. Jameson joined her, mirroring her pose.

"Rhy says you're ready to return—to come back home." She let that sit for a moment and asked, "How do you feel about returning?"

Jamey was silent for a few moments, giving the question the deliberation it deserved. "I'm not quite back to a hundred percent, Maddy." His hand scrubbed over his face. "I may never get there."

"No, you might not." Maddy watched the horses galloping through the pasture with no cares to slow them down. "But she believes you're damn near the best it's going to get, and she doesn't think it will affect your performance."

"Hmm," Jamey said, hoping that was true.

"What I need to know is not how you're doing physically, because I trust her to make that call. I need to know if your head's in the right place, Jamey."

Jamey bit his lower lip before answering. He watched Nizhoni enjoying her freedom, and he envied her. All she had to do was eat and run and give him a ride if he asked for one. She didn't have to deal with any of the emotional bullshit humans got mired in.

"Maddy, you know I won't lie to you." His dark amber gaze met her midnight blue one, waiting for her nod. "I'm in a helluva lot better place today than I was the day of the accident. My jealousy overruled my logic, and it nearly got us both killed. I give you my word that I won't ever let that happen again."

Maddy gave him a wry smile. "Emotions are funny like that, Jamey. Especially jealousy. Our best intentions mean little when our heart or our hurts get in the way."

His eyes returned to the pasture as he contemplated her words. "You're absolutely right." He picked at a sliver of wood on the top rail of the fence. "But I love her. I can be honest about that now. I won't ever do anything that will put her or any other member of our team in harm's way."

Jamey turned to face her. "I give you my word, Maddy. If our personal shit impedes the job, I'll ask for another partner immediately. I never want to put any of us in that position again. I live with the guilt of my poor decisions every day."

His eyes filled as he remembered the day that he nearly died. "What I put Danny through emotionally..." He cleared his throat. "The physical strain I put Rhy and Ferg through, and the emotional hell I put everyone else through, were selfish of me. I won't repeat it. You have my solemn vow."

Maddy was silent for a long time, watching the beautiful mares and the foals playing in the field. "You sure you want to leave the peace of all this behind you?" A smile lit up her face when she turned to him. "I'm not sure I'd want to."

Jamey grinned back. "Don't get me wrong. I love it here, but I can always return." He shook his head, sending his tail of hair over one shoulder. His voice was somber and his eyes begging when he said, "I miss my family, and I miss my home at the Sanctuary."

He turned away, clearing his throat. "I miss her, and I long to be near her."

A frown crossed his face, darkening his mood as something occurred to him. "Does she even want me as a partner anymore? Would it be easier for her if I didn't come back?"

"Oh, Jamey." Maddy stepped into him, hugging him tightly. Her arms didn't meet around the girth of him. "Of course she does. She's just never been good at showing her emotions or expressing what's going on in her head."

"No, she hasn't been." Hugging her back, he asked. "We'll have to work on that. When do you want me back?"

"How about the night of the Solstice?" Maddy gazed up at him with a question in her eyes. "Do you want me to tell her you're coming back, or do you want to surprise her?"

A cocky grin tipped his lips up. "I'd rather make a grand entrance as her escort for the ceremony."

"Perfect," Maddy said. "I won't say anything. I'll leave it up to you." She glanced at the carefree animals once more. "I best be getting back before Ronan sends out a search party."

"You're carrying precious cargo."

Maddy beamed up at him, rubbing her belly. "Yes, thank the Mother, I am."

75

A Woman's Wrath

Chantal and Blaze made it through one more day of hell before planning their break. Knocking lightly on Collette's door, they waited patiently for her to let them in.

Collette pulled the door open while towel-drying her hair. She looked at the two girls blankly as they pushed their way through her door.

"You're not ready," Blaze said, glancing around for her backpack.

"What are you talking about?" Collette asked her.

"Are you fucking kidding me? You forgot?" Chantal asked, throwing her hands in the air. "You came up with the fucking plan after that bitch beat the ever-loving shit out of us."

"Oh," Collette said, dropping her gaze. Acting purely on humiliation and rage, she had orchestrated a prison break with the other two yesterday. Because the trio couldn't imagine anything worse than the way Mistress Danyka had humiliated them in front of another class.

Collette had forgotten about their plans after her failed leap off the cliff—after meeting Lash. Tonight, she didn't want to go anywhere, knowing he was somewhere on the island. Her world felt safer knowing he was near. And she sure as hell didn't want to get sent back to the hell, she called home.

"I've changed my mind," Collette said softly, sitting on the window ledge in her room. "I'm not going, and I wouldn't recommend that you attempt it either." She rubbed her hair absently. "I doubt we'll successfully get off the island, and I don't want any extra duties."

Lifting her hair to her nose, she scrunched it up. "It's bad enough I can't get the smell of the stables out of my hair. I don't want to end up with a worse punishment."

"Who the hell are you? What changed since this morning?" Chantal asked in a pissy voice.

"And why were you late for self-defense?" Blaze asked, snapping her gum. "You seemed awfully flustered when you got there, and you appeared to have rolled through the leaves." One side of her lips quirked up in a cocky grin. "I want to know who you were rolling with?"

Collette's cheeks flushed, but she maintained her innocence. "I wasn't with anyone. I was running because I was late, and I fell on my way."

"Yeah, not buying it," Blaze said, popping a bubble in Collette's face.

"I don't care if you buy it or not." Collette stood and pointed to the door. "I'm sorry, but I don't want to get into any more trouble. If you're smart, you'll go back to your rooms. You can both leave."

"Malik and Regan are going with us, too," Chantal said, trying to sweeten the deal. "You always had a crush on Malik."

"That was a long time ago, and he's not a good enough reason to risk it."

"Well, if you're not interested, I just might be…" Chantal said in a singsong voice.

"Be my guest," Collette said, turning her back on them. "And shut the door on your way out. I'm tired. It's been a long damn day." Her muscles ached from the extra duties she was pulling in the stables. Physical labor was unfamiliar to her, and her body was making its discontent known.

Chantal and Blaze glared at her on their way out the door, slamming it as they left.

"Can you believe she turned down a chance to spend time with Malik?" Chantal asked in disbelief.

"Nope, and she gave you permission to take your shot," Blaze said.

"Well, I'm not staying here a moment longer than I have to," Chantal said fiercely.

"You sure this is a good idea?" Blaze asked, sounding whiny. "I really don't want to get in any more trouble, either. My parents will kill me if I humiliate my family while I'm here. As one of the founding families in our clan, the punishment will be severe."

"Do what you want. I've got a date with destiny," Chantal said disgustedly, slinging her pack higher on her shoulders. "I'll take my chances out there rather than being abused and treated like a slave here."

"Shoveling horse shit ain't exactly slave labor," Blaze said. "It's building character and making us think about our behavior and how the other half lives." She twirled her hair around her finger. "I actually like working in the stables. I don't feel stupid there, like I'm behind half of the class."

"Bless yer heart." Chantal drawled. "That's because you're dumber than a box of rocks," she said with a nasty sneer.

"And you can't fix ugly, bitch," Blaze snapped, stomping back to her room. "Have fun. I hope the hellhounds eat you."

"They're in the stables, idiot."

"Not at night, they ain't," Blaze reminded her. "I doubt they'd want you, anyway. You're too tough, no meat on your bones. I doubt Malik will want all your sharp edges for more than tonight, either."

"What do you know?" Chantal snapped, near to tears. It was her own damn fault. She'd started flinging barbs because she felt like they'd both abandoned her.

And Blaze always knew how to hit where it hurt. Chantal's self-image had always been her downfall. She wasn't pretty like Collette or sexy like Blaze. Her mother always told her she would grow into her angles. Chantal had her doubts because her mother had the same build and the same angular features.

"The hell with them," she muttered to herself, heading quietly down the stairs.

Without a sound, she turned the knob on the front door and was about to close it when Blaze snuck out.

"I thought you weren't coming?" Chantal sneered at her.

"I shouldn't have said that. I'm sorry," Blaze said, knowing she'd hit below the belt. "You know I didn't mean it. I don't want to get in trouble, but I don't want you to go alone either." Her voice was sincere.

"I'm sorry, too. You've got more common sense than the rest of us combined. Forgive me?" Chantal asked.

"Already done," Blaze said, giving her a hug.

"C'mon. We're meeting Malik in the gardens."

Running from shadow to shadow to conceal their passage, they made their way to the labyrinth garden. Across from the fountain was a small alcove guarded by two topiary lions. The girls entered the enclosure and settled in the corner far away from the blue witch fire lamps on the path.

Rustling sounded near the entrance. Blaze grabbed Chantal's hand, squeezing so tightly that Chantal cried out in pain. "Not so tight, Blaze."

A moment later, an enormous figure rushed into the alcove. Blaze's scream could've woken the dead, but Chantal cut it off by thrusting her hand over the other girl's mouth.

As the figure lumbered their way, he pushed his hood back, showing a heavy mane of blond hair.

"Malik," Chantal said, throwing her arms around him in a hug. "You scared us."

Patting her arm awkwardly, he said, "Sorry, something was moving in the maze behind me. I thought it was you."

"We just got here a few moments ago, and we didn't hear anything," Blaze said skeptically.

"How are we getting off this island?" Chantal asked. "You said you had a plan."

"There will be a canoe at the dock waiting for us," he said. Threading his fingers through hers, he pulled Chantal in for a quick kiss. "Regan bailed. You ready to go?"

Chantal nodded her head eagerly. "Yes, get me out of here."

"What about her?" he nodded toward Blaze trembling in the corner.

"I don't care if she comes or not," Chantal said, wanting him all to herself.

"What is wrong with you?" Blaze asked, her temper igniting. "I came so you wouldn't be alone, and you're just going to leave me here?"

"I don't mind two for the price of one," Malik said as his eyes lingered on Blaze's curves.

"Well, I do," Chantal's black eyes bore into his.

"Sorry, baby. My bad," Malik said, giving her another peck on the lips to placate her. "Let's go."

Malik stood up, pulling Chantal with him. Glancing over his shoulder at Blaze, he said, "Sorry, not today, red. She's got some jealousy issues. We need to work them out."

"I never wanted to go, anyway," Blaze said, following them out. She really didn't want to go, but damn, it hurt that Chantal hadn't even given her a second thought once he arrived.

When they reached the edge of the hedges, Blaze turned the opposite way, heading back to the foyer door. Tears slipped down her face at her friend's obvious betrayal. Turning the handle, it horrified her to find it locked. "No, no, no…" she chanted, praying it was just stuck. On her third attempt, the door opened, silently mocking her. Closing it quietly behind her, she made her way to the stairs.

Blaze gasped when she found Mistress Danyka and Mistress Madylyn waiting in the foyer for her.

"You made the right choice," Mistress SkyDancer said in a gentle voice.

"Smart call, kid," Mistress Danyka agreed. "Where are they going?"

Any sense of loyalty Blaze might have had vanished. "To the docks."

"Go to bed and speak of this to no one," Mistress SkyDancer said.

Blaze nodded, racing up the stairs and wanting this night to be over with.

Madylyn waited until Blaze was out of sight. "So how long do we wait to round them back up?"

Danny tipped her head. "I'd wait until they almost make it." She gave a soft chuckle. "Just when they think they can taste freedom, take it away."

"You're evil," Maddy said with a laugh.

"Who're you fooling? You were thinking the same damn thing."

"I was," Maddy snickered. "This class disappointed me. I can't believe it took them this long for someone to bolt. I have some new creations that want to come out and play. Let's see how they do tonight."

They took the stairs to the second floor and made their way to Maddy's office. Maddy used a small ball of witch light to guide their way. When they reached the window seat overlooking the garden, she settled into the corner facing the path the students were taking.

Danny opened herself up to her peregrine vision, helping her to see better than humanly possible. "I'll share a closer view if you let me in, Maddy."

"Happy to. I want to see their expressions when they curse this place."

"I want to hear their screams," Danny chuckled, creating a thread of air that carried their whispers to her and Maddy.

"Did you bring a flashlight?" Chantal asked Malik as the clouds covered the moon.

"Can't you even produce witch light?" he asked, sounding disgusted.

"Can you?" she retorted, pulling her hand from his.

"That's magic for girls." His scoff of disgust made it sound obvious.

"Didn't take you for such a male chauvinist," Chantal said, taking a step back.

Malik turned on her faster than he should have been able to. He backed her up against a tree and pinned her against it with his hand around her neck. Leaning his full weight against her, he gave her a brutal kiss. "That's all women are good for. And when we get away from here, you'll serve me best in silence on your knees."

Chantal's eyes grew wide, and her fear was palpable. When he kissed her again, she tried to turn her head and whispered, "No," but his hand on her neck prevented her from moving. His other hand made its way under the short skirt she wore, roughly gripping her mound. As his fingers tried to slip under the edge of her panties, she'd had enough.

Malik was over-confident and twice as ignorant, making him unable to pick up on the fact that fear wasn't the only emotion racing through her. Temper had jumped on board the emotional overload, and she was feeling feisty. Grabbing his shirt with both of her fists, Chantal yanked him closer, sealing her lips over his. Kissing him like her life depended on it, she bided her time. When both of his hands tried to push her thighs apart, she kneed him in the groin so hard that his testicles ruptured.

As he writhed on the ground in pain, her booted foot landed on his throat. Every primal urge in her body told her to finish him.

The surrounding air thickened, and she could have sworn she heard a whisper in the wind. *"I'll punish him. It's not your job to finish this, child."*

The voice sounded suspiciously like Mistress Danyka. Chantal was glad the warden had witnessed the near assault. She would gladly take any

punishment she deserved when she returned, as long as he never did this to anyone again.

Stepping back, she kicked him in the ribs twice instead. "Remember this the next time a girl tells you no. We're faster and a helluva lot smarter than you give us credit for. I don't need you to rescue me from this place, and I don't need your slobbering kisses to make me feel good about myself. I deserve better."

With one last kick, she walked away, yelling, "Before morning, every girl here will know what you've done to me, so you won't get away with it again, you piece of shit."

When the path forked, Chantal glanced forlornly at the right lane leading to the dock. Running away didn't seem like such a good idea anymore. A grouping of large stones sat in the middle of an intricate flower garden where the roads met. She crawled up on top of one and buried her head in her arms while tears ran down her face. Crying silently, she contemplated her options. Hating this place, she just wanted to go somewhere—anywhere else.

"Chantal?" A deep, concerned voice sounded in front of her. Glancing up, she found Galen Hill gazing at her with a frown. She recognized him from the village but had never spoken to the handsome young man.

Embarrassed to be found like this, she shook her head and let her hair cover her face, hoping he'd leave her alone. Unfortunately, fate had decided she didn't deserve even one break today. His broad form settled gracefully next to her on the enormous rock.

"Want to talk about it?" he asked in a gentle voice.

Chantal shook her head, her dark hair swinging wildly around her. "I already feel like a fool. I don't need anyone else thinking I am."

A large, calloused hand closed around hers. "We all make fools of ourselves at some point or another."

Chantal turned her head on her knee, studying him through the curtain of her hair. "Why are you being kind to me?"

"I'm not being anything. 'Tis just who I am." His blue eyes met hers. "I've always wanted to talk to you, but I've never had the courage."

"Why not? Am I that intimidating?"

"No, but you're so beautiful. I never thought I'd have a chance of you noticing me."

"That would make me two kinds of a fool tonight if I didn't see you through your kindness."

His thumb rubbed the top of her hand, soothing her.

"What are you doing out after curfew?" she asked him as she wiped the tears from her face with her free hand.

407

"I help Tobias in the stables in the evenings. We both enjoy working with animals, and Master Pathfinder doesn't seem to mind the extra help." His fingers still swept over her hand hypnotically.

His fingers gave hers a gentle squeeze. "And you? What are you doing out this late, other than feeling foolish?" His question ended in a teasing lilt that made her chuckle self-deprecatingly.

"Entertaining ideas of running away," she said in such a low voice that he nearly missed it.

"By land or water?" he asked, not making her feel foolish at all.

"Water."

"What stopped you?"

"I picked an asshole for a companion who thinks women are only available for his pleasure." Fury simmered beneath her cool response.

"Ah, I see you've met Malik, then."

Chantal laughed lightly, tipping her head so that her black hair fell forward, covering her face. "I didn't realize I was so transparent."

"You're not." His hand tightened for a moment against hers. "The bastard was bragging earlier that he would have you before the night was out."

Chantal pulled her hand away and covered her face with both of them, mortified. "Of course, he told everyone," she said in a horrified whisper. Her cheeks flamed in embarrassment.

"No. He just made the mistake of telling me."

Turning her head, she peeked through her fingers at him. "Why was that a mistake?"

Galen's jaw tightened, and his fists clenched. "Because I came out looking for you. If he'd hurt you, I would've killed him."

And just like that, Chantal's heart beat faster with interest. She pivoted to face him. Tipping her head, she studied him, then said, "Thank you for wanting to rescue me."

Galen chortled. "You didn't need me."

"How do you know that?"

"Because I found him near the river puking up his guts like someone had kicked his balls into his throat."

"I might be guilty of that," she said, shrugging her shoulders without an ounce of guilt.

Galen chuckled and his hand found hers again. "I was about to swear that as long as you're here, I won't let anyone hurt you. But you obviously don't need me."

"Including Mistress Danyka?"

"I won't interfere with the warden's punishments." His eyes met hers without judgement. "From what I've seen so far, everything they've handed out has been fair."

408

Chantal let out a long sigh. "You're right. We deserved what she gave us. It was just so mortifying."

"Don't look at it that way," he said. "Everything that happens to us here is a lesson to be learned."

Galen interlaced their fingers. "Magic isn't the only thing they're here to teach us. If you get your ego out of the way, you'll understand most of the lessons." He gave her a shy smile. "Admit it. If we weren't here, you wouldn't have given me the time of day."

It appalled Chantal to realize he was right. "I'm ashamed to agree with you." She took a shuddering breath, leaning into the heat of his body as the night cooled. "But I don't want to be that person when I leave here."

Galen leaned back until she met his eyes. His hand brushed the hair away from her face. "Good, I'd like a chance to get to know you before we leave this island."

"I'd like that," Chantal said, giving him a shy smile in return.

"Ready for me to walk you back?" he asked.

With a nod, they stood and followed the path towards the Castle. The trip back was quiet, both lost in their own thoughts. When they reached the foyer, he squeezed her hand and said, "Thank you for spending part of your evening with me."

"Thank you for being a friend when I needed one, Galen."

"It was my pleasure, Chantal. Mayhap we can do it again sometime." He gave her a wave and headed down the hall toward the kitchen.

"I'd like that, too," she whispered in a quiet voice full of wonder. Her night began with one man who offered her a change of scenery and ended with one who offered her a change of heart.

Chantal ran up the stairs and shrieked as Mistress Danyka stepped in front of her.

"You're out past curfew."

"I know," she said, unwilling to fight the obvious. "My apologies, Mistress. I'll take whatever extra shifts you assign me."

Mistress Danyka cocked her head to the side and studied Chantal for a long time. "You get a hall pass on this one. Don't let it happen again." Glancing out the window, she said, "Malik is limping up the hill. You know anything about that?"

"The only thing I know is that he's a misogynist pig, and he probably got what he deserved."

Danyka gave her a wide smile. "Well done, Chantal. I promise it won't be the only lesson he learns tonight."

The smile on her instructor's face almost made her feel sorry for Malik. Almost. Then she remembered his threats and his hands on her, and an evil smile crossed her face as well. "I'm glad. Make sure it hurts."

"I promise he'll get what he deserves."

"Thank you, Mistress Danyka." Chantal hung her head and said in a contrite voice, "I also want to thank you for teaching me a valuable lesson in humility earlier this week. It was long overdue."

Danyka nodded at her, proud of the young woman before her. "If you'd like a few extra lessons on self-defense, join me after class on Tuesdays and Thursdays. Bring some friends."

Chantal gave her a nod. "I'll see you on Thursday. I never want to feel that powerless again."

"No one should have to feel that way, Chantal. You are worth more than you give yourself credit for. Expect more from the men in your life because you deserve to be cherished and protected, not assaulted."

When Chantal's eyes filled, Danny pulled her into a rough hug. "It's going to be all right. We'll make sure he never thinks of hurting anyone else."

Chantal flung her arms around the petite instructor, nearly knocking her over. Danyka's hands patted her back awkwardly. With a shuddering sob, Chantal pulled away. "Thank you. I didn't think anyone would believe me."

"I believe you. Now get some sleep."

"Thank you, Mistress," Chantal said before running up the stairs.

Danyka observed Chantal's exhausted journey up the stairs before heading for Maddy's office.

"I'm almost disappointed they found some common sense," Maddy said, gazing out into the night. "I really wanted to let some of my nastier beasties off the leash tonight."

"Don't you worry about that, Maddy," Danny peered into the dark and pointed down the hill. "Right there. There's someone limping up the hill who needs a lesson on how to treat women."

"Clarify the lesson, please," Maddy's tone turned dark and menacing. Danny needed to calm her down before the lesson turned into something else entirely.

"Malik got a little handsy," Danny said, "and I hear he doesn't appreciate a woman's value."

"Anyone get hurt?" Maddy asked as her temper simmered below the surface.

"Nope, Chantal kicked his balls into his throat." Danny chuckled. "Did a hell of a job, too. He's still limping."

"Good." Maddy said, "Let's take the little prick on a longer return journey than he's expecting."

With a whisper of the word *exstinguere,* most of the witch light lanterns went dark. The path subtly changed, curving to the left, moving Malik farther into the darkness.

"Kyran," Maddy beseeched, *"I need heavy fog by the Sanctuary and covering the gardens."*

"Do I need to know why?" he asked.

"Not tonight."

"As you wish, Madylyn," Kyran replied.

The fog appeared, rolling in dense pockets that teemed with malevolence. Danny could see Malik easily as he ran towards what he believed was the light of the Sanctuary. But what he approached was nothing of the sort. The refuge of blue witch light he followed flickered and then faded completely.

Danny shared the images easily with Maddy through their link. "Perfect," Maddy purred as he stumbled into her topiary garden.

Malik stopped, hand outstretched, trying to create the witch light he had humiliated Chantal over. A small spark sputtered in the palm of his hand, but the density of the fog extinguished the spark every time he produced it.

Whimpering, his eyes sought any sign of light or life as he stumbled through the maze, wincing as his delicate bits protested when he tried to run.

There in the distance, he glimpsed dim light. Anything was better than this blinding fog. Lumbering along like a Neanderthal, he hunched over and cupped his throbbing nuts while bumbling along the uneven path.

"Fuck," he cried out as his toe caught an uneven patch of flagstone, pitching him forward onto his knees. He cursed even more creatively as he pushed himself up with one hand. When he lifted his head, he screamed like a little girl.

Right in front of him was a beast taller than the NightMares. A demonic unicorn reared up in front of him with glowing blue fire for eyes. Barbed wire surrounded the horn protruding from the center of its head. The wire spiraled around the horn. The sharp appendage glowed eerily with blue flames licking along the length of it.

Stomping a foot down nearly on top of Malik caused the terrified boy to scoot backwards, crab crawling in the most awkward fashion. He forgot about his damaged delicacies as he maneuvered his body away from the creature stalking him.

The unicorn stomped and bucked, and when the hoofs hit the ground next, they'd barely missed him again. Rolling to the side, Malik made it to his knees and hauled himself up on the edge of the ornamental water fountain.

He crawled around the perimeter of the enormous fountain, grateful for the illusion of safety it provided. The four-feet top edge of the fountain hid him from the creature, and he shuddered in relief. He kept his whimpers to a minimum until the demon unicorn appeared to lose interest.

Dropping his head down to the damp concrete edge, he tried to orient himself. Sweat poured down his face, mingling with the tears. As his body

sagged against the concrete, he noticed the statue in the center of the fountain.

A bronze mermaid emerged from the water. Flipping her head back, the artist captured the tendrils of her long hair in thick tendrils flowing above and behind her. Her golden-brown breasts crested the water as her hands reached for the sky. A long-bifurcated tail supported her beneath the water.

A splash on the far side of the fountain jerked Malik's head to the left. Peering over the edge, he noticed a dark shape swimming in the fountain, heading straight for him. Curiosity kept him there a moment longer than was wise.

A small mermaid swam in the fountain. Petite, the curvaceous beauty moved erotically through the water, her long red hair flowing well past her hips. Halfway around, her head peeked up, and she stared straight at him. Her red hair had an unnatural glow, and her eyes were backlit with the same demon fire the unicorn had exhibited.

Upon closer inspection, the mermaid's bifurcated tail was formed from braided ivy vines. The pattern continued up to her ample bosoms, leaving nothing to the imagination with little white flowers where her nipples would have been. As her eyes met his, she smiled, and razor-sharp teeth protruded from her mouth, dripping with green slime.

"Holy Mother of all," he whispered, ready to beg his creator for help, even if it meant fessing up to his poor behavior.

The creature took him by surprise by launching herself off the bottom of the pool and catching him by the front of his shirt. Yanking his torso into the fountain, she held his head under water until his arms thrashed at the sides for breath.

Letting him up for air, the creature hissed at him, and her mouth unhinged as her teeth elongated.

Malik struggled in the grip of a female less than half his size. The buttons of his shirt scattered as she yanked it open. Her hand around his neck pinned him against the statue of the pretty mermaid, frozen in time. He didn't miss the irony of his situation. And then the statue shifted behind him. A long bronze arm wrapped around his neck, holding him in place.

Claws sprouted from the smaller mermaids' webbed fingers as they trailed down the length of his chest. Her other hand trailed along his belt line and lower. His legs kicked out, trying to close and kick her away from him simultaneously.

Terror overrode the pain from earlier as her clawed fingers shredded the front of his pants. Garbled sounds emerged from his throat as fear rendered him speechless.

The shift in power made him realize the way he'd made Chantal feel, and guilt ate away at his conscience, overcoming even the fear swamping him. "I'm sorry, I'm so goddamn sorry for the way I treated her. I'll never do it

again. Swear on my mother's life, I'll only treat women with the utmost respect."

The mermaid's cold bronze lips brushed his cheek. The voice that passed through her lips was hoarse and thready, as if it came from the depths of the earth.

"Women are the future of your species. If you don't treasure them, I'll mark you with the pox so that all forms of affection will forever be out of your grasp."

"I'll treasure them, I swear I will…I will." His sobs echoed through the night as his bladder let loose.

The voice came again, whispering across his cheek. "I'll be watching you…" As her voice drifted away, the statue released him, and he splashed into the fountain. Glancing left and right, he tried to locate the little terrorist, but the water was still.

Stumbling over the side, he clawed his way to the path. Backtracking, he made his way down the path, returning to the fork in the road. The fog clung to him so thickly he couldn't see his hand in front of his face. Branches snapped behind him, and he heard the cry of a jaguar behind him on the left. Another enormous cat answered the cry on his right, and his panic amplified.

The bushes to his left moved, and red eyes tracked his movements. The same came again from his right, but closer this time. Running straight ahead and trying to keep his feet on the path, he refused to glance either way. Lungs burning and legs shaking, he never slowed until he caught sight of a blue sign on the right of the path.

There, straight ahead, brightly lit, was the sign marking the healer's shoppe. Mistress Rhyanna's clinic beckoned him. Paws padding behind him picked up the pace as Malik ran faster. Flinging himself up the steps, he pulled the bell outside for after-hours care. Yanking the rope repeatedly, his eyes shifted from left to right, waiting to be mauled by a cougar or one of the white tigers.

Telepathically, Mistress Rhyanna spoke to him. *"I be on me way. Please have a seat at the picnic table outside. I'll be there momentarily."*

"Hurry! Please, it's not safe out here," Malik begged.

Sliding behind the picnic table, he cowered under the bench. A loud thump sounded on the roof, making him shriek. Footsteps padded up the steps, and the shadows cast by the beast displayed long canines and raised hackles. Curling up into a ball, he was a sobbing mess when he heard something padding towards him.

Opening one eye, he peeked through his fingers, chanting, "Go away, go away…"

413

A loud purr sounded nearby, and it surprised him to feel soft fur brush his ankle. Jerking his foot back, he glanced down and found a house cat peering up at him curiously.

Relief flowed through him as he reached out a welcome hand and coaxed the feline to him. Picking up the ball of fur, he stroked its head as he waited for Mistress Rhyanna to arrive.

Witch light flared, lighting the lanterns on the path in front of the shoppe and the one by the door. Mistress Rhyanna and Master Kyran walked up the stairs hand in hand.

"Malik," Mistress Rhyanna asked curiously, "What are ye doing out after curfew?"

"C'mon out, lad, and let her get a good look at you," Kyran encouraged.

The boy stood on shaky legs and approached the pair.

Rhyanna studied him from head to toe with a critical gaze. "Want to explain why yer limping and the bruises around yer neck, lad?"

Shaking, he dropped to the bench and buried his face in his hands. "I acted inappropriately with a girl, and she kneed me in the balls." He whimpered a little before going on. "I think she broke something."

"She the one who clawed yer clothes up, too?" Rhyanna asked.

"No, that was…" his voice trailed off, and he shook his head. "You wouldn't believe me if I told you."

"Ye'd be surprised by what I'd believe, lad." Rhyanna stood, unlocking the front door. "C'mon in, let's get ye a hot shower and look at ye after ye tell me about yer ordeal."

Kyran ushered the young man in while she made him a calming cup of tea with lots of honey. While he drank it, he told them his wild tale. Neither of them said anything, just listened to him ramble on about unicorns, possessed mermaids, and demon cats.

Kyran ushered him into the shower while Rhy reached out to Maddy and Danny.

"Ye two have yer fun for the evening?"

"Would have liked to have had some more, but he found his way to your shoppe too quickly for my liking," Danyka said.

"Well done with the mermaid, Maddy. She sounds fecking terrifying."

"Aye, she was, both of them. Thank Kyran for the fog. It was perfect," Maddy replied.

"Will do. Gotta go check on me charge. Is the young lady alright?"

"She's just fine. Ego bruised a little, but in better shape than he is," Danyka said, sounding proud.

"Good, just wanted to see how much he should suffer over the next day."

"I'd make sure he remembers his ordeal with every step tomorrow, and I expect him in all of his classes. Do not give him a free pass, Rhy," Maddy said emphatically.

"I wouldn't dream of it," Rhy said. *"Night ladies, I've got an exam to perform, and I guarantee he won't enjoy it much."*

"Night," they both echoed back.

Danny's laughter rang out when they disconnected from Rhy. "That statue coming to life was fantastic."

"It worked out rather well, didn't it?" Maddy said with a grin. "I need to work on my kitties more, although their screams were damn near perfect."

The two women fell against the pillows on the window seat, laughing until they cried.

"You ever think we'll make it one year without needing to set examples?" Danny asked.

"I hope not," Maddy said. "It would ruin all my fun. I spend all year perfecting my little pets. They need something to do."

"And you say I'm demented."

"Well, you are. But you get more chances to take out your fury on men who deserve it. I have to enjoy the opportunities I get."

"Well, this is one for the record books," Danny said as she stood, stifling a yawn. "I'm going to bed."

"Me, too," Maddy said, rubbing her belly. "But I think I need a snack."

"You might talk me into a cookie run," Danny said as they headed downstairs.

"Good, I hate eating alone."

The foyer door opened, and Rhy stepped in. "I'll join ye for yer midnight sugar run."

"How's your patient?"

"He'll live." A giggle escaped. "Had to give him a sleeping draught. Ye really terrorized the poor lad."

"Poor lad, my ass," Danny shouted. "He'll think twice next time someone says no."

"Aye, that he will."

"Here's to a woman's wrath," Maddy said, raising a glass of milk.

"And a woman's creativity," Danny said, thinking of Maddy's creations.

"And to the woman stuck healing his balls," Rhyanna said with a cringe. "Teenage boys are disgusting."

Laughter filtered down the hall as the woman ate cookies and laughed at the folly of teenagers and the women in charge of them.

Maddy sighed, looking at the women she considered her sisters and was grateful for each of them. The night wouldn't have been nearly as much fun on her own. She loved her tribe.

76

Keep Yer Assets on Site

Fisher Jordan stood in line behind at least half a dozen men and two women who were signing up for the King's Poker tournament. They'd been here about an hour, and he'd only seen two people leave so far.

Christ a' mighty, it was gonna consume his entire morning just for the chance to play a game at the Court of Tears. He'd signed the sheet at the bar, but they'd required a formal meet and greet, as well. Figured the king wanted a peek at the folk who'd be roaming the halls of his court.

The tournament was the first hosted by King Varan's Court in quite a while. Fisher was itching to get inside and see what the palace looked like. The outside was damn impressive, a good sign of what the interior should be like. Smirking, he wondered if they would nail everything down, seeings how they were allowing degenerates like him inside.

Three-fingered Willie was entering now. With only eight fingers and one good eye, he came a close second to Fisher's mad skills at the poker table. Fisher often wondered if the patch he wore provided Willie with some kind of dark magic to help him win. Never could prove it, though.

The redhead in front of him was Scarlet Silver. Dressed in scarlet silk from the fascinator on her head to the Victorian boots on her feet, she dyed her clothing to match her hair. Pale peaches and cream skin were the perfect backdrop for large emerald eyes and scarlet lips. She was a looker as much as any viper could be. Just as likely to stab you in the back as smile atchya.

The woman had no tells except for the ruby hilt of a dagger strapped to her belt. Idly, she fingered it while waiting her turn. It wasn't much of a tell because she stroked it whether she won or lost. The feel of the gem and the cold metal under her blood-red fingertips must have soothed her and kept her emotions in check. Rumor had it she'd pinned a man's hand to the table once when she caught him cheating. Fisher didn't doubt it.

For so many in line, there was no chit-chatting going on. Everyone kept to themselves while side-eying the competition. Footmen abounded, providing refreshments to those in line. Fisher had himself a mug of ale, while Miss Scarlet sipped daintily at a glass of wine. Glancing behind him, he was grateful he'd gotten here early. The line went around the side of the building. But what could you expect? When the king offered to front the common man at a game of chance, every man who'd ever held a hand of cards had shown up.

The door opened, and four potential contestants exited. Thank the blessed Mother. Fisher was getting fidgety, and he needed to piss. He shoulda passed on the ale. The two doormen swung the doors open and ushered in the next dozen players, which thankfully included him.

The drop in temperature was instant as they entered the castle. Fisher sighed in relief in the cool air. The inside of the palace was as gorgeous as he expected it to be. Servants stood every four feet along the length of the hall. Some held trays, while others observed the visitors.

They led each of the potential players to a separate room in the long hallway. Today was his lucky day, he thought, when they ushered him into a posh room with one of the crown princes. Prince Kenn was more like one of the common men than royalty.

Fisher gave him a wide gap-toothed smile, sticking his hand out to shake the prince's hand. "Kenn, it's good to see you outside of a bar or brothel." His wide eyes took in the gold leaf on the ceiling, the hand-carved furniture, and Persian rugs. "Ye grew up here?" At Kenn's nod, he said, "Why in all the hells do ye prefer to come slumming with the lowest of us on the docks?" One eyebrow cocked while he tried to figure the rich prick out.

Kenn laughed at his statement. "I much prefer the games offered at the docks to the stuffy dinner parties offered here. I can be myself down there. Not sure how I got roped into doing sign-ups. Guess they figured you all would feel more comfortable with a familiar face." He gave Fisher a cocky grin. "I was hoping you'd show and wipe the floor with my old man."

"Plan to do me best, like I always do," Fisher said, returning the grin. "There's only one thing I've ever been good at, and it t'aint working."

Kenn chuckled with him, then motioned to another servant by the wall. "Have another drink with me while we get you officially signed up."

"Don't mind ifn I do," Fisher said. His mind refused to turn down free ale, although his bladder was making some mighty vehement protests. He hefted the mug to his lips and took a deep swig.

Kenn pushed a contract in front of him. "Sign here, and when you arrive for the tournament, the Court will provide you fifty dollars to start the game." He marked the line with an X and waited for Fisher to make his mark. Flipping the paper over, he said, "This is a non-disclosure agreement.

417

It states that you enter the property today and on the day of the tournament of your own free will. No one is forcing you to be here or play against your better judgment. Anything that happens at the Court of Tears stays at the Court of Tears. You get me?"

Fisher appeared confused as he dug a dirty finger under the greasy cap on his head. Scratching his head, he said, "Awfully formal to play a game of cards, t'aint it?"

"Father's rules..." Kenn said, dragging the offensive word out. "He doesn't want anyone coming back and claiming he forced them to gamble away their savings or the food they should put on the table for their kids."

"I see," Fisher said, although clearly, he didn't.

"You got any kids, Mr. Jordan?" Kenn's question was innocent enough, but it took him by surprise.

"We've never shared private details before. Why the interrogation?"

"No interrogation intended. Just realized that all the times we've played, I knew little about you. That's all." Kenn pushed the paper toward him for him to make his mark.

Fisher pondered his decision to join this tournament, something he'd never done before. Gambling was in his blood, a compulsive living thing he needed to feed almost as much as he needed to breathe. But something about this had his hackles up, and he couldn't put a finger on it.

"Would you like me to read the contract to you?" Kenn offered, wondering if he was illiterate. His voice held a smidge of compulsion to encourage the man to sign.

"No need, lad. Me eyes be perfectly fine." The compulsion won over his misgivings, and he made his mark a second time.

"Game starts promptly at midnight after the solstice celebrations."

"Perfect," Fisher said with a sly smile on his face. He stood to leave, then turned back to Kenn. "I've got me a daughter, a pretty little thing. She's staying with some friends, but I be picking her up on the solstice."

His gaze traveled the length and width of the room. "Mayhap I'll bring her along. She'd like a peek at the inside of the palace." A spark of evil lit his eyes. "Never hurts to keep all your assets on site should you need them, now does it?"

"No, sir. I guess it doesn't." Kenn's eyes met Fisher's as he spoke, trying to keep the urge to kill him where he stood from showing on his face.

Whatever Fisher saw there made his bowels cramp, and his bladder was damn near to bursting. "Good seeing ye, Kenn." He turned to the door and asked the servant, "Can ye show me to a water closet, if ye please?"

"This way, sir," the liveried man said, directing him to a small washroom down the hall. He waited outside for Fisher to exit.

"What, doan ye trust me to make me way out of here?" Fisher asked with a sneer.

"Not at all," the man thought, but he pasted on a smile and said, "Just don't want our guests getting lost, sir." He ushered Fisher out the front door.

Fisher stumbled down the steps, then turned and gazed up at the palace he'd soon be returning to. He'd grab Genny and then come here to win the top prize. When he won the king's gold, maybe he'd buy her a nice dress. They could enjoy a week here afterward, and mayhap she wouldn't hate him as much. A little culture couldn't hurt her prospects of getting back into the other game if he had her all gussied up.

The servant who escorted Fisher to the door entered the room that Kenn paced in.

"How the fuck didn't you kill that piece of trash?" Dashiel asked Kenn. "He smells evil, and the way he talked about his daughter." He shook his head in disgust.

"Genny is the girl rescued off the scuttled boat on Grindstone."

"Holy shit, and he's going to use her as an asset if needed?"

"Not on my watch," Kenn growled. "Word has it from Kyran that Kai has a soft spot for the girl."

"He always liked the wounded ones," Dash said.

"Yeah, he's always been good with them. He's the best of us all, but I wouldn't put it past him to kill Fisher before we can get any info out of him." His hand scratched the five o'clock shadow on his jawline. "I'll have Kyran give him a heads up and tell him to stand down. The fucker's worth more to us alive than dead."

"If anyone can keep it from turning it into a shit show, it'll be Kyran."

"I'm headed that way. You can take over for me here." Kenn eyed him from head to toe, taking in all the turquoise velvet and lace. "But for fuck's sake, take that horrible fucking outfit off first."

"Thank you. It's been fucking torture bowing and scraping like I mean it. Give me ten to get back into my leathers, and you can get out of here." Dash headed for the door.

"Hurry. I can't play nice with these imbeciles much longer."

Dashiel's chuckle came through the wall after he closed the door. Kenn kicked his feet up on the desk and pointed at the actual servant in the room. "Who's next?" he asked, emptying his mug of ale while waiting. It had already been a long fucking day, and it wasn't nearly over.

77

The Longest Day of the Year

The summer solstice dawned with a clear sky and temperatures in the low eighties. The community would spend the longest day of the year on Heart Island, prepping for the evening's celebration. Students didn't have classes today. Maddy posted task lists, evenly distributing the day's workload to help with the setup and decorating of the island.

Young women and girls from the Romani encampment gathered in the meadow to create daisy crowns for the maidens to wear and crowns of roses for the matrons. Woven mountain laurel branches with pale pink blossoms decorated arches leading into the gardens where the community would gather for the feast.

The menfolk prepared a massive bonfire near the Romani encampment. After digging a pit, the boys gathered large river stones to surround the perimeter of the hole. The men scoured the banks and forest for dead trees. Using horses, they drug trees to the beach and then cut them into manageable lengths for seating and to feed the fire. Landon raced up and down the shoreline with the Romani children, gathering dried grasses for tinder and driftwood. By midday, they'd finished. The pyre towered high on the beach, promising to light up the night sky until the next morn.

Mrs. O'Hare drafted a portion of the lasses to peel mounds of last year's potatoes and carrots. The solstice was a good reason to use up last year's leftovers before the new crops needed to be stored. Two pigs and a side of beef roasted over fire pits outside the massive kitchens. Pastries and decadent desserts waited on silver platters in the pantry, ready to be served.

Ryssa, Genny, Amberly, and Willow scoured the tables and chairs set up in nearly every available space. Regardless of their position, the community worked together by day and celebrated together come night. Wardens, the Romani, and the residents along the St. Lawrence would break bread, dining as one big, happy family.

Every island celebrated unique traditions for the solstice. This was Heart Island's way of giving back to their river community. It also made the locals feel more comfortable with the Wardens who governed them.

The view from Maddy's office overlooked her gardens and the main pathway. She watched Malik, Tobias, Galen, and Regan working alongside

the gardeners and carpenters to prepare for tonight's festivities. Galen kept throwing nasty glances at Malik, but other than that, they ignored each other.

The past week had passed by rather peacefully. Malik avoided Chantal, and Collette was exhibiting a softer side. Her change in disposition kept the rest of her classmates on guard as they waited for her haughtiness to resurface.

Everything was almost too peaceful, too easy. Maddy was on edge because of it. At midnight, King Varan's tournament would commence, and she prayed they would get the leads so desperately needed for Roarke's family.

With most of the preparations complete, the entire island took a four-hour siesta to rest and prepare for the evening's blessing.

Maddy was eager to see Ethelinda, the Noble Maiden of the Romani people. As always, she would sing the people's song and usher in the season of fertility.

During the Spring Equinox Blessing, she gave voice to her first prophecy. Events that had unfolded since then indicated she had been spot on—for most of it. Maddy wondered if they would receive additional pieces of the puzzle tonight. Rubbing her belly, Maddy smiled at the possibility of Ethelinda having a wee surprise for Fergus tonight.

Ronan walked up behind her and wrapped his arms over her softly rounded abdomen. "How are my girls?" he asked, nuzzling the side of her neck.

"We're good," Maddy said, melting into his arms. "Think we're ready for a nap, though." She yawned, emphasizing her words.

"Anything you need me to do?" he asked, wanting to lessen her burden.

"No, but thank you for checking." She turned, threading her fingers between his. "Where's Landon?"

"Cheveyo is wearing him out. He'll make sure that he sleeps for a few hours."

"Good, he'll need to if he wants to stay awake for the bonfire."

A knock on her open door had Maddy glancing up. Collette stood there, looking uneasy. "What can I do for you, Collette?" Maddy asked with a smile.

"Mistress SkyDancer, I was wondering if I might go for a hike before taking my afternoon break. I'm really excited about tonight, and I don't think I'll be able to rest yet."

Maddy studied her auric field for any signs of deceit. Finding none, she peeked at the clock. Four hours left until the evening started. "You have one hour and not a minute more. I want you bathed and relaxing for at least two hours before the ceremony. As I mentioned to everyone earlier, this is a

critical point in your stay here. I want you to meditate and determine what you hope to get out of the rest of your time here."

"Yes, mistress. I will. One hour and not a minute more." She was beaming as she turned to leave.

"Collette, wait," Maddy called, making a spontaneous decision.

"Yes, Mistress."

"Lash is welcome to escort you tonight, if you'd like."

Colette's jaw fell, but no sound came out. "How?" she stuttered.

"Nothing happens on this island that I don't know about," Maddy said. "If he makes you feel safer, he's welcome to join you tonight."

Collette's eyes filled with tears. "My family will be here tonight." Her fingers toyed with her shirt nervously. "It would be nice to have a friend by my side."

"So be it, lass." Maddy gave her a gentle smile as she stepped out of Ronan's embrace and walked towards her. Taking Collette's face between her palms, their eyes met, and gratitude radiated from the young woman.

Maddy kissed her forehead and whispered in her ear, "I won't let anyone else harm you if it's in my power to help. Come to me when you're ready to confide in me."

A tear rolled down Collette's face. No one had ever shown her this much consideration or kindness before. Swallowing the lump in her throat, she nodded.

"Now, go find Lash," Maddy said in a gentle voice. "I trust him with you."

"How did you know she's meeting someone?" Ronan asked, coming up beside her.

"Lash was one of our most promising students last year. His grandfather runs the River Patrol. He came to see me after Collette tried to kill herself." A shudder rolled through her as she thought about how hopeless the young woman must have felt to have even considered taking her life.

Maddy's eyes met his. "Their past life ties are very strong. Lash was having horrific visions of her succeeding. I've been keeping a close eye on her—and on them. He will take it slow with her. I've made sure of that. And since he's started having precognitive dreams, I'm pulling him back into classes for spirit training with Fergus."

Maddy sighed, leaning against Ronan once more. "I know she can come across as an entitled little witch, but I see great potential beneath her haughty veneer. Lash will provide her the sense of safety she needs to explore it. And he'll ground her."

"Her family?" Ronan asked. His voice was rough as his suspicions grew.

"I'll let her keep her secrets—for now. They'll come out soon enough."

"Before she leaves, I hope."

"I'll make sure of it," Maddy said. "I won't let her return to an unsafe environment."

"Want to fill me in on your suspicions?" he asked as his arm pulled her closer to his side.

"Not yet, but you'll be the first one I tell." She brushed a kiss across his jaw. "I'm taking a nap. What are you doing?"

"Joining you, of course," he said, lifting her into his arms.

"Put me down!" Maddy demanded. "I'm not an invalid yet."

"I know, but I enjoy carrying you in my arms."

Maddy rested against his chest, fatigue settling the matter for her. "Just this one time," she said groggily.

"Of course," he said, pressing a kiss to the top of her head. "Just this once."

He made his way to their suite, laying her on the bed and removing her shoes. Sliding in beside her, he pulled her back to his front and enjoyed having her wrapped in his arms.

This solstice would be the best one of his life because Ronan finally had the woman he loved, the family he'd longed for, and a community of friends and coworkers he loved being around. He enjoyed making a difference in the lives of the young men and women who were here for training. His family thrived on this island, and for the first time in a long time, he'd found peace.

Ronan sighed, pulling Maddy closer. He would fight for this place, his family, and these people. This was the community he spent decades dreaming of, and he wouldn't allow anyone or anything to ruin it for them.

Tonight symbolized different things for each of them. But for him, it was the consecration of everything he held dear. This would be the first ceremony he shared with his son, and he wanted to make sure the values Landon grew up with would last him a lifetime.

The people on this island already protected him as if he was their own. Landon was nearly old enough to understand what loyalty meant and how he could return the sentiment. Ronan would make sure his children were grateful to be a part of this beautiful community. Someday, he hoped Landon would become a steward of their world, making it a better place for future generations.

The sun shining through the window made his eyes droop, and within minutes, his body was heavy as fatigue from too many sleepless nights caught up with him. With his face buried in Maddy's hair, he slept better than he had in months. Dreamless and sound, his body took what it needed, and his soul was content with his other half touching him.

78

Rosella Diaries
Eleventh Entry

Steam billowed from the large soaking tub in the middle of Ella's room. With her head leaning against the high back, she tried to calm her racing heart and mind.

Shaelynn scrubbed Ella's skin until it glowed. A quick change of the bath water and Shae added essential oils to moisturize her skin and soothe her nerves. "I'll give ye a few moments, milady."

Closing her eyes, Ella let the water cover everything but her neck. Tears threatened, but she buried her fears and tried to find her courage. "I am strong enough to endure anything," she muttered under her breath. "Even if I hate every minute of what is coming."

A few deep breaths and she sought to find her center, failing miserably. The door opened and closed on the other side of her privacy screen. Knowing her time was nearly up, she ignored it. Eyes still closed, she prayed for a few more moments of solitude.

A shadow crossed her face at the same time that a hand trailed through the water at her side. Eyes snapping open, she found Pearl at the side of the tub, gazing down at her with a wistful expression. Dainty hands pulled up the long skirts of her gown as she settled onto the stool beside her.

Dark, soulless eyes stared into hers for a long time before Pearl spoke. "I can sense how much you hate me right now, Ella, and you're entitled to those feelings." Long, elegant fingers intertwined, and Pearl toyed with a massive emerald ring on her left hand.

"I remember what my first auction was like when I was little more than a child. I wish my owner had been kind enough to prepare me, even just a little." Her black eyes lost focus, transfixed by events in her past that obviously still tormented her.

Clearing her throat, she returned to the present and focused once again on Rosella. "Do you understand what will be required of you tonight?"

Rosella swallowed hard, not wanting to speak about this with anyone but her sisters or her mother. Options lacking, she gave a slight nod.

"I know the mechanics of the act." Nose scrunching, she continued, "But I have to confess, I have my doubts about the ability of an engorged

penis to fit inside of me." Cheeks flushing, she glanced away, embarrassed by her ignorance.

Pearl's lips quirked. "Every man is unique. As you've already seen, some are larger than others, while many men have more girth than length. Bigger isn't always better, but even the smallest of men can cause pain if that is their intention."

Long lacquered fingers trailed into the water, teasing patterns through the lavender flowers. "I don't know who will purchase the gift of your first time. But I can tell you, the more you fight them, the more exciting the conquest will be for them."

A sad expression crossed her face. "Many of the clients we serve find twisted pleasure in causing pain to young women their first time." Her voice thickened as she said, "I am truly sorry for that, and I hope for your sake, Ella, that your owner is kind."

Her fingers toyed with a lavender petal as she continued, "The best advice I can offer you is to relax. If you allow your body to accept what is coming—as much as you despise it—your muscles will relax, most importantly your inner ones."

Dark eyes pierced into Ella's soul. "No matter your man's size, they will all fit. Women are blessed and cursed with the ability to adapt."

"If they offer you alcohol of any kind, drink it. A glass or two will help you relax. Your body will be more pliable, and you will tear less."

Ella's face paled as Pearl tried to help her survive the approaching night. Her mind took a trip through the men she had serviced and the variety of shapes and sizes she observed during her lessons. She understood what Pearl was trying to tell her, but fear was crowding out her ability to reason.

"Do you have questions?"

Ella watched her for a long moment as one tear broke free, trailing down her face. "Do you have this talk with everyone?"

Pearl nodded as compassion appeared in her ebony eyes. "I try to. Some don't want to know or refuse to listen." Her trembling hand reached out and wiped away Ella's tear. "I know you think I'm a monster. I suppose, in some ways, that I am. But—believe it or not—I do care about each of you."

"I believe you, Pearl, but it doesn't mean I will ever accept this as my future. Giving in goes against everything I've ever known."

"You remind me so much of myself at your age." A chuckle emerged from her. "I fought my way through every stage. I'm trying to save you some of the pain and humiliation I experienced because of my inability to yield."

The sound of her silks sliding into place as she stood was loud in the otherwise silent room. "There are much worse places that you could have ended up than on my ship, Ella," she said as she leaned down and pressed a soft kiss on top of her head.

"Remember that when you hate me later. I saved you from being thrown into the stables on an ocean liner. A dozen men would have used you on your first night there and every night thereafter. I am trying to help you find hope amidst the darkness of this life. There are great opportunities to be had if you allow them, Rosella Gallagher."

Ella listened to the whoosh of her silks as Pearl made her way to the door, and she waited to hear the latch catch again as she left.

Pulling in a deep breath, she tried not to scream at the top of her lungs as the nightmare trapping her once again took a turn she couldn't foresee. Pearl knew who she was.

Every time she clung to her rage, Pearl did something that made Ella want to like her or respect her. What the hell was wrong with her that she could feel that way about a woman who was going to profit from her virginity? When had her survival become dependent on liking and respecting this woman?

How the hell did Pearl find out who she was? This information was more terrifying than her coming sale. Understanding the bargaining chip Pearl held, Ella's hands clenched on the edge of the tub. Her heart raced as terror seized her chest.

The only thing Pearl needed to keep Ella in line was her family. Now that her owner knew who they were, Ella's chances of escaping had just shrunk to zero because there was no way that she would take a chance on her sisters or nieces becoming pawns in this game.

Forcing a deep breath into her tight lungs, she pushed down her rage, hatred, and terror. She could protect the people she loved. If this was to be her life, then by the Mother, she would approach this game like any other puzzle she'd solved. She would examine it from every side and find the opportunities buried in this life, and learn how to exploit them to her benefit.

"Shae, I'm ready," Ella called out in a firm voice. Tired of cowering, she would face her future like a woman, not a child. She would hold her head high with pride, not hang it low in shame, because she had a purpose now.

If she were to be a pawn in a chess game, then she intended to make herself the most powerful piece. Ella was going to learn how to be the fucking queen.

Dear Diary,
Eleventh Entry

Weeks have passed, and I haven't been able to journal. My looming loss of innocence seemed to be my greatest fear until tonight, when the time has actually arrived.

Now, my greatest fear is that Pearl knows who I truly am. She can use that to manipulate me more or to threaten my family.

426

So, I shall spread my legs with a smile and pretend to enjoy the night. When they thrust through the only thing of worth I'm born with as a woman, I will grit my teeth and tolerate it without breaking their nose or kicking their balls into their throat.

Mother, help me. It shall be much harder than it sounds.

Rosella

79

I Missed You Too

Danny tied the corset laces on her sapphire-blue, silk tank. Tiny, embroidered forget-me-nots ran in vertical columns down the front of the silk. Her favorite flowers were the only reason she agreed to wear this getup.

Maddy talked her—no bribed her—into wearing a skirt for the solstice. Fingers tracing the fine needlework, she blinked back a moment of tears. The flowers reminded her of her father. She rarely allowed herself to wander through the dusty hallways of her memories, to remember the man who hung the moon for her as a child.

Focusing on her image in the mirror instead, she tipped her head, trying to decide if she liked the way she felt in this. Dainty and feminine were two things she rarely was. Thin straps anchored the tank to her shoulders, and the neckline dived into a deep v. The tank hugged her sides until it flared slightly at the bottom. A two-inch gap between the bottom of her top and the wide silk waistband on the skirt left the skin on her abdomen visible. The skirt gathered around her ankles, but slits on the outside of her legs to mid-thigh gave it movement and sex appeal.

Not that she was interested in sex tonight. There was only one man she had any interest in pursuing that activity with anymore. She doubted she'd find him in attendance this evening.

Running her fingers through her tousled, short, black hair, she contemplated her features. The ebony of her hair and smoky eyeshadow made her pale violet-blue eyes seem even lighter. Long fingers reached for a stick of kohl eyeliner, and she outlined her lashes. There, that was better, making her eyes pop even more. Her cheeks had a natural flush to them. A swipe of ruby red lip gloss moisturized her lips and gave her a sultry pout.

Danny reached for a sapphire pendant, hooking it around her neck. The teardrop shape nestled enticingly above her cleavage. She added the matching dangling earrings, loving the way they caught the light when they

moved. Jameson gave the set to her last yule, and she wished he could be here to see her wear them.

Slipping on her sky-high blue stilettos, she found her balance before reaching for a bracelet. A knock on the door announced that her primping time was up.

Anticipating Fergus or Kerrygan to escort her, she hollered, "Come in, I'll be ready in a minute."

Hurrying, she fiddled with the clasp for a moment before it latched. One last glance in the mirror, and she was ready. Stalking into her sitting room, she glanced around for a light wrap she'd set out earlier and said, "I'm coming. Sorry to keep you waiting."

Turning towards the door, she froze, not expecting to find the man she longed for to be standing there. "You're here?" Wide, luminous eyes tracked his movement as Jamey came closer. "You're really here," she repeated in a breathy voice.

Jamey studied the expressions crossing her face. Relief chased surprise before joy finally produced a radiant smile.

"I wasn't sure if you'd be happy to find me on your doorstep," he said, stepping closer. One hand cupped the back of her neck while the other traced the sapphire pendant she wore. "It suits you and is perfect for this outfit." His eyes roamed over her from head to toe. "Hellion, you take my breath away."

A light blush stained her cheeks at his words. "You don't have to say that," she said, swatting at his chest playfully.

Catching her wrist, he brought his lips to her knuckles. "You know me better than that." His thumb traced her cheek in a gentle caress. Half-lidded eyes memorized her features, lingering on her lips. His thumb traced her bottom lip, and she let out a gasp of longing. "If you don't stop me, I'm going to kiss you, Danny."

Jamey bent his head, waiting for her protest and praying it wouldn't come. He hovered for a moment before taking her lips in a heady kiss. There was nothing gentle about his mouth on hers. He poured all of his longing and need into the kiss.

Danny's arms wound around his neck, encouraging him. Her breasts pressed tightly against the muscles of his chest. She lost herself in the sensation of his lips moving against hers. The taste of him was intoxicating, like aged bourbon. His tongue stroked against hers in a primal dance that made her core tingle.

Their bodies melded together. Any misgivings she had evaporated when his hands encircled her waist. The feel of his palms covering the narrow band of exposed skin was sinful…and she wanted more.

Hands moving down his chest, she traced firm muscles, then clasped his hips. The hard length of him pressed against her belly insistently, declaring without words just how much he wanted her.

Reluctantly ripping her lips from his, she purred in a sexy whisper, "Last time, you focused solely on my pleasure. Tonight—after the ceremony—I want to focus solely on yours." Eyes wide and chest heaving, she met his dark amber gaze. His nostrils flared as he pulled her scent into his soul.

"Whatever we do tonight will bring both of us pleasure," he said, punctuating his words with a soft kiss. "I promise you that." His hands slid over her hips to her ass, and he pulled her tighter against him. "I'll give you whatever you want, Hellion."

"I want you, Jamey." Her lips crashed into his again as if she were trying to convince him she spoke the truth. "After the bonfire. I want you to make me yours."

His hands framed her face while he rubbed his nose against hers. Gentling the kiss, he said, "Hellion, you've always been mine. It's just taking you a while to realize it."

Not giving her a chance to reply, his lips toyed with hers in a kiss that spoke of sultry nights and silk sheet promises. Resting his forehead against hers, he said, "I'll let you take the lead tonight. If you're not ready or change your mind, I'll be just as happy to fall asleep with you in my arms."

His smoldering dark eyes watched hers darken to amethyst with desire. His hands roamed over her curves one more time. Stealing one last kiss, he forced himself to release her.

Danny stood there, chest heaving and heart racing. Her mind whirled at what she'd just set into motion. Straightening the collar on his shirt, her fingers lingered on the triangle of exposed skin. Tracing a pattern on his chest, she couldn't miss the thick rope of scar tissue on the left. Tears threatened when she thought about how close she came to losing him.

Jamey's hand closed over her fingers where they'd stopped. Giving them a squeeze, he said, "I need you to look at me, Danny." His tone was gentle, but his voice was firm.

Danny reluctantly met his gaze. His amber eyes glared down at her.

"What happened on Singer wasn't your fault, so get that shit out of your head right now," Jamey said with a bite to his tone.

Opening her mouth to protest, he stopped her with a finger against her lips.

"I broke protocol. You told me to wait, and I chose not to. That is on me." His eyes flashed at her as he spoke, drilling the point home. "You need to let it go. Stop pushing me away because of this." His hand rubbed her fingers over his shirt where it covered more scar tissue. "This is on me, not you, Danyka."

Danny stared at him, lost in his glowing amber eyes. His eyes only glowed like that when he was mad or aroused. Right now, he was both, and it turned her on even more. This was one man she couldn't intimidate, and she craved the way he met her head on.

Moisture pooled between her legs. Her eyes widened when his nostrils flared as he scented her desire. "God damn, I've missed you, Jameson." Her voice came out as a whimper.

"Not as much as I've missed you, honey," he growled. Giving her a tight squeeze, he formally offered his arm. "If you're ready, Mistress Danyka, we mustn't keep the others waiting."

Eyes wide, her hands went to her hair. "Do I look alright?"

Jamey's eyes slid appreciatively over her body. "You're fucking perfect."

Danny smiled at him as she wiped a smudge of gloss from his lips. He lightly caught her finger between his teeth, making her hiss when he sucked on the tip. Yanking her hand back, she curled her fingers into a fist, hoping it would stop the throbbing between her legs. "And you're a naughty tease."

"Only for you, Hellion." Threading his fingers through hers, he tugged her close and said in a whisper, "This night can't go fast enough."

The sparkle in her eyes told him she wasn't above teasing him back. Her other hand trailed down his chest, stopping at his belt line. She squeezed his hand, trying to convey how damn much she'd missed him and how happy she was to have him back home.

With a soft kiss on her temple, he whispered, "I missed you more."

80

Herding Cats

Maddy finished dressing for the Solstice celebration while Ronan bathed and dressed Landon. Lily helped her into a midnight-blue satin sundress with an empire waist that hid her expanding waistline. A band of tiny flowers embroidered with silver thread trailed under her bust and along the edges of her cap sleeves and hem. She was grateful her pregnancy gave her a reason to forgo the usual corset.

Lily finished pulling her hair into a loose updo. Silver ribbons sparkled throughout her dark hair, trailing through her dark curls. When Lily finished, Maddy painted blue swirls outlining her face and eyes. A labradorite pendant hung from her neck.

Opting again for comfort and safety with her pregnancy, she slipped on a pair of flat satin shoes that matched her dress instead of her usual heels.

"Yer a sight, Mistress," Lily said, taking her in from head to toe. "He won't be able to stay away from ye."

Maddy blushed. "That's reassuring." Although that's exactly what she was hoping to accomplish. Her body was changing, but Ronan still couldn't keep his hands off her. Grateful for that fact, she hoped she didn't lose his attention when she couldn't see her feet. "Let's hope it stays that way when I look like I've swallowed a watermelon."

"Ye've no worries, Mistress," Lily said as she fixed an errant curl. "That man adores ye."

Lily was right, Ronan adored her. It was a fact she was coming to terms with after many years apart. The steady presence of him holding her every night as she drifted off to sleep was something she couldn't imagine living without.

Male laughter coming down the hall made her smile. The two men she loved the most walked through the door, one a perfect miniature of the other. Their matching vests and boots made it even more adorable. Dark

blue brocade vests over pale blue shirts made their ice-blue eyes even more intense.

Landon's hair was slicked back, and Ronan had pulled his hair into a tail at the base of his neck. Her partner's eyes heated as he looked at her. "You're beautiful, darling," he said in a husky voice.

"Yep, Maddy," Landon added. "Yer lookin' real pretty." He tucked his hands into his breeches pocket and rocked back on his heels, the same way Ronan had a moment earlier.

Maddy gave them both a quick curtsy. "Well, thank you, kind sirs," she said with a smile. Reaching out her hands, she asked, "Shall we?"

Ronan entwined their fingers with one hand while Landon grasped her other. And just like that, her world was perfect. The little one she carried gave her first hearty kick, letting her know she was ready as well.

Eyes wide, Maddy pulled Ronan's hand to her belly. At his perplexed look, she said, "She just kicked for the first time."

Dropping to his knees in front of her, he placed a kiss on her rounded belly and said, "Hey, darling, Daddy's here." Another kick, stronger than the last, met his words. Eyes glistening, he stood and grasped Maddy's face between his palms. "Thank you, Maddy, for everything you've given to me."

With a gentle kiss, he released her to the sound of Landon's "Yuck."

Laughing, they clasped hands once again and headed downstairs to the sound of Fergus's bellowing and Jamey and Danny's laughter echoing off the walls.

Maddy's eyes widened when she spotted her Wardens. Jamey's arm circled Danny's waist possessively. Danny allowed it, leaning heavily against his side. Maddy's heart did a little flip for Danny, wanting to see her embrace the possibilities that existed between them.

Catching Fergus's eyes, she grinned, and he nodded at her. He'd noticed, too. Fingers crossed; the couple had been through the worst of it. Maybe tonight they could begin moving in the right direction.

Danny gave her a smile and blushed, knowing Maddy would recognize the step she was taking.

Rhy and Kyran joined them, looking like the perfect couple in similar shades of green. Rhy's sundress had thin straps and a corset bodice. It flared from her hips to a handkerchief hemline that swirled around her as she walked. She was radiant, and Kyran's appreciation was evident in his inability to keep his eyes off her.

The Sanctuary encouraged parents to join their students for this evening, and most did. For many, this was the first time their child had left home for an extended period of time, and they were eager to see them.

Landon broke free and ran to hug Danny. "Hey, little man," she said, leaning over to hug him back.

Fergus sidled up to Maddy and Ronan. "Dunno why he's infatuated with the Pixie," he growled. "She's got a mean streak, and she cheats. I'll have to give the lad a talkin' to sometime soon, so he kens what she's really about."

Danny glared at him. Covering Landon's ears, she said, "Is that because Uncle Ferg is a sore loser and can't shoot pool to save his life?" Lifting an eyebrow, she added, "Mayhap Landon and I will need to chat, too." Her eyes took in his getup and said, "About your poor fashion choices."

Eyes glittering dangerously, Ferg said, "Be careful, lass. Yer playing with fire." To prove his point, his fire drakes ran down his arm and hissed at her.

Fascinated, Landon ran over, reaching for the lizard-sized burst of color. "Can I hold one?" he asked, jumping up and down.

The drakes ran up and hid under Ferg's beard. The fire mage knelt down in front of Landon and said, "Give me yer hand." Closing his massive paw around the young boy's hand left none of the child's skin exposed. Fergus stared into his eyes and said, "I need ye to listen to me, lad. Wouldna want ye to get hurt. Yer da wouldna take kindly to it. Ye have to hold still fer me. Can ye do that?"

Landon nodded his head so hard his hair flew into his eyes.

"Ye have to be still and quiet, or ye'll scare the wee li'l beasties. Ye ready?"

Landon gave another nod as his entire body vibrated with excitement.

"Come, me wee friends, and meet this laddie," Fergus encouraged. Two of the dozen drakes that surrounded him were brave enough to come forward. Spiraling around his forearm, they crept closer to Landon. A blue and white colored one crossed Ferg's hand, then jumped to the child's sleeve.

Landon's eyes were wide, and he was trying extra hard not to dance around. A red and orange one followed, and they danced over the fabric of his shirt without marking it. Absorbing his nervous energy, they grew fat on his exuberance. A laugh erupted from the boy as their bellies grew. Terrified, they scampered back to Ferg. Landon's face fell.

"That's all we've time for, laddie," Fergus said. "Miss Maddy's letting me ken that it's time to head out to the gardens. We'll do it again sometime soon, Landon."

"Can I walk with Uncle Ferg?" Landon asked his father.

Ronan glanced at Maddy, getting a nearly imperceptible nod. "I don't see why not, but when we get to the Romani settlement, you have to stay with him and be quiet until after the dancing."

"I promise I'll behave," Landon said, taking Fergus's hand.

The man might have been a giant next to the boy, but they fit, whispering together. A smile crossed Maddy's face as she watched them, loving how easily her family accepted this child who had newly joined them. Not a one of them ever questioned whether he belonged at the Sanctuary.

They just opened their arms and their hearts and welcomed him into the fold. Tears stung her eyes as her heart filled with gratitude for the people in her life—her family of choice and circumstance.

Heading for the door, the Wardens passed the students patiently waiting in two lines in the foyer. Maryssa gave Rhyanna a grin, accepting the hug the earth mage offered as she walked by.

Collette fidgeted, twisting her hands together. She nodded at Danyka when she walked by, respecting the woman more with each passing day. Her eyes widened when she took in Danny's escort. The man was gorgeous. Where had she been hiding him?

When Maddy walked past her, the headmistress paused and whispered in her ear. "Relax, he'll be here." Collette shivered at the small infusion of magic that ran through her, but she was grateful for the way it calmed her nerves. She wasn't nervous about Lash showing. What she was terrified of was her family's arrival. The past few weeks had been a wonderful reprieve from the horror of her home life.

Exiting the foyer, they gathered outside. Collette glanced around anxiously and startled when Lash stepped into place beside her. Her eyes met his, and her heart melted when he grinned at her.

"I promised you I'd come," he whispered.

"I know you did." Cheeks flushing, she glanced down at her hands. Her breath caught when he reached over and entwined his fingers with hers.

"Everything will be all right." His voice was somber, but his dark eyes burned into hers as he vowed, "I won't leave you alone tonight."

Breath catching, Collette swallowed the lump in her throat. She gave him a nod, unable to speak.

Blaze's voice behind her purred, "Coll, where did you find him, and where can I get one?"

Lash laughed, while the question mortified Collette. "Ignore her. It's always the best course of action."

"Well, that wasn't very nice," Blaze hissed.

Collette tuned out her voice and glanced at the couple in front of her. Chantal was being escorted by…Galen? When had that happened?

The girls hadn't had time to speak after their failed escape plan. Their weekly schedules had changed, and even their meals weren't lining up as their training intensified.

Mistress SkyDancer's voice came down the line to them. "If you haven't already done so, please line up in pairs. I know every clan has a solstice ceremony, so I shouldn't have to tell you at this age how to behave. I want

you to enjoy the evening. You have worked hard to make it this far in your training. Tonight is yours. Make the most of it—safely."

The wardens led the way to the formal gardens. The heady scent of mountain laurel and early jasmine wove through the air. Tiny lanterns of witch light hanging from twine stretched between the trees. Fresh daisies and wild white roses were in short glass vases on each table, along with appetizers to hold them over until the feast.

Maryssa saw her mother and immediately ran into her arms for a hug. Even though Myranda had been working on the island, Ryssa rarely saw her. She was trying to get through the session the same way the other students were, without their families. "Mama," she said, hugging her tightly.

"How are you?" they both asked simultaneously.

"You go first," Myranda said with a laugh.

Finding their table, Ryssa popped a tart filled with meat and cheese into her mouth before answering. "It's not nearly as bad as I expected," she said as she reached for a piece of bacon-wrapped shrimp. "It's exhausting, frustrating, and absolutely exhilarating when things go right."

"It sure is." Myranda said, "I remember my training well." She sipped at a cup of iced tea before asking, "How are your classmates?"

"They're good." A snort escaped as she sipped her lemonade. "The only problems are ones I've expected, so that's nothing new." She glanced around and saw Genny standing by herself. "I want you to meet a new friend of mine."

Bounding off before her mother could reply, she approached Genny. "Is your family coming?"

"No. We don't speak anymore, and I don't want them here."

The sadness in her voice broke Ryssa's heart. "Well, good. Come with me because we want you to join us." She took her hand and pulled her towards their table.

"I don't want to impose on your time with your mother," Genny said.

"No imposition at all," Myranda said as they arrived. "Please join us."

"We were just talking about you," Ryssa fibbed. "Mama was hoping you would spend some time with us after our training is over. Mayhap you could join us for our Maybon celebration." She met her mother's eyes, raised an eyebrow and silently sent, *"Mama, she has no one. I really like her, and I hate to see her all alone. She lives here full time. I know they welcome her, but I think she could use some more friends."*

Myranda's heart ached in her chest for this young woman. Pride raced through her that her child took it upon herself to make her an honorary part of their family. "I think that would be lovely, Genny. We'd love to have you come if you're comfortable with that."

Tears filled Genny's eyes at their generosity. "I would love to join you." A heavy hand fell on her shoulder, startling her for a moment. When she glanced up, she found Kai standing behind her.

"You doing alright?" he asked. His eyes tracked the crowd and continued, "Lot of people tonight."

"I'm fine," Genny said with a smile.

"Kai," Myranda said, familiar with the young man. "Why don't you join us?"

"Thank you, I'd like that." He settled into the last remaining seat and accepted the tray Myranda offered him.

Ryssa watched Collette approaching a table near them and frowned. Her fellow student was deathly pale, and holding the hand of a Romani man as she approached her family. Abruptly, she dropped her death grip on his hand and crossed her arms over her chest. Troubled, Ryssa put it to the back of her mind as she returned to the conversation around her table. Mistress SkyDancer had joined them and was asking her a question.

"So, Ryssa, how is your work with Rhyanna progressing?"

"Wonderful. I love her class. We've been working on tinctures and poultices for healing this week."

Myranda laughed. "That should be easy for you."

"It is. I've been working with some of the other students." Ryssa said. "I enjoy helping them understand how it works."

"Thank the mother for her help!" Genny said with a laugh. "She's saved me a lot this past week."

Maddy walked over to Genny and put a hand on her shoulder, "Well, I'm happy to hear that you are getting the help you need, then."

Genny nodded her head, wholeheartedly agreeing with her.

Maddy stepped back. "If you'll excuse me, I need to welcome some of the other families." She walked away, grateful that Ryssa and Genny seemed to have connected. Her heart had nearly burst with pride for Ryssa and joy for Genny when she heard the Belmonts invite her for a visit after training.

Maddy excused herself, her inner radar going off when she noticed how pale Collette was. Hurrying towards the Creek's table, Maddy noticed the teen was shaking as she approached the people she should feel most at home with. She watched as her father, Adrian, gave her a hug, which Collette limply returned. Her stepmother barely acknowledged her, but the stepson, Eaton, was glaring daggers at where her hand clasped Lash's.

Adrian's temper was also rising as he checked out his daughter's escort.

"Mr. Creek, how nice of you to join us this evening with your family," Maddy said, welcoming them. "I wanted to tell you how well Collette is doing and introduce you to her escort, Lash. He is assisting her with her training."

"I bet he is," Eaton muttered loud enough for Maddy to hear.

"Thank you, Mistress SkyDancer. Please call me, Adrian." He gave her a wide smile while his eyes roamed the length of her.

The stepmother rolled her eyes without acknowledging Maddy at all. Eaton's fists clenched as he continued glaring at Lash.

"Sir," Lash said, offering a hand to Adrian while completely ignoring Eaton.

"You from the Romani encampment?" Adrian asked, with one brow lifted.

"Yes, sir. My family has been here since the Sanctuary began. We're proud to patrol the waters in this area."

Adrian grudgingly nodded at the young man's words. "Good people, your clan."

"Thank you, sir," Lash said with a small bow.

"Join us," Adrian said.

Maddy saw the horror crossing Collette's face at the only two seats available between her father and Eaton. Adrian stepped aside. "Lash, sit next to me."

Lash walked by Adrian but sat next to Eaton instead. "I'm sure you've missed your daughter, sir. I'll sit here so you can catch up."

Collette's relief was palpable, and Maddy knew who was hurting her. If she wasn't sure, the rage that Eaton was radiating confirmed it.

"Well, enjoy your time together," Maddy said, needing to make her way through the rest of the families attending. Her mind wandered through the ramifications and solutions to the girl's problem. Needing to focus on the event at hand, she put it away for the night. Lash would protect her.

"You alright, darling?"

"I'll be fine," Maddy answered. *"Something I need to figure out later."*

"Let me know if you need help. I'm here for anything you need."

"I know you are, Ronan. Thank you for checking in on me."

Making her way to the center of the tables, she amplified her voice. "Welcome to our Summer Solstice Celebration. We are grateful you've taken the time to join your young men and women and Heart Island's Wardens in celebrating the longest day of the year." With a huge smile, she continued, "It's our pleasure to invite you to join us as we make our way to the western shore for our ceremony."

Maddy headed for the rest of the Wardens. They gathered together, waiting for the procession to start. Her mind raced as she worried over Collette's predicament and Danny's and Jamey's situation. Even though it made her happy to see them together, she knew their path wouldn't be easy.

Reaching them, her brows furrowed, and she turned in a circle before asking, "Where's Fergus and Landon?"

A round of laughter was her answer. "He took Landon to change," Danny squeaked out before losing it.

"Why did he need to change?"

"He wanted to play with the wee dragons again," Rhy said, wiping tears from her eyes. "Well, his enthusiasm…"

"And impatience," Kyran said drolly.

"Yes, that, too," Rhyanna said, "caused a wee bit of a catastrophe."

"Everyone alright?" Maddy asked, concerned.

"Yep," Danny said. "But he scared the lil fellas again, and they went into defense mode."

"Caught his shirt on fire," Jamey added with a chuckle.

His words horrified her. Tears filled her eyes. "Landon?"

"Is jest fine," Rhy said. "Kyran overcompensated to put out the tiniest burn mark on his shirt, and Landon and Fergus got soaked."

"I didn't want the lad injured," Kyran said defensively.

"You nearly emptied the fountain," Danny cackled.

"Nearly," Kyran deadpanned.

"And you're letting Fergus dress him?" Maddy asked, nearly panicking. "Where's Ronan?"

"He went after them," Jamey said.

"Why do I feel like I'm herding cats?" Maddy asked. "And it's not the teens I have to worry about."

"Oh, sweet Goddess," Rhy whispered, gazing over Maddy's shoulder.

Maddy turned to see what had her attention and choked back laughter as all three of the males she was waiting on came down the stairs.

Fergus and Landon had matching black watch kilts on. A frilly light blue peasant shirt matched the color of their knee-high socks. Black leather boots came to their knees. A black sporran hung over their kilts. She knew Fergus's held a flask of whiskey. As the thought formed in her mind, Landon opened his, pulled out his own flask, and took a sip of something.

Ronan held out his hand, waiting to be handed the flask. Hair mussed and face flushed, he looked as exasperated as Maddy felt. But gazing at her son, she giggled. Landon looked adorable. Ferg with his scrawny chicken legs was less elegant, but at least the colors matched Ronan's and Maddy's.

"Mother, help me. Let's get this procession started before anything else goes wrong," Madylyn said, taking Ronan's arm and heading down the path. Glancing over her shoulder at Fergus, she said, "That better not have been the whiskey he was drinking."

"Maddy," Fergus said with a long-winded sigh, "give me a lil bit of credit."

"Special 'casions call fer bourbon. Dontchya knows that?" Landon asked, tipping his head at Maddy.

Maddy's eyes locked on Fergus's, threatening bodily harm.

"Swear, t'aint nothing more than flavored milk, lass," Fergus said, trying to placate her.

"Damn well better not be, or there won't be a drop of whiskey on this island for the foreseeable future."

Danny smacked Ferg in the back of the head. "Great, now we all will have to suffer because you got in trouble."

Maddy took Ronan's arm and moved down the path, swearing under her breath and trying not to laugh at this gaggle of lunacy she called her family. When she couldn't hold the grin back, she laughed, realizing she wouldn't want it any other way.

81

Surprise

Fergus was uncharacteristically quiet as they headed towards the Romani encampment. His mind drifted back and forth between the two women who had his stomach in knots.

Ethelinda, the Romani spiritual leader, might be carrying his child. He wasn't sure how he felt about that yet. At the Spring Equinox Blessing, Ethelinda predicted a child of their loins would become an important player for the light in the coming battles. The thought of creating a child as a pawn in the war of good versus evil still didn't sit well with him. But, taking one for the team, he'd put forth his best effort.

If she were pregnant, Ferg would make damn sure any child of his knew they were wanted and loved. Losing his father as a lad made him long for a child of his own. He would shower them with the love and time he wished he'd had with his father. But he hadn't found a woman yet that he wanted to fully commit himself to.

Carsyn, his favorite barmaid and current lover, was working her way into his heart without even trying. Their time together had been life-changing for him—even if so far, they'd spent most of their time in bed. She was the first woman he'd allowed to see behind the masks he always wore. She knew him without the layers of glamours he existed behind.

The illusions he chose didn't make him more attractive. If anything, they downplayed his physical strength and made him appear less of a threat. They made him blend in better with the average person.

One of the most gifted fire mages of his time, Ferg didn't want the attention his true appearance would bring. He didn't want the constant challenges and attitudes that also came with being a red-haired giant who was brawny as well. So, he made himself appear thinner, gaunter, and less attractive.

It wasn't his fault that through no intentions of his own, women flocked to him. Maybe it was the awkwardness of this character that drew them. He didn't fecking know. But he'd worn this mask for as long as he could remember. In some ways, it was more familiar than his true form.

Maddy was the only one of his fellow wardens who'd recognize his true appearance. He trusted his fellow wardens. But it was difficult to maintain the illusion if he was constantly switching back and forth.

Carsyn recognized the difference in him the first time they were together. It was a pleasant relief to let the illusion drop and be himself. He'd wanted her by his side tonight. Unfortunately, the solstice was one of the busiest nights at the tavern where she worked. All hands were required on deck for the solstice.

As if he'd conjured her in his mind, he heard her sweet voice behind him.

"Excuse me. Pardon me, have you seen Ferg?" Carsyn's voice asked from behind him.

As he turned to find her, she bounded up next to him. The shock on his face was obvious.

"Surprise." She gave him a brilliant smile, then the light faded at his stunned look. "Have I made a mistake in coming?" she asked, sounding uncertain. "I can go back and mingle with your other guests if you prefer."

Their relationship hadn't been public knowledge, not because he wanted it to remain hidden, but because they hadn't discussed it. Ferg gave her a wide grin and reached for her hand. "Nye, lass. Yer right where I wantchya. I invited ye, remember?"

Yanking her against him, he kissed her passionately. Aware of their audience, he released her lips much too soon for his liking. "Ye jest surprised me, is all. But tis a pleasant surprise. Thought ye'd be working all night."

"I called in a favor and got someone to cover for me," Carsyn said. "I wanted to spend the solstice with you."

Ferg kept his hand around her waist, grinning at her like a fool. "I'm glad ye made it."

Murmurs behind him caught his attention. Glancing over his shoulder at Danny and Jamey, he snapped, "Ye got a problem?"

Jamey gave them a grin and said, "Not at all." He nodded to Carsyn—his former lover—and said, "It's wonderful to see you, Carsyn."

A faint blush stained her cheeks as Carsyn gave him a curt nod. "You too, Jamey." Her eyes shifted to Danny, noting Jamey's hand in hers. Quirking a brow, she added, "Glad to see you finally found the sense the Mother gave you."

Danny swallowed down her snappy retort and a wee bit of jealousy that this woman had been with Jamey before her. "Aye, I finally pulled my head

out of my ass." With a smirk and a side-eyed glance at her. "A friend pointed out how stupid I was being."

"Must be a close friend," Carsyn said with a hint of longing.

"I'd like to think she is," Danny said. Tipping her head at Fergus, she asked her, "Seriously?"

"Behave, Pixie," Ferg hissed a warning through clenched teeth.

"I wouldn't be anything but happy for you both." Her hand motioned between the two of them, and her smile was genuine.

Danny knew the longings Ferg had for something more than a one-night stand. And she'd witnessed the devastation Carsyn experienced when Jamey called her by Danny's name while they were being intimate. It ended their friends-with-benefits relationship. Jamey may not have realized it, but Danny had known how badly Carsyn had wanted their relationship to progress into something serious. They both deserved to be happy.

"What's holding up the line?" A student asked from behind them. His deep chuckle had the rest of the line snickering, too.

Ferg threaded his fingers through Carsyn's, moving them forward quickly and catching up with Rhy and Kyran. He was grinning like a fool because his night had already improved significantly.

With regret, Ferg realized he would have to leave her halfway through the celebration. He needed to gain access to the ship where tonight's auction was being held. With any luck, they would have a direct lead to Roarke's sister and the network that had been abducting residents along the entire length of the St. Lawrence.

A reckoning was coming for the hell traffickers were still putting young men and women through. Fergus prayed he found his way into the highest levels of their network so he could help destroy the evil from inside.

82

Blessings and Warnings

The Wardens fell into line, followed by the students and then their families. Residents from the island and the surrounding villages brought up the rear. They made their way down the path as the sun began its descent in the western sky.

When they reached the hill above the Romani encampment, Maddy squeezed Ronan's hand and sent, *"We've come a long way since the Spring Equinox Blessing."*

"That was our turning point, Madylyn. That night was our new beginning." Pulling her hand to his lips, he kissed her knuckles while his eyes promised more intense kisses later. *"We triggered a melding—created new life."*

"I can't wait to meet her," Maddy said with a brilliant smile, rubbing her belly bump.

As the procession reached the western shore, they saw the lines of brightly colored Vardo wagons forming a massive circle. Madylyn entered the Noble Maiden's residence while the crowd patiently waited for their spiritual leader to appear.

Landon scuffed his boot against the ground, bored already. "Where did she go?" he asked Ronan.

"She has to pay her respects to the Noble Maiden, Ethelinda," Roarke said.

"Who's she?" Landon asked, glancing up at him with wide eyes.

"Ah, laddie," Ferg interceded. "She is a beautiful woman, full of magic and mystery. The noble maiden offers the blessings during our ceremonies by calling on the elements and the Earth Mother to help our community prosper."

Landon's tightly bunched brows showed he was more confused than previously. Ronan ran a hand over his hair and said, "She's an important advisor to our people."

444

"Oh," Landon said, scrunching his nose. "Like Cheveyo is back home?"

"Exactly. This is the reason he returned home this week. To lead your people through the Solstice." Ronan tugged at his hand. "C'mon, we need to take our places." Landon followed him eagerly, excited to do something.

A platform stood on one side of the pyre. Ronan led Landon and the rest of their entourage into forming a massive half circle several feet away from the stacked logs. The Romani and visitors from the mainland completed the circle.

Landon reached into his pocket, asking, "Is it time yet?"

"Not yet, son." Ronan glanced towards the periwinkle blue and silver Vardo wagon. He was just in time to see Madylyn follow Ethelinda and her assistants down the steps of the wagon. The two powerful women took their places. Ethelinda stood on the raised dais. Madylyn took her position to the woman's left, taking Ronan's hand as she closed the circle.

"Earth Mother, accept our offerings of gratitude and consider our requests as we celebrate your beneficence. We are grateful for the longest day of the year and the light that you share with your people."

Ethelinda started humming an old ballad, prompting Madylyn to step forward and lay one of her blue roses on the pyre. Ronan placed a prayer he'd written for the safe delivery of his daughter, and gratitude for the gifts of Maddy and Landon. Landon pulled a small piece of turquoise his birth mother gave him out of his pocket.

"Are you sure you want to leave that, Landon?" Ronan asked softly, not sure the boy understood he wouldn't get it back.

Landon gazed up at him solemnly. "You said it should be something that means something to me." His fingers rubbed the stone one last time. "This does. There are more back home—if I ever get to go back." His voice was sad, tinged with the memory of his mother's loss.

Ronan dropped to his haunches next to his son, uncaring that the procession was waiting on them. Placing his hands on the boy's shoulders, he met the child's eyes, so similar to his own. "As soon as I can make it happen, I will take you for a visit back to your village."

Landon met his gaze, and a deep shuddering breath exited his chest as he nodded his head. Gently, he put his offering on a piece of driftwood and returned to the circle. This time, he made his way between Maddy and Ronan, taking both of their hands.

"Maddy," he said, gazing up at her with adoring eyes.

Maddy gave him her full attention. "Yes, Landon."

"Thank you for letting me stay here with you."

Maddy's eyes welled. "You are most welcome to be here, Landon." She brushed her hand over his head before giving him a kiss on the cheek. "And we love having you here."

Landon flung his arms around her waist and said, "I love you, too."

Maddy met Ronan's gaze over his head, and the emotion in his eyes made her struggle not to cry more difficult.

Clearing his throat, Damian laid down his offering on the pyre. He'd intricately folded a letter for the Earth Mother into the shape of a tiger. Rhy and Kyran went up together, leaving a small basket woven from fresh reeds and a sand dollar. Danny left a circle of daisies, while Jamey placed a hand-carved bear. Fergus offered the mother a piece of volcanic stone, and Kerrygan left a falcon feather.

Maryssa slipped a letter between two pieces of wood before retaking her position on the perimeter. Each of the students made their way forth, leaving something of worth.

When they returned to their places, their voices joined Ethelinda in song. The ancient ballad spoke of love and loss tempered by hope. The joyous sound accompanied each offering that was freely given.

Fresh flowers and herbs sat beside letters and crystals, wreaths of grains and ribbons of hair. Carved statues and wooden bowls filled with nuts still in their shells perched on branches. The finest fresh vegetables and the bones of recently slaughtered lambs lie amongst the rushes.

Many of the offerings were reminiscent of the coming harvest and abundance the community would benefit from. Some were personal and private, as they ought to be. As the participants wove gifts throughout the pyre, the song ended on a note of joyful possibilities.

As the person to Ethelinda's right made her offering, Ethelinda closed the gift part of the ceremony by placing one of her silver bangles on the pyre.

Ethelinda picked up a large bundle of thyme from one of her assistants. "On the longest day of the year, we give these offerings to the Earth Mother. May she see fit to bless us."

Stepping down off the dais, she placed the thyme on the pyre. "May this please the mother, and in return, may she grant us the courage to face the long days of work coming our way.

"May she provide us with the strength to sacrifice time with friends and families while we take advantage of the extra light. We will generously assist our neighbors with their harvest. May our larders be full as we reap fresh produce, grains, meat, and gifts from the river."

Ethelinda accepted a bundle of sage next. Placing it farther down the pyre, she said, "May the Mother grant us strength and health, allowing those of us blessed with long lives the grace to appreciate it."

An apprentice handed her a large, fragrant, tied bunch of rosemary for one arm and a straw doll with a forget-me-not crown for the other. Standing before Danyka and Jameson, she spoke with her eyes locked on the two wardens. "Rosemary and forget-me-nots are for remembrance. When the

darkness takes you, remember who you are and what is most important to you. May the mother's love for us all remind you both that you're treasured and loved."

Her eyes settled on Danny. "Your fidelity is a gift for the right man. You will never regret giving him your trust or your love."

Shifting her gaze to Jameson, she continued. "If you pass on this opportunity, it shall not come around again. Choose wisely who is worthy of your love and your trust."

Gaze shifting back to Danny, Ethelinda handed her the straw doll. "When the time comes, your knowledge will come from the truth of your memories."

Goosebumps ran down Danny's arms. Ethelinda's eyes pierced into her soul. Her words confirmed Danny was making the right choice tonight, but her warning made her stomach twist. The memories she harbored weren't the kind she ever wanted to revisit.

Placing the rosemary in front of the couple, she accepted a bundle of basil. Ethelinda moved until she stood in front of the students. "May this grant us safe passage from evil and an abundance of wisdom as we enter the countdown towards darker days. May the chastity of these students be something they treasure, and not a gift that they try to dispose of too early." Her gaze touched on each of the young men and women standing before her. Quite a few of them looked away guiltily or glanced at their feet.

Lavender came next, a bundle so large it covered her chest. Squeezing it tightly against her chest, she said, "May this keep the harshest of words from being spoken, reminding us of the kindness and grace we should all act with." Rubbing her hands over the fragile blooms and releasing the calming fragrance, she set it on the pyre and turned to receive the final one.

The last bundle was a sheaf of hay, still green from the field. Ethelinda completed her circuit in front of the families and residents while speaking. "With this offering, may we all experience unexpected wealth. May all of our hard work come to fruition, providing us with the rewards we deserve. May we be prepared for the cold, dark days of winter."

"May the coming days be full of the perfect balance of sunshine and rain. With her grace, our bodies will have the endurance to complete the work needed to make the most of the crops we've planted. The animals we butcher, smoke, and prepare for long-term storage will be enough to keep our bellies full and the wolves from our doors."

"May the fresh water of the river be a blessing to all until it freezes over. The next few months will provide us with everything we need to survive the coming winter."

Reaching the raised dais, she stepped up onto it until she could see everyone gathered around the pyre.

"This day, the longest day of the year—the day that provides us with the most warmth and light—is a reminder of the Earth Mother's love."

"Even during winter's shortest days and in the darkest of times, she gives us the promise of light to help us make it through. When our lights flicker and dim," her eyes met Jamesons, "even then, there is light in the pain and loneliness of the dark.

"Turn to the person on either side of you. Memorize their faces and their names. Will you be their light in the dark if they need it?"

Everyone in the circle turned to their neighbors, and the gathering spoke as one. "I will be your light, should you have none."

Ryssa glanced to her right and saw Genny. She spoke the words, and when she turned to her left, she found Collette by her side. Meeting her eyes, she said the words, hoping that if the time came, she could abide by the promise she was making.

Collette's eyes locked with hers, and she gave a deep nod, acknowledging the debt they both now owed.

Ethelinda's six Romani assistants spread equidistance around the massive pyre, holding torches. At Ethelinda's nod, they lit the pyre. The herbal offerings filled the air with the deep earthy smell of thyme, sage, rosemary, basil, lavender, and fresh cut hay. Roasted nuts hissed and the pops from baskets of corn added to the festive feeling.

As the sun kissed the horizon goodbye, the noble maiden's rich voice filled the air as she sang the people's song of the solstice. The song told of long summer days spent in gratitude for the gifts the mother provided them.

The lyrics spoke of the hard work during the dog days of summer so that respite could be enjoyed at year's end. It held warnings of the bitter fist of winter knocking at the door and deep longings for spring.

The seasons resounded in her voice. Long lazy notes of summer, followed by the crunching leaves of fall. Winter cascaded in a groggy pitch of hibernation, followed by the blossoming warmth of a sweet, hopeful stanza of spring.

Thrice the circle went counter clockwise, dispelling negative energy and poor choices, then thrice clockwise for positive energy and wisdom. Couples paired up and danced together around the perimeter of the fire. Maddy danced a round with Ronan and then one with Landon. Rhyanna and Kyran swayed slowly together, barely moving, lost in each other's eyes.

Jameson offered a hand to Danyka, wanting it to be her choice. She took it without hesitation, making his heart swell. He'd been afraid Ethelinda's words might have set them back a few paces, but Danny reached out and grasped his hand without hesitation. Tugging her to him, he let out a prayer of thanks when she moved in close and wrapped her arms around his neck.

Next to them, Danny saw Lash offering an arm to Collette. The young woman took it with a shy smile, and Danny was happy for her. Lash was a good lad and would be good for the lass.

A young man came up to them as they danced and tried to cut in. Lash apologized and politely told him it wasn't his turn. The look of rage on the other man's face made Danny note his height and features for future reference.

"Are you flirting with another man while dancing with me?" Jamey asked, teasing her. He'd seen the interaction she witnessed as well. His arms circled her waist, pulling her tightly against his torso while his lips pressed against her temple. "We'll keep an eye on them."

One of Danny's hands stroked through the length of his hair, letting the silk strands slither through her fingers. The other clung to the straw doll, not knowing what to make of it. She started again at the nape of his neck, but this time, she pulled his hair, making him look at her. He quirked an eyebrow at her in question.

"Any second thoughts after what Ethelinda said?" Danny asked softly. Her eyes shuttered, hiding any emotion she might have been feeling, and she'd carefully muted their link.

"None." His lips grazed over her jawline to her chin, nipping lightly.

"I'm not a good bet, Jamey," she reminded him, giving him one more chance to back out.

"I've always loved the underdog," Jamey said. His lips brushed against hers as he moved them gracefully around the fire.

The distraction of his soft lips caused her to misstep, but his arms deftly picked her up, depositing her smoothly into the next step. Danny clung to him indecently, her body reacting to his strength, his smell, and his taste.

Her heart reacted to the way he took care of her without a second thought. He was always making sure she was safe, and he managed it all while kissing her like no one was watching.

His tongue stroked hers with gentle pressure. Danny thought she might come just from his hands and lips on her without either of them removing a single item of clothing. Her wishful thinking came to an abrupt halt when a small hand tugged on the side of her skirt.

Reluctantly, she came up for air and found Landon's expectant face staring up at her. She'd developed quite a soft spot for Ronan's miniature. With Jamey's hands still around her waist, she leaned down so that she could ask, "What can I do for you, little man?"

Landon's big blue eyes took up too much of his face and were so damn gorgeous and guileless. "Maddy and Rhyanna already gave me a dance. Kyran thought you'd be disappointed if I didn't save one for you, too." He was so damn earnest it was all she could do not to laugh.

"Well, he was right. I wouldn't want to miss a dance with my favorite young man. I think Jameson should go ask Mistress Rhyanna to dance so she doesn't miss out on him, too. What do you think?" She barely kept herself from laughing, knowing that she could cock block Kyran as easily as he'd done to her.

Gazing up at Jamey, Landon said, "I think that might work, if Kyran doesn't mind."

Jamey suppressed a chuckle. "I think he'll allow it. I'll see the two of you later."

Danny took his small hands. They bounced in a simile of a dance. She laughed aloud at the expression on Kyran's face when Jamey approached, bowing and begging for a dance with Rhy.

As they neared the prince, Kyran stepped in and asked Landon if he could interrupt. He sent him in search of Genny, then held out a hand for Danny. Surprised, Danny glanced at the hand he offered and then up into the cerulean depths of his eyes. "I promise, mistress, I don't bite."

"That's not what Rhy says," Danny deadpanned.

A flush made its way over his cheeks as he cleared his throat. "Be that as it may, I'm here to enjoy my dance with you while you gloat at outmaneuvering me."

Danny gave him a broad grin. "You're good for her."

"Thank you," Kyran said, surprised by the compliment. "I never expected your approval."

"Why not?"

"Well, most man-hating women don't approve of any men for their best friends or sisters."

"She's both, and so far, you've proven to be the exception." Her eyes drilled into his. "Don't give me a reason to change my mind."

Kyran's voice iced. "I don't intend to." He cleared his throat, and the storm clouds in his eyes scattered. "How are you doing, Mistress Danyka?"

His question surprised Danny. She tipped her head, studying him as she contemplated it. "For the first time in a really long time, I feel like I'm doing really well."

She paused, not sure how much she wanted to share, but realizing with his ability to sense emotions, he probably already knew. "I'm giving whatever this is between Jamey and me a chance."

Kyran watched her somberly as she struggled to express herself. "I still sense your doubts."

"I will always second guess my ability to have a successful relationship with anyone. It will take everything I have not to sneak out of his chambers in the middle of the night because I'm terrified of fucking it up."

"I sense the fear radiating off of you," Kryan said in a soft voice. "I can help you if you will allow me to."

His voice was soft, soothing, and didn't hold an ounce of pity, which was probably the only reason she said, "Why do you want to help me?" instead of rejecting him outright.

"You are both important to Rhy, and she is important to me. Does there have to be anything else?"

Danny just quirked a brow at him.

"Fine. You have grown on me, Mistress Danyka," Kyran said as he glided them around the bonfire. They were almost to where Rhy and Jamey were laughing and dancing. "You deserve to be happy. You give so much to the Sanctuary. And you help others learn to protect themselves. I would like to give you a gift. Will you accept it?"

"Did Rhy put you up to this?"

"No, she bloody well didn't. Why is it so hard to believe that I—on my own—might want to do something kind?"

"Because it's been my experience that few people do anything for nothing."

"The offer stands," Kyran said as he brought them to a halt. Handing her over to Jamey, he said, "I'll take my woman back, if you don't mind." He pulled Rhy in for a possessive kiss, wrapping an arm around her waist. Danny laughed and moved into Jamey's open arms.

As they moved away, Jamey asked, "What was that all about?"

"Not sure. He was being nice to me…like big brother, nice." She leaned her head against his chest as the music slowed. "It was weird, but sweet."

His large hands rubbed circles on her back as they swayed in place. Working his way up, his hands framed either side of her face as he stared into her eyes. The back-lit amber glow warmed her core, melting her where she stood. "I can't wait to be alone with you," he said in a husky voice, rubbing his nose against hers.

"Me neither," Danny said, although there was a small part of her that could admit she was a little nervous about the prospect. And that thought was all it took for her to reach out to Kyran on their link. *Do it. Take what you think I need removed.*

"Consider it done, Danyka," came Kyran's reply.

Ethelinda's songs ended, and her voice rang out clearly into the night. "The Heart Island Sanctuary invites you to join their feast and celebrations tonight." Smiling at her people, she added, "Please head up the hill and join us."

Jameson gazed at her with longing and regret when he released her.

Landon ran up beside them and tugged on Danny's hand. "Walk with me, please!" The boy jumped up and down exuberantly. Giving Jamey a little wave, Danny took his hand and headed up the trail.

451

"Tonight, she's mine," Jamey thought to himself, and a broad grin crossed his face as he joined Maddy and Ronan.

"Maddy," Ferg said, approaching them. "I needs see Ethelinda, and then I be off for me next job for the evening."

"What job's that, Ferg?" Jamey asked curiously.

Ferg's look darkened. "I'm off to see if'n I can learn anything on the dark side of the law."

"Good luck, and happy hunting."

"Aye, lad, I'm gonna need it."

83

Masculine Opulence

The summer solstice celebrations wound down on the beach at the Court of Tears. King Varan returned to the palace and surveyed the last-minute preparations in the ballroom. His queen had the palace busy decorating the ballrooms for the poker tournament taking place at midnight.

Varan's jaw dropped at the transformational magic Yareli had performed. Dozens of strategically placed poker tables dotted the room. The door at the far end opened into a smaller ballroom and held just as many pool tables. Both spaces felt like a professional gambling den.

The decor she selected from the court's attics and storerooms gave the appearance of subtle masculine opulence. Instead of the flowers and flash she would have used to decorate a ball, Yareli chose natural elements.

She'd gathered all the mounted animal heads from throughout the palace and strategically attached them to the walls. Varan didn't hunt, but his grandfathers loved collecting unique trophies. Deer, elk, caribou, antelope, elephant, pronghorns, sambar, and giraffe mounts currently adorned the walls.

Massive hides cured from the skins of lions, zebras, Bengals, and white tigers draped over the settees. Plush pillows made from mink and arctic fox pelts lined leather wingback chairs placed around the perimeter of walls for eliminated players. Cigar boxes, bottles of the finest whiskey, and glasses sat on nearby tables to console them after their loss.

Grizzly and polar bear rugs lay in front of the twelve-foot-wide fireplaces, facing each other on opposite sides of the room. Chocolate leather sofas and love seats formed places to commiserate when it was over.

Mountain laurel branches with their palest of pink—nearly white—blooms formed the base of arrangements on the mantles and sideboards. An enormous paper wasp nest sat in the middle, and antlers extended from

453

either side. Preserved butterflies and honeybees rested amid the branches. Small glass apothecary jars filled with fresh honeycomb settled amongst the blooms at the far ends of the arrangements. The entire effect was reminiscent of nature's gifts and summer's bounty.

Varan knew Yareli hated the fact that these trophies existed. But she had put aside her abhorrence of hunting and used what the palace offered to make the ballroom appeal to the players. Scarlett was the only woman who had signed up, and Varan doubted with her killer instincts that she would care about the mounted carcasses.

His gaze surveyed the room from corner to corner and then did it again. Each pass highlighted another feature he missed in the first round. Yareli was an excellent decorator. It was another art form to her. He had missed her subtle touches throughout his home. Varan welcomed the changes she'd made since her return.

His former queen, Meriel—the woman who destroyed his relationship with Yareli years ago—enjoyed a flashier approach. She drowned her court in sexual debauchery and fear. Leather and chains had accented the pain-steeped pleasure she reveled in. He shuddered at the memory of it and was deeply ashamed he'd done nothing to stop it.

Varan had been relieved when the Earth Mother banished Meriel to hell to pay for her atrocities. He would have preferred her death, but Mistress Rhyanna had shown mercy. If they'd consulted him, clemency wouldn't have been an option for the hell his family endured. They hadn't. He didn't know how long she'd remain there, but for right now, he felt safe with her out of the picture.

What he knew was that he was going to do his damndest to win Yareli back to his side. As if his thoughts conjured her, the woman who meant everything to him stepped into the room.

Spreading her arms to show her efforts, she said, "What do you think?"

"It's absolutely perfect," Varan said with a wide grin. "I can't imagine anything that could make it better.

"Has Tristan increased security?" she asked as she adjusted an apothecary jar on the mantle.

"He's tripled it. Most of the guards will blend in with the crowd in plain clothes as guests or as servers."

"How many are you expecting?" she asked.

"Hundred and a half," Varan said, crossing his arms over his chest. "Two hundred tops."

"That's a hell of a crowd you're sharing your home with." A delicate eyebrow raised in question.

"It is," he agreed. "But the tournament only lasts for a day, and we'll house the winner for a week. Then everything goes back to normal...or as close to normal as it can get."

Dark eyes met his pale ones, swirling with confusion, past betrayals, and longing. He moved towards her, drawn as he'd always been by her beautiful soul. His hand rose to cup her cheek, and this time, she didn't pull away. She met his challenge, stepping into the heat radiating from him instead of turning away. Her lips parted with a sigh, and he couldn't help himself.

Varan needed to taste her as much as he needed to breathe. Her shallow inhales echoed his. Gazing into her eyes one last time, he gave her the opportunity to protest, but she wrapped her arms around his neck and brushed her lips against his.

The boldness with which she kissed him was unlike the woman who'd studiously ignored him. One hand wrapped into her hair while the other settled in the small of her back, wrenching her against him. He let her lead their kiss, enjoying the tentative way in which she reacquainted herself with his mouth.

Hand clenching in the back of her shirt, he was the perfect example of patience, something he hadn't been in any area of his life. Unable to keep the moan from escaping, his tongue stroked hers firmly, shifting the power and control back to him.

"Yar," he whispered against her lips, "you can't possibly know how much I've missed you."

A purr escaped her as she nipped at his lower lip. "You'd be wrong about that. Unlike you, I've been celibate since I left you."

Varan's face blanched at her reminder of how he'd failed his entire family. Yareli placed a finger over his lips, silencing him. "I don't want to rehash our mistakes. I'm sick to death of the mess we made of things."

His large hands framed her face. "You have nothing to apologize for. I take full responsibility for my actions, regardless of how drugged I was."

Tears filled her eyes. "You're wrong about that. I should have stayed and fought for us." She gave a dainty sniffle. "I never trusted her. I always thought something was off with Meriel. She never should have been able to get that close to you." Her body vibrated with regret. "I should have fought for you, and I should have fought for our family. Our boys should have seen a united front, and Klaree should have had the chance to know her father better."

Varan didn't argue. Everything she said was true, except for the blame she was assigning to herself. "Honey, you couldn't have known. We can't live under the shadow of our mistakes. If we stay mired in the past, we'll never get the chance at a future together." Tipping his head, he grazed his lips over hers. "That's what I pray for every night."

Deepening the kiss, he tried to rekindle the love and heat that always existed between them. Wrenching his lips away, he growled, "What do you want from me, Yareli?" Her name was a rough sigh on his lips as he found

the courage to ask what was driving him mad. A long moment passed, and suddenly, he was terrified of her answer.

Dark eyes bore into his as her inner torment crossed her face. With a shuddering breath, she admitted, "I want you, Varan."

His hands tightened on her hips as she offered him the truth. "I've always wanted you. The longing for what we had is a constant ache in my chest." Her eyes filled as she stopped hiding her emotions from him. "I've missed you."

Yareli shifted away from him slightly, but his hands kept her close. "But we're not the same people that we once were." Her words were a sad truth that lay heavily between them. The years apart and the distance between them was a gaping chasm.

Varan closed his eyes as her unintended barb struck him. "You're right. We're not the same people we were then." When he opened them, his blue eyes bored into hers. "Mayhap we can be better than we once were."

The hope in his voice was fragile. He leaned his forehead against hers. Pulling her body flush against him, he eliminated the space she'd placed between them. His muscular frame trembled against her soft curves. The shock he felt was evident in his body's reaction to her words. "I didn't think you would ever give me another chance," he said in a raspy whisper.

Yareli let out a choked sound. "I'm not gonna lie. Some days I don't want to." She buried her hands in his hair. "I need to take this slowly. Can you accept that?"

"I'll accept anything you're willing to give me. And we'll take this as slowly as you need us to. You've got the lead this time." His lips found hers in a gentle caress, cementing their joint goal to find their way as a couple once again.

Clearing his throat, Tristan said, "Your majesty,"

Varan gave him a death glare and said, "I'm going to throw you in prison if you continue to cock block me, Tristan."

The captain of his guard smirked at him while Yareli chuckled against his chest. "Your presence is required in the courtyard, sir."

Varan eyed him with disgust. "Wait for me in the hall." When his eyes returned to Yareli's smirk, they narrowed. "What?" he growled.

"It's good to see your temper back, Varan. For too damn long, you've been apathetic. I took no enjoyment from the way Meriel emasculated you."

Yareli's molten chocolate eyes drifted down his body in a slow, smoldering path. "Go. Take care of your problem. We'll talk later."

"Promise?" he asked. Nipping her earlobe earned him a hiss.

Laughter bubbled out of her at his eagerness. "Go," she encouraged. "I'm not done with all the finishing touches, and I need to get the winner's suite prepared."

Varan kissed her hand and released it. "'Til we meet again," he said with a bow.

Yareli watched the man she somehow still loved exit the room. Rubbing a hand over her racing heart, she wondered if it was foolish to take a chance on him again.

Prior to Meriel, Varan had been her best friend, and he'd *never* strayed. Since they'd dethroned the woman who'd drugged him and taken over his court, she'd slowly witnessed his return.

Varan exhibited more consideration and patience—a trait he'd sorely lacked—than he'd ever done in the past. He'd always been gentle with her, but she'd witnessed his temper with others. The man didn't like to be denied the things he wanted, and he'd just clarified that he wanted her.

They'd always been insatiable in bed. That hadn't changed. Her core heated when she thought of his lips on hers. Her fingers traced the soft skin, remembering their kiss. Jerking her hand away, she realized the one thing that had changed was her willingness to settle for less than she deserved. With that in mind, she would keep a tight leash on her body's response to him. This time, she'd let her head lead the way.

Varan was always a consummate lover and rarely had a day passed that he didn't indulge in his need of her more than once. She missed their intimacy and the link they'd forged when they first pledged their love. Sensing his need for her in the past had fired up her own desperation, and they'd honed in on each other's location to scratch that itch.

The walls she'd erected around their link were still solid and secure. Yareli wasn't ready to remove them yet. Time would tell if his intentions were true. But until then, she would enjoy what they were trying to rebuild and having the power to tease him mercilessly.

A sultry smile crossed her lips when she decided on the dress she would wear for the tournament. The man wouldn't be able to take his eyes or hands off her. She would revel in the power that gave her and pray that she could keep her hands off him for a little longer.

Yareli might have all the control over their relationship this time. But Varan Tyde possessed the knowledge of her secret desires and the ability to bring her unending pleasure. The man was a walking sex god. He only needed to give her his panty-melting smile to make her want to strip for him.

"Just remember," she muttered to herself, "keep your clothes on and your hands to yourself. You can kiss him, but that is all…for now." She stomped her foot in frustration, realizing exactly how difficult this was going to be for her because, all excuses aside…she wanted him, too.

84

You See Me—All of Me

Madylyn studied the crowd, laughing, drinking, and dancing around the bonfire as they enjoyed the dregs of the solstice. After the feast, the crowd returned to the beach and lit the massive bonfire that would burn into the wee hours of the night.

Flames reached for the night sky in variations of red, orange, white, and gold tones. Occasionally, a blue flame would change up the color scheme. Benches surrounded the bonfire, and couples danced to the beat of the Romani music and drums. The sound of feet stomping, bells tinkling, and laughter filled the night air. A few children still raced up and down the beach, chasing the waves as they fought off sleep.

Landon had made some new friends from the Romani village. They hadn't stopped playing until they had gone home half an hour ago. As soon as Landon sat down and leaned against her, he had fallen asleep.

Long fingers drifted through the soft silk of Landon's dark hair. His head rested on her lap, where he'd fallen asleep a few minutes ago. The boy had worked hard and then played harder. The daylong celebration had finally worn him out.

The weight of his small body against hers made her smile. She loved this child as if he were her own and, as far as she was concerned, he was. That he trusted her enough to sleep in her arms was a big step. He could have gone to his father, but he'd come and cuddled up beside her, making her heart swell.

Kyran and Rhyanna headed back to their suite, so at least one set of chaperones was inside the building. Danny was playing poker with Damian and some of the Romani guards. She was smoking a cigar and hooting whiskey from a flask. Her grin was wide, and for the first time in a long time, she was relaxed.

Maddy tried not to laugh when she caught her sneaking glances at Jamey. Jamey was returning those heated looks with intense ones of his own. Before long, the two of them would be sneaking off.

Many of the students' families had already said their goodbyes and headed home. But a few lingered. Myranda was saying her goodbyes to Ryssa and Genny, hugging both of the girls.

The Creek family sat on a bench on the other side of the fire. Maddy could see their somber faces through the flickering light. Collette was pale, silently lost in reverie as she stared into the flames. Her father and Lash continued a conversation around her. Hands still clasped, she yawned, leaning her head against Lash's shoulder.

Eaton shot hateful glances at Lash, and when his eyes landed on Collette, they flickered between longing and disgust. Maddy's anger simmered as she studied him. Watching the family dynamics answered so many questions about Collette's behavior.

Her eyes drifted to the fire, and she witnessed the male bonding rituals of back thumping, raucous laughter, and more than one flask making the rounds. Kai and his brother Kenn were passing around a bottle of whiskey with Ronan, Damian, Roarke, Jameson, and some of the Romani men. Roarke was telling a story, and the men chortled at something he said.

Maddy gave a sigh of contentment. It had been a wonderful solstice, surrounded by the people she loved and the community they belonged to. Peaceful, there had not been one altercation, and she was grateful nothing had disturbed the perfection of the day.

"Thank you, Mother, for all our blessings and the young lives you trust in my care." Maddy's whispered words drifted on the wind. Moments later, she received an answer in the same manner.

"You're most welcome, Madylyn SkyDancer. Hold tight to those under your care. They will need your strength and guidance."

Maddy smiled, grateful for the communion with her creator. Stifling a yawn, her body swayed to the music as she continued stroking Landon's hair. Ronan glanced at her, checking in, and she gave him a brilliant smile. Returning it, he laughed at something Kenn said, but kept his eyes on her, constantly monitoring her fatigue and her libido.

Jameson took another swig of bourbon as his eyes met Danny's across the fire. She was sitting by herself, just watching him. Eyes locked on hers, he handed the flask to Ronan and said his goodnights before stalking towards her.

Extending his hand, he asked, "One last dance, Hellion?"

The music was softer and slower. The beat of the drums echoed his heartbeat as he anticipated their evening together. Danyka gazed at him for a long moment, then reached for his hand. He led her to a spot away from the other dancers, not wanting to share this moment with anyone.

His left hand on her lower back guided her until they could hear the music but were far enough away not to be seen. Stopping, he pulled her closer. Danny's eyes were luminous as her arms naturally went around his neck, trusting him to protect her while she let her guard down.

Their eyes locked, and their bodies swayed to the music, moving closer until there was no space between them. One hand rubbed her back while the other cupped the back of her head. His thumb stroked her cheek as he drank in the pleasure of her willingly in his arms.

Danny gazed up at him, idly noting how much taller and broader he was than her. She'd ditched the stiletto's earlier, and her head barely reached his chest. Long, silky strands of his hair slid through her fingers. She couldn't stop herself from spreading her fingers wide and running them through the gorgeous length. When she reached up to do it again, her hands fisted at his nape and drew his head towards her.

Jamey watched her lick her lips as she tugged his head down. He let her lead them, wanting her to know that with him, she was always in control. The heat in her eyes made his groin twitch and mouth water. Mere inches from her lips, she released her grip on his mane and framed his face, tracing his cheekbones.

"You're so goddamn pretty, Jamey," she whispered as her fingers moved lower and traced his lips. "But you're also pure masculine grace and power. Roll all that up with your sweet personality, and you are fucking perfect." The words rolled off her lips like a curse. She shook her head as she studied him. "I still don't know what I've done to deserve you." Her fingers pressed against his lips, stopping him from speaking.

"I don't believe that I deserve you yet. But I love you, and I'm gonna make sure you never regret placing your heart in my care." Her blue eyes widened as if she had surprised herself with that declaration. "Kiss me, Jamey."

Danny didn't have to ask him twice. Her statement elicited a low growl of pure masculine pleasure from him. She'd just declared him hers, and the animal in him needed her scent all over him as much as he wanted to mark her as his.

His lips crashed into hers with an intensity that mixed pleasure with a bite of pain. Arms settling beneath her ass, he hoisted her up, so that she was even with him. His tongue slid over hers with long, languid strokes, claiming her mouth in the same way he desperately wanted to claim her body with his cock.

Danny moaned, kissing him back with just as much ferocity. She tried to wrap her legs around his waist, but the length of her skirt made it difficult. She growled in frustration, making him chuckle.

Jamey pulled back with a groan. He gave her another gentle kiss but kept it light, even though he wanted so much more. Her nipples were drilling into his chest, and the heat of her against him made him want to forget about the party raging behind them. But he wouldn't. Never again would he allow her to be placed in harm's way because he'd let his guard down. "Hellion," he rasped as he sucked on the side of her neck, "This isn't the time or place…"

"Let's go," she said decisively. "We'll say our goodbyes and get the hell out of here."

"You're gonna have to give me a minute." He cleared his throat and nuzzled her neck. "I can't go over there looking like this." He pulled her tighter against him. She purred at the impressive erection pressing against her abdomen.

Feeling playful, she ran her hand down the length of him. A huge grin split her face when he cursed and pushed her away.

"You're not helping," he growled, stepping back.

Danny gave him a brilliant smile that softened the sharp planes of her face. She looked younger and happier than he'd ever seen her.

Danny was the perfect example of a woman in love. Jamey rubbed a hand over his heart where the ache used to be. She loved him. He saw it in her smile and felt it through their bond. For the rest of his life, Jameson Vance would remember the way Danyka looked when he realized she loved him.

"You're so fucking beautiful, Hellion." His words were only a whisper, but he sensed the moment she heard them by the sharp intake of her breath.

"That's because you make me feel beautiful, Jamey." The sheen in her eyes was obvious from where he stood. "You see me—all of me. And despite everything I've done to chase you away, you're still here, steadfastly loving me."

She blinked, and her stare was hungry, needy. "I'll meet you above the camp in fifteen."

"Ten," he snarled, not sure he could let her walk away without taking her. His grizzly prowled just beneath his subconscious, wanting nothing more than to claim their mate.

Danny picked up the sides of her skirt in both hands, then tossed him another one of those sultry smiles, making the blood throb in his groin again.

Returning to the fire, she was breathless when she leaned over Maddy's shoulder.

"Danny, you scared the bejeesus out of me," Maddy said with a hand pressed to her chest.

The pixie smirked at her, then gave her a kiss on the cheek. "I'm going to head out."

"Got someplace better to be, or someone better to run off with?"

"I just might, but I don't kiss and tell...until the morning after." They both laughed, and then Danny's face fell. She sat next to Maddy on the bench, glancing with surprised longing at the young boy sleeping on her lap.

"You don't have to rush this, Danny."

"I know," Danny said with a bite in her voice. "Maddy, I love him and want to be with him. I want him to make love to me." Her eyes met Maddy's, wanting to confess. "I told him I loved him tonight."

"That's an enormous step, Danny," Maddy said, studying her clasped hands.

"Yeah, it is." Danny gave a deprecating chuckle. "Funny thing though, I trust him, and I trust that, together, we will figure the rest of it out. Might not always go the way we planned, and I don't doubt he'll irritate the shit out of me as much as I will him. But in the end, it just feels right."

Danny glanced around and found him watching her from across the fire. "My heart won't let me ignore the ties to him any longer. I'm tired of fighting what I feel for him. I can't warn him away anymore. He knows everything."

Maddy listened to Danny working it out on her own. She took her hand and said, "Danny, he's the one you didn't think existed. But that man was born to be your partner in every sense of the word."

Danny's eyes never moved from Jamey. "I think you're right." On impulse, she turned and kissed Maddy on the cheek. "Thank you for never giving up on me and for not letting me give up on him."

Smiling, she said, "I'm gonna check in on that group of students farther down the beach, and with your permission, I'm done for the night."

Maddy let out a hearty chuckle, causing Landon to murmur in his sleep. "You've never asked me for permission for anything before, Danyka. Don't be starting now."

Danny gave her a tremulous smile and then headed down the shoreline. She moved down to where Ryssa, Willow, Genny, and Amberly sat with Tobias, Galen, Chantal, and Blaze. Halfway there, she heard her name on the wind and turned to find Collette and Lash moving quickly towards her.

"May we join you?" Collette asked her, glancing down at her feet.

"You can walk with me, lass," Danny said. "I'm just going to say goodnight to the rest of your friends, and then I'm heading in for the night."

"Oh." Collette seemed extremely uncomfortable. "I don't want to impose on them."

"You're not, lass." Danny stopped, then whispered in her ear, "An apology goes a hell of a long way."

A blush of shame lingered on Collette's face as they reached the others.

Danny felt a mite of sympathy for the young woman. Now that she understood what she was enduring, her animosity toward everyone else made sense. When they reached the group, she gave Collette a break. "I want to introduce you all to Collette's friend." She pointed to the swarthy young Romani man with a smile. "This is Lash. Lash was part of last year's training, but he's going to join us for the rest of this session. You'll be seeing him around a lot in the coming weeks."

Lash nodded and shook everyone's hand. Collette gave a curt nod to the group and stared at the ground.

Ryssa felt sorry for the girl's obvious discomfort. "Would the two of you like to join us?"

The surprise on Collette's face was easy to see. Blaze patted the ground next to her. "Sit your ass down, Collette. We've missed you."

Tears filled Collette's eyes, but she smiled. Glancing at Lash, she said, "We'd love to join you, but I need to use the washroom first. Save me a spot; I'll be right back."

"I'll go with you," he said, lacing his fingers with hers.

"No," Collette said in a faint voice. "Eaton's gone. There's no one left here to trouble me."

Lash searched her eyes to be certain. He squeezed her hand and released it. "I'll be waiting for you."

With a nod, she left them and made her way toward the small building housing the restrooms.

Danny watched her depart, then turned back to the group. "If you need food or drink, head over to the bonfire for snacks. If someone gets hurt, do the same."

She gave them a wink and one last piece of advice as she left. "Don't stay up too late. You get an extra three hours to sleep in, but that won't help much if you're up all night and finish the skins of wine and ale you've got hidden here."

"Yes, Mistress Danyka," a chorus of voices echoed behind her, followed by laughter. She laughed, knowing she would have done the same thing at their age.

Danny headed up the hill, following not far behind Collette. Her falcon sight gave her excellent night vision. She easily picked up the movement when Eaton's tall, dark shape stepped out of the tree line and followed the young woman much too close.

She dropped back, not wanting to be seen. She was close enough to intervene if needed, but she wanted confirmation of her suspicions.

"Jamey, I'm going to be a few minutes late. I need to follow up on something."

"Need help?"

"Nah. Just didn't want you thinking I changed my mind."

"Where you at, Hellion?"

Danny grinned, knowing he would always have her back. *"Heading up the hill near the washrooms."*

"On my way."

Danny's heart swelled at his declaration. Moving silently, she closed in on her prey. She wanted to hear the exchange between the two people in front of her, but she didn't want to alert them to her presence.

As Collette reached the building, Eaton grabbed a hold of her from behind. Yanking her around, he slammed her back against the building with enough force to cause Collette to cry out.

"You really think you can avoid me and parade a new man in front of me, you little cunt?" Eaton snarled, slapping her across the face. "Where's your pit bull now?"

Danny reacted immediately, reaching out to Lash. *"Get your ass up the hill. Her stepbrother stayed behind. It's getting nasty."*

Grabbing Collette by the hair, he dragged her around the back of the building. Flipping her towards the building, he kicked her legs apart and stepped between them. With one hand pinning her nape to keep her in place, he unlaced his breeches.

"No," Collette sobbed with her cheek pressed against the cold stone. "Stop it." She drugged in a breath and screamed. "I won't let you touch me again." She struggled against his hold. When his free hand groped the hem of her skirt, she shrieked. "HELP!"

Eaton knocked her head against the building, bruising the side of her face.

Horrified that this could happen here, where anyone could see her dishonor, Collette froze for a moment. But that was all she needed before the lessons Mistress Danyka had given them kicked in. She didn't have a staff, but she had other weapons at her disposal. Rearing back and to the right, she elbowed him in the face. The moment he loosened his hand, she swung away and kicked his knee to the side. With his pants half down, he lost his balance and landed on his ass.

"I'm gonna kill you," he sneered up at her. His rage turned his handsome face into the visage of a monster.

"You're going to have to go through me to do it," Danyka said, stepping between him and Collette.

"Who the fuck are you?" he growled.

"Your worst nightmare, asshole," Danny said, kicking him squarely in the balls at the same time Jamey came around the corner.

Jamey surveyed the scene and understood the situation immediately. Heaving the young man to his feet, he slammed him against the building and punched him in the face repeatedly.

The fury running through Jamey was unlike anything he'd ever known. All he could imagine was Danny going through this. The urge to kill the little fucker was compulsive. A weight on his back slowed him down, but then the scent of her hit him.

"That's enough, Jamey." Danny's words whispered in his ear penetrated his rage.

Jamey dropped his fist. Releasing his grip, the piece of shit hit the ground, bleeding, and was smart enough to stay there. He turned around, and Danny didn't flinch at the amber glow of his eyes.

Danny's hands framed his face, making him focus on her. "Look at me, big guy. Ignore him." She didn't release him until he hauled her against his chest and buried his face against her neck.

"Thanks for getting here so damn fast," Danny said. She felt him nod. "I need to check on Collette." Pressing his lips against her neck, he released her.

Collette sat on a bench while Lash examined the bruises on her face. The slap was causing the right side of her face to swell, but the abrasion on her left cheek was more concerning. Connecting with the building scraped a good portion of the skin off her cheekbone.

"She needs to see the healer," Danny said to Lash.

"I'll take her," he said. "Can you walk, baby?"

Collette nodded, leaning heavily on him. As they passed Eaton moaning on the ground, Lash stopped.

Lifting him by his lapels, he glared into the spoiled bastard's swelling eyes and said, "If you ever come near her again, I will kill you."

The even tone of his voice didn't camouflage the very real lethal threat. Spoken like a vow, he would follow through on his threat. Dropping him, Lash wiped his hands on his pants as if to remove the evil residue the man left on him.

Jamey hauled Eaton to his feet. "I'll take him to a holding cell."

"I'll update Maddy," Danny said, heading down the hill. Disappointment flowed through her at the disruption of their plans.

"Hellion," Jamey's growl made her turn back to face him. "Let me know the instant you're free."

Her smile and the desire flowing through their bond was the only answer he needed. Shoving Eaton from behind, he snarled, "Start walking, asshole."

Eaton stumbled but moved down the path, head bowed, and shoulders hunched. "What's the hurry?" He laughed maniacally. "I'm a dead man. If Lash doesn't kill me, Adrian will."

"Can you fucking blame them?" Jamey roared at him. This asshole was unbelievable. He wanted sympathy after what he'd done. "How long have you been abusing that poor girl for?" A growl rumbled through his chest. "You honestly didn't think there would be repercussions?"

"Don't let that little whore fool you." He spat a mouthful of blood onto the ground. "Every time she looked at me or smiled at me when she was younger was a fucking invitation. She silently begged me for everything she got."

Jamey clenched his fists, trying desperately to keep his hands to himself. He knew that if he grabbed Eaton again, he would end him. His inner switchboard lit up as Danny recognized his intent.

"He's not worth it, Jamey. Lock him in a cage and let someone else make that decision. Remember, I've got better things to do with you tonight than to visit you in a cell."

One deep breath and then another kept him from completely losing his shit. They reached what had once been a pump house. It provided the drinking water for the island and conveniently had half a dozen cells in the basement. Casting dim blue witch light in the first lantern they came to, Jamey stopped and drew a bucket of water.

Heading for the farthest, darkest cell, Jamey opened the heavy cast iron door and shoved Eaton inside. A pallet of straw and a folded blanket were in the far corner. Entering behind him, he set the water inside the cell opposite the corner where a bucket stood for waste.

Without a word, he slammed and locked the cell door, adding a magical lock to be sure it held. Heading for the door, he ignored the shouting from Eaton. The cell door rattled in its frame, and the young man's voice grew louder, but Jamey didn't care.

Exiting the building, he tuned out the wails and went in search of the woman he loved. This would be one of the best nights of his life, and he couldn't wait to spend it with her. With a grin, he headed down the hill to catch Danny as she returned from briefing Maddy, never expecting the turn of events the night still had in store for all of them.

85

Whatchye Waiting For?

McAllister gazed at his reflection in the dirty mirror of his rented warehouse. He spat on the glass and used the sleeve of his shirt to wipe it clean. Supple fingers traced the skin on his cheeks and neck, loving how tight and wrinkle free he was. A grin showed the dimples in his cheeks, and his teeth shone straight and white.

"Feck me. I'se never this handsome in me youth."

The charm he'd purchased was worth its weight in gold. He wondered what they were going to charge him for a more permanent one.

And the cherry on top was that he could pass as the notorious Roarke Gallagher at a quick glance. An evil cackle erupted from him that ruined the entire visage. The cackle transformed into a moist, wracking cough. His lungs were the one thing that could give it all away. Glamours were a superficial covering. They didn't fix the internal damage in the body or the soul.

With regret, he closed his eyes and removed the sterling silver charm in the shape of an anchor. When he opened them, his sunken, onyx eyes stared back at him. Greasy, graying hair was slicked back, and when he smiled, his rotten teeth formed a repulsive rictus.

Time was an evil bitch, and for those among them—like McAllister—who had very little, if any, elemental blood in them, it marched steadily along. Every breath, every step, every night turning to day, and every season that passed was a nail in his fecking coffin.

Well, this wee fecker on the bottom of the totem pole of longevity was going to suck this bitch of a body dry before he left this plane. With this thought firmly in place, he grabbed his silver-tipped cane, felt hat, and the remnants of his self-esteem and turned for the door.

His gaze landed on his newest acquisition, and the smile returned. A massive wrought iron cage sat in the middle of the warehouse. He'd ordered one for his associate "Sir" to transport dragon hatchlings in and decided it worked just as well for a miniature warden.

Large enough for a horse, but it only needed to be large enough for the littlest of whores. This would be her last home, and when he tired of tormenting and debasing her—years from now—he'd take even more pleasure in feeding her to the hounds.

Wide grin back in place, he exited and headed for the docks. His two associates for the Solstice's activities should be waiting for him on the docks by the time he got there.

The night was clear, and that boded both good and bad for their mission. Lots of boats would be in and out of the Heart Island harbor tonight, so the vessel he rented wouldn't be noticed. He'd also found a fire mage down on his luck and willing to do some under-the-table work for half price.

Tap, tap, tap. His cane made a consistent, melodic sound to his ears. Eyes darting back and forth on both sides of the docks, he searched for the men he'd hired. He found Sir first, leaning against the wall of the livery. The man was a beast. Six-and-a-half feet of muscle and jaunty attitude. He'd have to keep his eye on this one. Sir met his eyes and nodded, then waited for him to pass before following a few steps behind.

Closer to the vessel he'd be using, he found the card shark. The man was worth nothing more than a distraction, and that's what he'd pay him. Nothing.

Pointing his cane at him, he said, "Fisher Jordan?" The man gave a nervous nod. With a tip of his head toward the ship, he said, "Name's McAllister. Heard ye were seeking work."

"Yes, sir."

"Follow me." Tapping his way onto the deck, he made his way down to the captain's quarters and waited for them to come to him. Less than a minute later, someone tapped lightly on the door.

Fairfax sat there a minute or two more than was necessary, pleased to have someone waiting on him for a change. "Enter," he barked.

The thick door creaked open, and the large, squirrelly man he'd met in a tavern sauntered in. Size wise, he and Sir could be bookends. He'd cleaned up some and didn't appear nearly as exhausted or drunk as the last time Fairfax saw him. And per their agreement, he was sober. The man was a card shark, if Fairfax remembered correctly. He went by the name of Fisher...Fisher something. The name eluded him.

"Sir, what exactly is it ye aim for me ta do?"

"I wantchya to get yer daughter back. Seems only right to me that ye deserve to have yer flesh and blood in yer custody." Fairfax gave him a

crooked smile. "Me associate told me 'bout yer circumstance. I'se always one for the underdog."

"Thank ye, sir." Confusion pulled his brows together. "T'aint nothing I needs do for ye?"

"Well, ifn's yer willing, ye can help load some cargo afore we return."

"Happy to help," Fisher said, much too eager to oblige.

"Wait above deck," Fairfax said. "And send the other one in."

The door swung open, and Sir passed Fisher on the way out. They barely fit through the double door. "Ye got me a cage?"

Fairfax stood and tapped his way out the door. "Follow me." They made their way to the hold. He pulled back a tarp covering the cage. "This do?"

Sir walked around, inspecting the joints as he circled the iron box. "Aye, think it 'twill. Running his hand over the scruff of his beard, he said, "Surprised ye found one so quickly."

"Pays to have friends."

"Aye, it does, but old man, ye ain't got any." He chortled, holding his gut at his own joke.

Fairfax fumed. One night, that's all he needed him for. One fecking night. "Right ye might be, but it pays to have the right contacts jest the same." His gaze landed on his feet, afraid he might free the sword in his cane and use it on this arrogant fucker if he found him sneering.

"There're a dozen men on deck. They know what I seek. Ye just needs get them close enough to shore, and they will do what they'se supposed to."

"I can do that."

"Then yer free to pursue your own agenda."

"Boat will be here waiting when I'm done?"

"As agreed upon," Fairfax snapped.

"As agreed upon." Sir nodded, waiting for the slimy little bastard to shiv him. He shouldn't have poked at the bastard's pride, but he couldn't help himself. "Well, daylight be gone. Whatchya waiting for? Get this ship a moving!"

"If only you were the captain," McAllister thought sarcastically and then quickly shut that shit down. One thing you didn't want to do on the Solstice was put anything in motion you really didn't want. Bad vibes were bound to come back and bite ye in the ass with a vengeance.

86

Smoke Screens

"Rhy," Danny sent on their internal link. *"Collette needs your help. Lash is taking her to the clinic."*

"What happened?" Rhy asked, instantly going into healer mode.

"Eaton happened. Caught him in the act."

"Well, that certainly explains what I glimpsed," Rhy said.

"Yeah, it explains a helluva lot," Danny agreed. *"Sorry to bother you. Now I need to ruin the rest of Maddy's night, too."*

"No bother at all, luv," Rhy said. *"'Tis what I'm here for."*

Danny sighed, then reached for her thread to Maddy. *"Sorry to put a damper on the day, but we've got a problem."*

"Elaborate."

"Caught Eaton assaulting Collette outside the public bathroom."

"That little fucker," Maddy said vehemently. *"I knew something was wrong by the way he leered at her all day. Goddammit, I wanted to be wrong this time."*

"I stopped him before it went too far, but I can't help but wonder how long he's been doing this to her."

"Was it just physical?"

"Not sure in the past, but he was on the verge of raping her when I arrived."

"Where is he now?" Maddy's fury radiated through the link.

"Well, Jamey joined the party, and I think he would've killed him if I hadn't interfered." Danny paused, facing a hard truth. *"I wanted to let him...."*

"But you didn't allow it. That's what matters." Maddy gave her a moment to consider her words. *"Where is the bastard now?"*

"Jamey hauled him off to a cell."

"He need a healer?"

"The asshole doesn't deserve one."

"Didn't ask what he deserved. Does he need a healer?" Maddy repeated.

"I don't think anything is life-threatening or broken," Danny said petulantly. *"But she might want to take a peek."*

"I need to contact Adrian and have him return. It's going to be a long night and one none of us will enjoy."

"He's gonna want to kill him."

"Unfortunately, even though I completely understand, I can't allow him to do that….yet."

"What do you need from me?" Danny asked.

"I'll need someone to deal with Landon…" Maddy's voice trailed as a storage shed on the beach to the left of her exploded. *"What the hell?"*

"Maddy, are you all right?" Ronan, Rhy, Damian, and Danny reached out immediately.

"I'm fine. I need to check on the students." Another explosion rang out, this time on their right as a dock went up in flames.

"NO! I'll check on the kids on the beach. Get yourself back to the Sanctuary," Danny said.

"Maddy!" Ronan's voice interrupted on the common link. *"I want you protected in the Sanctuary. Whatever needs to be dealt with here, I will take care of it with the rest of the team. I'm headed your way and will take you and Landon back."*

"Ronan," Maddy argued.

"I will not take a chance while you are in no condition to defend yourself or our children."

Maddy allowed his demand to stand. After losing a child years ago, she wasn't about to place the one she was carrying or Landon in danger. *"I'm heading back now."*

Danny asked, *"You want me to go with you?"*

"I'm not completely without powers. I'll be fine," Maddy snapped, hating to leave others in the path of a potential threat. *"You're needed here until we figure out what's going on."*

Another blast came from the cliffs near where the dragons lived. Landon yelled, "Isabella…" as he got to his feet and raced down the beach.

"NO! Landon, come back," Maddy screamed, trying to run after him, but the child neither slowed nor answered. She picked up her skirts to run after him when Ryssa called to her.

"We'll get him, Mistress SkyDancer, and bring him back to the Sanctuary," Ryssa promised. "I know where he's headed. He showed me the caves."

Tears filled Maddy's eyes at her inability to chase him herself. "Be careful and stay together as a group."

Ryssa nodded. "I promise, we will."

Galen and Tobias had already raced off to help the Wardens with the fires. Ryssa locked eyes with the girls surrounding her. "Let's find Landon.

It's one thing we can do to help." The students loved the child as much as everyone else on the island. When she jogged for the path to the cliffs, the other girls filed into line behind her.

Danny hiked her dress up so she could run. She hurried down the beach to the burning dock. When she reached them, her keen eyesight noted three more burning in the distance where small boats were anchored for the Wardens' use. Why blow up the docks? Her answer came a moment later when she spied a shadow in the flames. With a flick of his hand, the fire mage set fire to the boats as well.

Eyes darting up and down the beach, she tried to focus on what was niggling at her. It was petty damage. No one had been hurt. Why scatter them? As that thought formed, she immediately knew why. Sending her message to all the wardens, she asked, *"Do you have any major damage on your end of the beach?"*

"No," Ronan replied. *"Just the shed and a few of the docks. A couple canoes are gone, too."*

"These are nothing but fucking smoke screens. They are distracting us by hitting us from multiple locations while they make a move. Who could be behind this?"

"And more importantly," Jamey chimed in, *"what do they want?"*

Silence ensued while everyone processed the unanswered questions.

In a panic, Maddy sent out a plea to Isabella, *"Mistress, I've need of your help."*

"What do you need, Madylyn?" Isabella's voice slithered through her head.

"Mischief is afoot, and we're not sure why. Landon was worried about you when he heard the blasts. He is headed your way, and I have students following behind to claim him. Please keep them there and protect them until I know it's safe to send for them."

"I'll protect them all as if they were mine," Isabella said. *"Alejandro was patrolling the shoreline. He noticed multiple small boats approaching not long ago. There are so many strangers here today we thought little of it, although they waited for darkness to arrive."*

"How many?" Maddy asked.

"Four boats. Two to three men in each."

Maddy sent out a command from the Headmistress of Heart Island to everyone on the island. *"Shelter in place! The island is under attack. Lock yourself indoors, preferably in large groups, until you hear otherwise from me. I repeat, SHELTER IN PLACE until further notice."*

Directing her thoughts to Ryssa, Maddy said, *"When you find Landon, stay in the caves with Isabella and Alejandro. They will protect you. Do not return until you hear from me personally."*

"Yes, Mistress," Ryssa said in a nervous tone.

"Where the fuck is Ferg?" Danny asked. *"I've got a fire mage in sight torching boats. I'm heading his way."*

"Ferg had another mission tonight," Maddy said cryptically. *"I've made it back to the Sanctuary. I'll be in my office when the rest of you return. Send me updates every fifteen minutes until then. Every one of you needs to keep this line open and responsive."* Maddy felt their assent through the Wardens' group link.

"Wait until I get there!" Jamey bellowed at Danny, already moving in her direction. *"I'm less than five minutes away."*

"I'll wait," Danny said, surprising him. *"But move your fine ass before I get bored."*

A smile crossed her lips as she felt his approval and his fierce concern coming at her. Her heart raced in her chest. Nothing turned her on as much as a battle did, and Jamey had already stoked her engine earlier.

Eyes tracking the mage's progress down the beach, she moved incrementally with him, keeping pace. So intent on his movements, she didn't pay as much attention to the rest of her surroundings as she usually would have.

Jameson was getting closer because her body was tingling with the awareness of him. Realizing she should be able to see him from this distance, she turned to look over her shoulder.

The blow came fast and hard, dropping her like a stone. The last thought that floated through her mind before the blackness settled in was, "I waited for you, Jamey, like I promised I would." With one last push of her will, she projected a thought to Jamey, *"Find me...."*

87

Please Don't Send Me Back

Kai's feet were dragging as he packed it in for the night. The alcohol he'd indulged in at the bonfire still burned through his veins. Carrying the last kayak into the boathouse, he stretched his tired muscles and wanted nothing more than a hot shower and his bed.

Fulfilling his earlier promise, he locked the doors to discourage students from taking unauthorized trips. For tonight's celebration, they had extended the time the boats were available.

Kai had taken two steps away from the building when it exploded behind him. The force of the blast flung him across the road. His palms and forearms were raw from where he landed, but somehow, he avoided embedding gravel into his face. Rolling to his back, he watched the building engulfed in flames.

Centering himself, he ignored the pain and pulled water from the river to douse the flames. Acrid smoke rose from the charred remains as he tried to process what had just happened. Before he could formulate a message to send to the team, Maddy's warning slammed into him. *"Shelter in place!"*

Worried about the students, he groaned, picked himself up, and started the long walk back to the castle, aching from head to toe from the blast. Moving as quickly as his battered body allowed, he pushed himself into a jog, even though every step jarred his body.

He tried to think of something pleasant to take his mind off the pain. A smile crossed his face as he remembered the joy Genny exuded when the otters came close enough for her to touch them a few weeks ago. The moment had been magical, especially when she had tentatively touched him. His thoughts turned to the night he helped her shift. The experience had been life changing. Kai couldn't wait to return to the water with her.

The path was dark. Gifted with excellent night vision, he didn't bother lighting the lanterns along the way. The dark embraced him like a lover, and

he would have enjoyed the peace following the large groups of noisy teenagers surrounding him most of the day if he didn't hurt so damn much.

Halfway up the steep hill, he paused. Scuffling to his left caught his attention. Stepping behind a large maple tree, he paused, expanding his senses to pinpoint the noise.

A loud thud followed by something dragging across the ground concerned him. His empathic senses picked up pain, confusion, then abstract fear…from Genny.

Closing his eyes, he used his other senses to locate the source. Someone was moving quickly, still to his left, but with a struggling companion.

Kai heard a slap and then a soft feminine moan. Forgetting his discomfort, he sprinted towards the sound, isolating the location easily. Almost there, he heard a shriek and then recognized the terrified voice crying pitifully.

"Lemme go! You gave up any rights to me when you sold me, you bastard."

Usually timid, Genny was terrified, but furious. A smile crossed Kai's face, proud of her for speaking up for herself.

Kai knew her father had contacted the Sanctuary, but Kyran told him she was terrified of returning home. Understanding flowed through him as well as rage. The audacity of the sick fuck. Thinking he could sneak in here at night and take her against her will.

Stepping into a clearing, he saw a man nearly his size, holding Genny by the throat with one hand. On her tiptoes, she struggled to breathe.

"Yer me chile, and that makes ye me property, ye li'l twit." Violently shaking her, he pulled her closer until they were nose to nose. "When ye didna drown on that ship, ye shoulda come home to me. They'se been looking for ye. I'se been offered double to return what was theirs."

His free hand came around and cuffed the side of her head, trying to get her to listen. "I'm gonna set ye down, and yer gonna follow me like a good lass, or I'se gonna put a leash on ye and drag ye behind me like a dog. Don't much care who sees. Choice is yers, lass."

Kai saw red. The calmest of the Tyde men, he was afraid he was going to kill the man when he got a hold of him. Wanting help nearby, if needed, he contacted Kyran. *"Genny's father is trying to reclaim his property. He's hit her at least once and punched her as well. Just want you to know what's about to go down."* His rage was radiating clear enough that Kyr would understand his message.

"Should I bring Rhy?"

"Not sure yet. Will let you know as soon as I do."

"On my way. Don't kill him. He might have vital information we need."

"That's why I called. Better get your ass down here before it gets real. Gotta go."

Genny's feet were back on the ground as her father released her. Choking, she tried to catch her breath.

"Alright, lass. Move in front of me, so ye don't get any bright ideas."

Genny spit in his face. "I denounce you as any part of my family. I refuse to return with you, and if you ever touch me again, I'll kill you." She bared her teeth at him and growled, daring him to come near.

The man backhanded her hard, knocking her to her knees. Grabbing her by her hair and dragging her close to him, he snarled right back in her face. "Ye little cunt, ye deserve everything they're gonna do to ye and more. Yer not worth..." His breath sucked in on a wounded gasp as her knee connected with his nuts. He hit the ground, and before he could curl up, she pulled her leg back and kicked him with all her might.

"I hate everything about you, you piece of shit." Genny danced around him, kicking anywhere she could land a shot. "I'll die before I ever return to that life or go home with you."

Tears rained down her face, mixing with the blood dripping from her nose. Damn, she was fierce. Kai was afraid she was doing more damage to herself than to the man writhing beneath her. Gently reaching for her arm, he didn't block when she swung around and hit him across the face.

As recognition set in, she gasped, and her rage turned to tears. Sobbing, she kept repeating, "I'm sorry, Kai. I didn't know it was you." She wrapped her arms around her middle as she took a step back.

It broke his heart to see her afraid of his potential retaliation. "Shh, honey. It's ok. You didn't hurt me." Unable to stand by and watch her cry any longer, he held out his arms and whispered, "Come here." He let out a massive sigh of relief when she flung herself at him.

Her momentum threw her arms around his neck. Wrapping his massive arms around her slight form, he lifted her up and against his chest while she sobbed into his neck.

Kyran entered the clearing with Ronan. Kai nodded at them, then left with Genny still clinging to him.

"Let me know if she needs further care, little brother," Kyran said.

"I will."

Kai followed the trail to the small garden they'd found together. Scattered throughout the beautiful foliage were wooden benches. Settling onto one, he held her, running his hand down the length of her hair with one hand and rubbing her back with the other.

"I can't go back with him, Kai. Please don't send me back. Please, I'll do anything. I can't go back to being their whore. I'd rather die. Please don't let them send me back. I'll do anything you want."

Kai sat there, stunned into silence. What the fuck was he supposed to say to that? This wasn't a negotiation.

Genny pulled back and sat there, shivering. Liquid pools of misery met his gaze as she began lifting her shirt. Voice breaking, she said, "I'll do anything you ask, as long as you don't let him take me."

Speechless and horrified, Kai grasped her hands before she bared her breasts. Yes, he'd had more than one fantasy about them, but there was no fucking way they were going there anytime soon—if at all.

"No, honey, don't do that," he said in the gentlest voice he could manage. His hands pulled hers down to her lap.

Her sobbing increased. "I'll do anything. There must be something you want or need that I can provide. Please. What can I do to earn your protection? Please, Kai."

Breath coming out in hiccupping sobs, she broke his heart as her forehead fell against his chest in defeat. Kai thought he'd had a pretty good understanding of her past prior to tonight but hearing her try to barter sex for his protection illuminated how fucked up this situation truly was.

Knowing what she'd been through, the only thing he wanted was to protect and cherish her.

Large palms framed her face as his thumbs wiped the deluge of tears falling from her tormented hazel eyes. Swimming with tears, the gold flecks were more noticeable.

Kai tried to speak and couldn't. Clearing his throat, he finally said, "Genny, I will never make you return to that life." He waited until she met his gaze and repeated, "Never."

Relief crossed her face, and the tears fell harder. Kai leaned down and kissed her forehead. "I don't care what you've had to do in the past. You never have to pay me for your protection. Your body isn't currency for me—or anyone else—to cash in on."

Her head shook violently in disagreement. "He's right. It's the only thing I'll ever be good at. Everyone will always see me as a whore, whether or not I was willing. People don't forget that. Sometimes, I wish I'd drowned on the boat with the rest of them."

Kai's heart broke at her words. How could he make her see that she was worth so much to him? He'd been trying to take it slow, knowing how fragile she was and not wanting to ruin the time they'd been spending together.

Defeated, she asked, "What kind of man will ever want me after this? How can they ever forget what they forced me to become?" Eyes closed tightly now, her entire body shook with her heartbreak.

Pulling a silk handkerchief out of his pocket, he wiped the blood slowly dripping from her nose. He wiped away her tears, although she no longer looked at him. When he finished, he took her face in his hands once more and said softly, "Please, look at me."

Shaking her head no, she tried to pull away, but he didn't let up. He held her gently, causing her no pain, but refused to allow her to leave before she heard what he needed to say.

"Please, Genny. I *need* you to look at me."

The hoarse desperation in his voice made her give in and glance up at him.

"You have fascinated me since the first day I met you in Mistress Rhyanna's shoppe. Even though I initially terrified you, you drew me in with your kindness." He kept his eyes locked on her surprised ones.

"You've said nothing."

"No, and I wouldn't have for a while, either. I knew your life hadn't been easy."

Her eyes closed, and shame colored her cheeks.

"I don't know all the details, but I can only imagine what you've survived. That fact alone would have made me keep my advances light, but you're so young, and I didn't want to take an unfair advantage by courting you while you were still vulnerable. I choose to be your friend, to take my time getting to know you. I didn't know if you would ever be interested in anything more after your ordeal."

He leaned his forehead against hers, inhaling the scent of her fear, sorrow, and there it was, a hint of hope.

"When I heard what Collette said to you outside Rhy's shoppe, it took all I had not to put her in her place right then and there. But I didn't have to. You did it gracefully and walked away looking regal."

His thumbs continued gliding along her face, offering comfort. He felt her relax on his lap, leaning into him, accepting his touch as her hands gripped his shoulders.

"Never doubt your worth or your place in this world because you are precious to me, Genny. This might not be the right time, but when you ask who will ever want you—you need to know—I want you. I want to be a part of your future in whatever capacity you have room for. I will never require your body to be a payment for our friendship or anything else we might become. If you don't see me that way…"

Genny's fingers pressed against his lips, stopping him from speaking. "Age is only a number, and I've seen more of life in my few short years than some who have decades on me. Please don't let my age keep you away. I would like to see where this could go, but I don't know when I will be ready for anything more than a friend. I don't want you trapped, waiting for the promise of a future that may never happen."

His lips pressed against her fingers in a soft kiss. "Let's just promise to be open and honest with each other about how we're feeling and take it from there."

Kai waited for her nod and said, "I'm in no hurry to change things. I'm not going anywhere."

Genny flung her arms around his neck and pressed tightly against him, needing to feel his arms wrapped around her. "I don't think I could survive this summer without you."

His hands stroked her back, but when he traced her right side, she pulled away, wincing. Putting some space between them, he pushed the hair back from her face. "I need to know how badly injured you are."

"Bruises, nothing more. I know broken bones, and I don't have any."

"I believe you gave as well as you got." He grinned at her. "Mayhap you did more damage to him."

"Is it evil to be happy that I hurt him before he could cause me more pain?"

"No honey, it's self-preservation, and I, for one, am proud of the way you fought like a hellcat."

A small smile crossed her face. "Thank you for being ready to rescue me."

"Didn't need to. You had it all under control."

"I think I'll join Grace when she trains with Danyka. I would like to be stronger, and next time, maybe he won't get me as far away as he did today."

"That's a great idea, but let's pray there won't be a next time. This one was bad enough."

"I agree." She yawned and settled against his chest, resting her head beneath his chin. "May I just sit here with you for a while? You're warm, and you make me feel safe."

Her words made him feel ten feet tall. "We'll stay as long as you need to, and then I'll walk you back to your room."

"Thank you, Kai." Her voice was soft, merely a whisper on the breeze.

"For what?"

"For still seeing me as valuable and worth saving, and for making me hope again. Thank you."

Kai pressed a kiss to the side of her head. "You're welcome." His arms wrapped around her, holding her closer, as he said a prayer of thanks that he had been in the right place at the right time.

88

Flesh Peddlers

Palms sweating, Fergus prepared to give the performance of his life. Staring hard into his strange dark eyes, he examined his physical appearance until he knew this reflection as well as he knew his own.

Big and burly, with long dark hair that hung loose to the middle of his back, he looked nothing like himself. He'd neatly plaited his long, dark beard. Eyes dark as coal stared back at him. His face was broader, jaw squarer, and he exuded more strength and arrogance than he'd ever possessed.

The air crackled with his nervous energy, and he tightened the leash on his power. The fire drakes weren't happy with him. The wee things were under Isabella's care until his safe return, knowing this place wasn't where the li'l fellas should run amok.

. Smoothing his hands down his silk button-down, he tucked it into his black and silver kilt. Nimble fingers fussed with the silver cuff links on his sleeves as a distraction from the queasiness he was feeling.

He rubbed his stomach, trying to relax. No matter how he tried to quell it, something was niggling his sense of security. Fergus was no stranger to dangerous situations, but he struggled to pinpoint his unease.

"Feck me," he muttered, deciding the entire package was making him uneasy. The kidnapping, assault, and sexual exploitation of women and children of both sexes was enough to make anyone lose their shit.

Fergus was *always* in control of his element, but he worried tonight would challenge his control. He wanted to eliminate everyone on this boat except for the victims. The desire to become judge and jury was so strong that Ferg choked down an inner battle cry.

480

He'd check his attitude at the door along with his brogue when he left this room. That kind of arrogance would get him killed. He'd be no help to those who needed it if he were dead.

Donning a pair of round glasses with a dark tint to hide the flames in his eyes, he was ready to face the auction. The flames in his eyes when he got angry would not be helpful, and this shit show was bound to push all the wrong buttons.

Embracing the man he needed to become, he pulled himself together and left his assigned suite. His swagger became more pronounced, and the tilt of his head held more arrogance than usual. Ignoring the staff, who stepped aside to let him pass, he spared none of his smiles for them.

Many of the guests had checked in early. Their security details were easy to spot as they made their way to the top deck for the main event. Enforcers dressed all in black followed their owners like dogs, alert and aware of everything around them.

Ferg made his way around the exterior of the deck, avoiding the crowds waiting to climb the stairs. Pulling an expensive stogie out of his vest pocket, he ran the cigar under his nose, appreciating the smell of the best tobacco money could buy. One large hand cupped the end while the other struck a match and lit the dried tobacco. He puffed slowly until a cherry ember glowed at the end. Inhaling the smoke deeply into his lungs, he embraced the burn and race of nicotine through his veins.

As the crowd ascended to the top deck, Fergus took a deep breath, waited his turn, and walked up the stairs to hell. Eyes surveying the crowd gathered, he felt sick. These people were the worst part of the problem. Without their sick desires, a market wouldn't exist for flesh peddlers.

Tamping down the urge to destroy them all, he climbed the stairs and forced his face to relax into the most neutral expression he could manage.

A server walked by, offering shots of bourbon and whiskey. Fergus gratefully accepted the whiskey, assessing it with his magic, making certain nothing extra made its way into his glass. Tossing the shot back, he allowed the burn to help him focus on the game at hand. Hip cocked against the deck rail, he observed the offerings and studied the enforcers wandering through the crowd.

Eyes flitting through the crowd, he noted a dozen respectably dressed men and, even more surprising, women who held bidding cards. Two women in front of him chattered like magpies. One was purchasing a girl for her husband's birthday festivities. The other was replacing a girl who hadn't survived the games she and her lover liked to play.

Deep, even breaths kept him from exploding. He took careful note of everyone able to bid, committing their faces to memory. When he returned,

he would visit Queen Yareli and beseech her to create sketches. Then, the wardens would begin hunting them down.

Six more offerings crested the staircase. Weighed down with diamonds, emeralds, and, in one case, rubies, they moved stoically through the crowd. The exquisite silks, satins, and gems couldn't disguise the terror in their eyes or the trembling in their hands. One by one, their handlers led them to places marked on the floor. The arrangement gave the buyers the best view of the young girls and boys on display.

Fergus's eyes passed over each of them, grateful for his perfect recall ability. He studied each of them, memorizing their hair and eye color, height, and any unique markings they exhibited.

As he reached the last group, his eyes widened. *"Feck me,"* he thought. There, in the last row, stood Rosella Gallagher, Roarke's sister. Somehow, he needed to get her off this boat and return with her. Roarke would fucking kill him if he left her here, but he didn't know how that was going to be possible.

Fergus was one of the most powerful fire and spirit mages in his own right, but they outnumbered him, and he was smart enough to realize it. At least two dozen guards wandered amongst the buyers, and he sensed at least four mages on board. The organizers had all the elements covered in case of any surprises. At best, this would have to be a reconnaissance mission.

The auctioneer arrived with a flourish, dressed in a black velvet tailcoat, and wearing a jauntily placed top hat on his tousled blond curls. Standing on a little platform built below the offerings, he spread his arms to welcome the crowd.

"Me fine ladies and gents," he said in a thick brogue. "Let me officially welcome ye to this month's gathering of similar minded folks with discerning taste and delicate palates." The lascivious smile he gave them resulted in a few delicate murmurs and grunts of appreciation.

Turning to the terrified offerings behind him, he said, "Shall we get the party started?"

A smattering of applause encouraged him to continue. "As always, we'll start the night with a preview of next month's offerings."

Each owner presented three to six virgins for the coming month. The master of ceremonies presented each with great care to their attributes and thinly veiled lust as he perused the offerings.

"If ye can't find anything at this auction or the next that strikes yer fancy," he drawled while quirking a brow, "then it doesn't exist. Before ye stands the finest and most beautiful offerings of untouched, unsoiled flesh ye'll ever come across. Yer purchase also includes the staterooms ye will use to enjoy the evening with yer guest or guests if ye choose to share. If yer seeking more permanent placements after this eve, then yer free to approach

the owners on the morn for a private sale." His lips twisted in a sardonic smile.

"But let's be honest with one another, shall we?" He paused dramatically before continuing. "Most of us like our toys to be intact."

Chuckles from the men and tittering from the women set Fergus's nerves on edge. Drawing deeply on the tobacco to keep himself calm, he listened to the description of the first child as his fists clenched and fury burned through him. It was gonna be a long fecking night.

89

Another Cage

Vibrant colors of pain woke her. Hot reds and burning oranges flashed behind her eyes as a bloody fucking clanging knocked on the door of her consciousness. Who in the bloody hell was making all that racket?

The sound of metal slamming against metal made Danny's head throb harder and her stomach roll over. Curled into a fetal position, her hands cupped her head, and she groaned. This was worse than her worst-ever hangover. The clanging came closer. Danny flung out her hand to grab the evil bastard, then cried out as her hand slammed full force into the metal. She curled her fingers around the cold iron, and her inner child began screaming in terror.

A cage. Someone had locked her in a fucking cage. Breath choppy, she began hyperventilating. Pushing through the pain, she pushed herself to her knees and skittered to the back of the cage, as far from the door as she could get. If they wanted her out of here, they were damn well going to come in and get her. Whoever attempted to remove her would wear her scars for life.

Half-focused eyes took in the dimensions of her enclosure. It was tall enough for her to stand in, so it had to be close to five feet high. Not quite as wide, but the length exceeded the height by at least two feet. A bucket sat in the far corner for her waste. The aroma it emitted suggested someone had recently used it.

Trembling from the pain and from the mind-numbing fear that she hadn't experienced in decades, Danny tried to shut the door on her past and remember her self-defense skills. She was a warrior, not some shrinking violet, and she wouldn't go without a fight. Intel—she needed to know what she was up against.

Eyes at half-mast, she peered around the room, trying to see how many men were here. A portly bald man sat a desk with a bottle of whiskey in one hand and the other rubbing his protruding belly. A lanky, dark-haired man

leaned against the door, watching her closely as he chewed on an unlit stogie. Smirking when he caught her eye, he hollered to another man behind her, "She's awake, boss."

"No shit, dumbass. I assumed that when she moved away from the door."

Danny's stomach plummeted, and the struggle to rise against the panic was real. This voice haunted her nightmares. Closing her eyes, she heard him once again as he reveled in causing her pain. *"Yer gonna be a good girl and tell me how much you want me to fuck ye, aintchya?"*

Fighting down the urge to wretch, she reached out with her other senses. *"Jamey…"* Moments passed, and when he didn't answer, she screamed, *"Jamey!"*

She waited for an answer, and when none came, she tried not to sob. Mayhap he thought she took off without waiting for him. *"I waited for you. I swear I did, but they hit me with something."*

And then there he was, his concern washing over her. *"Danny, where are you, honey?"*

Their unstable connection concerned her. The head wound could play into it, or a strong enough charm from a spirit mage could block transmissions. Despair filled her chest, and she did the only thing she could. She left the link wide open. Jamey would hear everything that happened to her and around her.

At that moment, the door to the cage creaked open. Eyes snapping open, she backed up against the bars behind her. The portly man wasn't much taller than her and could walk upright as he entered. A toothless grin crossed his weather-beaten face. "C'mon miss, let's na make this harder than it need be," he said as he reached for her.

Danny lunged. Snapping her fist into his throat and her knee into his groin, he was on the ground writhing as he alternated which part of his body his hands tried to protect.

The lanky one entered, kicking his cohort as he passed. "Get out of the way, Horace, if ye tain't able to help." He leered at Danny. "I likes me a hellcat. Go on and give it yer best shot."

Danyka emitted a feral growl as he came closer. He faked to her right, and in her addled frame of mind, she fell for it, nearly landing in his grasp when he sidled left. With a good grip on her ankles, he yanked, pulling her forward and causing her head to bounce against the concrete floor. White spots blotted her vision, but she had the sense to reach back and anchor her hands around the bars.

Lanky released her ankles and gave her a good kick in the ribs with his pointed boots. She felt a swift burst of pain as he broke two, and she sucked in a painful inhale. Legs free, she kicked his knee to the right, knocking his

legs out from under him. If pain was the game, she would give it back twofold. Rearing back, she kicked the same knee again, reveling in his howl. Backing up against the bars, she clutched her side and waited for the next assault.

The next round blindsided her. A hand reached through the bars and clenched a fistful of her hair, pulling it tightly so her neck extended. Before she could process what was happening, a thick piece of leather slipped around her neck, cutting off her oxygen. She reached up and tried to push her fingers under it to give her room to breathe. Failing to do so, she tried moving forward, then sideways. Nothing worked.

As her hands went limp, *his* voice whispered in her ear. "'Tis the same belt I used on ye as a child." Hoarse laughter floated around her. "Been waiting a long time to use it again, little lass." His tongue licked up the side of her neck. "Max was me brother. Ye tore his throat out, ye filthy little whore. I'm gonna take me time with ye. This won't go fast. Ye'll beg me for death afore it's over."

Danny managed a pitiful attempt at a laugh. "This filthy little whore doesn't lose any sleep over that raping bastard, and I won't lose any when I kill you either."

Lanky found his way to his feet. He slipped ropes around her hands and feet and then used them to pull her from the cage when McAllister removed the belt. If he made sure she hit all four sides of the cage on the way out, she couldn't blame him. He'd be limping for a hell of a long time.

A shadow fell over her as she exited the cage. Her jaw dropped in shock. This wasn't the man she remembered tormenting her. This was the face of a friend...or was it? "Roarke?" she whispered.

When he leered at her, she could see the difference in their features. This man was all cold, hard angles, nothing warm or welcoming. "Not Roarke," she said definitively, trying to warn the other wardens if her transmissions were getting through.

The Roarke imposter pulled off a medallion, swaying from his neck. There was the man she was expecting. Pure evil in a bag of flesh. This man haunted her dreams with countless others, but he featured more prominently than most. A cocky smile slipped across her face. "I'm gonna enjoy killing you."

McAllister backhanded her, then stepped on the fingers of her bound hands. "We'll see who gets the most enjoyment of the next few weeks. Me'se thinking it'll be me."

Danny spit at him, making him laugh harder. He grabbed her feet and drug her to a cot in the corner. "Who wants first dibs?" His voice thundered through the room. The two men she'd already injured were hesitant to take him up on that offer until he pulled a gold piece from his pocket and flipped it in the air. "Whoever's hard first gets a bonus."

The voices from her childhood started screaming in her head once again. As lanky pulled his pants down around his knees and stroked his flaccid cock, she geared up for another round of pain. There was no way in the seven hells she was going to make it easy on them. As he shuffled toward the bed, she pulled back her legs and kicked him in the chest, knocking him to the floor. Springing forward, she wrapped herself around him like a tick as her bound hands circled his throat. She was screaming as she reared back, and he choked beneath her. His face was turning purple, and she knew he was almost gone when she was cracked over the head again, harder this time.

Vision fading, she heard a multitude of voices. McAllister berated the portly man. "I want her conscious for this, ye dumb feck. Put her back in the cage."

Lanky was gasping for air and trying to say, "The filthy whore tain't worth a gold piece to feck. She's batshit crazy." His voice was hoarse, and she took perverse pleasure because she'd damaged his vocal chords.

Before all consciousness failed her, she opened her link one more time, and nothing. Opening herself to all the wardens, she sent out a distress call. *"Find me before it's too late. Beware of Roarke, not Roarke…"*

"I need you to focus for me, baby. Give me some indication of where you are. Any hint at all would help." Jamey's voice was a welcome balm to her shattered nerves and bruised body.

"Jamey, you can bring me back." Her waking mind was fading fast, but she needed to tell him one more time. *"I love you, Jameson. No matter what, I always will."*

At peace telling him how much he meant to her, she slipped into a place in her mind that no one was aware of. Deep into her memories, she drifted, going to the one and only place she'd ever felt safe in. Here she would remain until her mate came for her.

Regardless of the damage to her body, or the healing it received, he was the only one she would return for. She slipped further from the stream of reality and drifted into a place where there was no pain and no sorrow.

Danny kept going until nothing existed except for a clear summer sky and a field of forget-me-knots tickling her bare ankles. Dropping to sit crossed-legged amongst them, she gazed at the dark blue and purple blooms through the eyes of a child. Bumble bees buzzed nearby, but she knew they wouldn't harm her if she left them alone. Her fingers brushed the delicate petals, thinking they reminded her of joyful yesterdays.

Head tipping, her brows creased as an errant thought went through her mind. They also were the same colors as bruises she'd seen at some point…

Funny that bruises should cross her mind. Nothing bad happened here. This was her safe place as a child. Her long blond hair trailed over her shoulder. Deft fingers untied the blue ribbon in her hair that her da gave her

that morning. Swiftly, she picked only the prettiest of flowers to weave with the ribbon. Finished, she examined her handiwork.

"Perfect," she said, a wide smile crossing her delicate features. "I need to be perfect when he arrives." Tying the ribbon back in her hair, she felt like a fairy princess. The pale pink dress she was wearing caught her eye. "This is all wrong for today." With a thought, she transformed the dress to match the flowers in her hair. "There, now he'll know where to find me. I will wait in the place we will never forget. He will find me here. My bear always finds me."

90

Rosella Diaries
Twelfth Entry

They dressed Ella in white. From her lace garters and panties to her corset and lace gown, the color of purity adorned her from head to toe. Dainty pearl studs in her ears and a pearl choker around her neck created a double entendre. One signifying purity and the other ownership.

Ella noticed the girls fidgeting on either side of her. Nervous fingers twisted together and picked at the flowers woven into their braided hair. Struggling to keep calm, she gazed straight ahead, trying to ignore their fidgeting.

She wished she could have spoken to Gemma, but the poor thing refused visitors. Ella glimpsed her when she returned. Her eyes were vacant and dark bruises covered her face and arms. The sight had horrified Ella.

Pearl walked before the trio, dressed in an emerald silk gown. Luminous ebony eyes surveyed her property. The first girl she came to was younger than the others. She bent down and whispered in her ear, then wiped an errant tear away with a sad smile. She attached a leash to a small metal ring on the pearl choker and handed the excess to the girl's guard.

Moving on to Ella, she reached out and tucked a curl behind her ear as her eyes tried to convey courage, and her other hand clasped Ella's.

Ella met her gaze and gave her a brief nod, squeezing her hand. She lifted her head higher, and Pearl rewarded her with a smile. "I'm proud of you," she whispered into Ella's ear before she leashed her and moved on.

A paddle boat awaited them. Soft white lights ran along every railing and window, beckoning them. They boarded the vessel with Jonah and their personal guards leading them.

The guards wore black silk shirts and trousers accented with silver buttons running down the front and silver clasps on their knee-high black

boots. They'd pulled their hair back in slick queues. A handsome lot, every one of them. They completed Pearl's entourage beautifully.

Ella kept her eyes straight ahead, not glancing at Braden. Although she hadn't interacted with him, she couldn't miss the approval and desire in his eyes when he had assessed her before they left her room.

He'd reached for her face to reassure her, but she'd stepped back out of his reach. The hurt in his eyes was unmistakable, but she swallowed hard and shook her head.

Even Shaelynn had gaped at her when she rejected his touch. Shae could sense the attraction between them, but she'd never spoken to Ella about her suspicions.

Pearl and her entourage took their places on the upper deck. A raised platform awaited, and the girls walked up five steps to access it. Each guard led his charge to a numbered circle and left them there. Tall, freestanding candelabras emitted a soft glow behind them.

Pearl wasn't the only one to bring offerings. Five other groups of lasses were on display. Young women of all ages and a few prepubescent boys, wearing collars and terrified expressions, stood waiting. It horrified Ella to notice *children*—girls and boys—mixed in amongst them. A set of twins clung to each other. One of the toddlers sucked his thumb as his eyes darted around nervously. The bidding war for them was even more intense.

As terrified as she was of the unknown, her heart sank as she realized, in horror, they were all bound to meet the same fate tonight. Some of their bodies hadn't even matured, yet they were bound for an auction that would allow people to use them like common whores.

How, she wondered, confused by it all, had this become her life? Become any of their lives? Where was the Earth Mother's wrath now, she mused, when her youngest and most promising women stood leashed as chattel? When the youth of their race became slaves, what promise did the future of their people hold?

As the last girl—a child of no more than twelve—followed her guard to her circle, buyers began emerging from a door to the right.

Men and women of various ages, colors, and creeds stood perusing the delicacies on display as if they were appetizers they were about to devour. Ella stifled a nervous giggle at the thought, not wanting to appear daft or earn a public punishment.

Most of the girls appeared in versions of white, while the others stood in a demure display of pastels. They showcased the new girls one at a time, walking them on their leashes. Led by their owners to the center of the stage and turned in a slow circle to show their best attributes to future buyers, the girl's eyes remained downcast until instructed otherwise.

Finished with next month's prospects, the auctioneer went on to the girls available for tonight's entertainment. Ella stood transfixed by the man's booming voice as he listed each lot's attributes.

Pearl stood in the middle of the stage with an older girl who had accompanied them. Ella's vision was blurry, and she felt clammy as sweat dotted her forehead. Lightheaded, she tried to catch a breath as Pearl took her hand and led her forward.

A man in a black coat and tails stepped towards Pearl with his arm outstretched like a ringleader in a traveling circus she'd attended last summer. Ella stifled a giggle as she imagined how he would describe her.

"In this arena, ladies and gentlemen, we have an untamed beauty. Wild and likely to bite, she'll give ye a run for yer money and the ride of yer life. Best sleep with one eye open when yer done taking this li'l filly against her will because she's likely to slit yer throat while ye sleep afterward."

Movement to her left brought her attention back to the present as the announcer arrived by her side. "Last but not least, ladies and gentlemen, we have this delicate beauty. Hair like the sun frames delicate features. Firm, full breasts accentuate her tiny waist and luscious hips. She appears amenable, but there's a spitfire beneath all that grace. She will be a tough filly to break, but breaking this one will be a worthwhile challenge in the end."

Why did men insist on describing women like horses? Ella's breath came quicker as she listened to the man's description of her. He couldn't know those details without someone providing them.

Her thoughts raced as she imagined Jonah or Pearl selling her secrets. Why did it surprise her? This had always been her destination. She never had a chance of escaping this path. Squaring her shoulders, she lifted her chin and stared down at the small crowd of buyers.

If they wanted a challenge, then by God, she would give them one. If she was to endure pain for their pleasure, then she would take pleasure in their pain as well. Her eyes lit with a fierce determination, and she saw smiles crossing some of the men's faces. She knew who would bid on her just by the way they were leering at her now.

Pearl led her back to her spot. Gazing into Ella's eyes, she shook her head as she whispered, "Always the scrapper, Ella. I hoped I'd dissuaded you."

Her eyes were sad as she said in a resigned voice, "I can't help you now. You've thrown down a gauntlet. Now, they'll fight like gutter thieves to be the one to meet your challenge and knock you down a peg."

"I know, and I accept the consequences," Ella whispered back with a resigned smile. "It's who I am. Even you can't change me."

The master of ceremonies auctioned off the girls with humor and minute attention to the young women's attributes. Much too quickly, the spotlight returned to Ella.

Buyers who'd already made a purchase stepped back against the rails to watch the bidding war begin. Ella heard laughter and catcalls coming from the onlookers.

Four men remained. A barrel-chested ginger of average height opened the bid at a thousand.

A lean brunette with eyes so dark they blended with his pupils raised the bet to fifteen hundred as he stared at her with naked desire.

An older man dressed like a gentleman and trying to hide multiple jowls with silver mutton-chop sideburns doubled it to three thousand. Ella cringed at the thought of him touching her.

The last man, a lanky man in a kilt, stroked his beard thoughtfully. Eyes hidden behind dark spectacles, he had a mysterious air to him. His fingers continued stroking his braided beard while his jaw clenched as he gazed at her.

"Going once, going twice," the auctioneer said. "Four," the ginger said as his cheeks flushed with anticipation.

Ella gasped. The bid was already much higher than any of the other girls had sold for.

"Five," mutton chops shouted.

"Six," the brunette countered.

Pearl surprised Ella with a tight grip on her hand. Ella glanced at her profile, expecting glee at the prices, but the emotion on her face was unease. When the older man raised the bid again, Ella was sure she saw a flash of pure hatred cross her features. Pearl knew this man, and their dealings had not been pleasant.

Ella prayed to the Earth Mother that anyone but him would win her. The ginger had stepped back to the rail, hanging his head in defeat and removing himself from the bidding war.

Mutton chop's cheeks flushed darker as he shouted, "Sixty-five hundred." Gasps came from the crowd this time.

"Going once, going twice, going…"

"Ten," a deep voice countered. The man with the spectacles finally spoke up, as if he couldn't deign to begin the bidding war, but he intended to finish it.

"Sir, I doubt she's worth all of that!" mutton chops sputtered in outrage. Throwing his hands up in the air, he removed himself from their midst, grumbling the entire way.

"Going once, going twice," the auctioneer glanced at the brunette, who shook his head in disgust and turned away. "Sold to the man in the kilt, and may the ride be worth it, sir."

Laughter came from the assembled crowd. Proud new owners circled their prey, showing off their new acquisition to their friends and partners.

The man nodded, not saying a word as he waited for Pearl to lead her charge to him. Rosella was shaking with fear because the giant towered over her by more than a foot.

Pearl took her hand away and addressed her purchaser. "Her guard, Braden, will wait outside of the room if you prefer. He will not interfere." The glare she gave Braden was a warning to act appropriately.

Pearl handed the leather leash to her new owner and nodded at her. "I'll collect you tomorrow," she whispered. She was uneasy, but then her composure returned, and she left Ella in the possession of a stranger.

"Come, lass," the man said in a thick brogue, tugging on the leash. He was gentler than she expected as he led her down the stairs to claim her innocence.

"Dear Diary,
Twelfth Entry

I am quickly writing this to distract myself from the coming events. A man from the Highlands purchased me for ten thousand dollars.

I am terrified at what he will expect to make the evening worth his money. I must go now and pay attention before I trip going down the stairs in this stupid dress.

Mother, pray for me and give me strength.
Rosella

91

Devastation

Myranda raced back to Heart Island the moment Rhy contacted her requesting emergency assistance. She hadn't thought twice about answering the call, needing to reassure herself Ryssa was alright, too.

Entering the clinic, she was stunned to see the hive of activity and the distress and urgency on their faces. "What's wrong?" she asked as her mind instantly went to her daughter.

Rhy walked out of the clinic and gave her a curt nod. "I'm treating a girl for injuries sustained after a near rape attempt." Rhy's eyes watered, but she quickly blinked away the tears. "The island's under attack. It's jest been a long day for all of us."

Myranda gave her a quick hug and then, in an efficient tone, asked, "How can I be of help?"

Rhy swallowed thickly before answering. "I believe our assailant needs some attending to." Her gaze hardened. "Appears he fell down a time or two on his way to a cell."

Meeting Myranda's eyes, she said, "I don't think I can fairly treat him after seeing what he's done today and knowing what he's done over the past few months. I be more likely to kill the li'l bastard instead."

Myranda's eyes widened. Rhyanna was the gentlest of their healing guild. "I'll do it. How completely do we want the injuries healed?"

"Heal anything life-threatening. Leave the pain for him to stew in while he awaits his trial. He deserves it."

"So be it." Myranda picked up the leather satchel she'd brought with her and headed for the door.

Damian stood by the door. He opened it and stepped outside with her. "I'll go with you, Myr."

Myranda gazed into his dark, broody eyes and said, "It's unnecessary. I can manage this on my own."

494

"I know you can, but I don't want you alone with him."

Myranda quirked a brow at his concerned tone. "Lead the way."

He opened the door for her, and they headed out into the night. The solemn stillness of the night echoed the horrors of the past few hours. They walked in silence until they reached the pump house.

Damian released the wards on the door, and they entered the damp, musty-smelling stone building. Faint witch light flared from the end of the hallway, and they made their way towards it.

Eaton sat against the stone wall opposite the bars, caging him in. Damian opened the door and stepped inside. Myranda followed, stepping to his right.

"Mrs. Belmont will check your injuries," Damian said. "Act appropriately."

Eaton glared up at him. "Why should I? They are gonna hang me, anyway."

"Because if you harm her, I'll end you tonight. And hanging would be a mercy for what you've done."

Myranda walked forward, exhibiting no fear. She knelt beside the young man, examining him and healing the wounds still oozing blood. Her exam was cursory. Respecting Rhyanna's directive, she didn't take his pain away, merely staunched the bleeding and healed anything that might become life-threatening.

His life was in the court's hands now, and may the Mother have mercy on him because the Wardens would not.

Brushing her hands off, she stood. Reaching down for her bag, she caught the young man's eyes. The cockiness had evaporated, and fear was the predominant emotion peeking through.

"Thank you, mistress," he said as she left him there and walked out into the hall. "I didn't expect any kindness after what I've done."

"I've done what Mistress Rhyanna asked me to do," Myranda said softly. "It's my job to heal you, not to be kind."

Eaton's head dropped to his chest, and he said nothing more.

Damian reset the locks on the cell and the wards on the door as they exited the building. "The boy's damn lucky Rhyanna didn't ignore the directive. Eaton didn't offer Collette any kindnesses over the past few months."

He was angry, and his tone was sharp and unforgiving. But there was something else there lurking beneath the surface. Myranda stopped in the middle of the path and faced him. "Damian, I've known you for a long time. Tell me what's wrong."

Placing a shaking hand on his arm, she said, "You haven't been able to look at me all night. *What's wrong?*" Her voice cracked, and she clung to him. "Did you find him?"

Damian's expression was bleak. Shaking his head, he said, "No, we didn't find Mathyas, but I think we found some of his clothing."

"And?" she asked, as her heart pounded in her chest.

Damian's voice was gentle as he said, "His leather jacket is shredded and soaked in blood."

"But you didn't find his body?" she asked, still clinging to hope. "How do you know it's his blood?"

His gaze never faltered, but his eyes were full of sympathy. "I'll try to get the hellhounds to agree to track for us. They might find his scent on the jacket and be able to track him." He cleared his throat. "The Elemental High Court has blood samples of all the wardens. A forensic mage will verify if it's his blood or not."

The devastation in her eyes destroyed him.

"You knew." She threw the accusation at him. "You sat with us this evening for dinner, and you knew." A sob ripped through the night. "Why didn't you tell me?"

The hurt and disappointment in her voice cut deep. Damian ran a hand through his hair. "I wanted you and Ryssa to enjoy the solstice before I tore your world apart, Myr. And I didn't want to tell you in front of Maryssa."

Myranda stared at him as his words settled in her soul. "You think he's dead? Don't you?" Tears hovered on her lashes and then fell in a downpour down her face. She saw the truth in his eyes and couldn't face it. Closing her eyes, she shook her head.

When her knees collapsed, he stepped into her, letting her fall against his chest. His arms wrapped around her, supporting her. "I'm so fucking sorry, Myr. I hope that we're wrong, I really do. But I'm not gonna lie. It doesn't look good."

She clutched his shirt as she sobbed into his chest. "No. I can't believe it. It doesn't feel right here." She pulled away far enough to see his eyes. Her hand settled over her heart. "Why can't I feel that he's gone? Why isn't there a hole in my fucking heart?"

Damian framed her face in his hands and said, "I don't know, honey." He gazed into her pain-filled eyes, not backing away from her questions. "I'm so fucking sorry." He repeated the words, not knowing what the fuck else to say.

The tragic look in her eyes and the raw anguish she was radiating tore at his empathic gifts. He pulled her tightly against him, wrapping his arms around her and giving her a safe space to grieve.

They stood entwined for a long time, and when her legs gave out again, Damian picked her up and carried her to a bench. He sat with her for a long

time as she sobbed against him. When the surge subsided and her sobs faded to a quiet, steady cascade down her face, she tried to sit up, realizing dawn wasn't far off.

Sniffling, she said, "It's been a long day, Damian. You must be exhausted. Somehow, I need to get home." She wiped her face with her hands.

Damian didn't release her but gave her a gentle kiss on the forehead and said, "C'mon. I'll see you home."

She stared at him through bloodshot eyes. "You don't have to do that."

His dark eyes met hers, and he said in a gentle voice, "I know I don't have to, Myr." He wiped another trail of tears off her cheek. "I'm your friend, and I'd like to see you safely home. Will you permit me to do that?"

Devastated beyond reason, she nodded. "I don't want to be alone tonight."

"I'll sleep on the couch," he said.

Myranda took a shuddering breath as she nodded. "How am I going to tell Ryssa?"

"I don't know, honey. There's never gonna be an easy way to share this news with her." His hand rubbed over his stubble. "You could wait until I confirm what I suspect."

She shook her head. "I can't do that to her. I promised her I would be honest about anything we found." Her hands shook as she said, "I don't know how to do this."

Damian squeezed her hand. "Do you want me to tell her with you?"

"I don't know."

"Well, you can decide tomorrow."

He stood, cradling her to his chest. "Let's get you home."

"I can walk."

Letting her slide slowly to the ground, he waited until she found the strength to take a step. His arm went around her shoulders, and she leaned heavily onto him as they made their way to the portal.

When the doors closed, she glanced up at him with red-rimmed eyes. "Thank you, Damian, for being here."

"Anytime, Myr. That's what friends are for."

Exhausted, she leaned against him, letting someone else support her for a change. Heartbroken, she wondered at the devastation that she was about to wreak on her daughter. She closed her eyes, unable to face it tonight. Mother, give her the strength she needed to tell Ryssa.

Somehow, she'd staggered home on her own two feet. Numb, she hadn't said another word as her addled brain tried to make sense of the senseless loss.

She unlocked the door, and they entered the dark kitchen. Damian lit the inside lanterns with witch light, closing the door behind him. Gentle fingers pried the bag she'd forgotten she was holding from her hands, placing it on the table.

Without a word, he led her through the house and up the stairs into her room. She crossed the threshold, holding her breath as she tried to hold on to any dignity that she still possessed. Watching Damian pull the bedding back broke something in her because she'd never had another male in this room.

Blindly, she fell into bed, curling into a tight ball. The sobs tore through her as her reality shifted off its axis. All these months, she had been so damn sure that somehow, the man she loved had survived. How could she have been so wrong? Gentle hands removed the shoes from her feet, reminding her she wasn't alone.

Damian's heart ached for the devastation he'd caused. He knew there would be no easy way to present his finds. Some part of him had thought—mistakenly—that after all these months, mayhap she had expected this news. Setting her shoes by the closet, he turned back to the sobbing woman in the too-big bed.

This wasn't the first time he'd helped a woman deal with her grief. No, the first time had broken his heart when Maddy didn't return his feelings and then Ronan had returned to her. Mayhap there was still hope for Mathyas. Ronan was living proof of that.

"Damian?" her tortured whisper reached him in the dark.

Clenching his eyes closed, he begged the Mother not to let him make the same mistake again. "What do you need, Myranda?" he asked, even though he knew her answer before she spoke.

"Would it be too much to ask you to hold me tonight? Just hold me?"

Yes, it would be too much. He'd gone without the comfort of a woman for too long. And though he would never take advantage of any woman, women in pain sought comfort in ways they wouldn't normally consider on a good day. He let out a long sigh as he prayed for strength and walked to the bed.

Crawling in behind her, he wrapped his arms around her and pulled her in close. "No, honey. It's not too much to ask." He buried his head in the thick waves of her jasmine-scented hair. The smell of the bonfire smoke mixed with it, giving her an earthy scent that was so her. When her hand entwined with his, he let her, gently squeezing her fingers. "I've got you, Myranda. Try to sleep."

The sobbing continued. When she finally wore herself out and sleep claimed her, he let out a shuddering breath because she fit too perfectly

against him. But every time he closed his eyes, he saw Mathyas's face staring at him, reminding him they'd been friends once. And friends didn't poach.

Hell, he hadn't even been a good enough brother not to do that. But this time, he would keep his distance. His heart couldn't take another disappointment, and Myranda just needed a friend. So that's what they would remain—friends without benefits.

92

Where the Fuck is She?

"I want an update on the damages," Maddy snapped on her links to everyone. She paced back and forth in her office as reports filtered in. Her pregnancy might keep her confined to this building for safety, but damn it, she could still run the logistics from here.

"They destroyed the boathouse on the north side," Kai said.

"Anyone injured?"

"Bumps and bruises, but I'll heal."

"A shed on the western end and half a dozen canoes," Ronan said.

Jameson chimed in with, *"A dozen or more on the south side and all the docks on the main landing. Someone sure the fuck wanted us distracted and unable to follow."*

"Well, they didn't count on us following without boats," Kyran snarled. *"Kai, are you able to shift?"*

"Without a doubt."

"You up to a late-night swim around the perimeter to look for any additional surprises they've left us?"

"Let me drop Genny at the dorms, and I'll be there in ten."

"Where's everyone else at?" Genny asked timidly.

"They joined Landon on the cliffs, sheltering in place with the dragons until I give them leave to return," Maddy said.

"We're closer to the cliffs than to the shore. Can Kai leave me there with them instead? It would save him time," she asked, worried about her friends.

Maddy took a moment, trying to decide on the safest thing to do. *"Genny, I trust you to keep the students from making any rash decisions. I'm putting you in charge of the group there. If anyone gives you the slightest attitude about that, you tell them to march their asses into my office when this is over. We don't have time to worry about their petty misgivings right now."*

"Yes, Mistress," Genny said.

Maddy dropped onto her desk chair as physical and emotional fatigue overcame her. The entire day had been lovely as they celebrated with friends and family. Now terrorists were threatening everything she held dear.

Rage simmered in her gut, pushing out the exhaustion. How dare they come into her community—her home—and cause such destruction? When this ended, there would be hell to pay, and the punishments would be severe for those involved.

Needing to touch base with everyone under her protection, she sent out another message to the island residents. *"Continue to shelter in place until further notice. I will alert you when it is safe to resume normal activities. If you see any unusual activity, please notify me immediately."*

Supporting her head with her hands, she focused on what they knew and what she could do from the safety of her inner sanctum. Her promise to Ronan to remain here chafed, but she understood why he needed her to remain inside the castle walls.

Tears welled in her eyes as she thought about Landon and how frightened he must be. She was fucking terrified for the child. He was her child by the bonds of love they'd formed and by the promises she'd made to keep him safe.

Landon was wild and headstrong. He rarely thought of the consequences. He just dove in feet first. So much like his father, it hurt sometimes to look at him and see the young man Ronan had once been. She needed to keep him safe.

Considering her assets, Collette's ability to teleport came to mind. Powerful emotions triggered her gift. With the Mother's grace, she'd be able to use it in an emergency.

"Kai," Maddy called on her warden network.

"Yes, Maddy?" he asked.

"Swing by the clinic and see if Collette is fit to travel. Take her with Genny to the cliffs. She may be of use if needed."

"Nearly there, Maddy," Kai said.

"Excellent."

Reaching out to the River Patrol, she asked, *"Were you able to apprehend anyone?"*

"Not yet, Mistress," came a reply. *"But we're following several suspicious vessels."*

"Don't lose them. I want to know where they're going and how many are involved."

"Yes, Mistress," he replied. *"How do you want us to proceed when we have them cornered?"*

The question made her smile, reminding her how confident the Romani men always were. Truth be told, it wasn't just the men. The women were just as fierce and more than capable of magical protection—and the occasional curse, if needed.

501

"I want them on their knees in chains." Her vicious streak was coming forth, and it wanted to play.

"Yes, Mistress." His voice held amusement mixed with a hint of excitement. It was rare that they had to do much more than patrol the shores of the Sanctuary, but when called to battle, they met it gleefully.

"Roarke," she called, hoping to access his network of informants on the docks.

"Madylyn," he answered immediately.

"Have you left yet?"

"Aye, a while ago. Need something?"

"We've had multiple attacks on our shores in the past hour and would be grateful for any assistance you can offer, should it be needed."

"I'm heading for my ship. Will let you know when I'm nearby."

Closing her eyes for a moment to think about her next move, she pondered calling in reinforcements. Their unwelcome guests seemed to have departed in a hurry after the rash of vandalism. Until she heard more, she'd wait before calling in additional troops.

The office door across from her desk slammed open, hitting the wall behind it, and a furious Jameson stalked towards her. Madylyn's jaw dropped. In all the centuries she'd known this man, he had never once lost his temper in her presence. She'd seen him fighting with Danny, and with Ferg on rare occasions, but nothing like this.

Jamey was furious, and the only thing that came to mind was Collette's attack. More confusing than the fury she witnessed was the fear she felt behind it.

"Is she here?" he demanded.

Maddy stared at him, stunned, and asked, "Who, Jamey? You've got to give some more to go on than that. I don't know what you are talking about, and there's a lot going on right now."

"Goddammit, Maddy," he ground out, leaning over and placing his hands on her desk. "Where did you send Danny? Where the fuck is she?"

Madylyn gaped at the man in shock. Jameson never spoke to her in this tone. "What's wrong?" she asked.

"I can't find Danny. Where is she?" he repeated, this time fisting his hands and bringing the right one down on her desk, disturbing the papers on the surface.

Eyes wide, she watched his face turn red with frustration. He paced in front of her desk, clenching both fists.

"She was supposed to wait for me on the beach before engaging. When I checked in with her, she said she'd wait for me. I was nearly there. When I got there, she was gone."

502

Maddy heard the foyer door slam and boots on the stairs. She was afraid this would get ugly if he didn't calm down. Stepping around the desk towards him, she reached out to take his hand.

"For fuck's sake, Maddy," his eyes drilled into hers as he reached out and grabbed her hand like a lifeline. "The last thing she said to me was, 'Find me.' Something's wrong."

"Jameson!" Ronan's voice cracked through the air like a whip. "Release her," he growled. The threat of violence was a tangible thing between the two alpha men. Ronan had sensed Maddy's unease and came as quickly as he could. Jamey did as he requested with an apologetic glance at Madylyn.

The rarity of Jamey's raised voice brought others hurrying into the room. Rhyanna went to him immediately, grasping his other hand.

"Jamey, what's wrong, luv?"

"It's Danny. I can't get any response from her. She's in trouble." He rubbed his eyes. "They've camouflaged her scent. I followed her tracks on the beach, but they end twenty feet from the water. My grizzly can't track her either, and it's pissing him off."

"Pretty sure we picked up on that," Ronan said dryly.

Rhy watched him carefully even as she channeled soothing energy into him through her hands. Jamey had known her long enough to know what she was doing and tried to disengage himself with her. He didn't want to calm the fuck down. She surprised him when she only latched on tighter and pulled him towards her.

He took a ragged breath and let it slowly release as he closed his eyes in defeat, allowing her to hug him. He heard others enter the room and felt their concern.

"It's alright, luv," Rhyanna whispered. "We're here to help, but we can't if ye don't tell us what's wrong."

"She's afraid and in tremendous pain," he said, his voice like gravel. "This is the first time our link has been this wide open, but I can feel what she is experiencing."

Jamey turned to Maddy. "Reach out to her. Please."

Maddy focused on the link she'd formed centuries ago when she had rescued Danny. She took a deep cleansing breath, released it, and sent a stronger message through their shared link. *"Danny, I need you to answer me."*

Giving her time to respond, she waited. When nothing came through, she made it a command. *"Danyka, respond to me immediately."* Her shocked expression told him what he needed to know.

"I can't," she whispered. "She's intentionally blocked me." Tears welled in her blue eyes as she looked at Ronan. "She'd only do that to protect me."

Ronan pulled her into his arms, then looked at the rest of them. "You all have a link to her." He let that sink in. "Try to get a response of any kind, an

image, a location, anything at all. One at a time." He looked at Rhyanna. "You're like a sister to her. You're next."

Rhyanna closed her eyes and did as he asked. Her bereft expression said it all. Emerald eyes filled as Kyran wrapped his arms around her from behind.

Jamey ran a hand over his face as he met Maddy's gaze. "We rarely transmit physical pain. But tonight, I know she's in agony, and she's terrified."

"What wrong, and what can I do to help?" a deep voice asked from the door. Roarke Gallagher leaned against the frame and studied the occupants.

Jamey face him. "It's Danny. She went missing less than an hour ago. She's not on the island, and we need to find her.

Roarke's gaze was distant as he communicated with his network of eyes. "River Rats are on alert for anything suspicious and for Danny. If she's not on the river, we'll find her."

Jamey nodded. "Thank you." His gaze returned to Madylyn. "What's our backup plan if that doesn't work?"

Maddy turned to Ronan. "Rumor has it the hellhounds can track damn near anything."

Ronan shook his head. "I've heard it's been done, but I've never worked with them like that."

"Are you willing to try?" Madylyn asked him.

"As a last resort?" Ronan said, clenching his jaw. "Yes. We'll need something with her scent on it."

"I'll get it," Rhy said, hurrying to gather something.

"I need to meet Kai to secure the perimeter," Kyr said, walking out with her.

"The hellhound king will want something in return," Ronan said.

"We'll discuss terms if it comes to that," Maddy said, brows furrowing.

"I can't just sit here doing nothing," Jamey snarled.

"C'mon, we can start searching the docks on the mainland." Roarke tipped his chin at Jameson. "You're a shifter. If she's there, you should be able to pick up her scent."

"I'll try. Hopefully, they're not still masking it," Jamey said. "Let's go."

"Jamey," Maddy called as he neared the door. "Bring them back alive. Danny deserves to mete out her own justice."

Jamey's shifter eyes were backlit with an amber light, showing how close he was to losing control. "I'll try, Maddy, but I can't promise anything." He left, not waiting for an answer. Danny needed him, and he needed to find her.

His heart was racing, and his beast was prowling inside of him. The grizzly side of him wanted to kill someone, and Jamey hoped the human side was strong enough to prevent him from doing it. Because if they'd hurt

Danny as badly as he thought they had—there would be no holding him back. His grizzly would gut the fuckers and revel in their blood.

93

Games

Kerrygan entered the Court of Tears ballroom and let out a low whistle. Holy Shit. They had completely transformed the room into a luxurious gambling den. Varan must have one hell of a decorator. Conflicted, he felt both right at home and completely out of his league. Pushing up the dark glasses he wore to cover his disturbing eyes, he meandered through the room, observing the players.

To his left, eliminated players gathered around the bar. He noted a few of the River Rats from the tavern, admiring the fine sofas they sat on. If it hadn't been for the shitshow tonight had turned into, most of the men from the Sanctuary would have migrated here to join in the revelry.

He found King Varan and Queen Yareli studying their guests from across the room. Varan whispered in her ear, and she smiled up at him tentatively. Kerrygan hoped the king could fix the mess he'd made with his queen. He remembered a time when they'd been happy together. Wistfully, he wondered if it was possible to regain a sliver of what they'd once shown the world.

"What the bloody hell?" he murmured under his breath as his gaze fell on a face he didn't expect to see here.

Grace stood at a roulette table in a strapless black satin dress, showing deep cleavage. Hair in an intricate updo and makeup expertly applied, she appeared a decade older. A large sapphire pendant hung from her neck. He wondered how in the hell she could have afforded a stone that size.

Ruby-red lips gave the other players—mostly men—a heart-wrenching smile as she pulled her winnings in. She let out a sexy laugh at something the man beside her whispered into her ear. Generously, she shared her winnings with the other players.

Kenn sauntered over to Kerrygan, handing him a glass three-quarters full of whiskey. "Brought ya the good stuff, not the cheap shit they're handing out at the bar."

Kerrygan took it gratefully, drinking a third of it in one shot. This wasn't his usual gathering, and the burn helped settle him. "Maddy sent me. Hate to disappoint ye, but Fisher Jordan already be in custody. Ye won't get to play with him tonight."

"Fuck," Kenn said darkly. "Was looking forward to taking him apart a piece at a time. Now I'll need to find someone else to play with." Following Kerrygan's eyes, he honed in on Grace. "Who's the curvy little blond?"

"Works for Maddy. She's setting up the women's shelter near Sackett's Harbor."

"Single?" Kenn asked, undressing her with his eyes. "She's a pretty little thing."

"Don't think she's yer type," Kerry said, sharper than he'd intended to.

"You calling dibs?" Kenn asked, raising a brow.

"Feck no. Lass is a tad too crazy for me liking. I like me women willing and sweet. That one's got a mouth on her."

"So, you don't care if I give it a shot, then?" Kenn asked with a cocky grin.

Kerrygan didn't answer. His eyes locked on her lips, and when he glanced up, her eyes stayed on his. She stared at him, and even with the glasses, he felt like she was staring into his soul. Her smile and laughter faded. The thin line of those lush lips made him wonder if she'd heard him. Nye, she was too far away.

"I'm gonna take your distraction as a yes," Kenn said, taking a sip of his whiskey. "I ain't bout to get in the middle of whatever energy is passing between the two of you."

Kerry shook himself and finished his drink. "Have at it, brother. No dibs here."

"Your aura tells me a different story," Kenn snorted.

Grace's gaze snapped to him, and he knew without a doubt that she'd heard every word that he'd just said, and for some unfathomable reason, he'd pissed her off.

The siren stood up and glided towards them. Undulated might be a better word. Her movements were nothing like the clumsy ones he'd seen the day he met her. Tonight, she was sultry as fecking hell.

Reaching them, she smiled tightly at Kerrygan, but her eyes were cool. "Won't you introduce me to your friend?" She turned the charm on Kenn, giving him the brilliance of a genuine smile.

Kerrygan swallowed hard, jaw clenching. "Kenn, this is Grace." He left Kenn's title out, not wanting to encourage her.

507

Kenn took her hand, kissing the back of it softly. "It's a pleasure to meet you, Grace. I was just asking Kerrygan about you."

"I heard." She grinned, dimples showing as she said in a voice that went right to Kerrygan's cock. "I might be a touch too crazy for him, but I think I might just be the right flavor of crazy for you—sir." Her voice dropped and her expression changed, eyes dropping and body language becoming one of a submissive.

Kenn's eyes met Kerry's in a holy fuck expression. Kerrygan saw the conflict he struggled with. The man was salivating to have a go at the pretty young thing, but he didn't want to step on his friend's toes.

"Don't hesitate on me part, brother. If you need a new pet, she seems eager to play the part."

Kenn's eyes simmered, and Kerry thought he might have swallowed his tongue.

Grace placed a hand on both of their chests, the heat of her palm singing Kerrygan.

Batting her eyes at Kenn, she said, "If you boys gotta argue about it, I'm not your girl." She licked her lips, her gaze running up and down the front of him. With a small curtsy, letting him know she knew exactly who she'd been toying with, she said, "Perhaps some other time." Her long lashes lowered as the smoky sound of her voice wrapped around both men. "Forgive me for interrupting your evening."

Hazel eyes flashed to Kerrygan, and the smile faded. "I'm no one's pet, and you'd do well to remember it." With a lingering glare over her shoulder, she glided away.

"Fuck me," Kenn said, watching every glide of her hips as she sashayed away. "You think she was serious?"

"No fecking clue," Kerrygan said, wanting to reach down and adjust himself, but not moving a muscle. He shook his head in confusion. "Surprises me though."

"Why's that?"

"She survived the Grindstone wreck. Wouldn't think this would be her kind of playground."

Kenn's gaze narrowed. "Should have told me that to begin with. Those girls have been through enough. She doesn't need my brand of twisted pleasure."

Kerrygan frowned, rubbing a hand over his jaw. "Or maybe 'tis exactly what she needs."

Kenn shook his head, not willing to go there. "Not tonight, brother. Let's get another drink."

"Can't. Some shit went down on the island tonight. Gotta head back."

"Holler if you need a hand." Kenn winked at him and, a moment later, melted into the crowd.

Kerrygan left, heading straight for the portal, trying to keep those fecking ruby-red lips and flashing hazel eyes out of his head. Stepping inside, he heard a woman's soft voice behind him. "Please hold it for me. I need to get out of here."

Her voice was familiar, but he didn't glance back at her. He activated the portal the second she was through the door. "Where to, lass?"

Her head whipped around, and he realized too late that it was Grace. Her long hair was down, lipstick gone, and attitude checked. She looked nothing like the siren he'd seen inside. Damp eyes flashing, she turned back for the door to leave.

"For feck's sake," he said in a tired voice, taking off the glasses and rubbing his eyes. "Can't we take the same portal without any fecking drama?"

"That would depend on you," she said in a snide tone. "Got anything else you want to share about this Grindstone girl? Let's get it out and over with, falcon."

Now she was just being a bitch, slapping him with his humiliation.

"I was only trying to protect ye, lass." He let out a long sigh and wondered why he'd bothered. After her performance inside, the lass could damn well take care of herself.

"From what? You don't even know me." Her head cocked to the side, and her arms crossed over her chest. "I don't need a fucking chaperone."

"Ye got that part right. I don't know you. But what I ken is that man back there ain't into soft and sweet. He likes it rough, and he likes them meek, and I didn't want ye getting in over yer head, lass." His gaze wandered over her. "There ain't a meek fecking bone in yer body."

Grace continued glaring at him, and then she laughed in his face. "Yet, you title me a victim."

"I don't title ye anything. I stated a fact. Yer only a victim if that's what ye choose to be. I called you a survivor,"

"That why you're barely around? Hiding in your room, playing the victim from your own stupidity at being trapped in a cage?"

Fury shimmered in his eyes because she was striking a little too close to the truth. "And ye don't ken a fecking thing 'bout me, either, darling. Don't go believing the rumor mill. Lot more to it than that." His eyes narrowed in fury. "Tain't been around cuz I been assigned elsewhere this past week. What the feck do ye care, anyway?"

Irritation wound through him. Why the feck was he explaining himself to this wisp of a girl? And why did he care what she believed about his past?

"I don't." But her voice trembled, and her eyes remained on him.

Kerrygan pinched the bridge of his nose. When he glanced back down at her, mists swirled in his agitated eyes.

Grace glared up at him, not sure why she was picking this battle. After their first encounter, she'd watched the man discreetly from a distance, fascinated with the prickly shifter. He wasn't her type, so why the fuck was she poking this bear?

The answer slammed into her. On their first encounter, he was the first person who hadn't treated her with kid gloves. Her eyes shifted between those gorgeous, mutated eyes and his lips. Then he opened his mouth and broke the spell.

"What the feck is yer problem?" Kerrygan snapped, stepping into her space and backing her into the wall. "I don't have time to spar with ye, ye little twat."

He'd called her a twat, and while his words should have irritated her, she found herself turned on by his anger.

Kerrygan shifted closer, heat radiating off him. Bracing a hand on either side of her head, he leaned down so they were eye to eye. "While ye've been off playing games, li'l girl, the Sanctuary's been under attack. Genny's father tried to grab her, and someone assaulted a student. On top of that, Danyka's gone missing. So, lass, I don't have the patience or time to waste on an ungrateful child."

Eyes widening, she processed what he said with shock. But he didn't move, and his gaze dropped once again to her lips as he licked his. Grace's core heated at the carefully checked rage, realizing it wasn't all aimed at her. She wondered what it would take to break those restraints and set all of that anger free. Then his words repeated in her head. The bastard had called her a child. Well, she'd show him. Grabbing him by the lapels, she yanked him down and kissed him.

What the feck? Kerrygan thought. She'd jerked him completely off balance, flipped him, and then slammed his back against the wall. Guess the lessons with Danny had helped. Her soft lips on his were a cock tease he wanted to linger on, but he didn't have the time.

Grace clung to him as her lips moved over his, wanting him to respond. A moment later, he surprised her when he grabbed her arms. Instead of pulling her closer, he shoved her away so violently that she slammed into the opposite wall. His wild eyes stared at her like she'd lost her fucking mind.

"I'm not a child," she said in a breathy whisper.

Her clipped words slammed into him as hurt shimmered in those luminescent hazel eyes.

"That's a luxury I haven't had in a very long time," she said as a tear hovered on her lashes.

Kerrygan gave one slow blink, turned for the control panel, hit Heart Island, and initiated transport. When they stopped moving, he glanced over his shoulder at her. His smoldering eyes met hers for a long moment before

he strode from the portal with one last shot. "Then stop acting like one. Jest cause ye've had lots of sex doesn't make ye an adult."

Grace blanched as if he'd slapped her. Unable to witness the pain he'd inflicted rolling down her face, he left without another word. He'd meant what he'd said. So why did he feel like he'd just kicked a puppy?

94

River Rats

Roarke steered his vessel next to the dock. Deck hands secured the boat and lowered the ramp for Roarke and Jamey to disembark.

Roarke led the way through the maze of rickety docks and sloping walkways. Emerging beside a ramble shack warehouse, he walked into the building and pulled up a chair at the table. Jamey paced by the door, senses alert and praying to catch a whiff of her.

Gnarled hands, belonging to a wizened man, dealt cards to two other elderly gents on Roarke's. The old timer's face was a roadmap of wrinkles, detailing the long life he had lived. Bushy white eyebrows drooped over rheumy sapphire blue eyes. White hair stood up in contrary patches all over his head. A long braided white beard with silver bells hung nearly to his navel. The tintinnabulation of the bells, woven into his beard, tinkled when he sucked on his mahogany pipe.

Sucking hard, he narrowed his eyes at the newcomer and asked, "Ye in for this round, boy?"

Roarke grinned at the man and gave him a nod as he tossed a twenty in for his ante. "Yes, sir, I am." He picked up his cards and raised a brow. "How are things on the docks, Aalto?"

"Who wants to know?" he asked out of the corner of his mouth as he kept the pipe clenched between his teeth.

The grin faded, and Roarke said, "I do," in a dark, dangerous voice.

Aalto raised a bushy brow and tossed him two cards to replace the ones he'd discarded. "Been quiet past few weeks."

The man across from Roarke grunted, and he suspected Aalto kicked him under the table before he said anything.

Tall man to his right folded and pushed his chair back, wanting no part of what was to come. The one across from him did the same. The smell of

the river wafted from them as they stood. It was a damp, musty scent that never washed away.

"Aalto, we've been friends for how long now?"

"Friends?" the old geezer guffawed, reaching down to pet an old basset hound snoring at his feet.

"Acquaintances might be a better term," Roarke amended.

"Mayhap," Aalto said, puffing on his pipe. "Mayhap business associates be more accurate. Whatchya looking for this time?"

"Seen anything this afternoon worth my while?"

"Depends. Whatchya think it's worth?"

"C'mon old man, I ain't never cheated you." Roarke's voice chilled and his gaze turned to Jamey as a growl rumbled out of him. "That there grizzly shifter is looking for a loved one, and he ain't gonna be as generous as I am if you don't pony up some info."

"I gots no squabble with yer grizzly, and he ain't none with me."

Roarke pulled off several large bills and fanned himself with them. "He seeks the woman he loves. Don't think he'll care much who gets hurt trying to get to her. You feel me?"

The man's rheumy eyes glared at him. "Don't know if she's worth all that, but strangers been about this morning." A deep draw on his tobacco had him coughing noisily. "Strangest thing, we delivered two cages down the way," Aalto gestured to the south side.

"Big enough for a damned horse to live in." A dirty finger picked at a scab on his nose before continuing. "Me men loaded one of them onto that bastard's ship farther down."

"Which ship?" Roarke asked, peeling off another bill.

"One of them slaver ships on the last dock. All black one. Captain by the name of McAllister."

"Fuck me," Roarke cursed, remembering the sleazy little bastard from Wardens Court months ago. "What didchya do with the other cage?"

"Na, this is where things get interesting," the old geezer wheezed. "And pricier."

Jamey's growl escalated, the rumbling deeper, more threatening.

"Calm yerself, ye wee beastie," Aalto said to Jamey, giving him a shooing motion. "Yer both gonna wanna hear this."

Aalto's eyes dipped to the wad of cash Roarke still held. "Trust me, it be worth more than the ship."

Roarke peeled two more off and held them out to Aalto. When the man's dirty fingers closed on the bills, Roarke held them tightly. "If you're wasting my time, old man, I'll be taking it all back."

Aalto glared back at him. "I tain't ever disappointed ye Gallaghers yet," he said, referencing his long history with the Gallagher captains before Roarke's time.

"Out with it. We don't have time to waste."

"New captain been throwing his money and his weight amongst us peons. Pays good and demands discretion. Man be making a name for himself on the docks."

"Why would I give a shit about any of this?"

Cocking an eyebrow, Aalto said, "Cuz the man looks like yer twin and is going by the name of Roarke."

"What the fuck did you say?"

"Those of us who really know the Gallaghers can spot the difference, but he's been hiring men all week. Most of them don't give a shit who they're working for as long as it pays."

"Say what he's after?"

"Heard just this morning that he's got his eye on a sweet little thing out on Heart Island."

"I'll fucking kill him," Jamey ground out.

"Where didchya take the other cage?" Roarke asked.

Aalto's eyes dipped to the money roll, and Roarke wanted to beat the info out of him. "There are other informants I can go to," Roarke growled.

"But that'd take more time and money than what I'se asking.

The wily old fucker," Roarke thought to himself. He tossed two more bills on the table with disgust. "Spill."

"Rumors out that he was attacking the Sanctuary cuz they has something he wants."

"Elaborate."

"The tiniest warden. Said he was gonna make her real comfortable behind those iron bars."

Before either man could blink, Jamey's hand hit the table. Claws sprouted from his fingers, pinning the cash to the wood. "If you don't tell me right fucking now where you took that cage, I won't be responsible for the confetti I make out of this cash."

Aalto had lived long enough to recognize a predator on the verge of attacking. "'tween the tannery and locksmith. Don't know if it's still there, but that's where I'd start."

"Have you seen the girl he was talking about?" Roarke asked as he stood.

"Not yet, but they don'ts need to come by here to get to the tannery. From the ship, my crew wouldn't see them unloading anything."

Roarke clamped a hand on the old man's shoulder. "Thank you for your help."

"Ye's welcome." Blue eyes that had witnessed much in their time turned to Jamey. His gnarled hand reached out and nearly touched the claws

pinning his money to the table. "I'll be taking this now. Good luck finding yer girl."

Jamey snarled at him, but the claws retracted. "If we're too late because it amused you to waste our time, I'll be back."

The old man's chuckle followed them out the door.

"Maddy, send the troops to Clayton. We've got a lead," Jamey said.

"Let's go find your girl," Roarke said, clamping a hand on Jamey's shoulder.

A deep, menacing growl was the only response Roarke received.

95

I Need to Tell Someone

Kai and Genny arrived at Rhy's clinic as Lash and Collette walked out. Slight bruising on the side of Collett's face caught Genny's attention, but she didn't ask.

Kai shook hands with Lash. "Maddy wants me to take the girls to the cliffs with Isabella."

Lash glanced at Collette. "You going to be alright, baby?"

Collette gave Genny a quick glance before saying, "I'll be fine."

Lashed leaned into her, pressing a kiss against her forehead. "I need to help the river patrol. I'd like to see you tomorrow."

A flush crept across her cheeks as she looked at the ground. "I'd like that."

"We've gotta go," Kai said. "I need to join Kyran."

The three of them headed for the cliffs in silence. It was nearly a mile to the place set aside for the dragon family. Flames lit the sky as Alejandro patrolled in front of the cliff.

When they reached the fenced in pasture for sheep the dragons consumed, Genny said, "I know Kyran's waiting. We'll be fine from here. Alejandro will protect us."

Kai frowned, conflicted. He wanted to say he delivered them right to Isabella, but he didn't see any threats from here. "Promise me you'll stay together," he demanded, staring at both girls. Genny nodded, and Collette joined her.

Kai's eyes met Genny's, and he pulled her into a hug before brushing his lips over her temple. "I need to know you'll be safe."

"Promise," Genny said. "I won't do anything foolish. Go."

With a glance of regret, he left them and jogged down an adjoining path.

Collette watched him leave and then glanced at Genny. "He's quite the catch."

Genny wasn't up to another confrontation with Collette.

"He has been very kind to me."

Collette smiled at her. "I'm sure he has been."

Genny had just survived being abducted, and her patience was running thin. "I'm sorry he's not interested in you. I know you think after the things I've done that I don't deserve a chance with him, and maybe you're right."

Collette's eyes widened, and she said, "I meant nothing bad by that."

Genny took a breath and then kept on going as if she hadn't spoken. "But before you continue judging me, I want you to think about this." Her eyes welled as she spoke. "Do you think I wanted to be sold by my father, of all people, to someone who exploits young men and women? And do you think I wanted to be raped the first time I was with a man? Do you think I wanted to continue being abused by men I didn't know?"

Collette's eyes widened in horror, and she shook her head, not knowing what to say.

Genny helped her. "No, I didn't. Do you know how many times I wished I could just die so it would be over?"

This time, Collette nodded her head, and Genny was the one speechless.

A tear rolled down Collette's face. She swiped it away angrily, and then the dam burst, and she couldn't stop them. What were the chances that this was the one person who could understand what she'd been going through? And she had been so horrible to Genny about it?

"Yes, I understand more than you can imagine. I know all about the guilt and disgust you experience. I've spent hours in the tub trying to wash the filth of his touch from my skin, but it never goes away."

Genny's eyes filled as she listened to Collette's confession. "Who?" she asked in a gentle voice.

"My stepbrother, Eaton." Her voice was brittle as she spoke. "It started with subtle inappropriate touching. He enjoys leaving bruises where no one can see. I tried not to be alone with him, but he always found ways to corner me." Her eyes misted over again as her gaze grew distant.

"A month before I came here, he caught me alone inside of our boathouse. It was just before dawn." Her eyes closed as she remembered, "It was a warm morning. I was going to take a kayak out and watch the sunrise." Her throat closed, and she wasn't sure she could continue.

"You don't have to tell me any more," Genny said.

"I need to tell someone," Collette whispered. "I know I don't deserve your compassion."

Genny stared at her in shock. Swallowing the lump in her throat, she said, "I will witness your pain. I will hold space for you and bear this secret for you," Genny said solemnly.

Collette's face crumpled. With gratitude. "It all happened so quickly. He came in and closed the door behind him. From the look in his eyes, I knew it was going to be bad, but I never expected what happened."

Sniffling loudly, she forced the words out. "He was just coming home after a night of drinking when he saw me leave the house." Long fingers twisted a strand of her hair as she spoke.

"The bastard taunted me like he always did, telling me how I was always teasing him with the way I stared at him and how I dressed."

Her eyes darted to Genny nervously. "I never did, I swear. I tried really hard not to catch his attention whenever he was around."

"I believe you," Genny said, trying to soothe her.

"Eaton's much bigger than I am," she said. "He drug me to the back corner, away from the door." She stared at her feet as she remembered the horror of that day. "There's an old workbench back there." Her head tipped to the side as she re-lived that morning. "I tried to fight, but he hit me on the back of the head so hard that my knees buckled."

Collette swallowed hard, working up the courage to admit the rest. "With one hand he swiped everything off of the bench onto the floor. Then he slammed me down across the top of it. My feet barely touched the floor. I tried to kick him, but I couldn't get any leverage."

Genny's eyes swam with tears, knowing how this was going to end.

"He hit the back of my head again, and the pain was explosive." She touched the side of her head unconsciously. "I stopped fighting because it made me nauseous every time I moved."

"He yanked my leggings off." Collette stared off into the dark for a moment. The night surrounded them, another silent witness to her horror. "I remember the cool morning air on my skin. My mind screamed at me to do something, to fight back."

A tear dripped off her chin, but she didn't notice it. "I knew this time was going to be worse than the others."

Tears were streaming down Genny's face now. Silently, she wiped them away.

"He kicked my legs apart and stepped between them. I realized what was coming, but I couldn't stop him. I tried scrambling forward, but he was pinning me down. He laughed at me—told me to keep squirming because I was making it better for him."

Her voice faded as she recalled the loss of her innocence. "There was a window behind the bench. I could see our reflection in the window—the terror on my face and the glee on his. I wanted to rip that expression from his face." She swiped angrily at the tears, and her breath hitched.

"His cock tore its way into my body." Tears poured down her face, and she sobbed. "The pain was excruciating. He ripped me in places." Her arms

crossed protectively over her abdomen. "I wore his fingerprints for three days on my hips."

Collette was so pale, and she sounded hollowed out, but she continued narrating her assault. "He kept thrusting into me. Over and over…I didn't think it would ever end."

A pitiful laugh erupted from her. "And then it did. And all I could think was 'Thank the Mother, it's over.'" She giggled harder.

"But it wasn't. I lay there whimpering with him lying on top of me, telling me what a good girl I was and how much I had pleased him. I couldn't breathe with him there, but then, when I felt him getting hard again, I managed to drag in enough air to scream. He gagged me after that because he intended to keep playing."

There was a catch in her voice now. "I was so stupid, thinking it was over. He raped me two more times, taking me in ways that I won't speak about. When he got bored, he told me to go for a swim and clean up because I was filthy."

"I'm so sorry," Genny said, compassion shining in her damp eyes. She clasped Collette's hands, surprised the other girl allowed her. "Have you told anyone?"

All Collette's usual confidence had evaporated, and she hung her head. "He told me if I said anything, he would tell everyone I begged him to do it."

She chortled ironically. "That was worse than his threat to kill me. Appearances are everything…that's all I hear from my parents."

"You really think your father would have believed him?" Genny asked.

"I don't know, but after the first time…I was so ashamed. I didn't want my father to know what happened." She sniffled, wiping her nose with the back of her hand. "I just wanted to forget about it. I thought he'd leave me alone after he took what he wanted."

"He didn't though, did he?"

Collette shook her head. "No, he didn't."

"You need to tell someone," Genny said.

Collette let out a humorless laugh. "Everyone will know all about it soon enough." She wrapped her arms around her middle, hugging herself. "Mistress Danyka arrived just as he was trying to force himself on me outside the restroom."

Her words were matter-of-fact, numb even. A hint of a smile appeared as she said, "But I hurt him this time. I couldn't stop thinking, What would she do?"

"Who?"

"Mistress Danyka. I broke his nose with my elbow." A giggle escaped. "And when Danyka got there, she kicked his balls up into his throat. Then

Jameson nearly killed him. Don't think he'll be feeling up to hurting me anytime soon."

On impulse, Genny threw her arms around her. Collette stood stiffly for a minute before relaxing into the hug. "I'm so sorry you had to go through this," Genny said.

"I'm sorry you had to, too," Collette said. "I hated this place when I first got here, but it's made me rethink so many things. When I leave here, I don't want to be the same person I was." Eyes on her feet, she said in a whisper, "Honestly, I don't want to leave here at all. This is the only place I feel safe."

"I feel the same way, too. That's why I'm happy to call it my home. Everyone has been so kind to me here."

"Except for me," Collette said solemnly. "I'm so ashamed of the way I treated you."

"It was a deflection from the shame and pain you were experiencing," Genny said.

Collette met Genny's streaming eyes. The compassion in them broke something in her. "Now everyone will know what he did to me, and I'll be like…" Shame colored her cheeks as she looked away.

"You'll be like me," Genny said in a hoarse whisper.

"I was horrible to you."

"You were in tremendous pain."

"How can you justify the way I treated you?" Collette asked her, perplexed.

"Your entire life, everything you've wanted or done, has come easily to you. Friends, clothes, family connections."

Collette nodded ruefully.

"Then you arrive on the island, and here I am, a piece of white trash wearing handy me-downs from the kindness of strangers, and I had the attention of one of the Court of Tears princes."

"Please don't talk about yourself that way. I know what I said, and I've regretted it since it left my lips," Collette begged.

"You didn't want Kai because you liked him, and don't get me wrong, there's a lot to like about him. Kai represented someone more powerful, who could protect you from Eaton. You were desperate to have someone who could protect you when you left here."

Collette nodded guiltily. "I don't want to go home."

"I understand that. My father tried to force me to leave tonight." Her hand went to the bruised side of her face. "He sold me into that lifestyle the first time, and he intended to do it again. So, I really understand why you reacted so hatefully."

Sniffling, Collette said, "I'm not sure if it's better or worse that you're so damn nice?"

A genuine smile came over Genny. "I've never had friends my age before. Ryssa, Willow, and Amberly are wonderful. I would like it if we could be friends, too."

"I'd like that too. Ryssa and I were friends when we were younger. I've missed her, but I've been too proud to admit it."

"You're the only one who can change that," Genny said.

"I know. How do you know just what to say?"

"I've been in therapy since I arrived. Mistress Rhyanna has helped a lot." Genny cocked her head to the side and asked Collette, "So, what happens tomorrow when everything returns to normal? Will you ignore me and throw snide remarks when I walk by?" Genny said it jokingly. But honestly, she wanted to know what to expect.

"No. I'll never do that to you again. You know my secrets now. Can't get much closer than that."

"And you know more about me than most," Genny said, hugging her one last time. "We better check on the others."

They headed down the dirt path side by side. "Tell me about Lash."

Collette's eyes lit up, and her cheeks flushed. "It all started when I tried to throw myself off a cliff." She laughed at Genny's shocked gasp and shared another secret with her.

Heart lighter for the first time in months, Collette sent up a prayer of gratitude for the Mother's unexpected gifts. It was a relief having someone to confide in who really understood. And even if she still didn't think she deserved it, she was grateful to have Genny's friendship.

96

Count For Me

Danny's field of flowers faded. Instead of peace, she wandered through the fractured agony in her mind. Swallowed by the endless darkness, she drifted. In the distance, she faintly heard voices debating her fate.

"Don't see that the bitch is worth all this trouble," the lanky man said in a hoarse voice laced with pain.

"I wants no part in raping no one," the stout man said. "Keep yer money." Danny thought she heard a door slam.

Fairfax McAllister, the Roarke wannabe, said, "Drag him back here. He knows too much."

"Ye want him back, ye go fecking get him. I can hardly fecking walk," lanky man rasped. "Ye may wear the face of a young man, but you tain't got his strength. Feck this, I'm out, too." Fresh air wafted in as the door opened and then slammed again.

And then there was one, Danny idly thought, liking the odds better now. She needed to find clues to her location, but her eyelids were much too heavy, and the forget-me-nots beckoned once again. An approaching migraine was gonna be a bitch, and she didn't want to wait around to welcome it.

With that thought, she let herself slip under the cold, dark wave of pain, dragging her down like a tsunami swamping the coast. Like that monster wave, it tossed and flung her through hell as it carried her away. Darkness, deeper and colder than she'd ever experienced, embraced her. Her illusion of a safe place scattered as pounding agony overpowered the peace surrounding her.

The roaring in her ears grew louder, drowning out the exterior sounds. Thank the Mother for that. The sound of that despot's voice triggered her fight-or-flight response every time he spoke. The torment this man had put her through still brought her nightmares centuries later.

Fairfax McAllister was the bogeyman in her dreams. Finally, she had a name to go with the face. This was the man whose belt had bruised her neck for a week and left her unable to speak for much longer.

Many men had taken advantage of her and enjoyed causing her pain. But this man reveled in it. The last time he was with her, Danny was certain he was going to kill her. The guard, standing outside, getting off with him, was the only thing that saved her.

Her nightmares featured deviants of every size and shape. She remembered their faces and their physical characteristics, but she rarely heard their voices.

This bastard's voice haunted her. The mocking, nasally croak had demeaned her verbally as much as his hands and cock had physically. His voice in her child's memory was the sound of pure evil.

The wave pushed her toward the surface again, threatening to toss her back into the nightmare of her reality.

Something tugged at her wrists. She tried to focus, knowing every clue might help her. Large hands wrapped something rough around both of her wrists. The next thing she felt was her arm viciously wrenched above her head. The other arm soon joined it, taut enough that both of her joints protested.

A bucket of cold water jerked her unwillingly out of her stupor. Sputtering and blinking quickly to clear the water from her eyes, she tried to see where she was. Bright, overhead lights prevented her from opening her eyes fully. She squinted, inching her pounding head slowly to the right and peering through slitted lids.

Her wrists and ankles were bound. She lay on the cold, metal floor of the cage, spread eagle. They'd tied her to bars on opposite corners of the cage. Shivering from the cold, she became acutely aware of being buck-naked. The bastard had stripped her while she was unconscious. "No, no, no," she chanted as she tugged on her bonds.

The hemp ropes were tight and unforgiving, digging into her wrists and ankles painfully. As she tried to dislodge her bonds, she felt the pinch of a wide leather collar around her neck. His fucking belt was wrapped tightly around her neck, giving him complete control over her.

"HELP ME!" she screamed at the top of her lungs, grateful he hadn't gagged her.

"HELP!" Danny yelled again, praying someone outside would hear her.

An evil cackle came from the left of her. She didn't want to give him the satisfaction of glancing his way, but she needed to know how close he was to her.

Head slowly rotating to the left, she peered through the bars and saw her nightmare-made-flesh. He'd taken off his charm and sat there in all his naked glory.

Sallow skin covered his lean body. The years hadn't been kind to him. Wrinkled and hollow-eyed, he looked like shit. Her gaze traveled down his body, evaluating how much of a threat he posed to her at this age.

The old bastard possessed enough lean muscle to hold her captive on his own. He'd been smart to bind her hands and feet while she was unconscious.

Her eyes followed the movement of his right hand, stroking back and forth slowly. She gagged as she realized he was stroking his cock into fighting shape. Even at this age, the fucker could still get hard.

Danny tugged harder on her restraints, causing the binding to cut into her flesh, drawing blood. Her wrists were already raw, but she needed to get out of these restraints.

"Wontchya keep screaming, little warden?" he asked with a sly smile. "Perked me cock up when ye was screaming for help. Go on. Do it again. I'm nearly ready."

Danny met his gaze, pushing all of her hate and repulsion at him when she spoke. "Do your worst. My fellow wardens will take you apart one piece at a time after you rape and kill me."

"If they ever find me," he sneered. "Gonna be a long while before I puts you out of yer misery," He stood and ambled to the door of the cage, his long cock bobbing in front of him. "I aims to enjoy tormenting ye, ye little bitch."

The door to her cage creaked open, and Danny started screaming in her head. She wouldn't give him the satisfaction of hearing her do it again. Hyperventilating, she pulled tighter on her restraints, not caring if she cut off circulation in the process.

It took Fairfax a moment before his ancient knees lowered him to the floor between her legs. Dirty, wrinkled hands touched her inner calves. His eyes locked on her face, reveling in her repulsion. They moved higher, and he smirked at her twitching attempts to move.

In her mind, Danny started screaming at the top of her lungs. Sobbing inside, she kept repeating, *"Not again, not again, not again,"* as a mantra while trying to block all of her links.

When a gnarled hand slithered up her chest to latch onto the tail of the belt, she lost the ability to block anyone as she opened herself up telepathically to anyone who might help her.

"Help me, for fuck's sake, someone help me!" On the verge of passing out from pure terror, she screamed, *"Jamey, help me!"*

Black spots formed over her vision as she bucked, trying to drag air into her burning lungs. As her muscles relaxed, she stopped fighting him because death would be better than this.

McAllister loosened the leather just enough to bring her back around. Tears rolled down her face as his weight settled over her while she sucked in tortured breaths. His cock pressed against her inner thigh as he sneered at her and pulled the strap tight again. Spittle flew from his lips as he cut off her airflow once again, cackling in her face.

Fairfax leaned down and whispered in her ear. "I'm gonna do this all night long. I'll take ye to the brink of death and then resurrect ye just long enough to get yer attention."

His tongue licked up the side of her face, tasting the salt of her tears. He snickered. "Then I'll start over again, and…" he paused for dramatic effect. "Every third time, I'll fuck you until you're too damn raw to be worth anything to me."

"Now, be a good girl and count for me. I want ye to keep track, so ye can enjoy this with me, ye little bitch." The leather tightened slowly. "What number are we on, little warden?"

Danny shook her head, refusing to play his game.

"Ye'll fecking count, or I'll slam into ye right now," he said, knowing most women would do anything to postpone the inevitable.

"Two," Danny spat out through trembling, blue lips.

"That's me good girl," McAllister said, sliding his cock closer to her inner sanctum and loving the way she shuddered underneath him. Her body thrashed involuntarily, nearly seating his cock inside of her.

"I knows ye want this, but it's not time yet, ye second rate whore." He loosened the belt once again, loving the confusion and terror on her face and the way her body thrashed beneath him.

Choking someone while he fucked them was his favorite game. This wee thing was the one who'd gotten him addicted to it. He only used breath play with his disposable toys because, inevitably, he'd get too excited and kill the stupid bitches. Every one of them had been leading up to this—his reunion with his first victim. That she was also the tramp who killed Max was a fecking bonus.

'Twas harder to get young whores at his age. This was where his new charm would come in handy. The young captain was handsome and drew them like flies to honey.

A pitiful cough distracted him from his dreams of the future. Her lips were still blue, so he loosened the belt a smidge more.

Danny inhaled noisily, desperate to breathe and struggling to do so. Choking sobs echoed off the warehouse walls, mocking her.

Fairfax grinned, displaying his rotten teeth. "What number are we on?"

Danny sobbed, not wanting to say it. The moment she did, he would rape her. It wouldn't be the first time, or the worst thing, that had ever happened to her. She'd survived the physical and sexual assault before, but this time was different. This time, he was taking something that she'd promised to someone else.

Jamey was the only man she wanted inside of her. She'd never given him the opportunity to make love to her, and now he never would. Even if she survived this, she could never be with him now. She didn't even know if she could be with a man again without seeing this fucker's face over her.

"C'mon, ye little whore, ye know ye want this," Fairfax said, getting her attention. He shifted his hips. His cock was probing between her legs, seeking entrance the moment she opened her mouth. His face lowered to hers again. When his tongue snaked out to lick up her tears on the other side, she struck.

"Fuck you," she screamed as she reared up and bit into his neck the same way she had done years ago. The only weapon she had available was her teeth. The man was stupid to believe she wouldn't hesitate to rip his throat out the same way she'd done to his brother, Max. If she was going to die in this hellhole, this motherfucking predator was going with her.

Danny's momentum caused two things to happen that she hadn't anticipated. Fairfax's hips shifted, moving his cock closer to its destination, and his hand tightened on the belt as he tried to scramble off of her.

Wanting to puke at the feel of his swollen cock anywhere near her pussy, she tightened all her vaginal muscles, trying to prevent him from entering her. She clamped down harder, filling her mouth with the coppery taste of his blood.

In self-defense, McAllister yanked away from her, making her job easier when his retreat tore a chunk out of his neck. Hot blood splattered her face, but she was beyond caring. McAllister panicked, latching onto that piece of leather like it was a lifeline as he bled like a stuck pig.

As Danny's vision faded for the last time, she heard her grizzly roaring, followed by splintering wood. As she suffocated for the last time, she managed a rictus of a smile, knowing wrath had arrived.

"Three," she thought, knowing she wasn't the only one who was about to be fucked.

The field of flowers reappeared with her da waiting for her, hand outstretched. With a wide grin, she felt the warmth of the sun on her face as she ran to him, knowing she was finally coming home for good.

97

Let's See If He Can Fly

"Landon, something's wrong. Send help, please," Izzie's voice was scared as she projected the message into Landon's mind. Moments later, explosions rang out, and he knew he needed to get to her.

Landon ran as fast as he could, wishing he was bigger so that he could run faster. Sweat dripped down his bangs and into his eyes, making them burn. His fists rubbed at them, but his legs kept on pumping. The only thing he could think about was protecting the little dragons.

Izzie, the runt of the litter and her momma's miniature, had chosen Landon as her person. They'd communicated since the day she'd pushed her way out of her egg. It started with just shared images. As the li'l dragon learned and grew, they were progressing to conversations. Her plea moments ago had propelled him into motion.

"Landon, I can't get away from them…They need to hurry!" The fear in her voice as she repeated the message again made him go faster. He struggled to breathe, but he wouldn't fail her.

"I'm coming," he answered. His five-year-old brain didn't compute that she'd asked him to send help, not come himself.

Maddy's concern swamped over him as she reached out to him. *"Landon, honey, please answer me. Where are you, and are you safe?"*

"I'm fine, Momma," he answered. *"I'm nearly to the caves. The little ones need me. There's trouble there."*

"Stay there, and stay out of that trouble, Landon," she replied. *"Help is on its way. When Ryssa gets there, you listen to her as if she were me, okay?"*

Maddy's fear was a tangible thing, and he felt bad for making her worry, but Izzy needed him. That was more important than anything else in his world, even though he knew he would be in trouble when he returned.

"Yup," he said, not wasting any words.

He had a moment to wonder what his punishment would be this time. Would he have to stay inside for a week, work in the stables or, God forbid...read?

Landon didn't mind the stables. His father was fun to be around, and he got to see all the animals. The hellhounds and white tigers fascinated him, even though he didn't have permission to see them alone...yet.

Moonlight reflected off the rough-cut rock steps ascending the cliff in front of him. The steps were narrow—barely wide enough for a man to walk up. The erratic path had numerous switchbacks, as if its creator had changed his mind on the direction they were heading. Signs on the beach, warning against the dangerous trail and dragons at the other end, should have discouraged people from using the trail, but there was always someone who didn't believe the posted warning applied to them.

Hunching over for a moment, Landon tried to catch his breath. His chest burned, and his leg muscles were on fire from running the length of the shore.

From the corner of his eye, he caught soft flickering lights. Brows scrunching, he turned and found three small boats anchored just offshore. Lanterns attached to the bows bobbed up and down with the movement of the water. Empty from what he could see, they bobbed in the dark, awaiting their passengers' return.

Knowing he was running out of time, he raced for the boats. He extinguished the lanterns, not wanting them to find the vessels easily on their return.

Legs pumping, he headed back to the stairs, groaning at the thought of how many he needed to climb. Flames lit up the night sky as Alejandro hovered outside their lair. An enraged screech came from the dragon, and Landon climbed faster.

"Landon, don't come here. It's not safe for you either," Izzy sent to him.

"I'm coming. Where are you?" Landon asked, as fear settled in his chest.

"I don't know..." Izzie's terrified voice was on the verge of tears. *"They threw me in a bag. It smells like stale fish."*

"I'm almost there," Landon said in a ragged voice.

"Landon, where are you?" His father's voice was harsh. Landon wasn't sure if it was with fear or aggravation.

"I'm climbing the stairs." The child's voice cracked, betraying the brave young man. *"I gotta save her."*

"Landon, please wait where you are. It's dangerous," Ronan said in a strained voice. *"Please, son, wait for me. I'm coming to help."*

"I can't. Izzie's in trouble," he said, blocking off his link to his father. He was gonna be in big trouble later. But the link he felt to this fragile creature was as close as the ones he'd established to his new family.

He'd made it nearly three-quarters of the way up the stairs when he heard them. Rough voices arguing in front of him made his head snap up. He skittered behind a large rock to hide. Whoever was ahead of him was a bunch of strangers, and they didn't sound like nice men.

"Open the fecking bag," one of them screeched. "Afore the pissed off one gets a hold of us." The man was burly, with wiry red hair and shifty eyes.

"It is open, ye daft twat," another said in a gravelly voice. This one was lanky and bald. "Not me fault the dragon snatched Torvil up by his legs and bashed him upside the rocks, na, is it?"

Clinging to the rock cropping he hid behind, Landon glanced nervously behind him. His boots just fit on the ledge he stood on. If he backed up at all, he would plummet to his death. He swallowed hard, grateful it was dark so that he couldn't see how far down it was because he didn't like heights.

"If this one doesn't stop moving," the gravelly voice said, "I'mma bash it against the rocks to calm it down."

Landon gasped at his words. Peering around the corner, he saw two other men wrestling one of the little black and red dragons into a burlap sack. He thought it might be the one they called Sebastian, but he wasn't sure. Some of the hatchlings looked the same to him.

Another pair of men wrestled a writhing bag between them as they descended towards his location. "Calm down, ye little cock knocker. I aughtta kill ye fer what happened to Torvil."

"Izzie," he whispered on the simple link they'd formed. *"Can ye hear me? I think yer right in front of me."*

"They jest said they aughtta kill me," Izzie said with a catch in her voice. *"I'm scared, Landon."*

"Me, too."

Landon took a deep breath, wanting to be brave even though he was trembling. His father reached out to him again, breaking down his pitiful attempt at a wall in his mind.

"Landon," his father yelled at him, breaking down the wall he'd erected. *"Wait for me, son. I'm climbing the steps now. Please, don't do anything without me."* His voice was tense, scared even, but Landon was more afraid of what would happen if he waited any longer.

"They're gonna hurt her. I have to help her," Landon said, trying not to cry. *"You'll be my backup."*

"Landon! Goddammit, you wait for me!" Ronan yelled out loud.

Hearing his father's shout, he knew he was in big trouble, because Ronan never raised his voice to him. Guess it didn't matter now because he was gonna get it when this was over, anyway.

"Someone's coming," another voice said, sounding panicked. "We need to get the feck out of here."

"Ouch, I think the little bastard jest bit me," the man closest to him hollered.

"Feck this, Sir," his partner sneered. "Let's just toss the li'l bitch over the edge and see if she survives bouncing off the rocks.

"Landon, wait for your father," Izzie said in a trembling voice. *"I'll stop fighting, and they won't have a reason to hurt me."*

"For a wee thing, the li'l shite's heavy," his partner—the man he'd called Sir—grumbled. Sir was a large man with cold, calculating eyes.

"What are you doing with them?" Ryssa's shrill voice came from too far below him.

"'Tis none of yer business, li'l miss. Ye jest head on back the way ye came now," the burly man sneered.

"Ye don't want no part of this," gravelly voice said.

"You shouldn't want any part of this," Galen shouted as he and Tobias caught up with the girls. Taking the lead, he climbed the stairs two at a time. "That's one pissed-off Daddy heading your way."

The burly man's head twisted to his left and saw death headed for them. "Feck this," he said, dropping the bag. "This job t'aint worth dying for."

Gravelly stepped towards the cliff, dragging the wriggling bag with him. Balancing it on the edge, he addressed the winged death hovering before him. "Ye come any closer, and I'll toss her over. How close can ye get to this rock wall to catch her, na?"

Alejandro locked eyes on him and in a voice laced with fury said, *"I can get close enough to grab my daughter and disembowel you before I char you for my dinner."*

The man's eyes widened at the shock of hearing this creature in his head. One side of his lips lifted in a sneer as he responded. "Mayhap ye can, but can ye catch both of them?"

He turned towards the pair of men working their way down the first few steps and hollered, "Keep working yer way down. If that beast comes any closer, ye toss her over the side, ye hear me? Triple yer pay if ye make it to the boats with her."

"Can't triple nothin' if yer d-d-d-dead," a lanky dock worker said before dropping his end of the bag. "Fuck this. Ain't nothing worth dying for on this mountain. I gots a family to think of." He scurried down the stairs, heading straight for the group of students, nearly knocking Blaze and Chantal down as he barreled past.

Glancing back over his shoulder at the students he'd run through, he never saw Ronan coming. Turning, he barreled into Ronan's fist, knocking him out cold. Ronan took a moment to magically bind him, then left him there as he raced towards his son.

Landon clung to the rock as he peeked around the corner. The mean man was almost to him, dragging the heavy bag and thunking it down over each step.

He heard Izzie's grunts of pain, and it infuriated him. He took a deep breath, trying to be brave. His grandfather Cheveyo taught him it was important to be there for the people in his tribe. Isabella and her hatchlings were part of his tribe, and he wouldn't abandon them. He just couldn't.

Genny and Collette walked in silence as they neared the top of the stone stairs. Two sets of steps led down the cliff. The one to the left led to the dragon's lair and the one on the right to the beach.

Alejandro darted from the entrance of the cave, startling the hell out of both of them. His roar and the flames coming from his mouth terrified them. Flinging himself off the edge, he swooped down low, snatching something up and slamming it against the rock face below them. Then he rose into the air, swiftly gaining altitude. Moments later, the girls heard a scream and saw what once was a man falling from the sky.

Genny clasped her hand over her mouth as Collete gasped. Shouting from farther down the stairs distracted them from the horror they had just witnessed. Rushing to the top of the steps, they saw the chaos below.

Four men were struggling with burlap bags below them. From their vantage point, they could see Ryssa, Chantal, Blaze, Galen, Tobias, and Ronan racing up the steps from below.

The men were dragging the bags towards the edge as one of their partners in crime abandoned the scheme and raced down the steps.

"Justice was swift and deserved," Collette said in a whisper when she heard the distressed cries of the hatchlings.

"We've got to help them," Genny said, without waiting to see if Collette was following. Hiking her skirt up in both hands, she ran down the stone steps as fast as she could. Keeping her eyes on the melee below them, she gasped when Landon jumped out and launched himself at the man left wrestling the bag by himself.

"Let her go," the boy screeched, jumping in front of the man, and hitting his chest with his little fists.

"Landon, Don't!" Genny yelled, running faster, trying not to lose her footing on the dangerous stone stairway.

"LANDON," Ronan roared from further down.

The air was ripe with fear and rage as pandemonium followed his attack and the angry male dragon's return. The man Landon attacked grabbed him up by the shirt and hauled him close, shaking him.

With wild eyes, Sir weighed his options. His gaze took in the six people racing single file up the steps. There were very few places on the stairs where you could safely pass. The girls didn't worry him. He could shove them out of the way. But the three men were another story altogether. The younger two were as tall as he was and carried more muscle. The older one coming like a freight train had a dangerous glint in his eyes.

Turning the other way, he realized he was boxed in. There were two girls running down the stairs towards them, and his two comrades were in the way. Those two bastards were just as likely to toss him over the side as to help him for getting them into this mess.

Knowing he was out of options, he moved towards the edge of the cliff, dragging the bag with his right foot. The teens stopped in their tracks, not knowing what to do, but the man behind them pushed his way through.

Hands outstretched, the man begged him, "I'm Ronan, and that's my boy you're holding too damn close to the edge. Please don't scare him."

The boy sobbed in his arms. "Daddy," he said as he tried to wriggle away.

"Hold still, ye li'l shite," the man said, shaking him viciously.

"Please," Ronan pleaded, taking a step closer. "He's just a little boy. Put him down, and I'll make sure you leave here safely."

"Yer one of them feckin' Wardens, aintchya?" the intruder sneered, stepping closer to the edge. "Ye'll jest feck me with yer Island Law."

"I promise you I will arrange for clemency if you hand him over to me right now, unharmed."

"And ifn I don't,"

"If I don't kill you," Ronan said in an icy tone, "I'll let him do it." His gaze shifted over the man's shoulder.

The heat of the dragon's breath on his neck told him the only thing keeping him alive was the leverage he clung to.

A deep, dark chuckle emerged from his chest, and the sound of resignation chilled Ronan's blood.

The man took another step and dangled the boy over the edge. With his right foot, he kicked the bag, moving it closer to the edge as well.

"Ifn I'se gonna die here tonight, I'se taking them both with me," the burly man spit out at the group of students inching closer from below.

"Y'all stop right there," he screamed in a panicked voice, knowing he'd run out of options. "Ye hear me? Come any closer, and we'se gonna see if he can fly."

Ronan pushed past the teens and held his hand out, stopping their ascent. "Just give me my boy, and you walk out of here a free man. This is the last time I'm gonna ask."

"Whatchya gonna do? Rush me? Then we'll jest fly together," he taunted Ronan.

Ronan closed his eyes and reached out to Alejandro. *"What are our options? How do you want to do this?"*

"We're limited. The outcroppings will make it difficult for me to get close enough to catch them if he drops your boy or my Izzie. I might be able to get one, but I'm not sure I can reach both in time from this angle."

"There has to be a way," Ronan hissed. *"I'm not willing to lose either of them."*

"Neither am I, Beastmaster."

Out of the corner of Ronan's eye, he saw Collette and Genny descending into the mess above them. "Fuck me," he whispered, not sure how he was going to keep them all alive in this situation.

"Anyone available needs to get to the cliffs ASAP. There's trouble below the dragon's lair," Ronan said, sending the message to Kyran, Kai, Roarke, Lash, and the rest of the River Patrol. *"Hurry the fuck up."*

He intentionally blocked Maddy, knowing how much she was already worrying. His brain raced, trying to come up with a solution that brought everyone home safely.

"Back the feck up," the man threatening his son said. His grip loosened for a second as he focused on Ronan.

Ronan took a step back, watching horrified as his son took matters into his own hands. Rearing back, Landon bashed his head into the man's nose, then hauled his leg back and kicked him squarely in the gut.

Time slowed to a crawl as Ronan had a moment to be proud of Landon and then a moment of horror as the man released him, doubling over and trying to catch his breath. Lumbering forward, the kidnapper kicked the bag off the edge as he lost his balance, lurching to the right.

Alejandro's shriek echoed in Ronan's ears as he scrambled to get to Landon in time. Ronan watched as his boy's toes missed the ground. His little arms pinwheeled as he tried to regain his balance before realizing his feet were no longer touching the ground. The terror in his eyes as they met Ronan's gutted him. Landon screamed, "Daddy!" as he tumbled off the cliff.

Ronan's fingers brushed against the soft cotton of his shirt as he reached out for the boy, but once again, his world fell out from under him as his son slipped through his hands. "Landon…" he roared into the night.

His heart clenched as he watched the fear on Landon's face as his arms flailed. Alejandro flew as close to the cliff as possible, trying to reach both of their fallen children.

The bag holding Izzie plummeted faster than Landon because of her weight. Bouncing on a narrow ledge, the bag skidded to a stop.

"Don't move, child," Alejandro pleaded as he dove for Landon. *"Be still, and we will get you out of there."*

Landon struggled to breathe as the free fall snatched the air from his lungs. His hair flew in his face, and he was cold as the ground raced up to

meet him. His father's horrified face peered down at him, and he was sorry he hadn't waited for him.

It had been nice to have a family again. He'd never see Maddy again, or his pet rat, Tiny, or his skunk. Landon watched Alejandro diving for him and wondered if he'd finally decided to eat him. His eyes watered, and he had a moment to wonder how much it would hurt when he landed. Then everything went black.

98

Release the Beast

Jamey's amber eyes shifted back and forth, seeking his mate as he and Roarke made their way to the tannery district. Five of Roarke's sailors were joining them there, and the Romani patrols would join them there as well.

Even though they had manpower, Jamey wasn't feeling as comfortable as he would have with Danyka and Fergus by his side. He wondered where the fuck their fire mage had run off to. Fergus was the most powerful mage in the area, and his assistance would have been valuable. He also knew a minor mission wouldn't have kept him from helping his pixie.

"Spread out," Roarke said. "Keep your eyes and ears open for anything suspicious."

They turned the corner into the lower tannery district and walked past the half dozen buildings there. The acrid fumes from the tanning mills burned Jamey's nose as he inhaled deeply, seeking signs of Danny.

Nothing. Fists clenching and releasing, he slowed his pace and walked by each building, giving himself just enough time to discern her scent before moving on. He completed the first block. Frustrated, they started on the second.

Halfway down the last street, Danny's voice slammed into him. *"Jamey…"* The terror infused in his name staggered him. *"Jamey!"* The panic hit him as his hand clutched his chest.

"Danny, where are you, baby?"

He held up his hand when Roarke gave him a puzzled glance and opened his mouth. Before he could answer, they both received a distress signal from Danny on the warden's link.

"Find me before it's too late. Beware of Roarke, not Roarke…"

"What the fuck?" Roarke said.

Jamey ignored him when he got another message from her. *"I waited for you. I swear I did, but they hit me with something."*

Her voice faded in his head, but what he heard next made his grizzly fight for dominance. It took all his willpower to keep the bastard in check.

Danny left their personal link wide open, and he heard the surrounding voices, her shrieks of pain, and the incentive to be the first to rape her. His low growl warned everyone away.

When the beating ended and the men left, he reached out again, trying to get through to her before she passed out again.

"I need you to focus for me, baby. Give me some sign of where you are. Any hint at all would help."

"I don't know. I'm in a cage inside of a warehouse." Her voice faded off, and he thought she'd drifted away again.

"Jamey, you can bring me back."

"*Give me something to go on, baby,*" Jamey commanded, trying to keep her alert.

"I love you, Jameson. No matter what, I always will."

All sounds ceased, and he knew he'd lost her again. He glared at Roarke and said, "We're running out of time. The only reason they didn't rape her was because they knocked her out again. Let's finish this block and move on to the next."

Ferg's voice telepathically came through, *"What the feck is going on with the pixie?*

"*Someone took her. Where the fuck are you?"* Jamey snarled back.

"Middle of something I can't walk away from, no matter how much I wants to."

"Fuck me, Ferg. What if I can't find her?"

"Ye will, laddie. I ken ye will. I'll try tracking her from here and get back to ye soon."

"Make it snappy. The things they're gonna do to her, Ferg, will fuck her up again."

"On it."

A low, rumbling growl emerged as he and Roarke moved down the lane quickly. "If we don't find her by the last door on this street, we'll start over. This time I'll break down every fucking door in the district until I find her."

This motherfucker would pay. When Jamey found the man responsible for tormenting her, he would release the beast that lived inside of him and demonstrate what happened when you came between a grizzly and the woman he loved.

99

Rosella Diaries
Thirteenth Entry

Fergus's senses prickled as he led Rosella carefully down the stairs to the suite of rooms he had purchased for the evening. His auric field remained wide open in anticipation of any form of attack that might occur—physical, emotional, or psychic. The fear emanating from the young woman following him nearly drowned the empathic side of him. She stumbled behind him, and he turned, reaching for her, but her guard helped her first. The glances passing between the couple were heartbreaking.

Rosella radiated anger and fear, while the young Romani man exhibited sorrow, rage, and a sense of impotence. Fergus had noticed the romantic ties forming between them on the deck—and if he could see it, others would as well. The ties the two were forming could be helpful in more than one way tonight.

His guard, Samson, stood outside the suite. The massive man had ebony skin and brilliant blue eyes. Long, thin braids covered his head, reaching to his chest. Blue beads woven into the dark strands matched the color of his eyes. He nodded at Fergus. "Alls well, mon."

Ferg nodded at him, grateful that he'd been able to convince Roarke to stay behind and send his partner in his stead. Samson opened the door, standing aside and allowing them to enter. His gaze followed Rosella and his eyes widened, recognizing the similarity to her mother. A smile spread across his broad face when he met the icy glare of the young guard following her and his silent challenge.

"Sit down, lass," Fergus said in a soft tone as he headed for the bar cart. He poured four glasses of whiskey and passed them around. Rosella's eyes widened, and her hand shook as she took hers, but she didn't drink any of it.

Ferg looked at Samson and asked, "Ye checked for anything that will betray us?"

"Aye. I finds nuttin' dat will give away whats we says or whats we do inside dese walls."

Ferg nodded somberly, taking a chair in front of the young woman. Neither she nor her guard had taken a sip yet. The confusion and suspicion rolling off them was making him antsy. Clearing his throat, he leaned forward, resting his elbows on his knees to make himself appear less intimidating. He gave Rosella his full attention and pushed a thought at her. *"I be here to help you, Rosella. Can yer guard be trusted with all our lives?"*

The shock on Rosella's face confirmed that she'd received his message. She took a breath before nodding her head.

"Rosella Gallagher ye be, aintchya lass?" Fergus said aloud.

Her face paled, and she looked up at her guard, unsure of how to answer.

Braden raised a brow, and his entire body tensed. Not sure what to tell her, the dark-haired man took a step closer.

"Ya looks jest like yer maman, li'l miss," Samson said with a bow.

"How do you know my mother?" Rosella asked in a tight voice.

"I've partnered with yer brother Roarke. Catalina and me…be close," he said noncommittally. Clearing his throat, his gaze shifted away.

"You're her lover?" Rosella asked in disbelief.

"Dat's right."

"Where's her birthmark?" Rosella challenged.

"Which one?" Samson asked with a broad smile. "She's got dis one behind her left ear, and den dere's one behind her knee, and dere's…"

"Stop," Rosella said, not needing to hear more.

"We been searching for ye, lass," the dark-haired man said. "Me name be Ferg, although I'll not admit it to anyone else. This is the first lead we've had. Didna expect to see ye up on that stage."

"How are you going to get me out of here?"

A look passed between Samson and Ferg, and Rosella's hopes fell. "We're not ready for an extraction tonight," Ferg said. "'Tis no way to get us all out alive and still help the others trapped here, too. Ye ken what I be saying?"

Rosella numbly processed his words. "Roarke's ship isn't nearby?"

"Nye, lass. This whole world be locked down tight. Now that I've accessed it, we can return with a plan." He cleared his throat and rubbed a hand over his face in frustration. "It kills me to say this lass, but we'll need to come back for ye, if we'se to do it successfully."

Tears filled her eyes. "I understand," she said, even though she hated remaining in this nightmare. Gemma's battered face flashed through her mind, and she knew he was right. "I will not leave here unless you can free all the girls on Jonah's vessel."

"Fair enough. That's been our goal as well." His cheeks burned as he met her eyes. "That leaves us with one problem, lass."

"What's that?"

"I be sure that they'll examine ye on yer return. Ye canna return as ye left. Ye ken?"

Rosella's brows drew together in confusion. "I don't understand."

"I jest paid an exorbitant price for the privilege of yer virginity. Ye canna leave her with it still intact."

Heat rushed to Rosella's face as his meaning sank in, and a resurgence of fear flooded through her. "You're still gonna rape me?" she asked him in horror.

Fergus's face turned white in horror at her words. "Nye!" He cleared his throat, trying to find a dignified way of delivering what he was trying to say. "Can't help but see the ties between the two of ye. There be two rooms in this suite. We can give ye some privacy for the night if that be yer choice."

Rosella's eyes met Braden's and found a healthy dose of the same shock she was feeling and an equal dose of hope.

Swallowing the lump in her throat, she met the stranger's gaze. "I would appreciate that."

Fergus stood. "Sorry to be forcing this on either of ye, but there's only three options tonight."

"Yer maman'll roast me balls if I comes near ya, chile," Samson said, then added in a somber tone. "Me sister be going drough de same ding as ya are. Dat be why I be 'elping Roarke"

"I not be sleeping with teenagers, besides your brother would kill me," Fergus added, getting to his feet. "We'll give ye the room until morning," he said. "Besides, I've work of me own to do." The two men walked into the other half of the suite and closed the door softly behind them.

The soft snick of the door resounded in the small room. Rosella looked down at her hands, unable to look up at Braden. Her life choices were so far beyond her control that she didn't know what to do when offered a choice.

Braden cleared his throat, trying to find the appropriate thing to say. His hand shook as he reached out and tipped her chin up, forcing her to meet his eyes. "I'm so sorry for all of this, Ella."

"It's not your fault," she said, voice catching as tears threatened.

"What do you want me to do?" Both hands framed her face now, and his dark eyes bored into hers. He wasn't sure if he was seeking permission or absolution.

Ella lost herself in his gaze, taking a shuddering breath. "If I can have the choice of who will be my first, I choose you."

His eyes never left hers as his head bent, and he pressed a soft kiss to her forehead. "You've given me an honor, Ella. I promise to make it good for you," he whispered in her ear before tracing her jawline with his lips.

"I've fantasized about being the first man to touch you, but I never believed it could become a reality."

"I've fantasized about you, too," she admitted.

A nervous sigh escaped from her the moment his hands framed her face and his lips returned to hers. Braden kissed her as if they had all the time in the world and nowhere else to go. With gentle strokes of his lips against hers, he stoked their passion until she relaxed under his hands.

When her tongue darted out tentatively to stroke his, he let her play, encouraging her, stoking the fire until she pressed herself against him and fisted his hair in her hands. His arms moved to her back, rubbing small circles that became larger with each stroke until he was caressing her ass on the downstroke.

Braden came up for air, his eyes pools of molten blue desire. Deft hands on her hips turned her around so that he had access to the buttons of her dress. Leaving kisses along her spine as he unbuttoned what seemed like thousands of the damn things, he undressed her. He sighed in relief when he reached the last one. Gentle fingers slid the sleeves down her arms until the virginal white material pooled at her feet.

Standing in only her corset and garters, Rosella crossed her arms over her chest. Goosebumps rose on her arms, and she shivered nervously. She knew the mechanics of what was to come, but knowing wasn't the same thing as experiencing.

Expecting to be taken by a stranger, she'd anticipated fear, terror even. Braden didn't make her feel anything but a hot, aching need for more. She heard the rustling of fabric behind her, and her heart raced. Then his naked arms wrapped around her middle, and he pulled her back against his bare chest while placing soft kisses along her neck.

Dropping her head against his shoulder, she arched against him. One of his hands cupped her face as the other cupped her breast, kneading it through the silk of her corset. The pressure and the scrape of the fabric against her nipple created an erotic caress, and she moaned.

His teeth skimmed over her shoulder, biting down with just enough pressure to make her lean back into him more. His hand traveled lower across her abdomen, pulling her back against the hard length of him. Holding her in place, he circled his hips against her while his fingers slid into her panties.

Rosella gasped when his finger stroked the tender skin of her clit with gentle pressure. Her hips rolled against his as he continued drawing slow circles. One, two, three times, and then his long fingers dipped lower,

gathering her moisture and coming back for three more circles. Over and over, he repeated this until her knees were weak.

His lips brushed against her ear as he whispered, "It is a gift to introduce you to pleasure, Ella." His teeth caught her earlobe lightly before he continued. "Promise me you'll tell me if you don't like how I'm touching you." He waited for her to nod her head and asked, "Do you want more?"

"Yes, please." Her voice was raspy as she focused on his hand and the way their hips rolled together. The next time his fingers traveled lower, he traced the outside of her entrance before sliding the tip of his finger in.

Rosella jerked to a halt, expecting pain, but he paused, waiting for her to adjust before withdrawing and then continuing his previous motions.

"You're so wet," he groaned. Every time he slid down, he dipped his finger in just a little more, and on the fourth trip, he added a second and rubbed his thumb against the place that made her body tremble.

Her hips moved, riding his hand, seeking but unsure of what she was racing towards. "Braden," she whimpered. Ella didn't know what it was she needed, only that he could provide it for her.

"I've got you, baby." His fingers were firmer against her as her back arched against him. "Relax. Let yourself fall." His lips brushed against her temple. "I promise I'll catch you. Let everything go."

The sound of his voice and the promises he made threw her over the edge. Her pussy seized around his fingers as her first orgasm ripped through her, and he swallowed her scream of pleasure.

"That's it," Braden said, pressing a kiss against her damp temple. "I've got you."

Lifting her in his arms, he carried her to the bed and laid her down. Braden smiled as she flung her forearm over her face, trying to catch her breath. He removed her shoes but left the garter belt and stockings because they were so fucking sexy.

He grasped the sides of her panties, ripping them off of her. Before she could protest, he crawled between her legs and wedged his wide shoulders between her thighs.

"So fucking beautiful, Ella," he sighed as he gazed at her inner sanctum. Pressing teasing kisses up the inner skin of her thighs, he worked his way towards her center.

Embarrassed, Ella tried to push him away. Braden captured her wrists and held them by her sides. "I want to spend days worshiping your sweet pussy, but I only have a few hours." His gaze met hers, pleading. "Let me see all of you, Ella."

The erotic promises in his voice and the need in his eyes helped her relax her knees and open herself to him. Her eyes locked with his for a long moment before he gazed down at her.

541

Braden groaned, and his hips involuntarily pumped against the mattress. "Mine," he said before lowering his mouth and pressing a soft kiss on her labia. His fingers brushed her skin with gentle strokes as he familiarized her with his touch. Unable to wait any longer, he licked up the center of her and latched onto her clit.

Ella gasped as her hips came off the bed of their own volition. She couldn't decide if she should pull away or sink her hands into his hair and pull him tighter against her.

Moaning against her as he increased the suction, Braden was drowning in the taste of her. Sweet and succulent, her juices flowed freely over his fingers when he reinserted them. Pushing deeper, he monitored her for any discomfort. Her hips meeting his hand reassured him, and he pushed in until he felt her barrier.

Curling his fingers inside of her, he coaxed another orgasm out of her. Her knees clamped around the sides of his head as she sobbed her release.

Ella was a writhing, whimpering mess. Her core was still twitching, and she thought she might have passed out for a moment. She felt the bed move as Braden left her and heard him unbuckle his belt and the rustling of his pants hitting the floor.

She wanted to gaze upon him without witnesses so that she could appreciate his body as he had with hers, but she couldn't open her eyes.

The bed dipped again as he knelt on it. Without warning, he flipped her to her belly and attacked the strings of her corset vigorously. Freeing her from the contraption, he flipped her again to her back.

Ella's eyes popped open, meeting his pale blue gaze. The heat reflected made something inside tighten again, and she had the urge to clamp her knees shut, not knowing how much more she could take.

Braden settled between the cradle of her hips, resting against her. He framed her face, giving her a gentle kiss. His hands cupped her breasts, kneading them as he watched the expressions racing across her face. Bending his head, he took her nipple into his mouth and sucked on it before grazing his teeth over the tip.

Ella gasped, her hips rocking against his as he moved to the other stiff peak. The hard length of his cock pressed against her stomach, and the naïve part of her wondered how he'd ever fit all of that inside of her.

His teeth brought her attention back to him suckling her breast. A flush rose over her chest, up her neck, and onto her cheeks as her body responded. His hips began a gentle thrusting motion against her, and she wanted more.

Braden loved how responsive Ella was to his touch. She moved against him as if they had always been lovers. The urge to tip his hips and seat himself inside of her was overpowering, but she wasn't ready for that—yet.

Reaching down, he stroked her sensitive body again, sliding his finger in to make sure she was wet enough to make this pleasurable for both of them. His fist tightened around his cock, trying to stave off the growing sense of urgency his body was flooding him with.

With cock in hand, he guided it to her, stroking the length of her sex until he bumped into her clit. When he wrenched a moan from her, he repeated the motion until she called his name.

Ella arched her back, trying to get closer to the velvet touch taking her to the edge of paradise. Over and over, he glided against the most sensitive part of her. Grasping his forearms, she dug her nails into him. "Braden…"

"Baby, you're ready for me."

Her eyes snapped open, fear making a swift return as he notched his cock at her entrance. His lips crashed into hers, distracting her from the fears, as he entered her in a gentle glide. He swallowed her gasp at his invasion.

Braden leaned his forehead against hers. "You're so fucking tight."

"You're too big," she gasped as she felt him push further in. The sensation was foreign and uncomfortable. A strange burning sensation made her squirm when he stopped. "I can't…"

"Ella, baby, look at me," he said in a soft voice. "The gods created your body for me, and I promise, after we get through the next few moments, I'll make this pleasurable for both of us."

She blinked away the rapidly forming tears, wanting to be brave. Every woman went through this rite of passage. This was her transition from a girl to a woman.

Gemma's battered face flashed through her mind, and shame filled her. The other girls enduring this tonight wouldn't be as lucky. They were with strangers who possessed the authority to take them in any way they chose. Pain or pleasure was at the owner's discretion.

"Trust me, baby," Braden said, his lips brushing against hers in a gentle caress.

"I do," she said in a tight voice. Trying to distract herself, she threaded her fingers through his dark hair and kissed him as he shifted above her. He continued the gentle glide in and out and then thrust in to the hilt.

Braden swallowed her gasp of pain and halted. Seated fully in the soft, wet silk of her pussy, he felt her body tense. His body shuddered with the urge to move. He focused on the pleasure of her mouth, giving her body time to adjust to his intrusion.

"It's still too much," she whispered against his lips, and he tasted the salt of her tears on his lips.

"I'm going to move now and try to make it better for you, baby," he said as he withdrew partially and returned, but not as deep this time. Continuing

the motion, his eyes never left hers as he kissed away her tears. The fifth time he slid in, her hips moved with him. "Is it still painful?" he asked, trying not to slip the leash of his control.

"Not like it was," she panted.

"I promise you, it will only get better." His hand reached between them. "Are you ready for more?" he asked with another kiss. "You gonna come for me again?"

Ella gazed at him with complete trust. "I think so," she said. Her eyes widened as he rubbed her clit and began gliding in and out of her with steady strokes. The sensation was foreign, but that tightening in her belly and awareness of him in every cell of her body was making her climb into the abyss once again. She let him take her to the top, and when she was nearly there, he shifted.

"Hang on, baby." Braden bent her knees and held them there with one hand while continuing to stroke her with the other. His thrusts quickened and a sheen of sweat appeared on his torso. His eyes were like ice chips as they trapped hers so he could witness every nuance of her expressions. Thrusting deeper and moving faster, he tipped his pelvis so that he brushed against her clit with every stroke.

Ella panted as Braden brought her back to the pinnacle. She nearly forgot the pain. The only thing she could focus on was the coming implosion. He'd pinned her in place so she couldn't meet his thrusts. She was powerless to do anything but take every inch of him again and again, wanting more. "Braden," she wailed.

"Come for me, baby," Braden demanded. "Take me over the edge with you." Sweat dripped on her breasts as he thrust faster. His balls tightened painfully. After holding out for as long as he could, his own orgasm was barreling down on him.

He flicked her clit and groaned in relief when she bucked beneath him, her pussy trembling around his cock. Her muscles clamped down on his cock, sucking his release from him so intensely that his pleasure had a bite of pain mixed in with it. Good thing that's what he liked.

Braden groaned as he emptied himself into her, and Ella cried out his name as her body clenched around him. He collapsed to the side, keeping them joined but removing his weight from her. His arms wrapped around her in a tight embrace as she trembled with aftershocks.

His hands traced circles up and down her back. He waited until her breathing regulated, then pushed her hair back so that he could see her face. His lips found hers, and they lingered over a gentle kiss. "Did I hurt you badly?" he asked, afraid that he'd been too rough.

"No more than necessary," Ella said. "And you gave me much more pleasure than you did pain," she said, smiling against his lips.

His teeth pulled at her lower lip, and he felt himself stirring inside of her. "I'm glad to hear that. The night is young. I intend to wring every ounce of pleasure from you I can."

"Really, so soon?" She wrinkled her nose. "I didn't think it was possible."

Braden's grin was cocky as he grabbed her hips and moved her on his thickening cock. "With you, beautiful girl, I could do this all night."

Ella giggled when he flipped them, then huffed in disappointment when he exited her body. It was short-lived, though. He repositioned her on her stomach and pulled her hips back so she was on her knees.

"There's so many ways I want to make love to you, Ella," Braden said with a gleam in his eyes when she glanced over her shoulder at him. "And so little time."

"Then stop wasting it. Come back to where you belong."

Sliding his cock up and down her crease, he waited until she whimpered before sliding home. This angle allowed his cock to dive even deeper. The sensation was phenomenal. He started a slow glide as he bent over her back and pinned her neck to the bed.

In between kisses on her spine, he whispered, "This round, I'm going to take my time. Anytime you are in this position, I want you to remember the pleasure I gave you." And they made more memories as he wrung another orgasm from her.

Ella was helpless to fight against the pleasure. She sent up a prayer of gratitude because she would always be grateful that this was the man she gave her virginity to. A gentle lover who provided her with endless pleasure. But he was a man she needed to guard her heart with. No happily ever after awaited them.

Having Braden as her first lover had been a blessing, but tomorrow would turn into a nightmare. The next man who touched her could be a monster. After Braden, she didn't know how she would survive a forced, intimate encounter with a stranger.

Nearly asleep on his chest, her diary appeared in her mind.

Dear Diary,

Tonight, didn't turn out the way I expected. Anticipating being raped by a stranger, my owner stunned me by giving me to Braden. The man who purchased the rights for my first time may become my salvation.

My first night was everything I could have dreamed it would be. A man who adores me made love to me. He brought me more pleasure than I ever believed possible during this act.

Braden was a considerate lover, worrying more about my pleasure than his own. I loved everything about the encounter. Well, maybe not his first thrust as he seated himself.

The pain was fierce, but he quickly transformed it to pleasure. It will be difficult not to touch each other again, but it isn't safe for us to continue upon our return.

I have tonight. I will tuck it away and treasure it, reliving every moment in my dreams and fantasies to survive the rest of my captivity and further encounters.

A sleepy yet satisfied,

Rosella.

100

What Happened to My Son?

Ronan's knees hit the ground as he struggled to process what he'd just witnessed. His chest constricted, and he couldn't breathe. A fleeting thought of stepping over the cliff and joining Landon went through his mind until Maddy's frantic voice came through his link.

"Ronan, what the hell is going on? I feel your distress and Landon's terror. Goddammit, answer me."

Tears rolled down his face as he tried to figure out how to tell her she'd just lost another child she loved. Would they ever recover from this? His brain couldn't compute the events that had just unfolded, so how the fuck was he going to explain them to her?

The soft cries of the students behind him reminded him he wasn't alone. He was the only adult here who wasn't a villain, and he needed to get his shit together. But Ronan couldn't move, couldn't speak, and for fuck's sake, he still couldn't take a breath.

Tears rolled down Ryssa's face as she watched the heartbreaking scene unfolding in front of her. She didn't have any words for him, but she knew there was something they could do. Hesitantly, she neared the edge to the right of Ronan and peered down into the darkness. Not believing that all hope was gone, she searched for signs of life.

"Blaze," she called. "I need witch light. Can you provide me with enough light to see over the edge?"

Blaze stepped forward, happy to help. "Where do you want them, Ryssa?"

"If you could drop a few over the side so that we can peer over the edge and see if they could have landed on a ledge beneath us, that would be wonderful."

Closing her eyes to focus, Blaze formed half a dozen small balls and let them drift over the edge slowly. Ryssa laid down on her belly and slithered over the edge just enough that she could peer down.

Ronan finally recognized what the teens were doing, and even though he didn't want to see Landon's body broken on the rocks beneath him, he prayed for a miracle. Wiping his face, he dropped to his belly as well.

The witch light was bright enough to illuminate the side of the cliff beneath them. Ronan's eyes tracked from side to side, hopeful when he saw several small ledges beneath them.

"There," Ryssa pointed. "What's that?"

Ronan followed her gaze, noticing the burlap bag lying on a ledge about eight feet beneath them. The bag was still and much too close to the edge.

"Izzie," Ronan called, hoping she would answer him.

"I'm scared."

"I know you are, darlin'," he said in a soft voice. "We're gonna come get you, but you have to stay real still for me. Can you do that?"

"I want Landon."

Ronan's eyes filled, and he said, "I know, little one. I want him, too."

Ronan saw Alejandro drifting back and forth along the shoreline, no doubt seeking Landon's body. The immense dragon continued gliding low to the ground, occasionally emitting small bursts of blue flames. His eyesight was much better than a human in the dark. His chest tightened, and he couldn't look at the ground any longer, terrified of what the dragon fire would show him.

He would help rescue Izzie because that's what Landon would have wanted. Then he would hold his shattered self together long enough to return to Maddy and tell her in person of their devastating loss.

"She's too far for us to reach, and they tied the bag shut. I'm afraid if she moves too much, she'll topple off the edge," Ronan said, his voice gruff with suppressed emotion. "The ledge is too small for more than a child to maneuver on."

"I'll go," Genny said with a strength she hadn't possessed a month before. She gave them a wry grin. "I'm not much bigger than a child."

"I don't know," Ronan said, shaking his head. "Even if we get you down there, how are we going to get both of you back up?"

"I can help with that," Alejandro's deep, gravelly voice said. He turned his gaze to Genny. *"Do you trust me to retrieve you, little miss?"*

"I'd like to," she said aloud. "What do you need me to do?" Genny asked.

"Tobias, come here," Ronan snapped, wanting one of the largest boys to help him. They would have more control when they lowered her, so she wouldn't fall too close to the ledge when she landed.

"NO," a deep commanding voice said. Kai and Kyran finally arrived, emerging from behind Collette. "I'll help you," Kai said, not trusting anyone else with her. He stopped in front of Genny, sliding a piece of hair behind her ear and cupping her cheek. "You sure about this?" His voice when he spoke with her was gentle.

"Not gonna lie," she said self-deprecatingly. "I'm terrified of failing and terrified of heights. But I can only imagine how afraid Izzie is right now, too." She covered his hand with hers, rubbing her cheek against the warmth of his palm. "So, yeah. I'm sure."

Kai knelt on the ground next to Ronan, peering over the side. "Fuck me," he whispered under his breath. It was further than he'd originally thought. Even with them lowering her, it would still be a four-foot drop.

On his knees beside him, Ronan said, "Shift over about six inches, so we're dropping her in the middle of the shelf." They both shuffled over. "Tobias and Gaven, hang onto our legs."

Kai gave Genny a reassuring smile and reached out his hand for hers. "I'd like to tell you I won't drop you, but that's kind of the point," he said.

"Just a minute," Genny said, gathering the sides of her long skirt to the left. She deftly knotted it by her knee to keep it out of her way. Finished, she took Kai's hand, meeting his eyes. "I'm ready." Their gazes held, time stretching out at the unsaid words between them.

Kai clasped her right hand as she faced away from him, and Ronan held her left. With an arm under her armpit to stabilize her, they slowly lowered her down, making sure they'd centered her on the ledge. As they extended their arms, Genny was still too far above the ledge for his liking.

"I don't know that this is a good idea," Kai said, ready to pull her back up.

Genny glanced down and gripped their hands tighter. She'd have to maintain her balance and stick the landing, or chances were, she would topple off the edge, taking li'l Izzie with her. "I can do this, I can do this, I can do this, I can do this," she chanted.

Alejandro hovered beneath her. She could feel the updraft from his wings. Somehow, this reassured her. If she overshot the landing, she prayed he could grab them.

"I'm right here, child," his voice spoke gently in her mind. *"I won't let anything happen to you."* She felt his humor before he spoke again. *"You are very brave, Genevieve, and yes, you can do this."*

Genny wasn't sure why, but she believed the moody dragon. "I'm ready," she said. "Let me go."

Even though she thought she was prepared for this, the drop made her shriek. Her feet hit the ground, and her right ankle buckled. She cried out in

pain, dropping to her knees. Her hands hit the burlap sack, and instinctively, she pulled it closer to her when she heard Izzie's groan.

Ignoring the pain in her ankle, she worked at the knot at one end of the bag. It was tight, and she struggled to get it loose. "Damn it," she said as her fingers tore at the fabric in frustration. She glanced around, seeking anything with a sharp edge. Finally, she found a piece of jagged shale.

"Don't move, Izzie," she said. "I don't want to hurt you."

Genny used the shard to poke a hole in the bag large enough to get her fingers in. Grasping both edges with her hands, she wrenched the fabric, letting out a sigh of relief when it finally ripped down the front.

Izzie's big reptilian eyes gazed out at her with gratitude as she poked her head out of the bag. Climbing onto Genny's lap, the dragon was like a puppy trying to display her gratitude.

"You're safe now, girl," Genny told her, hugging her close.

"Thank you, Genny."

"Izzie," Alejandro's voice boomed beneath them. *"Have they harmed you, my daughter?"*

"No, papa," she said, gazing adoringly at him.

"Have you been practicing your flying lessons?"

"Yep, yep, yep. Every day."

"I want you to fly down to me, Izzie. Settle on my back between my wings, lass."

Izzie glanced up at Genny with enormous eyes. *"What about Miss Genny, Papa?"*

"We'll help get her down as well, lass. Now come to me."

"I have to go, Genny. But they'll save you, too."

Genny rubbed the ridges on the top of her pale blue and green head, making the little dragon purr. "Go, Izzie. I won't be far behind you."

"Genny, stay where you are," Ronan hollered to her. "We're sending someone down for you."

Genny waited, grateful she wouldn't have to leap off the ledge because she wasn't sure she'd be able to do that. Even if she trusted Alejandro to catch her, she didn't trust herself to take that leap on one foot.

She sat and waited, rubbing her bruised ankle and wishing she had Ryssa's basic knowledge of healing. A noise above her made her glance up. She wasn't sure who she expected, but Collette was the last person she thought would rescue her.

Kai and Ronan lowered her with a rope until she was right above Genny. A second rope dangled from Collette to her. "Wrap this tightly around your waist," Collette said, swinging the thick rope toward her until she grabbed it. "Make sure you knot it really well."

Genny double-knotted the rope and then balanced on her good foot. The tension in the rope increased until she felt it tug on her waist, lifting her off the ledge. She clung to the length in front of her. The ascent was quick,

with Kai, Kyran, Ronan, Tobias, and Gaven heaving on the ropes. She and Collette were back on solid ground in a matter of minutes.

Instantly sinking to the ground, she untied the ropes and put her head on her knees, catching her breath. Her body was shaking from the adrenaline rush. Her teeth chattered, and she didn't hear Kai approaching until he lifted her, cradling her in his arms.

Gratefully, she settled into the warmth of him. "Thank you for helping me," she said with a sigh.

"You're welcome," Kai said, pressing a kiss to the top of her head. "I'll always have you, Genny."

Genny looked up at him as tears filled her eyes. "Thank you," she said simply. She'd never had that from anyone before, and to be honest, she wasn't sure exactly what to do with this man who seemed so enamored of her. He confused her in all the best ways.

"Let's get you to Rhy." Kai turned and headed back up the stairs towards the dragon's lair.

Genny sighed, snuggling against him. "I'm sorry you have to carry me all the way back. I hate being an invalid."

"Trust me, it's my pleasure." His arms tightened around her.

"Wait a minute," she cried out. "We can't leave yet. Did they find Landon below?"

"What happened?" Kai asked, confused.

Tears fell down her cheeks as she said, "He fell off the ledge right before you got here."

Horrified, Kai turned back to see what he could do for Ronan. The man had been so collected when they rescued the dragon and Genny that Kai hadn't realized what he was going through. He sat Genny down near the other students and walked towards Kyran.

"Did you hear?" he asked his brother in a hushed voice.

"I did."

The brothers stood there watching Ronan stare into the darkness. With the stress of the other situation under control, Ronan's distress was obvious to them now. Their elemental gifts picked up his raw grief and heartache.

"Does Maddy know?" Kai asked.

"I don't think so. Not yet," Kyran answered.

Ronan stood, gazing out into the darkness. He heard the murmurs from the Tyde men and knew they were talking about Landon. Maddy needed to be told, but he wasn't ready. He wasn't able to…yet. He clenched his fists, unaware of the tears streaming down his face. The only thing he was aware of was the gaping wound in his heart where his son should be.

Alejandro was making one last pass, seeking Landon's body. The cliffs dropped sharply to the riverbank below. But the shoreline didn't come in

that far, so he couldn't have washed away. He swallowed hard, not able to think of how much damage his little body would have experienced on the way down.

The dragon returned, giving a long keening shriek as he turned and climbed towards Ronan. The sound cut through him—gutted him. He stepped back and shooed the students further from the edge as the massive beast landed before him.

Ronan moved into his space, and Alejandro lowered his head to Ronan's shoulder, nudging him gently.

"I've thoroughly searched the area, Ronan. I'm sorry, but I can't locate him."

"What do you mean?" Ronan said out loud, his voice rising in anger. "He couldn't have just disappeared."

"If he was below us," Alejandro said in as gentle of a voice as he possessed, *"even if I couldn't see him, I would scent him. I don't know if this translates well, Beast Master, but I still sense him."*

Ronan's voice bordered on panic. "I don't understand. What happened to my son?" He was yelling now, not caring about the students behind him or the men gazing at him with pity.

"Where the fuck is my son?" His hands fisted in his hair. "How am I supposed to tell Maddy I can't find him at all?" He paced like a wild animal. "We all watched him fall from here." His hands indicated the crowd behind him.

"Master Pathfinder," a scared voice came from behind him.

He turned to see Collette standing there, wringing her hands. "What?" he snapped in a hoarse voice, his mind and body emotionally exhausted and overwhelmed.

"I didn't mean to," she said, her fingers white as she clenched them in front of her. "When I saw him fall, I just wished him someplace safe. I didn't think it worked in time, and I didn't want to get your hopes up…"

Ronan stared at her agape as a flicker of hope kindled in his gut. Remembering the way she teleported Danny earlier in the season, he moved towards her. Taking her hands in his, he tried his best not to shout as he asked, "What were you thinking of, Collette, when he fell?"

Her eyes filled, and a tear streaked down her cheek as she said, "Alls I could think about was how much you and Mistress SkyDancer loved him, and how devastated you would be. I just thought about her and that I wanted to him to be safe with her…" A sob escaped, and she whimpered. "I don't know if it worked though…I don't know where he is right now."

"It's okay, Collette," Ronan said, pulling her in for a hug. "You were trying to keep him safe. Thank you for that."

Ronan thought about Maddy, and a smile crossed his face. He'd never answered her, and his woman would have badgered the hell outta him until he had or come to it herself—unless she knew everything was all right.

A shudder went through him as he prepared to reach out to her and confirm his suspicions. He was terrified to reach out to her, afraid to get his hopes up. It would destroy him all over again if Landon wasn't there. But he'd never know if he didn't ask.

"Maddy," he sent through their link, praying she'd respond.

"Yes," she answered.

Ronan couldn't sense her emotions, and that fucking terrified him. He could always feel her. For the first time in months, she'd blocked him intentionally. *"Landon,"* he began, not sure how to ask if the child that was supposed to be with him had magically appeared. *"Landon,"* he repeated, *"Is he…"* he couldn't finish; he couldn't form the words.

He felt her sigh before she answered him. *"Landon just fell asleep in my arms,"* she said. *"Had quite an ordeal, from what he's told me."* She was silent for a moment before adding, *"I'm guessing you've had quite the ordeal tonight, too. I think you have some explaining to do. Come home to me, Ronan. Come home to us. We need you."*

"I'm on my way, Maddy, darling," he said. *"Love you."*

"I love you, too."

Ronan walked over to Alejandro, meeting his ancient eyes. "You were right. He's not down there." Sobs tore through him, this time in relief. "He's with Maddy."

Alejandro once again leaned down into him, nudging his shoulder. Ronan leaned into his neck, resting against him for a moment as he released the fear and horror that had gripped him for the past hour.

"'Tis not easy being a parent," the creature said. *"I couldn't imagine my little Izzie being gone."*

"No," Ronan said with a choked laugh. *"It's the hardest damn thing I've ever done, and most of the time, I feel like I'm failing."*

"You're a good father, Beast Master. And your son is a good lad. He's growing on me."

"That mean you don't have the urge to eat him anymore?"

"Most days," Alejandro said as smoke drifted out of his nostrils. *"What will happen to the rest of the men who took part in this attack?"*

"Island Law. Madylyn, will happen to them."

"I want to be a part of this. I want my due."

"We'll see that you get it, Alejandro. You have my word."

"Go home to your family, Ronan. They need you, and I must see to mine."

Ronan patted his neck and moved away. Turning back to the crowd behind him, he said, "Landon is with Mistress SkyDancer."

He pulled Collette into a hug and whispered, "Thank you for saving him."

Collette nodded and squeezed him tight. "You're welcome. I'm just glad it worked."

"Collette and Genny both exhibited exemplary heroism tonight," Ronan said to the crowd. "The Sanctuary is grateful for their assistance." Pointing towards the top of the stairs, he said, "Make your way up the rest of the stairs and then back to the dorms. It's been a long day and one helluva night."

Glancing at Kyran and Kai, he asked, "Can you get Genny back to Rhy and take the prisoners to the holding cells?"

Kyran nodded. "We'll be fine. I'll draft the boys to help get them there. Go to Landon and Maddy. They need you."

"I need them," Ronan said, running his hand over his face and trying not to lose his composure again. "Good night. I'll see you both tomorrow."

Sprinting up the stairs, he ran the rest of the way back to the Sanctuary. Slamming through the foyer door, he checked the downstairs for his family before racing up the staircase.

Opening the door to his suite quietly, he entered, and his world fell back into place. Landon slept in his bed, clinging tightly to Madylyn. Ronan just stood there watching them as his heart unclenched and his soul relaxed. Kicking off his boots, he went to them, crawling in next to Landon.

Running his hand over the soft silk of his hair, he took in every inch of him, seeking injuries. Pulling him close, the tears returned once again, this time in relief that his boy was alive. He was safe and whole and, by the Mother, Ronan would dedicate his life to keeping him that way.

Shudders ran through his body. He felt Maddy's hand on his face and glanced at her. The worry on her face gutted him as he pulled her close and leaned his forehead against hers. "Thought we lost him tonight, Maddy," he whispered.

"I know," she said.

"Don't think I could've survived that," he whispered.

"I don't think either of us would've survived that," she whispered back as a tear rolled down her face at the thought.

Landon wriggled between them with a sleepy, "Yer squishing me."

They both laughed as they gazed into each other's eyes, realizing just how lucky they were. Ronan pressed a kiss to his son's head and said, "Go back to sleep, Landon. I love you." And if his voice broke while he said that—who the hell could blame him?

"Luv you, too, Daddy."

Maddy kissed Ronan and whispered, "I love you, too…"

They fell asleep clasping the child between them, needing to reassure themselves that, for tonight, he was safe from harm.

101

Storm Troopers

Jameson was gonna lose his shit. He and Roarke had just finished the last stretch of the final block in the tannery district and found no sign of Danyka.

Roarke peered through windows and knocked on doors, questioning anyone who answered. Jamey used his heightened shifter senses, trying to find Danny's scent or any indication that they brought her this way.

A quarter of an hour had passed since Jamey had last heard from Fergus. He paced, needing to do something—wanting to hit something. The woman he loved was in danger, and he couldn't do a fucking thing to help her.

Roaring into the night, he sounded every bit like the angry bear prowling inside of him. Whipping around, he pounded his fist into the wooden door behind him. Hurt like a motherfucker, but the cracks that appeared brought him some satisfaction.

"Easy there, big guy," Roarke said, keeping a safe distance between them. One thing he knew was wild animals, and right now, Jamey was more animal than man.

Jameson's eerie, backlit amber eyes landed on Roarke, seeking answers or an altercation.

"I'm not your enemy, Jamey," Roarke said, with his hands out, palms up in submission. "You got no beef with me. Save this shit for the men who took her."

Jamey shook his head, trying to pull his head out of his ass. This wasn't helping, and he knew it. But the helplessness he was experiencing was driving him insane. "I'm sorry, Roarke."

"I understand, Jamey," Roarke said, running a hand through his hair. "Hell, I've felt this way for months, trying to get a lead on Rosella." He gave

a rueful laugh. "Nothing emasculates you more than not being able to protect the people you love."

Jamey nodded. How could he have forgotten about Roarke's torment when he brought him along? The man had been searching for his sister for months. How the fuck did he keep going?

His lips parted to ask, but a pained moan emerged as he staggered, nearly driven to his knees by Danny's screams in his head.

"Help me, for fuck's sake, someone help me!"

Roarke's face blanched as he received the same terror-filled message. "Fuck me," he whispered.

Roarke had been working closely with the wardens since the spring equinox. He knew Danyka, and she was no shrinking violet. This woman was one of the toughest bad asses he'd ever known. For her to be in agony and begging for help, it was fucking bad.

Jamey's heart shattered at the pain and terror in Danny's voice.

"Jamey, help me!"

Danny's voice was loud in Jamey's head and for his ears only. She'd left their link wide open. He felt the pain in her head, her inability to breathe, and the fear of impending sexual violence.

Stomach rolling, he fought down the urge to be sick as he absorbed her emotions. The only thing keeping his human side in control was the fact that he needed to be rational until he located her. *"Rhy, I need you to be on standby when we find her. She's gonna need you."*

"Me bag's already packed. Don't drown in her pain, luv. It won't help you find her," Rhyanna cautioned.

"I'm trying. We'll be in contact when we have her location."

"We're only moments away, waiting on a location," Rhy said, pouring calming energy through their link.

Jamey welcomed the warmth and love that she sent. His grizzly settled down to a low growl, and his claws receded.

Walking towards Roarke, he said, "Let's start back at the beginning." They strode towards the head of the Tannery district. "Sure you can trust your informant?"

Roarke matched his stride and gave him a cocky smirk. "Hope so. He's my grandfather."

"And he makes you pay for information?" Jamey asked, stunned.

"It's not like that," Roarke explained. "He loves a good game, and I love to see if I can best him."

Jamey shook his head, trying not to focus on the time they'd wasted on his game.

As they neared the corner, Fergus's shaken voice came through to both of them. *"I got a lead on the Pixie when she screamed. Helluva way to get it. Take a left*

at the next intersection. Three streets down, make a left. I believe it's the second building on the right."

"Sucks to be them if it ain't," Roarke said.

"Sucks to be him if it is," Jamey said, the growl thickening his voice once again.

"Wish I was one of the storm troopers blasting through that fecking door," Fergus said. *"Give the Pixie my love when ye find her."*

"Without you, it would have taken a helluva lot longer to find her, Ferg. Thanks," Jamey said. *"Gotta go."*

The two men ran the three blocks, turning left on Hemlock Street and slowing only as they reached the second building.

A massive, wooden building loomed over them. Faded gray cedar shakes covered most of the exterior. Wind damage had removed pieces here and there, giving it the appearance of a smile that was missing teeth.

A solid oak door four-foot wide was the only point of entrance in the building's front. One wide window ten-foot off the ground was in the center of the wall to the left of the door.

"Let's go around and see if we can find an easier way in," Roarke suggested.

Unable to speak, Jamey followed. His vision was changing, eyes backlit with an eerie, amber glow. The beast inside was demanding to take charge. Following Roarke, they made their way around the side. There was no access point at the end of the building, so they kept moving to the rear.

Jamey drug a deep breath in, seeking her scent. Holding his breath, he processed the various nuances of the smells he encountered. Three men were here or had been here recently, and there it was—faint as could be— Danny's unique scent. Her usual contradictory scent of thunderstorms and innocence was mixed with pain and terror, inciting his grizzly.

Roarke stepped away slowly as Jamey's growl grew deeper and more dangerous. "I know you can still hear me, Jameson." He gestured to a window to the left of the door. "I'm going to peek in and see if she's here before we destroy the building. Okay?"

Jamey didn't acknowledge his question, but he didn't attack either.

Feeling hopeful that he would not die today, Roarke moved two crates under the window and climbed on top of them. He wiped at the cloudy film on his side, trying to better see inside. A small patch of visibility allowed him to gaze into the dimly lit building. On the left was a small office. Strategically placed in the middle of the warehouse was a steel cage.

Squinting, Roarke tried to make sense of what he was seeing. *"Rhy, get your ass down here as soon as you can. Hemlock Street, second building on the left. Cedar shakes. Come around back. All I can tell you right now is that there's a pool of blood. We're going in."*

Roarke swallowed hard as he gazed over his shoulder at his friend. He had fully shifted while Roarke's back was turned. "Jamey, if you're in there and can understand me, nod your head."

The massive animal's head bobbed slightly, his teeth clacking together.

"Danny's inside. She's on the floor of a cage." He paused, not sure how much of a warning he should give the man.

The rumbling growl decided it for him.

"There's a man on top of her, and there's a lot of blood. I don't know whose it is."

The grizzly raised up on his back feet, then pawed at the ground. His thunderous roar scared the shit out of Roarke. "Take the fucking door down. Go get your woman. Just be careful with her."

Jameson heard his words, but rage blinded the man and animal. Without another thought, his beast attacked the door, shredding the wood as if it were nothing but paper. With a thundering growl, he moved through the thick splinters and entered the room.

Danny's scent was stronger, as was the musk of the male lying on top of her. Jamey couldn't see her face or tell if she was alive. Frantically, he lumbered inside the cage and sank his teeth into the old man's leg, dragging him off her.

The human wore nothing on his skin, infuriating his beast even more. Jamey drug him clear of the cage. Enraged, he used his massive paws to roll the bastard halfway across the room.

McAllister landed on his back with a moist thud. A huge chunk was missing from the side of his neck. Jamey smiled inside, knowing his hellion hadn't needed him to save her.

The man's beady eyes were wide open, and there was still a glimmer of life left in them. Roaring in his face and hoping his bear was the last thing the man ever saw, Jamey swiped his claws across his groin, castrating him.

Fairfax McAllister watched the massive animal that had arrived for the warden. In the last moments before his brain shut down, he realized his bill had finally come due. There was a price for all the pain he had inflicted.

Pain was the price. His pain. The shredded remnants of his groin burned. He sensed that. And when the beast drew its claws slowly up his middle, spilling his guts on the floor, there was more pain. His mind was acutely aware of the trauma his body was experiencing.

If he could have drawn a breath, he might have laughed at the irony of it all. In avenging Max, he'd died the same damn way. As his vision began flickering, the creature lowered its massive head to his. Their noses touched. The dank breath of this brutal animal was one of the last sensations he would ever have. Because, in the next moment, the grizzly reared back and took his head clean off with one swipe of his sharp claws. Rolling like a ball, his head hit the back wall, and his debt was paid.

With the threat neutralized, his grizzly retreated, allowing Jamey to return to his human form. Exhausted from shifting, the only thing he could think about was his hellion.

Running to the cage, he found Roarke kneeling next to her. He was reaching for a leather belt around her neck when Jamey collapsed next to her. "Don't touch her," Jamey growled in a voice that was barely recognizable as human.

Roarke lifted his hands and leaned back. "She's blue, Jamey. We need to remove the belt."

Jamey instantly focused on Danny. With shaking hands, he loosened the leather. He removed the belt and tossed it outside the cage. Cupping her head, he tipped it back, trying to get her to take a breath. Her neck was a riot of bruises.

"C'mon, Hellion, I need you to breathe for me," Jamey begged. "I'm sorry it took me so long to get here."

Blood covered her face. "Here," Roarke said, pulling his shirt over his head.

Jamey used the shirt he handed him to remove as much of the blood as he could. "C'mon, honey. You've gotta breathe for me," he pleaded.

With his hand on her heart, he could just pick up a faint heartbeat, but it was fading fast. Prying her jaw open, he leaned down and breathed for her thrice. "Danny, you gotta fight. Don't you let him win."

Rhyanna burst into the room. "Get outta the way for me na, Jamey," she said, with no preliminaries.

Reluctantly, Jamey set her down as Rhy and Myranda entered the cage.

Quickly cataloging her vitals. Rhy shouted them out to Myranda. "Pulse is faint. She's na breathing. There's extensive bruising on her throat, and she's got broken ribs. Can't tell if he crushed her windpipe or if it's just bruised until I work on her."

Myranda immediately went to work. "I'll keep her lungs moving, while you work on her trachea." With her hands on Danny's chest, she forced air in and out of her lungs over and over. "Pulse is getting better."

"Well, he didna destroy it, but it's bruised badly," Rhy said with a sigh, closing her eyes and channeling energy into her.

Jamey's eyes were the only thing that hadn't quite returned with his humanity. Through them, he saw the energy both women were using to keep Danny alive. It flowed around them and through them into Danny, repairing and protecting her fragile system.

"Stop, Myr," Rhy said. "Let's see if she can breathe on her own now."

The four of them waited anxiously, praying that she would resume one of her most basic functions. A collective sigh of relief went up when her chest rose and fell on its own.

"Thank the Mother," Myranda said, relieved as Danny's lungs inflated on their own.

"Let's work on those ribs and bruises," Rhy said.

"Pulse is stable," Myranda said.

"I'm gonna ask ye both to step outside while I examine her more thoroughly," Rhy said with a glance at the men.

Roarke left without another word. But Jamey held his ground.

"I'm not leaving, Rhy," Jamey said in a hoarse voice.

"She would na want ye here for this exam, Jamey. 'Twill only take a few moments, and I swear, ye can come right back."

"Ye'll tell me what ye find?"

Rhy knew what he was asking. She nodded. "With her permission, I'll tell ye. Now give me some space."

Jamey closed his eyes, defeated, but knew Rhy had strict policies on privacy.

"Myr, go with him and give him a boost of energy. Lad looks like he's about to fall over."

"Let's go," Myr said as she followed him outside.

Rhyanna made a cursory exam, not seeing any evidence of forced sexual trauma. Gazing at Danny from the astral plane, she confirmed what she saw, much to her relief. This woman had already been through so much already in life. She sure as hell didn't need to deal with the trauma of being raped again.

"Jameson," she called.

Jamey came back in, his eyes locking on hers, silently pleading.

Feeling sorry for the couple—they'd been through so damn much recently—she put him out of his misery with a shake of her head.

His eyes closed in relief as he climbed back in next to Danny. "Can I hold her, Rhy?"

"Aye, ye won't harm her, and it will keep her warm until I get ye both back to the Sanctuary."

Jamey scooped her tiny frame onto his lap. Danny's head lay on his shoulder. Resting his chin on her head, he rocked her back and forth, so fucking grateful she lived.

Rhy covered them with a blanket she'd brought. "Are ye ready?"

Jamey nodded. He felt her hand on his shoulder and watched her place the other one on Danny. Moments later, they were in Jamey's suite. He didn't ask why they'd come to his room instead of hers, but he was grateful.

The turned-down bed beckoned to him, but they were both filthy, and he retained the musky scent of his bear.

Rhy's lips brushed against his cheek. "I needs to update Maddy," she said. "I'll be back later to check on ye." With a little elemental magic, she started the water in the bathroom.

"Tubs filling. Ye need me to help ye with her?" Jamey's arms tightened, making her smile at his territorial streak. Kyran was the same way with her. "Get cleaned up, and then ye both need rest. Make sure ye get some. Food will be sent up for ye as well. Ye'll need it."

Jamey nodded. "Thank you, Rhy. For everything."

Rhy patted his arm and shut the door on her way out.

Eyes drooping, he studied the woman in his arms. His gaze inventoried Danny, seeking any injuries Rhy might have missed. Smudges of dirt and blood streaked her face, but she was otherwise unharmed.

The scent of dried blood on both of them assaulted him. He felt disgusting as he carried her to the bathroom. The tub was already half full. With care, he stepped in and settled her body against his chest.

Danny didn't wake from the water, which disappointed him just a little. He desperately needed to gaze into her pale violet-blue eyes to reassure himself that she was all right. Well, as all right as one could be after her experience.

Handling her with care, he removed the evidence of her ordeal with soft strokes of his soapy hands. He washed her short, dark hair and her body thoroughly. When his hands passed over the faded bruises on her ribs, his fist clenched, and he wanted to kill McAllister all over again.

Letting out a ragged breath, he kept his mind on the task at hand. With a soft, wet cloth, he gently wiped the remnants of the day from her face. His eyes traced her delicate features.

After changing the water twice, Jamey finished washing and rinsing them off. Grabbing a brown bath sheet from a shelf next to the tub, he covered her from her shoulders to her toes. Naked, he carried her to the bed, cocooned in the soft cotton. He left her briefly to pull on some silk pajama bottoms.

A tray placed on the table in his sitting room caught his eye. He wolfed down two sandwiches and drank a glass of fresh grape juice and two of water. Snagging a blue silk button down for her to sleep in, he returned to the bedroom. From the door, he watched her sleep. Dark shadows, like bruises, had formed under her eyes from the ordeal.

The button-down he covered her in came to her knees. She didn't respond at all to him dressing her, which concerned him. With a thought, he turned off all the witch light—minus the one in the bathroom—and climbed in beside her. He didn't want her to wake up in the dark.

Pulling her back against his chest, he kissed the top of her head and nuzzled her neck. His arm wrapped around her, settling on her waist as he held her to him. "You're safe, Danyka. I've got you." He pressed a kiss to her temple. "Rest easy, Hellion, and then I need you to come back to me."

561

Eyes heavy and burning, he contemplated how close he came to losing her. He controlled his emotions, pushing them down, afraid of waking her. As he faded off, he wondered if this was what Danny went through when he nearly died.

'Til the day he died, he would never forget the hopelessness he'd felt when he entered that cage. It nearly destroyed him. "Hellion, I need you to come back to me. I can't lose you, not when I just got you, baby. Come back to me."

Repeating those words like a litany, sleep finally claimed him, offering the reprieve he needed. His woman was safe in his arms, and with the Mother's grace, she would wake up soon.

102

Forget-Me-Nots

Rhy tapped lightly on the door to Jamey's suite before entering. Concerned about them, the healer in her couldn't end her day without checking in on them once more. Not getting an answer, she carefully opened the door, not wanting to wake them if they slept.

Jameson and Danyka curled together as they slept. She faced him, head tucked beneath his chin. Her head rested on his shoulder, with one hand fisted in his dark hair and one leg sandwiched between his. His thick arm draped across her waist protectively.

Rhy observed them closely, not wanting to wake the exhausted couple. Danny's pale skin contrasted with Jamey's caramel tones. They were beautiful as they lay entwined. Their auras mixed, overlapping and caressing each other.

Going inward, Rhy examined them from the auric field. A sigh of relief left her as she studied Danny. The damage to her throat and ribs had healed nicely, and most of the bruises were fading.

The healer's relief was momentary as she examined the young woman's mental state. Danny's mental barriers were so tightly woven that not even Rhy could penetrate them. This concerned her. Gently, she probed through their personal link. Once again, static was all that she found. The only time she'd ever encountered this was with patients who were unconscious or catatonic.

Sending the Earth mother a prayer that exhaustion was the only thing causing it, she turned her attention to Jamey. Dark circles under his eyes testified to the physical and emotional strain he'd experienced the previous day. Otherwise, his breathing was deep and even, and his color was good.

As Rhy turned for the door, his eyes fluttered, sensing someone's presence even while deeply asleep. She stopped, meeting his half-lidded

gaze. Pressing a finger to her lips, she continued out the door. *"Go back to sleep, Jamey. All is well."*

His eyes drifted shut, and his arm tightened around Danny, pulling her closer. But his voice was clear when he responded. *"Thank you for everything, Rhy."*

"Always, luv," she said. Leaving them to rest, she left.

Jamey slipped back into the strange landscape of his dreams. Dreams were an important part of his culture, and while lucidly dreaming, he sought the meanings and hints they provided him. What he found often applied to his daily life in some small, meaningful way.

A strong wind blew warm air around him as he stood before an abandoned town. The gorgeous blue sky overhead was a stark contrast to the faded buildings before him.

Wandering through the remnants of a small ghost town, he walked the empty streets. Unsure of what or who he was seeking, he paid attention to the details of the quaint farming village.

A small mercantile across the street had lost a door and sported cracked glass and missing panes. A faded sign advertised strawberries for sale. The corner on his right was once home to the town's tavern. Batwing doors hung askew, creaking as they shifted in the breeze.

A raven perched atop a rocking chair on the front porch. Cocking his head, the creature studied him closely. Jamey wondered if the raven was a shifter. If so, why was he here? Ebony wings spread, and he took to the air, setting the chair creaking eerily behind him.

The scarlet glass in the lanterns mounted on the building on his left announced the local brothel. His skin crawled as he strode by, intuitively sensing it had once dealt in more illegal than legal forms of prostitution. His heightened shifter senses picked up the faded scents of fear, resignation, and despair oozing from the structure. Shuddering and trying to shake the sensation, he moved on, swamped in the hopelessness this place had left in its wake.

"Hello," he shouted, trying to find someone who could give him any indication of where he was. No one answered.

Jamey wandered through every block in the small town without seeing any inhabitants. Every building displayed the same deserted appearance as the main street. Broken glass from the windows and shudders torn from their hinges littered the streets. Faded, tattered curtains drifted in and out of the sad buildings, a testimony to the care and lives that once inhabited this place.

Making a second round of the small town and still finding no clues, he walked toward the edge of town. Jamey followed the only road leading out

of town. Acres of fields filled with blue and purple forget-me-nots grew on either side of the road.

The tiny, delicate flowers swayed in the breeze. Waves of blooms went on for nearly half of a mile until they met the tree line by the river. The sight was breathtaking. The town might be forgettable, but he'd always remember this view.

Slowly, he turned in a circle, his sharp gaze studying his surroundings. There was something here he needed to find. Intuition on high alert, his eyes shifted from one corner of the fields to the other, moving in a grid formation. Still nothing.

His mother's voice drifted through his mind as a memory from his childhood surfaced. *"Remember, Jameson, forget-me-nots represent true love and respect. Only give them to the one who earns both from you."* He'd been a boy then and didn't understand the full meaning of love or respect. But he did now.

Shading his eyes from the glare of the sun, he made one more pass. His head jerked as he stopped abruptly and moved in the opposite direction, seeking answers. There, in the middle of the field, something stirred. What was that?

The flowers shifted, disturbed by movements that were too big to be a small animal and too small to be a larger predator. Curious, Jamey moved closer. Silently he approached, not wanting to startle whatever was hiding amongst the foliage.

Moments later, the blond head of a young girl popped up amongst the flowers. A headband of flowers, matching the marbled colors of her dress, held back her wavy, blond hair and highlighted the delicate features of her face.

Facing away from him, he heard her chattering to herself in a sing-song voice. "Today is going to be a special day," she sang off-key, speaking to a faded stuffed animal seated before her. "Da told me afore he left for work 'twas a special day and I needed to look pretty."

Her head tipped to the side as if the faded creature were answering her. "Jest wait and see 'cause today he's supposed to come."

Jamey worked his way closer, fascinated by the child. She reminded him of someone, but he couldn't place her. Distracted, the petite little thing didn't notice him while he drifted closer, trying to see her profile.

His shadow cast across her, and she let out a startled gasp, scuttling away from him on her hands and knees. A safe distance away, she stopped and pivoted, glancing over her shoulder at him.

Jamey held his hands up, palms out towards her. "I mean you no harm, child," he said, watching the color drain from her face. Her chest heaved as she hyperventilated. "My apologies if I startled you."

Pale blue eyes watched him warily as she struggled to take a breath. "Who are you?" she gasped. "How did you get here?"

Slowly, he lowered himself to his knees to appear less intimidating to the child. "My name is Jamey." He gave her a gentle smile. "I'm not sure how I got here, but maybe you can help me figure it out."

"Jamey," the girl repeated, trying his name out on her tongue. A sad smile made its way across her face, and she tipped her head as she watched him. "You sound like someone I would have liked to have known," she said in a wistful tone. "Don't know how to help," the girl said with a sigh, twisting a lock of her hair between her fingers.

Jameson's hand went to his chest, pressing against the space where his heart clenched tightly. He knew that smile, and gazing into those changeable violet-blue eyes, he recognized the soul inhabiting this girl's body. His memory pulled up a conversation he'd recently had with his hellion, and sorrow nearly suffocated him.

"My blond hair was long and beautiful. It was kind of like Carsyn's, thick with slight waves. It was the only part of my appearance I was vain about. Well, as vain as you could be at twelve." Danny's words haunted him as he saw the softer version of her he never could have imagined. *"I cut my hair after I escaped and changed the color because I never wanted anyone to use it to cause me pain again."*

Dainty and sweet, without a care in the world. This version smiled and trusted him easily. She hadn't yet earned the wariness and cockiness the adult Danny wore like armor. This version of the woman he loved was gentle and open, conversing with a stranger without hesitation.

"Who are you waiting for?" he asked her in a soft voice.

"Me Da. This was the last place I saw him, but I know he'll come back for me someday. He promised I'd always find him in the forget-me-nots, but it's been a long time now…" She frowned, confused for a moment, her fingers brushing back and forth on the delicate blooms growing beside her.

Jamey nodded, going along with her theory. He knew the outcome of this day, and his heart clenched. "I hope you find him," he said in a rough voice. He kept the truth to himself, not wanting to break her heart.

Danny said nothing as she glanced down at the flowers her fingers plucked at nervously, shredding their delicate forms. "He promised to bring something that will protect me when he's gone."

"Do you know what he's bringing you?"

"No, silly. Then it wouldn't be a surprise." Her giggle was adorable. She turned back towards the stuffed animal that she'd left behind when he had startled her. Picking it up by one arm, the matted, brown critter dangled from her fingers as she approached him.

"Who's this?" he asked, pointing to her sidekick and wondering what it had once been.

"Why, this is Sir Vance, a bear from the kingdom of Wellesley." she said in a formal tone, offering the bear to him.

Jamey swallowed a lump in his throat as he bowed formally and reached for the offering. Her childhood bear had his surname and came from the island of his birth. Was this memory real or an attempt by her subconscious to merge her current reality with her childhood memories? To her inner child, he was a knight. He blinked rapidly, not sure he deserved such an honor.

His fingers carefully grasped the dingy, reddish-brown bear dangling between them. He wouldn't have known what it was if she hadn't told him. The well-loved stuffed animal had lost most of its stuffing and one of its eyes. But the detail that caught his attention was the left arm dangling by a red thread from the shoulder. Loose red stitches barely connected the appendage to the body.

His eyes met hers as goose flesh covered his arms. "What happened to him?" he asked in a choked voice as he pointed to the damage before handing him back.

Tears filled her eyes as she glanced down at what was obviously her favorite toy. "It's all my fault," she said in a voice thick with tears. "I was somewhere I shouldna have been." Her lips quivered as she told the tale. "I just wanted to play by myself next door."

Luminous eyes met his. "I was na supposed to be there. It was forbidden." Her voice was solemn, hinting of things to come. "We're to stay in the yard, but I was tired of minding all the little ones and wanted to be alone for a bit."

She bit her lip, glancing down at her feet. "I snuck through the neighbor's fence when they weren't looking and sat on the old swing in their maple tree."

"I loved their swing and wished we had one. It was the first time I'd been brave enough to use it." She stood and twirled her arms outstretched. "It was glorious. At the peak, I felt like I was flying." Her smile faded. "Until their dog charged at me."

Young Danny wiped her nose on the back of her hand. "A big black beast, he was, and I swear," her little hand went over her heart, "his eyes glowed ruby red." The gleeful pitch of her voice moments ago faded to a scared whisper.

Riveted to her tale, Jameson realized her subconscious had recreated the hellhound attack in a manner her inner child could understand.

"The beast grabbed his paw and wouldn't let go until Ole man Maguffin came out and beat him off." She hugged the bear to her chest tightly. "He nearly lost an arm."

Unconsciously, Jamey's right hand massaged his left shoulder as she recounted the tale. Glancing at the faded animal, he said, "Well, it looks like someone patched him up good."

Small fingers traced the red stitched x's that held his arm to his tattered body. "Mama tried, but she's not much of a seamstress."

Jamey noted the difference in her body language when she mentioned her mother. Tension racked her body, and her jaw tightened. When she spoke of her father earlier, it was with love and laughter. Her voice now held faintly disguised contempt.

"Where are your parents?" he asked in a gentle voice, hoping his question wouldn't upset her. "Are they in town?"

Those changeable blue-violet eyes darkened to a deep amethyst. He recognized the telltale sign that she was upset. The sky darkened overhead as her fists clenched and tears filled those hauntingly gorgeous orbs. "She left me here." The clipped words conveyed her rage.

"I don't know what I did to deserve the punishment she gave me. I tried to be good, helping with the little ones as much as I could." She sniffled, swallowing hard. "But it wasn't enough. She still s-s-sent me away," she stuttered, shifting from rage to devastation.

A tear slipped down her cheek, tumbling off her chin onto Sir Vance. She clutched the only source of comfort she had to her chest in a stranglehold as she sobbed out, "She gave me to the demons in town. 'Twould've been kinder to have drowned me in the creek."

Jamey's heart ached at her confession. He knew bits and pieces of her past from the few conversations about it they'd had and from the nightmares he'd witnessed. His eyes burned as he stopped himself from pulling her into his arms for comfort. This version of her didn't remember him as a man, and he didn't want to add to her trauma.

"Your Da?" he asked gently, trying to take her away from the pain of her mother's abandonment.

"He left me, too," she said in a trembling voice. "But he didn't want to." She added, clarifying that, unlike her mother, he had not abandoned her.

"Where did he go?" Jamey asked, sensing that she needed to purge the grief and fury out of her inner child's system.

Her streaming eyes shifted from his then. She pointed towards the river, and when Jamey followed her gaze, the landscape changed. The forget-me-nots were still there, but they originated from a freshly dug grave near a copse of oak trees.

"I'm so sorry," Jamey said in a choked voice. He couldn't imagine losing a parent, and he doubted they'd allowed her to grieve for long when this event occurred. "I know how much he must have meant to you."

Blond head nodding, she hid her face in the bear as sorrow overwhelmed her. "I don't have anyone, and I don't know where to go or what to do."

568

Jamey's heart broke as she stood there stoically, trying not to crumble completely. Unable to witness her pain and not reach out to her, he opened his arms to her and whispered, "Come here, honey."

She lowered the bear and took a step back from him, her sorrow shifting instantly to distrust. "You just want what every other man wants from me."

Her hand clasped the mound between her legs crudely. Fury rolled through those purple eyes, and her voice was icy with rage. "Think you can get it for free if yer nice to me, dontchya?"

"No," Jamey gasped in shock. "I don't want anything from you, honey."

"Honey?" She tipped her head at an angle and squinted her eyes at him, her demeanor once again changing. "Honey, sweetie pie, darling, little luv, my cherub, pretty little baby doll…" she sneered at him in a sing-song voice.

"I've heard all the sweet things that come out of men's mouths before they drive their dirty cocks into me, tearing me apart." Her lip curled and her features aged a bit—hardened. "You're all the same."

"That is not true," he said, trying not to sound defensive.

Voice hardening into that of a barker, she continued. "And let's not forget my all-time favorite line. 'Boys, yer gonna love this tight little virgin pussy. Ye'll never have better,'" she shouted as if advertising her attributes to a crowd.

Jamey's face lost all color. Cynical laughter erupted from the young girl who stood before him. It was such a contrast from the child he had been speaking with only moments before that it left him speechless.

"When they tired of that game," she continued, stalking closer, "I earned new names." She tapped her lips with her index finger as she remembered. "Twat, pussy, cunt, strumpet and the one I hated the most…" She paused dramatically. "Whore."

Lips curling in a rictus of a smile and eyes flashing dangerously, she shouted at him, "Why was I the whore when they purchased me from my mother without my consent? They abused and fucked me without my consent. They profited from my body without my consent. And they gang-raped me as punishment without my consent. So why am I the fucking whore?" she screamed.

"Danny," he protested, his hands out, trying to calm her. "Not all men are like that. I'm not like that."

"I don't know you, and I never told you my name," she scoffed. "You haven't earned the right to call me that. This is my safe space, and you don't belong here."

Jamey didn't know how this had all gone so wrong. Gaping at her, he was at a loss for words.

"GET OUT!" Danyka roared at him before dropping the bear she held. Shifting into her falcon, she took to the sky.

He caught the bear before it hit the ground. His eyes tracked her flight, but she didn't go far. Perched on the granite headstone, she watched him.

Walking slowly with his arms outstretched, he approached. Her angry squawks warned him not to come too close. Twenty feet from the grave, he knelt down, his eyes never leaving hers.

"I'm not leaving you here alone," he said in a gentle voice as he gently placed the bear on the grave. "I love you."

"You don't even fucking know me!" he heard on their line. ***"Get the fuck out!***

A sucker punch of energy slammed into him, throwing him out of her dreamscape.

Jamey awoke in a cold sweat, panting. Confused, he glanced around the room, trying to figure out where he was. The meadow was gone, and as his eyes adjusted to the dark, he realized he was lying in his bed.

Sucking in a painful breath, he peered down, trying to figure out what was piercing his skin. The past day came flooding back as he found Danyka still wrapped up against him. The pain he felt was from her nails clawing into his chest. Blood trickled between her fingers, and he felt the tension in her body against him, a testament to her distress.

Needing comfort, he ignored the pain, pulling her closer and tucking her head beneath his chin. His fingers feathered through her hair and over her cheek and still she didn't wake.

"Hellion, I need you to come back to me," he whispered. "I promise I won't leave you trapped there."

With a shudder running through his body, he reached out to Rhy. *"Have you got a minute?"* he asked, knowing there was no way to hide the pain in his voice.

"On me way, Jamey."

Giving himself a moment's grace, he allowed the tears burning the back of his eyes the release they were seeking. Gentle hands stroked her hair as he held the woman he loved and wondered if he could bring her back to the land of the living. Would he become just someone else she lost in the land of her forget-me-nots?

103

You Fucking Left her there?

Fergus returned via the Clayton portal from an undisclosed distant location. Dark thoughts ricocheted through his mind as he made his way down the worn docks to the Rusty Tap. His nerves were a fucking mess, and he felt like puking from the actions he had been forced to take over the past twenty-four hours.

Head hammering, he needed a drink—or ten. Hell, he might as well just grab a couple of bottles and drag Carsyn home with him if she was closing tonight. Mayhap he'd spend the night drowning his sorrows in his cups and finding oblivion between her thighs. Mayhap come morning, he might jest be able to look in the mirror without wanting to punch himself in the face.

Not that either option would help solve the dilemma he was facing. Goddamn it all to hell. Anyway you looked at it, they were fucked. He didn't know how in the fuck they were ever gonna save Roarke's sister and the rest of the young men and women scattered along the currents of the Saint Lawrence. The price for freedom would be high, with casualties on both sides.

Only paying attention to the chaos in his head, he smacked into the broad chest of a chap nearly his height. The warm glow of the Tap's gold lantern from the corner of his eye was calling to him like a siren as he opted for a quick apology.

"Sorry, man," he said, brushing the chap off without glancing at his face. "Wasna watching where I was going."

"Fergus?" a deep voice asked.

Ferg groaned inwardly. This was the last fucking person he needed to see tonight. Maddy needed an update before he confided in the sea captain.

"Roarke," Ferg said, trying to smile. "Good to see ye, lad. "

Roarke's brows furrowed. "What's up with you? You look like shit?"

"Thanks. Jest what every player wants to hear," Ferg said, trying to gain some levity in this situation.

"Anything I can do to help?"

"Feck me," Ferg muttered, running a hand over his face. His gray eyes met Roarke's, and he couldn't lie or mislead this man even though he wanted to. "Ye got time for a drink?"

A chill ran down Roarke's back at Fergus's cryptic behavior. "Is this about my sister?" he asked in an icy tone.

Ferg clamped him on the back and turned him back the way he'd come. "I need to talk to ye, lad, and ye ain't gonna like me when we'se done."

The muscles under Ferg's hand tightened, and the lines around Roarke's eyes were deeper as he gazed at the fire mage. "Stop pussyfooting around. Tell me what the fuck is going on."

"Inside," Ferg said, tipping his head towards the tavern. There was no fecking way he could have this conversation sober.

Roarke was silent as he followed the mage into the smoky atmosphere of the tavern. He grabbed a booth in the corner, away from the drunks and the gamblers. His nerves were fucking shot, and most days, he'd been drinking too much. Should have asked for a glass of water, but his sixth sense told him he was gonna need something stronger for this conversation.

Ferg returned with a pitcher of beer in one hand, a bottle under his arm, and two glasses dangling from his fingers.

"Think you missed your calling as a barmaid," Roarke said with a smile that didn't meet his eyes.

"Perhaps in another life," Ferg replied, not even attempting to grin. Pouring three fingers of whiskey for them both, he handed one to Roarke.

Roarke raised an eyebrow, concern swirling in his gut. He sipped at his whiskey while Ferg tossed the whole damn lot down without coming up for air. He followed it by filling his glass with beer and finishing that as well. When he reached for the whiskey, Roarke pulled it out of his reach. "Tell me what the fuck's going on, and I'll give you a refill."

"I paid for the lot; hand it the feck over," Ferg growled.

"Tell me where ye been the last few days because your absence was noted," the sea captain said in a cool voice.

"Checking up on me, have ye?" Ferg said, running both hands over his face. "Fuck me," he groaned, planting both hands on the table and meeting Roarke's pissed-off gaze head on. "I been undercover, trying to find a way in."

Roarke didn't need any clarification. He knew what Ferg was trying to find a way into—the human trafficking ring they'd been trying to find for months now. "Did you get in?"

"Ye haven't spoken to Samson yet?"

Roarke shook his head and quirked a brow.

"Aye, I got in." Ferg cleared his throat and gazed sightlessly at a point over Roarke's shoulder. "I worked security at one auction recently, watching as they auctioned young men and women off like chattel. I entered the second one as a buyer." Swallowing hard, he let the man across from him process that for a bit.

"What did you learn?" Roarke asked in a tightly controlled voice.

"I learned that this whole fecking thing is bigger and more connected than we can comprehend. I ken that this tain't gonna be a quick mission." Ferg stared wearily at Roarke. "And we can't sacrifice the entire operation for jest one lass."

Roarke's fists clenched on the table, and he was fairly certain steam was rolling out of his ears as he processed this info. "So, what you're telling me is that Rosella is an acceptable casualty until you decide otherwise?" His voice rose, and the threat of violence rolled off him.

"I met your sister, Roarke." Fergus's gray eyes met icy blue ones, facing the fact that he was about to lose a friend with the next words he uttered. He reached for the bottle, snatching it away from Roarke and chugging a generous swig straight from the bottle as Roarke's eyes bulged at him.

"You met her?" Roarke echoed in a monotone.

"They auction off their virginity in stages," Ferg said, ignoring his question. "Winning the bid for a young woman gives you the first two stages of their purity. You purchase the privilege of their mouth and their pussy. If you want to go around the world," his brow arched, making sure the man knew what he was talking about, "ye pay extra for the third."

Roarke's stony silence frosted the table. Ferg always suspected he was a strong water element, and the change in temperature was confirming it.

"Who won the privilege of raping my sister?" Roarke ground out.

Ferg met the man's tormented eyes with his troubled ones. He held the glass in both hands, rolling it nervously from one side to the other before saying, "I did."

Roarke's eyes clamped shut at the images those words put in his head. When they snapped open, a latent fire element flared behind his gaze. "Did you enjoy breaking a fifteen-year-old girl?"

"I didna enjoy any part of this, Roarke. Not one fecking minute of it." His fingers were turning blue where they sat on the blistering cold table.

"Didchya fuck my sister, Fergus?" Roarke asked, his lip curling in disgust. All that frost started melting just as quickly as it came as his body heated with the waves of rage radiating off him.

"No, lad. *I* didna." Ferg met his glare head on, knowing the fury was about to break loose.

"Then who the feck did?" Roarke growled.

Fergus wasn't nearly as inebriated as he appeared. His eyes were clear, and his mind was firing on all cylinders. He knew what Roarke needed to hear and what he needed to do. Roarke needed to blow off steam, and the fire mage was going to let him use him to do it. "Her guard."

Roarke's fists pounded against the table. "You let him fuck her? You let him be her first?"

"Nye, laddie, she let him," Fergus said, digging his claws into the wound. "There was no way she could leave that room a virgin. Healers are on deck to act as witnesses and to verify the auction fees when the night's over. Woulda blown me cover had she remained untouched."

"So, you let some random man take what he wanted from her?"

"Nye, I didna," Ferg repeated. "There are links between the two of them." When Roarke lifted his brows in a question, he added, "She has feelings for the lad, and he for her."

"And that was enough for her to spread her legs and let him in?" Roarke asked.

"I gave her a choice, and she chose him," Ferg said in a tight voice. "There were no good fecking choices, man. I'se jest trying to keep her alive."

"Where is she?" Roarke demanded. "I want to see my sister right fucking now."

Ferg shook his head. "No can do, laddie."

"You call me lad one more time, and I'm gonna fucking pummel you."

"Yer gonna pummel me either way," Ferg thought as he nodded at Roarke.

"Where the fuck is she?" Roarke shouted, not caring who heard him now.

Tensing because he knew what was coming, and a part of him welcomed the distraction from feeling like a failure, he told Roarke the truth. "There was no way to extract her safely."

"So, you tie her up, gag her, and toss her over your shoulders, but you don't fucking leave without her!" Roarke was standing now, fists clenched and vibrating with fury.

"The lass refused to come without some of her friends who were on another vessel. She cared enough about the bigger picture not to leave them behind even though she knew how much it would hurt ye." Ferg never glanced away from Roarke's eyes, waiting for the first strike. The man frothing across from him didn't disappoint.

Roarke reached across the booth and hauled Fergus out of his seat. "You fucking left her there, you piece of shit." He held him with one hand while his fist pounded into the side of Ferg's head.

"What kind of all-powerful mage are you? You couldn't figure a way to get one little girl out?" With each sentence, he punched him again. Yanking

him out of the booth, he slammed him again, letting him fall to the floor this time so he could straddle him.

"How could you walk away and leave her there?" Roarke roared at him.

"I did it because she begged me to," Ferg roared back, reaching into his shirt in between blows. "She sent you a letter." He waved a wrinkled piece of paper in front of Roarke's face.

Roarke's ears were ringing as he tried to process what Ferg had just told him. He was trying, but he couldn't wrap his brain around how close this man had been to sweet little Rosella. Then he abandoned her. His head and his heart couldn't take the shock.

Chest heaving, he sat back on his heels, glancing up at the crowd gathered around him. "WHAT?" he roared at them. "Mind your fucking business," he said as he staggered to his feet and collapsed back into the booth.

Fergus lay there, bleeding on the floor. *"Mother fecker,"* he thought. The man could throw a punch. Roarke broke his nose and, running his tongue around his chompers, Ferg found a few of them loosened. The fecker had split his lip, and his ears were ringing. He wasn't sure if he could sit up without vomiting. But he felt better, and he'd helped Roarke work off some of the guilt and rage.

Dragging himself off the floor, he slithered into the booth opposite Roarke. Carsyn appeared with a bar towel wrapped around a chunk of ice and a disgusted look for Roarke.

Roarke didn't even notice, too caught up in the message in his hand. He couldn't wait to open it but was terrified at the same time. Reaching for the bottle, he upended the glass, finishing the last third of the whiskey.

"Why didn't you fight back?" he asked Ferg in a rough whisper, not looking at him.

"Because ye needed this, and I needed ye to do it."

Roarke's head whipped around, and he glared at him.

"Ye gonna open it, or ye want me to do it fer ye?" Ferg asked, trying to staunch the blood cascading down his face.

Roarke ignored him, his thumb brushing back and forth across his name on the front of the envelope. "She's always had beautiful penmanship," he told Ferg. Taking the pitcher and filling his glass, he downed it before pulling the paper from the envelope.

Roarke,

I know this letter will bring you sorrow, and I am truly sorry for that. Please don't take it out on Mister Emberz when I am unable to return with him. He was nothing but kind to me and saved me from what could have been a terrifying ordeal.

Mr. Emberz was in an impossible situation, but he allowed me to have some say in who would be my first. I chose Braden. I've wanted him, but never dreamed we'd have the opportunity to be together. Braden has been my guard for the majority of my captivity. He's become a dear friend—and a bit more. I care for him deeply, and he returns my feelings.

My innocence has long been gone now. I am no longer a child. So, please stop thinking of me like one. I willingly gave him the gift of my body. If I were to only have one thing I could control, losing my virginity would be it. So please don't hold my decisions against anyone. Braden took me through a woman's rite of passage with respect and, dare I say…love. I would choose him again if the choice were mine to make—every time.

Had we met under different circumstances, we would have courted properly. But as circumstances are, this is the life I've had to adapt to, and I've learned how to survive in this world. I listened to Maman's advice and will do whatever I have to until you finally arrive.

Even with this distance between us, I sense the guilt you have of not meeting me the day I was abducted. So please, lay that burden down. I know how many things you take on that are not yours to carry. I would have canceled my time with you to spend time with Manfri. So, this journey was always going to be mine to take.

This is my fate—for now, although I have no doubts that you will find me and bring me home.

Be prepared to rescue more than me. Options are very limited for many of those in my position and for those who labor on board this vessel. If you come, you must help us all…I won't leave if you don't.

I love you, Roarke. Give Maman and the rest of the family my love. I am as well as can be expected. More importantly, I am alive, and I will never give up. So don't give up on me, and please don't judge the things I need to do just to survive here. I have to go now, someone approaches.

With all of my love,
Your favorite sister,
Rosella

Roarke's eyes were streaming as he read the letter again. He could hear her sweet voice speaking the words in his mind as his fingers traced over the letters in front of him. By the Mother, his little sister was one of the wisest souls he'd ever known.

Wiping his face with his hands, he leaned his head back on the booth and faced the barely recognizable mage. "Why didn't you at least defend yourself or zap me with some of your hellfire?"

Fergus snuffled, his nose congested and the blood still trickling down his face. Clearing his throat, he choked out, "Ye needed this, and to be honest, so did I." Bleary eyes stared at the man across from him. "Killed a part of me to leave her there, ye ken?"

Roarke nodded. "I know. Would've done the same to me. Don't think I could've done it."

"If it would've gotten ye all killed, ye could've." He pinched the bridge of his nose and tipped his head back. "There were no safe options. That's the only reason it went down this way."

"Sorry," Roarke said, waving his hand at Ferg's face.

"Don't be. Rhy'll fix it right up."

Roarke flushed at the healer's name.

Ferg cocked an eye at him. "Tough one to get over, t'aint she?"

"Toughest yet," Roarke said in a tortured whisper. "Both of them."

His voice had shifted from wrath to sorrow in mere seconds. The pain this man was suffering was visible to Fergus in more ways than one. But this time, there was nothing he could do to ease this individual's journey. And for that, he was ashamed.

104

Let Me In

Jamey carefully disengaged himself from Danyka and slipped from the bed. He used the bathroom and waited in the sitting room for Rhy to arrive. Mindlessly, he picked at a tray of food the staff left for them.
The selection of meats, cheeses, and fruit was precisely what his body needed as it recovered. Nibbling on a piece of dried fruit, he heard a light knock on the door.

"Come in," he said, waiting before the warmth of the fireplace in nothing but a silk pair of lounge pants.

Rhy entered, followed by Kyran. It didn't surprise him to see both of them. The water mage might come in handy, too. She hugged Jameson tightly. When she let go, Kyran gave him a nod and not-so-subtly pulled Rhy under his shoulder.

"Possessive little fucker," Jamey thought idly, but he couldn't blame him. He could be the same way with Danny even knowing it would make things worse.

"Have a seat," Jamey said, remembering his manners and gesturing towards the couch. He settled on the loveseat across from them with his elbows on his knees as he stared at the floor.

The healer in Rhy studied him, noting the fatigue still in his eyes. Shirtless, her eyes traveled from his torso to his hips, assessing the scars from the hellhound attack. Shiny white lines marred his creamy caramel skin, but they were thinner than they had been last time. This was good. She'd been afraid his shift at the warehouse would have reopened old wounds, but they appeared stable.

"Were ye able to rest at all, Jamey?" Rhy asked him.

Clearing his throat, he ran his hands over his face and through the length of his hair, pushing it behind him. "A little," he answered, not sugarcoating it. There was no point—she'd know if he was lying.

"And Danny?" she asked, raising a delicate brow. "Has she woken?"

Closing his eyes, he shook his head. Pinching the bridge of his nose between his thumb and forefinger, he tried to wrangle his meandering thoughts. He nearly laughed aloud, thinking it was about as easy as corralling mustangs.

"What do you know of shared dreamscapes?" he asked the couple.

Kyran spoke first. "They're rare from what I've read. But they are powerful and nearly as realistic as we are, sitting here right now."

"Aye," Rhy agreed. "Typically, both parties be linked in some way— friends, family, or lovers." She waited for his nod and continued. "They both view the same scene and interact within it. One participant controls the dream and can end it at will."

"That be the truth right there," Jamey said, laughing mirthlessly. "She booted my ass right outta there."

"Will ye tell me what ye saw, lad?" she asked in a gentle voice.

Jamey gave her a sad smile, realizing she was using her version of his horse-whisperer voice. Clearing his throat, he began.

"I stepped into the dream in a ghost town, nothing but dilapidated buildings and a dirt path running down main street. Forget-me-nots surrounded the place, and I found her there amongst them."

"Danny?" Rhy said for clarification.

"Yeah, our Danny, but not our Danny." His gaze lifted to hers. The pain and anguish in his eyes slayed her.

"Playing in the field was a child. Long blond hair and all girly; she wore a dress. Dainty and delicate, she was polite as hell." He laughed at the irony of his description. "She carried around this pitiful stuffed animal—a stuffed teddy bear with its left arm dangling by a thread."

Rhyanna gasped and reached for Kyran's hand.

Jamey's tormented dark eyes stared into hers, and he continued. "His name was Sir Vance, and he was from the Kingdom of Wellesley. And to top it all off, her neighbor's dog had mauled him, nearly yanking his arm off." He ran a hand through his hair. "The dog had red eyes."

"Holy shit," Kyran muttered. "Her subconscious worked your attack into her memory so she can cope with it."

"I understand that," Jamey said. "But she doesn't seem to recognize me as an adult."

"Ach, na, Jamey, that must have broken yer heart, seeing her so," Rhy said sorrowfully.

"Sure the fuck did." His shoulders drooped in defeat.

"What woke you?" Kyran asked, brows furrowed. "Usually, all members of a dreamscape wake simultaneously."

He coughed out a caustic laugh. "She booted my ass out."

"Why?" Rhy asked.

Jamey's brows furrowed. "Still trying to figure that out. I think I triggered it by calling her 'honey.'"

Rhy and Kyran looked at each other in surprise and said, "What?" as if on cue.

"I offered her comfort. She spoke about her father's passing and what her mother had done." He gazed at Rhy intensely, not wanting to air Danny's past in front of Kyran.

"I understand," Rhy said without going into detail.

"I opened my arms and told her to come here, and she lost her shit," Jamey said, standing and pacing once again. "Her appearance changed as she ranted. She aged slightly and was harsher in both appearance and speech."

"So the older version of herself jumps in to protect the wee one when she feels threatened."

"Exactly. How am I supposed to get her to trust me enough to come back if I can't get past her protective shell?"

"How did she kick you out?" Kyran asked

"She shifted to get away from me and then bitch slapped me with some wicked powerful energy. It didn't just toss me into another dream, it woke me up instantly."

"Bruise you?" Kyran asked.

"Didn't think to check, but I don't think so." He glanced down at his chest. "I don't see any new bruises."

"Ye ken by now what li'l Danka endured, dontchya, Jamey?" Rhy asked. Danny's past had been a closely guarded secret.

Jamey's fists clenched. "Weeks ago, she confided in me that after her father's death, her mother sold her to a brothel. She's told me a good part of all that entails," he said, giving the condensed version. "And I've spoken with Maddy about it as well."

Kyran whispered, "Fuck me," and hung his head. "Explains why she is so fiercely independent and made no attachments before you," he said, glancing at Jamey.

"It's not been easy for either of us," Jamey said. "But she's worth it." His voice was soft and full of love. "The girl I saw today hates men. After the things she said today, I can understand why."

Neither of them asked him to go into the details on that.

"Ye said she shifted, Jamey?" Rhy asked a few minutes later, brows furrowed as she tried to figure something out. When he nodded, she asked, "Into which one of her forms?"

"Her favorite, the peregrine."

"And she had something representing ye already in the dream?"

"A stuffed teddy bear that's seen better days."

"Are ye capable of changing yer clothing and surroundings when ye lucid dream?" she asked him.

"In my dreams, yes."

"Next time ye arrive, see how much control ye have in her world. Add a bear pendant or change the color of something minor and see if it works afore ye find her."

"I'm willing to try anything," Jamey said.

"Can you shift in your dreams?" Kyran asked.

"Sometimes."

"Try that, too—even a partial shift. Danny is afraid of what you represent as a man." He ran a hand over his jaw. "Someone who terrorized her as a child nearly raped her again yesterday. That one act tore down centuries of safety she's come to know at the Sanctuary. He took away her confidence and replaced it with terror. She won't want to trust men anytime soon."

Jamey hung his head, devastated.

Kyran continued. "You have two things going in your favor. She reached out to you when she was in trouble, and you saved her. And she trusts your animal. Work with what she's comfortable with."

"So, you think if I can't reason with her as a man, I need to give her the comfort and protection of my unpredictable grizzly?" Jamey looked at him as if he was daft.

"If she fears yer grizzly, lad," Rhy said, "she can jest fly away. She still retains her sense of safety." A huge grin crossed her face. "Danyka loves yer grizzly. When everyone else was terrified of him, she rode ye like a pony."

They all chuckled at the thought of that.

"As a shifter, you are a natural part of the animal kingdom and one that is no threat to her," Kyran said. "Yes, you're a predator, but I don't believe you typically go after birds in that form. Do you?" Now he was the one giving Jamey a dumb ass look.

"No. And I doubt I could catch one if I tried. She's one of the fastest creatures on this planet."

"Exactly," Kyran said, making his point. "She keeps her ability to protect herself by fleeing."

Rhy's lips quirked. "Funny, isn't it? Our little scrapper in real life prefers to flee in the dream world."

"I want to try again," Jamey said, encouraging them to leave by standing. "Thank you both for coming."

Rhy gave him another fierce hug, then grasped his face in her hands. "Be careful in there. She can still harm ye," she said. "I'm gonna peek in on her afore I go."

Jamey nodded, giving her permission—not that she needed it.

Kyran stepped forward and offered him a hand. "If you'll allow me, I can drain some of the raw emotions you're drowning in from the past few days. It will allow you to be less aggressive and to focus better when you're in there. You'll be less emotional and more analytical, which may prove helpful."

Jamey locked eyes with him for a moment, wondering if his emotions were motivating him to keep going at this stage. But one glance at the door to the bedroom and he knew better. Danyka was why he kept going. He would *not* lose her.

"Does it harm you?" Jamey asked.

"Not at all. I transmute it into something productive. It won't affect me physically or emotionally. And it won't affect her either," Kyran said, knowing what the next question would be.

"Do it."

Kyran grasped his hand in a firm grip. An electrical shock ran up Jamey's arm, but it wasn't painful. It throbbed and then faded away. He felt lighter and clearer than he had since the Solstice.

"Thank you, Kyran."

"You're welcome."

They both turned as Rhyanna rejoined them. Her sad eyes told them there had been no change.

"Call me if ye need me, lad," she said as she opened the door.

"I will, Rhy. Promise," Jamey said, shutting it gently behind them. Nibbling on some more of the snack food, he thought about their conversation and wondered if it could be so simple.

Pouring a glass of wine, he took his time drinking it as he stared into the flames in the fireplace. He wished Fergus were here. He'd know what the fuck to do or come up with some hare-brained scheme to fix it.

Jamey trusted Rhy, and her suggestions were sound. He just missed Ferg. He finished the last of his wine and returned to his bedroom.

Danyka slept deeply, seeming so damn tiny in the middle of his bed. But he liked the way she looked there, and he didn't want her sleeping anywhere else.

He slid in beside her, lying on his side. His eyes traced every inch of her features, memorizing how relaxed and peaceful she was in sleep. Her features were delicate—more so now, without her usual scowl.

When he moved closer and wrapped an arm around her waist, he waited for her to stiffen in his arms. But her body instinctively recognized him and moved closer to his warmth. Danny snuggled into the same position she had earlier.

A weight lifted from his heart, and he placed a gentle kiss on her temple before resting his forehead against hers and whispering, "Let me in, Hellion. Please, just let me in."

Jameson fell asleep repeating the litany over and over, praying she'd hear him and open the doors.

105

What Have Ye Done?

Fergus woke to every muscle in his body screaming. He was curled around Carsyn's back, and he took a moment to appreciate the expanse of creamy soft skin under his hands. Stroking the curve of her breast absently, he cataloged his healing injuries.

Roarke had pounded the fuck out of him, and Fergus didn't blame him in the least. If someone had left his cousin Elyana in a hostile environment, he would've wanted to kill the fecker, too. Slipping his arm out from under Carsyn, he rolled onto his back. His fingers gently prodded at his nose. He was pretty sure he'd reset it last night, but he'd have Rhy check on it later today. 'Twas still tender.

The earth wench would probably re-break it jest to make him suffer for not seeking her out when it happened. But Fergus didn't want to face her yet. He needed to see Madylyn before he could talk to anyone else about what he'd experienced.

He sat up carefully, wincing and praying that his stomach would stop rolling and his head would stop throbbing. The pounding was incessant and only partly his fault from drinking. Roarke could take credit for the other half of his misery.

A cold shower cleared the webs of sleep from his head and made him appreciate the value of warm water. Turning the faucet off, he dried and dressed in the dark blue kilt and gray sweater he'd worn last night. His dirty clothing matched his dreary mood.

Boots on, he pressed a kiss to the lovely Carsyn's brow. Her light green eyes blinked up at him blearily. Her fingers traced a gentle path down the side of his face, mindful of his injuries. "Leaving so soon?"

Ferg bent down and kissed her. "Aye, lass. I've got appointments that won't wait." He brushed his lips against hers again, wanting nothing more

than to slide back under the warm covers and into her. "See you tonight, then?"

Carsyn gave him a shy smile, "I'd like that," she said drowsily. She yawned, pulling the covers back up to her chin and snuggling against his pillow.

"Go back to sleep, luv," he said, heading for the door. "Jest make sure ye dream about me."

Lighting a smoke, he drew the tobacco deeply into his lungs and made his way to the Clayton Portal. Exiting at the Stag Gate, he made his way to the castle, eyes watching the daily hustle and bustle as he went. A stable hand was in the pasture working with a young horse, and another was feeding the white tigers in the pen next door.

Kitchen hands stoked the massive outdoor fires, preparing them for the spits of meat they would roast for the evening meal. Nearby, scullery maids peeled mountains of potatoes. Everyone was in good spirits, calling to him and waving as he passed. He got more than one questioning look about his battered appearance, which he completely ignored.

Taking the stairs two at a time, he reached the second floor and headed for Maddy's office. The door was open, and he heard Kerrygan and Maddy talking.

"I need you to go to Sackett's Harbor. Figure out the warding needed for the perimeter. Elyana needs measurements for the gates and the perimeter fencing," Maddy said.

"Wouldn't Fergus do a better job of this than me?" Kerry asked, sounding grouchy at hell, which was unlike him. The falcon had solemn and sulky down to an art form, but he rarely questioned an order.

"Fergus is handling other matters for me," Maddy said decisively, ending the conversation. "While you're there, you can give this to Grace for me." There was a hint of humor in her voice and from where he stood, he saw her holding back a smirk.

Kerrygan's jaw clenched, and Fergus frowned again, wondering what the hell was up with him. The safe house was a brilliant idea. All the wardens had pitched in to clean the place out and volunteered their time for once it was up and running.

So why in the seven hells would Kerry resent going there? Fergus drew on his cigar, knowing he was going to catch hell for smoking inside. He meant to put it out but forgot upon entering. All these new fecking rules since Maddy got pregnant. He shook his head in disgust. This was his home, too.

Kerrygan took the letter and gave Maddy a brisk nod before leaving. He cocked a brow at Fergus, asking, "Eavesdropping again, flame thrower?"

"Nah, jest like watching ye pout, falcon."

585

Kerry's scowl turned into a snarl, reminding Fergus that some days, the man was less human than the rest of them. His display made Ferg chuckle, which probably didn't help the situation. Oh well, he wasn't in a people-pleasing mood today.

"My turn?" he asked Maddy, dropping into a wing-back leather chair in front of her desk before she could answer.

"About time you dragged your scrawny ass in here," she snarled. Her eyes roved over him. "Been meaning to ask, who beat the snot out of you?"

Fergus blew out a disgusted breath, realizing he'd forgotten his glamour and said, "Roarke. And before ye go all mama bear on me, he had good reason."

"I'm listening," Maddy said, steepling her hands and tapping her forefingers lightly. Her eyes narrowed, noticing the smoke. "And put that damn thing out."

Ferg drew in another drag before walking to the window and tossing the butt outside. "Sorry, I forgot."

Plopping his ass back down, he ran his hands over his face and filled her in on the auction he attended, the young girl he purchased, and the brother he'd pissed off. When he finished, he sat there in silence, waiting for her to hand his ass to him, too.

Maddy's eyes locked on his for a long time. "You did the right thing, Ferg. As difficult as it might have been and as wrong as it must have felt, you had no other choice. You were there to gather intel. You were alone, and you were not prepared to extract anyone."

She stood, pressing her balled hands into her lower back as she moved around the front of her desk. Leaning against it with her hands braced on either side of her, she faced him. "Much as it pains me to admit it, you have fantastic instincts."

Fergus chuckled at her back-handed compliment.

"You were right about Sabbath—so far. We'll have to wait and see if that partnership holds up long term." Maddy's eyes narrowed at him. "Will you be able to get back on board for the coming auctions?"

"I believe so." Ferg tipped his head, considering the question. "Unless there's something unique for each one that I'm not aware of, I don't see why not." He grinned. "And I've got an undercover warden on the inside."

"An agent. That's interesting." She rocked in her chair. "Well, put the auctions and showcases on your dance card. You're about to become a regular at these events." Her voice sharpened and her eyes narrowed as they snapped to his. "And work on your poker face. I'm sure you'll see a lot worse before this is over."

Ferg said nothing, staring back at her without a sound. "I'll do that." He stood and made his way to the door. "To hell with what it costs me." His voice was solemn, resigned.

Maddy's shoulders sagged. "I know what it costs you, Ferg, and I hate it. But you're our only way in. When we find another way, I'll take you out of there."

Her voice was so soft he barely heard her. Ferg turned back to her and shook his head. "No. Ye won't, lass. This is mine to bear." Taking another step, he heard her clear her throat.

"Ferg, there's one more thing we need to discuss."

"Don't mean ta be rude, Mads, but me head is fecking pounding."

Maddy's tone was apologetic, which scared him more than their last conversation. He raised a brow at her, waiting for the other shoe to fall. "You're going to be busier than usual with this problem and with helping Elyana." Her fingers worried the bracelet on her wrist, and she wouldn't meet his eyes.

A sinking feeling hit his gut. "What have ye done, Maddy, luv?"

She took a steadying breath and met his eyes. Fidgeting, he knew the next words that came out of her mouth were gonna piss him off.

"Morganna will be here tomorrow to take over your duties on the island for the summer." She rushed through the explanation, seeing the scowl forming. "You're welcome to jump in any time you are free. This is only temporary."

Fergus stared at her—glared at her might be more accurate. "Only temporary, my ass," he said. "That wench has been waiting for any opportunity to get her foot in the door here, and ye jest invited her in."

Shaking his head, he ran a hand through his hair. "I'se always trusted ye to have me back, Maddy." Ignoring the way her face fell, he continued, "Didn't expect ye to stab me in it."

"Ferg, wait..." she pleaded. "It's not like that."

"Keep telling yerself that, lass." Scuffing the toe of his boot on the floor, he shook his head. Without another word, he walked away, tossing over his shoulder, "Why in the ever luving feck did ye think I'd be ok with her on the same continent as me?"

Ferg didn't give her a chance to answer. He just stomped down the hall. Last, he knew his nemesis had been in Europe. With one sentence, Maddy had sent him reeling. "Mother fecking Morganna," he muttered. "What did I fecking do to deserve this?"

106

Island Law

Madylyn SkyDancer sat in a captain's chair behind a table on the raised dais. This was the courtroom where she represented the Elemental High Court. From her perch, she stared in disgust at the men in chains seated before her. An emergency Warden's Court had been called in the name of Island Law.

Island Law was a form of justice that could be called on by anyone who had been grievously injured or attacked. Island Law did not apply to petty theft, arguments, or land disputes. But it applied in cases of kidnapping, aggravated assault, manslaughter, and rape.

Today, they were addressing all four of the charges in a rare, closed-door session. Madylyn had been the Head Mistress of the Heart Island Sanctuary for four-hundred years, and she dreaded where this day would take them. But it was her duty to stand witness and mete out sentences.

Wilmont Curly, Arno Shore, and Fjord Smyth stood before her with their heads hung low. They had just confessed to being hired by Sebastion, "Sir," Barrow to cause a ruckus on Heart Island. They all denied knowledge of the theft of the hatchlings before they docked.

All three of the men balked at antagonizing the dragons. Only under extreme duress—in the form of threats to their families—did they finally agree to help Sir. Sir neither denied nor confirmed their accusations.

"Each of you shall serve a term of two years upon a prison ship. Your families are welcome to meals in the public dining hall anytime they wish during your incarceration. You will work on the ship to provide additional support to assist with their housing."

"Was it worth it?" Maddy asked, staring at them as they shook their heads. "You broke the law for a quick profit, and now your families will suffer your loss. You will suffer whatever whim the captain believes suits your crimes." She gave them a moment for that to settle in. "Be grateful the

dragons are allowing you to live," she snapped, having no sympathy for the imbeciles.

She did, however, have sympathy for the women and children they were leaving behind. 'Twas not their fault that their men made such poor choices. "They have fifteen minutes to say their goodbyes outside, and then they will be remanded to the captain waiting at the docks."

The bailiffs led the men and their weeping families out of the courtroom. Lachlan Quinn, her law guardian, called for Sebastian Barrow to step forward. He shuffled forward, his leg chains rattling as he moved.

"Mr. Barrow," Madylyn said, trying with great difficulty to stay professional. There was no one else nearby to try the case, so she could not recuse herself. "You stand accused of trying to abduct two of the dragon hatchlings. In the process of committing this crime, a man died, and a child, Landon Pathfinder, nearly died. How do you plead?"

"I'se jest out for a stroll with a few friends. They'se the ones that wanted the wee ones to sell in the dark circles. I'se jest along for the ride." He had the audacity to bat his eyes at her.

"I interviewed the three other men charged, individually, yet all three of their stories are identical." She picked up a stack of papers and slammed them on the table. "I have eyewitness accounts of the events that unfolded the evening of the solstice, proving that you are lying."

"You gots a bunch of kids who will say anything ye tell them, too," he sneered. "'T'aint reliable."

"Mr. Barrow, do you deny holding a child over the edge of a cliff and kicking a burlap bag, holding a small creature, over the same cliff?"

"I'se jest trying to save the wee lad. He tripped, and I grabbed for him to help him find his balance." His voice was trite with the assumption that he could weasel his way out of this situation.

Madylyn's eyes glittered dangerously at his lies. "Did you not say, and I quote, 'Come any closer, and we'se gonna see if he can fly.'"

Sir chuckled, his chest rattling in a moist cough. "Yeah, I mights have said something like that."

"Doesn't sound like much of a rescue to me. Sounds like you threatened to harm a child—my child. You also harmed an innocent creature under my protection."

Sir stared at her, his hostile eyes glowering dangerously. He offered nothing further in his defense, but this mere slip of a woman wouldn't cow him.

Maddy studied him, grateful he wouldn't survive the night. This man would have become a deadly enemy if he lived. "Sebastian Barrow, I find you guilty of threatening the welfare of a child and the dragon hatchlings under my care. Your punishment will be determined by the injured parties."

She picked up her gavel and slammed it down. The sound of finality rang out.

"Ronan Pathfinder, how would you like this man's sentence carried out?"

Ronan stood, not wasting his time, glancing at the man in chains. "I would like Sabbath to verify our findings, and then I want him to know exactly what my son experienced as he fell off that cliff. Then I want him to comprehend the anguish I felt."

Sebastian cackled. "That's the best ye got? Pussy."

Ronan turned his head and met the man's eyes. "I wasn't done, you arrogant prick. When the NightMare finishes with him," he smiled then as the man before him paled, "I will be satisfied with the outcome after Alejandro and Isabella have their due. They have claimed parental rights for their hatchlings, whom you abducted. They nearly perished because of your actions."

"'Tis not right allowing those animals to decide me fate, Mistress…" Sir whined as he exhibited the first indications of fear.

"You acted like an animal, so it's only appropriate that the ones you wronged end your life. And so, it is." Maddy's gavel came down once again, cementing the man's fate. "We will carry out your sentence at dusk tonight."

"Ye'se no right to sentence me, ye cunt. How's that fair when that's yer man, and it was yer brat that's involved?"

Maddy stood, her fury evident by the gale blowing through the room. "You've received a much fairer sentence than the one this cunt would've given you." Her midnight blue eyes blazed with the fire of righteousness. "I would've made you suffer for months before I gave you permission to die. Be grateful I was not the one in charge of your sentencing." She nodded to the bailiff, who led away the man who'd nearly destroyed her world.

"This next case involves a minor. I'll have the room cleared of everyone but the necessary parties."

Taking her seat, she accepted the next file that Lachlan handed her. She dreaded this one the most, knowing the pain it had already caused one of her students. The trial and conviction would surely add additional trauma, and she hated that Collette's testimony was necessary to prosecute Eaton. Maddy took a moment to gather her thoughts before beginning.

"Eaton Sparks, I charge you with the ongoing physical and sexual assault of your stepsister Collette Creek. How do you plea?"

"Not guilty, Mistress." Eaton stood rod-straight, eyes meeting hers and chest out proud as he faced his fate. "My stepsister and I had a consensual sexual relationship that she initiated when we both were under the age of consent. She loved every minute," he said with a side glance at Collette.

Maddy steepled her hands under chin as she listened to the lies this young man was spouting. She knew he lied by the tone of his voice and the

energy surrounding him. The horror and revulsion crossing Collette's face only confirmed her suspicions.

Collette's father sat there silently, holding his daughter's left hand. Lash held her right. The tic in Adrian's cheek and his clenched fist were the only signs of how much control he was exerting to remain seated. His wife sat next to her son on the other side of the room. Tension swirled between the two halves of the family, thick and ugly.

Adrian Creek had been inconsolable when Maddy explained what happened the night of the solstice. The agony radiating from him when he realized his only child nearly killed herself because of the ongoing abuse pierced her heart as a parent.

Today, Maddy could see the ravages of guilt and rage etched in the lines of his face and the hollows beneath his eyes. His lack of attention to his daughter created a chasm between them that hadn't been there when her mother was alive. His negligence at home took an immeasurable toll on their relationship because his daughter no longer felt safe coming to him. Collette paid a painful price for the woman he brought into their family and her sadistic son. Maddy doubted he'd ever forgive himself for not being there for her.

Lash's eyes simmered with fury as Eaton continued speaking. "The first time she snuck into my room, I awoke with her lips around my cock," he said, trying to look ashamed and failing miserably. "I tried to fend her off, but…" The smile returned as he added, "She was so persistent, I didn't want to disappoint her."

Collette shrieked in protest, trying to go over her father to get to her lying abuser. Adrian gathered her in his arms and whispered in her ear, calming her as angry tears slid down her face. Lash's glare promised retribution at a later date as he stood staring into Eaton's eyes. "Justice will be served," he hissed, a sound that barely reached Maddy's ears. "I promise you will regret ever looking at her."

"You're just jealous I got there first," Eaton retorted.

"ENOUGH." Maddy's voice cracked through the air like a whip. "Take your seats. I will not tolerate your disrespect in my courtroom. This court isn't a sparring ring. Save it for outside." She gave Lash a pointed glare. He gave her a curt nod, understanding what she was saying. Lash would get his turn. He took his seat, wrapping an arm over Collette's shoulders and whispering soothingly to her.

"Do you have anything else to add to your defense?" Madylyn asked Eaton.

"I responded to Collette's advances like any other hot-blooded male would." His words were callous, amused even. "With every glance and every

sway of her hips, she invited me in. Every tight piece of clothing she wore was meant to tease me."

His eyes were glossy with lust as he thought of Collette. "The fantasies she projected on our link called for me to satisfy her heat." His chained hands rubbed at his crotch, getting off on the memory. "When she finally came to my room, I knew she was ready to take our relationship further."

The young man was delusional, and Maddy's disgust was obvious. She no longer tried to hide the way this man made her feel as she clenched her jaw and her eyes narrowed.

Eaton smirked at Adrian. He knew this would not end well for him, but he'd be damned if he was going out without sharing some of the blame. "We're not related in any way that matters. Collette was afraid of what her daddy would think if she gave in." His voice dropped to a pouty whisper. "But Daddy was too busy fucking everything but my mother to pay attention to his lost little girl."

His mother gasped beside him, but Eaton straightened his shoulders, his cold, empty eyes meeting Madylyn's. His voice hardened. "It was my duty as her brother to give her the attention she so desperately needed." His voice changed to a silky leer as he turned back to Adrian and continued. "You told me that the first time we met."

Horror crossed Adrian's face as Eaton continued in a mockery of Adrian's voice. "You'll have a little sister, and I'll need you to look after her for me when I can't be there." His lips quirked in a smirk as he glanced at his stepfather. "And you were rarely home."

Adrian's face lost all color as Eaton continued with his cruel lies. "And believe me, Daddy, it was my *pleasure* to be there for her when you neglected us. I looked out for Collette, and I looked in on her late at night while she slept—and she sleeps so deeply."

Eaton licked his lips. "I'd slip in and pull the sheets back just so I could do what you told me. If I jerked off while I was there, who could blame me?" His eyes flicked to Collette. "She's a beautiful little tease."

Collette's fists clenched in silent fury.

Eaton gave her an indulgent smile. "But I showed her what it takes to make a man happy. I taught her she needed to keep her mouth shut and her legs open anytime I wanted her. And I anticipated the days when she fought back because then she earned the consequences of disobeying me."

A blur passed as Adrian vaulted over the aisle and grabbed Eaton by the neck with one hand and started swinging with the other. The court watched in shock, and Maddy let it go on for a few moments before calling for the bailiffs to break it up.

Adrian's face was purple, and he was breathing hard when they pulled him back to his seat. He sank to the bench, elbows on his knees and hands tangled in his hair as he tried to regain control over his volatile emotions.

Eaton choked on his own blood as Maddy peered down at him. "Have you no control over your courtroom?" he shouted. "Charge this man with assault," he roared, glaring up at her.

"I'm sorry," Madylyn said, tipping her head. "I didn't see anything." Madylyn gazed at the crowd. "Did anyone witness this assault? Can anyone in attendance back up his claims?"

No one, not even his mother, came to his defense. Maddy cocked an eyebrow at him. "Do you have anything to actually offer in your defense? Any witnesses?"

"My mother witnessed Collette's enticing behavior. Tell them," he growled at her.

Lachlan swore the woman to truth telling and took his seat. Ashlyn Sparks-Creek stood up and faced Madylyn's piercing gaze.

"Do you have something to add that will help in your son's defense?" Maddy asked in an icy tone.

"*Tell them*," Eaton growled at her.

The woman jerked as she gaped at her son. "This won't help your case, Eaton," she whispered, begging him with her eyes to let it go.

He bared his teeth at her and snarled. She jerked back; her fear clear as she stepped away from him. "I d-d-did see them together," she finally choked out.

"Where did you see them and what were they doing, Mrs. Creek?"

"In her room, late one night." Her gaze turned on Collette with sad eyes. "I walked in, thinking she was asleep. You see, I wanted to leave a note for her to find the next morning." She swallowed a lump in her throat, trying to continue. "Collette was on her knees with her mouth on Eaton. He'd pinned her against the bed with his legs, holding her arms at her sides as he slid in and out of her mouth." Her voice trailed off as she remembered the scene.

"Did Collette seem to enjoy herself during this encounter?" Madylyn asked.

Ashlyn's face crumpled. "No. Tears were streaming down her face, and bruises covered her forearms from where she'd struggled against him. Vile things spewed from his mouth."

"Why didn't you stop him?" Maddy asked with thinly veiled disgust.

Shoulders sagging, she wrung her hands. "He screamed at me to keep my mouth shut, or he'd kill me." She sobbed, covering her mouth with a dainty handkerchief. "I believed him. I don't know how I ever gave birth to such a monster."

"She was a child, and you did nothing?" Adrian roared. "I would have protected you if you'd come to me."

Ashlyn sobbed harder, eyes pleading with him. "Forgive me, Adrian. You're right, I should have come to you."

"Forgive you? I can't even fucking look at you without wanting to strangle you right now."

Madylyn didn't know if she believed Ashlyn or if the woman was playing on Adrian's sympathies to save her marriage, but she'd heard enough from her. Collette deserved the opportunity to tell her story. Gazing at the young woman, she asked gently, "Would you like to say anything?"

Collette nodded, stepping forward and meeting Lachlan. Sworn in, she kept her eyes on Maddy, refusing to give him any power over her.

Collette laughed ruefully. "The first week after they moved in with us, my father told Eaton he was to be in charge of the household whenever he was gone." Her lips quirked in a wry grin.

"Daddy reminded Eaton constantly that he was the man of the house when he left us to take care of business. Eaton took that title to heart and created reasons to discipline me when Daddy left..." Her voice faded away as her eyes recalled the horror of living with him.

"My stepbrother found every excuse to cause me unimaginable pain. When he first moved in with us, it was minor bruises at first. A pinch here or a slap there because I misbehaved."

"As we got older, he was a lot bigger than I was—taller, stronger. He watched me like a predator, always waiting until I was alone or until I walked out of a room." She laughed humorlessly.

"He'd lurk in the shadows outside the dining-room door. Covering my mouth to keep me quiet, he'd bite down on the muscle of my shoulder or squeeze my arms so hard they bruised while he eavesdropped on our parents as they squabbled."

Her hand went to her left shoulder, rubbing as if it still hurt all these years later. "Sometimes he'd pin me to the wall while he ground his groin against me, whispering all the nasty things he wanted to do to me."

"I thought he was bluffing, just trying to scare me more," Collette said in a choked whisper. She blinked, unaware of the tears rolling down her cheeks. "But I was a naïve fool because he started acting out those threats about six months ago. Stealing into my room in the middle of the night, he'd touch me, using his fingers to probe into places that didn't belong to him." A shudder rolled through her.

Collette wiped her nose with the back of her hand. "He'd make me use my hands on him or my mouth." Sniffling, she went on. "He loved to be in control, and to decide whether I was allowed to breathe while he choked me with his cock," Colette said. "Sometimes he'd cover my nose at the same time until I was on the verge of passing out. He'd let me take one breath, and then he'd start all over again."

"After he started visiting me in the dark, I could count on a visit from him every night unless daddy was home." She didn't glance at her father

when she heard him curse behind her. "He wasn't home much." Her voice faded to a monotone.

"Just weeks before I came here, he raped me for the first time—actually, it was thrice in the boathouse. He threatened to tell everyone I begged him to fuck me if I tattled." A shudder ran through her, and her voice cracked. "I was so ashamed, so I told no one. He took my silence as permission to rape me every chance he could thereafter."

Clearing her throat, she continued. "If Mistress Danyka hadn't stopped him, he would have taken me against the wall outside of the restrooms on the night of the solstice. 'Twas the first time I fought back." Her head turned to Eaton then. "It was good to give back some pain instead of always taking it."

Clearing her throat, her eyes met Madylyn's. "I don't know what else to say or how much detail you need me to go into. But the one thing I swear to you is that I never encouraged him by anything I said or did. This wasn't what I wanted, and I'm tired of hearing it was."

Collette faced Eaton and said in a clear, firm voice, "I won't give you another thought when you're gone because you don't deserve to take up space in my memories."

The room was silent as she returned to her seat. Adrian pulled her into his arms as she approached. Collette let him hold her for a moment before sitting back down next to Lash. He reached out a hand—palm up—and waited for her to interlace her fingers with his. He pressed a kiss against her knuckles, letting her lean her head against his shoulder.

The air was rife with misery. Heartbreak radiated from Ashlyn, knowing her son wouldn't live to see the end of the day. Eaton finally recognized that things weren't looking good for him. His expression was a cross between fear and outrage.

Waves of guilt and rage were drowning Adrian. Collette, on the other hand, was at peace, knowing Eaton would never hurt her again and that she would get her due.

Madylyn sat for a few more moments before reaching a verdict. It wasn't difficult, but she gave the appearance of thinking about the testimonies she'd heard. "Collette Creek, I am truly sorry for the pain this man has caused you. Mistress Danyka corroborated your story about the events that she witnessed, as did Master Jameson Vance. Neither could be here today, but I have their sworn testimonies about the evening in question."

"Eaton Sparks, I find you guilty on multiple counts of statutory rape and assault." Maddy's gaze glinted dangerously at him. "Say your goodbyes today, for you're out of time. Island Law will take effect come sunset. Collette Creek or her father, Adrian Creek, as is his right as the parent of a

minor, will enforce this order. The Creeks have permission to castrate you and end your life in any way they please."

Ashlyn wailed at her son's side, one hand covering her mouth as she sobbed in horror. Despite being aware of the penalties handed down to rapists, she never expected to see her son convicted of this heinous crime.

Adrian stood up unexpectedly and addressed Madylyn. "Forgive me. But if it pleases the court, I would also like to petition for the dissolution of my partnership with Miss Sparks. Under the guise of ignorance, she knowingly allowed her son to repeatedly harm my daughter. I can no longer cohabitate, nor will I continue to support her."

Ashlyn's sobs grew louder. "Adrian, please don't do this. I love you, and I love Collette.

His head whipped around at her words. "If you had one ounce of love for her, you never would have permitted her to be harmed. Do not speak to me again. You are dead to me. Be grateful that I don't petition the court for your death tonight as well for allowing these atrocities."

His gaze returned to Maddy. "If it pleases you, Mistress, I wish to legally sever all my ties to this woman. I need to focus on my daughter."

Adrian bowed deeply, praying Maddy would take pity on him and settle this manner right now. He couldn't face the thought of a long separation and future court dates.

Maddy tapped a nail against her lips. She rarely presided over family court matters during criminal court. "Because of extenuating circumstances, I grant your request. All ties—personal, legal, and otherwise—are hereby dissolved. You are both free to live your lives separately—one from the other.

"The court denies alimony. Miss Sparks, had you cared for anyone other than yourself, the outcome of so many things could have been different. Your lack of action has altered the course of multiple lives."

Maddy shook her head in disgust. "I sentence you to find your own way. You leave this building with the clothes on your back and nothing more. Should Adrian choose to ship your belongings to you or provide any additional financial assistance, that will be at his discretion. This court absolves him from any financial responsibility regarding you."

Madylyn stood. Striking her gavel, she said, "Court's dismissed."

The bailiff came for Eaton. As he dragged him by Collette, Eaton looked at her and sneered. "I'd do it again. You were the tightest fuck of my life."

His dark chuckle echoed in the courtroom. "And in the dark of night, when the stairs creek and your door glides open, letting in that tiny sliver of light, will you see your lover joining you, or will your heart race in fear? Will you see my face in the dark when he slips inside you?" His chuckle was evil. Eaton knew where to hit her and how to torment her even after he was gone.

Before Adrian could react, Lash beat him to it, pounding the ever-loving fuck out of him. And if the bailiff stepped back and let it happen, no one would hold it against him. The father of three daughters, he'd have done the same.

The courtroom emptied. Ashlyn wailed as she trailed behind her condemned son. Maddy paused as she made her way past the Creeks. Taking Collette's hands in hers, she said, "I didn't make it a court order, but you will seek counseling. Rhy will set it up. This is non-negotiable."

Collette's eyes flared for a moment, but then her defiance faded. "Yes, Mistress SkyDancer."

Maddy nodded, glancing at Adrian next. "Whatever she needs, you damn well better provide for her. You have a lot to make up for. If you fail this time, she will become my ward."

Adrian nodded, pulling Collette closer. "I won't fail. I just hope I can earn her trust and get the chance to do better."

"Lash," Maddy said, holding out her arm. "I'd like you to escort me back to my office."

"My pleasure, Mistress," he said. Turning to Collette, he said, "I'll see you later." His gaze landed on Adrian, but he didn't ask for his permission. Adrian nodded at him.

They walked away, and when they exited the room, Maddy said, "She's going to need a lot of extra care."

"I understand that."

"Collette needs to regain her self-esteem and her self-respect. It may be a long time before she's ready for another physical relationship. How do you feel about that?"

Lash gave her question the consideration it deserved. "I've waited a long time for her to appear in my life. I'm in no hurry. We'll take our time. I'll help her in any way that I can."

They'd reached the top of the stairs. Maddy turned to him and framed his face in her hands. "You are our future, Lash. You have a good heart and a sense of decency many lack. I trust you with her, but I worry about the toll this relationship may take on you."

Lash's eyes crinkled, and he brushed his lips against her cheek. "She's worth it, Maddy. Thank you for your concern."

Maddy smiled at him and stepped back. "That's all I need to know." She tipped her head towards the stairs. "Go to her."

Entering her suite, she stripped, wanting to shower and get the filth of the courtroom off of her. She would need to do it again later tonight after the execution, but she refused to wait that long. This was one of those days that reminded her how difficult it was to hold the power of life over death.

597

But when it came to anyone abusing children, the penalty in her courtroom would always be torment and death.

107

Demons In My Head

The peregrine falcon perched on the headstone until the intruder faded away from her world. Had he even been real? Danny waited half an hour before gliding over the field of flowers and shifting back into her inner child form.

In reality, her body had matured. But here—in this world—in her safe place, she retained the innocence and hope that they had savagely stripped from her in her youth.

The sky cleared as her mood calmed, and she thought herself a new dark purple dress. The color brought out the complexity of changeable colors in her eyes.

A canopied bed popped into existence in front of her. The soft-white curtains blew gently around her as she climbed onto the soft, down featherbed. Pulling a white duvet up to her neck, she rested her head on the fluffy pillow and closed her eyes. Nearly drifting off in the warm cocoon, her eyes popped back open.

Where was Sir Vance? Did the strange man take him away? Breathing raggedly as panic set in, her eyes scanned the flowers, hoping he'd dropped her bear somewhere nearby.

But wait, what was that over there by the headstone? Memories of him walking with his arms outstretched skittered through her mind. Her falcon observed as he gently placed her bear there for to reclaim. His actions confused her. Was it a trick?

Scrambling off the bed, she raced for the bear. Snatching him up and hugging him tightly to her, she ran back to the bed. Climbing back in, she pinned him to her chest and snuggled down into the hollow she'd created earlier. Warm and safe, she closed her eyes and let her tired mind drift off into a sound sleep that she desperately needed, praying that the voices of her past and the demons in her head would remain silent for just a little while.

Walls slammed up in her mind to protect her while she slept. As she faded from consciousness, she thought she heard his voice again. The man from this morning.

Gently, he spoke to her with care and mayhap love. Longing filled his voice as he whispered a phrase over and over to her.

"Let me in, Hellion. Please, just let me in."

Her inner child didn't know how to feel. Jamey seemed nice, polite even. But harsh lessons had taught her that men lied, and they made promises they never intended to keep. The child burrowed deeper into her safe place.

Meanwhile, the scarred woman buried deeper inside of her also heard his voice. She longed to reach for him because he sounded so sad. His voice warmed a part of her, and she remembered why he felt safe, warm, and right. He felt like home.

But the trauma from the past few days prevented her from responding to him. Battered too many times, her mind and body had shut down. The fucker reappearing from her past had shattered not only her sense of safety, but all of her self-defense mechanisms were gone.

Danyka was sick of picking herself back up and dusting herself off. She was so fucking tired of it all. The inner walls protecting her were thicker now and getting higher, muting his pleas. She lay in the dark, trying to drown out the horrors in her head.

And then the demons of doubt woke and began whispering to her.

"You're not good enough for him. He deserves better than a washed-up whore like you."

Then her sister, the demon of incredulity, piped up. *"What kind of Warden are you? Do you hate your partner that much? If he's lucky, mayhap next time you'll actually get him killed."*

Their voices slithered through her psyche like maggots in her brain, destroying any self-esteem she'd regained since his accident. They called on their sister demons, who chimed in like an ill-timed chorus in a tragic play.

"Do you honestly think you can be faithful to any man? Ye'll give him the pox."

"He'll never love you…"

"Jamey needs a woman who doesn't talk and fuck like a sailor in a strange port."

"He'll want children. What kind of mother would you be?"

"How many men have you fucked?"

"Ye'll get bored with someone that nice."

"Jamey and Danny, sitting in a tree. Danny runs off and fucks a stranger for free."

"He'll get tired of cleaning up your messes the morning after, especially when you've been out all night without him."

"How many times is he willing to have a threesome so you can get your jollies?"

"He'll never love you…never ever ever."

"Yer just a puzzle he wants to put together, a problem for him to fix—then what?"

"Jameson Vance deserves better than a woman one step away from a mental breakdown."

"How many nights will your nightmares let him sleep?"

"He'll get one feel of your overused pussy and realize you're not worth all this bullshite."

"He'll never trust ye when yer out alone."

"He'll never love you...nope, nope, nope."

On and on they went until she curled tighter into herself, covered her ears with her hands, and started screaming to drown them out. When her voice gave out, she rocked herself back and forth, chanting, "They're not real, they're not real, they're not real…"

A maniacal laugh escaped her occasionally as her inner asshole jumped up and asked, *"How the fuck would ye know what's real anymore? Look around, twat. Taint much real 'bout where ye'se at."*

The voice quieted for a moment before leaving her with one last thought. *"Girl, ye either needs to get on board this crazy train or jump the fecking tracks. Yer running outta time to linger in the in-between. Clock's a tickin'.'"*

And there in the distance, she saw a massive grandfather clock. Ornate, like the intricate walnut one in the drawing room of the Sanctuary, it mocked her from afar. Lightning arced back and forth between the dark cumulonimbus clouds surrounding it.

The enormous timepiece perched precariously on top of a mountain. A massive pendulum swung back and forth, making the base rock on the unsteady foundation. Pebbles cascaded from beneath it every time the weight shifted, making it lean heavily to the left.

The muted ticking, coming from its haphazard movements, was off-key and barely recognizable. Thick tendrils of fog caressed the scratched glass on the face of the clock, obscuring the time and teasing her with glimpses of the hour hand.

But Danny knew what time it was. Her gut knew the truth—the time for her to resurface was running out.

108

You Won't Need These Where You're Going

Collette stood on the dock, watching the sky change colors. Day's end was upon them. The time had come to claim her pound of flesh.

Her hands shook as she thought of all the horrible things she wanted to do to Eaton. It should be enough that he would never hurt her again, or hurt anyone, for that matter.

But it wasn't. She wanted him to suffer as she had suffered. Collette needed him to experience the pain, trauma, and shame that she still felt.

Working in the stables as a punishment had brought her into contact with Sabbath, the NightMare queen. They had bonded in some freakish way that Collette didn't want to examine too closely. All she knew was that the mare brought her comfort when her demons raised their heads.

Hell's equine listened to her this afternoon when she'd gone there seeking comfort. Sabbath offered to absorb her rawer emotions, and Collette accepted the offer, needing to focus on what came next, not what was past.

Sabbath explained how her gifts worked and how she could use them to help others or to drive them bat-shit-fucking crazy. Collette's words, not Sabbath's.

The young woman spent most of the afternoon contemplating the loss of life justice demanded and what she *needed* this event to provide her—vengeance.

Eaton's death would give her peace of mind because he could no longer inflict pain on anyone. But her inner voice questioned if she'd ever find peace.

Would slicing off his body parts have the same effect as fucking with his mind over years? She didn't know the answer to that, and she wasn't sure what it said about her that she'd contemplated his endless torment.

Maddy called Collette into her study earlier, making sure the legal system understood the victim's requests. The Elemental High Court would carry

out her wishes tonight, and its Head Mistress had been happy to oblige Collette's special request.

A shadow fell across her, and she sensed more than saw Lash stepping into her. His arms came around her middle, pulling her back against his front. His chin rested on her shoulder, his soft breath tickling her neck. They stood there in comfortable silence for a few moments before he said in a solemn voice, "Baby, it's time."

"I know," she whispered. "Will you come with me?"

"Do you want me to?"

Her head nodded, and she squeezed his hands tightly. "Am I asking too much? I might scare you away after this." A wry laugh escaped.

Turning her in his arms, he cupped her face and gazed into her luminous eyes. "There is nothing in this world that will scare me away." He brushed a light kiss across his lips. "Not even you, baby."

Collette laughed. "We'll see."

They stopped by the stables. Ronan led Sabbath out by her reins. Placing a hand on Collette's shoulder, he gave her a solemn nod and asked, "Are you ready for this? There is no shame if you don't want to see this through. I promise he will get his due."

Collette nodded her head. "I need to finish this. I need to know it's really over before I can move on."

With a nod of understanding, Ronan led the way, with Sabbath by his side. They walked down the path leading to an isolated clearing used for these events. Hidden in a secluded part of the forest, it was far from where the students or residents could hear anything.

Maddy scanned the area for souls who didn't belong. The Romani children had an eerie fascination with Island Law. She wouldn't put it past the boys to sneak in to witness the executions. Erecting a bubble of air over the area to ensure the screams didn't travel, Maddy glanced at the crowd gathered as witnesses.

Two logs stripped of bark had been driven into the ground before them. Eaton stood, his hands manacled and chained above his head. Naked except for the chains, he stood there defiantly, glaring at them.

Sebastian Barrow, aka "Sir," stood to his left, shackled in the same manner.

Adrian waited with Madylyn for the rest to arrive. Ronan joined her, brushing a kiss over her cheek.

Collette took her place before Eaton. Lash stood on her right, and her father took his place on the left. She stared at her tormentor, trying to find something redeeming in him—just one reason to request mercy.

Eaton's dark eyes mocked her, traveling up and down her body. Leering at her, he still believed she was to blame for his sick needs. Even with the crowd watching, his cock twitched excitedly.

Kyran and Rhyanna joined the somber crowd as witnesses. Ashlyn Creek stood in front of them, silently weeping. Rhy wondered if it was for her son or for her lost fortune.

Ronan stood in front of Sebastian Barrow, with Sabbath beside him. Dust churned as Alejandro and Isabella landed behind the crowd to claim their due. Any cockiness Sir might have had evaporated as he gazed up at his doom.

The dragon's eyes glowed as their rage ignited. Steam rose from their nostrils as they patiently waited for their turn.

Madylyn stepped forward, desperately wanting this night to be over with. The rulings had been fair, and the judgments were righteous. Even knowing this, she didn't take lives without a lot of forethought and guilt.

It was a burden to possess the power of life over death. But she also had the power of mercy, which she had used on a rare occasion. Neither of these men qualified for her mercy.

Sir nearly killed her son, and even if it had been someone else's son, the ruling would have been the same. This man's flagrant disregard for the safety of a child and the sanctity of his life condemned him. Madylyn had no mercy in her heart to give him.

Eaton tortured and tormented a young woman without mercy. Collette's bullying stemmed from the physical and sexual abuse at his hands. The psychological and long-term ramifications of his abuse were yet to be seen.

After watching Danyka struggle for centuries, Madylyn had no mercy for anyone who abused men or women. And she vowed long ago that those who used their bodies as a weapon would know pain before they left this world.

"Sebastian Barrow and Eaton Sparks, you are guilty of crimes resulting in a death sentence." Maddy's voice rang out loud and clear. "I will not dignify your actions by reciting them once again. You know what you are being punished for. The opportunity was provided for you to say your last farewells. The time has now come to execute the sentences assigned to you through the Elemental High Court."

She stepped closer to the accused. "Acting on my authority as a lawgiver for the Elemental High Court, I sentence you to the following."

Maddy turned to Ronan and reached for Sabbath's reins. The massive NightMare walked towards her with what could only be called dainty steps. Maddy turned to the mare and leaned her head against the animal's forehead.

Sabbath reached out to Maddy, *"Your sentence is just Madylyn SkyDancer. Neither of these men would have changed their ways. Their thoughts are dark, and evil dwells within them. As an agent from Hell, I recognize their kind."*

"Thank you for your reassurance, Sabbath." The mare's words took the tiniest bit of guilt she felt at ending any life and transmuted it by carrying it away. *"When you requested a parlay from me through Fergus, I wasn't sure how you could have been of use to us. Then you proved yourself when you assisted us after Jamey's accident. The Sanctuary is grateful for your help."*

Maddy paused, knowing she needed to be respectful and yet firm when dealing with this queen. *"I apologize for the delay in setting up a parlay. You've requested to be of service on the island in a way that is beneficial to us both. And you've requested a place where you may roam freely."*

"Aye, Madylyn, that I have. No creature likes to live in a cage."

"There is a pasture on the bluff near where Alejandro and Isabella are raising their brood. Will you coexist in peace?"

"I have no ill intents towards the flying beasts. Let's be honest, if I piss them off, they'll torch me."

"Something tells me you are impervious to flames," Maddy said wryly.

Sabbath's amusement came through as a deep chuckle in Maddy's mind.

"Hmm." Maddy thought. *"I require your assurance that you will NOT tamper with any of the residents' or visitors' minds or fragile emotional states. Even one hint of impropriety will throw you all back into the stables."*

"Ye of such little faith, Madylyn. I will be an exemplary prisoner, as will my herd. You have my word."

"I'll hold you to that," Maddy said and then shifted the subject to the matter at hand. *"Do you understand your role in these proceedings?"*

"I do. You want these men to suffer in the same manner in which their victims suffered."

"Yes." Maddy gazed into her flame-red eyes and asked for clarification. *"What will they experience?"*

Sabbath's demeanor changed as she tapped into their mental grids. *"The old one will take Landon's place in the free fall. He will experience his terror. I will also show him what he put Ronan through."*

The horse let out a huffing sound and said, *"He is guilty of many more things, some of them quite vile. Should I make him share those experiences also?"*

"Absolutely," Maddy said. *"And the young one?"*

"Will come to experience the pain he's caused to Miss Collette. He will sense fear, self-doubt, shame, and the brutality and humiliation of being raped repeatedly. Have I missed anything?"

"No, Sabbath." Maddy swallowed hard, not wanting to be on the bad side of this creature. *"Will this harm you in any way?"*

The equine's humor resurfaced. *"Thank you for your concern, but this experience for me will be the equivalent of a good bottle of brandy for you. It will leave me warm, happy, and just a little giddy when it's over."*

Maddy shivered at her comparison. *"We have a compact, then?"*

"Yes, Mistress SkyDancer. We have a formal compact."

"Thank you, Queen Sabbath." Maddy bowed to the equine, showing her the respect due one of her status. *"Take it away."*

Maddy turned and led the mare forward, dropping the reins and returning to Ronan's side. He took her hand, squeezing lightly as she leaned against him. Maddy stared straight ahead, unwilling to look away from the punishment she imposed.

Sir shrieked and jerked in his chains. Arms flailing, he cried and pleaded for it to stop. His voice was shrill as he screamed, "I didn't mean to kill her. It was an accident."

Bruises in the shape of fingerprints appeared on his neck, and Maddy struggled to believe it had been an accident. Minutes passed, and he was finally silent, dangling from the chains as his knees gave out, no longer able to hold his weight.

Maddy raised a brow, unaware that Sabbath could manifest physical as well as mental damage. It was a fact the wardens needed to add to their literature. They knew too little about the mares and hounds from Hell. Every encounter taught them how much more fucking terrifying Hell's creatures were than originally believed.

Maddy waited until the sniffling began, then waved at the two bailiffs waiting nearby. They strode forward, uncuffing the middle-aged man. Unable to get his feet under him, they drug him quickly behind the rest of the crowd that had gathered. A hole opened, and they made their way through it until they stood in front of the dragons.

Following them, Maddy met Alejandro and Isabella's gaze. "We've finished with him. Do with him as you will." With a formal nod, she left them to their new toy. Isabella grabbed his foot in one talon and rose into the air with grace. Powerful movements of her wings helped her gain altitude. She continued climbing and then released the man.

His body fell quickly, his screams piercing the air. Just before he hit the tree line, Alejandro appeared, grabbing him just in the nick of time. Flapping his enormous wings, he climbed back up and tossed him to Isabella in midair. Nausea rolled through Maddy as she watched them toy with their prey, but she pushed it down.

This continued for a dozen more times until they grew bored. As Sir fell for the last time, Alejandro opened his maw, allowing fire to burst forth, charring the man. His screams faded away as Isabella caught him in her mouth. With three bites, the man ceased to exist, and his sentencing was complete.

Sabbath's glowing red eyes settled on Eaton. His head kicked back against the pole as bites and bruises appeared on his body, mirroring bruises Collette had once worn.

Adrian blanched as he glanced at his daughter with unending guilt and sorrow. Collette met his stare without flinching. She didn't offer him forgiveness. He hadn't earned it yet. When tears cascaded down his cheeks, she reached up and wiped them away.

"If I survived it," she whispered in an icy voice, "you can bear witness."

Her father nodded, clasping her hand tightly. His gaze turned to the man before them, noting the blood running down his thighs. Adrian choked back the bile rising in his throat as Eaton screamed in agony, much like Collette must have screamed for him. His body jerked as a phantom rapist violated him.

Collette remained unfazed and unwavering as she watched the man who stole her innocence being tormented in front of her. Numb, she felt no vindication, relief, or glee as she witnessed his torment. When he hung there spent, she stepped forward and picked up the thin curved blade waiting on a stump for her.

Grasping the blade, she faced the man who haunted her nightmares. She locked eyes with him and tried to find any redeemable quality in their pale depths. It was an exercise in futility.

Hands shaking, she took a breath. Both of the men behind her stepped forward. Her father whispered in her left ear, "You don't have to do this, Collette. Let me take this burden from you."

Her head whipped over her shoulder, and she glared at Adrian. "This isn't a burden. I am regaining my freedom." She kissed him on the cheek. "Thank you, Daddy, for the offer. But I'm taking back my power."

Without another word, she stalked forward until she stood nose-to-nose with Eaton. Bruises covered him from head to toe, as they should have. Blood leaked from numerous places on his body, as it should have. Lackluster eyes dulled with pain stared into her dark brown orbs.

The side of his mouth twitched, and she knew he was trying to leer at her, but she ignored him. When she just stood there, he snarled at her. "What else do you want from me, you little slut?"

And there it was, the spark she needed to ignite the tinder beneath her rage. Her wrath bubbled up, filling her with vengeance. She leaned in next to his ear as she reached down with her left hand and clasped his genitals tightly in her right.

"Oh, baby, that's good. You remember how I like it," Eaton said in a sultry whisper.

"Mother fucker," Adrian snarled from behind her at the same time that Lash growled, "You son of a bitch."

But Collette didn't give them a chance to intervene. With her lips nearly touching his ear, she said, "You better hope you're dead when the

hellhounds find you. Rumor has it they like to fuck their prey before they play with it."

"What the fuck are you talking about?" Eaton asked. "I'm gonna die standing right here. Are you gonna slit my throat with that knife? Maybe you'll let your *daddy* do it. Which is it gonna be?"

The way he sneered *"daddy,"* tripped something inside of her the same way it had when he sneered it in the courtroom. "I don't need a man to do anything for me anymore. You made sure of that. It's the only lesson I'll take from my time with you."

An evil chuckle erupted from him. "I'm imprinted on your soul. You won't find it so easy to purge me from your nights, li'l Lette. You don't have what it takes to kill me."

Collette smiled then, the first genuine one she'd managed in a long time. She hated that nickname. He'd always used it when he was about to hurt her. Her grip tightened painfully on his partially swollen cock and balls, pulling them towards her. "You won't need these where you're going," she hissed.

Before he could blink or process what she said, she brought her right hand down, slicing through everything that made him a man. Blood poured from the wound, drenching the ground in front of him and splattering the clothing she wore.

Eaton screamed in agony and sagged in his chains as his knees buckled. His eyes locked on the blood spurting from where his cock should be. The bits and bobs floating in the puddle beneath him quickly deflated.

"You fucking bitch," he snarled at her. "I curse you to know no pleasure of any kind. You will end up alone, wishing you had me to touch you because you will run everyone else off. You…"

His voice faded as Lash punched him in the face, stopping the curse from finishing. The Romani kept at it until Collette placed her hand on his arm. Shaking out his hand, he stepped back.

"Maddy, tell the hellhounds I left them something to play with in the forest," Collette said in a clear voice. Before Maddy could respond, she grasped Eaton's hair and jerked his head back, meeting his gaze.

"I may not have what it takes to kill you, but they do. After this moment, I will never think of you again, you piece of shit."

Before he could taunt her more, she released him, and he disappeared. She stood there breathing heavily as a weight lifted from her soul.

Collette wasn't foolish enough to think the nightmares would stop instantly. But during her waking hours, she wouldn't allow him to take anything else away from her. Eaton had taken enough.

Cool fingers grazed her right hand where she still gripped the knife. Lash's melodic voice said, "Baby, let me have this."

Her fingers relaxed, and she dropped the metal as if it had burned her. Turning away from the pole, she met her father's eyes. Collette saw pride

shining in them, and when he opened his arms, she stepped into them, finally allowing him to provide her with comfort.

Giving them a moment, Maddy gazed at Ronan, interlacing her fingers with his. *"Are you satisfied?"*

His fingers tightened on hers. *"I am. Didn't know dragon tossing was a thing,"* he deadpanned.

Maddy snorted next to him, trying to cover it with a cough. *"Why do I feel like I had very little control over the execution of this sentence?"*

"Are you disappointed? Think they got off too easy?" Ronan asked her with an arched brow.

"On the contrary. I wish I'd thought of it myself," she said with a grin as she headed for Collette.

"Are you all right?" she asked the young woman. "Are you satisfied?"

"I think so," Collette said, not really sure how to answer that question.

"If you need help to process anything that's happened recently…"

"I'll see Mistress Rhyanna," Collette answered, rolling her eyes.

"Come see me tomorrow. We need to discuss your abilities," Maddy said.

"Yes, mistress," Collette said. Scrunching up her nose, she asked, "Am I in trouble?"

Maddy rubbed her arm, giving her a smile. "No, but there's a time and place to use those gifts. We need to discuss some boundaries."

109

Time's Running Out

Jamey slept fitfully. He entered her dreamscape many times, not getting far before she kicked him out the moment she caught sight of him—each and every time. Physically and mentally exhausted, he showered, trying to relax so he could make another attempt.

Rhy came by every six hours to check on Danny now. Her body was struggling and needed nourishment. A healer could only keep her in suspended animation for so long before the body failed, and hers would soon.

His eyes burned, but he pushed his emotions down, refusing to give up hope. Finished, he grabbed a towel and roughly dried himself before slipping on a clean pair of silk sleep pants. Ripping a comb through his hair, he avoided the mirror, not wanting to acknowledge how rough he looked.

Dark circles under his eyes made his cheekbones sharper. That he'd only eaten the bare minimum over the past few days was evident in his lean appearance. Rhy had already been on his ass about it.

Didn't matter. Bringing Danny back to them was the only thing that did. If she didn't wake soon…. He refused to consider that option. Failure was not an option. He wouldn't lose her.

Mindlessly, he grabbed a few things off the tray in the sitting room to eat so that Rhy would stop bugging him about it. He drank three glasses of water, recognizing his body's need for hydration.

Walking into the bedroom, he leaned against the doorframe. His gaze lingered on the woman curled up in his bed. The view should have soothed him, but the only thing he could focus on was how frail his warrior appeared.

Danny had no extra weight to spare on her petite body, so going without food for days was taking a toll on her. Her gaunt cheeks concerned him, as well as the way her ribs were becoming more obvious.

Rhy had given her a sponge bath and changed the shirt she slept in, replacing it with another one of his. This one was a black. He loved seeing her in his clothes, but the stark color against her chalky skin was too much of a contrast.

Maddy dropped by earlier. She cuddled behind her for a while, holding her and singing to her. He left them alone, understanding she was trying to break through the barricades in her mind that Danny had slammed up in self-defense.

Hours later, Maddy left with tears in her eyes, heart aching for the woman whom she'd raised as a child and over the centuries had become like a sister to her.

Scrubbing his hands over his face, Jamey's shoulders drooped as he sat on the end of the bed, trying to formulate a plan before entering the forget-me-not world.

He closed his eyes, imagining the things that Danyka loved. They flashed like bullet points in his mind.

Danny's smile and the peals of laughter as she rode on Nizhoni, racing him across the fields of Wellesley. She always won. Her lighter form was easier on the animal. And his horse preferred her, if truth be told. A wry smile crossed his face.

Running the pool table with a cocky swagger and even cockier attitude as she took everyone's money.

The image of her with Maddy and Rhy, laughing and poking fun at the male wardens and men in general as they drank.

Listening to her and Fergus fighting over who was cheating this time became one of his favorite pastimes.

Then he jumped to the memories of them…

The first time she shifted into a falcon and soared high above him, screeching like a banshee because he couldn't catch her.

The first time they sparred, and she kicked his ass.

And there was the first of many times they got drunk together.

Their very first mission—and all the ones that came after as partners. Even in the thick of danger, the woman made him laugh. She always had his back and the first round at the bar afterwards.

Reluctantly, he witnessed their last mission together and how he'd nearly ruined everything with his jealousy. But they worked through it and came so close to finally having it all.

Jameson loved her more every day—even on the days she hurt him and tried to push him away. His mind drifted towards the intimacy they were developing.

The night Ronan and Maddy triggered a melding, they'd masturbated together in one of the hottest solo sessions of his life.

611

He'd never forget the sensation of her body melting against his when they danced together at Maddy and Ronan's pledge celebration. The familiarity of her body pressed against his when they'd never danced together before was a balm to his soul.

There was the first time he gave her an orgasm without even touching her, quickly followed by her bursting into tears and running away. Then she compelled him to forget on the same night when she opened up about her childhood abuse. *"I love you too much to let you remember my heartache."* Damn good thing he couldn't be compelled.

His body reacted to the images of the first time Danny kissed him—kissed anyone—straddling him on the beach after Rhyanna nearly died. Her petite form in his arms was like a dream come true. As they sought comfort in each other without taking their clothes off, he found hope that they just might have a future.

The scene at the Seaway popped up. That evening, he found her with someone else, but she let him in again. After sending her useless partner away, Jamey had given her multiple orgasms, taking nothing for himself because it was what she needed.

His only mission in life was to take care of all of her needs. Later that night, he'd taken his pleasure in the shower. Jerking off to the memory of her writhing in his arms had been beyond satisfying.

Danyka told him she loved him on the solstice and that she wanted him to make her his. She was already his, but she never let herself believe she was worthy.

And then McAllister took her and kept her in a fucking cage.

Eyes popping open, a plan formed. Maybe if he brought all of her favorite things to her...the thought trailed off as he climbed in next to her, pulling her close. His long fingers brushed her dark bangs off her forehead, and he pressed a kiss to its center. They trailed down over her sharp cheekbones, concern settling in his gut. The physical changes were becoming more visible. Her essence was fading.

Closing his eyes, he leaned his forehead against hers as he breathed in the heady scent of her. He began his litany again as his exhausted body relaxed into her. "Let me in, Hellion. Please let me in." This time, he added another plea. "I need you to come back to me Danny, time is running out."

A single tear trailed down his cheek. When the droplet reached his chin, it hovered for a moment before splashing onto her lips.

110

Rosella Diaries
Fourteenth Entry

Ella knocked on an ornate door leading to Pearl's private quarters. A maid opened the door and ushered her in. Head bowed, she stepped over to the side, awaiting further instructions.

Pearl sat behind a sleek, narrow desk in the corner of her sitting room. "I'll be right with you, Ella," she said without looking up.

A small table and chairs awaited them in the center of the room. A centerpiece of fresh, white lilies floated in a glass bowl, surrounded by tea lights. The aroma of fresh bread wafted to her from a covered basket, and Ella's stomach growled. Nerves had prevented her from eating this morning. She regretted that decision.

Trying to distract herself from her grumbling stomach, she observed her surroundings. Daylight streamed through sheer curtains along an entire wall of glass. Sheer valances hung over most of the windows, and floor-length sheers adorned the ends. The delicate fabric pooled on the floor atop a cream-colored, embroidered carpet, exquisite in design and execution.

She spied a massive king-sized bed through an archway on the right, leading to another room. Ella turned away as unwanted pictures of Jonah and Pearl ran wild through her mind. Images she couldn't unsee flitted across her mind's eye as she tried not to picture dainty little Pearl dwarfed beneath massive Jonah.

"Ella, you've my full attention now." Pearl's light melodic voice came from behind her.

Ella turned, surprised at her proximity because Pearl hadn't made a sound as she approached. Glancing down at the thick carpets and Pearl's bare feet, she understood why.

Pearl waved to the chair closest to her as she walked around the other side of the table. "Sit."

A bottle of wine sat chilling on the side. With a flick of her fingers, the young woman almost forgotten by the wall came forward to pour. Condensation formed on the outside of the glasses as they waited for her to finish.

"Leave us," Pearl instructed, reaching for a roll. With a raised eyebrow, she asked Ella if she wanted one.

"Please," Ella said as the tantalizing aroma tortured her. Slathering whipped butter onto the bread, she waited until Pearl took a bite before indulging. The salted butter and lightness of the roll were delicious. A moan of pleasure escaped before she could stifle the sound.

A hearty laugh erupted from her companion. "I love when you girls enjoy your meals. It's one of the slight comforts I can offer you. We've hired a new baker, and I'm assuming your reaction means you approve."

Wiping her mouth with the linen napkin, Ella nodded heartily. "I haven't had anything this wonderful since..." Her words died off, not wanting to bring up the last time she had been so lucky. "It's been a long time since I've enjoyed food this much."

"Well, don't be shy. There's plenty more. If you think the bread's good, wait until dessert!" Pearl's enthusiasm was childlike, and the genuine smile made her appear younger.

Removing the heavy sterling silver lid from a platter of food, Pearl set it to the side, then dished out tender pieces of filet mignon, buttered asparagus, and creamy whipped potatoes.

Pearl fed her girls well, but it wasn't as extravagant as this. Ella's mouth watered at the sight of the plate set before her. Waiting for her owner to begin, she cut a small piece and then closed her eyes in bliss as the first tender piece of beef met her tongue. Seasoned perfectly and medium rare, the meat was perfect.

"Tell me about yourself, Ella," Pearl said as she lifted a glass of wine to her lips. The glass dangled from her hand as she swirled the rich ruby liquid and waited for her to answer.

"What do you want to know?"

"Anything you'd like to share."

Ella chewed thoughtfully, not wanting to share anything with this woman but realizing she needed to answer her.

Keeping as close to the truth as possible, she said, "I'm the youngest of five. I excelled at school, and I enjoy music. I play the piano, violin, and mandolin, although I'm not much of a singer." She kept her voice soft, even though speaking of life before Pearl was painful.

"I wanted to be a teacher. Botany was my specialty. I loved spending time in the gardens at home and along the river." Glancing at Pearl, she thought she saw compassion in the woman's eyes.

"I miss walking outside most of all." She didn't add, "since my abduction," but she wanted to. No sense in poking a bear when there was nowhere to run.

Pearl was silent for a long while, staring into the wine that she swirled in her glass. Her voice was sad and held a hint of nostalgia when she spoke.

"I understand what you speak of more than you realize, Ella. I, too, loved being outside. The sensation of blades of grass between my toes with the sun beating down on my face made me feel so alive. I longed to lie out at night and watch the constellations, searching for falling stars."

Lifting the glass, she took a dainty sip and then finished the remaining wine before refilling it halfway. "I hated every moment of my first year in captivity."

Ella was silent but couldn't stop her eyes from widening in shock. She waited for Pearl to continue, wanting—no, needing—to learn more about her enemy.

"My tale differs from yours. My father lost my freedom in a game of cards and." Transfixed by the candlelight, she continued, "Yes, mine is different, but equally horrifying and tragic."

Ella sat there, stunned. Pearl never confided in her. Not knowing what to say, she waited without a sound, wanting to learn more.

Pearl's eyes were distant, remembering a time and place Ella couldn't see. "Much like you, I fought my first night in captivity. I spent my time in isolation, vacillating between fear and hatred. I was younger than you are and didn't understand their intentions for me."

Tapping her fingers against the glass, she continued. "As I realized where my life was heading, my hatred grew. Not wanting to remain a pawn for my entire life, I watched, and I learned. I worked my way up through the ranks until I became one of the most sought-after girls because I tolerated anything from the people who purchased me." Dark eyes flashed up to Ella's.

"Not because I wanted to do them, but because I needed powerful connections. I saved everything I earned. I hid my intentions from everyone because I trusted no one."

Brow raising, she met Ella's eyes. "That's a lesson you've yet to learn," she said with a sad smile, "but you will."

Ella swallowed hard, wondering who in her inner circle would betray her. Braden? Shaelynn? They were the only ones she ever confided in. The comment put her on edge, and she was loath to examine it too closely right now. She gave Pearl a nod, acknowledging the warning.

615

"I collected allies and enemies—powerful ones of both. They came to appreciate my business sense and my vision."

Long fingers idly played with her jade necklace, twisting the pendant between her slim fingers. "Then I found the muscle I needed to make it all happen." She laughed at the expression on Ella's face.

"Youth allows you the luxury to be swayed by outward appearances. Maturity teaches you to seek what's beneath the mask. I'm aware of the horror you view Jonah with, and I understand your fear of the man. His scars make him unattractive to you, ugly even. I see so much more in the man now than I did when he was, what you would call, handsome."

Ella lowered her eyes, unable to deny her statement. She'd heard the other girls whispering and wondering about the companion Pearl had showered with adoration. The comments were unkind to the man and to the couple. Although Ella didn't take part in the conversations, she understood their comments. "I recognize the genuine affection between the two of you."

Pearl cocked an eyebrow, surprise evident in her expression. "I'm glad someone does. Our relationship was a long time in the making. He was my guard before his disfigurement. We fell in love. Our relationship was fast and fierce, and we thought we were so clever in hiding how we felt. Touching's forbidden unless you're a paying customer or being rewarded for spectacular service."

She refilled her glass and took a long sip before continuing. "We were creative in the moments we stole to be together. And that's all they were— moments out of a never-ending day. Sometimes the mere touch of his fingers on my arm made me want so much more, but I was afraid."

"I wasn't afraid of what they'd do to me—I'd already survived their worst. I'd been beaten, raped, and harmed in so many ways I'd never imagined. After every assault, I learned to smile when I wanted to stab someone and beg them to fuck me harder when I wanted to cry. I took whatever form of degradation they gave me with grace."

A laugh escaped. "They threatened to kill me, and I smiled and begged them to bring it on because death would have been a welcome relief from the hell I lived in."

"But I feared what they would do to Jonah, and I wouldn't take a chance on his life. We planned, and we dreamed about a life of our own choosing. Jonah wanted to settle far from here, where no one knew either of us. He dreamed of a small farm and a family, and I became a part of his dream. This sweet man gave me hope." The nostalgia in her voice was hard to miss, as was the anguish as she continued.

"Hope was the most dangerous gift he could've offered me because it made me careless, and I let our intentions slip to someone I trusted."

Her tone sharpened as her story took a dark turn. "For almost a year, we subsided on long looks and barely-there touches. The night we finalized our plan to leave, I offered myself to him, wanting him to make love to me." Pearl's dark eyes were luminous as she gazed at me. "It was the first time I'd ever *wanted* a man inside of me."

"Jonah tried to refuse, wanting to wait until we were safely on our way, but I was persistent, needing something that was mine. It took little coaxing for him to give in. He loved me so beautifully and gently that our captivity ceased to exist. We explored each other, loved, and laughed together." A tear slipped down her cheek as her memories overwhelmed her.

"I fell asleep in his arms—a stupid mistake with devastating results. It could have cost us our lives, and in the end, my selfishness cost him his looks and…"

It was as if she'd flipped a switch. Pearl sat up straighter, cleared her throat, and the sad reminiscing ceased.

Shrewd ebony eyes stared at her. "I've never shared that with anyone, but I see a lot of myself in you, Ella. Heed my warning because I've been where you are. I'm not heartless, but I've worked hard to build up my business and earn my freedom. I'll not have it compromised by anyone."

Ella nodded at her as tears slipped down her cheeks. "I'm sorry for your life, Pearl. Truly I am."

With a nod, Pearl dismissed her. Ella walked woodenly to the door and turned the knob. As the latch released, she couldn't resist asking one last question. "Was there no other way to earn your freedom than by stealing freedom away from others?" She didn't expect an answer and was shocked to hear her whisper.

"First off, I didn't take you, Ella. Hamish abducted you of his own free will. If I hadn't purchased you, someone else would have."

Ella turned and looked at Pearl, wanting to witness the woman's expression as she so casually spoke of taking advantage of Ella's bad luck.

"No, you didn't abduct me, but you could have returned me," Ella said in shock.

"Have you ever considered that I treat many of the girls I employ here better than their families or the streets treated them?"

Pearl waited for an answer Ella didn't have before continuing. "I feed them three meals a day. Ask around and find out how many went hungry regularly before they joined me. Not all of us were as blessed with the luxury life of a ship captain's family as you were, Rosella."

Her tone was sharp, but it gentled for a moment. "We play the hand we're dealt, Ella. The deck of life is often stacked, and we're forced to play the cards we're dealt. Folding in this world is a watery grave."

"I'm a survivor first and foremost. I don't expect you to understand, but I expect you to think hard about the advice I've just given you."

Ella's knuckles turned white from clasping the knob so tightly in her hand. She said sadly, "My family loved me and treated me well. I appreciate the upgrade your employment may be for many of the girls. But it isn't for me." Ella watched Pearl's eyes narrow before softening her tone.

"I'm grateful for the beautiful meal and for being treated like a trusted companion. But I can't change who I am, Pearl. Not even for you."

Pearl chuckled. "I'm well aware of that fact, Ella. It's one of the many reasons I respect you."

A warning crept into her voice as she said, "I respect your intelligence enough to squash your inner voice—the one constantly reaching for hope...and rebellion. Please don't make me squash it permanently."

Her voice frosted as she added, "Please don't make me squash those who trust you, too."

Ella's breath hitched as she shut the door behind her and tried to keep her face from showing any distress. Braden silently fell into step beside her.

She ambled through the halls and returned to her rooms. What she wanted was to race through the halls and slam the door behind her, but she moved slowly, methodically. She smiled at the people she passed and kept herself from screaming out loud.

Pearl had all but told Ella she knew what they were up to. If she disobeyed, she would pay a steep price, and the people surrounding her would pay a steeper one. She thought of her night with Braden and knew she wouldn't do anything to harm him.

Saul's face flashed in her mind, and horrified, she realized how much she truly stood to lose and how grateful she should be for her current situation.

With dawning horror, Ella realized she needed to let go of her past, adapt to her circumstances, and learn everything she could because she finally understood. To not only survive, but thrive in this world, she needed to become as cold and calculated as Pearl.

Dear Diary
14th Entry

She knows who I am—my given name. With this knowledge, I will do anything she asks to keep her away from my sisters and my nieces.

I don't know who to trust, and it's breaking my heart. Pearl knows about Braden and me. I am sure of it. The witch all but told me so and compared her story to mine.

The bit of joy I felt with Braden has turned to sorrow and regret, and the hope I found after the auction now brings me nothing but fear. Because unless Pearl and Jonah end up incarcerated or dead, there is no safe place for me to go.

Hopeless and helpless,
Rosella

111

Wildflowers and Wild Horses

Jameson entered the dreamscape from the edge of town, leading Nizhoni by her reins. Making his way down the dusty lane, he walked through town. The forget-me-not fields stretched before him, exhibiting signs of distress, much like Danny was in the real world.

The fields on the edge of town were brittle and brown, the petals dried flakes on the stems. Jamey swallowed hard, concerned when he saw how quickly they'd gone from vibrant and healthy to withered and drab. He continued down the road, hoping to find her near her father's grave site.

The blight crept across the fields. Where he once glimpsed a flourishing river through the distant trees, the rocky riverbed was now desolate and cracked. As Danny's body faltered, her dreamscape was unraveling.

Clicking his tongue, he encouraged Nizhoni to follow without tugging on her reins. A southern wind blew, stirring up dirt dervishes that danced down the lane.

His eyes tracked the movement, wondering what her mood was for the wind to be kicking up so strongly. He stopped close to her father's grave, squinting into the sun and seeking any sign of Danyka. Finding none, he eased closer.

A child-sized tea table and chairs sat next to the grave with chipped cups and saucers. Sir Vance sat haphazardly, listing to the left while live animals cheerily settled on the other three chairs. A squirrel nibbled on a small bowl of nuts, while a brown hare munched on miniature carrots. A raccoon occupied the last chair. Standing on his hind legs, he clasped a tiny porcelain teacup in both hands. Upending the cup, he used his tongue to chase the honey-drunk ants around the porcelain.

Jamey grinned at the scene but couldn't locate the child he sought. The crunch of dead foliage behind him gave him hope. Turning, he found young Danny standing in the middle of the road, gazing longingly at his horse.

Curious, wide violet-blue eyes met his. "Is she yours?" the child asked, taking a step towards him.

Inclining his head, he said, "Yes. Would you like to pet her?"

"Really? You'd let me?" She moved closer, chattering as she walked. "Papa always says that ours are work horses and we're not supposed to treat them like pets." Her mouth turned down when she spoke, but she asked, "What's her name?"

"Nizhoni," Jamey said, reaching into the saddlebag. He pulled out an apple and offered the fruit to her. "She loves attention and treats. Would you like to give her one?"

"Yes," she said, bobbing her head up and down.

He stretched his hand out to her, palm up, hoping she would trust him.

Danny studied him for a long time, eyes shifting between him and the horse before giving him a shy smile and taking his hand.

Jamey grinned back at her, and hope bloomed in his chest. Leading her to Nizhoni, he gave her the shiny red orb. His hand stroked the horse's nose, and he said, "Hold your hand out flat and offer her the apple."

The mare delicately plucked the fruit from her hand. Danny's laugh was carefree as Nizhoni's tongue licked her fingers, seeking more. She stroked the sides of the mare's neck, nuzzling against her. "Sir Vance had a horse named Nizhoni," she mused, giggling as the horse licked her face.

"Would you like to ride her?" Jamey asked, hoping he wasn't pushing his luck.

"Yes, I would," she said, glancing away shyly.

"May I help you mount?" he asked, wanting to make every decision her choice.

Little Danny eyed him for a moment, unsure.

Jamey knelt down and interlaced his fingers, creating a step for her. "Reach up and grab the saddle horn," he instructed. "I'll give you a boost."

Danny stood on her tippy toes until she could reach the saddle. Clinging to it, she allowed him to lift her until she could throw a leg over the horse. She leaned over the mare's neck, reassuring her. Tiny hands stroked Nizhoni's mane. "We are going to have a lovely ride," she whispered to the horse.

"Hang on tight," Jamey said, taking the reins to lead the mare away. Heading down the lane—back towards town—he was grateful she wasn't paying attention to their destination. Too enamored of the horse and the joy of riding, she wasn't watching where they were going.

Jamey needed to get her away from the constant reminder of her father's loss long enough to break through to the older version of Danny. They moved down the main street slowly. An enormous mercantile took up the

entire block on their left. Her animated chatter ceased, making him glance up at her and ask, "How are you doing?"

Danny's eyes were wide, and her hands clutched the pommel so hard he could see the whites of her knuckles. "Why are we here?" she asked in a scared whisper. "It isn't safe here."

"I promise, Danyka, that you will always be safe when I am with you," Jamey vowed with a hand over his heart.

Her eyes morphed into a dark purple as they met his. "Is this some dirty trick?"

"I swear it's not," he said, stopping for a moment to give her his full attention. "There are friends of yours in the next building who miss you and want to see you. They are throwing a party in your honor."

"For me?" The confusion on her face was heartbreaking. "Why would they do anything nice for me?" Her dirty hands pushed the tangled hair back from her face, and she glanced with dismay at her dust-covered skirt. "But I'm not dressed for a party," she wailed.

"You can pick a new dress," he said. "There are dresses waiting for you inside," Jamey said in a soothing voice. He grinned at her and said in a mock whisper. "I made sure there's lots of cake and cookies." Hopefully, Danny's weakness for sweets would work to his advantage.

"I'm not supposed to come to town," Danyka said in a wobbly voice. "There are wicked men in town—mean men. We're not to go with them because they'll hurt us." Her voice trembled in fear as they neared the intersection between the tavern and the brothel. "That place is evil." She pointed to the building on the other side of the intersection—the brothel. "Please don't make me go in there." Her legs tightened instinctively around Nizhoni's middle, making the horse dance nervously.

The whimpers coming from her gutted him. He had absolutely no intention of taking her in there, but he needed to get her into the tavern before she bolted. "I don't like that place either," he said.

"Can you hear that?" Jamey asked, trying to distract her. He pointed to the tavern doors swinging in the breeze. The sound of a player piano choking out an off-key tune drifted out to them. Laughter rang out from inside the building.

Jamey had made sure this structure appeared inviting before he searched for her. He transformed the dilapidated building into a happy, thriving place. Pastel pink paint adorned the clapboard siding. White trim and shutters turned the tavern into an oversized dollhouse.

Jamey imagined Ferg coming through the doors in a pink kilt, and he did.

"Jameson Vance," the red-haired giant said, "who be this wee princess on yer noble stead?"

Danyka giggled at the strange man. She glanced down at Jamey and asked, "Does he realize he's wearing a dress and that it's pink?"

"Sad thing is, Miss Danyka," Jamey said in a conspiratorial whisper, "he does." He offered her an arm. "Shall we join the party?"

Once again, she glanced down forlornly at her outfit. "I'm not dressed for a party," she said.

"Well, me wee lass," Fergus said, producing a wand in his right hand. "Me has a mite of magic, and I be thinking ye'd look lovely in a pink dress."

Danyka's face lit with excitement. "With pink bows?"

"Of course, little miss," Fergus waved his wand theatrically. "Close yer eyes."

Danyka closed them and felt the shiver of his magic wash over her.

"Whatchya think, lass?" Ferg asked.

Danyka's eyes popped open, and her fingers grazed over the soft satin material of her skirt. Her hands were clean, and when she reached up, her hair was clean and curled softly around her face. "Are you a wizard?"

Fergus winked at her and said, "Aye, something like that, and I promise, someday, we'll be the best of friends, lass."

Jamey's eyes burned. He knew Fergus had joined them in his bedroom because he hadn't imagined this. Their family had linked to Danyka through Rhyanna. They would play their own parts for the rest of this scene. His heart was so full of gratitude for the people in their life that he nearly missed her question.

"Will you help me down?" Danyka was gazing into his eyes, a concerned look on her face. "Are you all right?" she asked him. "You look sad." Her nose scrunched as she studied him.

"No, Miss Danyka," Jamey said, "I'm fine." She took the hand he offered and allowed him to help her dismount.

Her brow furrowed as she asked, "Why do you have the same surname as Sir Vance?"

"I'm not sure, Danyka. Mayhap someday you can tell me."

Clasping her tiny hand in his, he led her up the wide stairs. She halted in front of Fergus, her wide eyes taking him in from the top of his head to the fugly boots on his feet before she said, "Mister, you need to let someone dress you. You're not doing such a great job of it yourself."

Fergus threw back his head and guffawed. "Ye might be right, me wee lass, but I loves me a colorful wardrobe."

Serious eyes studied him for a long moment before her lips quirked. "I'm jest not sure it loves you back."

Jamey choked back a laugh because every word she said was true.

Fergus chuckled, and his fire drakes ran up and down his arms, changing colors as they absorbed his joy. One of them ran down his hand, settling in his palm as she stared at it in fascination.

Danny tipped her head to the side, brows pinching. "Why does this feel so familiar—like I've met you before?"

Jamey's heart sped up as his heart ached. This scene was like the day that Danny first met Ferguson. He remembered Fergus telling him about it one night when he was drunk.

Ferg knelt down, meeting her eyes, "Mayhap ye have, lass." Extending his arm towards the door, he said, "You've got folks who luv ye jest waiting inside."

She brushed a kiss over Ferg's cheek, surprising Jamey, then pulled him towards the swinging doors, still clenching his hand tightly.

Jamey pushed open the door on the right, waiting for her to enter. Using her child's preference for color, he'd kept everything in soft pastel shades, trying to make her feel at home.

Hooks on the wall displayed several frilly little girl dresses he thought she would've liked as a young woman. They hung next to leather vests and breeches she preferred as an adult and silk dresses she'd recently worn. Below the dresses, an array of footwear in children's and adult sizes sat waiting. Ballet flats and shit kickers competed with heels and sandals. Her favorite long leather duster lay over the back of a chair.

"These are all for me?" Danyka asked, fingering the dresses but gazing longingly at the leather pants and boots.

"Yes, everything here is for you."

The young girl's eyes widened as she gazed around the room. The walls were a dusky pink. White lace balloon valances hung on the windows, the bottoms tied up into frilly, scalloped sections, like icing on a cake. Darker pink and white buffalo check tablecloths covered small round tables scattered throughout the room.

Each table offered one of Danny's favorite meals or sweets. The left side of the room held chunks of rare prime rib with a creamy horseradish sauce. Thickly crusted fried chicken was arranged next to mashed potatoes with a pool of butter on top. Ham and cheesy scalloped potatoes sat alongside pasta dishes.

The only thing she wouldn't find here were vegetables other than spuds. Danny hated vegetables, no matter who prepared them. And salad, in her opinion, was best left for the rabbits and the deer.

Danyka's eyes widened as she took in all the choices before her. The right side of the room was a child's sugar-coated fantasy. Candy of every kind sat in glass bowls on the bar top. Frosted cookies and pastries filled platters just waiting to be enjoyed. Intricately decorated desserts—a white cake with buttercream frosting and pink roses, a truffle with fresh whipped

cream and strawberries, brownie bites with creamy peanut butter rosettes, and luscious caramel cheesecakes awaited her selection. A seven-layer rainbow cake, frosted pink with crushed peppermint candy sprinkled on top—waited on a taller pedestal table, beckoning her.

Jamey led her through the sugar temptations. Straight ahead were two more rectangular cake tables. On the left, taking up nearly the entire surface, was an enormous cake in the shape of an island. Nearly four-foot high and tiered to exhibit the terrain, the edible diorama was lifelike.

The bottom tier represented the Saint Lawrence River. Thick swirls of frosting represented the shore break. White sprays of waves crashed against the gray stones.

Blue spruce, red maples, and mighty oaks decorated the sides of the second and third tiers. The perimeters of each tier's surface displayed local flora and fauna. Jamey incorporated the animals from her tea party.

Additional squirrels, rabbits, raccoons, and grizzlies nested and scampered around the edge in playful scenes. Since Sir Vance was from Wellesley, he hoped this would help trigger her memory and correlate him with the bear.

He'd imagined the top to represent the kingdom of Wellesley. Victorian houses perched along the waterfront. Local stores and shops were easy to recognize. Horses stood in the stables next to the portal. Cookie crumbs formed the road leading from the gazebo through the green landscape.

Wide eyed, li'l Danyka stepped closer. Her gaze roamed over the scene before her, and Jamey witnessed the recognition sparking behind her eyes.

Stepping closer, she pointed to the gazebo with the letters WELLESLEY painted on the side facing the water. "Sir Vance lives here. The portal is downstairs." Her head shifted to the right, brows scrunching as she found the stables nearby. "You board Nizhoni here." A grin crossed her face. "We race our horses down the road." Her finger trailed over the path they took to…

Danny's breath caught when she saw the sign towering over a narrow road. The painted white letters on the brown sign read, "*Vance's Horse Farm.*" Danyka's head tipped as she peered up at him, and her features changed just a smidge, aging her.

"You always win when we race," Jamey said softly, not wanting to break the spell.

"I think you let me win sometimes," she said, and her voice changed. Layered with a smoky, sultry sound that he missed so fucking much, it was a woman's voice.

"Sir Vance is from Wellesley," she said, frowning. "Is this his home?" She pointed at the lane under the sign, her finger trailing above the dirt path cutting between horse pastures and barns. Horses grazed on both sides of

the road, making her pause for a moment. Figures were working outside of the barn, and she bent down to get a better look at the woman and the three men working side-by-side.

"Her name is Kateri," Danny said suddenly, running a hand through her hair as if it hurt too much to think about this place.

"Yes," he whispered. Jamey took a deep, shuddering breath as he contemplated his answer. "My full name is Jameson Vance, and I live there, too. Kateri is my mother."

His eyes roamed over her face, letting out a relieved breath when *his* Danny stood beside him.

"And your father is Kuruk, and you have two brothers." The memories came rushing back so fast they made her gasp. "Where did I come up with Sir Vance from?" she whispered to herself. "I never had a stuffed bear as a child. But he made me feel so safe…"

Still holding her hand, he tugged her closer and stared into her confused eyes. "You know how you shift into a falcon when you need to flee to safety?"

A small nod of her head was the only sign that she heard him. "I shift into a grizzly to protect the people I love."

The fog of confusion was lifting from her eyes. But he could sense the panic just below the surface.

"Please don't force me to leave," he pleaded, clinging to her hand. "At least not until you meet the rest of the people who came for your party."

Danny gave him a stiff nod, even though she trembled with the need to bolt. Movement in her peripheral vision made her eyes shift to a hallway on their left. A beautiful blond woman walked towards them with a gentle smile on her face and kind emerald eyes.

"I know you," Danny whispered. "You heal people, and we're friends?"

"Aye, lass." Rhyanna laughed, and the sound was like sunshine. "We be a mite closer than that, more like sisters." She stepped forward and hugged Danny, whispering in her ear. "Ye needs come home to us, Danyka. 'Tis been too long, na."

Danny returned her hug with one arm, still clinging to Jamey.

A tall chestnut-haired man with startling pale blue eyes stepped forward and gave her a bow. "Danyka," he said with a smile.

"You helped me when I was hurting in here," Danny said, tapping on her head. "You were kind to me when I needed it."

"I tried to be, and you helped me when I needed it." Ronan gave her another bow and said, "We miss you, Danny girl. Come home."

The sound of an ivory ball ricocheting off of fifteen others made her snap her head to the right. The red-haired man stood behind a cloud of smoke, sucking on a foul-smelling cigar while he peered at her over a pool table.

"You cheat," she called out.

Fergus just gave her a crooked grin and said, "Ye need to come back, lass, and prove yer accusations. Yer the little cheater, Pixie."

A dark laugh erupted from her. "Lying bastard," she said cockily.

Jamey's heart was beating double time as he watched the woman he loved reemerge. Her fingers tightened on his. He was trying so damn hard not to get his hopes up, but goddamn, he'd needed this. The backs of his eyes burned as he watched her come to life, confident and full of herself.

The sound of heels on the wooden floor jerked her head back to the left again. She took in the woman with long, dark, curly hair and midnight-blue eyes walking towards her. Danny's eyes filled as she stared into the eyes of the woman who'd rescued her from hell. "My avenging angel," she whispered as a tear spilled over.

"You know who I am?" Maddy asked her somberly. Her dark eyes pierced into Danny's and the commanding voice demanded the truth.

Another tear fell down Danny's cheek as she answered. "You're my angel, my mother, my sister, and my friend."

"Do you trust me, Danny?" Maddy asked just as somberly, reaching out and wiping the tear away.

"I trusted you with my life then, and I always will," Danny answered.

"Who else stands with you?"

Danny felt a tug on her hand. She glanced up, meeting Jamey's dark eyes, now backlit with an amber glow. "Jameson Vance stands with me."

"Who is Jameson?" Maddy asked, still compelling her to remember.

Danyka's eyes darkened to that amethyst color he loved as she stared at him. "He's my friend, my partner in crime, and my soon to be lover." She swallowed hard as she faced him and brought her free hand up to his cheek. "He's the man I love."

"Do you trust him?" Maddy asked.

"I trust him completely."

Jamey closed his eyes at her words and rubbed his cheek against her hand.

"I need you to trust both of us. You need to leave this place with us now," Maddy said in a somber voice. "It's not safe for you here anymore."

"Why?" Danny asked.

Jamey could sense her momentary panic as she turned back towards Maddy.

Maddy clasped Danny's face between her hands and hissed, "This place isn't real. And the longer you remain here, the more damage you are doing to your body. If you don't return with us soon, honey, I don't know if you can ever return."

627

Her voice was full of sorrow as she wiped the tears running down Danny's face. "The threats you ran away from no longer exist. It's safe to come home. Just walk out that door with us and come back home, baby girl."

Danny shuddered, remembering another woman saying that to her recently. Maddy led her to the cake diorama on the right. Similarly decorated on the sides as the Wellesley one, but the landscape was different. A yacht house, pump house and castle stood on the island instead of the gazebo and horse farm.

She recognized The Pit, the weapons shed, and the castle housing the Sanctuary. The nearby stables had two white tigers lounging outside. Hellhounds and NightMares roamed the pastures with horses, dragons, and unicorns.

Mrs. O'Hare worked outside in the kitchen garden. The labyrinth maze was lit with sparkling white fairy lights. A table in the garden held figures of all of them having dinner together. Landon ran around the table, laughing.

Danny's eyes glanced from Maddy to Jamey. "I remember this. I remember all of you." Her gaze traveled to Rhy, Ronan and Fergus. With a sob, she said, "But I don't know how to get back."

"We'll show you," Maddy said, pulling her towards a door.

Jameson recognized Maddy's mistake the moment she took them through the door facing the brothel.

"No, no, no, no," Danny shrieked, trying to pull her hand away. "I won't go back there."

"Danyka!" Maddy's voice snapped her attention back to her. "I'm your avenging angel. Am I not?"

Danny's body trembled with fear, but she nodded her head weakly.

"It's time for our vengeance, my child." Maddy's voice was kind but firm.

Fergus stepped in front of them, handing Jamey and then Madylyn a torch. With a flick of his fingers, flames burst to life on the soaked ends. Danny's eyes widened as the orange-blue flames grew higher.

Maddy turned to her. "This place can't harm you if it's no longer here. Don't you think it's time you took back your power, Danny?" She gave her a moment to process what she'd just said before continuing. "It's time to burn this hellhole to the ground." She extended her torch to Danny. "Do you want to do the honors?"

Danny gazed at the dilapidated building through the flames. Painful memories burst to life in her mind. The horror of her mother selling her to the proprietor of this building. The first time the proprietor sold her, and an old man raped her. All the subsequent times men raped her flickered through her mind. Every person who took advantage of her innocent body caused another chink to form in the armor she wore around her heart.

Their disembodied faces floated before her. Displayed in each pane of the nine-pane windows—they mocked her. The windows on both sides of the house, both upstairs and down, were full of her demons. She knew if she walked around the building, evil would fill the rest as well. She studied some of the many faces mocking her.

They had laughed, gloated, and degraded her in so many ways. The chorus of their evil voices still taunted her, echoing in her head.

And there, in the final pane, she found a tormented version of herself. This weak, apathetic version turned to alcohol and faceless men to drown out the horror of her childhood. She was ashamed of every man she picked to have unsatisfying sex with as an adult. She couldn't even look at them when she fucked them because she was so disgusted by what they were doing.

Danny's gaze returned to the front step of the brothel. Standing there and gazing at her with the saddest eyes was the child she'd once been. She'd buried this damaged part of herself so far down in her memories, but she still existed. She rarely gave her a thought except for when she awoke screaming from her nightmares.

The little girl with tangled blond hair and a dirty face gazed up at her with luminous eyes. Her eyes shifted to the torch Danny held. "Are you going to burn me up, too?" she asked as tears created sooty trails down her face.

Sir Vance dangled from her fingers, and the forget-me-not dress was in tatters. "I'm so tired of being alone here," the little girl said with a hiccupping sob.

Danny's chest tightened. She stumbled forward and knelt before this miniature version of herself. "You're not alone anymore," she said, gazing into pale violet pools of misery. "I'm taking you with me." With a glance over her shoulder, she looked back at her tribe. "And you have all of them. They will protect both of us and love us."

Li'l Danyka gave her a sad smile and said, "May I?" as she reached for the torch.

"Here," Jamey said, stepping forward and handing her his.

Danny extended her left hand and said, "We'll do this together." The child clasped her hand tightly. In step, Danny and li'l Danyka stepped forward. Danny tossed her torch through the open door of the brothel, and li'l Danyka followed suit. They stood witness as the flames licked across the floors and climbed the tattered curtains.

Maddy, Rhyanna, Fergus, Ronan, and Jamey all strode forward, torches in hand. Walking the length of the building, they made sure the entire structure was aflame before returning to li'l Danyka and Danny.

The inferno erased the horrors that destroyed their innocence. The hovel that ruined any hope and self-esteem they might have once had collapsed in

on itself. This was the place that framed her sexual experiences as an adult and destroyed any pleasure she experienced during the act—until Jameson.

The woman and the child held hands in the street, watching the flames embracing the building. Windows cracked as the flames melted the faces of their tormentors. The conflagration jumped to buildings on either side and, within moments, engulfed the entire town.

Danny gazed down at her inner child and asked, "Are you ready to go home?"

Trails still ran down her soot-covered face, and her chin quivered, but the little girl wiped her nose on the back of her hand and shook her head. Danny's brows met in confusion. "I don't understand."

The little girl glanced over Danny's shoulder. She threw her arms around Danny and hugged her tightly. "Just don't forget me." The child's gaze returned to the lane leading out of town to the riverbank. "And don't forget them."

Li'l Danyka gazed up at her with a wobbly smile. "It's time for me to go now," she said, surprising Danny. The child pointed over her shoulder. "My papa is waiting."

Danny's heart shattered when her eyes found her father standing behind all of her siblings. "They might need your help, too," li'l Danyka said.

Guilt ate at Danny, but she nodded solemnly as her eyes met the little girl's. "I promise I won't forget. I'll find them and protect them as well."

When Danny glanced back up, her father was standing alone amongst the forget-me-nots. Her heart clenched at the vision of him young and healthy, smiling and happy, with his arms outstretched.

Tears of sorrow rolled down Danny's face as she clasped li'l Danyka's hand tightly. Swallowing past the lump in her throat, she walked with li'l Danyka towards him, knowing she needed to see this through. She needed to know her inner child was safe.

There were so many things about her father that she'd forgotten since his death. His smile was crooked, and his eyes were the same unique shade as hers. Blond hair hung in unruly waves over a high forehead. He was taller than she remembered—built a lot like Jamey was.

One of the strongest memories she had was of the way he made her feel cherished when he hugged her. When he smiled and opened his arms, she didn't hesitate, but stepped right into them.

Tears blinded her as she sobbed into his chest. His arms closed around her. The smell of pine and wood smoke surrounded her, taking her back to happier times. "I miss you," she hiccupped.

"I know, lass," he said in a soothing voice. "And I, ye." He pressed a kiss to the top of her head before framing her face in his hands. "I'm so proud of you, me li'l Warden. Ye've made a good life for yerself, me Danyka."

He glanced over her shoulder towards the burning town. "I wantchya to promise me something, lass." His voice was solemn as he trapped her gaze in his.

"Anything, papa."

"Ye need to let us go. Let this place go. It does ye na good." His hands tightened on her cheeks. "Ye, grab onto that man—he's a good un—and ye hang on tight." His lips pressed against her forehead, lingering for a moment. "I'se gonna take the wee one here with me." His eyes shifted to the child beside her. "She shouldna be alone here no more."

Danny shook her head. "No, she shouldna."

"I wants ye to consider one thing afore ye leave, chile." His somber voice made her eyes snap to his.

"Anything, papa."

"It wasna right what they forced ye to endure as a child, lass. Never forget that. Yer Mam did what she had to do for the good of the whole, but it wasna fair to ye. I won't ask ye to forgive her, but I'll ask ye to think on yer siblings. Mayhap ye could check in on them. Ye ever think that they might need help escaping their lives, too?"

Whatever Danny had expected, this request hadn't been it. Anger and guilt overwhelmed her, but he held her still. "Ye've all the rights in this world to yer anger chile, but ye ever think that they mights be trapped in the same hell ye were?"

Danny's face paled, and she stared at him in horror. He had to be wrong. Her sacrifice had to have been worth something.

"I love ye, Danyka. Dontchya ever doubt nor forget that," he said, wrapping her in his arms one last time. Danny hugged him back, not wanting to let him go. But time was short, and she sensed the tethers to this world drifting with the smoke from the fire she'd started.

With tears in his eyes, he released her and reached down for li'l Danyka. Hoisting her up on his hip, he ruffled her hair and asked. "Ye ready to go, me li'l pixie?" He tickled her side, eliciting a loud giggle.

"Yes, I've been waiting for ye to come back," she scolded.

Li'l Danyka glanced down at Danny. Her guileless violet-blue eyes lingered on hers for a long moment. Unexpectedly, she reached out a finger and wiped a tear away from Danny's cheek. "Thank ye for coming back for me." She glanced down at the bear she clutched and offered it to Danny. "I don't need him anymore. Sir Vance will always protect you."

Danny's chin quivered as she reached out with a trembling hand and accepted the beloved, tattered critter. "I promise I'll clean him up and take good care of him."

Li'l Danyka giggled. "No, silly. You need to love him as he is and, more importantly…" she trailed off and said somberly, "you just need to let him

love you exactly where you are." Her ancient eyes drifted over to Jameson. "Because he already does." Danny's heart skipped, knowing who spoke to her through this child. The Earth Mother's advice was the best confirmation that she could have gotten, telling her it was time to go.

The pixie face turned back to their father. "I'm ready to go now. She doesn't need us anymore." They gazed at Danny and Jameson and the people who surrounded them.

"She's got her own tribe na," her papa said, pressing a kiss to his child's head. "They'll take care of her." With a wink at Danny, he turned, and they walked away.

Tears fell harder as Danny watched her father walk away. He diminished, his form becoming transparent, before he and her inner child disappeared into the ether.

Taking one last look around, Danyka reached for Jamey's hand. They turned around to see their friends fading as well. Rhy blew them a kiss, Fergus saluted, Maddy smiled, and Ronan winked before they faded into the smoke pouring out of the town.

Jamey's fingers tightened on hers, supporting her without rushing her. Glancing up at him, she gave him a tremulous smile and asked, "Can we go home now?"

Jamey brushed a chaste kiss over her lips, whispering, "I thought you'd never ask." He pulled her in close, his forehead pressed against hers. The forget-me-nots mixed with a riot of colors as new wildflowers bloomed, and the blight faded away.

With a hitch in his voice, he begged one last time, "Come back to me, my Hellion. Please come back."

112

Helpless

Jamey woke slowly, with Danny still wrapped in his arms. He knew instinctively that they weren't alone. His grizzly's enhanced sense of smell picked up on the rest of the team in the room.

Rhyanna sat at the foot of the bed between them, with a hand on each of their legs, confirming his suspicions that she had pulled the entire team into the dreamscape. Kyran stood behind her with his hand on her shoulders, boosting her power. Maddy, Ronan, Kyran, Damian, Mrs. O'Hare, and a bruised Fergus gathered in the room behind them. Each of them sat or stood near enough that they could touch Rhy's arms or her back. Their contact helped her link them to the dreamscape.

They'd become as much of the dreamscape as Jamey had. He and Rhy had speculated about it one time he'd been conscious. She wasn't sure if it would work, but he'd wanted all of them there, supporting Danny and urging her to come home.

Danny's body felt so right in his arms, but she'd lost more weight. He kept his eyes closed because he was a coward. He was terrified of opening them to find her still sleeping. With a ragged breath, he opened them, and his heart sank. Her eyes remained shut, and the toll this was taking on her body was more evident every time he returned alone.

Eyes burning, he pressed his lips to her forehead as he rocked her in his arms. Discouraged and heartsick, he didn't know what else he could do. Sorrow overwhelmed him, and he didn't know how he was supposed to let her fade away into the dark.

But then he stopped breathing because he could've sworn she moved. Her tiny hands were touching his chest, but he felt the pressure against his skin change as if she were pushing against him.

In a hoarse whisper, he said, "Hellion?" His eyes studied her face for any sign she could hear him. Her hands curled deeper into his chest like claws, digging in and keeping him in place.

He didn't care how uncomfortable it was because she was moving, if only this little bit. His thumbs rubbed her temples lightly as her brows scrunched. "Honey, I need you to look at me." He kissed her forehead, smiling as they furrowed more. "Please, Danny, open your eyes for me?"

The room was silent as everyone waited. Anticipation and hope were thick in the air. Hands clasped, tears pooled, and gasps of relief rang out when she finally pried her eyes open and saw him.

Jameson broke the moment he saw her violet-blue gaze meeting his. Unashamed of the tears trickling down his face, he pulled her tighter against him, never breaking eye contact. Her hands came up and framed his face, wiping the tears as fast as they fell.

"Don't cry, Jamey," she said in a hoarse voice. "I'm here, and I'm not going anywhere." Her lips kissed the trails down his face until she met his lips. She brushed a chaste kiss against them, then glanced around the room.

"I heard you in there," she said, coming back to him. "I remember every attempt you made and every word you said." Her gaze went to the bottom of the bed, seeing the people she loved coming together for her. "You all were there. I felt your touch and your words. They made me want to come back and be with all of you."

There wasn't a dry eye in the room. Danny was a beloved member of their team, and they weren't about to lose her without a fight. Jamey scooched up against the headboard and pulled her into his lap, keeping the blankets over her legs as he moved. His arms wrapped around her, pulling her tightly against him, needing her close.

Spying Mrs. O'Hare, she gave her a sly smile. "I'm starving. Do you have anything quick I can snack on 'til breakfast?"

Rhy piped up. "She can have broth tonight, and water."

"You can sneak me up some chunks of cheese and fruit when Rhy isn't looking," Danny said in a conspiratorial whisper to Mrs. O'Hare. "Or some chocolate."

"Trust me, lass," Rhy admonished in a stern tone. "Yer body will not be happy if you eat anything heavy so soon. It's been days since ye've eaten. Take it slow."

Danny paled. "How long have I been out?"

"Nearly a week," Maddy said.

"And a terrifying one at that, Pixie," Ferg added.

"Kyran kept ye hydrated, but we couldna get nourishment into ye," Rhy said with a hitch in her voice. "Ye scared me, lass. Dontchya be doing it again!"

"I'm so sorry." Danny's voice trembled. "Time had no meaning there." She scrubbed her face with her hands. "If you hadn't come for me, I never would've found my way back," she said. She tipped her head up and met Jamey's eyes, then glanced around the room again. "But you all helped me find my way home. I am grateful for every one of you."

Danny covered her mouth as she yawned. She didn't think she should be tired, but she was exhausted.

Rhy stood and gestured to the rest of the clan. "Say yer farewells and let her rest."

Danny gave her a grateful smile and accepted hugs and kisses from everyone as they left the room. She pulled her knees up to her chest on Jamey's lap and rubbed her head over his heart. He'd been quiet while everyone else was here.

Jamey's hands trailed up and down her back, rubbing in soothing circles while his cheek rested against the top of her head. They sat there in comfortable silence while she toyed with the ends of his hair. Now that he had her to himself, he wasn't sure if he wanted to break the spell they were under.

He didn't want to close his eyes as he struggled to believe she was back. He didn't want to miss one moment with this woman who held his heart.

Danny yawned and then shivered in his lap. "You cold?" he asked, breaking the silence. He reached for the blanket bunched beneath them.

"No."

Her eyes met his, and he knew he could drown in her mystical depths if she'd let him.

"I'd like to brush my teeth and take a bath, though, if you don't mind."

"I don't mind at all." His hand rubbed her back. "I'll help you."

She nodded, visibly relieved. "I'd appreciate that. Not sure how steady I'll be on my feet."

"I've got you, Hellion," he said, starting the water in the tub with a thought. He stood with her in his arms. "I'll always have you."

Danny's gaze never left his as he walked to the bathroom. "I know you will, Jamey. I never doubted you."

Jamey swallowed hard, realizing he'd finally earned her complete trust. He sat her on the edge of the tub as he grabbed fluffy towels, shampoo, and conditioner. Standing before her, he reached for the buttons on her shirt. His eyes met hers as he asked, "May I?"

Danny nodded, grateful for his help. "I'm not much use, yet."

His fingers made quick work of the buttons, grazing gently against her skin. She let out a hiss, and he jerked back, not wanting to make her feel uncomfortable. His eyes snapped to hers, expecting anger, but he found something else dancing in those amethyst depths. He found interest.

Slipping the shirt over her shoulders, he kept his gaze above the neck. He scooped her up and bent down over the extra-long tub, settling her in the water.

Danny grabbed the sides to keep herself upright. Her arms shook as she reached for the bar of soap, and her hand fell into the water. "I've never been so helpless," she whispered.

Jamey had seen enough. Stepping into the tub in his sleep pants, he settled behind her. Gently, he pulled her back against him.

Danny plucked at his pants. "You could have taken these off," she said, glancing up at him.

"I didn't want to make you uncomfortable."

"Don't treat me with kid gloves, Jamey," she said in a lost voice. "Please don't pussy-foot around with me." Her eyes were sad when she spoke. "That's not who we've ever been."

"All right," he said. "I'm just trying to be considerate."

"You're always considerate."

"Close your eyes, Hellion," he warned as he poured a pitcher of water over her head. His large hands lathered up the shampoo before covering her short, dark hair with it. He massaged her head gently, and she let out a moan that went south of his brain.

"That feels so good," she said, melting into him.

He smiled down at her, loving her reaction. They'd have to make this a habit. He rinsed her hair and reached for a cloth.

"Did you prefer me as a blond with long hair?" she asked in a timid voice that was so unlike her.

"I don't know you as a blonde," he said. "I fell in love with a dark-haired pixie who turns into a hellion." He pressed a chaste kiss to the side of her neck, making her giggle. Jamey was enjoying this playful side of her.

Soaping up the cloth, he quickly washed her back and her chest with efficient movements, reaching forward and doing her legs. When he was done, he handed her the cloth. He cleared his throat and said, "I'll let you finish."

When she did, he rinsed her from head to toe and bundled her up in a towel. A quick stop at the sink to brush her teeth made her legs shake. Scooping her up again, he carried her into the sitting room and placed her in a plush chair, handing her a steeping mug of broth that was waiting on a tray for her.

Jamey found a thick sweater and a pair of pants with a drawstring for her to wear. Snuggled into the warm clothes, she sat sideways with her back against the wing of the chair and her knees to her chest. Sipping on the broth, she let out one of those delicate moans that made his body shudder.

He sat across from her, eating a roast beef and provolone sandwich with a horseradish cream sauce and greens. Potato crisps sat on the side. He

wolfed it down until he felt her eyes shooting daggers at him from across the room.

Danyka glared at the crumbs left on the plate. "You didn't even offer me a bite," she said, appalled.

"I'm glad you don't have your daggers right now," he said with a grin. "I think you would've pinned my arm to the chair and fought me for it."

"You're damn right," she snarled, sipping at the warm, seasoned water. Mrs. O'Hare's broth was damn good, but it wasn't nearly as good as her roast beef.

Jamey's elbows were on his knees as he watched her savoring the broth. He enjoyed seeing the flush in her cheeks as she drank something nourishing.

"Can I ask you something?" His tone was hesitant.

"What?" she asked, voice wary as she peered through the steam rising from her mug.

"Come home with me for a while. Stay with me while you recuperate." His jaw clenched as he waited for her answer.

She frowned, brows nearly meeting in confusion. "On Wellesley with Kateri and Kuruck?" she clarified.

"No." He chuckled, running a hand through his hair. "I want you to stay with me, in my home."

Danny's eyes widened. "Where is your home?"

"I have a cabin on Wellesley that was given to me by my grandfather. It's on a plateau above the farm. The view is amazing. It's quiet, peaceful."

Danny was silent for a long time, her expression giving nothing away as she studied him. He was about to retract the offer when she sighed.

"Yes." Her smile was genuine, missing her usual cockiness. "I would like that."

Jamey grinned back at her, feeling the rightness in this moment. The two of them, relaxing together at day's end. This was what he'd always wanted—what he needed.

637

113

You Don't Know How to Let Me Fall

With Maddy's permission, Jamey and Danny left for Wellesley Island two days after Danny woke. Skittish around him by day, she was slowly regaining her strength. But by night, she still sought comfort and safety within his arms, and Jamey was grateful for it.

Nizhoni and a gelding awaited them at the stable next door to the portal. Danny's eyes lit up when she saw his horse. The mare walked up to her, nuzzling Danny's neck. She nickered, seeking a treat and knowing she'd get one. Danny laughed, pulling an apple out of her bag and feeding it to the horse.

Jamey slung his saddlebags over the gelding, surprising her. He mounted, glancing down at her with a raised brow. "Ready?"

"Really?" she asked with a smile, immediately reaching for Nizhoni's saddle horn.

Her pure, unadulterated joy made him grin, and he said, "She's yours to use while you're here."

Danny's face lit up with joy, making him chuckle. "But don't be spoiling her all the time. Too many treats, and her saddle won't fit."

"Shush," she admonished. "She can hear you. There'll be no fat shaming in our vicinity."

Nizhoni tossed her head as if in agreement.

"My apologies, ladies. Although I do like women with curves."

Danny shot him a coy glance from under her lashes. "Well, guess that rules me out. I'm all skin and bones these days."

His eyes met hers, and the heat in them nearly melted the panties she wasn't wearing. Jamey had been very respectful of her personal space, and she wasn't sure how she felt about that. Prior to her abduction, she'd needed him to touch her, to soothe the raw ache inside of her. But so much had

changed. If his gaze was any indication, he still felt the same way? But was this what she still wanted?

Shaking the long bangs out of her eyes, she wasn't ready to examine those thoughts too closely. Leaning down over Nizhoni's neck, she whispered, "Let's see if you've got wings on today, love." The mare took off, and Danny cackled with glee. Nothing she loved more than the wind on her face and a fast horse between her thighs. The utter freedom of riding was exhilarating, and for the first time in days, she felt like herself.

The sound of the gelding closing in made her encourage Nizhoni to go faster, and for a few moments, they were neck and neck. But Nizhoni carried the lighter passenger, and the other horse was tiring.

Danny slowed for the entrance to the Vance Farm, breathing hard while she waited for Jamey to join her. Her cheeks were flushed and her eyes leaking from the wind in her face, but she felt good. No. She felt fucking fantastic. She was alive with the sun on her face, air in her lungs, and the man she loved gazing at her like she was everything he needed.

The events of the past week had forced her to rip the scab off an old wound. When pain and fear festered for that long, it hurt like a mother when it finally came to a head. And Danny's past had been festering for a long time. The sense of abandonment from both of her parents in different ways made her inner child believe she was unworthy of anyone's love or protection long-term.

As an adult, she'd crafted a version of herself who needed no one. Her heart and her emotions were untouchable. Her body became her greatest weapon, and in the process of becoming, she created her greatest champion—herself.

But no matter how deadly of a warrior she was and who she could take down, she hadn't been able to outrun her past. Until she stopped running and faced her inner demons, they would keep coming for her when she least expected it, preventing her from ever being happy.

The running stopped now. Releasing the baggage that had hung like an anchor around her neck wouldn't happen overnight, but she'd be damned if she lost the only good thing she'd ever had because she was a coward.

When she said goodbye to Rhy yesterday, the healer handed her a pamphlet for weekly meetings Grace was starting. She'd created a group for abuse survivors. Rhy suggested she join in on one when they began. Danny promised to consider it. Shaking her head to clear the cobwebs of the past, she brought her attention back to the present.

Following Jamey, she studied the casual grace with which he rode a horse. His broad shoulders naturally moved with the gait of the animal, and his hands loosely held the reins, rarely using them to direct his animal.

Thickly muscled thighs straddled the gelding, controlling him gently with the slightest movement of his legs.

A few strands of his banded hair had come loose, and the thick chestnut tendrils drifted on the breeze. When he glanced back over his shoulder at her, the chestnut length caressed his sharp cheekbones as he winked at her and gave her a sexy smile.

Danny smiled back, feeling a blush hit her cheeks as she wondered if he'd caught her staring. The man was *hawt*—and he was hers. Her heart beat faster, finally accepting how much Jamey adored her. The sensual inner woman whom she'd neglected for too long stirred—waking and taking notice of the healthy male before her. Purring, her inner goddess wanted him.

Instead of heading for his parents' homestead, Jamey took a barely noticeable path on the left that wandered up into the hills. Danny followed slowly behind him, letting Nizhoni pick the best way up the narrow trail.

Wiping the sweat off her brow, she glanced at the sun's position on the horizon, gauging the time. Nearing midday, it explained why her stomach was growling and her lips parched. She uncapped a canteen and drank half of it down.

A riot of wildflowers dotted the terrain, and as they neared the top of the bluff, she viewed the lush fields butting up against the banks of the Saint Lawrence. Massive willows anchored on the riverbank swayed in the breeze, their long tendrils dancing in the wind.

Herds of horses grazed in the pastures below. This year's foals frolicked alongside their watchful mothers. Her keen eyesight picked out ranch hands, fixing fences and training horses. The day-to-day life of a horse farmer played out on the stage beneath her.

Cresting the plateau, his home came into view. Danny's breath caught at the porch wrapping around the gorgeous two-story log cabin like garland. The structure sat on a basement formed from large river stones. Stone fireplaces climbed the walls facing north and south, while walls of glass faced east and west.

In her mind's eye, she imagined them enjoying this place through all four seasons. She envisioned them snuggled under a blanket—her on his lap with a cup of cocoa—watching the sun rise and set. The thought didn't terrify her at all. In fact, it created a longing in her soul for something she hadn't known she needed—a home of her own—a place to share with their friends and family.

Nizhoni neighed, bringing her back to the present. The horse knew she was home and due to be fed. She automatically headed for the red barn tucked behind the house. Dismounting, Danny worked in silence next to Jamey as they unsaddled their mounts and led them to their respective stalls.

Hanging the tack on the wall, Danny shouldered her bag. Jamey grabbed his saddlebags and offered her a hand. "Would you like a tour?"

Danny gave him a shy smile, then interlaced her fingers with his. The heat in his eyes made her incredibly aware of her body's reaction to his proximity. "I'd love a tour of your beautiful home."

Jamey tugged her closer until there was barely a space between them, then leaned down and brushed his lips over her jawline before whispering in her ear, "When you're ready, I'd like you to think of this as our home."

Her breath hitched from the heat radiating off him, and her eyes met his, not shying away from what he offered. The air was thick with the sexual tension between them. But, always the gentleman, he took a step back. Danny found herself disappointed by the distance.

With a tug, he led her through the back door. Kicking off their boots in the foyer, they walked into a large kitchen. An enormous stone hearth took up one wall, and a twelve-foot island sat in the middle with a marble sink at the end.

"Kitchen," he said, stating the obvious as they moved through, "Dining room, living room, and bath on this level." Leading her up the stairs, they came into a split loft. Pointing to the right, he said, "There's a guest room down there, and my room is over here."

Jamey released her hand and carried his bag into his room. Danny stood there, not sure what to do. He hadn't invited her to stay in his room, although that's where she'd spent most of the last week while she recovered.

Not wanting to assume that's what he wanted, she dropped her bag on the bed in the guest room. Extra wide French doors leading onto the deck beckoned her. Danny pushed the left one open so she could step outside.

Closing her eyes, her head dropped back, and the warm breeze caressed her cheeks. The air element within called to her, missing her. She let a shaky breath out, releasing tension she hadn't realized she was still carrying from her incarceration. Lifting her arms shoulder height and palms up, her falcon beckoned.

Without another thought, she shifted. By the time her clothing hit the deck, she was climbing high, then soaring and setting her soul free. She glided over the beautiful island, automatically checking the perimeter for danger. Categorically, she noted the strengths and weaknesses before soaring for pure pleasure.

Keen eyesight observed the people and animals in the pastures below. She saw Kateri shield her eyes and track Danny's flight over them. Danny shrieked and tipped to the side, acknowledging her. Kateri smiled and waved at her. Making her way to the river, she soared, climbing higher, needing to expand her view of the river valleys below her.

The lush emerald pastures of the island contrasted with the ripe fields of hay and wheat waiting to be cut. Forests opened into meadows where spotted fawns played. A few farms dotted the landscape but were far enough apart to enjoy privacy.

Docks lined the riverbanks closer to town, and small boats bobbed on the gently flowing water. The gazebo gleamed in the sun as she glided above, remembering the night Jamey took her there, giving her more pleasure than she'd ever known was possible. Longing for more of that pleasure warmed her blood and made her head back.

As much as she hated to admit it, her body was still recovering, and shifting this soon hadn't been her brightest idea. She turned back, reaching the riverbank near the Vance homestead. Returning to her human form, she hugged her naked knees, watching the river flowing by as she conserved what little strength remained.

A shiver ran over her body. Trembling, her body struggled to create heat, and her teeth still chattered. Her head whipped to the side at the sound of movement behind her.

"Goddammit," she snarled to herself. It had been irresponsible to come out alone when she couldn't protect herself. She quieted her breathing, hoping whatever was there would pass her by.

When the bushes parted, a large animal lumbered onto the bank beside her, dashing her hopes. Heart racing, she let out a laugh, realizing that it was Jamey. In grizzly form, he dropped something in front of her and settled next to her with his head on his paws.

Danny rested her head back on her knees with her head turned toward him. Pale violet-blue eyes locked on his animal's amber gaze. "Always so damn considerate. What am I gonna do with you?" She reached for the small satchel with the clothes he'd carried for her.

The grizzly chuffed, and Danny quickly dressed, then leaned her back against his side. For the first time, her nudity seemed inappropriate. As shifters, they'd seen each other naked hundreds of times. But as a potential lover, she felt like she was flaunting something at him she wasn't sure she was ready to follow through with.

They sat there in silence as the sun disappeared beneath the horizon. Her stomach growled, and she laughed when he stood and nudged her with his head.

"Ok, I'm going," Danny said, walking back towards his cabin. They were farther from his home than she'd realized. Partway back, she yawned, and her steps dragged heavily.

Jamey nudged her again, settling onto his belly and staring at her expectantly.

"You don't have to carry me," she grumbled.

The only answer she received was a low growl of admonishment. With a defeated sigh, she pulled herself up onto his back, straddling him and leaning over the nape of his neck. Fingers fisting in his coarse hair, she snuggled onto him, closing her eyes, knowing he had her.

Jamey's voice whispered through her mind, *"Hang on, Hellion. I don't want you to fall."*

"You don't know how to let me fall, Jamey," she said, yawning.

A low growl of agreement or a purr of satisfaction—she wasn't sure—rumbled underneath her, making her smile. Her fingers dug in tighter as he made his way up the steepest part of his mountain. When they reached the porch, he dropped again, allowing her to slide off.

Danny staggered into the house, starving and exhausted. Heading straight for the kitchen, she pulled out the fixings for sandwiches. Both shifters needed fuel.

Smoked turkey, ham, and a chunk of cheddar landed on the island behind her as she tossed ingredients over her shoulder. Lettuce, tomato, onions, and bacon followed. Grabbing a glass jar of milk, some mustard, and mayo, she turned and nearly dropped them as she ran into Jamey.

"Careful," he said in his gravelly voice. He took the milk and condiments from her, then turned and set them on the butcher block island. "There's fresh marble rye and some whole grain rolls in the bread box behind you."

Danny grabbed the baked goods and joined him at the island. She pulled herself up on a stool and watched him prepare their dinner. Salivating at the mountainous sandwich he was creating, she grabbed a roll and shredded it. Nibbling slowly on the small pieces she'd torn off, she tried not to eat too fast, knowing she'd regret it later. A glass of milk followed as she eyed the meal he was making her.

Plating up two halves of the ham on rye, he added two dill spears before sliding it in front of her. A bowl of grapes appeared, and she tossed three in her mouth, relishing the pop as her teeth scored the skin. The sweet rush of the juice hit her tongue, and she moaned in pure pleasure.

Jamey tensed beside her for a moment, then took a huge bite of his sandwich without looking at her. She finished before he did, and without a word, he made her another one before returning to his meal.

With only two grapes left, she sat back. Rubbing her belly, she said, "I know it's pitiful, but I can't finish them.

Jamey reached over and grabbed them, tossing them into his mouth with a wink. "I gotchya, Hellion." Picking up her glass and plate, he carried them to the sink and washed them. Drying his hands on a linen towel, he turned back and gazed at her.

Danny met his eyes, finding only amusement there. She wanted to say something snappy, but another yawn ruined the effect. He grinned at her,

somehow making it worse. Sliding off the stool, wanting to make a quick exit, she lost her balance and stumbled.

Before she could make a sound, his arms were on her waist, steadying her. Her hands automatically grabbed the front of his shirt, pulling him closer. Their breaths mingled, and Danny's chest tightened—not in fear— but in anticipation.

She waited, hoping he'd kiss her, but Jamey took a step back, and she felt bereft when his hands dropped from her waist. Blinking quickly, she turned away, heading for the guest room he'd shown her earlier. She mumbled, "Good night," as she headed up the stairs without looking back, even though she wanted to.

What the fuck was wrong with her? She'd never been afraid to ask for what she wanted. But it had never been Jamey she'd been asking. His gaze burned into her back as she walked away. She let out a groan as she entered the guest room, pushing the door shut behind her.

Chest heaving, she caught her reflection in the mirror on the wall across from her. The first thing she noticed was the lack of fear. The second was the faint flush of color heating her cheeks. And the third was the feverish shimmer in her amethyst eyes. It was the color of desire diluted with denial. Because once again, she had proven—when it came to this man—she was a coward. She turned and leaned her head against the door, inhaling his scent through the wood.

Jamey was close. She would have put money on his hand touching the door. She placed her palm on it, imagining his mirroring it on the other side. But he wouldn't push her, and he wouldn't come to her unless she asked him to. And tonight, she wasn't ready to face the possibility of starting something she couldn't finish.

Disgusted with herself, she walked to the bathroom, stripping as she went. Turning on the shower with a thought, she stepped under the water and let the ice-cold stream wash away the tears of disappointment streaming down her face.

Danny knew nothing about being a couple. She didn't know how to talk to Jamey about what they'd gone through together. It was a conversation they needed to have, but she didn't know how to start it. And she sure the fuck wasn't selfless enough to let him go.

Toweling dry, she donned an old pair of shorts and a soft cotton shirt. Dropping onto the bed, her fist connected harder than necessary against her pillow, trying to beat it into the shape she wanted. But no matter how many times she hit it or flipped it over, it still didn't feel like his shoulder under her cheek.

"For fuck's sake," she growled to herself, "Just ask him if you can sleep with him." She nodded, agreeing with her subconscious, but it still took her another half hour to work up the courage to leave her room.

Tip-toeing down the hall, she paused outside his open door, listening to his even breathing. She couldn't tell if he was sleeping or awake. Backtracking one step, she stopped when his gravelly voice reached out to her like a lifeline in the dark.

"Come here, Hellion," he said in a raspy voice.

Danny hesitated another moment before taking the last three steps to his bed.

Jamey pulled the comforter back and patted the mattress by his side. "I warmed up your spot," he said, his voice a low growl.

The view of him lying in that bed beckoning her made something coil low in her gut. The moonlight hit his caramel skin, making it glimmer. Thick strands of his long, dark hair trailed over his chest. She wanted her fingers tangled in his hair and her head on his shoulder.

Her confused eyes met his dark gaze. Ever the gentleman, he waited patiently for her to decide.

"I've been waiting for you, Hellion."

His words settled into her soul, warming her. He'd expected her, and any anxiety she was experiencing melted away as she climbed onto the bed and took her place in his arms. Her thigh slid between his legs, her head found the hollow on his shoulder, and her fingers tangled in the long strands of his hair.

Luminous eyes locked on his back lit amber orbs. They didn't speak out loud. There was no need. She was where she belonged, and she felt the tension in his muscles relax beneath her.

Pressing a gentle kiss on her forehead, his chin found its spot on the top of her head. His voice whispered, *"Sleep, Hellion,"* through her mind.

Danyka let out a long sigh that she hadn't realized she'd been holding and snuggled in closer.

Her eyes drooped, and as her fingers traced over the scars on his chest, she whispered back, *"I love you, Jamey."*

Jamey tensed for a moment beneath her before answering. *"Good thing, because I love you too."*

Smiling against his skin, she soaked in the shared energy pulsing between them—in the magic they created together and in the cocoon of safety he offered her.

As she drifted off, she thought about the magic of this place and of his people. People of the earth, they offered everyone they came in contact with a safe place to land—and healing if needed. Part of the magic of Wellesley Island was that you always left feeling better than when you arrived.

Wellesley Island welcomed broken souls. She dusted them off, offered them a purpose and encouraged them to follow their dreams with a gentle push and the knowledge that they were welcome to return at any time. This

place had been home to many—some for a short period of time and others who became lifelong residents.

The magic of Wellesley was that she brought out the best in you and helped you to give your best back to the world. Danny wasn't sure what her best would be, but she was going to stop for a while and find out.

114

Hope

Collette's eyes flickered open as the sun peeked over the horizon. For the first time in a long time, her dreams had been peaceful. Her eyes traveled around her room, noting the changes that she had come home to after the night on the cliffs.

The dingy gray walls were now an abalone shade. The pearlescent white walls shimmered with streaks of blue, purple, and green. Accents from the ocean—her favorite place—scattered throughout the room. Shells, sand dollars, pearls, and starfish sat in a basket on her dresser. In the corner, a macrame swing hung.

Sea grasses grew in a far corner, and her tiny cell-like windows transformed into French doors that opened onto a small beach. A cushioned bench beckoned from the stone patio. Last night, she had spent hours out there listening to the crashing of distant waves as she soothed her soul.

Days had passed since her hands held the knife that castrated Eaton. Sometimes she still felt the weight of his flesh in her hand and his blood dripping down her fingers. The sensation scared her because she felt no remorse or guilt that he had suffered or that he no longer existed. She just felt safe.

On the wall opposite her bed, a blackboard hung. Words appeared on it the night she had teleported Landon to safety. The list continued to grow, and she read each word before she climbed from bed in the morning. This was who she wanted to be. She would never return to the vapid bitch she'd been upon her arrival.

The words written in delicate script gave her hope. HUMILITY COURAGE, STRENGTH, FIERCE, SELF-LOVE, FRIENDSHIP, TALENTED, WARRIOR, LOVED, KIND, LOYAL. Today, there were

two new ones. PEACE had appeared, followed by HOPE. She took a moment to ponder what those two words meant to her now.

Hope—the sensation of waking and looking forward to a new day and the possibilities it held—she'd forgotten what that was like. It was how she felt when she sensed Lash's gaze upon her, as well as the warmth of his hand in hers and the promise of a future they might create. It was the relationship her father was trying to recreate with her. It was the sound of birdsong filtering in through her open doors and the kiss of the wind on her skin, reminding her she survived to enjoy another day.

Peace—the ability to walk the halls and the trails on the island without fear of evil stepping in front of her. It was knowing she could return home without being stalked and preyed upon. It was the dissolution of the despair and pain she had experienced on the day Lash found her. It was the rage and horror pounded into grains of sand by the crashing waves and swept from her soul. It was the ability to breathe deeply and find a quiet place inside of her—a place that she wanted to explore.

Blinking back tears, she threw off her white bedding and pushed through the gauzy white curtains draping her bed. Entering the bath, she grinned. She loved the airy beach house feel of her bedroom, but she *loved* the bathroom.

Large flagstones covered the floor. Heat radiated from the blue-gray stone. The bluestone continued out the back wall to a path leading to natural hot springs. She smiled with anticipation as she performed her morning ablutions, knowing her bath was always ready.

A massive piece of obsidian extended from the sand. Walking down the rough-cut steps, she made her way to the deep end of the natural pool. Reclining against the glossy black stone, she bathed in the morning sun. The pool was enormous, big enough to swim in. But her favorite place was a natural shelf she could settle on. She leaned back against the rough-cut ebony stone, warm from the sun, and relaxed. A screen of woven reeds on one side provided a sense of privacy.

Gentle waves lapped at the beach in front of her, and she grinned at the seagulls fighting over scraps on the beach. This was the best way to start her morning.

Nights brought an entirely different experience. The sun beating down on the ebony grotto all day maintained the water temperature in the dark. She let her day drift away under a moonlit sky with waves crashing close enough to see the sea foam sprayed on the edges of the dark stone forming her tub. Natural hollows on the edges held candles that softly lit the way. The tang of the salt water and the watchful eyes of the stars released any tension from her day. Collette struggled to stay awake in here at night, not wanting to leave her oasis.

Closing her eyes, she thought about how much had changed in mere weeks. She cringed, remembering the words on the dingy gray walls the first time she entered her room.

"Thoughts create your reality, and deeds create your world. To create a more beautiful world, change your thoughts and your deeds."

Her reality had been dingy and mean. Collette could admit now that she deserved what the Sanctuary had originally chosen for her. She deserved it because she took her pain, guilt, and shame out on everyone else.

By placing others before herself, she had earned this change, and she didn't want to do anything to jeopardize not just this place, but her soul. She never wanted to return to the shallow, callous shell she had once been.

Bathed, dressed, and starving, she headed for the dining room. Butterflies fluttered in her stomach as she headed down the stairs. She had seen none of her fellow students in two days because she had needed the time to heal and process her experiences.

Mistress Rhyanna had been to see her twice a day. Collette was grateful for her kindness and healing. She would continue to see the healer weekly for therapy. She didn't resent the forced counseling as much as she originally thought she would. The Warden was easy to speak with, and every time she left, Collette's soul felt lighter.

The chatter from the dining hall was comforting. She paused as she stepped into the room. They had removed the round dining tables. Large rectangular ones replaced them, representing how the students were coming together as a unit. Ryssa, Amberly, Willow, Galen, Tobias, Chantal, Blaze, Kai, and Genny sat together with some of the other students Collette didn't recognize.

Swallowing uncertainly because she still wasn't sure they had truly forgiven her for her behavior, she glanced nervously around for empty seats. Rubbing her hands on the sides of her leg, she found half a dozen available. Heat infused her cheeks as she realized she couldn't decide where to go.

"Collette," Genny's voice called to her.

Collette turned to see Genny smiling at her. She'd never not known what to do, but for the first time, she didn't know her place in the pecking order.

"Join us," Genny said, tapping the chair to her right. "I saved you a seat."

And with those five words, a weight that Collette didn't realize she was still carrying lifted. Genny, in her infinite kindness, reminded her that in this world, there was no pecking order. They were all enduring trials and tribulations, but they were doing it together. Tears burned in the back of Collette's eyes, but her smile was brilliant as she took the seat.

"Good morning," she said softly to everyone seated. "How's everyone today?"

Multiple voices chimed in, welcomed, and answered her question. Movement to her right startled her. Her eyes darted to the handsome young man beside her, and her heart fluttered.

"Good morning, beautiful," Lash said as he picked up a basket of muffins. Choosing a blueberry one, he passed it to her.

"Good morning," she said with a shy smile. She took a banana-walnut one and passed the basket to Genny.

Galen chortled as he told a story about the hellhounds, and Tobias chimed in with more details. Laughter rang out, and Collette joined them.

The realization that this place was becoming her home, and these people were becoming family, slammed into her. She may have reclaimed her life and found peace. But this place, and more importantly, these people, had given her hope.

115

Healing Magic

Danny woke before Jamey. She stared at him, studying the angles of his high cheekbones and his full lips. Her fingers itched to trace them, but she wouldn't wake him this early. They'd been here a week, and neither of them were sleeping through the night yet. Her nightmares still woke her, and she, in turn, woke him. He rocked her until she relaxed enough to fade off, but she knew he was awake long after she drifted off. The tattle tale shadows under his eyes told on him every morning.

It was still dark, but dawn was nearing. In the distance, she thought she heard drumming. Carefully extricating herself from beneath his arm, she slithered out of the bed without waking him. Wistfully, she studied him, wishing she knew how to paint so that she could capture his masculine grace and beauty. Sighing, she forced herself to move away from the bed before she intentionally woke the slumbering man. She wanted to watch the sunrise on the water.

A quick and quiet shower later, she walked down the mountain trail, eating an apple as she went. Nizhoni had whinnied at her, wanting to go for a run, but Danny's body needed to move. The meals she'd been gorging on had been high in fat and protein, helping her body to rebuild the muscle she had lost, but her endurance needed some attention.

At the base of the trail, she found a path leading to the river. Following it, she came to a clearing on the riverbank. Large river stones formed an enormous circle around a stone lined firepit. Dried grasses and logs formed a small pile ready to be lit. Around the stones was a wide band of mowed grass four feet wide. Mats woven from dried rushes sat a foot apart around the perimeter.

Brows nearly touching, Danny walked the perimeter of the circle, trying to puzzle out its purpose. Symbols on the ground between the mats and the

651

buzz of energy around her were overwhelming. Feeling like an interloper, she turned to leave until a phrase whispered through her mind.

"Stay, my child. This ceremony will do you good."

For the third time this year, her creator addressed her. "I don't think I can," Danny said aloud, ready to bolt.

"This is what you need to move forward—for you and for him."

Those words stopped Danny in her tracks. She'd promised herself yesterday that she would stop running from her demons.

Her keen hearing picked up the sound of movement coming from a path on her left. Eyes alert, she clenched her fists and automatically reached to her side for a dagger. But she didn't have one on her. She shook her head, silently reminding herself that she was safe. This island was a refuge, this clearing was safe, and there was nothing here that she couldn't fly away from.

Giggles reached her moments before something more terrifying emerged. A gaggle of women entered the clearing. The drumming drew closer, setting a rhythm in her soul. Women of all ages took their places around the circle. Some were young, lithe, and beautiful, and others showed the generations they'd lived with the wrinkles on their faces and the silver peppering their dark hair.

Women of all sizes and shapes lowered themselves onto a mat, shifting until their sitting bones were comfortable on the ground. A toothless smile greeted her as one elder slapped her hand on her thigh and cackled at something the young woman to her right said.

Unconsciously, Danny backed away from the gathering. Four more women took their places around the circle. Danny recognized Kateri and was surprised to see Grace had been drawn there as well.

On the edge of the river, two women settled cross-legged with drums and strikers. They hadn't missed a beat as they sat down on the bank. The younger woman with a long dark braid started a new rhythm. Her striker slapped the doeskin hide stretched taught over the rim in a slower pattern. Feathers hung from the striker, swaying with each blow. The other woman, a middle-aged version of her, joined in, chanting.

Danny felt the rhythm deep in her soul. Her body wanted nothing more than to lose itself in the music's beat—more than she wanted to leave. Kateri caught her eye and motioned to an open mat next to her. Her brow lifted, challenging her to join them. Curious and unable to back down from the challenge, she sat.

The elder at the head of the circle was directly across from Danny. She bobbed her head in welcome. Danny nodded back. A young woman in her early twenties sat between her and Grace. She smiled at Danny and said, "Good morning."

Across from her, the toothless woman's eyes were half-closed as she drew heavily on the cigar dangling from her lips, puffing away until the tip was heavy with a thick ember. Reaching down for an enormous sage smudge stick at her side, she touched the bundle against the cigar until it was well-lit and smoking. Passing the cigar to the woman on her right, she cupped the sage bundle and blew on it until the smoke wafted around her.

After waving the bundle over her head and down both sides of her torso, the ancient woman passed it to the woman on her right, who repeated the sequence and passed both items to the next woman.

Danny watched as some drew on the cigar and others passed it on. The red edge of the smudge bundle drifted farther down, consuming the sage as each woman blew on it, repeating the cleansing ritual.

Fascinated with the differing amounts of smoke and the unique shapes forming over and around each woman, Danny observed closely. Watching so intently, Kateri surprised her when she tapped Danny's arm, offering her the cigar. Feeling the need for a hit of something, she welcomed the burn of the acrid smoke into her lungs.

Passing the cigar to the woman on her right, she reached out with shaking hands and accepted the smudge offering, blowing gently on the end. Dense smoke surrounded her, irritating her lungs more than the cigar had. She waved the sage around her head. Thick smoke made her eyes burn as she moved it down to her sides. Intuitively, she stopped in front of her torso for longer than she had anywhere else.

The smoke settled heavily in front of her over her heart center—the center of her emotions and her pain, her sacral chakra—the center of her sexuality, and then lower to the center that should have made her feel safe, her root chakra. She'd been around Rhy long enough that it didn't surprise her to find those energy centers needing attention.

The smoke took on a burnt orange cast in front of her, and she wasn't sure if she should be concerned or not. When the tightness in her chest loosened and she could take a deep breath, she handed the sage to the woman next to her.

As the sage moved once again, Danny watched the trails of smoke also flickering low on Grace's torso near her tailbone before slithering around to settle over her heart. Grace handed the sage off, and the ritual continued until it returned to the ancient one. The smoke was the lightest in her form as she closed her eyes, mumbling a prayer in a language that Danny didn't understand.

Joints popped as the crone stood. Walking around the circle, she purified the group while uttering a creaky, guttural indigenous chant before returning to her place in the circle.

"I call on our four brothers, who willingly offer us protection as we enter the vulnerability of the healing circle. Come forth and receive the Mother's blessing."

Four men stepped out of the surrounding forest. Danny's eyes widened because she had sensed none of them, and she was even more stunned to note that Kerrygan was one of them.

The men lined up in front of the woman, bowing their heads and thanking her as she smudged them. "Return to the cardinal points, keeping your eyes open and your senses alert to evil spirits trying to enter this haven. Nothing crosses your path. Call on the kings and queens of the cardinal directions and energetically close the exterior circle."

They nodded, expressions grave as they resumed their posts. Danny's brow arched. She could have sworn Kerrygan had given Grace a side eye as he passed. Grace had definitely been aware of him. Her entire body tensed in his presence. Kerry had shown no interest in anyone since his return. When Danny's eyes darted to Grace, she noted the pinched look and clenched jaw. Interesting.

Kerrygan returned to his position in the east, facing the rising sun. Out of her peripheral vision, Danny saw his head tip to one side as if listening, but he didn't turn, remaining steadfast and focused on his sacred duty. His mother was part Mohawk. Danny hadn't realized he had reconnected with his clan upon his return.

After he helped her cope with Jamey's accident, he'd become a ghost. Outside of his sanctuary responsibilities, he barely spoke or spent time with any of them. Guilt washed over her as she realized what a shit friend she'd been, not recognizing the pain he was in.

The ancient leader's craggy voice brought her attention back to the circle as she reclaimed her seat. The woman's energy reminded her of Rhyanna. She must be the tribe's eldest healer—their crone.

"Welcome to my healing circle. Every month, the circle is open to all in need, male or female. The Strawberry Moon's circle is open only to the women who find me. I never know where this month's circle will take me. The Earth Mother sends me on a journey at sunrise, just like the one she sent to all of you."

A warm smile lit up her face as she gazed at her audience. "Welcome. I'll open our time together with gratitude." Her wrinkled eyes closed, and she raised her palms up in supplication.

"Earth Mother, thank you for pulling on our heartstrings this morning. It is your will that we gather for this time of healing and fellowship. We are grateful for your wisdom and your love. Thank you for helping us survive our individual ordeals—even when we don't understand the purpose or lessons that were intended by enduring them."

"We seek the courage to offer our humble stories and share what needs to be spoken today so that we might lance the wounds that fester beneath our skin. Telling our stories may help one of our sisters who bears witness to our pain."

Her round body swayed from side to side with the drumbeats. "We will treat each other with the utmost respect as we trust our sisters to keep our words in their hearts and minds and off their tongues. The sacredness of this circle is reliant upon the safekeeping of one another's stories. Mother, grant us the ability to accept the healing as it is offered—freely. And so, it is."

Ancient dark eyes opened and stared into Danny's soul. The medicine woman's dark eyes nestled amongst the crags and crinkles of her wrinkles. They shifted, traveling over each woman's face. Stopping again at Danny's, she bowed deeply before saying, "Welcome, our warrior sister. I have been waiting for you."

Danny's breath caught, and she didn't know what to say. Bowing in return, she said in a confused voice, "Thank you for allowing me to join you today. How did you know I would come?"

A toothless grin appeared. "A falcon told me," she said, chuckling. Her attention moved to Grace. "Another soul in need." She bowed to her as well. "You offer so much of yourself in the care of others. My sister healer, it's time you lanced the wounds you hide."

Grace paled and swallowed a lump of shame. "I'm not sure today is the time for that."

"If not now, then when?" The healer's eyes held hers. "The mother will only give you so many chances to face this on your own before she forces you to see the truth in the mirror of your soul."

Danny felt guilty watching her, but she realized everyone's attention was on her.

"We gather once a month to honor our bodies and cleanse our minds and souls of the pain, grief, or horror we've experienced."

"This ceremony welcomes survivors of many forms of trauma. Those of us gathered here today are women the Mother has chosen and sent to this time and place. Today, we welcome our sisters from neighboring communities and from the other side of the river."

"It is my honor to join you on this journey. Some of your faces I recognize, and some of you are new here. Let us begin." As she brought her hands down, a shield of air surrounding them snapped into place.

"Our words shall only travel to each other, and to the river where they will be transmuted into a soft release. Our emotions will softly flow from our wounded souls, providing us with an opportunity to reclaim the space pain and rage have taken up and to fill that space with the healing power of her love."

She glanced around the circle, and sorrow now clouded the fathomless depths of her eyes—the Mother's eyes. "Today's healing will be but a drop in a nearly full bucket for some. For others 'twill be the first step of many yet needed. This is an opportunity for some to put their demons to bed."

"You may be resistant or unwilling to speak, and that is your choice. We will honor your silence. But we will also raise you up in prayer and hold space for your unspoken wounds, your inner pain and humiliation, and for any loss of innocence or self that you have endured."

"The mother who brought us into the world with nothing more than a sigh stands witness. She cradles all of us in her arms, holding us close to her bosom and crying for our wounds. Her hands stroke our hair and our backs, soothing our souls in the way only she can."

The hair on Danny's arms rose as she felt the caresses against her skin, and on her hair. Tears pooled as she felt the overwhelming power of her creator's love washing over her. The women gathered, took a collective breath, and she heard more than one sob emitted.

"With a gentle inhalation, she extracts the horrors, the beatings, and the assaults on our bodies, our emotions, our spirits, and our wombs. She siphons away the pain, the damage to our psyches, and the barricades we've put up against ever allowing any man or woman to come that close again."

Her voice wobbled as she continued. "She claims our pain as her own, pulling it into her heart and hating that she could not prevent our anguish. She experiences every blow, every unkind word, every time they raped and humiliated us, and every time we felt unloved. Her wrath for us coils like a serpent seeking something to strike."

Picking up a rattle made from the shell of a snapping turtle attached to a wooden handle, she shook it in time with the drums behind her. Her expression sobered, becoming one of sorrow and loss. "I come to this circle to find relief for the burden time has placed on my body and my mind. My joints ache something fierce when it rains, and my mind wanders so far that I'm worried that I won't find my way back to my people." She chuckled along with two older women in the circle.

Her smile fell, and her eyes spoke of grief. "I seek relief from the constant ache of grief. My mate's been gone for three months now, and my days have no rhythm without him." She cleared her throat as she continued to shake the rattle. "Would anyone else like to share their joys or sorrows?"

A middle-aged woman to her left, with a sleek chin-length bob, hazel eyes, and bruises on her arms, said in a meek voice, "I can do nothing right. When he drinks, he reminds me with every blow what a disappointment I am as a mate. He won't leave me, and he won't let me go because he won't allow me to humiliate him. He's afraid everyone will see the truth about him."

Dainty head tipping to the side, her tears fell off her chin as a sad smile graced her face. "But in the dark, he seeks comfort between my legs because that is the one thing he says I'm good for." Her voice chilled with icy rage. "I'm too afraid of him to refuse. But every time he sinks his cock into me, all I can think about is stabbing him to the rhythm of his thrusts."

Her lips curled into a sneer. "And when those thrusts bring me soul-shattering orgasms, I'm not sure who I hate more—him or myself for drowning in his dark pleasure and knowing I'll never leave that."

No one spoke, but a healing chant rose from the women drumming.

A young woman barely out of her teens, sitting between the woman with the bob and Kateri, spoke next. "I was in my first trimester when my son slipped from my womb without a sound and without a breath."

Her sobs came out in hiccupping breaths. "I don't mourn the loss of the child because I never wanted him." Tears rained down heavily, soaking her shirt. "I know that makes me a horrible person.

"My father forced me into a loveless, arranged marriage to seal a business deal. I'd finally worked up the courage to leave my husband for my lover. I realized I was pregnant the day I packed my bags."

As she remembered, her eyes watered. "My lover made it clear our first time together that he didn't want children and would not be burdened with one. Carrying this child would take away the only thing I'd ever wanted for myself."

White knuckles stood out on her clenched hands. "I tried to end the pregnancy and nearly bled to death. My husband found me on the bathroom floor. I barely survived, but I lost the child the next day."

A breath wheezed out of her. "He knew it wasn't his child because we hadn't had sex in months. Furious, he kicked me out. I sought shelter with my lover, only to have him laugh as he, too, turned me away. My family refuses to acknowledge me. I've found a place to stay with the kindness of strangers."

The sad smile that crossed her face was heartbreaking. "I see him in my dreams—the son I didn't want. He is so sweet and joyful, and..." her voice faded as she sobbed, "and...forgiving. I have so many regrets about what I did. I can't sleep most nights."

She gave a wry laugh. "Mayhap it would have been a blessing if I'd bled out with him." Her voice was a portrait of regret and self-loathing.

They heard her confession in silence. The only sound they could hear beyond the drums was the communal dripping of tears hitting the ground.

The ancient leader's voice held depths that no human could utter when she spoke. "Every life is precious, including yours. Your son rests in the shelter of my care until you join him a long time from now. Your actions did not bring on the miscarriage. He wasn't strong enough to survive to full

term. Let me carry your guilt. You will only find happiness if you learn to love yourself. Only then will I lead you to someone who will love you."

As each woman spoke, Danny experienced their sorrows, grief, rage and pain. She realized as much as the Mother was helping them individually, they were helping each other carry their inner burdens.

"I-I-I wasn't innocent when they abducted me," Grace struggled to get the words out. "I freely admit—without guilt—that I enjoyed sex immensely, and sometimes I preferred it with more than one man."

She paused, waiting for the condemnation, and when it didn't come, she continued. "But when they broke me, they turned my body against me."

Speaking in a monotone, her voice dropped to a whisper. "My master trained me to enjoy pain with my pleasure—not just to enjoy it, but to crave it. They turned me into a submissive when I'm anything but—and I've the scars to prove how much training it took to break me."

Grace's head kicked back. She stared sightlessly at the peaceful blue sky as trails of tears rolled down her face. Letting out an anguished wail, her entire body was taut as her gaze dropped to the flames before her. "I never wanted to enjoy what they turned me into." She chuckled darkly. "But I ended up fucking loving it, and I can't forgive myself for that."

She swiped angrily at her tears. "Now my biggest fear is how is any 'normal' man ever going to want me like this? I'm terrified of intimacy with anyone, terrified of my inner freak slipping out." Angry eyes flashed at the ancient one, witnessing her pain, and she lashed out verbally.

"Mayhap you can tell me. At what point should I mention, 'Oh, by the way, I'll never have an orgasm if you don't cause me intense pain or bring someone else in to join us?'"

When nothing was forthcoming, Grace glared at the woman, and finally said with a sneer, "What, no words of wisdom for me, Mother?" Her sarcasm was sharp and challenging.

"The only thing I have for you, Grace, is a question." Her timeless voice was full of dark power. The ground beneath them trembled for a moment, causing the drumbeats in the distance to miss a beat. "Why do you want a 'normal man' when you are anything but normal?"

"I don't understand the question," Grace said, her voice trembling with fear as she waited to be struck down for her insolence.

"You are beautiful, fierce, and protective towards all the women under your care. You are a warrior and a damn fine advocate for everyone you come in contact with. When will you do the same for yourself?"

"I don't have the time to take care of myself. There's too much to be done, too many people who need help."

A low chuckle made the hairs on her arms rise. "Will you play the victim for the rest of your life? You know what brings you pleasure. Own it."

The voice offered no quarter as it continued. "You quickly adjusted to your circumstances, and you survived. You didn't hate having sex with strangers. No, you hated them because you believed they changed the way you experienced pleasure."

The ancient keeper's brow rose, challenging her. "Your darkest fear isn't that they changed you, but that this is what you craved all along. They simply unleashed your inner siren, and you hate them because you are ashamed of your desires. You never allowed yourself to admit that you crave more than one man. There's never any shame in that if everyone is a consenting adult."

"Buttt," Grace sputtered, mortified and unable to come up with a retort.

"Take some time to pleasure yourself—you may find that you are not as conditioned to extreme pain as you believe you are."

Grace's horrified gasp echoed among them as her cheeks flamed, and the elder chuckled.

"If you're still unsure, find others who enjoy the same flavor of intimacy as you. There is no shame in exploration and no shame in loving more than one person—again, as long as it's mutual. But whomever you choose to experiment with, have the courage to do so with complete honesty.

"Don't settle for a lifetime in a lukewarm bed with a man who knows he is failing you. Own your sexuality. No one can take that from you unless you allow them to."

The creator's advice surprised them all. No one spoke. They all sat there in stunned silence at the simple acceptance and love that she gave them.

The stories continued, stories of losses, abuse, trauma in many forms, and of grief. They wept together and occasionally they laughed.

After a few moments of silence, their leader asked, "Would anyone else like to share?" Her gaze went round the circle, stopping on the women who'd remained silent.

Two women shook their heads, passing up the offer. But Danny felt the tug on her heart to unburden herself.

With a shuddering inhale, she whispered. "I don't know where to begin. There are so many wounds and betrayals. They grew teeth with time, biting and clawing at any self-esteem I might have had." She blew out a breath that shifted her long bangs. "But they all stemmed from my father abandoning me."

A caustic laugh erupted from her, and she wiped angrily at the tears streaming down her face in his memory. "Well, to be honest, he didn't abandon me in the traditional sense. He died. I guess I can't really blame him for that. But his loss triggered a series of events that changed the course of my life."

Her voice hardened. "My mother sold me to ensure the survival of my younger siblings, and although as an adult, I can understand the 'why' of it. I

will never understand how she could do it so callously, with no explanations, words of compassion or even a last hug on the day she left me in a brothel."

Danny's tears slowed as rage rolled through her. "I want to kill every man that raped me—and some I have. I want to castrate and eviscerate every man who purchased my body, intending to use it for pleasure—and someday I will. But I loathe my mother more than any of them. I despise her for not trying harder to do anything—even offer herself up—before she resorted to selling me.

"I don't know if I have the capacity to love the way I should." Her voice was thick as she swallowed the lump in her throat. "There is a man who loves me—a good man who deserves someone who can meet him where he is at physically, emotionally, and sexually."

Pale violet-blue eyes filled again. "I love him. Truly, I do in the limited capacity that I am capable of. But I'm so fucking terrified of failing him—and his family—badly." She turned to the left, meeting the eyes of the woman who could be like a mother to her.

Kateri's eyes met hers in understanding and sorrow. She said nothing, but tears rolled down her face, not just for her son, but for Danny.

"And what kind of mother would I be if I could even have children?" she asked acridly. "Any time they pissed me off, I'd probably threaten to sell them. Am I capable of the warmth and love that they deserve? Will I resent them when they need more than I can give?"

Her eyes were luminous again as she choked out, "He'll be a wonderful father, and he deserves the opportunity to become one. But I don't know if I will ever be stable enough to give him the children he will eventually long for."

Her fists clenched as she sat there shaking. A moment later, she felt Kateri's hand clenching hers, silently offering her strength.

"But, Goddammit, I deserve to be loved, too, and no matter how afraid I am of where this will end up, I'm begging the Mother to give me the courage to reach for it all. After everything I've lost, I'm begging for the opportunity to cling to him and love him with everything I've got."

Sniffling, she added, "Please give me the faith I need in myself to at least try." Danny wiped her nose on the back of her hand and swiped at the tears rolling down her face as she finished.

The Mother's voice emerged once again, answering Danny's request. "You already possess more courage than ten women, Danyka. Don't beg me for this, child. The opportunity has always been waiting for you to reach out and grab it. Anytime you doubt your commitment, close your eyes and imagine your life without him. That will immediately set you back on track."

Danny's eyes were streaming, but the hope filling her chest was new. She pulled her knees up, hugging them tightly, still clasping Kateri's hand.

"One more thing, li'l Danyka. When *you* decide you are ready, you will be an amazing mother. Any children you might have will adore you. You will love and protect your offspring fiercely. Never doubt your capacity to love your children. Your mother's last gift to you was making sure you would be nothing like her.

"Faith in yourself, Danyka, is something you must work out on your own. But you can always trust me—as you do Jameson—to catch you when you fall."

Silence filled the void between the stunned sisters gathered around. Ancient eyes scanned the circle, seeking any others who needed to unload the guilt, shame, or horrors they were clinging to.

"The Strawberry Moon Circle offers us the opportunity to release what no longer works for us anymore." Her gaze traveled the circle, meeting each of the women's eyes. "Decide which of your burdens you would like to give up. Let them go. Give yourself the gift of peace."

Ancient dark eyes met each of theirs, peering into their souls and challenging them to reclaim their lives. "This time is often associated with fertility, love, and sensuality…" She waggled her eyes at them and grinned, making them all chuckle. "Enjoy your bodies. Take lovers that know how to make your blood boil and your core weep."

They all laughed at that, and the mood lightened. Swollen knuckles struggled with the ties on a leather pouch that sat beside her. Tugging it open, she reached in and fumbled around for a moment before pulling out a rough piece of amethyst. Tears filled her eyes as she passed the pouch to the next woman.

"The Mother always knows what we need. She offers us a piece of her heart to aid us on our journey. The Mother offers us a symbol of her love and support." Their leader rolled the rough-cut amethyst between her fingers. "Amethyst for consolation will help calm my wounded heart and bring me tranquility."

The woman with a bob who hated her mate chose next. She pulled a pale green tower out of the bag. Pinching the three-inch tower, she gazed at the healer quizzically.

"You have stated that you hate the abuse you live with, yet you enjoy the pleasure he gives you so much that you will not leave him." There was no judgment in the ancient voice.

"If you want a different life, you must find the courage to leave your current situation. If you choose to stay, this stone, Peridot, will help you transform your fury into calm clarity so that you might avoid acting on your enraged impulses."

The woman nodded, fingers stroking the pretty tower over and over.

The young woman, who'd lost a child, pulled a large, white oval stone with black marbling out of the bag. She stared and traced the lines with her finger. Glancing up, she raised a brow.

"Howlite will help you transform your self-hatred into gentle tranquility. This stone will teach you to be patient with yourself as you process your negative emotions. This process will take time, but if you meditate with this stone, you might learn to like yourself once again. It will also help with your insomnia, calming your mind and giving you a few hours of peace."

The woman nodded, mumbling, "Thank you, Mother."

Kateri pulled an amethyst point for inner peace and protection.

Danny pulled a beautiful blue-green stone the size of an egg from the leather pouch. Another stone dropped beside it. "I'm sorry," she said, picking it up. She reached for the bag to return it.

"No, child." The elder said. "They are both meant for you."

A gnarled finger pointed at the first stone. "Azurite is not only beautiful, but it will absorb the negative energies that cling to you from traumatic events. In addition, this stone can help you clear emotions that no longer serve you. It will help your body to release the trauma and emotions trapped inside." The elder smiled at Danny. "Azurite can help you make room in your heart for the man you love."

"The dark blue stone is a raw piece of lapis lazuli. Keep it on you. It will help you move past your emotional wounds and give you the courage to move forward."

Danny's eyes filled once more, but this time it was in relief. The woman next to her pulled a raw piece of citrine to assist with inner wisdom. She passed the bag on to Grace.

Grace reached into the bag carefully, as if afraid something inside might bite her. She wasn't sure she understood the purpose of using the crystals, although she was very aware of the healing power of nature. Her fingers grazed a smooth crystal that seemed to call to her. Pulling it from the pouch, she examined the crystal she had selected.

A long faceted, mostly opaque crystal with a point on the end lay in her hand. Translucent in places and the color of a stormy sky in others, her soul settled as she ran her thumb over the pointed tip.

"Ah, my child, you've got a good one there." The elder smiled so wide her eyes vanished in the wrinkles surrounding them. This woman had lived hundreds, if not thousands, of years. Earth wisdom oozed from her pores even after the Mother had left her body.

"Child of the Earth Clan, this crystal will provide you peace while you work through your fears. Let it ground you as you balance your emotions and release the rage that is strangling your heart. This also offers protections from negative energies that plague you. Open your heart to its healing qualities and regain your self-confidence and your sensuality."

Grace closed her fist around the stone and hugged it to her heart, wanting all the healing it could offer—even if she wasn't sure she believed in it.

She passed the pouch to the woman next to her, who pulled fluorite for connection and protection. The next woman received a piece of obsidian for anxiety and insomnia. The last woman held a massive chunk of rose quartz that was bigger than the bag she pulled it from, to assist with the loss of a young child.

The healer joined the musicians in their chant as Kateri swayed from side to side, occasionally joining in the closing song. When the beats ended, the silence in the clearing was oppressive.

With another deep bow to each of them, the woman said, "It has been my pleasure to lead you in this month's healing circle. You are welcome to join any of our monthly gatherings. Thank you for making it through the entire ceremony."

Smiling at them, she said, "The Earth Mother is with you always, even when you are at your lowest and can't feel her. She wants you to be happy, safe, and loved. If you are not safe at home, please see Grace, and she will give you information on the shelter she will soon be opening."

They all stood, talking quietly amongst themselves. Kateri turned to Danny and opened her arms. For the first time, Danny didn't hesitate to step into the woman's warm embrace. "You know he needs you as much as you need him."

Danny buried her head in the woman's shoulder for a moment, breathing in the maternal waves rolling off her. She nodded her head, not sure what to say. "I'm going to try to make him happy."

Kateri pressed a kiss to her cheek and said, "Then you will." And with those simple words, and a heap of faith that Danny hoped wasn't misplaced, they turned and walked away from the circle.

Danny glanced around in wonder once again at the healing power of this place. She imagined a life on this island with the man she loved. Smiling, she walked faster, ready to take the steps necessary to make it happen.

116

Prove It

The healing circle had concluded. Most of the women had already left. Two women approached Grace, seeking information about the shelter. She provided them with the location and reassured them that protection would soon be in place. The location of the shelter was a closely guarded secret to keep the residents safe.

The last of the women headed home, and Grace sighed in relief. This morning had been an emotional one, and she was craving time alone. She wanted to ponder the Earth Mother's words on her own.

Opening her fist, she gazed down at the beautiful crystal she'd received and let out a sigh. It seemed crazy, but her chest didn't feel as tight, and she didn't feel so damn angry. Mayhap it was working. She turned the piece in her hand, gazing at the different facets and thinking it would make a beautiful pendant.

Footsteps made her glance up, and for the first time, she didn't feel agitated to see Kerrygan standing in front of her.

"The Mother gave ye a beautiful gift. May I?" he said, reaching for the crystal.

Her hand tightened protectively around it, and she realized she was being ridiculous when his eyes narrowed. "I picked it out of the bag."

"Ye always receive the one the Mother wants you to have." He held it up to the light, turning it slowly. "If this were mine, I'd wrap it in a silver cage and wear it as a pendant."

"I was just thinking the same thing," Grace said, giving him one of her rare genuine smiles.

Kerrygan's eyes widened, and his heart beat faster. God dayum. The woman was beautiful when she knocked the chip off her shoulder.

"Wish I knew how to do it," Grace said, frowning. "Maybe I can find someone in town."

"I'd be happy to do it for ye," Kerrygan said, wondering just what the fuck he was doing. It had been a long time since he'd created jewelry.

"Oh," Grace said, surprised he offered. "I don't want to impose."

Kerry ignored her, still peering at the stone from every angle. His eerie eyes narrowed, and she wondered how different his vision was from hers.

"It's not polite to stare," he snarled.

"I'm sorry. Didn't mean to, it's just…" she trailed off, shame flushing her cheeks.

"That I'm a freak of nature?" he supplied, glaring down on her.

"Not at all," she snapped back. "You've got the most uniquely gorgeous eyes I've ever seen." She didn't miss the way his eyes flared in surprise.

A slow smile crawled across his face as if he had forgotten how to do it. "Ye think I'm gorgeous," he drawled. His smile deepened, showing off deep dimples on his cheeks that took him from dark and dangerous to darkly devastating.

Grace's mouth watered, but she controlled her urges. "No. I think you're an ass," she said dryly. "Give me my stone back. I don't want it picking up any of your bad juju."

Kerrygan had about eight inches on her. Gazing lazily down at her, he wondered just how riled up he could get her. "I'm not done looking at it."

"I don't care. Give it back." She wasn't sure why she was so upset about a damn rock. Rage roiled up from her gut, and she slammed both of her hands on his chest, knocking him back a step.

His eyes narrowed, and he snarled at her. "That was uncalled for." Then, just to taunt her, he held it over his head. "If ye want it. Come and retrieve it."

Grace glared at him, having the sudden irrational urge to burst into tears. Nothing about this conversation was rational, and it was pissing her off. At least anger was better than tears. Her eyes met his, and the humor in them settled it for her.

She jumped once more, and when he still held it above his head, she pounced. Reaching up and grabbing his shoulders, she hoisted herself up, wrapped her legs around his waist, and shimmied until she could reach her stone.

Kerrygan groaned at the heat radiating from her body. His free hand landed under her ass, keeping her in place above his waist, terrified that when she shimmied back down, she would feel his reaction to her proximity.

Grace's left hand steadied herself on his shoulder while the other took the stone from his slack hand. Victorious, she glanced down at him and sucked in a breath.

Eyes wide and breathing ragged, he stared at her like the predator he was. His unique eyes locked on hers as her head moved closer to examine the

intricacies of those gorgeous orbs. The hand with the crystal touched his cheek, and the other one framed the opposite side of his face.

His quick breaths filled the air between them, caressing her chin. Horrified, Grace realized she had wrapped her legs around his torso, and the muscles beneath her were twitching at her position. The hand on her ass squeezed, and the other snaked into her hair, grasping her nape and hauling her closer.

"This is a bad idea," Grace mumbled.

"Goddamn right 'tis," Kerrygan said, tugging her head even closer.

"What are you doing?"

"Hoping that if I taste ye just once, I'll get ye out of me fecking system."

"Didn't know I was in your system," she panted, rocking her hips against him.

"Feck, lass," Kerrygan said, nipping at her chin. "Ye weren't even in my peripheral until ye climbed me like a fecking spider monkey."

He groaned as she rocked against him again. His hand fisted tighter in her hair, knowing it had to hurt, but he didn't care because the witch wasn't backing down. And then she moaned at the bite of pain.

Four awkward steps later, he slammed her against a tree, letting her slide down his torso just enough that she touched...

"Just what every girl wants to hear," she snarked. "That nobody's noticed us."

Kerry rocked his hips against her core and snarled, "Not what I meant, and ye ken, Grace."

"I know nothing about you, Kerrygan." Her teeth snapped awfully close to his full lips.

"Whatchya wanna know?" He slid his nose along hers, willing to take the chance that she'd bite him just to kiss her.

The claws on the last two fingers of his hands dug into her scalp, and she arched back, shuddering at the feel of his brute strength pinning her to the tree. Her eyes lit with an evil glow when she whispered in his ear. "Anything south of the border change when your eyes did?"

"Nope. Everything be working jest fine." He hovered just above her lips, not wanting to make the first move.

"Prove it," she taunted, rocking against him once more.

"Feck it," he roared, and his lips crashed into hers as he yanked her down against the hard length of him. And feck him. The taste of her was sweet and tangy, like a granny smith apple. She shuddered in his arms, and his hips thrust against the heat of her core.

"Yes," she chanted as his hand squeezed her ass tight enough to make her moan louder.

Warning bells were going off in his head. He knew she would feel fucking fantastic wrapped around his cock, but the aftermath would be

detrimental to both of them. "Stop," he roared, stepping back and dropping his hands. "Get off me."

The tone of his voice was like an ice-cold bucket of disgust thrown at her face. The implication horrified Grace as she lowered her shaking legs to the ground and walked away from him. Her vision blurred as she ran away as fast as she could.

Kerry roared as she took off. He'd wanted to explain to her why he was slowing down, but she didn't give him the chance. His hands fisted in his hair as he prowled the clearing. Needing a drink, he turned to go, then stopped in his tracks.

Laying on the grass right in front of him was the smoky quartz crystal they'd been fighting over. It was important to her, and he'd upset her enough that she'd forgotten about it.

Shaking, Kerrygan picked it up and put it in his pocket, wanting to return it to her and to apologize. Another thing he sucked at. "Feck me," he growled again and stomped off.

117

Do It Again

Danny followed Kateri back to the family homestead. They'd returned in companionable silence, both contemplating all that they'd seen and heard.

Raised male voices at the barn had both women shading their eyes to see what was happening. All the Vance men were shirtless and unloading bales of hay. Sweat slicked down their bodies, and if Danny hadn't already handed her heart to Jamey, any of these men would have been a welcome distraction.

Danny's gaze locked on Jameson. His banded hair hung down his back, and his bronze skin glistened in the sun. When he caught her eye, he grinned. Those fucking dimples got her every time. The man was gorgeous, and he was hers.

Kateri purred next to her, and Danny turned her head to see the woman's eyes locked on her mate's form. The man was an older version of Jameson, and other than a few wrinkles around his eyes, one would think them brothers instead of father and son.

Danny smirked, happy to see that centuries hadn't dulled the libido of the woman beside her. Kuruk, sensing his mate's interest, glanced over and gave his mate a sly grin.

Kateri returned it and grabbed Danny's hand. "Would you mind helping me in the kitchen? They must be starving."

Danny blinked. She'd been sure that the woman was going to drag her man off into the haymow and have her way with him. "Sure," she said, lifting a brow at the woman.

Kateri drug her into the kitchen, where they prepared a platter of sandwiches, a gallon each of switchel and water, and a bowl of fresh berries and cream. Filling a deep picnic basket and adding fresh fruit to their bounty, Kateri looked at Danny as she added one more thing. A glass jar

that Danny recognized as one of Rhyanna's with a pump on top went into a pocket on the inside of the basket.

"Jamey won't admit it," Kateri said, narrowing her eyes at Danny, "but he's going to be hurting after he's done out there. I usually work this into his shoulder to ease the pain and loosen the tightness that comes afterwards."

Kateri threw a handful of cloth napkins on top of the sandwiches. "His back also bothers him something fierce. Make him lay down and work this in from his shoulders to his hips." She turned, giving her the full weight of her stare. "Because you're so petite, it will be easier if you straddle his hips to work on him."

Danny gaped at her in shock. "Straddle him?"

Kateri gave her a shit-eating grin. "Yup. You know, like when you mount a horse, one leg on either side of him…"

"I know what it means to straddle something," she snapped back at the woman. "Is it necessary?"

Kateri's grin faded to a sad smile. "Don't know. See if you can reach the entirety of his back, sitting at his side. I can, but I've got eight inches on you, Pixie, and a much longer reach."

The gaze locked on hers hardened. "Is the thought of touching him so abhorrent to you, Danny?" Kateri asked in a deceptively soft tone.

She knew Kateri wanted to know her answer not only as her friend but also as the mother of the man whose heart she was playing with.

Danny's jaw dropped. "No, of course it's not. I spend most nights wrapped around him while we sleep."

Her statement made Kateri smile. "It takes time, Danny. I know that. Truly, I do, and I respect the horrors of what you endured. But sometimes, the little things are what it takes to reconnect. I'm not asking you to ride him like a stallion…"

"You did not just say that," Danny said, covering her face. "I can't discuss this with you. You're his mother, for fuck's sake."

Kateri roared with laughter. "You'll find, Danny darlin', that there's not much off limits in my family. My boys always come to me instead of their father. I know most of their dirty little secrets, but I don't tell. Sex is one of the most natural things in the world. There should be no shame or guilt involved in a conversation about it."

"Sweet Mother," Danny choked out. "Enough. I'll rub his back while I straddle him."

Kateri gave her a sweet smile. "Thank you." Her gaze found her mate through the window. "Because I intend to do some massaging of my own, down by the river."

"Not another word," Danny said in a strangled voice. "I do not need those images in my head when we walk out there."

"Shall we?" Kateri grabbed the large basket and a smaller one that was sitting nearby.

Danny grabbed the two gallon jugs and followed behind, hoping the flush had left her cheeks. She couldn't even glance at Kuruk when they sat down at a picnic table between the house and the barn.

"Let's eat!" Kateri hollered. Her shout caught the men's attention.

"Almost done," Kuruk yelled as they tossed the last half-dozen bales to the men in the mow. He jumped off the hay wagon and swaggered towards them. His eyes glittered as they met his mate's. Pouring a glass of switchel, he drank it down and then refilled his glass with water. "Thanks, baby. I needed that."

His arms slid around her from behind and he nuzzled the side of her neck, dragging a deep breath into his nose and no doubt scenting her intentions for the rest of their afternoon. His hand slid down to hers and he interlaced their fingers, tugging her behind him.

"There's no rain on the horizon, so you can finish the other wagon tomorrow, boys," Kuruk said without taking his eyes off Kateri. "Take the afternoon off and enjoy." He glanced at their mother and said in a sinfully deep voice. "I intend to."

Tobias coughed like he was trying to clear a hairball and then dug through the basket to see what offerings were inside. He grabbed two sandwiches and an apple. They were gone in less than a minute. Filling his glass twice with the switchel, he patted his stomach and declared. "I'm ready for a nap. Then I might find Sheera and see if she wants to spend the afternoon with me."

"Good luck with that," Jamey said, pointing his half-eaten sandwich at him. "Last I heard, you'd pissed her off, and she wasn't speaking to you."

"Well, we kissed and made up. I brought her some flowers and chocolates and made some promises that I damn well intend to keep this time around."

"What did you do to get on her shit list?" Danny asked, curious.

"Well, I might have fallen asleep after promising to spend an evening with her, and I never made it."

"Oh, shit." Jamey laughed at him. "Bet that went over well."

"Let's just say I won't be doing that again. I swear it would have been easier if she'd found me with another woman on my lap at the bar instead of believing I'd forgotten her." He pulled a banana out of the nearly empty basket, stepping backwards toward the house. "And just what do the two of you plan to get up to?"

Jamey's eyes met Danny's and neither of them answered him. They heard his chuckle as the kitchen door slammed behind him.

670

Danny sat next to him, facing him as she straddled the bench seat. She pulled out the bowl of strawberries and cream and handed him a spoon, setting the bowl between them on the table.

Taking an overly big spoonful of berries, some of the cream dribbled down her chin. She lifted her hand to wipe it away, but before she could, Jamey caught her hand.

His dark chocolate eyes were backlit with amber, and his voice was a growl when he rumbled, "Let me."

Danny gasped. Expecting him to wipe it with his napkin or his hand, she hadn't expected him to lean in and use his tongue to lick up the drop. The swipe stopped at her lower lip. Her gaze shot toward his, and there was no mistaking the banked desire in his eyes.

She swallowed hard and stammered, "I-I-I'm supposed to rub some of Rhy's oil into your shoulder and back."

Jamey's nostrils flared as he scented her nervousness and her response to his tongue. "Let's go," he said in a guttural growl, tossing everything back into the basket.

"I'm not done with the strawberries," Danny snapped, reaching for them.

Jamey beat her to them, pulling them away and saying, "We'll save them for later." His dark eyes challenged her to argue. "You'll enjoy them more then."

Danny found she was no longer hungry as she stared into the depths of his gaze. Well, that was a lie. She was starving, but it had little to do with food.

He grabbed the basket, and she grabbed the beverage containers. They dropped them on the kitchen table. Jamey dumped the berries into a glass jar with a lid and handed them to her as they left the house.

"Wait," Danny said, running back in and grabbing the bottle of oil.

The gelding Jamey rode to the farm grazed in the pasture. A massive beast, he could easily carry them both. He led him out with a braided rope slung around the animal's neck. Boosting Danny onto the gelding's bare back, he quickly joined her, leading the animal with nothing more than his knees and the rope.

The ride back to the cabin was quicker than usual. Danny had relaxed into the heat of Jamey's chest behind her, aware of every movement he made. Every time the muscles of his thighs tightened against hers to control the horse, she tried not to purr. His palm rested on her stomach, sending butterflies racing inside. When they reached the barn, he dismounted and helped her down because her hands were full.

Danny still felt the warmth of his hands on her hips as she walked into the kitchen and placed the berries in the icebox. Shaking her hands out, she

paced like a caged animal, not sure whether to stay or fly away. A moment later, her options dwindled when Jamey stalked inside.

More amber backlit his eyes as he walked into her space, pinning her against the counter. "Want me to take a shower first?" he asked, leaning in and placing his hands on either side of her hips. "I'm covered in dust."

"If you want to." Her voice was pitifully high, and she was trying so damn hard not to pant.

"Do you want me on the bed or the floor?" he asked in a rough voice, trapping her gaze with his.

Danny nearly swallowed her tongue. His eyes were those of a predator and her heart raced, liking the way his gaze traced the contours of her face, lingering on her lips.

How was she supposed to answer that question? *"Well, we could start on the bed, and then move to the floor...against the wall might be nice..."* Her rampant thoughts were naughty, taunting her with the various positions she wanted to try only with him.

She settled on, "What's most comfortable for you?"

He tipped his head, thinking about it for a moment, and then growled, "The floor will give you more stability."

"All right then, see you when you're finished cleaning up." And then, unbidden, the image of him in the shower—of his large hands tracing soapy trails down his broad chest and narrow waist...

His lips twisted up in a crooked grin, and she knew, somehow, he'd seen what she'd imagined. She slammed the walls up in her mind, not wanting to give away anything else. *"Peeping, fucking Tom,"* she sent through their link.

"Danny," he said, chuckling at her comment.

His voice grabbed her attention, and she couldn't stop the guilty blush. "What."

"There are some extra blankets in the chest in the living room. You could pad the floor, so it doesn't bother your knees." This time, he groaned at the images in his head and abruptly left her alone in the kitchen.

She heard his shitkickers pounding up the stairs and tried to stay away from the dirty images of him cleaning up. Shaking herself, she found the blankets and created a pallet on the floor. The leather breeches she wore didn't seem appropriate, so she ran upstairs and raided his dresser once more.

With a short sleeve button down and a pair of silk sleep shorts, she felt properly dressed to tackle her assignment. She brought in the oil and grabbed a couple of towels from the downstairs bath—just in case. In case of what, she didn't know. But it made her feel prepared.

The water upstairs stopped running, and her heart was pounding in her chest as her palms grew clammy. Taking a deep breath, she rubbed her

hands on the shirt and turned to wait for him. She could do this. They were both adults.

But nothing could have prepared her for the moment he came down the stairs in nothing but a form-fitting pair of shorts, highlighting every damn asset the man had to display. His damp hair hung over his shoulders, and her eyes traced a drop of water that ran down over his pecs.

"Ready?" he asked and tried not to smile when all she could do was nod.

Jamey laid down on the padded floor and thought, *This is gonna fucking kill me.* Her nerves were obvious, but she hadn't run off, so he took that as a good sign. He'd jacked off in the cold shower, trying to make it so that he could endure this without a raging hard-on. But he was afraid that once she put her tiny hands on him, it wouldn't make a difference.

Knees cracking the floor, he smiled at her. "If you're not comfortable doing this, Hellion, we don't have to." He gave her a cocky smirk. "I'll be fine without it for a day."

Danny's eyes darkened to an amethyst shade, and she whispered, "Lie down."

Without another word, he lowered himself onto his arms in a plank position and then settled on the blankets. He heard the pump depress on the bottle and her hands sliding against one another, and he waited anxiously, anticipating that first touch.

"You're thinking too hard about it, Hellion. Just work it into my skin." His raspy voice made it sound as if he was thinking too hard about it.

He heard a long sigh, as if she were working herself up to it. Then he felt her small hand in the middle of his back as she balanced there. And fuck him—she straddled his back, settling on his hips. The heat from her core scorched him through the thin shorts she'd scavenged, and he was uncomfortably hard again.

Jamey hissed, and she instantly tensed against him.

"Am I too heavy?" she asked nervously, bracing herself to leave him.

"Not at all." Her leg lifted from his right, and he reached back and grabbed the outside of her thigh. "Don't you fucking move." His voice was tight, and he could imagine her teeth biting her lower lip. "I'm fine, Hellion," he said in a guttural growl. Whispering a prayer to the mother for control, he lowered his head and waited for the torture to begin.

Danny shifted nervously against him, then leaned forward and placed her hands on his shoulders. Rubbing the oil over his skin, she took the time to trace his muscles and the scars she could reach from back here. His shoulders were tight from the labor earlier, so she applied pressure and worked through the tension and knots she found.

Jameson let out a low moan under her ministrations, and the sound made her smile, thinking she was doing something right. It also made moisture

pool at her core, and she prayed he couldn't feel it through the thin shorts she wore. She shifted, reaching for the oil, and the muscles beneath her clenched. Oopsie.

Bronze skin gleamed with the oil slicking it. Slowly, she made her way down his back, taking her time and massaging everything she could reach. Reaching his lower back, she scooted down, so that she settled on his taught ass. One more pump, and she worked the tight muscles in his lumbar region. Starting in the middle and sliding her fingers out to his sides, she repeated the motion slowly until he moaned beneath her.

Jamey was in hell. There were no two ways about it. Her hands felt amazing on his skin, and some of his muscles had relaxed, but every goddamn time she moved forward, her hips shifted on his ass, and she pressed her sweet little core against him.

His cock throbbed like a bitch, and he worried the skin might split because he was that fucking hard. Every time she rolled against him, he moved with her, thrusting his hips against the blanket, grateful for any friction he could muster. Fingers clenching the blanket, he couldn't hold back the moan as she rolled her hips again.

"Am I hurting you?" she asked in a soft voice.

"Not in the way you think," he answered, not going into details.

Danny did it again, and his moan was louder. The little fucker was doing it on purpose, he realized as she stifled a giggle. So, she felt up to playing. Well, two could play that game. The next time she lifted and rolled her hips, he flipped over underneath her.

Danny gasped and planted her hands on his chest so that she didn't fall. Jamey smirked at her, placed his hands on her hips and said, "Hold on."

In a seamless move, he sat up and scooted back against the couch. She still straddled him, but this time, her core nestled right where he wanted it to be. "You need to reach my shoulder," he said innocently when dark amethyst eyes locked onto his in surprise.

Swallowing hard, she nodded and glanced around for the oil. The bottle was on Jamey's right just out of reach. She stretched, half leaning off him and driving him fucking mad. When she plopped back into position, he nearly exploded, slamming his eyes shut so she couldn't see how badly he wanted to be inside of her in this position.

The squelch of the pump depressing and the whisper of her hands sliding against one another prepared him for her touch. Or rather, he thought it did. But when she reached for his left shoulder, she shifted against him as she lifted, sliding against the monster hard-on he was trying to control.

Her touch was gentle as she mapped out his shoulder and chest. Her fingers traced the silvery sheen of scars against his bronze skin, and the sexual tension eased as he felt her guilt return for what had happened to him.

Jamey let her continue for a while until the pressure she was using gentled to a light caress. The change in mood helped him get his body under control, but his hands still gently held her hips. His fingers stroked the soft skin of her lower back.

Danny's tongue slipped out and wet her lips as her brows drew together and her tentative gaze met his. "Does it cause you much pain?"

She'd pushed the guilt down, and he was grateful for that because he didn't want to reexamine that bullshit again. It wasn't her fault. Shit happens, and that happened to be his day for it. End of story.

Jamey shook his head, meeting her eyes, so that she could hear the honesty in his voice. "Not usually. When I overexert myself—like what I was doing earlier—it aches a little."

His fist chucked her under the chin so he could see her eyes. "But Hellion, that happens every hay season. Tain't nothing new. Ask my father and Tobias how much they hurt come tomorrow."

Her violet-blue eyes remained on his, and he knew she wanted to apologize again, but she didn't. Pride welled up for her courage. Her fingers traced over the claw marks once more, and then she broke his gaze by leaning over and pressing a tentative kiss to his damaged skin.

Letting out a long hiss, his right hand clamped on the back of her neck. Wide eyes met his with a question in them. Amber eyes glowed as he dragged her head closer and begged, "Do it again."

A feline smile crossed her face, and keeping her eyes on his, she did. But this time, her tongue traveled the length of each scar, tantalizing him without mercy.

His right hand tightened on her neck, and his left pulled her hips tighter against him. He lowered his head until his nose brushed against hers. "Hellion, I need to kiss you. If you don't want me to, you should stop me now."

He waited for her answer, but he didn't have to worry about her stopping him because her lips crashed into his. They both moaned at the contact, and when her lips opened for him, his tongue was there a moment later, needing to taste her.

Danny met every stroke of his tongue, hips sliding over his lap, leaving little between them but the thin scraps of silk that magnified the erotic caress. Thick and hard, his cock bumped into her clit every time she moved, and like that day on the beach when they'd dry humped each other to completion, he wouldn't do anything to break this spell.

He captured her cry and her moan with his lips as she chased something she rarely caught.

"Jamey," she whispered, eyes wide with an expression close to panic.

"Tell me what you need, Hellion. I'll give you anything."

"Your hands, baby. Touch me with your hands." She nipped at his bottom lip and whimpered, "Please."

"Don't gotta beg me, sweetheart," he said as he shoved his hand under the too-big leg of his shorts. He found her soaking wet, her cleft slick with her moisture. Sliding a finger inside of her, he caught her mouth with his, mimicking his finger's movement with his tongue.

She was breathless and so fucking beautiful in his arms. "Jamey," she pleaded. "I'm so close."

Adding another finger, he pressed his thumb against her clit. Her body bowed back over his arms as she screamed her release and bucked in his arms. His fingers kept moving as he coaxed another one from her. This time, his hips thrust with her, gliding against her core. Moments later, he came with her, soaking his shorts.

Their ragged breathing filled the air as she collapsed against him. She buried her fingers in his hair as she nestled against his neck. His arms banded so damn tightly around her that he wondered if she could breathe. He kissed her temple, grateful that she trusted him with her body again.

"Thank you. Thank you. Thank you..." she chanted into his neck, making him chuckle.

"Anytime, Hellion," he said with a shit-eating grin. "Any fucking time."

Danny chuckled with him. "Guess we needed that," she said.

"You do not know how badly I've needed that after spending my nights wrapped around you." He nuzzled her neck, and his lips found hers again. This time, their kiss was gentle and sweet, a reconnecting of their souls—a remembrance of where they had been headed before McAllister.

"I love you," he whispered against her lips as his eyes pierced her soul, refusing to let her ignore his words.

Her gaze didn't drop. Meeting his challenge, she brushed her lips softly against his and said, "I love you too, but I think you need another shower."

Roaring with laughter, he held her tighter, so damn grateful that this felt easy, and it felt right. They had so much more to look forward to, and he couldn't wait for round two.

676

118

Hurt So Good

Kerrygan stared down at the cloudy stone in his hand and felt the hurt radiating from Grace through it. "Feck me," he said for the umpteenth time this hour. Pain was the one thing he'd been hoping to spare her. The look of horror on her face as she left had gutted him.

But he was different and not just in appearance. He knew he wasn't what most women would choose as a lover, and he'd learned to live with that. His sexual predilections had thinned the pool of willing lovers long before they'd trapped him in a cage.

His cock pulsed, still at full attention, long after Grace had gone. He didn't think he was ready for slow and gentle yet. Spending the night of the solstice in Ethelinda's bed had helped reacquaint him with how to appreciate a woman's body. She'd also soothed a fear he'd had by proving that everything worked exactly as it should—repeatedly.

One night with the Romani noble maiden was a lifetime gift. She had blessed Kerrygan with her attention multiple times. Every night he spent with her was unique, as if the spiritual leader was trying on a new skin and experiencing a woman's pleasure from every aspect possible.

He toyed with the crystal, once again examining the facets, seeking the prettiest one, knowing what he needed to do and hating it. Apologizing wasn't his forte, nor was soothing the emotional wounds of an injured female. His gaze found the sky, and he ached to take flight and let the mother's breath blow the pain from his soul. Rhyanna's warning and her threats kept him on the ground. Their team had taken enough of a hit lately, and he didn't want to do anything else to traumatize them.

Walking at a quick clip, he headed back towards town, needing to return to Heart Island and find his metalsmithing tools. He'd neared the end of the path when he heard light sobbing coming from his left near the river. He let

out a sigh, dropping his head, hating that he caused her pain. An ache settled in his chest. Pushing the stone into his pocket, he tracked her scent, pulling the smell of jasmine and sunshine deep into his lungs.

Grace sat on a rock ledge with her knees pulled tightly against her chest, arms banded around them and forehead resting on her knees. Long blond hair fell around her, hiding her face from him. On silent feet, he approached her without her knowledge. Dropping to his knees in front of her, he placed a hand on either side of her hips, caging her in.

Grace sucked in a ragged breath as the awareness of him hit her. She could still feel the sexual heat rolling off him, and the smell of him made her core even wetter. But he rejected her, and she really didn't want to see him. "Go away, Kerrygan. I don't want to deal with you right now."

His thumbs pressed against her legs as he muttered, "Me friends, call me Kerry."

"But we're not friends, are we?" she snapped back, anger helping to stem the tears.

"Might like to see what we could be," he said, surprising himself with his honesty. His hands touched her sides, and he felt the deep inhalation that she took.

"I think you made it pretty clear that you wanted nothing to do with me just a few minutes ago." An ironic laugh rang out. "Thanks for the verbal slap, by the way. I needed to gain some perspective."

"I'd like to explain," he said in a soft voice that tugged at her heartstrings. He sounded so unsure of himself when he wasn't growling at her, like he couldn't remember how to be polite. "Please look at me, Grace."

The way he whispered her name was like a benediction. His voice had trailed off into a sexy whisper, and she couldn't deny him.

Wiping her tears and snot on the inside of her shirt, she lifted her head. Thick waves the color of wheat fell around her heart-shaped face. Her hazel eyes met his mutated ones and couldn't glance away.

"Yer wrong Grace. I wantchya. Hell, baby, I'm still hard just breathing ye in."

She sucked in a shocked breath, his honesty unnerving her. She might have preferred him lying to her to assuage the hurt and sending her on her way with a pat on the head—or her ass. Her brows nearly touched as his eyes traced her features before finally lingering on her lips.

Kerrygan didn't know what the fuck he was doing. He sure the fuck didn't know what to say. She stared at him with eyes that reminded him of a startled doe one second and a courtesan the next. He couldn't speak, but he couldn't stop the soft caresses on her skin.

His hands traveled up her torso, barely grazing the outside of her breasts, and she didn't stop him. He expected her to. Reaching up, he used both

appendages to brush back the thick mane of hair from her face so he could examine the gold flecks in her eyes better.

Gathering all her hair in one hand, he held it back while running his other thumb along her jawline. "So fucking beautiful," he murmured, not realizing he'd said it aloud. His thumb brushed over her lower lip, a mere graze of his finger. He felt her soft exhale against his skin and moaned.

Grace sat there, still as stone. She didn't know where this was going and for the life of her, she couldn't decide if she wanted him to stop or not. His words curled low in her gut, and she wanted to hear more from his gorgeous lips. Her eyes kept flicking to them, and when his tongue flicked out to lick them, she wanted to taste him again.

His hand tightened in her hair, pulling her head back so that she would stop teasing him by staring at his lips. When she let out a soft gasp, he relaxed his grip, realizing he'd caused her pain.

"I'm sorry," he said, relaxing his fingers to remove them.

She growled, grabbed his hands to stop his retreat, and begged, "Do it again—harder this time."

His eyes snapped to hers, and the desire he found there destroyed any chance he might have had of walking away. "Are ye sure, baby?" he asked, giving her one more out. "If we do this, I won't be fucking gentle."

Her small hands found their way into his dark locks, grasping near the base of his neck just as tightly. His sharp inhalation and the way he pushed his hips between her knees—rocking that beautiful hard cock just where she needed it—told her he liked it just as much as she did. She nipped at that full lower lip of his, then said, "I don't want gentle. I want you to make it hurt."

Hazel eyes challenged him, and when her legs clamped around his hips, he accepted the challenge, crashing his lips into hers and drowning in the taste of her. His body bucked against hers as he tried to untie the laces of her pants. She tugged his shirt over his head, tracing the scars on his chest. He paused, hearing something banging in his head.

"What the feck," he growled, trying to figure out what was interrupting them. His eyes popped open, and he found the ceiling over his bed. It had been a dream, nothing but a fucking dream. But when his cock twitched, he remembered how good her legs felt wrapped around him.

The pounding on the door resumed, followed by Fergus's voice. "Ye've had enough of a nap for today, my falcon. It's time fer whiskey. Get yer ass out here."

"I'm coming," he grumbled, sitting up and rubbing his gritty eyes. Protecting the women's circle always used a lot of energy, and he'd been exhausted when he'd returned. Sleep also offered him the opportunity to escape how he'd left things. He glanced down at his clenched fist and when he opened his hand, he saw he'd been clasping her crystal tightly while he

slept. It was glowing, and part of him wondered if she had been thinking of him as well.

"I'll meet ye downstairs in thirty."

"Fifteen, lad, or I leave without ye."

"Feck off," Kerrygan shouted as he walked to a desk in the corner of his room where he kept his wire and pliers. Finding his favorite facet, he took his time, knowing Ferg wouldn't leave until he was ready. He twisted and turned the metal, creating a beautiful silver cage around the smoky quartz. He crafted the cage in a way that left most of the stone visible, enhancing the beauty of the piece. With a final twist, he examined his handiwork, pleased with the finished product. He only hoped that she wouldn't hate that he'd done it without her permission.

Adding a fine silver chain to the pendant, he placed it in a black velvet bag and tucked it into his pocket. Picking up the cleanest shirt he could find on his floor, he slipped it over his head and tucked a knife into the sheath of his boot.

Loping down the stairs, he met Fergus's grin with a glare and said, "I need to make a stop on Sackett's Harbor first."

Fergus raised a brow. The nosy bastard.

"I need to drop something off, and it's yer turn to work on the wards. Don't know where ye been mucking about, but it's time your lazy ass did something out there."

Fergus's eyes flashed in warning, and his fire drakes made an appearance, hissing at him. "None of yer business where I been, laddie. I pull me weight. No need to worry about that. If ye need an excuse to see Miss Grace alone, all ye gotta do is ask." He raised a knowing brow and turned his back on Kerry as he walked out the door.

They portaled to the harbor and quickly made their way to the massive estate housing the shelter. Fergus didn't say a word as he worked his way around the perimeter, examining the wards they'd started.

Kerry walked in the front door, grateful the powerful energy recognized him. He'd been afraid Grace might have locked him out. Long strides took him down the hall. He found a light on in her office. Leaning against the door frame, he studied her for a moment. The mass of her thick hair was in a messy bun on top of her head, and she wore a pair of glasses that made her look studious and sexy as hell.

Grace glanced up from her paperwork, sensing him in her space, and her features remained carefully neutral as if she hadn't climbed his body earlier today.

"Can I help you with something?" she asked in a clipped tone completely at odds with her outward image of polite interest.

"Ye forgot something when you ran off," he said, pulling the velvet bag out of his pocket. He walked towards her slowly, wanting to drag this

moment out because when this was over, he would have no reason to linger, and he wanted more time with her.

Grace stood and met him in the middle of the room. He opened his palm, extending the pouch to her. Her eyes met his, warily. She reached for the bag, and when her fingers met his palm, he closed his large hand around her smaller one, tugging her against him.

She gasped as her chest met his, but she didn't pull away. Kerry leaned down and whispered into her ear, "Me stopping this afternoon had absolutely nothing to do with ye and everything to do with me fecked-up head space."

His free hand came up beneath her chin, lifting it and making her meet his eyes. "Yer so fecking infuriating. But the only thing I wanted to do was feck ye as brutally as I could against that tree. We both would have come out of it bruised and mayhap a little bloody." He cocked a brow at her as she sucked in a gasp, and his lips drifted closer to hers.

"It might have been just what we both needed, but ye had just left a healing circle. There was a reason ye were there. And before ye ask, I didn't hear nothing that was said. But I think ye might have needed some time alone to process everything. And me thinks maybe ye needed something gentler than I could offer."

Before she could protest, he kissed her. It wasn't gentle; it was a claiming, a reassuring that she shouldn't doubt how she'd made him feel. He'd enjoyed every touch and sound she'd made. When he released her, she gaped at him.

"I hope ye like that," he said and gestured to the pouch she clasped tightly in her hands. "If not, I'll return it to its original condition." Without waiting for an answer, he walked out the door. He'd nearly made it to the end of the door when he heard her gasp of pleasure.

"Kerrygan," she said, running down the hall after him. She grabbed his hand and said, "It's absolutely beautiful. Thank you for taking the time." Squeezing his hand, she gazed up at him for a long time and then asked in a sultry voice, "Do you have scars on your collarbone?"

Kerry's cock twitched. "I do. Why do ye ask?"

A pretty blush stained her cheeks. "I just had this strange dream this afternoon."

His full lips twitched into a sexy grin, and he whispered in a gravelly voice, "Did ye ask me to make it hurt in this dream?"

The pink on her cheeks turned a deep scarlet, and she couldn't look at him. "I might have…"

"Well, baby, next time ye say those words to me, make sure ye mean them." Her gaze collided with his as he leaned down and stole another kiss.

"Because the next time ye make me that offer, I'm gonna spend days making it hurt so fecking good."

Grace grabbed him by the front of his shirt and dragged him down for another kiss, demanding as much from him and maybe a little bit more. When his hand snaked into the hair at her nape, pulling a little too tightly, she moaned. He released her as if she'd burned him.

"Later, sweet thing. Don't got time to play with ye tonight. Got plans for this evening." He chucked her beneath the chin with his fist and swaggered out the door, adjusting himself as he went.

An enraged gasp came from behind him, and he grinned, punching Fergus in the arm as they headed back to the portal.

A book sailed by, narrowly missing his head. "Listen, you arrogant asshole. I didn't ask you to stay and play, and it will be a snowy day in hell before I do."

"Keep telling yerself that, darling." He turned to her and gave her a cocky grin, then blew her a kiss.

"What the feck are ye doing, laddie?" Fergus asked him with a raised brow. "That wee lass will fry up yer balls for her breakfast."

"I know," Kerrygan said, giving Ferg the first genuine smile he'd managed since he returned to his human form. "She's fecking magnificent."

"She's a shitload of trouble if I've ever seen one. Tread carefully, lad." Fergus was uncharacteristically somber as he glanced at Kerry. "She's got a lot of fecking baggage that she hasn't even begun to unpack."

Kerry stared at him for a moment before saying, "Don't we all, brother?"

Ferg blinked and then nodded. "And she's nearly jailbait."

"Nearly, but ye try telling her she ain't old enough when y'all let her run that shelter."

Ferg nodded. "Yer right. With all those lasses been through, ain't none of them close to their birth age."

Kerry nodded and reached for his stogie, drawing hard on the lit tobacco. "Got that right. Now, let's go. Ye owe me a fecking drink for waking me from one of the best dreams of me life."

The mood lightened, and they laughed as they headed down the lane. But Kerry's mind stayed on the dainty woman with a mean throw and glittering hazel eyes that would haunt his sleep for days to come.

119

Keep Loving Me

Jamey staggered up the steps as twilight fell. Exhausted, he dropped on the top step and thought about the path this day had taken while watching the stars appear.

Danny had fallen asleep in his arms after their interlude. He'd carried her up to his bed and tucked her in, then taking another shower, reliving the way her slight body had felt sitting on his hips while she massaged his back.

He'd done his chores, and when he found her still sleeping soundly, he'd gone back down to the farm and helped Tobias unload the last load of hay. They'd downed a couple of beers and sat bullshitting for an hour before he came home. He'd bedded down the gelding, whom he needed to name, and was too damn tired to move right now.

The sounds of summer enveloped him—bullfrogs and peepers, racoons chittering, this year's cicadas. A deer coughed near the barn and stomped its hoof against the ground in warning. A bobcat screamed, and in the distance, he heard the faint howl of a coyote. The silky whisper of the wind caressed his face as the weather changed, cooling down. He didn't scent rain yet, but it was coming.

A light came on behind him, and he heard the upstairs shower running. Hauling himself to his feet, he went straight to the downstairs bathroom for his third shower of the day. He would have skipped it, but he didn't want to drag the dust and stale sweat into his bed with Danny.

Kicking off his boots, he stripped and lathered up. Turning the water as hot as he could stand it, he stretched his arms overhead and let the water massage away some of the hurt. He stood there with his head and forearms against the wall and could have fallen asleep that way, but the hot water ran out, and the cold snapped him out of his doze.

Pulling the shower curtain back, he stepped out and wrapped a towel around his narrow hips. He pulled a tortoise-shell comb through his long hair and swore when it knotted at the bottom. With a sharp yank, he pulled the comb through impatiently.

The dark chestnut strands falling over his shoulders nearly touched his waist. He'd thought about cutting it. But every time he did, he remembered Danny's hands running through the loose strands when she'd kissed him for the first time. She loved his hair, and the thought of her controlling him with it made his cock flare to life again.

Pushing those images away, he stepped into the living room of the cabin, intending to head upstairs to his bedroom. Instead, he froze, his breath stolen by the vision awaiting him.

Danny lay on the floor in front of the lit fireplace. Her upper body was bare, with a blanket covering her from the hips down. A thick pallet of blankets cushioned her petite frame from the floor. The bottle of the massage oil she'd used on him sat nearby.

Large violet-blue eyes met his dark ones as he stood there, stunned. The exhaustion evaporated, and his mouth watered at the thought of licking every inch of her skin.

Not wanting to break the spell, he reached out on their inner line. *"What are you doing, Hellion?"*

Her gaze was steady, but he sensed her nervousness. *"You were so relaxed after I worked on you...I could sense the pleasure you were receiving from my hands, even though you tried to ignore it.*

A flush stained his cheeks, not in embarrassment but in desire. He loved the way she was so in tune with him. The connection between them added another ember to the internal fire simmering low in his gut. He swallowed hard, watching the firelight dancing across her pale skin. *"You read that correctly,"* he said, not sure how far he should push this. *"What are we doing here, Danny?"*

She needed to say it, to voice her wants and needs. He wouldn't encourage this if she weren't ready. There were so many landmines they needed to navigate. He wanted her to know she was always in control of anything they did and how far they were going to take any form of intimacy. She could always put the brakes on, and he would respect her choice.

She gave him a lazy blink as her eyes tracked the water dripping off his hair and running down into the low-slung towel. Tongue darting out, she licked her lips, and inwardly he groaned. The scent of her desire hit him, and there was no stopping his body's reaction to her, so he stopped fighting what she was doing to him.

Her gaze grew wider as it traveled lower, taking him in and making him throb like a bitch. Eyes returning to his, her breath came a little quicker when she finally formed a coherent thought.

"I thought we could…I mean, I would like to try…Aw, fuck Jamey, I'm not good at this." Her eyes welled with frustration, making him step towards her.

"Just tell me what you want, Hellion, and I'll give it to you. Tell me what you need."

"Touch me, like I touched you." Her breath caught as she started second-guessing herself. *"But only if you want to."*

The doubt in her eyes slayed him. How could she not know how badly he needed to put his hands on her after this afternoon? "I want to," he finally said aloud in a ragged voice. "I've wanted to for a very long time."

He moved until he was standing next to her. "Where do you want me to sit? In front of you? Beside you? Straddling you?" He knew by the flare of her eyes she wanted the last one, but again, he needed her to say it.

"Straddle me, Jamey, like I did you," she said in a breathy whisper.

The warmth of the fire left a fine sheen of perspiration on her back. He wanted to run his tongue up her spine, but he would behave, even if it fucking killed him. And it damn well might.

He slid the oil closer to her. He straddled her, gathering the bath sheet between his legs, and hoping to cushion his erection so it didn't dig into her every time he moved. "This all right?" he asked in a husky voice.

Her body tensed as he lowered his hips to hers, carefully settling where her hips met her bottom. He was massive next to her and took his time, lowering his full weight onto her. His thighs tensed, ready to lift back off at any moment.

Danny sensed his concern. *"I'm good,"* she said through their line. *"I'll let you know if I'm not."*

"Promise me."

"I promise, Jamey. The moment I need to stop, I'll tell you."

The oil was already warm from its time near the fire. He pumped a small amount into his hand and rubbed his hands together. Taking a deep breath to calm the desire raging through him, he leaned forward, running his palms over her shoulders and down her arms. She stiffened, and he paused for a moment, waiting for her skittish nerves to settle. The internal battle she was fighting with herself transmitted easily through her tense muscles.

Jamey nearly stood but waited for her to call it. Stroking small circles with his thumbs, he worked the area on either side of her neck gently until he heard a soft sigh escape her.

Danny lay there, overwhelmed by the gentleness of his touch. Make no mistake, there was power and strength in his hands, but the reverence and gentleness he touched her with was incredible. Her body melted under him, her muscles relaxing and her heart thudding harder in her chest.

Jamey waited until her body told him she was ready for more. As she sank deeper into the blankets beneath her, he made wider strokes with his

thumbs and began using his fingers and palms to work her tight shoulders. *"This too hard?"*

"No…harder."

A smile crossed his lips as she responded the same way he did with a deep tissue massage. He continued his ministrations as her body relaxed completely beneath his hands. He took his time working down over her back, wanting to enjoy every moment of this, not knowing if he would get another opportunity. As he worked along her ribs and the outside edges of her breasts, he paused. *"Anything you don't want me to touch?"*

"Not so far." The voice in his head was a whisper and so fucking sexy.

His fingers stroked her sides and as his fingertips pushed the boundaries, she writhed beneath him. Sucking in a deep breath, he backed away from an obvious erogenous zone for her and tried to keep his body in check.

Danny tried not to gasp as he brushed against the sensitive edges of her breast. Fuck. She wanted to beg him to do it again, but she wanted him to work his way over her body in his own time. She was so turned on that her hips pushed back against him, and there was no mistaking his body's response to her.

Jameson was hard against her, and no matter how he'd bunched that towel to camouflage it, she could feel the feral heat of his cock against her ass, and it made her fucking hotter. She wasn't sure she would survive this encounter, but she was going to enjoy every second before she went up in flames.

Jamey reached her lower back and couldn't help himself. He leaned forward and pressed feather-light kisses along the length of her spine. Dainty hands clenched into fists on the blanket, and he smiled against her back. His hands massaged her lower back as far as he could without stroking himself, but he was gonna need to do that sometime soon. Trying not to groan, he sat up straight with his fists clenched at his side.

"Do you want me to stop here…" he asked in a tight voice.

Danny was quiet for a moment before her hips shifted against him once again, causing him to bite off a curse. *"I want…more, please."*

Fuck yes. He lifted his hips and shifted back, moving the blanket with him until he settled lightly on her thighs. Picking up the bottle of oil, he poured some directly into the hollow at the small of her back and then drizzled it like honey over her buttocks, letting a tiny stream of it pool in the crack between her cheeks.

Danny moaned long and low, not caring if he heard—hoping that he heard—what he was doing to her. She needed him, and tonight, she wanted all of him. Everything he was doing was lighting up all her pleasure centers and none of her fears. So, she was going to enjoy this as far as they could take it. Her soaked pussy and her throbbing inner walls wanted him inside of

her. But she would not rush this encounter. No, for the first time in her life, she was going to enjoy the slow ride.

Her long moan nearly made him cum, and the way her upper body undulated when he massaged the pooled oil out over her hips and down over her ass. Goddamn!

He took his time slowly working down over those beautiful, tight globes. As he reached the edge where they met, his hands kneaded and gently pulled them apart, watching as the oil slithered into all her crevices. He monitored their inner link, but all he felt was a deep sense of contentment, intense desire, and a hint of curiosity about what he was going to do next.

Danny's breath came in short bursts as she tried not to pant. The sensation of his hands on her was amazing. When he grasped the cheeks of her ass, massaging and pulling them apart to tease her, the throbbing of her inner walls intensified.

This was something she hadn't ever done willingly—never thought she would want to—but he made her want to try anything he wanted to explore with her.

Jamey took his time loving on her ass. As he pulled her cheeks apart once again, he felt her intake of breath, but still sensed no fear. He gently stroked his thumbs along that inner crease, coming closer to....

"I've heard some women enjoy playing there..." Danny said, trailing off as if embarrassed.

"Some do," Jamey said, his voice even deeper. *"Many women find it quite pleasurable with the right amount of patience and prep."*

His fingers teased even closer, and her muscles involuntarily clenched in nervous anticipation.

"Do you want me to stop or move lower?"

"Do what you want to do to me, Jamey. I trust you to know what's too much."

The complete trust she finally gave him staggered him. She had been through so much, and that she could even stomach him touching her like this was a tremendous step for them.

With one hand spreading her cheeks apart and the other drizzling more oil between them, he felt her moan. He used his forefinger to spread the lubricant up and down between her crease, grazing her tight hole, giving her the opportunity to stop him. The sensations radiating at him from their link encouraged him to continue, but he had other plans for tonight.

Pressing a kiss on her gorgeous ass, he moved his hand lower, traveled along her inner thigh to where it met her heated core, inching closer to her dripping entrance.

"We're gonna save that for some other time. Tell me what you want, Hellion," he growled at her. *"I won't do anything until you ask me for it."* The command in his voice was so unlike anything he had ever used with her before. It was the

687

equivalent of her compulsion. She wanted to answer him, she wanted to please him, and she desperately wanted him to keep touching her.

"Please touch me, ease the ache inside of me." Her body squirmed beneath him as her desire ratcheted higher.

His thumb glided through the moisture she was shedding. Shifting his left leg, he moved it to the inside of her thigh, spreading her legs wider and pulling her hips up slightly. His thumb stroked the length of her from back to front, his thumb gently bumping against her clit.

"Yesss," she hissed out as her body moved against his touch, trying to get closer to the pleasure spiraling tighter and higher inside of her.

On the next stroke of his thumb, he slid it between her lips, pressing against the sopping entrance of her pussy and whispering, "Hellion, do you want me to make you come on my fingers? Look at me."

Danyka's head turned, and her eyes found his over her shoulder. The amethyst orbs were half-mast and sultry as hell. Her flushed cheeks and the teeth marks on her lower lip where she had obviously been biting them added to her sultriness. The command was back in his voice, and she loved the way he bit off the words, forcing her to claim her own pleasure. "Make me come, Jamey. Any way you can."

He gave her a sultry smile, accepting her challenge as he settled into place. He intended to make her scream his name multiple times, even if he didn't get to join her. Danny needed to realize what she'd been missing, and he fully intended to savor this night, giving her such intense pleasure that she couldn't decide whether to beg him to stop or give her more.

His thumb kept tracing that path up and down her slit until she whimpered. On the next pass back, he pressed it gently into the center of her, moaning at the feel of her tight, velvet walls sucking him in. He stroked her slowly until she squirmed beneath him, begging him, still unable to reach the climax she needed.

Needing to make her come as badly as she needed to get there, he removed his hand. She gasped in displeasure until he flipped her over onto her back. Wide, glazed eyes beseeched him for more. Her need radiated through their bond, and it was a physical ache that was damn near painful.

"I'm going to take care of you, Hellion. You all right with that?"

Danny hesitated for a moment, and he felt a whisper of uncertainty coming through her.

"I won't do anything you don't want me to do, I promise you that."

Danny blinked as her hands ran over her abdomen and then moved upwards, massaging her breasts. She arched her back, needing him to touch her. *"I don't know what I need, but I trust you to know what I can take."* Luminous amethyst eyes begged him silently as she said, *"Jamey, please…"*

Jameson knew she didn't beg lightly. He wasn't torturing her to be an asshole. This wasn't a power trip for him. He just needed to know if he needed to slow down or back the fuck off completely.

With her gaze on him, he pulled her knees open and settled between her thighs. His muscled shoulders opened her thighs wider as he cupped her ass in his hands, glanced up, and dragged his tongue up through the center of her. Her back came up off the floor, but he placed a hand on her stomach, holding her down. He cradled her in place while he lapped up the juices flowing from her sweet pussy.

Moaning, he took his time before finding her clit, sucking it into his mouth, and plying it with his tongue. The mewls coming from Danny made him harder. He dug his hips into the floor, grateful for the blanket to rub his cock against. He'd lost the towel when he flipped over but was determined to make this experience all about her pleasure.

Her body trembled beneath him. Sucking on her clit, he slid a finger into her pussy, slowly fucking her with it. Her hips kept trying to punch up to meet him, but he wouldn't allow it. Adding another one, he kept up the same slow speed until she was mumbling incoherently.

When her inner walls clamped down on his hand, he curled his fingers and stroked the upper side of her walls, causing a gush of fluid. Danny screamed his name as she violently came.

Danny exploded. That was the only way to describe what he'd just done to her. Bursts of colors streamed behind her eyelids. Her limbs twitched and flailed as she keened his name.

Still twitching, she realized he hadn't even slowed down but continued to move his hand as if nothing had happened. His fingers curled inside of her once again, and she rolled under that tidal wave of pleasure even deeper and darker than before. Her entire body bowed, and she wailed his name again, trembling from head to toe.

Jamey wiped his face against her inner thighs, and the feel of his cheeks there made her sensitive skin twitch. She couldn't breathe. Her chest was too tight, and she tried to suck air into her lungs. Lids struggling to open, she glimpsed his amber eyes watching her intently, backlit by the desire he had for her.

He peered up at her from between her legs, his expression so intense that Danyka reached down and stroked the side of his face tenderly. "Thank you, baby. I needed that."

"Know you did." He gave her a cocky grin. "But we're not done yet." Before she could protest, he leaned back down and started again, playing her body like a fine instrument, over and over until she reached that crescendo.

Orgasms later, she gasped, "What about you?"

"Tonight isn't about me. It's about you, Danny."

Danny's eyes watered at his willingness to take nothing for himself, only seeing to her pleasure. "But you always make it about me. What if I need to feel you inside of me? Will you deny me that?"

Jamey looked at her for a long time. "You sure you're ready for that, Danny?"

"I want to try." Her voice was low, hesitant, and he detected a hint of fear in it. Not fear of him, but fear that she would fail at this.

She opened her arms to him and simply said, "Come here, Jamey. Keep loving me."

Jamey was grateful that she realized that was exactly what he was doing. This wasn't fucking. He didn't want that tonight. With every touch, he showered her with love, placing his heart in her hands and his hopes into her keeping.

Pushing to his knees, he slowly stalked up her body, giving her the opportunity to change her mind. He watched her eyes widen as she took in the full sight of him engorged.

"Kiss me," he ordered, taking her thoughts off the size of him. Her lips met his hesitantly. "Close your eyes, Danny." He waited for her and then gently brushed his lips against hers. Her hands came up to frame his face as she remembered his exquisite taste.

Jamey took his time distracting her with the feel of his tongue stroking against hers as he settled between her thighs. Her hands wrapped into his hair, pulling him closer, making him moan at the bite of pain she caused by fisting his silky strands.

Gently, he glided his cock through her moisture, making both of them moan. He nudged her entrance, not entering, just settling against her. He studied her intently as he kissed her again, making sure that she was comfortable. Too many men had caused her pain in this position. He refused to be another one.

Danny continued kissing him as he nudged a little more insistently against her until the crown of his cock glided inside. Her eyes flew open, amethyst orbs staring at him. Jameson held himself in place while his tongue stroked hers.

"I want this, Jamey. I want you so badly," she said in a wobbly voice, but he noted the tension in her body.

He pushed in a little deeper, encouraged by her words, but the moment he did, tears filled her eyes, and her entire body tensed beneath him. He stilled over top of her as his thumbs wiped them away. "We don't have to do this, Danny," he whispered as he withdrew.

"Wait!" she cried out. "Do that again, just a little."

Jamey slowly slid in again, watching her expression the whole time. "Is this painful?"

"No, it's not that." She cried, looking devastated. "I think I could enjoy it—I want to. But every inch of my body wants to fight against you, and I don't know why."

"It's ok, honey. I know why."

"Let me roll over and you can take me like that," she begged, trying to flip to her stomach.

"No!" His voice cracked through the room. Her eyes jumped to his, and fear hovered there. She was afraid that he would force this on her. His hand caressed her face gently as his lips took hers again, softly, sweetly.

"I don't want to take you the way you've taken every other man who's fucked you. I want you looking at me when I glide inside of you, and there are other ways to accomplish that.

Pulling out of her, he rolled to his back and pulled her astride him. Her hands landed on his chest, and she stared at him, lashes wet as she blinked back tears of frustration. Framing her face with his hands, he pulled her to him, brushing his lips over her eyes and capturing her tears.

"No need for that, Hellion," he said in a voice that was pure sin. "We're going to try a position that gives you all the power. You all right with that?" He waited until she nodded. With his hands on her hips, he slid her moist cleft over the length of his cock. "Kiss me, Danny."

Danny watched him, and he could see the uncertainty and frustration in her eyes.

"Kiss me," he said again with a hint of that command. She placed her hands on either side of his head, then leaned down to brush her lips over his. His hands ran up and down her back as she kissed him while her lower body started moving intuitively on its own against him.

Jamey groaned as she picked up speed, moving her slick heat against him. His fingers grasped her hips tightly. *"If you want me inside of you, then take me, Hellion. As much or as little of me as you want, or not at all. Make yourself come using my cock any way you choose."*

Danny's eyes met his, and he saw the fleeting moment of gratitude in them for giving her options and not forcing something that wasn't working. On her next forward slide, she tipped her hips and stayed there a long moment with the tip of him nestled against her opening. She panted, gazing down at him. The love shining back at her calmed her erratic breathing and stilled the chaos swirling through her mind.

Jamey caressed her thighs, reassuring her. The sensation added to the desperate need she had to feel him inside of her. With her hands on his shoulders, she slid onto him, her eyes wide as he stretched her beautifully like she always knew he would. Slowly, steadily, she worked the head of his cock into her, then paused, acclimating to his impressive girth. His hands tightened on her legs, the only sign of how close he was to losing control.

Danny wanted to see him lose control, and she wanted to be the reason he did. She rose and when she slid down this time, she took half of him in, and it was fucking amazing.

His shaft was so thick that he challenged her body to accept his cock. The more she took, the more she wanted. She rose again and saw his jaw clench painfully. *"Need me to stop?"* she asked as a frown crossed her face, afraid that she was doing something wrong.

"I want you to do whatever you want with me."

"Not what I asked, Jamey. What do you want from me?"

His backlit amber eyes met hers and he gave her the truth. *"I want you to sink down on my cock and ride me, Danny. That's what I want."*

As his words sank in, her body swallowed his entire length. She released his shoulders and sat back with her hands on his thighs. His body was fucking perfect beneath her, and she could feel her inner walls already clamping tightly around him.

His right hand shifted from her hip to her clit, and she moaned at the sensation as her body took over for her. Hips moving slowly at first and then faster, she rode his gorgeous cock with her head kicked back and her eyes closed.

Jamey played with her clit, and palmed her breasts, watching her body above him and moaning her name.

Every stroke brought her closer and closer to the precipice she needed to fly from. And when she glanced down at him, the pure masculine pleasure he was radiating as he gazed up at her through half-closed eyes made her come all over him.

Jamey was in fucking heaven. Pure bliss rolled through him as she took that slow ride on his cock. Her core throbbing around him made it so hard to keep his shit under control, but he would *not* cum before she did. This was all for her, and if he enjoyed it, too, that was a fucking bonus.

Her long moan and gasping breaths told him she was close, and when her sheath clamped around him and she screamed his name, he grabbed her hips and slammed her up and down on his throbbing member, thrusting deep inside of her as her orgasm erupted, taking him with her. He pulled her tightly against his chest as he crushed his lips against hers and kept sliding her up and down on him. His arms banded around her as tears rolled down her face.

"Hey, honey, what's this?" he asked as he brushed them away with his lips.

"I didn't know...I didn't know it could be so fucking beautiful." She sobbed in his arms, clinging to his neck. "Thank you for showing me what it should be and for not getting frustrated when I couldn't..."

"Shh. No, Hellion, thank you for giving yourself to me." His lips grazed her forehead, then her temples before working his way down and gently capturing her mouth once more. "Honey, thank you for trusting me.

With exquisite tenderness, he showed her without words how much she meant to him. When her body moved on him once again, they made love slowly. Jamey sat up and wrapped his arms around her. Danny's legs wound around his waist. Slow and sweet, their orgasms this time were even more powerful in the gentleness of their coming together.

"There are so many ways that I can make love to you," he whispered against her lips. "I don't need to pin you down and make you feel helpless for us to enjoy each other. I can prop you against the wall."

Jamey kissed her neck. "Enter you on our sides or," his lips moved to her collarbone, "if those positions don't make you scream my name, we'll try another, and another, and another." His lips punctuated his words until she was laughing with him. He lay back on the floor with her tracing patterns on his chest, his heart thumping madly in his chest.

His soul was at peace for the first time in weeks. Jamey laid there watching the firelight dancing on her slick skin while her fingers glided through his hair. Eyes heavy after a very fulfilling day, Jamey fell asleep on the floor with Danny splayed on top of him.

120

Always Take What You Need

A ray of sunshine flickering across his face woke Jameson. He stared at the ceiling, trying to orient himself. This wasn't his bedroom. Last night came rushing back, bringing with it a torrent of lust. Danny had finally trusted him enough to let him make love to her—multiple times.

His eyes closed as he relived every beautiful moment, and his cock swelled. What the fuck? His eyes flew open as he realized he was lying there alone. Scrubbing his hands over his face, he let out a long sigh. He was well aware of their dance by now. Two steps forward and twenty back. He stood up and headed for the shower, wondering how far she'd gone this time.

The cold shower cleared his head and deflated his cock. With a towel wrapped around his waist, he headed for the kitchen seeking caffeine. The smell of a fresh pot hit him the moment he walked out of the bathroom. A smile crept across his face as he realized she hadn't left him.

Through the kitchen window, he saw her curled up in a blanket in a wooden chair that dwarfed her. Dainty hands clasped a mug that he knew held half cream and half sugar with a splash of coffee.

Pouring himself a mug and adding cream, he joined her on the deck. He stood behind her, his eyes on the view before them. He took a healthy sip of the rich brew before asking, "Did you sleep well?"

Violet eyes glanced up at him, and her cheeks flushed a warm pink. "Best night's sleep in a long time," she whispered. Her gaze dropped to his lips, and that was all the invitation he needed.

Setting the mug on the table next to her, he took hers and set it beside his. Reaching down, he scooped her up, making her shriek in surprise. He took her seat and settled her across his lap.

Danny rested her head on his shoulder and nestled into him, inhaling his clean scent. "And you?" she asked coyly, peeking up at him.

"Best night ever." He cupped her face and tilted her head up for a soft kiss. "Morning."

"Morning." Her eyes lingered on his before she wrapped her hand in his hair and tugged him back down for a smoldering one. His body hardened beneath her, and her hand reached under his towel to stroke him.

Straddling him, she wrenched the towel out of her way and positioned him at her entrance. Hovering there, she said, "I woke up needing you." The words whispered against his lips, as if asking permission.

"You should have taken what you wanted." His teeth tugged at her lower lip. "You have my permission to always take what you need."

"Yeah?" She kissed him as her slick heat engulfed the tip of his cock.

"Yeah..." He moaned as she lowered herself onto him fully.

Leaning her forehead against his, she reveled in the power she had over this male and the way he cherished her. With every kiss, every stroke of his tongue, every caress of his hands, and every thrust of his hips, he showed her again and again how much she had been missing and how much they had to look forward to.

With every movement, Jameson Vance exhibited his adoration and his love, reaffirming the connection between them. This man was the light to her dark, and the hope she'd found in the bleakest of days. Her bear rescued her from the depths of despair with the remembrance of what it meant to be loved. Danyka knew without a doubt that her mate would steadfastly remain through the joys and challenges life would present.

Epilogue

Fergus brooded in the dark, with a half-empty whiskey glass in one hand and fire drakes circling his other. Dangling from his fingers was the latest piece that he'd just finished carving. A ship with its sails fully inflated sailed into a deadly riot of waves. Roarke stood at the helm, guiding the ship into the coming storm. Lines of grief and rage were etched on his face.

"Feck me," he muttered. "The man's been through enough already." But this image told him that more heartbreak was ahead for the ship captain. Question was, would it be a physical storm he faced or a metaphorical one?

Running his hand through his wild hair, he thought about the missive he'd received this morning. The Fire Clan historian couldn't verify a death certificate or burial site for his grandfather. The information made him want to vomit. Seems the evil bastard might still be kicking. Horrified that he was related to the man who'd tormented Ronan, he hadn't told Maddy yet.

The last fecking month had been a fecking shit show all the way around. The nightmare of the auction still haunted him with all those kids he couldn't save. Their faces had become a slide show, flickering through his mind whenever he closed his eyes.

He'd even turned Carsyn down tonight, not wanting to keep her up half the night with his tossing and turning. She'd tried to hide her disappointment, but he'd felt her hurt. Tomorrow, he would apologize to his beautiful lass. She'd been one of the few good things that had happened to him.

His thoughts drifted to the attack on the island. The multiple hits had blindsided them all. They'd become complacent, thinking they could protect the Sanctuary with nothing but fear of the Elemental High Court backing them.

Fergus hadn't been there, and the guilt of not being able to help or prevent the pixie from being taken still stung. They had nearly lost her to her past and almost lost Landon as well. He wiped his eyes as he remembered her withering body in Jamey's bed.

And Roarke was barely speaking to him. The captain had reluctantly allowed Samson to take his place the night of the auction. Fergus had finally

convinced Roarke that there was no way that he could keep his shit together when he saw what was about to go down on board those ships. They couldn't afford any mishaps. Roarke regretted that decision now.

Fergus expected his rage when he returned without his sister, but he had welcomed the pain Roarke dealt him. The guilt he already felt embraced the beating he felt he earned.

Ferg hoped he'd regained a little of his trust when he delivered Fisher Jordan to Kenn Tyde this morning for an interrogation. Kenn agreed to allow Roarke to help him inflict some pain.

And then there was the cherry on top—Maddy's little bombshell. Morganna. A demon from his past. His fingers curled into his palms, piercing the skin. An enemy from long ago, he didn't know if he could remain on site if she stayed for long. Neither his soul nor his pride could thrive in her presence.

Slumping further into the deep armchair he'd settled in, he closed his eyes and let himself drift onto the astral plane. His elemental gifts showed him the astral plane in a way similar to Rhyanna's healing gifts.

Rhyanna's gifts showed her injuries to the body, mind, and spirit. Fergus's ethereal gifts allowed every link he'd ever created with another soul, or any trackers he'd placed on others, to become visible. The shimmering lights of each individual stretched out and away from him across the plane. At will, he could reach out a whisper of his power against an individual's string and divine so many things about them.

At worst, the gift was an invasion of privacy if misused. But at best, it could aid in healing or function as a warning system for coming trouble. It was also one of the best tracking systems in existence, second only to the hellhounds.

Tonight, he wanted to check in on the newest string on his ethereal light show. With a featherlight touch, he caressed Rosella Gallagher's string, sending just a glimmer of his power through it. Slowly and carefully, he traced her line, trying to find her. He was alert, trying to avoid any traps that might exist in the young woman's aura.

Allowing his astral body to soar, he drifted above the strings, narrowing his attention until only hers was visible. Expanding his vision, he allowed the landscape below him to come into view. Mountain ranges, small towns, and the river lay beneath him. The view was hazy, but he sensed they were west of the Sanctuary—quite a ways west.

Fergus let the shimmering gold light that represented Rosella tug him closer. Senses on high alert, he noticed nothing that concerned him until he slammed into what felt like a brick wall. He hit the barricade so damn hard that it knocked him off the ethereal plane.

Groaning, his hands cupped his head, finding a goose egg in the center of his forehead, the seat of his inner power. "Fecking hell," he growled as his head throbbed like a bitch.

Instantly, Fergus rebuilt his mental shields and barricades, setting traps in the many layers that protected not only his mind and body, but his location and the people he loved.

Sending tendrils of his power out, he examined all the wards surrounding the island and the castle. Nothing seemed amiss, but he reinforced them, adding additional layers to the intricate wards in place. By the time he finished, sweat was dripping from his brow.

Hauling himself to his feet, he staggered to the bath. Wetting a cloth with ice-cold water for his head, he waited for the throbbing to subside. Banging on the door made him wince. Irritated, he shuffled back into his sitting room.

Yanking the door open without checking for an energy signature was his first mistake. Allowing this visitor to see him in pain was his second. Standing on the threshold was the woman who once had been his teacher, became his best friend, and a bit more, before breaking his fecking heart.

"Hello, lover," a smoky voice said. Emerald eyes glittered dangerously at him. The auburn-haired amazon with a permanently abrasive attitude glared at him. "What the feck didchya do this time, ye bloody fool?"

And with that one statement, the beautiful woman in front of him reminded him once again why he still fecking hated her.

Acknowledgements

Eric for always believing in me, and for being a combination of all my sweet, sassy, and sexy book heroes all rolled into one. I am so grateful for all the ways you support me while I take this journey.

Kassie Wilber for always being my first beta reader, and for encouraging me to keep going. I appreciate all the marketing assistance you provide as well as your wish list of plotlines that you want changed, and characters you want eliminated. Thank you for your contributions to the playlist and for challenging me when things don't seem quite right.

Dianne DeCarlo for listening to my frustrations and celebrating my victories when I finally figure out how to fix a plot fiasco. I love you for wanting to save the magical creatures that I threaten to put down, even when they are evil.

My beta readers: Barbara Barnhart, Lisa McVaugh, Nicki Wilber, Carroll Adams, Anita Barnhart, Liane Miksits, and Jen Kupcho for falling in love with my characters and this world. Your input is invaluable and greatly appreciated.

Rebecca Chen for the time we get to spend together, the support, encouragement, and the laughter.

Josie Carter for being my biggest fan and for checking in every few weeks to see how my world is progressing. Your enthusiasm keeps me going! Thank you for your patience and encouragement, even when I wouldn't tell you if Jameson lived or not.

Cori Preston for another beautiful cover. I think this is my favorite one so far! Thank you for your infinite patience when I format incorrectly and need to adjust all the sizes.

Emily Hostetter for the ability to edit my chapters out of order and still make sense of my meandering, ever-changing journey. For never making me feel like the world in my head is too much. I'm so glad to be on this journey with you!

Author Info

A member of the RWA, AnnaLeigh Skye loves to read and write spicy dark romantic fantasy. She lives on a working farm in the Endless Mountains with the man of her dreams, their lovely daughter, four possessed felines, and her extended family.

River of Remembrance is the third novel in the Heart Island Sanctuary Series.

www.annaleighskye.com

RIVER OF REMEMBRANCE